Jennifer Lang is the autho[...] four of them on the history of London guilds and livery companies, and one previous historical novel, the highly acclaimed THE PEACOCK AND THE PEARL, also set in the reign of Richard II. As well as writing, she has worked as a secretary in the House of Commons and in the Savoy hotel as a press officer. She now lives in Gloucestershire with her sporting-agent husband.

Also by Jennifer Lang

The Peacock and the Pearl

The Crowning City

Jennifer Lang

HEADLINE

First published in 1994
by HEADLINE BOOK PUBLISHING

First published in paperback in 1994
by HEADLINE BOOK PUBLISHING

10 9 8 7 6 5 4 3 2 1

ISBN 0 7472 4494 4

Typeset by Keyboard Services, Luton

Printed and bound in Great Britain by
Cox & Wyman Ltd, Reading, Berks

HEADLINE BOOK PUBLISHING
A division of Hodder Headline PLC
338 Euston Road
London NW1 3BH

To my husband Richard
whose encouragement, love and enthusiasm at all times
keep me going.

THE CROWNING CITY

Who hath taken this counsel against Tyre, the crowning city whose merchants are princes, whose traffickers are the honourable of the earth?

The Lord of hosts hath purposed it, to stain the pride of all glory, and to bring into contempt all the honourable of the earth.

Isaiah 23: 8–9

PRINCIPAL CHARACTERS

The Court

Richard of Bordeaux – King Richard II of England.
    Ann of Bohemia – his wife
    Juetta Seward
    Gisela   } her ladies-in-waiting
    Isabella of France – his second wife
    Madame de Courcy – her Mistress of Ceremonies

The King's uncles, sons of Edward III:

John of Gaunt, Duke of Lancaster
    Henry of Derby, Earl of Bolingbroke, Duke of
        Hereford – his son
Thomas of Woodstock, Duke of Gloucester
Edmund of Langley, Duke of York

King's Party

Robert de Vere, Earl of Oxford, Duke of Ireland
Michael de la Pole, Earl of Suffolk
Roger Mortimer, Earl of March – heir to Richard II
    Lady Mortimer – his wife
Earl of Salisbury, poet, scholar, soldier and Lollard
Thomas Holland, Earl of Kent   } Richard II's half
Sir John Holland   brothers
John Fordham, Bishop of Durham
Sir Robert Tresilian, Chief Justice of England
Sir Simon Burley

Lords Appellant

Earl of Arundel
Thomas Mowbray, Earl of Nottingham, Duke of Norfolk
Earl of Warwick
Henry Bolingbroke, Duke of Hereford, King Henry IV
Duke of Gloucester

Knights

Sir Piers Exton
    Esmon de Linbrok – his squire
    Crispin Greyshot – his squire
    Guy de Luval – his squire

French Challengers: **Jean de Boucicaut, de Roye, de Sempy**

Stephano de Corsini – an Italian

Sir Thomas Swinford – half brother to Henry Bolingbroke

Mayors of London

Richard Whittington, mercer. Mayor 1397–98, 1406, 1419
    Alice his wife
Sir Nicholas Brembre, grocer. Mayor 1377, 1383–86
    Idonia his wife (sister to Margaret Bamme)
Nicholas Exton, fishmonger. Mayor 1386–88
Adam Bamme, goldsmith. Mayor 1390–91, 1396–97
    Margaret his wife (sister to Idonia Brembre)

Others

H. Vanner, vintner
    Margery his wife (sister to Idonia Brembre and
      Margaret Bamme)
William Gryffard – Merchant of the Staple at Calais
    Adam Stickleby – his Steward
    Nicolette de St Pierre – his natural daughter
    Lisette – her maid
Giles de Bourdat – his partner in Calais
    Jeanne de Bourdat – his wife
The widow Wendegoos – a whore

Those marked in bold type are recorded in history.

PART I
1386–1388

'Only to see her whom I love and serve
Though it were never granted to deserve
Her favour, would have been enough.'
Geoffrey Chaucer, *The Knight's Tale*

CHAPTER 1

Caen, 1386

'A bastard an abbess?' he exclaimed. 'Surely that's impossible.'

'Her mother was a noblewoman,' the Abbess replied. He scowled and she added quickly, 'And her father is a man of great wealth and if his conscience can match his worldly state he should be able to help her rise to the head of her house – in time.'

He stared at her warily and took a sip of wine from the fine silver goblet she handed him, prepared for a hard tussle.

'There is nothing in the Augustinian rule against a bastard becoming a nun,' the Abbess continued. 'Indeed, I can think of no more fitting life for such an unfortunate than to try to expiate the sin of the parents by devoting her life to God.'

'No indeed,' agreed William Gryffard, the bastard's father. 'Is she good enough for such a task?'

The Abbess looked at him sharply, as if she suspected mockery, but he stared back enigmatically. The grim severity of her patrician features softened as suddenly she smiled. 'Your daughter Nicolette is an angel,' she said and there was no doubting the sincerity in her voice. 'She is devout, accomplished, willing and able in all things to please. We all of us love her dearly. Ever since her mother's death she has been waiting only for you to come so that she may take her vows and enter fully into our life here. We have waited five years for this day,' she added reproachfully.

'Well, I am here now,' he said. 'But I cannot see why you could not have gone ahead without me. I have not been consulted over much before.'

'There is the question of her dower,' murmured the Abbess.

'I sent you money.' He had made a mistake when he was twenty years old in the full flush of youth and a slave to his passions, which he had long since learnt better to control. Mistakes had to be paid for. He knew that.

'The money you sent helped with the cost of keeping your daughter fed and clothed but before a nun can take her place in an ancient foundation such as we have here at Caen, we have to have some substantial contribution towards the future of the house.'

He studied her with ill-concealed mistrust. She was tall and stately and could perhaps have been handsome but for the severity of her nun's habit and her features with the strong nose, unyielding mouth and firm jaw. A formidable woman, he decided, with the calm assurance of a noble-woman, sure of herself, of her place in the world and her right to command.

'It's not easy for me,' he began. 'I'm no landed nobleman with manors I can make over to the abbey.'

'You have money – which is easier to bequeath.'

'My money is the tool of my trade,' he protested.

'Is it not written that one-tenth of what we have should be given back to Our Lord?' she chided.

The accusation made him angry. All very well for her, secure in her well-tended abbey, wrapped in sanctity and protected by generations of aristocratic patronage, to lecture him on charity; she had no idea how difficult money was to come by. He longed to make this aloof and critical woman understand some of his problems as an international trader. She was intelligent enough, a practical woman of the world for all the unworldliness of her calling, and he needed to justify himself as well as to get as good a bargain as he could.

'I trade in wool,' he said. 'I buy it in England and I ship it across the Channel to Calais and sell for the best price I can get for it. Simple enough, you might say. But to buy best Cotswold wool I first have to compete with the great Italian merchant princes, people like the Mannini, the Guinigi, and the Alberti, all of whom have established branches in London. Unless I can buy in advance, there is nothing left when the Italians have done. Sometimes I have bought while the wool is still on the sheep's back and then when the clip is shorn it turns out to be unsatisfactory.'

4

'But as a merchant of the staple surely you have an advantage with the customs and subsidy.'

'Then there is the problem of getting the wool to Calais,' he continued, ignoring her interruption. 'All these years that England and France have been at war has made the Channel a battlefield and no merchant likes having to carry his goods across a battlefield.'

'I thought your Duke of Lancaster had negotiated a truce so he could go off and make war in Spain,' she said.

'There is still the danger from the pirates. Only last week a merchant in Prato had a wheat ship sunk by a privateer under Genoese command and lost his entire investment.'

'But you can insure your cargoes,' she persisted.

'Then once I get it to Calais I still have to sell it,' he continued, 'and the tax on wool is now so high it is killing the trade. My profit is less than ten per cent – a small enough return for so great and so prolonged an effort.'

'Then why don't you sell cloth,' she said with a small shrug. He did. He traded in anything he could buy when the price was right and a market could be found. He belonged to no craft guild and was one of a rare breed who traded across national boundaries, unfettered by the guild regulations that controlled and protected the majority of merchants. He looked at the Abbess and knew that it was useless to try and gain her sympathy. She was too used to getting her own way in the tiny world she ruled over. He thought of the money he had brought with him from Venice after settling his second wife's affairs. With regret he thought of what it could buy – how he might have used it to make more. It was a pity. But his daughter had to be dowered and the Abbess knew how to drive a hard bargain.

Dinner was served in the Abbess's own quarters. It was a fine meal – pieces of lamb in a spiced sauce, white bread, good wine, local cheese, and it included a dish of sweetmeats which Gryffard felt sure were made for the Abbess's personal indulgence and not for the rest of the convent.

Over dinner the Abbess took pains to explain to him her own difficulties, pointing out that the Abbey of Holy Trinity was old, having been founded by the wife of William the Conqueror for her daughter Cecilia, and expensive to maintain. All this William Gryffard did not need to be told.

He had noticed, because he was a man who missed nothing, the elegant simplicity of the cloisters with their carved stone foliage, the orchards laden with fruit, the well-tended gardens with the great pine growing in its central lawn, the fountain splashing musically in an inner court. He had put a value on the magnificent gold and silver vessels which adorned the Abbess's table, noticed the caged larks in the corner of her parlour in direct defiance of the Archbishop of Rouen, and smiled wryly to himself as he reflected that a woman in charge of her own abbey had greater freedom and power than any of her more worldly sisters outside.

By the time dinner was finished, it was agreed he would pay for the building of a new refectory in memory of Marguerite de St Pierre, Nicolette's mother, and endow a chantry with prayers to be said night and morning for the repose of her soul. 'To which we shall add your name when your own time is come,' the Abbess promised, adding with one of her rare smiles, 'until then we shall pray God to deliver you from shipwreck, piracy, land robbers, dishonest agents, closed ports, pestilence and deterioration of wares – all the things which might come between you and the just reward for your labours upon earth.'

William drained his goblet, aware that in the battle of wits he had definitely been bested, and suddenly he felt tired. He had been travelling hard for many days and had many more days' riding before he reached Calais.

'And now,' continued the Abbess, 'perhaps you would like to see your daughter.'

He did not care whether he saw his daughter or not. She was a mistake which had cost him money already and now, to be rid of her once and for all, it was costing him far more than he was willing to pay. But the Abbess, without waiting for his acceptance, was already dispatching a nun to fetch Nicolette.

Impatiently William eased his tired body and cursed the injustice of fate which had left him childless after two marriages and yet inflicted him with this bastard child he did not want. His first marriage to a young and beautiful mercer's daughter should have provided the children, but he had been unlucky with Mariota. Her first two babies had died and she had been killed through her own folly during the Peasants' Revolt. His second marriage to a prosperous Venetian merchant's widow had been more fruitful commercially, but

6

there were still no children. His second wife had died in the spring of the year. So here he was at the age of thirty-five with a flourishing business and the only fruit of his loins a devout postulant, whose abbey would quickly swallow every groat he gave her. He was not yet ready to part with his wealth. He never liked parting with anything. He had no curiosity about this child he had never seen. She was a nuisance, that was all; of no possible use to him that he could see.

When Nicolette arrived he was startled to find she was not at all what he had expected. Instead of the quiet, devout creature he been led to expect, there stood before him a young girl so stunning he felt suddenly invigorated. Even in her ugly postulant's habit he could see that she was a beauty. Her face was a perfect oval, the jaw line a clean sculptured curve above the severe confines of the bulky linen of her veil. Her nose was small and perfectly shaped, her lips ruby red. But it was her eyes resting upon him with such a look of complete confidence that impressed him most. Face to face for the first time with his own flesh and blood, he recognised in her a quality he would have given all his wealth to win. Her confidence was as natural as any lady's in her castle, her belief in herself shone from her eyes.

'You see,' the voice of the Abbess broke through his confused thoughts, 'is she not everything I promised you? She has been well educated, can read and write, sing and sew, and has learnt to exercise the strictest discipline over the demands of the flesh. She will be a credit to you and to the abbey. When she has taken her vows.'

William continued to stare at his daughter. She did not seem perturbed by his intent scrutiny but bore it with the kind of calm serenity he only associated with the nobly born. A sweet, slightly hesitant smile touched her lips and William caught his breath as a bolt of pure joy flashed through his soul. Here in this most unlikely place he had found what all his life he had been looking for – the perfect tool. Confident, disciplined, talented, beautiful and, above all, loyal. For what could be more trustworthy than his own flesh and blood? He turned to the Abbess.

'I've changed my mind,' he said. 'She'll not be taking her vows. There'll be no new refectory nor chantry either. Nicolette will be a burden to you no longer. I'm taking her with me to London.' More than anything he enjoyed being able to take someone by surprise and as he watched the satisfaction and pride drain from the Abbess's face, he congratulated himself on as bold a stroke of business as any he had done in a long time. He had saved himself a knight's ransom and gained at the same time a pearl beyond price.

Nicolette could not believe the evidence of her own ears. Ever since her mother's death, here in the abbey, she had looked forward to the moment when her father would come. She knew nothing of him except that he paid for her to remain at Holy Trinity and that he was wealthy – the nuns had left her in little doubt about that. That she was a bastard she knew but it troubled her not at all. Bastardy had little stigma in a sheltered environment such as this. Her mother had been a nun and so obviously her father could not marry her, that was all. To Nicolette it was a story as noble and poignant as that of Abelard and Heloise.

Born and brought up in the abbey, the only child in a community of women cut off from all the joys and woes of family life, she had been the pampered pet of all the nuns. She had grown up surrounded by peace and security in the measured calm of a well-ordered and disciplined life, singing and praying for much of the day, taking for granted the affection she received and accepting the self-denial she was forced to practise, happily unaware of any other kind of life. Naturally quick to learn, she benefited from all that the nuns could teach her and could think of nothing better than to spend her days praising God and perfecting the tasks she had been taught to perform. Her mother had been a frail, sad beauty whom Nicolette could barely remember – except for one cold winter's night when she was ten years old and she had been dragged from her dorter to attend her mother's deathbed. The last words of the dying woman had made an impression on her then as irrevocable as any curse.

'My little star,' Marguerite had said, struggling for breath. 'You'll never be a failure like me.' The rasping agony of each tortured word had sunk deep into the child's mind like tablets of stone. After that Nicolette had redoubled her efforts to please, desperate to erase the memory of the poor, faded beauty who had languished so ineffectually and to make up for her mother's wasted life. To her natural talents she added an extra determination which enabled her to excel in everything she did, as all the time she strove to be worthy of the shadowy, insubstantial ideal of her father – when at last he should come to the Abbey.

Now at last he was here. She had borne his scrutiny sure of her own worth and unafraid of those penetrating eyes of his which seemed to pierce her very soul. But he must have seen there something which displeased him; she was not to remain at Holy Trinity, not to take her vows. The moment she had spent her whole life preparing herself for, the first real test she had ever had to meet, she had failed and she did not know why.

'Am I not good enough to be a nun?' she cried, turning in anguish to the Abbess. The Abbess was angry, Nicolette could see it; she should not have spoken, should not have questioned her father's decision. Immediately she fell down on her knees. 'Forgive me, Reverend Mother, I am unworthy.'

'Do not blame yourself, my child,' replied the Abbess, glancing at William. 'It is not your fault that you are not to take your vows. It would appear that your father has more important things to do with his money than to enable you to fulfil your vocation. But I would remind him of the story Our Lord told of the rich man who had so much he pulled down his barns to build bigger and better barns to house all his fruits and his goods and how he said to himself, "Soul, thou hast much goods laid up for many years; take thine ease, eat, drink and be merry." But God said unto him, "Thou fool, this night thy soul shall be required of thee, then whose shall those things be which thou hast provided? So is he that layeth up treasure for himself and is not rich toward God."'

Nicolette, still trembling on her knees, did not dare look at her father. So the Abbess was not angry with her, it was her father who had erred, but Nicolette still could not accept what was happening. There had been some mistake; surely the Abbess who was infinitely wise and good could make it all come right again.

'We shall leave at dawn tomorrow,' William said, apparently undeterred, and Nicolette was horrified that her father seemed not to realise the terrible risk he took in incurring the Abbess's displeasure. 'She will need some female to accompany her. Will you arrange it?'

Ignoring him, the Abbess raised Nicolette to her feet. 'It

seems God has another purpose for you, my child,' she said, looking down into the girl's shocked face and smiling reassuringly. 'It is not for us to question God's will. Remember what you have learnt here and you will not come to any harm. You will succeed in whatever you do, I know that. Now stay and talk to your father while I make arrangements for your departure.'

Nicolette gazed at her father while dismay and disappointment threatened to overwhelm her. He had defied the Abbess and instead of being struck down by an instant bolt from heaven he was standing there with a distinct expression of triumph on his face. She could not believe that this sallow-skinned little man with the darting eyes and cowled head poking out of his stooped shoulders as if he had no neck could possibly be her father. He was not at all the sort of dashing merchant prince who went about the world seducing young noblewomen. She had imagined him handsome, distinguished, bejewelled, and he was old and careworn. It made her mother's failure seem even worse. Remembering her mother, she decided to make one last plea.

'Father,' she said, 'could I not please stay and be a nun, like my mother would have wanted?'

'No, my dear, for you would be wasted in a convent,' he replied, studying her thoughtfully. 'Now we must decide who you are. I think we shall say that you are a distant kinswoman of mine. You will keep your mother's name of Saint Pierre – it is a fine old French name. Your father died in battle, I think, and your mother went into a convent where you were born and brought up. On her death I discovered your whereabouts and brought you to England. Does that sound plausible?'

He had such shrewd, watchful eyes, he made her feel guilty, but what had she done? 'It isn't true,' she said, even more bewildered.

'We do not want the world to know you are a bastard, it can make marriage difficult.'

'You want me to lie?' she asked carefully.

'Not all the time, and never to me, you understand. But just in this one instance, yes, I want you to lie.'

'Why?'

'Because I ask it. I thought you were schooled in obedience.'

10

It began to dawn upon her that he was not taking her away from the abbey because she was not good enough but for some purpose of his own.

'I expect you to be a good daughter,' he continued. 'As good a daughter as you would have been a nun.'

With an enormous effort she repressed all the disappointment she felt. It would be difficult being a perfect daughter to such as he. But she would do it – all the more so because it was so very difficult.

CHAPTER 2

For fifty years France had been at war with England, but the young English knight riding across the windswept, inhospitable plains of northern France did not fear a French ambush. The war which had gone on so long was now being pursued in Spain. A year ago King João I of Portugal, with the help of English archers, had won a crushing victory at Aljubarrota, which established Portuguese independence for good and crippled the military power of France's most useful ally Castile. A new twist had developed in the long-running war which gave England a chance to triumph against France by destroying her staunchest ally, and Sir Piers Exton now hurrying through enemy territory with such confidence was anxious to be part of it.

It was growing late. The sun had sunk into a massed bank of cloud over an hour ago and darkness was gathering. Sir Piers scanned the road ahead for any sign of the turreted walls of a monastery or an abbey but he saw nothing save deserted wasteland with here and there a lonely tree leaning sideways like a supplicant serf in permanant thrall to the prevailing wind from the west. It was August and quite warm enough to sleep beside the road. The horses could graze the scrubland which stretched with such unvaried monotony to the horizon and doubtless find plenty of food, but Piers had seen little sign of wildlife – no rabbits, no streams leaping with fish, nothing to quench his thirst or satisfy his hunger and it was a long time since he and his squire had last eaten. He glanced at the boy. He was slumped in his saddle, almost asleep. The war horse he led, taking advantage of the slackening rein, stopped to grab a mouthful of grass and he jerked awake with a start.

12

'Tired, Esmon?' asked Piers. Immediately the squire sat bolt upright and gave the destrier a fierce jerk on the rein to punish him for having caught him napping. Piers grinned at him. 'We'll stop as soon as we can find some shelter for the night,' he said encouragingly. The boy swore that he was ready to ride on all through the night if need be but Piers continued to scan the way ahead for some sign of habitation. He did not believe in pushing others to the limits of their endurance when it was not strictly necessary.

A little later his keen eyes spotted a most welcome sight almost on the horizon – a wooden building with a long pole sticking out in front of it.

'We're in luck, Esmon,' he exclaimed. 'Saint Christopher be praised, there's a wayside tavern not more than ten leagues ahead. It may not be much of a place, and flea-ridden I dare say. Pray God it's not rat-infested as well.'

'Who cares about rats, or fleas either?' declared Esmon as they spurred their horses forward. 'So long as there's a supper to be had – my stomach's so empty I'd not mind eating their rats as well.'

Too late the knight remembered his dwindling resources; they should have stopped at the abbey they had passed in Caen some hours ago. But when they drew rein in front of the tavern, he knew that for the rest of his life he would give thanks to the divine hand which had led him along this of all the roads in France, to choose this most ordinary of taverns, and to stop here at this very hour. For standing in the middle of the square of well-trodden earth in front of the tavern was the most beautiful girl he had ever seen. She was wearing a simple garment of some sort of thick grey cloth rather like a nun's habit, but her head was uncovered and her yellow hair, bright as new-minted gold, was braided in a tress behind her back a yard in length. He gazed at her dumbstruck and she returned his gaze gravely, as stately and as self-possessed as any queen, then modestly lowered her eyes while he stood and watched her like one in a trance. A man appeared at the door of the inn.

'Nicolette! Stop dawdling,' he shouted and disappeared into the tavern. Swiftly she obeyed the summons.

It was some time before Piers came out of his trance, but when at last he did, he noticed that the yard was full of horses

13

and men-at-arms. Clearly a man of some standing had also stopped at the inn and Piers guessed it was the fellow who had called to the girl. He wondered what relation she was to him. Then he noticed a forlorn heap of human misery still perched upon the back of one of the horses. She was young but far from lovely, her face badly scarred by the pox and her body sturdy as a packhorse. She was clearly so exhausted from her journey that she was unable to dismount and nobody had thought to help her down. He went to her aid and it was as well that he was strong for she was no lightweight. She thanked him effusively in a patois so broad that he understood barely one word, but her beaming smile, which showed an unfortunate mouthful of missing and misbegotten teeth, made her gratitude plain enough. She said something about her mistress Nicolette and beamed at him again while she hung back shyly. So he took her by the hand and escorted her into the tavern as ceremoniously as if she had been the mistress and not the maid.

Inside, the tavern was dark and filled with smoke from the open fire in the middle of the room. It smelt, as all taverns did, of a mixture of grease and smoke and body odours, but penetrating the unfavourable stench was the more welcome one of cooking meat which made the knight's mouth water. A haunch of beef was hanging above the fire being turned by a spit-boy. Regretfully, Piers put all idea of it out of his head and instead bought for himself and his squire a hunk of bread and some ale, adding a pastie for Esmon. Piers, too, would dearly have loved a pastie for he was very hungry but he was used to fasting – any soldier who had endured a siege soon learnt how to bear the pangs of hunger – and growing boys needed feeding. He and Esmon took their meagre rations to the communal table. Piers looked round for the girl. She was sitting at the far end with a bowl in front of her. Piers sat down opposite and watched her enchanted, marvelling at the graceful way she scooped the meat out with her bread in small dainty mouthfuls, spilling not one drop of gravy on chin or gown or table. He wondered if she would look so perfect when she smiled or whether her smile might be spoilt as so many were by missing or uneven teeth. He tried to think of something to say to make her smile but he had little experience in the ways of winning a lady's smile.

'Have you come far?' The man who came and sat down

beside Piers was stooped and had a pointed sharp look to him rather like an inquisitive rat. His gown, however, was of finest wool, richly trimmed with fur, and pulled down over his hood he wore a hat of best beaver. A merchant, thought Piers, and a prosperous one.

'From Tuscany,' replied Piers, averting his eyes from the large slices of charred beef covered with a generous helping of delicious smelling gravy on the other's plate.

'A soldier of fortune,' commented the merchant.

'Sir Piers Exton,' replied the knight, looking at the girl, 'at your service.' She didn't look up. Piers took a bite of his bread, chewing carefully to make it last.

'The warring Italian city republics make good paymasters now that the war in France is no longer profitable,' commented the merchant.

'My father is a Cheshire knight,' Piers told him. 'I'm the youngest of four brothers and have to make my own way in the world. When I was fifteen, Sir Guy Fortinbras took me as his squire. Sir Guy joined Sir John Hawkwood's White Company.'

'I've heard of Sir John Hawkwood. The son of an Essex tanner, wasn't he, who made enough money to marry the natural daughter of Bernabo Visconti, the tyrant of Milan. How did he do it?'

'He's a good soldier,' replied Piers with a shrug. 'He knows what a well-trained and disciplined band of Englishmen can do if well led and he put his company at the disposal of first one warring Italian city republic and then another.' The girl had finished eating but still she did not look up and he could not tell whether she took any interest in the conversation or not.

'It's a profitable business, for a knight. You must be an experienced warrior by now.'

Piers was too fascinated by the girl to pay much attention. She sat so still and quiet and composed. If only he could make her smile.

'May I buy you a plate of cooked meats?' asked the merchant, suddenly taking out his money bag.

'I'm not in the habit of accepting gifts from strangers,' Piers said with a grin, 'so perhaps you'll tell me your name.'

'William Gryffard, merchant of the staple in Calais.' He looked Piers up and down, balancing his money bag as if on an imaginary scale. 'Are you too proud to accept charity from a merchant?'

Piers looked pointedly at the girl. Gryffard made no attempt to introduce her. 'A knight is never too proud to accept a gift from a merchant,' Piers replied, 'I'd be glad of some beef, if you'll also buy some for my squire.'

The girl smiled. Her teeth were small and white and even between her rosy lips, and Piers felt his heart leap in his chest.

'How long were you with the White Company?' Gryffard persisted once the meat had been brought.

'Three years.' Piers was not interested in the merchant's questions. He was too busy watching the girl, hoping that she would look at him. He thought that if he could but make her smile again, or look at him, he would die happy.

'Three years with the White Company and nothing to show for it. I'm surprised Sir John Hawkwood could afford to let you go.' There was no mistaking the merchant's scorn. Piers, now happily wolfing down the roasted beef, did not care in the least what the merchant thought of him. But his squire did.

'Sir Piers did very well,' put in Esmon hotly. 'Only he chose to give away his money to a traveller we found being attacked on the way. Stripped naked and robbed and bleeding to death of his wounds, he was. Sir Piers drives off his attackers and then takes him to a tavern and leaves him with all his money – that's the sort of thing Sir Piers is always doing.'

'We had a picture of the Good Samaritan in our church at home,' said Piers, embarrassed. 'It always fascinated me. I suppose I was just trying to see if I couldn't be like him.'

'What a wonderful thing to have done,' said the girl. Piers thought he had never heard a voice so magically low and sweet and imagined an angel could not sound more enchanting.

'A very perfect, gentle knight,' said William Gryffard, unimpressed. 'If that's the way you go about the world I doubt if you'll make your fortune this side of paradise.'

Piers, all too conscious of the girl's candid gaze resting on him in approval, felt that had he needed a reward for his act of charity, he had it now. Willingly would he have given away twenty bags of gold just for such a moment. The merchant glared at her angrily and she hurriedly dropped her eyes.

'It was stupid of me,' said Piers to placate him – for the girl's sake. 'I dare say the tavernkeeper turned him out and kept the money as soon as my back was turned. I should have stayed with him until he was fit to travel. I didn't do enough.'

'Why didn't you stay then?' William demanded.

'Because I was in a hurry to get to England to try to join John of Gaunt's army before he leaves for Spain.'

'I doubt if the Duke of Lancaster's Spanish ambitions will make your fortune for you,' William said. 'He's raised armies at great expense and marched them about the fair land of France more than once but the French have been too cunning to fight a pitched battle. He has returned home empty-handed every time.'

'This time it'll be different. He isn't fighting the French, he's going to help the Portuguese against the Spanish.'

'Ever since he married the exiled daughter of the dethroned Don Pedro of Castile, Lancaster's had his eye on the Spanish throne.'

'And why not?' demanded Piers. 'If Constance were to be restored to her rightful place as Queen of Castile, John of Gaunt could then claim the crown as her consort and bring Spain to his nephew's aid against France. With Spain on our side we'll be able to conquer France once and for all.'

'And what if we do?' scoffed William. 'In good King Edward's reign the English won a whole string of resounding victories – Crécy, Poitiers. The Black Prince captured King John of France and burned France to the very gates of Paris; England controlled a third of the country. But the Black Prince is dead, King Edward is dead, and his grandson King Richard II is surrounded by his powerful uncles.' William wiped his eating knife carefully on his trencher bread before sheathing it at his belt. 'Now all that is left is Calais, Brest, Bordeaux and Bayonne.'

Piers looked away uncomfortably. He knew that what the merchant said was true. The war against France had for a long time been going badly. The French and the Spanish between them controlled the English Channel. There were raids on English ports; merchant shipping was burnt at anchor as near to London as Gravesend, and invasion fears were rife. He knew well that there were no longer any spoils of war to be had from fighting the French. The French would not fight pitched battles against the English any more. It was why men like Sir Guy Fortinbras went to work for Hawkwood and his White Company. Piers as his squire had had no choice but to go with him. He had served his apprenticeship in war, been knighted and acquired a squire of his own. At eighteen he was an experienced warrior, as William Gryffard had guessed, but he was never at heart a mercenary. When news of the Portuguese victory had reached Florence it had made him restless. Not long afterwards Sir Guy was killed in battle and the only call upon Piers's loyalty had been broken. In Venice he learnt that an army was being raised once again in England. Here at last he felt was a cause worth fighting for. England was going to the aid of a damsel in distress – Don Pedro's daughter – and in addition, John of Gaunt had the blessing of Pope Urban VI who had named him 'Standard Bearer of the Cross for the Pope and the Roman Church'. This gave the expedition against Spain something of the nature of a crusade and fired Piers with enthusiasm to be part of it. As soon as he could, he had sought permission to leave the White Company and set off in haste for England. But he did not think this calculating merchant with the heavy money bag and watchful eyes would understand.

'I want to fight for something nobler than the disputes over the monopoly of trade which is the only concern of the merchant princes in Italy,' said Piers. 'To shed my blood for someone more worthy than Bernabo Visconti, the tyrant of Milan.'

The girl looked at him, a quick shy glance and then down again at the table. But Piers thought he caught a gleam of approval in her eyes.

'You may be too late,' William said as he drained his ale. 'I heard the Duke of Lancaster has already sailed for Spain.'

Piers was shaken. Until that moment he had not con-sidered the possibility that the army might not still be in England.

'Of course I may be wrong. They'll know for certain in Calais. That's where I'm bound. I'll tell you what, if you'd like to come with us, I'll pay all your expenses. Two of our horses went lame today and we had to leave one of our men behind. I don't like being short of men-at-arms travelling through France, especially with two women to slow us down.

I'd ride much easier if I knew I had one of the White Company with me, and in Calais you can get sure news of the whereabouts of the Duke and his army. What do you say?'

'There's nothing I'd like more,' exclaimed Piers, watching the girl for her reaction. But she no longer seemed interested in him. She was looking at the merchant a little apprehensively, Piers thought, and he longed to know what she was to him. But it did not matter. Nor did it matter that William Gryffard thought he could be bought. All that mattered was that he had found his lady and was to be allowed to protect her all the way to Calais.

CHAPTER 3

It took them five days' riding to reach Calais. For Nicolette it was five days of painful challenge. Never having ridden a horse, her back ached and her body was rubbed sore wherever it came in contact with the saddle. She tried to concentrate on a perfect vision of Christ's love, which had always worked when her knees had complained after too much contact with the hard stone floor of the chapel at Holy Trinity, but she found it impossible to achieve the necessary detachment when bouncing about on the back of a horse, with Lisette riding pillion and moaning behind her. The road was rough and uneven and the patient white palfrey her father had procured for her, although quiet and amiable, was inclined to stumble if she did not watch him carefully, nor did he seem as anxious as she to be done with this journey; he would seize any excuse to pause for a mouthful of grass if she did not keep urging him forward. She started out at the beginning of each new day with every muscle and bone in her body protesting from the day before but determined to conquer her feeble flesh; alas by nightfall even the recollection of Christ's agony on the Cross could not lift her mind above her aching limbs and all she could think of was the comfort of her hard mattress on its rope springs back in the novices' dorter.

In addition to her physical discomfort, she was struggling with new and disturbing sensations. She was disconcerted by the stares and admiring glances she encountered both from the men-at-arms who rode with them and from the people they passed on the road – drovers with their wool trains, merchants with their packhorses, travelling pedlars selling their wares, even the friars with their begging bowls; all of them looked at her with such blatant admiration it made her feel hot and uncomfortable.

Most confusing of all was Sir Piers Exton. At Holy Trinity Nicolette had seen few men, only the serfs who toiled in the fields and, on his twice yearly visits, the Bishop, who was old and paunchy. Sir Piers was young and strong; his shoulders were broad and his legs bulged with muscle; his hair was dark and close-cropped and curled vigorously round his well-shaped head. With his gleaming armour, his prancing war horse and his devoted squire, Sir Piers Exton was a glamorous and exciting figure and he watched Nicolette with such soulful fervour in his brown eyes that she felt more hot and confused than ever.

By day she was all too conscious of his presence as he tried to make the journey easier for her with little acts of kindness. When she fell behind he loitered by her side, ready to prod the recalcitrant palfrey when he baulked or seize the animal's bridle and lead him firmly back to the path when he strayed. When they passed a stream, he would leap from his horse and fill his helm with clear cool water for her to quench her thirst. When towards evening they passed a likely looking tavern or religious house, it was always Piers who suggested breaking their journey, although William would insist on continuing until nightfall.

When at last they did stop and Nicolette was so stiff she could not dismount, Piers was always there to lift her gently off her horse and deposit her carefully on her feet; then he would hurry away before she had time to thank him properly. At such times her confusion was like an insurmountable barrier. She was grateful for his care but she was not used to being the object of so much chivalry and at a loss to know how to respond. She sensed that Piers was as confused as she was, that he longed to talk to her but did not know how. She wanted to put him at his ease, but she had not been taught how to converse with a man. All she knew was how to be quiet and modest and self-effacing.

William Gryffard did not confuse her with his admiration. On the contrary, she soon became aware that her father was not at all pleased with her and she studied him closely to try to discover what it was she was doing wrong. His closed, pinched face gave nothing away. He was her father, but he

21

was a complete stranger and she had no idea what he wanted from her. All he seemed to want was to get to Calais as quickly as possible, and to please him she was determined to ride on to the limits of her endurance, ignoring the dust and the heat and her aching bones and trying to dredge up enough sympathy from her exhausted spirit to console Lisette whose sufferings, to judge by the stream of vociferous complaint, were even worse than her own.

On the morning of the fifth day they finally came within sight of Calais and for the last hour of the ride had to contend with a steadily increasing number of people going to and from the town. Bemused and somewhat unnerved by the noise and bustle, Nicolette clung to the palfrey's mane as Piers forged a way for her through the crowd. They entered the walled city through a wide stone arch and plunged into what seemed to Nicolette a scene of utter confusion. Long trains of mules and donkeys carrying sacks of wheat or wool struggled past prosperous merchants and their well-armed servants. Fishermen with buckets of fresh fish hanging from a yoke across their shoulders and farmers herding swine or geese shouted abuse at all who got in their way. A strong wind blew in their faces, bringing with it the tang of the sea and the all-pervading smell of raw wool mingled with fish. A sudden gust whipped the palfrey's mane across Nicolette's face and flung her skirt round the scabbard of a young man as he pushed impatiently past. He swore at her incomprehensibly, but Nicolette smiled a quick apology whereupon he fell to staring at her like all the others and said something in a completely foreign tongue. Piers swung round and shouted something equally incomprehensible back.

'What did he say?' asked Nicolette as the man retired crestfallen.

'It doesn't matter,' Piers replied.

'What language were you using?' she asked, still curious.

'English – he'll be squire to one of the knights from the garrison,' Piers told her.

English? she thought in panic. It sounded gibberish. 'I wish you were coming with us to England, Sir Piers,' she said wistfully. 'Then you could teach me some of this English on the way.'

'You needn't be afraid, damoiselle,' he replied swiftly. 'French is the language of the court. Any true-born gentlewoman speaks French in England, albeit with some difficulty. Among them you will be able to shine.'

Her panic left her and she followed him full of eager anticipation, enjoying the wonder of the shops open to the street, the cobbler, saddler, tailor, goldsmith, barber, all plying their trades in the public eye. Between the small, dark, wooden houses sheltering beneath the battlements were little square plots of green planted with onions, leeks and beans. A weaver sat in a doorway with her loom; the fruiterers and fishmongers sold their wares at open booths; before the butcher's shop a sheep's throat was cut in the open street while the purchasers stood by, bargaining over the entrails. In the cobbled square below the castle were a great variety of traders shouting their wares in a language as unintelligible to Nicolette as the cry of the sea birds swooping in the wind above her head.

'The Blessed Virgin protect us, did you ever hear the like?' sobbed Lisette, clutching Nicolette round the waist in terror.

'Be calm,' replied Nicolette with more reassurance than she felt. 'We're almost there, I'm sure.'

Where they were going she had no idea, but her father was pushing his way confidently forward through the throng. Presently he stopped in front of a large house, three storeys high, of stout timbers and whitewashed plaster. William dismounted and climbed the steep outer staircase at the side of the building. A tall, bony man dressed in a gown of dark brown fustian appeared at the head of the steps and embraced William warmly.

'Welcome back, my friend,' he said. 'Jeanne and I have been worried about you. We've been expecting you for at least a week.'

'Let me present my kinswoman Nicolette de Saint Pierre,' said William. 'She is the reason I've been so long in getting to Calais.'

Nicolette's heart sank. Her father obviously regarded her as an impediment despite her best efforts not to slow him down.

'I cannot think of a better reason for delay,' said her father's friend, smiling at her as he descended the stairs.

Somewhat comforted, Nicolette smiled shyly back. William introduced him as Giles de Bourdat, his partner of many years, and disappeared without further preamble into the house, leaving Nicolette to introduce de Bourdat to the knight.

'You must be tired after your journey, damoiselle,' de Bourdat said as he escorted her up the stairs. 'And hungry too. I'll call my wife and see what she can find for dinner.'

The door at the top of the stairs led into a large rectangular room with a high raftered ceiling. It was cool and the rushes on the floor clean and sweet-smelling. Nicolette took a deep appreciative breath and de Bourdat smiled at her sympathetically.

His wife came hurrying into the room. 'Here at last,' she cried, holding out her hands in welcome to William. 'We'd almost given you up, hadn't we, Giles? I had a sheep slaughtered for you in readiness more than a week ago now, but at Mass this morning I saw a swallow skimming in and out of the Lady Chapel and just knew you'd be here today. So as soon as I got home I had it put on the spit and it's been roasting ever since. It will be ready to eat as soon as you want it.'

'There's no hurry for dinner,' William said. 'I'd like to read my letters first and Sir Piers Exton here is anxious for news of the Duke of Lancaster's army.'

Mistress de Bourdat seemed to notice Piers for the first time and instantly bobbed him a curtsey. She was as short and stout as her husband was tall and thin and her simple gown of grey worsted was almost entirely covered with a clean white apron. Piers swept her a low bow as if she were a fine lady and she dimpled and coloured with pleasure.

'Let me commend to your care my kinswoman Nicolette de Saint Pierre,' William went on impassively. 'She has endured a long and tiring journey without complaint and might like to rest. Giles, you and I will go to the counting house and you can inform me of what has been happening since I've been away.'

Nicolette felt cheered by her father's words. It was a crumb, but the first sign of approval he had shown. She raised her eyes to his face in gratitude but he was already hurrying from the room.

Jeanne de Bourdat led her upstairs and ushered her into a small chamber overlooking the street below. 'You can lie down and rest here, damoiselle. I will show your maid where she can draw water for you to wash.' Madame de Bourdat withdrew quickly and Nicolette was left alone for the first time since leaving the abbey.

She gazed around her, marvelling at the large comfortable bed with its embroidered linen hangings, which almost filled the solar, at the table in the window littered with an assortment of trinkets. Hanging on one wall was a piece of polished steel and as she idly looked at it she was startled to catch her own reflection peering nervously back. At Holy Trinity the nuns had not been permitted anything so encouraging to vanity as a mirror, and Nicolette studied this first reflected view of herself with all the wonder of a new discovery. She noticed that her face was dirty and framed by wild tendrils of hair which had escaped the long braid hanging down her back, that her hood and cape were deplorably travel-stained and her grey serge kirtle hung loose and baggy – but not that she was beautiful. She decided that it was a sad, dishevelled picture she presented; no wonder her father was displeased.

When Lisette appeared bearing a jug of water she was full of all the wonders she had seen in the Calais house. 'There's a separate building just for the kitchens,' she said. 'Set all apart in the midst of an orchard of sorts, with apples and quinces growing up out of the kitchen wall. And another chamber even bigger than this off that room downstairs, with a bed in it and all. 'Tis a grand house, this, and no mistaking. Oh, if only Father could see me now, wouldn't he burst himself with pride!'

'He would indeed,' said Nicolette struggling out of her travel-stained habit. Lisette's father was one of the abbey's serfs, the unfortunate begetter of five daughters and no sons. He had jumped at the chance of ridding himself of one of the burdens with which an unjust Creator had seen fit to saddle him. Lisette was an unlikely choice for the task of maid-in-waiting but she had been as glad to escape the crowded hovel she shared with her family as her father was to let her go. She bent and picked up the discarded habit but seemed uncertain what to do with it.

'See if you can clean some of the mud off for me, Lisette,' said Nicolette, as she shook her hair loose.

'Can't I help do your hair first,' Lisette pleaded. 'I never seen hair such as yourn – so long and soft and thick as week-old cream.'

'If you like,' replied Nicolette startled. It took Lisette some time to find the comb among all the fascinating trinkets on the table and Nicolette waited patiently. It was not the girl's fault, she told herself, as Lisette tugged inexpertly at the great curtain of hair which fell to her waist. Lisette had been brought up working all the hours of daylight upon the land, her only shelter a one-roomed peasant's cot which she shared with the animals as well as her family. The journey and these strange surroundings were far more daunting for the maid than they were for herself.

By the time Nicolette's hair was combed and braided, Lisette was close to tears of frustration. 'I never thought hair could be so hard to get straight,' she sniffed. 'It be more lively than a kicking sheep at shearing time.'

'We both of us have so much to learn, but if we just try and perfect one thing at a time, it'll come in the end.' Suddenly Nicolette wondered whether the Abbess had chosen Lisette precisely because the girl would make such an inept maid – to be her private scourge, a hair shirt to keep her from being corrupted by temptation. If only she knew how much I miss the abbey, Nicolette thought, she would not have worried about temptation.

They set about cleaning and brushing the habit, and as soon as she was dressed again, Nicolette went to look in the polished steel hanging on the wall. She was still studying her reflection when Madame de Bourdat came to summon them to dinner.

'You look well rested,' she said, beaming goodnaturedly. 'I hope the bed was comfortable.'

'Yes, thank you, madame, I do feel better,' Nicolette replied, unwilling to admit that she had spent so long restoring her dishevelled appearance.

'If there's anything you lack, you have only to ask and I'll try and find it for you,' promised Madame de Bourdat holding the door open and standing aside for Nicolette to precede her. It was the first time in all her fifteen years that Nicolette had been treated with any hint of deference and she found it unnerving.

She felt even more unnerved when they entered the communal room below. A dozen or so men were gathered round the trestle board, all of whom looked at Nicolette curiously. Eyes downcast, trying furiously not to blush, she took her seat beside her father. Giles de Bourdat was busy carving from a side of mutton at one end of the table and at the other his wife began to ladle a sticky mess of frumenty into bowls. Opposite sat Sir Piers Exton, his eyes warm with approval. Remembering the image of herself she had seen in the polished steel, Nicolette felt a tiny glow of pleasure. It was an entirely new sensation and she smiled at him more confidently.

'Have you had any news yet of the Duke of Lancaster's army?' she asked. Without his armour he looked strangely vulnerable, she thought, noting how his fustian tunic was sadly worn. He was gazing at her longingly, but it was William Gryffard who answered.

'I'm afraid Sir Piers has come too late to take part in the Spanish adventure. John of Gaunt sailed for Spain more than a month ago.'

'More than a month?' she exclaimed softly, full of sympathy for Piers. 'Are you sure?'

'I met a merchant in the town just newly arrived from Brest,' Piers told her. 'He owes his liberty and probably his life to Lancaster. Brest's been besieged all summer by the Duke of Brittany, who to prove his new-born loyalty to France has been besieging the English garrison there. The besiegers built two forts, one uncomfortably near the walls of the town, from which they've been harassing the garrison. But word of their plight reached John of Gaunt as he left for Spain and he thought nothing of making a detour in order to land his men and allow Lord Fitzwalter to storm the forts. The siege was raised and the Duke continued on his way to Spain. The merchant was very glad to be able to escape unscathed from Brest.'

'At a cost of some valuable lives, I don't doubt,' muttered William disapprovingly. 'It's just the sort of thing the Duke of Lancaster would do. An extravagant waste of money and time and lives. He'll never get to Spain if he goes on like that.'

'But noble,' murmured Nicolette, dipping her spoon into her bowl of steaming frumenty.

'That's the sort of overlord to have,' declared Piers. 'Maybe I could catch up with him. I'd like to serve under such a man. Do you think I could get a ship to take me to Spain?'

'I doubt if any of us will find a ship to take us anywhere,'

27

William said gloomily. 'Nearly all our English merchant ships have been pressed into the Duke's service, I'm told, and even then the Portuguese had to send a naval force of ten galleys and half a dozen smaller ships to help. A force that large poses a huge transport difficulty.'

Piers looked so crestfallen that Nicolette felt compelled to come to his rescue. 'Why don't you come with us to England?' she said without thinking. The look of joy on his face was her reward.

'What would you do in England, Sir Piers?' demanded William, frowning at Nicolette.

'I don't know.' Instantly the knight was downcast again.

Nicolette applied herself once again to the frumenty in her bowl, aware that she had displeased her father again.

'Of course King Richard needs swords,' William said thoughtfully.

'He has the Earl of Arundel, with his castles on the March and fiefs in Sussex, or Thomas Mowbray, Earl of Nottingham, whose family is an ancient power in Northumberland and Norfolk, or Warwick, who may be the most powerful of all,' Piers objected. 'He doesn't need me.'

'The King doesn't trust them, they're too powerful.'

'If they're so powerful, why did the King let the Duke of Lancaster go?' asked Nicolette, trying to understand.

'Because Lancaster is the one the King fears and distrusts the most,' William explained. 'When the King took an army to Scotland last year, Gaunt's men numbered nearly half as many again as the King's own levies, more than three times those of his brother the Earl of Buckingham and five times as many as those of the Earl of Northumberland.'

'You're very well informed,' said Piers. 'I've been away from England for so long I hardly know what's going on in my native land any more. The news we got in Florence and Venice was always very confused. We never knew who to believe.'

'Information is the most important weapon a merchant can have,' replied William. 'Prior knowledge of events is all that stands between me and my rivals. I pay well for good information and even better if the news is bad. Disaster brings the biggest losses, but there is profit, too, to be made in times of trouble – with prior knowledge.'

Nicolette watched her father in fascination, for his pallid

28

features were tinged with colour and for the first time he seemed almost animated. He caught her looking at him and bent over his bowl of frumenty, scooping up the boiled wheat with pieces of his trencher bread and popping them into his mouth while the sweetening honey dribbled down his chin. From time to time he darted quick penetrating glances round the table, reminding her of a spider busily spinning a web for the unwary. She thrust the thought firmly from her as Giles de Bourdat picked up a jug of wine and began moving round the table filling goblets.

'I thought the King had healed the breach with Gaunt,' said Piers. 'I thought he needed Gaunt to keep his other uncles at bay.'

'He does, but I'm afraid he so distrusts Lancaster that he has forgotten the others.' William turned to look at Nicolette. 'But the Duke of Gloucester is hungry for power and a troublemaker, and the Duke of York might throw in his lot with anyone who forced him to it. With Lancaster off on this wild goose chase to conquer Spain for his wife, who knows what mischief might be brewing?'

'You don't think the Duke of Lancaster will succeed?' asked Nicolette.

'With ten thousand men?' William impaled a hunk of mutton on his eating knife and pointed it at Piers as he leant across the table. 'You're the soldier, what do you say? Can you conquer a country the size of Spain with ten thousand men?'

'It's enough to prolong the war there against the King of Castile and his French allies,' replied Piers, 'but no, not enough to conquer Spain.'

It was strange, Nicolette thought, that the knight could be so tongue-tied with her and yet when he was talking to her father he was self-confident and at ease.

'Does Lancaster want to be King of Spain?' she asked him.

Again it was William who answered. 'The Duke of Lancaster has always wanted to be a king. First he thought he might rule England, but he gave up that dream, probably when he married the Queen of Castile. Through her he believed he could become King of Spain. He has invaded Spain before but it was not a success. Now he's older and, who knows, perhaps may even have learnt something from his many military failures. This time he has left his heir

Henry Bolingbroke behind and taken his daughters. Perhaps after sufficient time has elapsed he will attempt to do by diplomacy, through the marriage of one of his daughters, what he cannot do by force.'

'If the Duke means to make peace with the Castilians through diplomacy, why take an army?' asked Nicolette. 'Isn't it all a great waste of money?'

'You may well be right.' William turned to look at her again, smiling at her almost warmly and she felt relieved that she had pleased him a little.

'It won't be a waste if it brings peace,' replied Piers. 'A show of force such as the Duke brings with him will make his diplomacy more effective than any negotiations or beauty on the part of his daughters.'

'I agree,' said William. 'But Lancaster's absence leaves the King dangerously exposed. He has no army of his own, remember, only what the magnates bring into the field at his command.'

'What would you do if you were me, Master Gryffard?' asked Piers. 'Should I seek to become a retainer of the King's or one of his magnates?'

'I'd apprentice myself to a good master in an important city such as London, learn a trade, marry his daughter and set about making a fortune,' said William with the glimmer of a smile.

'I don't want a fortune,' said Piers, and William looked genuinely shocked.

In the embarrassed silence that ensued, Nicolette leant forward and asked the knight softly, 'What do you want?'

'Adventure . . . a cause worth fighting for.' He was gazing at her longingly again. Whatever it was Piers felt for her, it wasn't disapproval, that she knew, and it made her feel all warm inside. Her heart skipped a beat as she held his glance and decided he did not look vulnerable after all but noble somehow in his simplicity.

'He wants dragons to slay,' William interjected harshly. 'You'd better offer your sword to King Richard, he has plenty of dragons you can slay for him.'

Nicolette felt guilty – her father was displeased. Was it because she had tried to be kind to Piers?

'How long do you think it will be before we can set sail?' she asked.

'I don't know. The wind is rising and they say we're in for a storm. First we have to find a ship, and a master bold enough to take us to England. With the greater part of the English marine engaged in the Duke of Lancaster's service, it leaves the seas dangerously open to the French and the pirates.'

'I wouldn't worry about the French, or the pirates either. They'd be useless against a few good English archers properly deployed,' reassured Piers.

'I shall fear nothing if I have you and your squire to protect me,' replied William and Nicolette glanced at him in surprise. But he wasn't smiling and Piers looked crestfallen so she supposed her father hadn't meant it as a compliment after all. Couldn't he just occasionally be a little encouraging, she thought and smiled sympathetically at Piers, to make up for her father's sarcasm. Piers blushed with pleasure but William was unimpressed.

'No doubt you can find lodging for yourself and your squire with the garrison,' he said. 'Perhaps you would find out for me how ready they are to withstand a siege. If the French attack Calais, we cannot count on the Duke of Lancaster to come to the rescue as he did at Brest. If Calais is to fall into French hands, I want my business out of here long before. When the storm subsides, come and find me here. Meanwhile, Giles, you and I must conduct our business as expediently as possible.'

Nicolette relaxed as she finished her dinner, looking forward to at least a few days of comfort and rest under Madame de Bourdat's motherly care. She was glad that Piers was to accompany them to England. She looked at her father timidly, hoping for some sign that he was glad to have her with him at last. He returned her look, eyes narrowed.

'Giles,' he shouted down the table to his partner in a voice for all to hear. 'Ask your wife to find this child something to wear. She cannot go around in that ugly postulant's habit any longer. I'm sick of the sight of her in it.'

All Nicolette's joy vanished, quenched like the flickering flame of a candle beneath the snuffer, and she hung her head in shame. Would he never be pleased?

CHAPTER 4

A week later, on the eve of Holy Cross Day, Nicolette stood on the quay dressed in a robe of bleached linen covered by a surcoat of rose damask edged with fur. Her hair was braided into two neat coils on either side of her head and hidden by a wimple which framed her face becomingly.

William had found a ship. A Genoese galley bringing wine from Bordeaux to London had been blown off course by the storm and forced to seek shelter in Calais. The storm had abated now and the *Santa Maria Nuova* was getting ready to put to sea again. The quay had been as busy as a hive of bees since dawn but now the activity had reached a frenzy which betokened that the tide was on the turn.

Piers had persuaded a half-score of English archers to travel home to England at William's expense in exchange for their protection on the way. Now he was standing fully armed watching anxiously while his horse, with much high pitched whinnying, was slung aboard the galley. A train of packhorses were resting from their labours, while William stood fussing over a pile of bulky packages being loaded onto the galley. Giles de Bourdat waited anxiously by his side, a sheaf of papers in his hand.

At the foot of the rickety ladder hanging over the ship's side, the other passengers had gathered. Nicolette gazed at the great expanse of restless water stretching into the blue horizon. There was something exhilarating about the sea, about the mysterious contrast between the smooth blue tranquillity of the ocean and the violent turbulence of the waves hurtling themselves with such relentless force upon the long ribbons of white sand stretching out of sight on either side of the harbour. Across that living blue-grey mass with its little flecks of white lay England and her unknown future.

'I wish you were coming with us, Jeanne,' she said, turning impulsively to the stout little woman at her side.

'Bless you, child, you don't need me in England.' Jeanne de Bourdat smiled. 'William Gryffard's house in London is far too grand for the likes of us.'

'But how shall I manage without you there to guide me?' For a moment Nicolette's spirit quailed.

'You'll manage, for you're quick to learn. Already you're a different young woman from the travel-worn little novice who arrived in Calais barely a week ago.'

It was true, thought Nicolette. This morning when she had peeped at herself in the polished steel on the wall of the solar she had been pleased at what she saw. She was getting used to looking at her reflection and the thrill of surprised enjoyment it gave her. Her father had been right. The habit she had worn at Holy Trinity was horribly ugly.

'I wish there was something I could do to thank you,' she said.

'I don't need thanks,' declared Jeanne, enfolding her in a warm embrace. 'It was easy.'

'You can't say teaching Lisette to sew was easy,' laughed Nicolette as she hugged her back.

'No, that wasn't easy,' Jeanne agreed, 'but I think she's learnt something. You must be patient with Lisette and persevere with her. If you take the time now to teach her well you will gain in the end. A maid's no good to you if she can't mend and remake things as well as wash and clean. Everything she knows she must learn from you and that will be your reward in the end. She's already devoted to you and she speaks your language. You will be grateful for that during your first months in England.'

'Master Gryffard doesn't seem to mind that I don't speak English,' Nicolette replied swiftly.

'Master Gryffard can be proud of you whatever,' Jeanne declared.

Nicolette glanced over her shoulder at her father. She had not been long in the house at Calais before she realised that Giles and Jeanne de Bourdat were much in awe of him. Jeanne had confided, one day when they were busy at work in the solar on Nicolette's new kirtle, that her husband had come to Calais, like William himself, a penniless apprentice and like him had attempted to set up business in France. But Giles was less fortunate, or less shrewd, than William; he had failed in all his ventures and had been imprisoned for debt. After his release he took service under William. 'For eight years he dwelt with Master Gryffard at a fixed salary with which he bought his own clothing and food, sharing half his bread with his brother and his brother's children who were as misfortunate as he and whom he loved better than himself.'

'What happened to his brother?'

'He and his family went to be Master Gryffard's agent in Bruges and that was when we were able to be married.'

'How kind Master Gryffard is, although I don't think he likes people to know it,' said Nicolette, eager to discover good in her father. 'I suppose he thinks people might try to get the better of him if they thought he was too easy.'

'William Gryffard is as careful with his kindness as he is with everything else,' said Jeanne attacking the rose damask with quick sharp jabs of her needle. 'He was lucky to find someone like Giles, for you could not get a more loyal or more honest man. For twelve years he has been Master Gryffard's partner without adding a penny that was not due to him to his share of the profits. Even when Master Gryffard began to prosper and Giles shared in the profits, his first thought was to pay off his old creditors. He desires neither riches nor advantage and he will not rest until each man has been fully recompensed.'

'I think that Master Gryffard secretly admires such nobleness of spirit,' said Nicolette. 'Look how kind he has been to Sir Piers who has beggared himself with his generosity.'

'Ah, now Sir Piers is a true knight errant.' Jeanne put down her needle and gazed at Nicolette. 'He would make you a wonderful husband.'

'A husband? Sir Piers?' exclaimed Nicolette, completely taken aback.

'Anyone with half an eye can see that he is head over heels in love with you.'

Nicolette looked up from the seam she was sewing and stared at Jeanne in bewilderment. Marriage was something she had never even thought about. 'Do you think my—' she was about to say father but stopped herself in time, 'my kinsman wants me to marry Sir Piers?' she asked, her thoughts in a whirl.

Jeanne shook her head sadly. 'William Gryffard would

never let you marry a landless knight. But maybe he intends to help him to a fortune. You never can tell with Master Gryffard what plans he has in mind. What is certain is that if he's befriending that young man, it's for some purpose of his own.'

Nicolette bent over the damask and tried to concentrate on making small neat stitches as she thought about marriage to Piers. He was certainly interesting, young and strong and apparently devoted, but until a week ago she had been entirely committed to becoming a nun. Piers was the first young man she had ever met and the thought of marriage was both strange and frightening. To calm herself she asked Jeanne to tell her more about William Gryffard, but Jeanne merely shook her head.

'Don't try too hard to find out about him,' she warned. 'He likes his secrets. Much better not to pry.'

Now, standing on the quay waiting to depart, Nicolette watched her father poring over documents with Giles. Even now, she thought, at the moment of departure, he was still hard at work. She supposed that it was his infinite capacity for taking pains that had helped to make him so successful and it made her feel more proud of him.

Piers was scrambling up the ladder over the ship's side. In full armour it was not an easy exercise and he could not help looking ungainly, rather like a crab hauling itself over the rocks, she thought. The other passengers were following Piers: two Italians looking far too hot in their robes of velvet, some vintners accompanying their wine to England and a pardoner who had been plying his trade until the very last minute and was probably even now hoping to sell more ecclesiastical indulgences to the sailors aboard the galley. The master bellowed from the galley to hurry. William thrust the papers at his partner and beckoned Nicolette to follow as he hastened to obey the master's bidding. Jeanne embraced Nicolette again.

'May God and His blessed saints go with you and keep you safe until you reach London.'

'I know He will,' Nicolette replied.

'I'll light a candle to Saint Nicholas – he's the sailor's saint – and keep it burning day and night until I learn of your safe arrival,' Jeanne promised.

Giles came hurrying over. 'This is a sad day for us, damoiselle,' he said. 'The house won't seem the same now.'

'I shall never forget your many kindnesses,' Nicolette said, smiling at him. 'And I'll miss you too, you and your wife. I wish you were coming with us to London.'

Giles turned away abruptly and rounded on Lisette who was clutching Nicolette's travelling cloak in her arms and viewing the *Santa Maria Nuova* with the gravest misgiving.

'What's the matter, Lisette?' he demanded with uncharacteristic brusqueness. 'You aren't afraid of the sea on a beautiful sunny day like today?'

'I don't trust the weather and I don't trust the water neither,' declared Lisette with a sniff. 'And least of all I don't trust that there ladder.'

'I dare say Sir Piers can arrange to have you slung aboard like his horse,' answered Nicolette laughing gaily as she seized hold of the ladder. 'Come on, Lisette. It's much easier than riding that dreadful horse.'

The master of the galley, a burly Genoese built like a bull, escorted them to his cabin and told them to stay there since a ship at sea was no place for women to be wandering about. Nicolette had a brief glimpse of a row of slaves chained to their oars in the waist of the ship, of a loosened sail flapping in the gentle breeze, of the archers grinning down at her from the castellated poop before she was shown into a small stuffy enclosure no bigger than a closet. It was not what she had expected but she thrust aside her disappointment and resigned herself to comforting her maid, who was already on her knees and at her prayers.

'Courage, Lisette,' she said as she settled down on the hard bed fixed to the wall. 'Lie down here with me to rest and when we wake up we'll find ourselves in England.'

'The Blessed Mother save us, there's no rest to be had travelling about the world,' muttered Lisette.

It was not long before Nicolette reluctantly wondered whether Lisette might perhaps be right, for despite the bright sunshine and gentle breeze, the recent storm had left a heavy swell and the galley began to pitch and roll as soon as they were out of the harbour.

'Blessed Saint Christopher, we shall all be drowned,' cried Lisette as the *Santa Maria Nuova* shuddered and slid down to the bottom of a wave.

Nicolette closed her eyes and murmured a swift Hail Mary while the ship settled in the trough for what seemed eternity before beginning to climb out of it with another stomach-churning lurch. Lisette groaned. Nicolette clutched her beads to her breast and added a Paternoster as the ship gave another lurch, shivered and plunged into the next trough with a roll which knocked Nicolette sideways on to the bed. It did not seem possible that the ship would recover but with another sickening lurch she did, and after several more Nicolette realised that the *Santa Maria Nuova* was as buoyant as she was lively.

As time went on Nicolette detected a certain rhythm to the pitching and rolling, and began to feel exhilarated by the galley's wild dance with the waves. By this time poor Lisette was retching into a leather bucket, presumably provided for the purpose, but Nicolette was relieved to discover that she did not feel sick. She longed to be out on deck away from the stench of vomit, to feel the salt wind on her face, to be able to watch the mighty sea in all its restless energy, but she did not dare disobey the master. Instead she made Lisette lie down on the bed beside her and urged her to forget her sufferings in sleep.

Nicolette did not know how long she slept, but she awoke immediately aware of a different tempo in the dance. The pitching and rolling seemed less violent, but the *Santa Maria Nuova* appeared to be moving through the water faster. To the noise of creaking timber there was now added the steady beat of a drum, the sound of men shouting, and running feet. The door burst open suddenly, bringing with it great blasts of invigorating air. 'All the men who aren't fighters get in here with the women,' shouted the master, snatching down a rusty breastplate and helmet hanging on the wall.

'What's the matter? What's happening?' Nicolette cried, jumping up in alarm.

'An alien ship,' announced the captain, as William, the two Italians, the pardoner and the vintners stumbled into the cabin like a lot of frightened sheep.

'Is it the French?' she asked, bewildered. 'Surely the French wouldn't attack a Genoese.'

'The pirates or the French, it doesn't much matter. She don't mean to be friendly,' retorted the master with an oath. 'Would to God I'd never let you persuade me to bring all that cloth from Arras instead of more men-at-arms,' he added, stabbing an angry finger at William. 'It'll be your fault if we're taken.'

To Nicolette's dismayed surprise, her father did not attempt to remonstrate, just stumbled over to the bed where he collapsed, white and shaking.

'What of Sir Piers Exton?' Indignantly Nicolette challenged the master. How dared he blame her father!

'What indeed! If he's the young knight who's been puking his gizzards out ever since we left Calais, he can't make it from the poop to this cabin, let alone stand up and fight,' said the captain in disgust. 'Here,' he added, flipping a coin at the pardoner, 'it looks as if I'm going to need remission for my sins sooner than I thought.' So saying he locked them in and departed.

The smell of fear in the tiny cabin was stronger even than the stench of vomit as they all began to pray and make vows. The Italians prayed to St James and vowed to go on pilgrimage to Compostela in Spain if he would but save them. The vintners prayed to St Martin and promised to build a chapel in his honour. The pardoner did a brisk trade selling pardons but Nicolette doubted whether he had enough faith in them, for his face was the colour of his own parchment and his hand shook so much he could barely get the coins they gave him into his money bag. As Nicolette listened to their desperate promises, she realised with a thrill of exaltation that she was not afraid. Her conscience was clear, her belief in her salvation absolute. There was nothing to be afraid of but fear itself. She had lived all her life so close to God that the thought of meeting Him now did not worry her.

She looked at her father, remembering the Abbess's aweful, angry words: 'Thou fool, this day thy soul shall be required of thee,' and trembled at the swift accuracy of the prophecy. Was it too late for him to repent, to promise the refectory and the chantry and to send her back to Caen? William sat with his pardon clenched between his shaking hands and trembled from head to foot as if with an ague. With a shock of dismay Nicolette realised he was so afraid he could not even pray. What should she do? Did she dare remind him of the Abbess's words? If ever she were to persuade him to let her go back to Holy Trinity, now was the moment.

'I don't want to die. Not yet. Now now,' sobbed Lisette.

Nicolette put an arm round the maid and tried to think of some words of comfort. But her mouth had gone suddenly dry. The fear in the cabin was very contagious. I don't want to die either, she thought. Not now, not just when life is beginning to be so exciting. And I no longer want to be a nun. Was such a thought blasphemy on the brink of eternity? She crossed herself quickly. Remember what you have been taught, the Abbess had said, and you will come to no harm. Nicolette had been taught to pray. It was as natural to her as waking and sleeping, and so she knelt upon the heaving floor of the cabin, clutching at the edge of the wooden bed for support, and started with the night office, lauds and matins, then progressed to prime, terce, compline and the Angelus, repeating out loud the familiar words she had learnt as soon as she could talk and had repeated day in, day out since childhood.

Outside the cabin the master uttered a series of hearty curses as he watched the sail clearly visible above the white crest of the waves. Piers leant against the mast, held upright by his squire, also watching.

'Can't you stay out of the way?' the master bellowed. 'I've a mind to lock you in my cabin with the rest of them, only I doubt there's room for any more and they don't want you puking all over 'em.'

Piers paid no attention. His eyes were fixed on the white sails of the pursuing ship. 'Do you think they'll catch us?' he asked.

'It looks like it. They're a cog not a galley. They've more sail and they're running before the wind.'

'Can't you alter course?'

'It won't do any good. The only thing that'll save us is if the wind drops, and there's no hope of that this side of nightfall.'

'You could throw the cargo overboard, it might lighten us a bit,' said Piers, frowning.

'What would be the use? It'd only give us a few more miles, they'd still catch us in the end. Better to keep the cargo. If they're pirates they'll be happier if they get a good haul and they'll likely treat the women better. Though I don't hold out much hope for that pretty young thing in there. She's a tasty morsel for any man.'

'Then we'll make a fight of it,' announced Piers.

'Six archers can't do much,' replied the master. 'They'll have three score men at the very least. My sailors'll do their best after they board us but I doubt they'll be much use against trained men-at-arms, and I daren't unchain the slaves. We're done for. Merciful Jesus,' he swore as Piers doubled up and retched helplessly. 'Can't you do that with your back to the wind?' But Piers was slumped against the mast, his face the colour of saffron and his armour flecked with vomit, gasping for breath.

With another oath the master ran down into the waist of the galley where the slaves laboured at their oars in time to the beat of the drum.

'The devil take you for a whore's bastard,' he shouted

at the slave master. 'Can't you go faster?'

The drumbeat quickened and the slave master screamed at the rowers as he brought the thick hide of his lash across their backs. The oars flashed in and out of the water as the slaves redoubled their efforts, but in this sea and with this wind, the captain knew it was a waste of time. He watched helplessly as the pursuing ship closed the gap. He could not recognise the flag which fluttered from her masthead but he could see the men gathered along her rails, grappling irons in their hands. There was no doubting their purpose. In desperation he looked up at the crenellated poop and uttered a string of obscene profanities in French and Italian and English. The knight had his helmet on now and was standing with drawn sword, a lonely and ridiculous figure of defiance. Their pursuer plunged and reared towards them across the restless sea, her many sails straining taut in the wind, sweeping nearer like a charging war horse in pursuit of an ambling palfrey.

'Sir Piers says to stop the rowers.' It was the squire, standing by his side.

'What?' The master stared at the boy, about to argue.

'Do it!' Esmon shouted urgently and without waiting for a reply ran back across the plunging deck towards the poop. With a resigned curse the captain passed the order. The slaves were about to collapse anyway. It would make no difference now.

Up on the poop, the English archers knelt behind the low parapet with only the tips of their longbows showing, while Piers with raised visor bent double in an agony of retching.

'How much longer?' grumbled one of the archers fitting an arrow to his bow. 'By the bones of Saint Michael, they'll be upon us before you're done.'

'Wait!' Piers gasped, straightening up, eyes streaming. 'We can't afford to waste arrows, or time, once they come within range. They'll be an easy target all gathered together in the waist like that. But you'll have to be quick. When the rowers stop, that'll be our chance.' The cog was almost level when the beat of the drum suddenly ceased. The slaves slumped exhausted over their oars. The galley crested a wave, hung poised at the top looking down on the other ship.

'Now!' shouted Piers.

Six long poles bent like saplings in the wind as the archers' muscles bulged and arrows flew swift and straight to find their mark. Men fell but the archers did not wait to see them drop. They fitted fresh arrows, bent the bow, released the string again and again and again, all in one continuous rhythmic movement, pouring a constant hail of murderous fire into the midst of the attackers. The galley wallowed in the trough of a wave. A crossbow bolt flew overhead.

'Shall I start the rowers?' asked Esmon.

'Wait,' said Piers, then to the archer nearest him, 'do you think you can reach the helmsman?'

Esmon ducked as a crossbow bolt glanced off Piers's steel breastplate. The archers continued to fire from bended knee, pouring wave after wave of arrows into the crowded waist of the enemy, while most of the returning crossbow fire fell harmlessly into the sea between. Suddenly the sails of the cog began to flutter uncertainly as the helmsman staggered backwards, an arrow through his helm. The ship began to lose way as she came off the wind.

'Start the rowers!' yelled Piers, leaning over the side of the poop. This time the master leapt to do his bidding. As the drumbeat began again, the slaves bent willingly to their oars. The galley gained a little ground.

'Give them hell!' shouted Piers.

The archers sprang to their feet, still pouring their deadly fire into the confusion on the cog's deck. Their quivers were emptying fast.

'Enough,' said Piers, holding up his hand as arrows began to drop into the sea. 'Save them in case she comes again.'

But their pursuer had had enough. When at length her sails filled once more, it was to turn away in search of easier prey. The captain crossed himself. 'God and Saint Nicholas be praised,' he muttered as the galley began to pull away, rising and falling in the heavy swell. A cheer rose up from the poop.

'The English!' muttered the captain, shaking his head in baffled relief. 'Madmen, all of them.' The archers were holding their bows above their heads in triumph but Piers was slumped against the parapet, endlessly voiding his empty, tortured stomach.

On the eve of St Matthew, the *Santa Maria Nuova* anchored in the River Thames. Nicolette emerged thankfully from the stuffy cabin and stared across the water in wonder at the city. It seemed to be made of turrets and towers, the light of the setting sun gilding their spires so they glowed like a hundred candles. 'So many churches,' she murmured. 'And that one on the hill above all the rest, its spire must stretch up almost to heaven itself.'

'Saint Paul's Cathedral. It's the biggest in the city,' said a voice behind her and she turned to find Piers regarding her gravely. It was the first time she had seen him since they had left Calais and she was dismayed by his sorry appearance. He had laid aside his armour and, in his old fustian tunic, looked ill and somehow helpless. Filled with pity for him she turned away, wanting to comfort him for his failure to overcome his seasickness but not knowing how. She did not know, because the Genoese captain had not thought it worth mentioning, that they owed their deliverance to the presence of mind of one seasick knight and the skill of a few English archers. The Italians were convinced that a vision of St James the Apostle had appeared above the masthead and frightened away the enemy. The vintners that St Martin had intervened. Nicolette thought that perhaps her prayers had something to do with it. A miracle was a miracle. It did not do to question whence it came.

Spanning the Thames like a great wall a short way upriver was a bridge with massive arches and buttresses and houses leaning out over the water.

'Is that really just a bridge?' asked Nicolette.

'London Bridge, the finest in England,' Piers told her. 'With a gatehouse and a drawbridge and even a chapel.'

As she gazed at it in awe, a line of rowing boats came skimming between the arches towards the galley to help with the unloading, darting in and out of the more stately sailing barges tacking to and fro. Then suddenly there came from every part of the ship the sound of men's voices raised in song.

'What is it?' she asked, startled.

'The traditional hymn of praise to Saint Nicholas,' Piers replied. 'It's the custom whenever a ship reaches port safely.'

Nicolette stood listening to the chant coming from the throats of the rough men who earned their livelihood on the sea and from the slaves who toiled in captivity. It was simple, moving and all the more poignant after their miraculous escape. 'I used to think the singing in the abbey was the finest sound in all the world but this is even more beautiful,' she said, turning to smile at Piers impulsively.

'Nothing could be more beautiful than the way you look now,' he said. 'I shall carry the memory of it in my heart until we meet again.'

She felt warmed by the fervour in his eyes and her pity for

him was touched with regret. 'Aren't you coming with us into London?' she asked.

'Not at once. Master Gryffard wants me to see to the unloading of his arras cloth and then there's my horse and the archers. It will all take time. But if there is any way in which I can ever be of service, you have only to send for me and I will come.'

She turned away from his ardent gaze to hide a smile. His fine words fitted so ill with his gaunt appearance. The boats were now clustered round the galley like a colony of industrious ants and Nicolette could see her father hurrying towards her, driving Lisette before him like a flustered sheep. She turned to Piers, aware that she would miss him.

'How will I know where to find you?' she asked.

'I'll keep in touch,' he promised.

When William reached her side, he was in a hurry as usual. 'Over the side with you, Lisette,' he said, ignoring the knight, 'and you too, Nicolette. We want to be in the city before nightfall.'

She held out her hand to Piers, but he backed away from it. 'Aren't you going to help me on to the ladder?' she asked, unable to suppress the tiny thrill of conquest at the helpless longing on his face. He sprang forward, but it was William who grasped her hand and steadied her as she climbed over the ship's side and scrambled down the ladder into the boat waiting to ferry them to the bank.

They were rowed ashore to the sound of the Angelus. Nicolette bowed her head and counted her Hail Marys as first one church bell then another and another came pealing across the water in a great cacophony of joyous harmony. Her soul thrilling to the magic of the bells and her mind clouded with excitement, she forgot Piers as she gazed at the jumble of buildings crowding down to the water's edge and drawing nearer with every stroke of the waterman's oars. Perched on the edge of the river bank but standing remote and aloof just outside the city wall was a huge white-walled fortress. When Nicolette asked what it was, William told her it was the Tower of London, the King's stronghold, a place of imprisonment and of execution, and also a palace. She shivered. 'It looks impregnable,' she breathed, gazing in fascination at the great stone walls rising almost out of the River Thames.

'It was built to be impregnable,' William said, 'and yet it fell to an army of peasants back in the fourth year of the King's reign and the Archbishop of Canterbury and the

King's Treasurer were brutally beheaded by the mob.'

'Were you there?' she asked, troubled by something in his face.

'I was in the Tower that fateful day, yes,' he said, crossing himself. 'But I escaped, by the grace of God.' She longed to ask him all about it, but the waterman was bringing his boat up to a crowded wharf and there was no more time for questions.

Leaving the warehouses and the wharves of the river bank, they walked at first through narrow little lanes which became wider and more salubrious as they left Billingsgate behind. London was so much bigger than Calais that here the various different crafts had whole streets to themselves. The candle-makers were all concentrated in Candlewick, the bakers in Bread Street, the sellers of fine imported silks and velvets in the Mercery, and the goldsmiths' booths were lined up all along one side of the wide thoroughfare of Chepe. William Gryffard had built his house on a plot of land just south of the Priory of St Helen's in the north-east part of the city between the Church of St Andrew Undershaft and St Peter's Upon Cornhill.

On entering the great hall, Nicolette gasped at the sheer splendour of its painted walls, tiled floors, and lofty timbered roof. It was bigger than anything at Holy Trinity and much more colourful. The walls were painted with hunting scenes: Atalanta hunting a wild boar; Diana, dressed in a mantle of bright green, mounted on a stag and holding a bow and arrow with a sickle moon and hounds at her feet. It is pagan, thought Nicolette, shocked.

A thin, stooping man in a gown of grey fustian came forward to greet them, whom William introduced as his steward Adam Stickleby.

'This is my kinswoman, the Damoiselle Nicolette de Saint Pierre,' William said.

Nicolette smiled uncertainly and held out her hand. The steward bowed over it humbly and Nicolette felt a quiver of excitement. All her life she had been taught to be humble, penitent and obedient. Now here in this grand mansion of her father's the steward was bowing to her.

'We shall have supper in an hour,' William declared. 'From tomorrow the damoiselle will have the ordering of the household.' He repeated the words in French to Nicolette and her elation evaporated. The nuns had not taught her how to run a household, only how to read and write, sew and sing.

The steward was marshalling the various members of the

44

household into a long line to meet her and she gazed at them bewildered. There were so many of them. How was she to manage them when she could not speak their language and did not even know what they were all for? With longing she thought of Jeanne de Bourdat and wished that warm and friendly woman was here to advise her now. They were all looking at her expectantly, including William, whose watchful eyes narrowed. Then she remembered him white and shaking as he clutched his pardon between his clenched hands in the cabin of the *Santa Maria Nuova*. She had not been afraid then and she had not been sick; and would not let him get the better of her now. She felt hot and dirty and tired after the long walk from the river.

'Perhaps I could be shown to a chamber where I might rest until supper,' she said in French. Her father was pleased. She could see it in the brief twitch of his lips which was his apology for a smile.

He led her out of the hall and up a wide stone staircase to the solar above. It too was richly and lavishly furnished, oppressively so. Nicolette looked at the large bed with its many pillows and silken hangings, at the carved table in the window embrasure, the prie-dieu in the corner, the painted chest at the foot of the bed, the polished steel hanging on the wall between the gilded prickets with their beeswax candles. 'Is it all really necessary?' she whispered, shocked by such extravagance.

'Of course it's necessary,' William retorted, throwing open the lid of the painted chest. 'Just as it is necessary for you to wear fine clothes and learn to dress in the height of fashion. You must be able to hold up your head among the people who count in this city.' She watched as he carefully unpacked the contents of the chest and laid them one by one upon the bed. 'All these belonged to my first wife, Mariota,' he said. 'She was about your age when I married her.'

'Was she very beautiful?' asked Nicolette, sensing some great tragedy.

'Yes, she was beautiful and she thought she was in love with a handsome knight. But her father was in debt to me and so I bought her. She married me to save her father from ruin – because she was good and obedient as well as beautiful.' His face showed no emotion.

'What happened to her?' Nicolette persevered, determined to find a way to his heart.

'Mariota died – in the Peasants' Revolt.'

'Did you love her very much?'

45

'Love,' he scoffed. 'There's no such thing. Love's just a trick dreamt up by minstrels for foolish knights to justify their need to practise fighting.'

Nicolette gazed at him miserably. Surely he did not mean what he said. He was hurt, so deeply hurt by Mariota's tragedy it had made him bitter.

'I married Mariota because I lusted after her,' William went on. 'And because I thought her father might one day become Mayor of London. He could have been very useful to me. But Mariota died and her father chose the wrong side in the battle for power in the city. Because of his foolishness I had to leave London for a time. The second time I married I did so for good, sound commercial reasons. She was the widow of a prosperous Venetian merchant and brought me some very useful trade concessions. She died in the spring of this year, which is why I've come back to live in London again.'

'But my mother,' she cried out impulsively. 'You must have loved my mother.'

'Your mother made a mistake!' He glared at her fiercely. 'You were that mistake, which is why your mother had to become a nun.'

Sweet Jesus! Jeanne de Bourdat had warned not to pry into his secrets! 'Could you not have married her?' she whispered, shame driving out her sympathy.

'I was a young wool merchant struggling to make my first fortune and your mother was nobly born. It was foolish.' He turned away abruptly, bent over the coffer so she could not see his face. It was clear that he was not going to confide in her. Perhaps when he knew her better, trusted her more, he might allow her to come closer.

'Mariota was a little smaller than you are,' he said, throwing another bundle of silk upon the bed, 'but you are a good needlewoman and should be able to alter it all to fit. The jewels I'll bring tomorrow.'

Nicolette gazed at the mantles trimmed with fur, scarlet silks, pale pink taffetas, embroidered surcoats, veils, head-dresses, girdles woven with silver thread. She could not believe she could be expected to need so much for her personal adornment. It was against all her training and upbringing, completely foreign to everything she had been taught. 'What am I to do with it all?' she asked, bewildered.

'Do?' he exclaimed, seizing her by the wrist and dragging her to the polished steel hanging on the wall.

'Make the best of yourself, of course.'

She peered at the image of herself in the fine new clothes she and Jeanne de Bourdat had toiled to perfect. 'What is wrong with the way I am now?' she asked, genuinely perplexed.

He stood close behind her and studied her reflection with a deliberation which made her tremble. Then he leant forward and carefully unwound the wimple which covered her head and neck, exposing the exquisite line of her throat. His eyes met hers in the mirror then dropped to the edge of her low-cut kirtle which barely covered the small mounds of her young breasts.

'You are a rare beauty, my child,' he said, 'and beauty has its price. But it needs to be polished and refined like a fine jewel to bring it to perfection. You must learn how to set off your beauty.'

'Why?' she asked, stung. 'Why must I? Sir Piers thinks I'm quite beautiful enough as it is.'

'By the Blessed Virgin!' he exploded. 'What has Sir Piers Exton to do with the matter?'

'Don't you want me to marry Sir Piers?' she asked, crestfallen.

'A landless knight?' He laughed mirthlessly. 'No, I most certainly do not want you to marry that young man.'

If Piers was so unsuitable, why had he bothered to befriend him? She gazed at her father bewildered but the face in the mirror gave nothing away.

'The knight is a redoubtable fighter, I dare say,' William went on. 'But he has no money. And money is power. Remember that, my child. Beauty fades and lust is soon satisfied. Might has to be paid for. The only thing that endures is money. I could do nothing to help your mother because I had no money. But I have money now and I can help you, just as you can help me.' He let her go and turned away abruptly, leaving her confused and dismayed. It was hard, so hard to please a man who was so secretive. All she knew was that he was her father and she was determined to be his perfect daughter.

'What do you want from me?' she burst out.

He put a hand beneath her chin and turned her round to face him. 'It is not for you to question what I want,' he said, 'but to obey me in all things. I thought you had been well trained in obedience.'

She hung her head, penitent, baffled and afraid. What would become of her if she failed to please him?

CHAPTER 5

The next day Nicolette discovered what it was she thought her father wanted. She had gone with him to the first Mass of the day at St Peter's Upon Cornhill, a beautiful stone-built church no more than a short walk from Gryffard's Inn. On the walk back to his house he said, 'The Mayor is to give a great feast, on Saint Michael's and All Angels. Anybody who is anybody in London will be there.'

She looked at him. He was not an imposing figure, she thought, despite the velvet fur-trimmed gown and jewels on his fingers. He was bent with care and his face, so pale and pointed, seemed designed by nature to express fear rather than joy. Yet in the church this morning he had been greeted by many with deference and in some cases warmth.

'Does that mean you?' she asked.

'It means us,' he said, pausing to examine her critically. 'I want you to outshine them all.'

She held her head up and tried to appear confident. 'Will the King be there?' she asked nervously.

'I don't know. He might. Sir Nicholas Brembre, the Mayor, is a great favourite of the King's.'

'He must be very important,' she said, as they walked on down Cornhill.

'Sir Nicholas Brembre is the most powerful man in the city,' he told her. 'He has been Mayor four times in all and is master of London with the support of the King. If he should notice you, be careful not to displease him.'

She walked along thoughtfully. 'Has Sir Nicholas a wife?' she asked suddenly.

'Sir Nicholas is married to Idonia, one of the four

48

daughters of John Stodeye, a vintner and a man of great wealth and influence.'

So he did not want her to marry this Nicholas Brembre. 'Is she beautiful, the Lady Mayoress?'

'She doesn't have to be beautiful,' he said taking her arm to draw her away from the centre of the street as a shutter was flung open above their heads. 'What you must understand, Nicolette, is that the city is controlled by a close-knit inner circle, who by marrying each other's sisters, wives and daughters keep the government of London in their hands.'

With a sense of disaster narrowly averted, Nicolette watched the contents of a chamber pot being emptied from the window above into the gutter running down the middle of the street. There seemed a great deal about the city she was going to have to learn, and quickly.

'The daughters of John Stodeye all married merchants of standing in the city of London,' William continued. 'Idonia is the eldest. Then there is Margaret, whose second husband, Sir John Philpot, now alas dead, was Mayor several times and a hero in his day.'

'Like Sir Nicholas Brembre?' asked Nicolette drawing her skirts more carefully above her wooden pattens as they walked on.

'No, not like Sir Nicholas. Sir John Philpot was a hero because he helped to rid the seas of a notorious Scottish pirate, which made the English Channel safer for us merchants to get our goods across. Whereas Sir Nicholas Brembre rules by fear.'

'He sounds a bad man,' she said.

'He's dangerous,' William agreed, 'ruthless and tough, riding headlong into danger when others urge caution. But he's been very successful.'

'You're more successful than any of them,' she said, hoping it would please him. 'One day you'll be Mayor.' But to her surprise he shook his head.

'I cannot be Mayor since I am not a member of any guild,' he said. 'I cannot sell my goods within two miles of London without being a member of a guild, which I am not. The arras cloths I brought from France I shall sell to a mercer and he will put them in his shop. The guilds guard the monopoly of their respective trades closely and it is from their ranks that the Mayor and sheriffs who govern the city are elected.'

So he did not want Brembre's help to make him Mayor. She did not understand, not really. Why was it so important that she should please this terrifying Brembre? Perhaps, she thought with a shiver half excitement, half fear, she was to redeem the wicked Sir Nicholas Brembre with her beauty and goodness.

It did not seem impossible, not then. She had slept soundly in the feather-bedded softness of her luxurious chamber, the sun was shining out of a clear blue September morn, she was filled with spiritual confidence after the Mass, uplifted by the belief that God, who had plucked her from the quiet seclusion of the abbey at Caen and delivered her from much peril at sea, was looking upon her with special favour. She felt strong and confident and full of grace. Today anything seemed possible.

She was not so sure when she arrived at the Guildhall on the morning of 29 September for the Mayor's feast.

The women were to eat separately from the men, as was the custom on such festal occasions; Nicolette found herself separated from her father and banished to a splendid upstairs chamber which was rapidly filling with well-dressed women exchanging greetings and visually measuring each other's jewels. None of them paid the slightest attention to Nicolette. Alone and ignored, she backed into a far corner against the wall, bemused by the babble of English voices, ashamed that she was unable to understand a word they were saying, afraid, looking round at their elaborate headdresses and embroidered surcoats and voluptuous fur trimmings, that somehow in spite of all her efforts to look her best she had got it wrong.

She was dressed in a sheath of rose-coloured silk tightly moulded to her slender form. On her head she wore a jewelled filet and her hair hung in a loose shining mass of gold to her waist. She wore it thus because she was proud of her hair, and because neither she nor Lisette knew what to do with all the elaborate headdresses they had found in the painted chest. William had not commented when they set out for the Guildhall and she had assumed that he had been satisfied with her appearance. She was beginning to learn that he was swift to criticise but parsimonious with his approval and to be thankful if he said nothing. But now, as she studied the bared necks and plucked brows and hair entangled in cunningly wrought coils of the women around her, she was agonisingly aware that she looked different from the others. She stared down at her feet, clenching her hands tightly and swallowing hard.

'Don't look so sad. You're here to enjoy yourself.' Nicolette did not understand one word, but the voice sounded sympathetic. She looked up shyly. A lady dressed in aldermanic scarlet, with solid gold buttons down the front of her low-cut sleeveless surcoat and a little Negro boy slave to carry her train was regarding her with curiosity. 'You must come and meet my sister. Is she expecting you?'

'I come with Master Gryffard,' replied Nicolette, stumbling over the unfamiliar tongue and blushing beneath the other's inquisitive stare.

'So you're his wife from Bruges!' exclaimed the lady, her bright eyes twinking with mischief. 'I had no idea William had married a child. I thought she was a widow with a flourishing dye yard. You don't look old enough to be a widow or run a business of your own.' She spoke in French but so strangely accented that Nicolette had difficulty recognising her own language. Nevertheless it was a relief to find someone she could talk to.

'My name is Nicolette de Saint Pierre.' She took a deep breath and half expecting a bolt from heaven told the lie she had practised so carefully with her father. 'I am kinswoman to Master Gryffard. My father died before I was born and my mother went into the Abbey of the Holy Trinity at Caen.'

'De Saint Pierre. It has a noble ring to it,' the other cocked her head on one side like an inquisitive robin, 'and Master Gryffard hasn't one drop of noble blood in his veins, I'd swear by the Rood.' No bolt from heaven, but a disbeliever, thought Nicolette, frightened as she again looked down at her feet. 'You don't look like a nun,' went on her tormentor with a little trill of laughter. 'There's some mystery here. How I love a mystery.' Nicolette looked up startled. 'Are you his mistress perhaps?' said the woman, bright eyes twinkling with mischief.

'Don't be absurd, Margaret. Why, she's little more than a child.' The imposing figure in close-fitting gown adorned with heraldic symbols who had come to her rescue was so

51

majestic that Nicolette instinctively dropped a curtsey. 'Don't pay any attention to my sister, she's a terrible tease. You must be William Gryffard's kinswoman – he told me he was bringing you.' The Mayoress's French was bad, much worse than her sister's, thought Nicolette, and she was definitely not beautiful. Her headdress, an elaborate artifice with two openwork tubes on either side of her head through which her plaits of hair were drawn up, emphasised the square jaw and bulging, prominent brow. Nicolette smiled uncertainly at the lady, unable to think of anything to say. 'Don't let Margaret upset you,' the Mayoress went on with a haughty glance at her sister. 'She's jealous, that's all. She can't forgive you for being able to wear your hair like that.'

'Only very young girls and brides ought to appear in public with their hair unbound,' said Margaret, tossing her head.

'Exactly,' laughed the Mayoress. With sinking heart Nicolette watched Margaret sweep away, her head and her colour high. Her father would never forgive her if she upset this powerful and important family. She looked fearfully at the Mayoress, wishing she knew what she had done wrong.

'Poor Margaret, she hates anyone to be more beautiful than she,' said the Mayoress complacently. 'Now we must find you somewhere to sit. Come with me.' She seized hold of Nicolette's hanging sleeve, dragged her over to a table at the side of the room and, leaving her in the care of two aldermen's wives, turned away to her other guests.

The two women seemed disposed to be friendly enough but spoke not one word of French and as Nicolette's English was still very limited, it wasn't long before they were talking over her head, busy recounting the details of their latest lying-in to each other and totally ignoring her. Laid out on the table was an array of varied and splendid dishes – a heavily spiced eel stew with cheese, jellies in every colour of the rainbow, sugared chicken with rice flour and almond milk, a tart made in the shape of a crenellated castle, with chicken-drumstick turrets and the Mayor's coat of arms gilded with gold leaf, and a roasted swan sewn back into its skin complete with feathers. Never had Nicolette seen so much food. The women reached across each other gossiping and chattering and attacking the dishes with relish, while a bevy of pages ran about the room filling the wine goblets. Nicolette was used to eating her meals in silence. At Holy

Trinity she had done it all her life and she was content to be ignored at first.

As the feast progressed, the women grew more flushed and noisy, sauce ran down their chins and on to their fine clothes, the tables were littered with bits of meat and spilt wine and the floor with discarded bones. From time to time they tried to include Nicolette in their conversation and she did her best to look as if she understood, but it was very difficult. It seemed to her that the feast would never end.

At last the dishes were removed, but it was only the first course. With the second course, a minstrel came to entertain them with a song of love. Although Nicolette could not understand much of the minstrel's tale, there was no mistaking the languorous looks he cast in her direction and she was at first amused. By the time the dishes of the third course appeared upon the table, she could eat no more. She was hot and thirsty. The rich, heavily spiced food was beginning to make her feel queasy. The chamber, lit with hundreds of beeswax candles, grew stuffier as the feast progressed. One of the aldermen's wives pressed against her, laughing uproariously. Nicolette could feel the warmth of her overheated body, damp and unpleasant through the fine silk of her gown. The minstrel's attentions became more pointed and she began to feel embarrassed. She sipped her wine but it did not seem to quench her thirst. Her head began to swim. The jewelled filet weighed heavily on her head, pressing into her brow. Altogether it was a relief when at last the ladies left the disordered chamber and went down into the great hall to join the men.

The hall was large and lofty, hung with colourful tapestries and lit with even more candles than the upstairs chamber. Merchants in flowing velvet and liveried gowns mingled with knights and their squires in colourful short tunics emblazoned with their arms. Nicolette fought a strong desire to turn and run. The noise, the colour, the sheer unrestrained splendour of it all made her feel more of an outsider than ever. In vain she searched the crowded hall for a glimpse of Piers, hoping that perhaps he might by some miracle be here. She so longed for a friendly face, someone who could speak her native tongue with ease, a protector who would save her from making a fool of herself. But there was no sign of Piers. She was alone and friendless. She shrank back into the shadows watching nervously for William, aware that she was failing him dismally.

With the appearance of the ladies, the musicians in the gallery high above had struck up a lively jig and soon the hall was filled with men and women dancing. Nicolette, alone and, she hoped, unobserved, listened to the music with surprise. The only music she knew was the plainsong of the abbey and she had loved its soothing, subtle harmony, its unhurried certainties. This music was quite different. It did not soothe or reassure. It was a wild, catchy sound, galloping along with an insistent tunefulness which made her forget her troubles and long to join the dancers. Fascinated, she watched the twirling figures as her feet began to tap to the merry rhythm of fiddle, pipe and tabor.

'Do you not dance, mistress?' A young boy of about her own age appeared at her side. He was dressed in a tunic with wide sleeves belted tightly at the waist, which stopped short above long shapely legs encased in particoloured hose. His merry blue eyes regarded her admiringly.

'I'm afraid I don't know how,' she said in French.

'Then I'll show you. It's easy,' he replied in the same tongue. He seized her hand and before she could stop him had swept her off into the dance. She stumbled and tripped over his feet at first but her natural balance and well-trained ear helped and before long she was able to follow him without too much difficulty. He was right. Dancing was easy and it was fun.

When they were both out of breath, he stopped and let her rest. To her polite inquiries he told her that he was squire to Sir Hugh Daintry, a knight who lived in the Vintry.

'Why are you not in Portugal with the Duke of Lancaster?' she asked him.

'Sir Hugh's not a retainer of Lancaster's, he's liegeman to the Duke of Gloucester,' the squire replied and proceeded to put her more at her ease by paying her pretty compliments. He was good at compliments, but he was soon ousted by a master fishmonger. Other partners followed in quick succession and she danced with them all, her feet flying with the music and her heart as light and untroubled as the soaring notes of the fiddles. When the musicians paused to rest, tumblers and jugglers entertained the company. Nicolette watched, full of delighted incredulity at their resourceful daring, while her courtiers gathered round her, vying with each other to bring her wine, beg a dance, win a smile, pay her homage. She laughed at their foolery while at the same time enjoying it, experiencing for the first time in her life the knowledge that men were fighting for her favour. It was heady wine for a girl of barely sixteen summers just out of a convent.

'Come and meet the Mayor.' Suddenly William appeared at her side. She gave a guilty start. She had forgotten all about the Mayor; forgotten why the rose silk of her gown was moulded so tightly to her body, why the front was cut so low it hardly covered her budding breasts, why Lisette had brushed her hair until it shone, why she had to endure the weight of the wide gold band pressing on to her brow. Now when she looked at all these frightening ladies with their elaborate headdresses and coats of arms embroidered on their surcoats she felt foolish and absurd. The Mayor could not possibly want to meet her.

With sinking heart she followed William through the dancers to the dais at the far end of the hall. A number of merchants and one or two knights were grouped around a strong, powerfully built man in a short tunic decorated with the same green hooded falcons she had seen on Lady Brembre's gown. His legs in their green and white hose were well muscled, his hair a rich red brown, his moustache luxuriant.

All this she had plenty of time to observe while she stood beside her father, waiting for the great man to notice them. Sir Nicholas Brembre did not look wicked, she decided, but he did look powerful. Big and strong and handsome, towering above the others, he looked every inch the master of London. She would have known him for the Mayor even without the device on his tunic and the gold chain of office round his shoulders.

She shivered and held her breath expectantly as she waited for him to turn and see her. But he did not turn round. He just went on talking, showing no sign that he was aware of their existence. She let out her breath in a small sigh, feeling impatience for the first time in her life. Would he never look round? William's hand closed tightly round her wrist, restraining her. She cast a quick glance at him. He was listening intently to what the Mayor was saying, and his hooded eyes gave nothing away. If it had not been for the hot dampness of his hand, she would not have known that he, too, was nervous.

'Who's this, William? Your wife?' Suddenly Brembre swung round to stare at Nicolette. Eyes that were brilliant blue and hard as agates swept over her from head to foot impatiently.

'My wife died,' William explained apologetically. 'This is my kinswoman, Nicolette de Saint Pierre, from Caen.'

'French, is she?' His eyes bored into hers and she knew she ought to look modestly downwards as she had been trained to do. But she could not. She was at his mercy, like a rabbit bewitched by a stoat, unable to move, or breathe, or think. 'You'd better go and talk to my sister-in-law Mistress Bamme,' he said. 'She speaks French like the true English-woman she is.' He gave a short bark of laughter and turned away to resume his conversation.

Nicolette found she was shaking all over. The thunderbolt had struck but it had not come from heaven. She felt helpless. In that brief hard glance she had been seen, measured and rejected. He did not want her. She stood with her head bowed, beset by a turmoil of conflicting emotions, chief of which was fear – fear of herself, of the uncontrollable thoughts which were whirling through her mind, of Sir Nicholas Brembre, that he would turn and look at her again, that he would not, of her father's anger because she had made such a bad impression on the Mayor. She stole a frightened glance at William but he was not looking at her. His eyes were on the Mayor's broad, implacable back and his face was expressionless.

William was quite content to be forgotten and ignored; waiting and listening was how he learnt his secrets.

'Suffolk's been dismissed. Along with the Bishop of Durham, the King's Treasurer.' Suddenly Brembre swung round and confronted William. 'Is it the Duke of Gloucester's doing, do you think?'

'The Duke of Gloucester is hungry for power,' he replied cautiously, 'and may be trying to rally the King's enemies in Lancaster's absence.' He broke off, uncomfortably aware that he was not telling Nicholas Brembre anything he didn't know. 'The Earl of Suffolk looks as if he's to be the scapegoat. The King won't like it but he may not be able to prevent Parliament from impeaching the Chancellor,' he finished lamely.

'We can't have that, Suffolk's too good a man to lose his head,' retorted Brembre.

'He may escape with a large fine,' William suggested, but the Mayor turned his back on him again.

William watched him warily. He had been useful to Brembre in the past and the Mayor had made it well worth his while but William found him a dangerous man to serve. To be dependent on such a man was like riding on a tiger's back. It needed nerves of iron and William was not a brave man. Once, he had tried to get off the tiger's back. He had changed sides when Brembre had fallen from power, thinking himself safe. But Brembre had come back and to survive William had had to make himself very useful indeed with several acts of betrayal. Since then he had absented himself from London to give time for wounds to heal and men to forget, and if today was anything to go by, they had forgotten. Nobody had thrown his past in his face today.

'Arundel and Warwick will support Gloucester,' Brembre said. 'Will Derby and Nottingham side with the King or his uncle?' The question was addressed not to William but to the other men surrounding him.

William watched and listened to them arguing, wondering what it was that Brembre wanted now. In a few days' time, Nicholas Exton, a member of the powerful fishmonger's guild, would be Mayor in Brembre's place, but Exton was Brembre's pawn. He would do what Brembre told him. Was the city of London too small a conquest for a man of Brembre's overpowering ambition? Was he about to become embroiled in the King's struggle with his magnates? If that was the case, thought William, Brembre might become very powerful indeed. Far too powerful for me, the still small voice of caution urged. Yet it would be well worthwhile keeping the favour of a man so determined upon reaching the highest pinnacles of power. But how? He needed something more than his ability to be first with the news to satisfy a man like Brembre.

He was all too aware of Nicolette standing obediently by his side, her eyes modestly lowered. He gripped her more tightly by the wrist and studied her thoughtfully beneath his hooded lids. She turned her candid eyes to his and smiled sweetly. Suddenly he was gripped by an entirely new emotion. It was pride. She was his own flesh and blood, and today she had surpassed his expectations. Although young and inexperienced, she had held her own among the best in the city. Not only held her own, she had shone. He had seen the men both young and old paying homage to his daughter, his bastard, his mistake. He was proud of her. This rare creature was his, to mould, to keep, or to use to buy Brembre's favour.

The Lady Mayoress was approaching the dais. William prepared himself to be ingratiating. He knew she did not like him. Idonia never bothered to hide her feelings. She did not play games, not like her sister Margaret.

'Have you come to chide me for not dancing, my lady?' Brembre demanded.

'I've come to rescue the Damoiselle de Saint Pierre,' Idonia said. 'She looks frightened and bored. This is her first feast, she tells me, and I'm sure she would be happier dancing with the young squires.'

'Is that true?' Sir Nicholas swung round to stare at Nicolette again. 'Am I boring you?'

Nicolette shook her head in obvious confusion and looked anxiously at her father.

'She speaks no English as yet,' William explained hastily. 'The child has been convent reared and has little experience of the world.'

'Then you'd better get her to come and talk with you, my dear,' Nicholas said to his wife. 'Your French is sadly in need of improvement. You can teach each other.'

Idonia frowned and glared at William as if challenging him to come to her rescue. But he looked at the bent head of his daughter and said nothing. He did not dare interfere between husband and wife.

'You can spare her, can't you, Gryffard?' Brembre was always at his most bullying when he thought he was not about to get his own way. 'Of course you can. You've only just discovered her. Now, damoiselle, my wife tells me you're longing to dance.' He held out his hand to her. 'You can dance with me.'

Nicolette hesitated and again looked at William. An emotion gripped him and he knew it well for he had fought it all his life: possession. Here at last he had something with which to tempt Brembre, but he did not want to lose his jewel. She was young and innocent and trained in obedience. If he let Brembre have her, would she lie and deceive for her father out of filial piety? Were ties of blood strong enough for that? Or would she become Brembre's tool instead?

'Well, Master Gryffard?' Nicholas Brembre was glaring at him almost as if he had read his thoughts. 'Does she have your permission to dance with me?'

William put her unresisting hand into Brembre's and told himself that he had no choice. Whatever Brembre wanted he would take.

CHAPTER 6

'I won't do it!' shouted the King. 'I won't do what my uncle of Gloucester s-s-says. Why s-should I?' He hurled a gold goblet across the chamber; it spilled its contents in an arc of red wine and left a trail like splashed blood on the tiled floor. 'I'm the King, aren't I? Well, aren't I?'

They would not look at him. The two men seemed far more interested in watching the large hairy wolfhound licking up the spilt wine. It made Richard even angrier. He drew his dagger and flew across the chamber to pounce upon his old tutor Sir Simon Burley, seizing him by the high-necked collar of his velvet gown. 'By Christ's mercy, am I the King or no?' he demanded as he pressed the point of his dagger up against the old man's throat.

'Sire, nobody is denying it,' Burley replied.

Meeting his calm gaze, Richard uttered another oath and flung his dagger after the goblet. The hound leapt for his life with a yelp of terror. Richard released his Chamberlain. 'Then why must I s-s-send S-Suffolk to the Tower? I don't want him to go. He's my Chancellor.'

'Sire, Parliament has impeached the Earl of Suffolk,' Burley replied. 'He has to stand trial.'

'I know that.' Sometimes his old friend and counsellor seemed to forget he was no longer a child but a man of twenty-one, fully grown. 'What do you s-say, Robert?' he demanded, rounding on the other, younger man.

'I say let Parliament go hang. You don't need Parliament.'

Richard looked at the exquisite young man in his surcoat of oriental cloth of silk, lined with vermilion linen. Robert de Vere had been his playfellow and his closest companion since

60

childhood. He had made him Earl of Oxford, then Marquess of Dublin and now, at the beginning of this Parliament, Duke of Ireland.

'I need Parliament to grant me money – to keep you, Robert, in jewels and c-c-c-cloth of gold. Isn't that right, S-Simon?'

'It's too late for you to dissolve Parliament,' said Burley. 'Parliament has set up a commission of regency, you haven't the power, Sire.'

'Well, what can I do?' He wished Burley would not look so solemn. He always looked solemn when things went wrong. It was Robert who could be relied on to cheer him up. He wanted to be cheered up. But he also wanted to help Michael de la Pole, the Duke of Suffolk, and the Bishop of Durham, his Treasurer, who had also been impeached. He wanted to assert his authority. That was why he had left Westminster and come to his palace at Eltham in Kent with his friends. To decide what to do. Only his friends weren't being much help.

'What will they do to Michael de la Pole?' he said.

'Confiscate his goods. Imprison him, pending a fine, which is bound to be exorbitant.' Sir Simon Burley looked more serious than ever.

'They'll ruin him. I don't want Michael to be ruined,' said the King. 'He's been good to me, I can always trust de la Pole.'

'You can trust us, Sire,' said the new Duke of Ireland, retrieving the dagger and handing it back to the King.

Richard took the weapon and turned it over in his hand. Its hilt was of chased silver of a delicate and particularly fine design. It had been a gift from Robert de Vere. 'Of course I can trust you. Everything you have has come f-from me,' he said as he slammed the dagger savagely into its sheath. 'But it'll be your turn next.' That ought to make him come up with something! 'They won't be content until they've taken away all my f-f-friends.'

Robert turned pale, chewing at his fingernails and casting furtive glances at Simon Burley, who tut-tutted in the way he used to do when Richard couldn't get his Latin verbs right.

The King felt his frustration mount. What use Latin at a time like this? What he needed was an army, not Latin. They wouldn't have dared to treat his father, the Black Prince, so.

'I wish my uncle of Lancaster hadn't gone to Spain,' he said suddenly. 'He would never have let them do this to me.' He glared at the two of them, waiting for some response, but they looked defeated. It made Richard feel all the more helpless. Robert was fun but he was no use at a time like this and Simon Burley had no fire in his belly. The silence lengthened and he gazed about him looking for something else to torment. A log fell from the fire on to the hearth with a mighty crash and the King kicked it viciously. The dog watched warily from the window embrasure.

The Keeper of the Guard appeared at the door of the chamber. 'Sir Nicholas Brembre is here, Sire,' he said.

'Send him in,' said Richard, pleased at the diversion. He was getting tired of baiting de Vere and Burley. 'I want to see Brembre. I need to borrow some more money from him.'

Sir Nicholas Brembre came striding into the chamber a few minutes later and bent his knee in an act of obeisance. He was dressed in chain mail surmounted by a surcoat emblazoned with his coat of arms, and a long sword dangled from his hip.

'Welcome, Sir Knight,' mocked the King. 'You look ready to do battle. Have you come to rescue me from my wicked uncles?'

'I've come to offer my services,' replied Brembre.

'How many retainers did you bring? I need deeds, not words. And money. Did you bring money, Sir Nicholas?'

'How much money do you need, Sire?' asked Brembre, getting to his feet.

'Enough f-f-for an army. If you can buy me an army, I'll make you a duke like Robert here.'

'I haven't got that sort of money, but I could raise some four thousand pounds from the city for the defence of the realm. After the attempted invasion of the south coast by the French, the citizens are very nervous.' He smiled sardonically.

'What makes you so s-sure the Londoners'll do what you s-say? There's s-s-some in the city after your blood as well. The mercers and s-some of the other guilds brought a petition against you in Parliament. It s-s-seems they don't like s-s-s-some of your methods.'

'My methods, with your support, Sire, have kept me in power these last three years and more. I came here today to tell you that London will support you in whatever you do.'

He was a cool customer, thought Richard. Not easily ambushed. 'You aren't the Mayor any more,' he said, pushing him further.

'Nicholas Exton will do what I tell him.' There was arrogance in Brembre's cold, hard stare.

'If Nicholas Exton is s-so biddable, what makes you think he won't do what others tell him too?'

'If he does, then I shall replace him with someone else. The city is still mine to do what I want with.'

The fellow's self-assurance was remarkable, thought the King. It made him feel better, having someone to advise him who wasn't terrified of upsetting everyone all the time. 'What am I to do?' he asked.

'Defy Parliament,' Brembre said. 'Refuse to accept the commission of regency. You're the King. Dismiss Parliament with a declaration of your prerogative. Compel the judges to declare the commission illegal. Chief Justice Tresilian will do what you tell him.'

'By the rood, you're right, Sir Nicholas. I am the King. I'll have S-Suffolk released. Use f-f-force if necessary. Raise the Cheshire levies. They're the best archers in England.'

'No armies,' interrupted Simon Burley. 'Sire, you must be careful not to push the country into civil war. You are too young to remember but it's not so long since your grandfather Edward III had to fight long and hard to restore order after the deposition of his father Edward II.'

'Deposition!' shouted Richard, rounding on him furiously. 'D-Don't you d-d-dare threaten me with d-d-d-deposition. You're as bad as my uncle of Gloucester. When I told Parliament I would bring help f-from F-France if they did not obey me, my uncle reminded me of what happened to Edward II.'

'Sire!' The old man fell down awkwardly on his knees at the King's feet. 'You are the rightful King appointed by God. May He strike me down now or do you take my head from off my shoulders here in this very chamber if I so much as think of setting aside the anointed King.'

'I wish my uncle had as much respect for my divine right,' said Richard, much mollified by the old man's obvious distress. 'The thought of deposing me has obviously entered his head.'

'The Duke of Gloucester is surely only trying to frighten you,' said the old man, struggling painfully to his feet again. 'He is loyal in his heart.'

'All the same, Sire,' said Brembre, 'you must exert yourself now, before it's too late. Show them you're no longer a child. If you act quickly with London's support, the rest of the country will rally behind you. Remember how easy it was back in the Hurling Time at Smithfields. You saved us then, when we were at the mercy of the whole peasants' army. "I am your King, your leader and your chief," you said after William Walworth had killed Wat Tyler. "Those of you who are loyal to me should go immediately into the field." Do you remember? And they followed you. All they want is someone to follow. You are the King. Lead and we will follow.'

By St George, thought Richard, delighted to be reminded of his finest hour, the fellow had found a way. He was a tough rascal and aimed high, for a merchant, but he had guts.

The part played by Brembre in encouraging the King to defy his overbearing uncle was soon being widely discussed throughout the city of London. William Gryffard mingling in the nave of St Peter's Upon Cornhill with the mercers, corn merchants, knights and men of substance who lived in the vicinity found opinion divided as to whether the King would succeed. He returned home to break his fast more worried than reassured. If this latest daring act of Brembre's were to lead to disaster, how many of the King's friends would suffer? And if one of them was Brembre, what then? Was the great man about to fall at last?

Perhaps he ought to put a stop now to Nicolette's frequent visits to Brembre's Inn. He said a quick prayer of thanks to the Blessed Virgin that for the time being at least it was Idonia Brembre, not her husband, who seemed interested in Nicolette. According to Nicolette, Brembre was hardly ever at home. William believed her. He did not think she had learned yet how to lie. He was reluctant to put a stop to the visits, for Idonia had taken a great liking to the girl and was doing her much good, teaching her how to dress and wear her hair. He could not teach his daughter these things. Besides, Idonia was a very powerful woman. Her patronage was of immense value. With Idonia as a friend, Nicolette would soon be accepted by anyone who was at all important in the city.

No, William decided, for the time being it was better to let Nicolette's visits continue. Sir Nicholas was too preoccupied with the King's affairs to want to complicate his life with seducing an innocent young girl under his wife's nose, and if the King should be victorious in this latest struggle with his barons, then Brembre would be all the more powerful.

Nicolette did not feel innocent at all, not since Sir Nicholas Brembre had made her dance with him at his feast. It was as if at that moment a candle had been lit within her which burned with an unquenchable flame. She had tried, with prayer and constant visits to St Peter's, to put out that flame but it only seemed to burn the stronger. She knew that she ought to go to confession, but she could not bring herself to promise not to think of him or, worse, to forgo her visits to his house in the Royall. She told herself that she went there to please her father and Lady Brembre, that since Sir Nicholas was hardly ever at home and when he was seemed unaware of her existence, it did not matter. But she suspected that the Abbess would call it a sin, for the way her pulses raced and her heart lifted every time she went to Brembre's Inn, for the trouble she took each time to look her best, because she knew that she did not do these things for the Lady Brembre but for Sir Nicholas, in the vain hope that one day he might be pleased to notice her again.

She was looking her best when she set out for the Royall with Lisette one morning late in November. It was a cold crisp day and Nicolette walked with a spring in her step and colour in her cheeks, laughing and joking with Lisette, her spirits fuelled by hope that Sir Nicholas might be at home. Reaching the Royall, she saw a knight and his squire riding abreast down the wide, clean, cobbled street and drew back under the archway of the Tower Royal, a massive stronghold from which the street took its name. The horse's caparison was covered with three red trefoils on a cream field. Surprised Nicolette recognised Piers' arms. She had not seen him since they parted company on the *Santa Maria Nuova*. At first she had been disappointed and a little hurt that he had made no effort to keep in touch. But that was before the Mayor's Feast and her meeting with Sir Nicholas Brembre. Since then she had forgotten Piers.

'It's good to see you again, Piers,' she said when he reined in beside her. 'We wondered what had become of you when you never came to see us, didn't we, Lisette?'

'I came, once or twice, but Master Gryffard did not make me welcome and I didn't want to be a nuisance – not until I'd found my feet as it were.'

'I'm sorry,' she said embarrassed at the thought of him being turned away from their door. 'I didn't know.'

'It doesn't matter. I knew you were safe and well and not in any immediate need of my services,' he said looking down at her with such fervour, she felt overcome with guilt, knowing she had not thought about him at all. He was her first friend after all.

'You look very dangerous in all that armour,' she said laughing up at him to hide her dismay. 'Who are you going to succour now?'

'I'm on my way to practise tilting at the lists on Smithfields,' he said, beginning to dismount.

'Please don't delay, not on my account,' she said swiftly.

'There's no hurry. First let me escort you wherever you're going,' he replied. 'Lisette, you look well. Do you like living in this big city?'

'I likes it well enough,' Lisette replied. 'Apart from the noise – the 'prentices calling their wares by day and the watch ashouting by night and them bells aringing all the time.'

'Yes, I suppose it is a good deal noisier than the abbey at Caen,' he said, handing his reins to Esmon and turning towards Nicolette with eager solicitude.

'There's no need for you to come with us, Sir Piers,' she said. For reasons she did not herself quite understand, she did not want him coming with her to Brembre's house. 'We're almost there.'

'I'll walk with you,' he said.

'In all that armour?'

'If I can fight in it, I can walk in it,' he said, grinning at her. 'Especially since you're almost there.'

'Have you found a cause to fight for yet?'

'No. But I've found somewhere to live – here in the Royall.'

'At Brembre's Inn!' she exclaimed and then blushed when he looked at her sharply.

'No, not with Sir Nicholas Brembre,' Piers replied. 'With Richard Whittington.'

'Whittington?' she said hurriedly. 'Who is he?'

'A mercer. He has a house at the far end of the Royall close by Saint Michael's de Paternoster. He sells silks and velvets to Robert de Vere, the King's favourite.'

'You've taken up with a mercer?' She could not help feeling disappointed. 'Don't tell me you're going to take Master Gryffard's advice after all and turn to trade.'

'No, I'll not do that. I've already learnt my trade.' He was looking at her thoughtfully, and the anxious look in his eyes made her feel uncomfortable.

'Perhaps he has a daughter – well dowered?' she said lightly, hoping to distract him.

'Master Whittington hasn't any children,' he replied.

'But he is your friend?'

'He is my friend. Is Sir Nicholas Brembre yours?' The sudden question caught her unawares.

'No!' she said to the cobblestones.

'Is that where you're going?' he asked. 'To Brembre's Inn?'

'Yes.' She raised defiant eyes to his face. 'What is wrong with my going there?'

'Be careful of Brembre, he has an unsavoury reputation.'

'What for? What has he done?'

'He's a man who takes what he wants – by force if necessary.'

'Don't you all?' she retorted. 'Isn't that why you're going to practise tilting at the lists in Smithfields?' The horses were growing impatient, pawing the ground and snorting at the contents of the gutter.

'I like to think I use my skill at arms to defend the weak, not to prey upon the defenceless,' he said.

'Sir Nicholas Brembre doesn't prey on people. He's a member of the King's Council.'

'Master Whittington says that Sir Nicholas Brembre has no respect for the rule of law, that he filled the Guildhall with armed men to ensure his election and then when the citizens rioted in protest he had their leader beheaded in Chepe without trial. He's a murderer.'

'You're making it up.' She did not want to believe him. What did Piers know of such things? He was only a landless knight with a head stuffed full of impractical dreams.

'I'm not making it up. The mercers and other crafts brought a petition before Parliament listing Brembre's crimes. Whittington told me.' Piers was staring down at her, his eyes searching her face in an agony of uncertainty.

She made herself meet his gaze 'Well, I come here to see Lady Brembre, not Sir Nicholas. To teach her French but in truth to keep her company. I think she's lonely in that big house all by herself. Sir Nicholas is hardly ever at home and they have no children.' She began to walk and he fell in beside her, Lisette and Esmon with the two horses following in their wake.

They proceeded thus in silence, until Nicolette could see the outline of the substantial stone house set back from the street in its own large gardens where Brembre lived. She glanced at Piers. He looked so dejected she began to feel ashamed of herself. She did not have so many friends in the city that she could afford to hurt a devoted admirer like Piers.

'Would you like me to ask Lady Brembre to speak to Sir Nicholas for you?' she asked. 'He might be able to put you in the King's way.'

'Master Whittington is going to seek the help of Robert de Vere when the King comes back to London,' replied Piers.

But Nicolette was no longer listening. A horseman, accompanied by two men-at-arms, was trotting rapidly towards them and she recognised the falcons on the flapping saddle cloth. She walked on quickly, her head bent, hoping for once that Sir Nicholas Brembre would not see her, that he would sweep on in through the arched entrance of his house and that she could get rid of Piers and slip in unobtrusively after him. But perversely Brembre did not ride on by. He brought his horse slithering to an abrupt halt as he came abreast of them. His eyes swept over Piers in his armour, standing protectively at Nicolette's side, Esmon fighting to control the two prancing destriers, Lisette staring, mouth agape, and came finally to rest on Nicolette who could feel herself blushing furiously right up to the edges of her fine Venetian veil.

'Good morning, Damoiselle de Saint Pierre,' he said. 'What have you found in the Royall to frighten you so much that you bring an armed escort with you when you come to visit us?'

'Sir Piers Exton is on his way to the tilting ground on Smithfields,' she explained hastily.

'Exton?' he demanded, fixing Piers with a piercing stare. 'Any relation to the Mayor?'

'A distant kinsman,' replied Piers. 'I'm living with Master Whittington who has a house here in the Royall.'

'Dick Whittington?' Brembre frowned. 'The apprentice who married his master's daughter? Done very well for himself, for a landless younger son of a knight.' Nicolette clenched her hands tightly in the folds of her fur-trimmed mantle. Brembre sounded angry. 'What does a master mercer want with a knight in his household?'

'I don't know,' replied Piers. 'I only know that he has been very kind and hospitable.'

'Give Master Whittington a message from me,' Brembre growled. 'Tell him to take this petition of his guild and use it to . . .' He broke off and glared angrily at Nicolette while she wondered miserably what she had done to offend him so. His hard blue eyes swept back to the knight standing defiantly at her side. 'The mercers'll get nowhere with their complaints, not now that Parliament has been sent about its business – you can tell Master Whittington that. The King has taken the country into his own hands. He doesn't need Parliament with its plague of petitions and commissions.' His ferocious gaze swung to Nicolette. 'Come, damoiselle, if you're on your way to see the Lady Brembre, you don't want to be loitering out here all day in the cold.' Clapping heels to his horse he rode off.

Nicolette smiled a little nervously at Piers. 'God go with you, Sir Piers,' she said and held out her hand. He took it gingerly in his mailed fist. 'I hope you find a worthy adversary to practise against at Smithfields.'

'I don't doubt I shall,' he replied staring grimly after Brembre. 'Remember, if ever I can be of service, you have only to send to Master Whittington. He will know where to find me.' He was still holding her hand, cradling it as if it were a wounded bird and gazing at her soulfully. Before she met Brembre she had thought that Piers's devotion was a little exciting. But now that she knew what excitement was, she found his talk of chivalry and service sadly dull. She removed her hand, thinking that Piers was a great one for high ideals but he had little to show for all his fine talk, whereas Brembre was a man who took what he wanted and was very successful. With her heart leaping, she followed Brembre into the house.

Sir Nicholas stood with his back to the fire blazing in the great hall, talking to his steward, but he watched Nicolette as she entered. She paused just inside the entrance and her eyes locked with his. The room was, as usual, full of people – members of the household coming and going about their daily tasks, men from the city with their attendants waiting patiently to see the great man. There was no sign of Lady Brembre, who would doubtless be in her solar.

Brembre raised his hand and beckoned commandingly. Slowly Nicolette began to walk towards him through the crowd, her stomach churning and her heart hammering in her chest. By the time she reached his side, she was breathless as if she had been running. He finished with the steward, dismissing him with a peremptory wave of his hand.

'Who is Sir Piers Exton?' he asked her, his hard cold gaze searching her face.

'He's the younger son of a Cheshire knight sent into the world to make his fortune.' She had to struggle to keep her voice steady. 'We met him on the road to Calais and Master Gryffard befriended him for a while.'

'And now Whittington. I wonder why.'

'Perhaps it makes them feel good – helping him,' she said. 'Sir Piers is full of chivalry you see, but poor.'

'Whereas I am rich but wicked, is that what he told you?' His eyes scanned her face and in their cold blue depths she thought she detected a faint glimmer of flame. She took a deep breath.

'I didn't pay any heed to what Sir Piers said. He's jealous,' she added impulsively.

'Jealous?'

'Of your success.' The flash of triumph in his eyes made her look down fearfully at the floor. He said nothing and she was terrified that she had said more than she should.

'How is my wife's French coming along?' he asked at last.

'Very well,' she replied.

'Don't lie to me, Nicolette de Saint Pierre. You're not very good at it.'

'A convent is not the best place to learn how to lie,' she

retorted, with a quick upward glance at him. 'But I'll get better with practice.'

He gave a bark of laughter. 'I can see you've learnt a lot since you've been coming here to teach my wife – far more than she.'

'If I am benefiting, it is because I have a lot to learn,' she replied, eyes lowered modestly.

'And Lady Brembre has nothing?'

'The Lady Brembre is not used to receiving instruction,' she said, looking at him again with her sweetest smile.

'No, my wife is far more accustomed to giving orders.'

'I have much to be grateful to Lady Brembre for,' Nicolette told him. 'She is helping me turn Lisette into a proper tiring woman. She now knows how to braid hair and to arrange all kinds of elaborate headdresses.'

'That's a pity, for you have beautiful hair,' he said, staring at her almost fiercely. 'I'd far rather see it hanging loose the way it was the first time I saw you.'

Sweet Jesu, he had noticed, she thought, elation sweeping through her.

'Do you think my wife's French good enough to hold her own at court?' he asked suddenly.

'I don't know, I've never been to court,' she replied, taken aback. Then, because she thought she might have been less than kind, added, 'I'm sure the Lady Brembre could hold her own anywhere.'

'I think you could hold your own anywhere,' he said and there was no mistaking the approval in his voice. She glanced quickly up at him and found him smiling at her for the first time. Her heart gave a great bound and she swallowed nervously. 'The King has summoned us to spend Christmas at Westminster Palace,' he went on. 'My wife will need a gentlewoman to accompany her. Someone who speaks the language of the court fluently. You'd better come with us.'

She could scarcely believe her ears. He thought well of her, enough to invite her to go with them to spend Christmas at the palace! 'I must ask Master Gryffard first,' she said, assailed by doubt, afraid suddenly of so much good fortune.

'Master Gryffard will do as he's told,' Brembre replied and her heart soared at the supreme confidence of this man. It was so different from the careful, worried, painstaking persistence of her father or the idealistic dreaming of someone like

71

Piers. Sir Nicholas Brembre took what he wanted and got what he wanted whenever he wanted it. *He* would never fail, of that she was very sure.

CHAPTER 7

William received the news of Nicolette's good fortune with his customary suspicion.

'Why would the Lady Brembre want to take you with her to the palace?' he said. 'I would have thought she would choose one of her sisters' children to accompany her.'

'It was Sir Nicholas Brembre who said I was to go,' replied Nicolette proudly.

'Sir Nicholas?' William looked, if anything, more suspicious than ever. 'I thought you told me that Sir Nicholas Brembre was hardly ever at home when you went to the Royall.'

She bit her lip and stared at her feet. 'Today was the first time I have spoken to him,' she said. Would he refuse to let her go?

'But already he lusts after you?'

'No!'

He stretched out his hand, raised her bent head, forced her to meet his gaze. 'I told you never to lie to me, Nicolette.'

'I don't know what he feels,' she stammered, blushing beneath his watchful eyes.

'But he asked you to spend Christmastide with him at court?'

'To accompany the Lady Brembre. I think because I speak French. I thought you would be pleased – that you wanted me to be a success.' Then, because he continued to stare at her so suspiciously, she added, 'If you do not want me to see Sir Nicholas Brembre, I will not go there any more. I only went to please you.'

He was frowning thoughtfully as he released her. 'Sir

Nicholas Brembre is too powerful a man to cross,' he said. 'All the more so now that he advises the King. You'll have to go. It is too late now to undo the damage.' She did not understand what he meant.

'Then I am to go to court at Christmastide – it is what you want?'

'I'm not sure you're quite ready yet to appear at court, not without me there to guide you.' He was pulling at his straggly beard and peering at her speculatively.

'The Lady Brembre will be able to instruct me in all things.'

'If the Lady Brembre wants you and you're to go as her gentlewoman-in-waiting, I suppose we cannot disappoint her,' he said with a sigh.

'I'll do my best not to let you down,' she said, her heart lifting.

'Stay close to the Lady Brembre at all times, and beware of Sir Nicholas. Do nothing to inflame him further, do you understand?'

'Of course not,' she said.

He caught hold of her wrist, jerked her towards him. 'Be careful that you don't fall in love with him,' he warned.

She looked away, wishing that he did not always think only the worst. What was wrong with love? she thought. As long as it was pure and good and self-sacrificing.

'Remember, Nicolette,' he said, 'you will be little use to me if you are a slave to your own desires.'

'You need have no fear.' She forced herself to meet his searching gaze. 'At Holy Trinity we were taught to subdue the flesh to overcome all earthly desires.'

'With fasting and prayer,' he said drily. 'You might find it harder to practise the disciplines of the abbey amid the temptations of the King's palace at Christmastide.'

She dropped her eyes hastily. If only he did not share her doubt. If only he had more belief in her, then she might be able to believe in herself. The nuns had always given her confidence; their faith had been so strong. It had been so easy to be good at Holy Trinity.

Long before Christmastide was upon them, Nicolette began to dread the approaching visit to the palace. William frightened her with unceasing advice on how she was to

74

conduct herself with dignity and restraint, how she must not gossip, or flirt or allow her head to be turned by pretty speeches. He tried to teach her about precedence and the correct forms of address, of the importance of memorising badges and coat armour so that she would know at a glance who people were.

Christmastide drew near and Nicolette became so alarmed at the thought of all that she could do wrong she began to pray to the Virgin to send something to prevent her having to go after all.

No divine intervention occurred, perhaps because her prayers were not sufficiently heartfelt, and on the day before Christmas, William took her to Brembre's Inn not long after noon.

The distance from London to Westminster was little more than three miles, but their progress was slow for the horses were laden with many panniers and Idonia, who was no horsewoman, preferred to be carried in a litter. Because Westminster was the centre of administration as well as the King's palace, the halls and buildings extended over a large and complicated area along the river bank. There were law courts as well as state apartments, a great central hall where Parliament met, a white hall, gardens, and Westminster Abbey whose bell was ringing the Angelus by the time they arrived. Nicolette gazed about her in awe at the jumble of stone towers and low timbered buildings, the buttressed walls of the abbey and the church of St Peter which housed the sacred shrine of St Edward the Confessor.

A plump red-faced man in gold-embroidered robes riding on a large grey horse, whose retinue filled the paved courtyard, was dismounting. A page clad all in white proffered a jewelled mitre. As the bishop donned this symbol of his office, Nicolette instinctively dropped to her knees.

'There's no need, damoiselle, to dirty your fine kirtle on the cobblestones,' Brembre chided her. 'You're not in the abbey at Caen now.'

Feeling foolish, Nicolette scrambled to her feet, and found herself face to face with the bishop. Her training still urged her to abase herself before so important a personage, but Brembre's gaze challenged her even as he bent his head to acknowledge the bishop's blessing and so she bobbed a curtsey instead.

'The Damoiselle de Saint Pierre has been convent bred,' explained Brembre, 'and she is finding it harder to put off the instincts of a nun than to discard her serge habit.' The hard blue eyes were regarding her mockingly and Nicolette looked away embarrassed and afraid. The bishop surely would be angry. But to her surprise he merely smiled at her vaguely.

'A loss to the Church but a gain to the world,' he said, taking Brembre by the arm and sweeping him away through the crowded courtyard, smiling and raising his fingers in blessing as he went.

'Who is he?' Nicolette asked Idonia as she descended from her litter.

'John Fordham, Bishop of Durham, one time Treasurer.'

'He seemed very friendly,' said Nicolette, 'for a bishop.'

'Well, he ought to be friendly,' replied Idonia with a toss of her head. 'But for my husband he'd still be in the Tower.'

The bishop's patronage had not gone unremarked. A chamberlain was soon bowing at Idonia's side, ready to escort her to their lodgings – a room at the top of one of the towers to the east of the central hall. It was far smaller than the solar in Brembre's own house, but the bed curtains were of silk embroidered with the red leopards of England, and the ewer and basin were of silver. 'The damoiselle can lodge with the Queen's ladies-in-waiting,' the chamberlain informed them as he withdrew. 'I will send a page presently to show you where to go.'

It was some time before the panniers had been brought in and unpacked and Idonia could be arrayed in green velvet with a long train and open-sided surcoat trimmed with ermine. Then her brown, rather lifeless hair had to be brushed and rebraided and the new Bohemian headdress arranged to her satisfaction. Nicolette, surveying the effect of the balanced crescent moon above Idonia's well-plucked brow, felt it was an unfortunate fashion for someone with quite such a square face as the Lady Brembre. By this time the page had arrived to escort Nicolette to her lodgings. There was no sign of Sir Nicholas.

The page hurried Nicolette down the winding stone staircase and across a number of small courtyards connected by narrow passageways. Nicolette, following him breathlessly, thought that the palace was far more cold and inconvenient than the well-planned merchants' houses she had become accustomed to – more a very grand monastery, in fact – and wondered whether she would ever be able to find her way back to Lady Brembre's lodgings again. The page darted across a small garden with heraldic symbols in clipped yew, under a stone arch, down one more passageway, up a final flight of stairs, and pushed open a stout oak door. Then with a wink and a flourish of his hand he left her. Nervously, Nicolette hesitated on the threshold. Two girls – one dark haired and slim, the other solid-looking with flaxen hair coiled in two thick braids on either side of a smooth, round face – were chattering by the fire. They stopped and stared at Nicolette in silence. The low-vaulted chamber was strewn with veils, surcoats, discarded sleeves, which a tiring woman was listlessly trying to restore to the open coffers lying about the rush-covered floor. Nicolette was pleased to see her own panniers propped up among them. With a nervous smile at the two ladies watching her from the fire, she set about removing her travel-stained garments and making herself presentable for supper. William had warned her not to flaunt herself, so she chose a fur-lined surcoat to wear over her kirtle of fine blue wool to protect her from the chill of all those open courtyards, but which was still sufficiently low in front to reveal her unmarked white skin.

'My name's Juetta Seward. What's yours?' said the dark-haired girl suddenly.

'Nicolette de Saint Pierre.'

'Who do you attend?'

'The Lady Brembre.'

'Brembre?' The girl had a small pointed face and bright hazel eyes which she turned on Nicolette like an inquisitive squirrel. Nicolette busied herself with the buttons down the front of her surcoat.

'There's a merchant of the staple at Westminster called Brembre,' said the fair girl. 'He rents a house from the Comptroller of Customs.'

'A scribbling wool counter?' exclaimed Juetta. 'Surely he wouldn't be invited to the King's palace at Christmastide?'

'I don't know if Sir Nicholas Brembre is a stapler, I only know that he has been Mayor of London four times and is now adviser to the King.' Nicolette found herself rushing to his defence.

'Of course, Sir Nicholas Brembre,' the girl Juetta nodded

brightly. 'He's rich, isn't he? Rich enough to lend money to the King. Perhaps he gets it all from the wool customs at Westminster.'

Don't gossip, William had warned. Nicolette bit her lip and set about unbraiding her hair, determined not to be provoked again.

'You must be French, for you speak it like a native,' the big fair girl said.

Nicolette smiled and went on struggling with the long shining mass of her hair, hoping that if she seemed preoccupied they might leave her alone.

'I too am a foreigner in this land. I came with the Queen from Bohemia.'

Lulled by the sympathetic friendliness in the girl's placid blue eyes, Nicolette permitted herself a small confession. 'I was born in the Abbey of Holy Trinity at Caen. My mother was a knight's daughter and my father was killed on the battlefield before I was born,' she said.

'Where was he fighting when he was killed?' asked the Bohemian. 'Was it with van Artevelde? No, if he was French he would be against him. He wasn't Flemish, was he?'

'Don't be stupid, Gisela,' put in Juetta. 'How old are you, Nicolette de Saint Pierre?'

'Sixteen,' replied Nicolette, bemused by so many questions.

'Her father could not have been fighting for van Artevelde, not if he was killed before she was born.'

'Of course, Juetta. How clever you are. Where was he killed?'

Mother of Mercy, Gisela had the dogged perseverance of an ox, thought Nicolette nervously. How difficult it was – to lie – at court. Here she was, in spite of all William's careful preparation, already in trouble. 'I don't know. My mother was so heartrent by his death she would never talk about it. I think it was somewhere in Spain.'

'The French do not make war with Spain.' Gisela was quite certain.

'On a crusade.' Desperation helped. 'Against the Moors.' To her relief they accepted it. Juetta was investigating the contents of one of Nicolette's panniers and held up a belt of silver thread with an ornamental buckle. 'That's a pretty girdle,' she said. 'Will you wear it?'

'Not with this surcoat, it's too bulky,' replied Nicolette smiling. 'Would you like to borrow it?'

Beaming with pleasure, the girl tied the belt round her hips while Gisela admired it. Before long they were both delving into the contents of Nicolette's panniers, trying her veils and headdresses and jewels, like sparrows descending on a fallen sheaf of corn, while Nicolette, for whom possessions still had little meaning, struggled with her hair, wondering how she was ever to get it into the cauls without Lisette to help her. Then Juetta ordered one of the tiring women to help and Nicolette felt a glow of pleasure that perhaps the Queen's ladies-in-waiting had accepted her. She knew it when, ready at last, they took hold of her hands and ran chattering and laughing down the winding stone stairs and across the chilly open courtyards to the great central hall for supper.

The vast stone-vaulted hall was already filled with a great number of men and women seated at rows of trestle tables. At first Nicolette was aware of nothing but a blur of colour and noise – music from the gallery above the great west door, the scent of crushed herbs masking the usual body odours, pools of light from the flickering torches and hundreds of candles. The chamberlain waved them to a side table with scant ceremony.

'The King has not yet come in,' said Juetta pulling Nicolette down beside her on to the hard bench. 'The Queen will not like to be kept waiting too long.' At the far end of the hall a long flight of steps led up to a dais and a large beautiful window of coloured glass. Here, sitting at the high table beneath a golden canopy, was a youngish-looking woman with a jewelled golden circlet above her floating veil. The great carved chair beside her was empty.

'She looks kindly,' said Nicolette, a little disappointed that the Queen was not more beautiful. 'Is she easy to serve?'

'No more than any other,' replied Juetta with a little shrug of her narrow shoulders. 'She's amiable for most of the time – for a queen – and when she's not it's usually because the King is being difficult, which he is quite often.'

Nicolette glanced about her nervously at this indiscreet speech but the sudden sound of trumpets made her jump. The huge oak doors at the far entrance to the hall were flung wide. Gusts of cold air swept through the chamber. The brightly coloured banners fluttered on high, the torches flared alarmingly.

'Richard, King of England and France enters!' a herald declaimed from the doorway. The trumpets sent another great triumphant call, like a whinnying stallion, echoing through the hall. To the sound of wood scraping against stone the company rose in a billowing wave of colour like a banner unfurled. Nicolette craned forward eagerly but could see nothing except a frieze of hoods and hats and headdresses until the King mounted the steps to the dais. Then she saw a slim, handsome figure in jewel-encrusted velvet, his hair as gold as the crown on his head, bounding up the steps towards the Queen who smiled happily as he kissed her hand before seating himself in the carved chair. Nicolette let out her breath in a long, slow sigh of wonder. The King was everything a king should be, the royal couple as happy with each other as they had any right to expect. It was like a tale told by the troubadours, and she could scarcely believe that she was here to play her part, however humbly, in this great and glorious world.

A cleric in richly embroidered cope and jewelled mitre said Grace.

'That is the Lord Neville, Archbishop of York,' Juetta said as they sat down again. 'And the handsome young man next to the King is Robert de Vere, the new Duke of Ireland. Whatever you do while you're at court, do not fall foul of young Robert. He's the King's old playfellow and whenever His Grace gets into one of his sulks, only Robert can be sure to bring him round. The Queen values him greatly,' Juetta added with a grin. 'The solemn old goat at the far end of the table is Sir Simon Burley, the King's tutor. Once he was a retainer of the King's uncle Lancaster but, in spite of that, the King trusts him absolutely. His loyalty is beyond question. The man in the sable hat is the Earl of Suffolk, he that was once Chancellor of England until Parliament sent him to the Tower for corruption. But now the King has released him. I don't know the man next to him.'

'Sir Nicholas Brembre!' exclaimed Nicolette, surprised and at the same time proud to see him seated up there at the high table among the mightiest in the land, looking as arrogant and masterful as at his own table at home.

'So that's Sir Nicholas Brembre.' Juetta's eyes bright with curiosity, were almost popping out of her head. 'He looks rich – and cruel. Like a pirate. Is it true he murders people who cannot repay him what they owe?'

'I do not know,' said Nicolette, fighting back a strong desire to defend him. She felt sure that anything she might say to her companion would be squirrelled away into that dangerously well-stocked memory for some future use.

'Is that his wife, the unhappy lady in the new fashioned Bohemian headdress at his side?' went on the irrepressible Juetta. 'You must persuade her it is not for her – she looks like a horned cow.'

Nicolette could not help laughing as she looked again at the high table. Idonia, ignored by her husband, was gazing rather belligerently out into the hall as a long line of servants staggered towards the high table bearing the dishes of the first course.

'Has he a mistress, the wicked pirate? He looks as if he might make an exciting lover.'

'I don't think Sir Nicholas is interested in women,' replied Nicolette firmly. 'Who is the severe-looking man in scarlet with a white coif next to the Lady Brembre?'

'Sir Robert Tresilian, the Chief Justice. He it was who helped the King hang all those wicked peasants after the rising. He does all the King's dirty work for him.'

Nicolette glanced at Juetta alarmed, unable to tell from that maiden's lively face whether she was teasing or not.

'By Saint Michael,' exclaimed Gisela nudging Nicolette and pointing at a table almost directly opposite. 'The King has a new retainer and he has eyes, it seems, only for you.'

Nicolette looked across to the table where some of the King's retainers who had accompanied him into the hall were now seated. Among them, with the white hart of the King's badge upon his sleeve, sat Sir Piers Exton, gazing at her with longing.

'He's very attractive, do you not think?' whispered Juetta, plucking at Nicolette's sleeve. 'Such curly dark hair and those eyes,' she gave a little shiver of desire. 'Are they not made for love? I wonder who he is.'

Nicolette looked away quickly. Some of the other young men were also taking a lively interest in her and she was embarrassed.

When the dishes of the first course came down from the high table, the ladies-in-waiting who had been attending the Queen were released from duty. They came fluttering down the hall like birds of paradise to settle at the table reserved for the Queen's ladies and soon they were all busily discussing the King's new retainer, chattering and laughing as they exchanged smiles and covert glances with the young men opposite. Nicolette tried to concentrate on eating her food and sipping her wine, listening to the music and keeping her eyes down, taking no part in the talk all around her.

When supper was over and the King and Queen had withdrawn for the night, the young men from the table opposite came flocking over and the chattering and laughing grew much bolder.

'Here is a knight I know wants to meet you. The Chevalier de Real, Nicolette de Saint Pierre,' Juetta said, fluttering her eyelashes at a good-looking young man. 'He's fun but he's married and the biggest rake at court, so be careful.'

'Cruel fair one,' replied the chevalier, rolling expressive eyes at Nicolette. 'She spurns me because I did not wear her favour when I unhorsed the Saxon knight at the tourney last Michaelmas. You would not be so unjust, damoiselle.'

'No indeed, I would expect you to wear your wife's favour when you fight,' said Nicolette.

'Oh, my wife. She is older than I am by some ten years and at present confined to my manor, which adjoins with hers, expecting our fourth child. Three girls already – will you not light a candle to the Blessed Virgin for me that this time it will be a son?'

'Perhaps it is God's punishment for your infidelity,' said Nicolette with a mischievous smile. Really he had such merry eyes it was impossible not to tease him.

'Ah, damoiselle, you have the face of an angel, do not be so cruel.'

All this time Nicolette was conscious of Piers standing silent and shy. Among these assured young men he looked awkward and aloof. But good manners alone required that she acknowledge him.

'Well met, Sir Piers,' she said, smiling as she gave him her hand.

'Well met again, damoiselle,' he replied, clasping it

fervently and then, as if not knowing quite what to do with it, dropping it awkwardly.

'You know him?' Juetta accused. 'Why did you not say?'

'I wanted to surprise you,' said Nicolette, laughing as she introduced Piers to Juetta and Gisela. He bowed respectfully but made no attempt to engage any of the women in conversation.

'Are you married, Sir Piers?' Gisela inquired.

'No,' replied Piers looking at Nicolette.

'Piers is a younger son and landless,' the Chevalier de Real explained. 'He hopes to make his fortune fighting for the King.'

'Perhaps he will begin by triumphing at the tourney,' said Juetta, making eyes at him. 'I wonder, Sir Piers, whose favour will you beg to wear in the lists?'

Nicolette, exchanging bright smiles with the chevalier prayed that Piers would not embarrass her further by renewed declarations of service. To her relief he remained silent, while the young men clustered about her with their flowery speeches and languishing glances. It was all very polished and charming but although Nicolette was not used to such talk she knew instinctively that it was nothing but a game.

'Damoiselle de Saint Pierre,' the Chevalier de Real beseeched Nicolette, 'will you not come out in the pleasaunce with me? There's a troupe of jugglers practising for tomorrow and a performing bear you might like to see.'

'No, thank you. It's too cold for walking outside,' she said primly, but she did not lower her eyes as she had been trained to do in the convent.

'The poor child's tired after her long journey from the city, she wants to go to bed,' Juetta protested.

'Then at least let me escort you across the courtyard, damoiselle,' he replied.

'I shall escort Damoiselle de Saint Pierre to her lodgings,' said Piers. De Real looked at Piers in surprise but there was something about the quiet determination on the knight's face which brooked no interference.

'So strong,' whispered Juetta, casting up her eyes. 'Will you be safe, do you think? Shall I come with you?'

'I shall be safe,' replied Nicolette. It never occurred to her not to go with Piers. He was her protector and she knew she could not be in safer hands. The other young men fell back to let her pass but then suddenly she found her way barred by Sir Nicholas Brembre.

'What do you think you are about, damoiselle?' he demanded angrily. 'You have not come here for your own pleasures but to attend the Lady Brembre.' There was no mercy in the cold, hard gaze. All Nicolette's enjoyment vanished in a wave of guilt and fear. She had inflamed him, not with desire but with anger. And his anger was justified, for in truth she had forgotten all about Lady Brembre. On her very first day at court she had failed in the most important thing of all – her duty to her mistress. She raised pleading eyes to his face.

'I'm sorry, Sir Nicholas,' she stammered. 'I did not mean . . . forgive me.'

He seized her by the wrist, dragging her after him between the deserted tables towards the dais. At the foot of the steps, he stopped and jerked her round to face him.

'Strumpet!' he hissed. 'I did not expect these lewd ways or I would never have brought you here. Now go and attend to Lady Brembre.'

She fled up the long flight of stone steps, gulping back tears, terrified by the anger in his face and utterly ashamed. It had all been so innocent. She had meant nothing by it.

Idonia was still in her place at the high table, sitting alone; she did not appear to have enjoyed her first taste of court life.

'There you are, Nicolette,' she said. 'I was expecting you to come back to our lodgings before supper, to carry my train.'

'I meant to,' Nicolette felt even more ashamed than ever. 'It is just that the palace is so big and it takes so long just to get from one place to another, and I was not sure of the way.' Even to her own ears it sounded a poor excuse.

'If you do not feel able to perform your duties, perhaps one of the Queen's ladies would be prepared to help me instead.'

'Oh no, no. I'm so sorry, Lady Brembre, please forgive me,' cried Nicolette, falling down on her knees by Idonia's chair. 'I truly wish to serve you and I will try harder. I promise. It is just that it's all so new and different.'

'We must all try hard to fit in here,' said Idonia with a sigh as she got up. 'I thought I might depend on you to help me, Nicolette.'

'And I will,' said Nicolette as she picked up Idonia's train. 'I swear by the Holy Rood, everything that I can do, I will do.'

CHAPTER 8

It was a promise that Nicolette found hard to fulfil. She seemed to be perpetually on the run, fetching and carrying for Idonia, darting between the guest tower and the Queen's apartments. And she was torn between her duty to Idonia who was ill at ease and unhappy in these unfamiliar surroundings and her own enjoyment with the Queen's ladies-in-waiting.

Idonia found it hard to settle into the ways of the court. She was unable to understand or to take part in the women's quick-witted, gossipy French chatter, although Nicolette translated as best she could, unwilling to resign herself to the role of silent spectator. She was used to ruling in her own world and it was Nicolette who had to bear the brunt of her desire to dominate. She bore it patiently because she found it sad that Idonia, who had been her mentor and from whom she had learnt so much, now seemed a little ridiculous, a lonely and frustrated figure without her own small court of family and friends to queen it over.

It was good to be able to escape at mealtimes and at night to the much more congenial company of the Queen's ladies-in-waiting. Among these well-educated young women, who spoke French, sang well, and read well, Nicolette did not feel out of place, for they reminded her of the other novices at Holy Trinity, and it made her realise how much she missed the companionship of those days. Like the novices at Caen, the Queen's ladies were daughters of landed families, but they were being prepared for marriage, not dedication to God. One day they would be expected to marry whoever their parents chose for them. In the solar, the talk was nearly always of marriage or love, and Nicolette very soon discovered that the two were not the same.

Marriage was for healing disputes over land, acquiring manors, uniting dynasties. Love was a courtly, stylised game. A lover should be prostrated by his mistress, wounded to death by her beauty, killed by her disdain, bound to an illimitable constancy, marked out for her dangerous service. A smile from her was all that such a lover might expect as reward for years of painful adoration. It was this love that the troubadours sang about, this love that the jousts and knightly pursuits were all designed to embody. Nicolette realised that it was this love which Piers had to offer her and although she was pleased by his homage and the envy it caused among her companions, it was not what she wanted. What fascinated her was the other, darker and more exciting kind of love, the secret, illicit, adulterous passion which the ladies whispered about in the privacy of the solar when snuggled up in their shared beds together at night. Nicolette recognised this love all too well for it was what she felt for Sir Nicholas Brembre and it was all the more compelling because she knew it was wrong.

On Christmas Day the whole court attended Mass in Westminster Abbey. All the abbey clergy came out to meet the King in procession and the court vied among themselves to make notable offerings at St Edward the Confessor's shrine. The King was confessed by the anchorite monk who was attached to the abbey and afterwards came out, refreshed, to enjoy himself anew. Nicolette had expected, in so holy a place, to find a spiritual answer to her inner turmoil but although the Church of St Peter had been filled with the most beautiful singing, a multitude of magnificently robed clerics, as well as the entire royal household devoutly prostrate before the shrine, Nicolette had not been moved, or soothed, by any mystical visions.

It was barely six months since she had left the convent but already the quest for perfection had become hopelessly entangled and she did not know what she wanted any more. In her heart she knew she had failed to live up to the ideals instilled by the Abbess at Holy Trinity. She did not pray enough, she did not fast. She would like to have gone to confession, but although the palace was full of clergy, from the Archbishop of York downwards, and every noble lord had a monk or a friar as his own private confessor, yet she did not know who to approach. She was afraid that she might no longer be able to subdue the promptings of her sinful flesh, if tempted.

She lit her candle and asked to be given the strength to resist temptation. But no sooner had she placed her candle in front of the shrine than it flickered in the draughts swirling about the lofty church and went out. Nicolette crossed herself nervously. It was an evil omen. Did it mean that she would fail to resist Sir Nicholas? Or that he would not put her to the test? She got up from her knees realising that she did not know what to pray for any more. Confused, frightened, filled with doubt, she left the sacred precincts of the abbey unconfessed and unconsoled.

It snowed after Christmas, covering the courtyards with a pure white carpet deep enough to add to Nicolette's difficulties in trying to be several places at once, but not deep enough to deter the men from riding out each day to hunt with hawk and spear and bow. Nicolette spent many days closeted with Idonia in the little chamber in the guest tower, either reading to her or sewing. One day when Idonia was sleeping off the effect of a heavy dinner, Nicolette sat gazing out of the window. After the snow had come clear frosty weather and the river sparkled in the late afternoon sunshine. Idonia would be asleep for a long time yet and when she awoke, the short winter day would be over. Seizing her chance, Nicolette slipped out of the chamber and down the winding stairs to the courtyard below.

There was nobody about. She wandered, happy to be for once alone, breathing the cold air with delight after the stuffy, smoke-filled chamber. Enjoying the peace and the cold and the rare opportunity to take her time, she wandered towards the Queen's small garden with its gryphons and unicorns and other weird animals all intricately contrived in clipped yew. She was so absorbed examining these exotic heraldic symbols that she was unaware that somebody else had come into the garden, until she came face to face with him. It was Sir Nicholas Brembre.

'What are you doing here?' he demanded.

She gave a guilty start. 'Just walking. Lady Brembre is sleeping.' She waited for Sir Nicholas to upbraid her for failing in her duty, but he did not scold. He stood, gazing at her with the cold, hard look she knew so well.

'Are you sure you haven't come here to meet someone?'

'Only you.' She did not know why she said it. She was so confused and startled by his unexpected appearance that the words popped out of her mouth before she had time to think.

'Don't flirt with me, Nicolette de Saint Pierre.'

'I don't flirt with people,' she said and blushed as she lowered her eyes hastily.

He was silent and as if compelled by some force beyond her control, she peeped at him mischievously through her long lashes. The effect on him was quite alarming. With a hiss of indrawn breath he lunged for her, held her hard against him and kissed her crushingly on the mouth. It was not at all what she expected. Her lips were bruised, her mouth filled by his searching tongue, the breath knocked out of her. She struggled frantically but the more she struggled, the more inflamed he became. Her cap came off. Her long heavy braids uncoiled from round her head. There was the sound of tearing cloth. Just when she thought she might suffocate, he flung her violently from him. With her hand pressed to her bruised lips, breathless and dishevelled, she stared at him horror-struck.

'Why do you hate me so?' she asked.

'Is that what you think? That I hate you? Sweet Jesu, damoiselle!' He lunged for her again and she, thoroughly unnerved by the look of what she took to be rage on his face, instinctively stepped back, caught her toe in her unwieldy train and fell at his feet.

He glared down at her and she held her breath, terrified of what he might do next. A sword grated on a stone somewhere behind her. She heard a startled exclamation, glimpsed a pair of sturdy, steel-clad legs.

'Touch her and you are a dead man.'

She looked up and saw Piers Exton, dressed in chain mail, beginning to draw his sword from its scabbard.

'Piers, no! You don't understand.' Hastily she scrambled to her knees.

'I understand all too well,' Piers said, guarding her like a dog with a bone as he faced Brembre, bristling with challenge.

'How dare you interfere with me?' Brembre demanded hotly. 'You shall answer for this, Sir Knight.'

'I shall be glad to meet any challenge you care to mount at the tourney on Epiphany.'

For what seemed to Nicolette like an eternity, the two men stood facing each other in the garden and if Brembre had been dressed for it, she was certain that they would have come to blows then and there. But he was fashionably attired in a long-skirted tunic, a velvet, fur-trimmed houpland, with only a dagger at his belt, which perhaps was why, with a muttered oath, he turned abruptly on his heel and strode off.

'Are you harmed, damoiselle?' Piers held out his hand and helped Nicolette to her feet.

'No. Just my coif. It has fallen off.'

He bent to retrieve her linen cap. She was so shaken and ashamed she did not dare look at him. It was all so different from what she had expected – even in her wildest dreams. She did not know what had made Brembre attack her like that, but it was certainly not love, she thought. She became aware that Piers was standing with averted gaze, holding her cap reverently in his hand. She began winding her two long braids round her head with hands that shook, praying that he would ask no questions. Whatever it was that had occurred between her and Brembre, it was not something she wished to discuss with Piers.

'Shall I escort you to your solar?' he said, handing her the coif.

She dragged her scattered wits together. She wanted to run somewhere and hide, to be alone to think, to recover, to pray – for forgiveness, strength to resist temptation, deliverance from evil? Where could she go? The solar was tempting but she did not feel able to face the curiosity of the Queen's ladies-in-waiting. She thought with longing of the abbey church but remembered with a stab of guilt Lady Brembre.

'I must return to Lady Brembre. She may have woken up by now,' she said, not daring to look at him.

He did not argue with her, did not question her at all. Just waited patiently while she put on her linen cap and pulled her cloak together where it had been ripped from its jewelled clasp at the neck. She tried not to think of the expression on Sir Nicholas's face when he strode out of the garden, or what she would do the next time she saw him. She had meant to be so cool and dignified and aloof and instead she had probably lost him for ever.

When she was ready, Piers walked with her to the foot of the guest tower. She could not bring herself to thank him for his interference. He had made Brembre look a fool and it was all her fault. She would never be forgiven for that.

'Is Lady Brembre in her lodgings?' Piers asked.

'Yes. I left her sleeping. I only went out for a little. To get some air. It looked so beautiful this morning.' She knew she owed Piers some sort of explanation. He made no comment, and she was grateful to him for his silence. He bowed and took his leave and she went to wait on Lady Brembre, not knowing how she was to face her, or Sir Nicholas, or Piers ever again.

Lady Brembre was far too concerned with her own problems to notice anything wrong and by the time she was ready to go down to the hall for supper, Nicolette had recovered a little of her composure. Her worst time was when she came face to face again with Piers. He did not show by so much as a raised eyebrow that anything untoward had occurred and she was glad that he was so strong and silent. She knew she could depend upon him utterly. But she was tortured by doubts and fears and shattered illusions. Brembre had frightened her. His kisses had been brutal, painful, unpleasant even. She longed to know if kisses were supposed to be like that. When the ladies lay in bed at night whispering together about the dangerous delights of un-bridled passion, Nicolette longed to ask them what they meant, but she did not dare. Nothing had been at all as she had meant it to be. Sir Nicholas did not come near her, but she was aware of his presence even at the other end of the crowded hall. She was torn by a longing for him to notice her and terrified of what to do if he did. But most of all she was afraid that he would not forgive her.

On the Feast of the Epiphany a tourney was to be held, when all the knights were to display their skill in a splendid clash of arms, which would be followed by a great feast in celebration. From early in the morning the knights and their squires were busy arming while the King and Queen with the rest of the court flowed out of the palace and down to the greensward by the water's edge to where tiered stands had been erected on either side of the lists.

Nicolette was not at all sure what happened at a tourney, never having been to one, but from the chatter among the Queen's ladies-in-waiting she had learnt that knights liked to have a lady to fight for, whose glove or ribbon or piece of hanging sleeve they would attach to their helmets. Piers asked her for a favour to wear but she refused him, turning away from the hurt in his eyes, irked that he paraded his love so openly. The other ladies teased her for being so cruel to her true knight who was so eager to fight her battles for her, but Nicolette was terrified that Piers was not playing games, like the other knights, that he meant to fight for her in earnest against Sir Nicholas Brembre. She could not face the spectacle of the two of them fighting over her in front of the whole court and so she stayed away from the tournament altogether, telling Idonia that she needed the time to make everything ready for the evening's feast. The night before, Idonia had tripped going up the steps to the high table and torn the front of her best gown. She was beginning to feel a little more at home and was quite prepared to do without Nicolette at the tourney if it meant she would be able to wear her best gown at the feast.

Left alone in the Brembres' chamber with her sewing and her thoughts, Nicolette tried to make some kind of sense of the confusion which possessed her. Tomorrow she would be leaving the palace to return to the city and William Gryffard. What was she to tell him on her return? There was nothing really to tell, she told herself, stabbing at the Lady Brembre's torn gown with her needle. Except that Sir Nicholas Brembre was so displeased with her he would probably never speak to her again. Should she tell her father that? Was it what he wanted?

She did not know what her father wanted except that she should not become a slave to her desires. At which thought she cast aside her sewing and threw herself down on her knees to pray. She began the chant for matins but it was so different alone in the Brembres' bedchamber, kneeling on the cushioned prieu-dieu instead of the hard stone floor of the abbey chapel. There was no repetitive plainsong soaring into a vaulted roof to uplift her thoughts and take her mind away from her bodily discomfort to a contemplation of God. There was instead the sound of the trumpet calling the knights to come forth and do battle. At its sound she could not concentrate on her prayers any longer, but jumped up and ran to the slitted window. She could see the lists on the greensward by the river and the banners of the contending knights fluttering from the wooden stockade. She strained her eyes for a glimpse of Piers's red unicorn or the green falcons of Sir Nicholas but it was too far away to recognise individual devices. All she could see was a blur of colour. 'Blessed Mother preserve him,' she whispered, as she sat down by the window and took up her sewing once more.

As if in direct answer to her prayer, the oak door was flung open and Sir Nicholas Brembre strode into the chamber. Nicolette shrank back on the window seat, fear – and something else – robbing her of breath. He was not dressed in armour for the fight, but in a short tunic embroidered with his arms and tight-fitting particoloured hose. He closed the door carefully and leant against it, staring at her with brooding, sombre gaze.

'The Lady Brembre gave me permission to stay behind,' Nicolette said nervously. 'I had work to do on her gown.' She held it up in front of her like a shield.

'I have come to you, Nicolette de Saint Pierre, because I want you. More than I have ever wanted any woman. You are the most beautiful girl I have ever seen and if I do not have you I think I shall go mad.'

Her heart began to pound like a drum. She shrank back further against the cold stone of the window, unable to move, unable to think – except that it was sin.

'Your wife?' she whispered.

He came to stand in front of her. Took his wife's gown from her lifeless hands, threw it on the floor behind him.

'Come, Nicolette, you have been at court long enough to know that marriage has nothing to do with what a man such as I and a woman such as you feel for one another.'

She could scarcely breathe, her heart was pounding so. He bent forward, pulled her to her feet and kissed her hard, but not so crushingly as before. Almost, she thought, somewhere in the dim recesses of her bemused mind, I might grow to enjoy it. But she must not enjoy it! With a supreme effort of will she prised her hands free and tried to push him away. He stopped kissing her and she sank down on to the window seat, trembling all over.

'I thought you hated me,' she said.

'I did, I do, for the power you have over me,' he said, beginning to undo the row of buttons down the front of her surcoat. 'No woman has ever tormented me as you do.'

It was hardly a declaration of love. She ought to tell him to stop. She tried to but she was mesmerised by his fingers on her buttons. Her surcoat fell to the floor and his hand was inside the low-cut front of her kirtle. It was wrong, she knew. His fingers found her breast. Blessed Mother, what to do, what to say? His fingers were sending shivers of exquisite pleasure through her whole body. 'No,' she moaned. 'Please. You must not. I can't.'

He laughed and kissed her on the lips. She opened her mouth to protest and he held her crushed against him, kissing her deeply, while from outside the window came a blare of the heralds' trumpets and the roar of excitement from the spectators at the tourney. She made one last desperate effort to free herself, struggling and beating at him with her fists. He laughed and dropped random kisses on her while she fought him. She paused, panting, and he grasped her clenched fists and forced them behind her back, holding her hard against him. She could feel the heat of his body through the fine silk of her kirtle; the pounding of her heart was no greater than his.

'Sweet Jesus, damoiselle,' he said gazing down at her fiercely and his eyes were no longer cold, but dark with passion. 'I have imagined you many times thus but the reality is far, far better than any of my visions.' He was holding her so tightly she could hardly breathe and she knew that to struggle further would be useless. She thought of her father and all his warnings. She thought of the nuns at Caen and all their teachings. Nothing had prepared her for this! Her clamouring flesh was defying her, but her mind still clung to the idea of chastity.

'I am in your power, Sir Nicholas,' she said, trying to keep her voice steady, to instil into it something of the Abbess's aloof authority, only he was tugging impatiently at the heavy braids of her hair and it was difficult to sound aloof and cool and dignified with her hair tumbling down, like the walls of Jericho. 'Surely you won't force me to commit a mortal sin against my will?' she begged.

'I'm no slave to chivalry like that foolish champion of

94

yours, Sir Piers Exton,' he said. 'When I want something I take it.' As if to prove his point he picked her up, carried her over to the bed and threw her down upon its velvet cover.

Nicolette closed her eyes and waited for him to take her, telling herself that she had failed. She did not know what she could have done to avoid this terrible moment but there must have been something. Her father had warned her, Piers wanted to protect her. Here in this great palace filled with so many people, she should never have got herself into such dire trouble. But all the time her flesh was glorying in what he was doing. Soon she forgot that it was sin, that he was a wicked man and Idonia's husband, all she wanted was to please him, to make him hers for ever. Then there was pain and she struggled. It seemed to inflame him, so she struggled more until the bed was a mass of fighting, thrashing limbs.

'Tell me now,' he panted, suddenly rearing up above her, 'that I am taking you against your will.' Her protests were smothered by his kisses and, scarcely knowing what she did, she kissed him back fiercely. He was a big, heavy man and he lay on top of her, crushing her. There was more pain but she welcomed it. Pain was necessary to subdue the flesh and she wanted to subdue her flesh to his demands. To give him what he craved. When the pain seemed almost more than she could bear, he gave a great cry and with a long shudder was still.

She lay beneath his panting, heavy body trying to make some sort of sense of the thoughts seething in her over-wrought mind. Suddenly Brembre raised himself on one elbow, stared down at her wildly.

'Dear God,' he said seizing great handfuls of her hair and burying his face in it. 'I thought that if I could but have you, it would kill the longing, but now I find I want you again.' He kissed her and she wriggled beneath him, feeling the weight of his body pressing her down into the feathery softness of the bed. His kisses grew more demanding and she kissed him back, feeling an urgency of her own swelling within her, sweeping her up like a great wave racing towards the shore. She dug her nails into his back, clinging to him, not knowing what she did, riding the wave until with a great crashing roar it broke against the shore, leaving her floating in still, calm waters, at peace for ever.

'May God have mercy,' he muttered, lying exhausted at her side. 'No woman has the power to move me as you do.'

She did not know whether it was success or failure; all she knew was that the struggle to resist him was lost and that it was an exquisite relief.

CHAPTER 9

The feasting after the tournament went on long into the night. There was a huge amount to eat and drink, dancing, jesting, and as the drink flowed and the merriment reached its pitch, there was a great deal of lewd revelry, in marked contrast to the formal chivalry of the tournament. The King and Queen remained in the hall until almost midnight and the King threw himself wholeheartedly into the pranks and jests devised by Robert de Vere. Nicolette and the Queen's ladies-in-waiting were besieged by knights and their squires who seemed none the worse for a day's hard fighting in the tournament. Nicolette danced and laughed and flirted with them all, so full of warmth and good will that she was able to be kind even to Piers.

All the ladies were eager to be kind to Piers, who had acquitted himself well in the tournament. Although he had been unhorsed in the mêlée, he had fought on foot so furiously and with such skill that he had helped to carry the day for the King's retainers against those of the King's half-brother, the Earl of Kent. Nicolette could not fail to see the great purplish swelling on his hand where a blow had caught him, nor help to notice that when he tried to dance with her he was even stiffer than usual.

'Poor Piers,' she said feeling sorry for him. 'Don't dance if it hurts too much.'

He shook his head, smiling at her ruefully. 'I'm sorry if my dancing isn't up to much.'

She returned his smile absently because she was not listening to a word he said. She was looking over his shoulder watching Sir Nicholas who remained talking earnestly with the rest of the King's councillors on the dais. It was only a few short hours since they had been parted and she was surprised at how much she pined for him. But already he seemed to have forgotten all about her. She remembered the talk in the solar, of the girls who had driven their lovers mad with desire by their modesty and reticence, of the love potions which had been slipped into many a man's drinking cup. Nicolette had been amused but she had not thought it mattered. Now she wished that she had paid more attention to the art of seduction.

She went to bed that night in a confusion of hope and fear, hope that on the journey back to the city Sir Nicholas would make some sort of tryst with her, and fear that he might not want her again, but mercifully she was so exhausted that she fell instantly into deep untroubled sleep.

She awoke with hope in the ascendant and dressed with great care, choosing a close-fitting velvet gown trimmed with fur and a wimple of fine lawn. The Queen's ladies-in-waiting teased her, telling her she was preparing for a journey not for a tourney and that her fine clothes would soon be spoilt by the dust and mud of the road. But Nicolette only laughed as she fitted a chased silver girdle round her slender hips, saying that she needed something to make her feel cheerful now that Christmastide had come to an end.

She danced out of the solar, her blood singing in her veins, but when she reached Idonia's chamber she was overwhelmed by guilt. Idonia was in a good mood this morning, happy to be going home, and warm in her praise and gratitude to Nicolette for all she had done to ease her life at court. It made Nicolette feel terrible. She was all too aware that in giving herself so joyously to Sir Nicholas she had committed a sin; it would have to be confessed, and many penances performed, before it could be absolved. As she helped Idonia prepare for the journey home, she could hardly bring herself to look at the silk-curtained bed in which only yesterday she had betrayed her mistress's trust. She was thankful that Sir Nicholas had, as usual, left the chamber long before his wife was ready to rise. At least she would not have to meet him again here in this room.

They went down to the outer court and found Brembre's small retinue waiting. Nicolette helped Idonia into the litter and by the time she had her settled comfortably, and the panniers had been loaded on to the packhorses, Sir Nicholas came striding into the courtyard. He was deep in conversation with two knights and walked straight past Nicolette without so much as a glance. The squires brought the knights' horses and they began to mount. With a sinking heart Nicolette realised that if they were to accompany Brembre to London, there would be no chance of a word with him in private.

She stood shivering beside her palfrey in the bright cold of the wintry morning, wishing she had been more sensible and worn her thick travelling cloak. How foolish she had been, how weak. She had let Sir Nicholas Brembre take what he wanted and now he had no further use for her. She was a failure. She resolved that as soon as she was home again she would go to confession, accept whatever penance the priest imposed and begin a new life of penitence and grace.

Suddenly Sir Nicholas broke away from his companions and came towards her.

'Good morning, damoiselle,' he said. 'Is my wife safely bestowed in the litter?' It was an innocent question, one fit to be heard by anybody in the crowded court, but the way his eyes raked her from head to foot made Nicolette's heart leap and she was glad that she had dressed so carefully to please him. She found she was holding his glance longer than necessary.

'Your wife is ready and looking forward to the journey, Sir Nicholas,' she said and looked away quickly. He lifted her on to the palfrey, and turned away almost immediately. But just the feel of his hands on her body, the masterful way he had lifted her off her feet sent Nicolette's blood racing. She was overwhelmed by guilt. How could pardon and absolution be achieved when her flesh – her once obedient, self-denying flesh – was crying out to sin again?

She watched Brembre climb on to his own strong gelding and ride out of the court with the two knights on either side absorbing all his attention, but she knew he still wanted her. She had felt it in the way his hands gripped her when he lifted her into the saddle; she had seen the hunger in his eyes and knew that it matched her own.

She no longer felt cold. She felt invigorated, more truly alive than ever before. Bright sunlight sparkled on the water of the Thames; the fields running down to the water's edge were white with frost. The pace was slow, because of Idonia's litter, but Nicolette was content to amble along watching Sir Nicholas riding ahead, remembering the feel of his body crushing the breath out of her and the wonder of his kisses. How could she refuse him anything? she wondered. But she would try. She had to try, although deep down she knew that Sir Nicholas Brembre would stop at nothing to get what he wanted. It was one of the reasons he fascinated her so.

When at last they reached London, Sir Nicholas drew rein and let the knights ride on into the city while he waited for her beneath the great stone arch of the Lud Gate.

'Will you ride back with us to the Royall, damoiselle?' he asked.

'I don't think so,' she replied, not looking at him but very conscious that he had brought his horse so close his shoulder was almost touching hers as they rode together through the gateway into London. 'I think it would be better if I went straight home to Master Gryffard who is doubtless expecting me. Lady Brembre will be able to manage without me, once she is at home again.'

'What of me? Do you think I can manage now without you?' he replied harshly.

'I hope not,' she said, so startled she blurted out the truth. He was glaring at her almost vehemently and it thrilled her to realise that this man, who wielded such power in the city, was angry because he could not take her home with him.

'If you won't come today, will you come tomorrow?' he demanded as they rode on side by side up the steep, cobbled street towards St Paul's Cathedral.

'If you want me to,' she replied so softly he had to bend his head to hear.

'I can't seem to stop wanting you,' he said. 'But it won't be easy to find a way. My wife is a very good housekeeper. There is nothing that happens in her household that she does not know about.'

'I thought you never let difficulties stand in your way,' she said, emboldened by the hunger in his eyes.

'By the Rood, no!' he cried, laughing. 'Is that why you love me?'

'You assume too much, Sir Nicholas,' she said, lowering her eyes, to see what a little belated modesty might do.

'Don't dissemble, Nicolette,' he retorted. 'It's one of the reasons I love you – for your refreshing simplicity.' She was undone. Riding beside him with his eyes, which once had appeared so cold, blazing down into hers and his thigh brushing against the velvet of her skirt, she could think of nothing save how she could please him.

'Master Gryffard is often away from home,' she suggested tentatively.

'William Gryffard must know nothing,' he said sharply, 'and he will be the hardest to fool. He is my eyes and ears and keeps me informed of everything that goes on in this city and beyond. Well I know how good he is at winkling out secrets.'

'Then you must trust him, surely,' she said. 'Would it matter if he knew?'

'He must not know.'

Suddenly Nicolette felt afraid. She would have to lie to her father. Another sin, another promise broken. She felt as if she had plunged into a dark, impenetrable forest, full of unknown terrors. She glanced at her lover. He was trouble. Instinctively she sensed that nothing about this man would be easy. She had been warned that he was ruthless. She knew that he was the most powerful man in the city. In pleasing him she might not be able to help hurting others.

'If William Gryffard finds out about us, he might send you back to that abbey in Caen,' Sir Nicholas said smiling at her, 'and you wouldn't want that now would you?'

She knew that if she did not go back to Caen she was lost, had been lost since yesterday when she had lain with him; she also sensed that soon she would have to choose between her lover and her father and wondered which one she could bear to deceive; worst of all, she knew that right now all that mattered was that Sir Nicholas still wanted her.

William came hurrying into the hall to welcome her back. 'Clearly life in the King's palace suits you,' he said, his watchful eyes scanning her carefully. 'There's a glow about you which wasn't there when you left.' Casually, she walked over to the fire, held her hands out to the leaping flames, launched swiftly into a detailed description of the lavish entertainment, the rich and wonderful food, the sumptuous clothes, the costly jewels and all the glories of the King's palace.

'The cost!' he exclaimed with a shudder. 'The King's extravagance will be the undoing of us all.'

She wondered if, like Sir Nicholas, he had lent money to the King. Sir Nicholas did not seem worried by the King's extravagance. She would like to have reassured her father but did not dare mention Brembre's name. William was staring at her moodily. She told him about the Queen's ladies and how they had befriended her. To her relief he began to show an interest in the King and Queen, to question her as to how often the King visited the Queen's apartments and in particular how the Queen's health appeared. When she realised where all these careful questions were leading she was able to inform him that she had it from the Queen's ladies that Her Grace was definitely not with child.

'Four years married and still no sign of an heir,' he said looking even more glum. 'Was Henry Bolingbroke there?'

'No,' she said, surprised.

'A mistake. It would do the King no harm to have had Lancaster's heir under his eye, especially while the Duke is away in Spain.' He wanted to know which great lords and which bishops had been with the King and she recounted them all, hoping that he would be pleased with her for having remembered their names and titles so exactly, but all he did was to look graver than ever.

'No Warwick? No Earl of Arundel?' he asked. 'The King overlooks his enemies. There are plenty of ambitious men waiting to see what will happen now that the King has defied his uncle of Gloucester. Men like Warwick and Arundel may support either side. The King would do well to make friends of the waverers instead of always surrounding himself only with those he knows he can depend upon.'

She could not understand his morbid determination to see disaster round every corner. Sir Nicholas was not like that, she thought. He took risks all the time and won, because he was courageous. He was indestructible because he did not believe that he could be destroyed. Her heart swelled with love at the thought of him. Tomorrow, he had said. She would see him tomorrow and somehow he would contrive a way for them to be alone together.

'Nothing is likely to happen to the King,' she said gaily. 'He is in excellent health and spirits and leaves Westminster now to go north to rally the country behind him. Everybody at court thinks he has successfully triumphed over his enemies.'

'What about Sir Nicholas Brembre? Does he go with the King?'

'No. Sir Nicholas has returned to London.'

'Any trouble from him?' He slipped it in so quickly she was almost caught unawares. He was watching her, but not so closely as before. His eyes were hooded, almost sleepy-looking, but she was not deceived. He was watching her, still and patient. She felt repelled. Her father did not love her, he only wanted to use her for some mysterious purpose of his own. Nothing she could do would ever please him. Whereas Sir Nicholas . . .

'No,' she said, with a bright innocent smile. 'No trouble. Sir Nicholas was so taken up with the King's Council that I hardly saw him. Only once, on the first night, was there trouble. He was angry with me because I spent too much time with Sir Piers Exton and neglected my duties to Lady Brembre.'

William took the bait and set off in pursuit of Piers, wanting to know what he was doing at the palace. Happily Nicolette told him all about Piers and his touching devotion, thinking that it was easy to lie, if you kept as close as you could to the truth. Much easier than she had ever imagined. Instead of being consumed with fear at having deceived her father, she found she was rather excited. It was a challenge to succeed in keeping something from a man who knew so many secrets.

It was spring before William Gryffard learnt the truth. He returned from a trip to Calais to find an urgent summons to Brembre's Inn and hurried to the Royall, anxiously turning over in his mind what Sir Nicholas might want. News had reached him recently that the Earl of Arundel had captured the La Rochelle wine fleet at Cadzand off Margate. It was news that William had kept to himself just until he had stocked up his warehouses with grain and wool and cloth. Arundel's victory would give the English control of the Channel again. There would be much less risk in shipping cargo across to France and Flanders and William wanted to be ahead of other merchants. As he entered the Royall, he wondered whether Brembre was angry with him for not having passed on such significant news, and then thought that with his close connections with the King and the court, he would surely have known already.

Sir Nicholas was not in the great hall; in fact he was not at home at all, William was told. It was Lady Brembre who had sent for him.

Relieved that he was not to account for the shipment of wine he had sold to a vintner at twice what it would be worth once the spoils of Arundel's captured wine fleet reached the city, he followed the steward out of the hall, carefully observing, as he always did, the wall-hangings, the array of silver and gilt cups on the board at the far end of the hall, the fragrant smelling freshly laid rushes on the floor, and in his mind comparing it to his own splendid house. There was nothing, he decided with pride, that gave cause for envy. His own house was newer, better built and Nicolette was learning to be every bit as assiduous a chatelaine as Idonia Brembre.

He entered the solar feeling relaxed and pleased with himself, totally unprepared for the onslaught of abuse which assailed him as soon as the steward had withdrawn.

'How dare you send that harlot here,' Idonia accused as soon as they were alone. 'That Jezebel!'

'Harlot?' he echoed, utterly bemused.

'Nicolette de Saint Pierre is a harlot,' she shouted at him. 'And what's more, I don't believe she's your kinswoman at all. My sister was right, she's your mistress and now she's my husband's.'

'I don't believe it,' he said, aghast.

Even in her anger Idonia could not mistake the genuine astonishment on his face. 'You mean you didn't know?' she taunted him. 'I thought you knew everything. My husband calls you his eyes and ears, yet you did not know what was going on right under that long, inquisitive nose of yours. He and that strumpet have made fools of us all, it would appear.'

He was speechless. He hated to be caught unawares and she had caught him so unaware that he was unable to think how to defend himself. It was important to think, to collect his scattered wits and decide whose side to take. But all he could think was that Nicolette had deceived him utterly and completely. His perfect tool, whom he had thought to fashion entirely to his own ends, was being used by another, and that other was Sir Nicholas Brembre. He began to tremble as he realised how foolishly trusting he had been.

'I'm glad to see it grieves you to have to share your mistress,' Idonia said.

'She's not my mistress,' he said, clutching at straws. 'She knows nothing of men. Why, she's barely out of the convent.'

'But not too innocent to bewitch my husband,' Idonia declared.

'Bewitch!' he crossed himself involuntarily. 'It's not true. I don't believe it. How do you know?' He still could not accept he had been so badly betrayed.

'I caught them in bed together, in his chamber, after noon when I thought Nicolette had gone home and I had gone to rest here in my solar.' So there was no mistake. 'What do you propose to do about it?' Idonia demanded.

'What do you want me to do?' he asked, playing for time.

'Send her to a nunnery,' she said, glaring at him.

He knew that he must not think about Nicolette, but of what to do. If Nicolette was Brembre's mistress, would he want to keep her? Would he acknowledge her openly or cast her off to placate his wife? Idonia, too, was powerful. Her sisters and their husbands might take her part. Could Brembre risk losing the support of men such as Henry Vanner and Adam Bamme and Thomas Goodlake? Did he care? Or was the King's favour protection enough?

Groping through his anger, William tried to think how best to turn this crisis to his advantage. He did not want to make an enemy of Idonia, but he could not afford to lose her husband's support. Somehow he must play for time until he could find out what Sir Nicholas thought about it all. Nicolette was nothing but a pawn, he reminded himself. But pawns could threaten kings if used skilfully enough. So he allowed himself to be abused and shouted at by Idonia, begging her forgiveness, humbling himself, until she was soothed by his capitulation. Eventually he got himself out of her solar, promising to punish Nicolette and to keep her fasting and penitent and confined to her chamber, well out of Sir Nicholas's way.

The first thing he did when he got home was to tie Nicolette to the bedpost in her chamber and beat her. She did not weep, or scream or beg him to spare her, even though he beat her until his arm ached and he was out of breath. When he stood back panting, she bowed her head and said it was no more than she deserved. He left her on her knees, still tied to the bedpost, and went to his counting house to think.

What did Brembre want? How much influence did Idonia have? William closed his eyes and was instantly plagued by a vision of Nicolette kneeling in penitence at the foot of the bed; despite himself he was moved by the simple dignity with which she had accepted her punishment. Angrily he told himself that she had lied to him, concealed her secret with consummate skill. She was no use to him if he could no longer trust her.

The sound of bells pealing joyfully penetrated his confused mind. It swelled to a great cascading wave of continuous sound and he listened to it in a kind of bemused stupor until he realised what it meant. The bells were celebrating Arundel's great victory over the French. Arundel and Gloucester – the King's enemies. This victory would make the Earl of Arundel a popular hero. Would Gloucester use it for another trial of strength with the King? If fighting broke out, the city would be expected to raise money for an army to support the King. Suppose the King, heaven forfend, should fail? What then?

William's head ached. The sound of the bells hammered out all these unanswerable questions, sending them pounding through his tired mind like prophets of doom. He thought of the loans he had already made to the King, which would be forfeited should the King fall. His goods and property might be confiscated. He wondered for the first time whether it might be more profitable if he were to throw in his lot with the Duke of Gloucester, the Earl of Arundel and the disaffected barons who supported them. But immediately he rejected the idea. His financial empire was built on the city of London and London supported Brembre who supported the King. Could Idonia with her powerful family connections persuade the city to desert Brembre? But if Brembre was ruined, Idonia would be destroyed with him. She would not be so foolhardy. Everything depended on Brembre.

He came three days later. William received him with exaggerated courtesy and took him into his own chamber off the hall. Brembre wasted no time in announcing that he wanted Nicolette for his mistress and was willing to keep her in his house in Westminster where she would want for nothing. 'As you know,' he said, 'I succeeded as Mayor of the Staple of Westminster upon William Walworth's death last year.'

'Lady Brembre?' William murmured, pouring wine into a silver goblet and offering it to his guest.

'Lady Brembre has no objection as long as Nicolette is out of the city.'

'Banishment!' exclaimed William. 'I had hoped to do better for her than that.'

'From the city but not from court,' Brembre told him. 'As you know, I am frequently sent for by the King and will take Nicolette with me when I go. She fits in well at court, far better than my poor wife and is popular with the Queen and her ladies. What better can you hope for than that?'

Before his arrogant stare, William quailed. What choice did he have? He needed this man's favour, however much he might wish it otherwise. He was riding on the tiger's back and could not in any safety dismount. He agreed.

'You can visit her whenever you wish,' Brembre promised tossing off his wine. 'I'd be glad of your help with the staple. It's taking up too much of my time now that I'm away so much on the King's business.'

As William agreed he felt his spirits rise a little. Perhaps his relationship with this difficult and dangerous man was about to improve. This was, after all, the first time that Brembre had sought him out in his own house, instead of peremptorily summoning him to the Royall. It was a promising sign.

But when he broke the good news to Nicolette, she was not at all grateful. 'Won't you send me back to Caen?' she said, falling on her knees at his feet. She was wearing the grey habit she had worn at the abbey and her hair was hanging in one golden braid down her back. He had kept her locked and fasting in her chamber and he realised at once that it had been a mistake. She was beginning to take the role of penitent seriously. 'Please, Father,' she said her eyes eloquent with appeal. 'Let me expiate my sin.'

'I thought I told you never to call me by that name,' he snapped, angry with himself as well as with her. She hung her head but the stricken look on her face made him angrier still. 'You should be thankful that a man such as Sir Nicholas wants you. Don't you realise what you've done?' he shouted at her. 'You've brought the most powerful man in London here to my house, asking me for favours.' She did not smile or look up. Even in the shapeless postulant's habit, which he thought she had disposed of in Calais, she still looked beautiful. But she had lost her confidence and she would need it again if she was to be of use to him.

'I'm proud of you,' he said.

She looked up, startled. 'Are you Master Gryffard? You weren't before.' She wasn't making it very easy for him.

'I only beat you because you lied to me,' he tried to explain. 'You will be no use to me if I cannot trust you, Nicolette.'

'And I am of use to you if I am Sir Nicholas Brembre's mistress?' she asked. Just for an instant he quailed before the look of horror on her face.

'I cannot afford to cross Sir Nicholas, not while he is master of London.' He wanted her to understand that he had no choice in the matter, but he was not in the habit of explaining himself to anyone. 'I warned you not to become a slave to your desires and you did not heed me. If Sir Nicholas wants you, it is your own fault and you must do your best to please him. When he tires of you, as tire he must, then you may go back to Caen if you still wish.' To his surprise she sprang to her feet.

'Sir Nicholas won't tire of me,' she said, her face now flushed with defiance. 'I can promise you that.'

'Men like Sir Nicholas are as hard to hold as they are to resist,' he told her. But she threw back her head and stared at him, her eyes now bright with challenge. He felt truly proud of her now. She had spirit, a quality he knew he lacked and for that reason much admired. It would be more use to him than obedience, he thought with a shiver of foreboding, if calamity were to strike.

CHAPTER 10

Nicolette lay in bed and listened to her lover's steady breathing. He lay on his back, spread-eagled in the middle of the bed, satiated after their lovemaking. She clung to the edge, resisting the urge to snuggle up against him and lay her head on his shoulder. Once desire was satisfied, he liked the bed to himself and hated her to cling to him.

Carefully, she eased her cramped limbs, sinking down into the feathery softness of the bed, savouring the languid peace invading her body, drifting towards sleep. His breathing deepened. She smiled to herself in the darkness. Soon he would begin to snore. She had driven from his mind all his worries and preoccupations, had made him forget, even here in the King's castle at Nottingham, the cares of the kingdom.

It was not easy being the mistress of Sir Nicholas Brembre. But she did not expect or want it to be easy. When he had carried her off in triumph from William Gryffard and set her up in the house he rented at Westminster, Nicolette had been filled with a confusion of guilt and remorse and fear, haunted by the knowledge that what she and Nicholas were doing was mortal sin. She had feared some kind of divine retribution from above. A thunderbolt seemed the least she might expect for such a fall from grace. But in place of God's wrath, there was nothing but joy. Instead of leaving her to endure loneliness and isolation during his long absences on the King's business, Nicholas had insisted in taking her with him.

She had been afraid that the King would refuse to receive her, had expected the Queen to be shocked, but instead the King had been amused and the Queen delighted, saying that she had found Lady Brembre a very dull person to have at her

109

table. The Queen's ladies had welcomed Nicolette warmly, overcome with curiosity and extremely envious of her improved position as Sir Nicholas's mistress. There was no denying that she was a success and it was all because of her lover. He was very powerful. The King's right hand, the only man who could promise London for the King.

Juetta was to be married soon to one of the King's retainers, a knight a little older than Sir Nicholas, and she had asked Nicolette how to keep her husband as much in love as Sir Nicholas. What charms did she use, what potions? But Nicolette had laughed and said she did not know. It was true. She seemed to be in the grip of a powerful force sweeping her along like a runaway horse. The mercy of it was that Nicholas seemed to feel the same. That he was a demanding and difficult lover she did not mind. As long as she was still able to please him, that was all she cared about now.

Sometimes it troubled her that when she went to church she was no longer able to take any pleasure in the Mass. She could not now meet a pardoner without feeling compelled to purchase his wares, but in spite of the pardons and indulgences she bought, it made no difference. Her prayers were nothing but repetitive, empty phrases, she was sure that God must be angry with her. She had lost her confidence in the certainty of her salvation, but it was the price she was prepared to pay for her success.

She awoke when the first beam of sunlight penetrated the chink in the bed curtains. Nicholas was lying on his back staring wide-eyed at the gold stars painted on the green of the tester above. She raised herself on one elbow, let her hair fall on to his chest in a cascade of golden silk. He looked at her, but his eyes this morning held none of the dark intensity of the night before. She moved closer, kissed him inquiringly. Then drew back, waiting.

'Not now,' he said. 'I must catch the King before he goes hawking.'

'Surely the King's Council doesn't sit this early.'

'The King's Council wouldn't sit at all if left to the King. The King hates taking difficult decisions. He'll take half a morning choosing the right colour for his new wall paintings but he won't spend a paternoster time trying to save his kingdom.'

She lay back, realising that for now she'd lost him. His

mind was already far away, grappling with the burden of being the trusted adviser to a wilful young man of twenty-one who wanted to be an absolute ruler without an army at his back. Soon he would be gone, summoned by the King or one of his Council and she would see him no more today except at dinner perhaps, seated far away from her above the salt, for mistresses did not receive the same precedence as wives, however well they might be treated in other respects. But he would come back sometime, either exasperated or exhilarated depending on how his plans had gone. She never pestered him with questions or tried to offer advice. But she listened when he wanted to talk. She was a good listener, quiet and sympathetic and attentive. Sometimes he wanted to know what was being said in the Queen's solar tower where she spent her days, and she would tell him everything the ladies talked about as they whiled away the time sewing, reading and making music while they waited for the men. Gradually she would woo him from the cares and challenges of his chosen path, until his pent-up enthusiasm for action and excitement was transformed into passionate lovemaking. That is what she knew he craved, and that it was her duty and her pleasure to give him.

He got out of bed and she rolled over into the warm hollow where he had lain. Screened by the bed curtains, she lay listening to the murmur of voices in the chamber, drifting in and out of sleep, uneasily aware of a mounting nausea. She willed herself to stay calm, fighting it back, holding on until Nicholas and his attendants should have left the chamber. But he was taking so long to dress and her need was becoming urgent. At last she heard the chamber door slam, the voices receding. She tore aside the curtains, leapt out of bed and ran along the narrow passageway to the privy.

When she returned to the chamber, white and shaken, Lisette was busy setting it to rights.

'You looks poorly, mistress,' she said, staring.

'I shall be better soon,' Nicolette replied, sinking down on the platform round the bed. 'I don't know what it is about this place but ever since we've been here, I've lost my supper in the morning. Do you think someone in the castle is trying to poison me?'

'By Our Lady no!' exclaimed the maid. 'Didn't the nuns teach you anything about anything?'

111

'What nonsense you talk, Lisette.' Nicolette laughed and jumped up. As suddenly as it had come, the nausea had gone. 'Now, what shall I wear? Something cool, I think. It looks as if it's going to be another hot day. My Lincoln green?'

With a disapproving shake of the head, Lisette disappeared into the adjoining closet and returned a little later saying, 'It's childbearing you be and nothing surprising in that, seeing what's been going on these months past.'

'Childbearing? Don't joke with me, Lisette. I'm not in the mood for it this morning.' But Lisette didn't smile and Nicolette sat down rather suddenly on the bed. Childbearing was something she knew nothing about, except that it was the natural consequence of a man and a woman lying together.

'No monthly courses these three moons past,' Lisette went on knowingly, 'and them breasts apopping out of your gown like ripe plums bursting on the tree after a storm of rain, and now sickness in the mornings. I tell you, it's childbearing you be.'

Nicolette stared at her maid feeling foolish and afraid. Lisette came from a large family; her mother had borne five daughters. She knew what she was talking about.

'If I am with child, is it anything to grieve over?' she asked anxiously.

'What's to become of us when he finds out? That's what I'd like to know.'

'You wouldn't tell him, would you, Lisette?'

'Of course not. Any secrets of yours are safe with me. Don't you know that by now? But he'll have to know one day. You can't put it back where it came from.'

Nicolette stared down at the twin mounds of her breasts swelling above the line of her low-cut gown. They did seem bigger. Nicholas should be pleased. He often told her she was too young, that he couldn't wait for her to get rounder, fuller, more voluptuous. Would he be pleased that she was to have his child? Idonia had borne him no children. He ought to be pleased. She smiled at Lisette.

'Don't look so glum. He'll love it, you'll see. It will bind him closer than ever.'

'All very well for you to say that now, but wait until your belly's swollen out to here and you be not so lively in there,' Lisette said with a jerk of her head towards the bed with its

112

rumpled linen. 'Men are animals when all is said and done and a bull's not that interested in the cow once he's got her in calf.'

'When do you think it'll be born?' Nicolette asked as the sleeping monster of fear which lurked beneath the surface of her success stirred.

'It's August now.' Lisette's brow furrowed as she counted the months off on her fingers carefully. 'Sometime between the end of Christmastide and the beginning of Lent, I should think,' she pronounced.

Nicolette opened the casket which contained her jewels. Perhaps Lisette was right and she ought not to assume that Nicholas would be as pleased as she was at the thought of this child. She would have to be careful, tell him when a good opportunity presented itself. She selected a fine French enamel on a gold ground to fasten her cloak. She shivered. What was to become of her if Nicholas no longer wanted her? The end of Christmastide – that was many moons away. There was plenty of time yet.

In the great chamber the royal household was busy with the elaborate ritual of the King's daily rising. Richard sat on the edge of his canopied bed studying a scroll, while his gentleman of the bedchamber fastened the laces of his short linen shirt and a kneeling squire eased his shapely legs into long woollen hose. It took some time, for the hose were tight and difficult to fit, but Richard did not mind. It did not worry him that the chamber was full of men coming and going while he dressed. He would have felt lonely had there not been all these people here.

He ignored them all, absorbed by the picture on the scroll. It was a design for a painted window in the hall. Nottingham Castle was an ancient stronghold built long ago in the time of William the Conqueror to consolidate the Norman's conquest of England. It was a great fortress, but spartan. Richard had had the idea for the window in the hall the last time he had stayed in the castle and Robert de Vere had found him a designer. Richard studied the scroll with a sense of pleasure. There was nothing he liked better than choosing designs. He stood up to let the squire tie the tops of his hose to the points of his shirt and waved the scroll at Robert de Vere, who was lounging on the raised bed platform.

'It's good, Robert. I like it,' he said. 'Fetch the man to me. I'll speak to him now.' Robert grinned cheerfully and got up. 'And tell the falconers to make ready,' the King shouted after him.

'The hawks and hounds have been ready and waiting this hour past, Sire,' replied the favourite, bowing gracefully as he withdrew to perform his errand.

'Good.' Richard liked to keep people waiting. It made him feel more like a king. The Earl of Suffolk had been waiting a long time already, hovering in the window embrasure with an anxious air, obviously wanting to unburden himself of something troublesome. But Richard had no intention of noticing him until he had finished dressing.

He was arrayed in a short jacket with red and white roses on a pale yellow ground. Standing in front of the mirror, he studied the widened shoulders and the way the full skirted jacket set off his shapely, slim hips. Someone brought a jewel-encrusted girdle and belted the jacket tightly at the waist. Then the gentleman of the bedchamber reverently placed upon his head a scarlet hood with such long points they nearly reached the ground. The King smiled. He was a good-looking young man and the image of himself in the polished steel was, as always, pleasing, a tribute to the interest he took in fine clothes and beautiful jewels. He sat down to have his long pointed shoes put on and let his eyes roam casually over the squires, pages, knights and noblemen all crowded into his chamber waiting to be of service.

'Well, Michael?' he said, holding out the scroll and condescending to notice the Earl of Suffolk at last. 'What do you think of that?'

Suffolk came forward, studied the drawing, giving it the serious attention he gave to everything. 'Very pretty.'

'It's f-for the hall. I'm going to have the window glazed with coloured glass. It s-should brightened the place up a bit, don't you think?' Suffolk did not look very taken with the idea. 'The window can be taken out and s-stored when I'm not here,' Richard added persuasively.

'Sire, Sir Nicholas Brembre is waiting outside. He wishes to speak to you.'

Richard already knew this, had known as soon as he woke up that Brembre was outside the chamber. His gentleman of the bedchamber had told him.

114

His eyes swept the room more broodingly. His chamberlain and his household steward, whom he had recently ennobled, were standing on either side of the bed, anxiously alert. Simon Burley was waiting grave and patient by the great carved stone fireplace. The Archbishop of York was watching him with a somewhat pious air – did he expect him to go to Mass? Robert de Vere was coming back with the glazier. Richard beckoned to him, relieved.

'I think perhaps there's too much blue in it,' he said, holding up the scroll and staring at it at arm's length. 'What do you think, Robert?'

'I think that if we don't go hawking soon it'll be too hot for the falcons to fly well,' replied Robert.

The King ignored him, turned to the glazier. 'Do you think you can make Our Lady's mantle a different colour?' The man looked at his feet and muttered something about how he didn't think Our Lady's mantle was ever anything but blue. Amused, Richard began to argue the point with him, aware that all the time Suffolk was growing more and more impatient. He shot a quick conspiratorial glance at Robert, but he was looking out of the window and it was obvious that he was longing to go hawking. Suffolk had a disapproving look on his face, so did Burley. Richard hated to be disapproved of.

'Well, Michael,' he said. 'What's the matter? Don't you think I s-should make Nottingham Castle more habitable?'

'Of course, Sire. But that can wait, whereas Sir Nicholas Brembre has already been waiting since prime.'

'S-so have the f-falconers and Robert thinks it will s-soon be too hot for the hawks to f-f-fly. Isn't that s-so, Robert? I dare say the Archbishop thinks I should f-first go to Mass. Which of you am I to please this morning?'

'Sire, you have a hawk waiting outside whom you need to hunt down your enemies. Shouldn't you at least listen to what he has to say?' said Suffolk.

Richard scowled, robbed of his pleasure in teasing them. Here in Nottingham Castle he was safe, surrounded by friends, guarded by loyal retainers; but he knew that outside in the rest of his kingdom there were forces to be reckoned with. The situation between him and the Duke of Gloucester was deteriorating sharply. Soon his uncle might try to usurp his power. The Earl of Arundel was supporting him. The

Earl of Warwick was rumoured to be about to join them.

The King walked over to the window, stared down into the court below where the hunting party waited. The horses' heads were hanging as they dozed in the bright sunlight; the falconers, their hooded predators mounted on their fists, stood about in groups; the hounds sat or lay patiently waiting. Richard sighed, remembering his cousin Henry Bolingbroke, his uncle of Lancaster's heir. They had played together sometimes, when they were boys, and Henry had been fascinated by hawks. Richard did not trust Henry at all.

Beyond the court, the steep stone walls of the battlements rose rugged and uncompromising. Nottingham Castle might be grim but it was unassailable, which is why Richard had summoned his Council here in the first place. He saw that the last of the early morning mist was beginning to clear from above the keep. The sun shone down out of a clear blue sky. He turned away from the window.

'Robert, you can dismiss the f-falconers,' he said. 'Tell them I s-shan't go hawking this morning. It's too hot. You'll have to think of s-s-something else to amuse us.' He noted the disappointment on his favourite's face with a trace of glee, and swung round to confront Suffolk. 'Now are you satisfied?' he asked.

When Robert had gone, the King threw himself on the bed. 'Get rid of all these fools,' he ordered, 'and bring the wool pedlar in.'

When Sir Nicholas entered the chamber a few moments later, Richard wondered what it was about Brembre that always made him feel uneasy. Suffolk and Burley were a bore at times, especially when they were being disapproving, but they'd been with him a long time, throughout his childhood. He knew where he was with them. The Archbishop of York was a nobleman by birth, Robert de Vere was his friend. The rest of his Council he could manage. But this upstart from the city was different.

As Brembre went down on one knee before him, Richard thought he looked more like an angry bull than a hawk and told himself that he only put up with him because he was the representative of London. He kept him bowed before him just a little longer than was necessary before allowing him to rise.

'You'll have to get rid of Arundel,' said Brembre going

straight into the attack as soon as he was upright again. 'He's too popular since his victory over the French.'

'Get rid of him?' said the King. He was too belligerent, that's what was wrong with this fellow.

'Arrest him, before he becomes too powerful.'

'On what grounds?' But belligerence was what he needed. Certainly the other members of his Council had nothing better to offer.

'What about treason? It's always a difficult charge to refute,' said Brembre with a sinister smile, 'and if it can be proven, the sentence is irreversible.'

'Wouldn't that drive the Duke of Gloucester into doing something rash?'

'Not without Arundel's support. He hasn't the forces on his own.'

'Gloucester brought thirteen hundred men into the field when we went to Scotland,' Suffolk reminded the King.

'And the Earl of Warwick five hundred. An attack on Arundel might bring Warwick into the field,' warned the Archbishop.

'The country will not support the Duke of Gloucester on his own. Not against the King. The Duke is not liked,' argued Brembre. 'It's the Earl of Arundel we have to fear. Act now before it is too late.'

'But I am acting,' protested the King. 'The justices have proven that the Duke of Gloucester's Council of Regency had no right in law. I'm the King, aren't I? They cannot question my right to rule.'

'You cannot rely on the law to vanquish them. They're not sufficiently afraid of the law. You must act now, do something daring before they are ready to move against you. The kingdom is waiting to see which side is the stronger. The Duke of Gloucester has thirteen hundred men, Arundel maybe more, Warwick five hundred. Together it is a formidable force. But you, Sire, have the Cheshire levies, and you are the King. Show them that you are not afraid. If you can pick them off one by one, you will succeed. But you must start now, with Arundel, before it is too late.'

'What of London?' asked Richard.

'I can promise you London,' Brembre said, and the King believed him. Standing in the middle of the great chamber with his head thrown back and his cold blue eyes holding the

King's with all the arrogance of a man used to getting his own way, Sir Nicholas Brembre was very convincing.

'Suppose we fail?' It was the Archbishop who spoke but the King knew that he voiced the doubts of the others as well. 'If we try to arrest the Earl of Arundel and don't succeed, we may be worse off than we are today.'

'We most certainly s-shall be,' replied the King angrily. 'If I cannot arrest one of my noblemen f-f-for treason I might as well abdicate here and now. Do I rule in my own kingdom or does the Earl of Arundel?'

'The King needs constant pushing,' Brembre commented to Nicolette as they lay in bed together that night. 'He doesn't like unpleasantness but he's not a coward. Anybody who saw how he behaved in front of the peasants' army back in the fourth year of his reign when he was only a boy of fourteen knows that. But Burley and Suffolk lack the stomach for the sort of fight he's got on his hands. De Vere's a court jester, Archbishop Neville's a priest, Tresilian's only a judge when all's said and done. Not one soldier among them. I can't think why the King surrounds himself with such a chicken-hearted lot.'

'Perhaps to make him feel more comfortable.'

'And sends for me to do his dirty work.' He was lying on his back staring up at the painted tester, as rigid as a knight in armour. Nicolette leant across him, trailed the mantle of her hair over his body, teasing him gently.

'And what of the others, did you convince them in the end?' she whispered into his ear.

'It was the promise of London which persuaded them. London has no army but it is where the money is, and money buys men.'

'Will London support him?'

'If the King arrests Arundel now.'

Always so sure. She wished she had such an unassailable belief in herself. She kissed him gently on the lips, rested her breasts against his naked flesh so that her nipples brushed against him as lightly as butterfly's wings. He did not stir. His mind was still in the King's great chamber, his body cool and unresponsive.

'What happens if we fail?' She felt helpless, consumed by her hunger, her flesh rebelling against the need for patience.

118

'We won't fail. London will do what I tell it.'

How she loved him – for his certainty, for his ability to ride headlong over any obstacles. It made her feel more daring just to be with him. She began to explore his body with her lips, moving slowly and tenderly, with infinite care, until with an oath he seized her, drew her down on top of him, kissed her hungrily. He was ready for her now. Eagerly she returned his kisses as he rolled her over, crushed her beneath him, venting his feelings of frustration and anger in a passion of violent lovemaking which left her panting, bruised, but triumphant.

CHAPTER 11

The attempt to arrest the Earl of Arundel failed. He proved to be too powerful and after joining forces with the Duke of Gloucester and the Earl of Warwick was, by the end of the summer, openly under arms. Sir Nicholas Brembre took the news of the calamity calmly and Nicolette was both thrilled and reassured by his courage in the face of adversity. Nor did the foreigners who came to the house in Westminster that autumn seem to be unduly perturbed. They were used to feuds and power struggles between nobles; it happened all the time in their own countries. A prudent merchant confined himself to selling his goods to both sides and never became embroiled in the quarrels of princes.

The house in King Street, Westminster, which Brembre leased was a simple timber building within sound of the abbey bells and Nicolette found it reassuring to hear them ringing the hours for prayer. Occasionally she would be woken in the night by the bell calling the monks to matins or lauds and for a moment think she was back at the abbey in Caen. Sometimes she would even struggle out of sleep mentally preparing herself to get up for the night office, then as realisation came she would snuggle back down again in her warm bed, drifting contentedly into sleep comforted by happy memories of Holy Trinity and untroubled any longer by an uneasy conscience. Life was too sweet to let guilt upset her and God was good.

The house had a narrow frontage on to the street, with the living quarters – a small hall and a chamber adjoining – on the first floor and the kitchen in an open yard behind. Nicolette took pride in making it as warmly welcoming for her lover as she knew how. She and Lisette worked hard to ensure that the bed linen was always freshly laundered, the hall clean and strewn with sweet-smelling herbs every day, the cooks hard at work preparing delicacies, the fires brightly burning, the candles well trimmed.

The ground floor of the house was entirely given over to the work of the staple. Nicolette had grown used to seeing the yard full of laden packhorses and the house full of men. Wool was what brought them – sacks of shorn wool and bales of fleeces on the hide – woolfells – all of which had to be weighed and graded before it could be taxed. The woolmen and merchants often grumbled about the amount of tax they had to pay but English wool was the best and so they paid what Brembre's staplers demanded.

Sometimes when Nicholas was there, he would invite one or two of the merchants to dine with him. Nicolette did not mind, for they were interesting and appreciative, especially the foreigners, the Flemings and Italians. She welcomed them prettily, conversing with them easily in their common language which was French. She enjoyed making them comfortable, knowing that it amused and excited Nicholas to think that although they always treated her with respect, there was not one who did not envy him greatly. From time to time she would smile at him, knowingly, confidently, and his eyes would light up with the pride of ownership, watching her as she flitted among his guests, shining like a bright newly polished jewel, bewitching them with her youth and beauty. It was good to know that he was pleased and proud, and that as soon as all the woolmen had gone he would prove it in the big canopied bed in the chamber off the hall.

There was only one man Nicolette did not feel entirely at ease with and that was William Gryffard. Her father was now on very good terms with Nicholas Brembre and often conducted the business of the staple for him when he was away. She knew, because Nicholas frequently told her, that William was doing well from the Westminster staple, but whenever he came to the house he always plied her with so many questions that she could not help feeling that he was using her to spy on Nicholas. She was relieved, when they got back from Nottingham, to learn that he had gone wool buying.

On 13 October, Nicholas Exton was re-elected Mayor of

London. On the morning after the Feast of SS Simon and Jude, he came riding through Westminster on his way to the palace to make his oath to the King. It was a splendid and colourful procession; all the city's guilds in their different liveries, with banners, musicians, torch bearers and singing priests, came riding down King Street. Nicolette, watching from her chamber window, saw Nicholas; he was arrayed in scarlet robes like the rest of the aldermen, mounted on a magnificent stallion covered from head to toe in a sweeping caparison emblazoned with the hooded falcons of his crest. Beside him the Mayor paled into insignificance and to Nicolette, gazing down proudly on her lover, there seemed no doubt that London would do what Nicholas wanted and that with the city's help the King would triumph eventually. Nicholas looked up, staring at her fiercely as he rode by, and her heart beat all the faster as she wondered if he would dare snatch some time with her after dining at the palace, before he had to return with the Mayor to the city to pray at the Church of St Thomas of Acon and afterwards at St Paul's Cathedral.

She dined early that day and then went into the chamber to prepare for him – just in case. Lisette brought warm water from the kitchen and added a handful of rose petals. Nicolette washed carefully and put on an undergown of Lincoln green whose loose folds clung to her body and swirled about her as she moved. Her hair she left unbraided, hanging in a gleaming curtain to her waist, with her only adornment a garland of entwined silver gilt round her brow. If he came he would be in a hurry and she did not want to waste a moment.

She looked round the chamber humming a French love song to herself, full of confidence that it was as perfect a love nest as she could make it. The fire burned brightly, the beeswax candles on the wall prickets kept the grey autumnal gloom outside at bay; on a table by the window was a flagon of wine and a silver goblet gleaming in the light from the candles, the bed behind its deep red draperies waited full of promise. Nicolette picked up her embroidery and sat down by the window impatiently to wait.

Soon, too soon almost, she heard footsteps and a voice asking for her in the hall outside. Before she had time to rearrange her expectations, the door was thrown wide and a servant showed William into the chamber.

'Master Gryffard!' Nicolette exclaimed, leaping up and scattering embroidery silks in surprise. 'I thought you were in the Cotswolds buying wool after the autumn shearing.'

'I was, but the news was so bad I thought it best to get back to London,' William replied. 'Sir Nicholas has gone too far this time. The Earl of Arundel has defied the King and we who supported him are lost.' She was dismayed by how pale and haggard he looked. Often he appeared worried, but never so much as now.

'Sir Nicholas doesn't think so,' she said, determined not to let him wear her down with his anxiety and mistrust. 'He still thinks the King can win.'

'Sir Nicholas will be the first to fall if the King loses,' said William, glaring at her. 'They won't be content just with Suffolk this time. They're going to impeach de Vere, Tresilian, the Archbishop of York and Sir Nicholas too, of that I'm certain. And he knows it.'

'Sir Nicholas doesn't even think of failure,' she insisted.

'If he's so sure of winning, why has he made over all his personal property to his brother-in-law, Henry Vanner?' asked William, producing his nugget of bad news with a gleam of triumph in his watchful eyes.

'Even the lease of this house he has made over to Agnes Fraunceys, the widow of a business partner.'

'What Sir Nicholas does with his property is no concern of mine,' she said, but she was shaken.

'By the Rood, it should be,' he retorted. 'Don't you see what it means, you poor deluded child? He's afraid of losing. He's trying to save his assets.'

'I don't believe it. He was worried perhaps that if Nicholas Exton was no longer Mayor, if they chose a mercer or goldsmith in his place, things might go badly. But not any longer. Why, he's more confident than ever now that Nicholas Exton is still Mayor. He said it was the turning point. Now he could be sure of being able to deliver London for the King.'

'And yet it was not until after Exton was re-elected that he made over all his property to Vanner and his goods and chattels to four others. He's preparing for ruin and spreading the risk among as many as possible, men unconnected with the present government of London.'

She sank down on the window seat, feeling suddenly weak. It did not occur to her to question his information, nor how he came by it. William always knew things. But he was frightened, badly frightened, she could see and it made her feel less sure.

'The King will protect him,' she said, clutching at straws. 'He has before.'

'If Brembre made over all his goods it's because he knows the King cannot help him now,' he almost shouted at her. 'They'll be out to ruin him and he's trying to save what he can. Nicolette, don't you see, if anything happens to Brembre, I could fall with him.' He was standing in the middle of the chamber staring at her wildly and it reminded her of the way he had been in the cabin of the *Santa Maria Nuova*. He had been out of his mind with fear then, but they had survived that peril, she reminded herself firmly.

'You could leave London, before it's too late,' she suggested, 'if you're so afraid.' Try as she would, she could not keep the scorn out of her voice. 'You'll be safe in Calais. You can run your business from there, like you used to before.'

'And lose everything I have built up here in the city of London? What about my house, what about my wall paintings, my glazed window, my orchards and the dovecote? I can't take it all with me to Calais.' He was almost weeping in his frustration and despair.

'Can't you do what Sir Nicholas has done and make over your goods to another?'

'What other? Unlike Brembre, I have no family.'

'You have a partner in Calais,' said his daughter. 'Giles de Bourdat is an honest man.'

'No successful merchant is an honest man. I've taught Giles de Bourdat everything he knows. Too much perhaps. I think at last he has learnt to appreciate money.' He gazed at her thoughtfully and she noticed that he had stopped shaking. 'Now, if you had a husband . . .'

She got up, went to the table for the wine she had put out in case Nicholas should come. William bent down and began carefully picking up her scattered embroidery silks. She poured wine into the silver goblet and carried it over to him.

'In all my life,' he said, 'I've only met one honest man, a man who had no use for money.' He stretched out his hand

and took the goblet from her. 'Sir Piers Exton.'

'Piers!' She was so surprised she at first did not guess where the conversation was leading.

'And Sir Piers is truly noble,' William continued, watching her speculatively. 'Is he noble enough to take you even though you are Brembre's mistress?'

'You can't trust Piers. He's such a fool he'd give it all away,' she said, appalled at what William seemed to be suggesting. 'Besides, isn't he a retainer of the King's? Suppose the King himself should fall, where would you be then?'

'Piers would have to change sides, of course.'

'A man who'd change sides for money wouldn't be an honest man,' she said scornfully.

'Not for money,' said William, watching her slyly, 'for you.'

'Do you really think I can be bought, by Piers, with your money?' she flung at him.

'Piers is so very anxious to rescue you from your folly,' he murmured.

'What folly?' she demanded. 'You were happy enough to give me to Sir Nicholas when it suited you. Now you want me to abandon the man who loves me if he should fail. But he will not fail and I shall not abandon him.'

'If Brembre falls, you will be ruined,' he reminded her. 'He has done nothing to safeguard your position. Even the lease of this house he has passed to Agnes Fraunceys. What is to become of you when the Widow Fraunceys throws you out into the street? What will you have left? Nothing. You might as well don the scarlet hood of the harlot and ply your trade in the stews with the rest of them.'

'I could become a nun – like my mother,' she said, drawing herself up and staring at him accusingly, but he showed no sign that the taunt had touched him.

'Your mother was a woman of noble birth and well dowered,' he said. 'Whereas you, my daughter, have nothing unless I choose to give it to you. No convent would take you without a dower.'

'Perhaps I could become one of the Queen's ladies,' she said. 'The Queen is fond of me, I'm sure. If Sir Nicholas were to ask the King for me, I'm sure it could be arranged.'

He studied her carefully and thoughtfully for the time it

might take to say an Ave Maria. 'Are you not forgetting,' he said at last, 'that you are with child?'

She turned away from his penetrating stare, fighting down panic. She had told him nothing about the baby, yet he knew. He always knew. The spectre of failure cast its sinister shadow over her bright confidence like a huge dark cloud blotting out the sun's light. William was sitting slumped on the window seat, pulling at his straggly beard with a hand which trembled. Once she had vowed to be the perfect daughter to this man. But that was before she had given herself to Sir Nicholas Brembre. Her father was frightened and full of doubt, but he would be the first to come running to claim her support when Nicholas triumphed. It was to Nicholas she was now committed body and soul and she could not allow herself to believe that he could fail.

Having imparted his unwelcome news, William did not stay long. When he left, Nicolette sat for a long time with her embroidery untouched in her lap, alone with her unpleasant thoughts. William had sown the seeds of doubt – in her lover, in her own worth – and try as she might she could not cast them out. At first it was the thought of Idonia triumphant which hurt most. Nicholas had taken care of his wife's future, but thought nothing of hers.

She put her hand on the small mound of her belly beneath her gown. She could feel the baby kicking. Nicholas knew nothing of the baby. Maybe if he did he would have done more to safeguard their future.

Suddenly another unpleasant thought struck her. William would tell Nicholas about the baby, just as soon as it suited him to do so. Blessed St Mary, why did I not tell Nicholas from the very first? she thought. She would tell him now, if he came. She did not want him to learn her precious secret from William Gryffard.

She looked out of the window longingly. If only he would come. She could not rest until she had seen him again although she knew in her heart that it was already too late, that he would not be coming today. She waited for him long after the procession would be on its way back to London, feeling lonely and longing for reassurance. It was an entirely new emotion.

He came a few days later, as the abbey bells were ringing for compline. He was alone and came striding into the chamber to sweep her off her feet and into his arms.

'By the Mass, I've missed you, my sweet angel,' he said, kissing her fiercely.

'I've missed you too,' she said responding eagerly. 'I thought you might be able to get away from the palace for a little while, before riding back to the city. I was ready and waiting, but you didn't come.'

'I've carried the sight of you leaning out of your window and smiling down at me these five days past, but I couldn't come until now.' He took off her fine lawn coif and held her at arm's length. 'Jesu, but you're beautiful. No woman has the right to be as beautiful as you.'

'William Gryffard was here,' she said, reaching up to release the long braids of hair coiled round her head.

'What did he want?'

'What he always wants. Information.'

'What did you tell him?'

'What you wanted me to tell him. That the King would triumph over his enemies.' He was kissing her bare throat, following the line of her low-cut gown with his lips. 'You believe that don't you?' she said to his bent head. He did not answer. He was too busy with the buttons down the front of her gown, releasing her breasts.

'So warm and round and soft,' he murmured. 'I vow they get bigger by the day.' As his hungry mouth fastened on her nipple, guiltily she wondered whether he'd seen William, whether he knew yet about the baby. If he did, he showed no sign of it. So many secrets between us, she thought, fear and panic making her freeze. He raised his head.

'What's the matter. Don't you want me any more?' But he wasn't angry. He was amused. He slipped his hands round her waist, held her hard against him, looked down at her with arrogant certainty. 'Feel how I want you,' he said. She closed her eyes, gave him her mouth, and he kissed her hungrily. He tore off her gown but she found to her dismay that she could not respond instantly as she usually did. She wanted so much to surrender to his passion, to let desire conquer her doubts, her intrusive thoughts. But although she could surrender, she found she could not make her senses leap, could not lose herself in him, could not give herself completely, because she no longer trusted him. William had sown his seed of doubt too well, she thought, and shivered in spite of herself.

'Cold?' he asked, staring at her in surprise. 'Or has Gryffard said something to upset you?'

'Master Gryffard is very frightened. He's afraid that if . . .' beneath his hard stare she faltered, 'if things go wrong for the King, it'll bring down all those who supported him. He wants to save himself from ruin.'

'Gryffard's a coward, he runs if a cow farts,' Nicholas said. 'You don't want to listen to him. He's always seeing disasters, never stops worrying.' He kissed her again but all she could think of was how he had made over everything to Idonia's family. He began to take off his doublet. Usually she helped him undress, laughing and teasing and calling herself his squire, but today she went straight to the bed, jumped in and pulled the cool sheets up to her chin. He came and stood looking down at her, frowning.

'What's the matter, Nicolette?'

'Nothing, I'm tired.'

'You're not tired. You've never been tired. You don't love me any more. You think I'm going to lose – that's it, isn't it? Gryffard has frightened you into thinking I'm finished. Merciful Jesus, Nicolette, not you too.' He was staring down at her and she was shocked to see in his face not his usual ruthless confidence but for the first time doubt. She could not bear it.

'Why did you make over all your property to your brother-in-law?' she cried.

He sighed. 'So that's it. Gryffard has been busy probing with that long nose of his.' He sat down on the edge of the bed, pulled the sheet away, ran his fingers almost absently over the swelling curve of her breast.

'Why?' she demanded, trembling a little beneath his touch. 'If you don't believe you can win, how can I?'

'I had to do it. I had to get the city's support for the King.'

'But why? Nicholas Exton will do what you tell him. Isn't that why it was so important for him to be re-elected?'

'Not just the Mayor, I need the aldermen and the Common Council as well. The city is divided. There are men in the city who always want to play safe. I had to get all the support I could and that included Vanner and the others. It's not Idonia, it's her family. I need their support, that's all.'

She felt better. It wasn't Idonia herself he cared for, merely her influence. Should she tell him about the baby now?

He was looking at her almost triumphantly as he stroked her naked breasts. 'You need not be afraid, my sweet dove,' he said. 'The Mayor and the aldermen and the Common Council have taken an oath of allegiance to King Richard against all those who are or shall become rebels to his person or royalty. The city will support the King.' Not now, she thought, not when he had so many more important matters on his mind. 'The King is coming to London. He has summoned Gloucester and Arundel to his presence. I expect they will come in force. The city will have to raise an army.'

'War?' she said, staring up at him frightened and at the same time fascinated by his calm acceptance of calamity.

'Perhaps. I don't know if it will come to actual fighting. But Gloucester and Arundel have to be beaten once and for all if the King is to be more than a helpless puppet. It's risky and the next few months will be difficult and unpleasant. But you do not become ruler of a turbulent land such as England by playing safe. The King knows it and I think I have persuaded him to act like a leader at last.'

She lay and looked at him wonderingly. He was so brave, so daring, so different from her worried, frightened father. Trouble never seemed to daunt him.

'Trust me, my sweet light,' he said gazing down at her intently. 'I must have someone I know believes in me.'

She was completely convinced. He was a god among men and the miracle of it was that he needed her still. She stretched up, wound her arms round his neck, drew him down on top of her. 'I do, my love, my only, own, true love. I do, I do,' she said kissing him fervently. He made love to her then, savagely as if trying to combat the violence threatening from every side. But she did not mind. She gloried in his raw passion, matching his savagery with a frenzied onslaught of her own as she tried to absorb his power and his strength to fortify her in the difficult days to come.

CHAPTER 12

William Gryffard left the house in King Street with one object in his mind – to find Piers. He had to journey as far as Chester where the King's retainers were helping Robert de Vere raise the north for the King.

The outer bailey of the castle was full of horses and men when William arrived, weary and mud-splattered from his journey. Gazing about him anxiously at all the steel-clad figures he was relieved to see a knight with red unicorns and wings of gold embroidered on his tabard. His long hazardous journey had not been in vain. Having tracked him down William wasted no time in approaching him.

'A word with you, Sir Piers, if I may – before you leave,' he said.

Piers looked him up and down contemptuously. The knight had avoided him ever since Nicolette had become Brembre's mistress and William guessed that he held him to blame. It suited him that Piers should think Nicolette was an innocent victim. He watched the knight covertly, aware that Piers was struggling between desire to tell him to go to the devil and his natural chivalry. In the end chivalry won.

'In what way can I be of service to you?' Piers asked.

William looked about him at the crowded courtyard, at the horses fidgeting and pawing the ground, at the men in chain mail shouting orders, at a group of knights laughing and jesting together as they waited. At Esmon, holding his master's shield and helm, watching curiously. It was scarcely the place to negotiate a marriage.

'Isn't there somewhere a little quieter?' he said. 'My business is a matter of great delicacy, but I think you will find it interesting.'

Piers handed the reins of his horse to his squire and led William out of the court. They passed through a second cobbled yard, more crowded than the first, and then through a low arched doorway into a long stone passageway interspersed with small embrasures large enough to accommodate an archer beneath the narrow slits. By one of these Piers paused. 'Is this quiet enough for you?'

It wasn't ideal, but it would have to do, thought William, squeezing into the small cavity and leaning his back against the wall. Then without preamble he offered Piers Nicolette's hand in marriage, promising to dower her with his magnificent house in Cornhill and all the goods and chattels therein.

The effect on the knight was all that he could possibly have hoped for. Joy, disbelief, gratitude were writ plain on his innocent young face and William smiled wryly to himself as he thought how easy it was to conquer contempt with the right weapons.

'Why me? Why now?' Piers asked as disbelief threatened joy.

'Nicolette needs rescuing. You want to slay dragons, don't you? Brembre is your dragon. Rescue Nicolette from him and you shall have my house in London and all that it contains.'

'I'd take her in her shift,' declared Piers hotly. 'If she'd have me. But I can't just ride up to that devil Brembre and murder him in cold blood, and I doubt very much whether he would agree to joust with me. I tried that once before and he failed to take up my challenge.'

'If the King's forces are defeated in the coming struggle then Brembre is a ruined man,' said Gryffard. 'The five lords appellant have impeached him for treason along with the King's other close advisors. If the King loses then Brembre will have to stand trial. Nicolette will be alone and friendless. You must rescue her.'

Piers rounded on the merchant, surprised and defiant. 'And if the King triumphs?'

William suppressed a trickle of fear at the light of battle in the knight's eye. 'Then you will have to go on waiting for your lady a little longer,' he said with a shrug. 'Doubtless you will be well rewarded for the part you have played in the

131

King's victory and will have something more to offer the damoiselle than your faithful heart. Sir Nicholas is a married man with a wife and family of his own, he can offer Nicolette nothing but dishonour, whereas you, Sir Piers, are young, brave and anxious to make her your wife. If the King is victorious it is up to you to try and outshine Sir Nicholas. It should not be too difficult.'

A shaft of autumn sunlight fell on the knight's face and William peered at him from beneath the brim of his close-fitting hat, wondering if he had presumed too far. Piers was looking thoughtful.

'I'm very much afraid the King may not triumph,' William continued. He glanced cautiously up and down the empty corridor, then laid a hand on Piers's mailed sleeve. 'If the King loses then you can only be of service to your lady if you change sides in time,' he whispered. Piers started and turned away, but not before the merchant had seen the revulsion in his face. 'What's the matter?' he asked. 'Is your honour worth more than love? Is my price too high? Surely you did not expect to get a pearl such as Nicolette for less?'

Piers shook off the hand on his sleeve. 'I have vowed to serve the damoiselle in any way I can,' he said with simple dignity. 'I would sacrifice my life for her, if need be.'

'I am not asking for your life,' retorted William. 'Can you bear that others might think you a coward?'

'A man's courage is something he has to prove to himself, not to others,' Piers replied.

'It is not your courage that will be tested so much as your judgement,' William reminded him. 'Nicolette will be ruined if the King is defeated and Brembre falls, but if the King triumphs and you have deserted him, it will be you who will fall.'

'Then you will have to find another dragon slayer,' said Piers. 'You should never have allowed her to fall into that evil man's clutches.'

William hung his head, feigning penitence. 'Alas, I had no choice. Sir Nicholas Brembre is a dangerous man to cross. May I rely on you to save her for me?'

Piers was smiling again, the joy in his face as bright as his shining armour. 'You can count on me, Master Gryffard,' he said. 'There is nothing I would not willingly do for her.'

Such eager confidence, such nobleness of spirit, thought

132

William. But would he make the right choice, or was he too good, too innocent to carry off the difficult task before him? He wished he did not have to rely on someone so hopelessly romantic as Piers, but then he told himself that only a chivalrous fool would take Nicolette should the worst befall.

William left the castle immediately, eager to get back to London before the King's forces and those of his rebellious magnates started roaming the countryside. He had risked enough to try to save himself and Nicolette from whatever might befall. But as he left the city of Chester he wished he did not have to rely on knights to fight his battles for him. Once before he had tried to use a knight – Sir Tristram de Maudesbury, the handsome young man Mariota believed she was in love with. But he had underestimated Sir Tristram's stupidity. Mariota had died in the Peasants' Revolt and William had been humiliated by her sister – Sir Tristram's wife. He hoped that Piers might prove more worthy of his trust, but he doubted it.

To Piers, the promise he had made did not seem a hard one – not at first. In the time he had been a retainer of Richard's, he had seen enough of the life at court to make him question whether he had found the answer to his quest for glory. Robert de Vere had been made Duke of Ireland for doing little more than play the fool, or so it seemed to Piers, and as he became more disillusioned and frustrated, he began to question his own destiny. What had he to show for his nineteen years? He had accomplished nothing, slain no dragons, found no Holy Grail. If he died he would leave nothing behind – no wife, no sons, no legacy of any kind. Once he thought all he wanted to do was die in battle. That was when he believed Nicolette lost to him for ever. But now William Gryffard had given him hope.

Should he change sides now, he wondered, before his courage was brought into question? But he did not really believe that the King could be defeated. Better to help the King to victory; that way he could win glory, honour and perhaps some rich manor in recognition of his loyalty. He cared nothing for riches or manors for himself but he would do anything for Nicolette. If the King were to reward him, he would be able to make an honest woman of his lady with Gryffard's blessing, and at the same time keep his honour.

Sustained by this rosy prospect, Piers left Chester with Robert de Vere, and an army of four thousand men on 14 November. They marched towards the Severn Valley, intending to join forces with the King coming from London, but discovered from their scouts that the way was blocked at Northampton by the forces of the five lords – Henry Bolingbroke Earl of Derby, Thomas Mowbray Earl of Nottingham, the Duke of Gloucester, the Earls of Arundel and Warwick – now united against the King. Instead of giving battle de Vere marched them on southwards through Stow-on-the-Wold. It was a foolish move, but the Duke of Ireland was so impressed by the importance of his title and sole command of such an army, he was unwilling to listen to any advice. In the long, weary march southwards, when it became plain that Robert de Vere was determined to avoid any contact with the forces sent to oppose him, Piers began to lose heart.

Then on 20 December, scouting ahead of the main army, Piers sighted the enemy as he crested a hill overlooking the River Thames at Radcot Bridge. A small party of men were hard at work attacking the stones of the bridge with picks, clearly bent on destroying it, guarded by about two score archers and three knights. It was a raw foggy day but despite the cold, Piers felt sweat begin to seep into the thick padding he wore beneath his hauberk as his worst fears were realised. Their scouts had told them that Banbury, Chipping Norton and Chipping Campden to their rear were occupied by the opposing forces, cutting off their line of retreat to Chester. They had marched straight into a well-devised trap.

Esmon, with their packhorse and two battle chargers in tow, came up the hill behind him. As he drew rein beside Piers his eyes widened at the sight of the enemy working on the bridge.

'There aren't very many of them,' he said, making the best of it.

'No,' Piers replied absently. He peered through the swirling fog at the view in front of him. The river was wide and fast-flowing, swollen with weeks of heavy rain. The bridge was narrow and what remained of it unlikely to be safe for more than one horse at a time.

'Do you think they'll be difficult to dislodge?' asked his squire.

'Perhaps,' said Piers, but he wasn't really thinking about the military options, he was wrestling with a quite different set of choices.

As he stared down at the impassable river and the busy men working on the bridge, he knew that the moment had come to choose. Or had he already left it too late? He cursed himself for a fool. He should have gone before. Should have known that under such a weak and vacillating leader their cause was lost, that de Vere's obstinate belief in his own infallibility and frivolous tendency to underestimate the enemy must lead to disaster.

He looked back at the approaching column he was scouting for. Somewhere among them was the 'lance' of six mounted archers and three foot soldiers that he had brought with him from his father's manor. His father had been proud of him then. 'You're well mounted, my boy, and I've found you some of the best bowmen in the land. I've done my best, now it's up to you. I know you'll not let me down. God and Saint Michael protect you and lead you to victory over the King's enemies.'

Piers had ridden away full of confidence in his own ability and those of his lance to give a good account of themselves in battle. They trusted him and were proud to go with him to fight for the King. Could he desert them now?

He stared down at the badge he wore on his surcoat embroidered with the King's white hart. Was defeat inevitable? He did not need to prove anything to himself or to his fellow men, but his instincts and his training were to fight; the tighter the corner, the greater the thrill when the battle was won. Could he forgo such a chance as this to test his skill? He thought of Nicolette – her lovely image was never out of his mind for long. Did he love her enough for that?

With his mind still unresolved, he tugged sharply on the reins, wheeling his horse to face his companions in arms. He raised his hand and pointed over his shoulder in the direction of the bridge. He saw Robert de Vere moving out ahead, followed an instant later by a knight whose red wolf rampant fluttering from his pennant was recognisable even at a distance of a thousand paces – the flamboyant crest of the Chevalier de Real. They spurred their horses up the hillside, scattering the sheep grazing on the rough winter grass, and as they approached the crest, Piers gestured for Esmon to move out of earshot.

Robert de Vere and the Chevalier de Real reined in beside Piers and silently gazed down at the frenzied activity around the bridge. The chevalier was the first to break the silence.

'Henry Bolingbroke's men, I don't doubt,' he said. 'By God, that man moves fast. He must have outflanked us in the night.'

De Vere said nothing, transfixed by the sight of the bridge with its guard of archers and men-at-arms lined up on the far river bank. He was young and good-looking but his face was puffed and there were dark circles under his eyes. He hadn't slept for nights and Piers thought scornfully that the hard life of a soldier was proving too taxing for such a pleasure-loving creature. It did nothing for his confidence in him.

'What do you intend to do, my lord Duke?' asked the chevalier.

'Do?' With a visible effort de Vere tore his gaze from the view below. 'Intend to do?' he repeated, looking from Piers to the chevalier in consternation. 'Take the bridge, of course. There aren't very many. We should be able to storm it – shouldn't we?' He did not sound very certain.

'In time perhaps, and with many casualties,' replied Piers. 'But a handful of archers could hold that bridge for a long time. Even then, once we've cleared it, it will take hours for us to get our forces across. It's narrow and we don't know how unstable. Somewhere in the Oxfordshire countryside on the other side of the river will be the main bulk of Bolingbroke's forces. We shall be vulnerable to attack from both sides.'

'Time is something we haven't got,' de Real pointed out, unnecessarily, Piers thought. 'We've got Arundel advancing behind us. We're trapped.'

'Then we'd better attack the bridge straightaway before they demolish any more of it,' said de Vere. 'We have to get across the river and join up with the King.'

'It would be madness to try to attack that bridge with Henry Bolingbroke's army waiting on the other side. We'd be playing straight into his hands. Our only hope is to attack the forces coming up behind,' urged Piers.

'But we're hopelessly outnumbered,' objected de Real.

'Numbers don't count so much as skill in deploying them,' said Piers, 'as was proved at Crécy, and at Poitiers.'

'That was because the French were no match for our English bowmen. But the forces against us now have longbowmen too, remember,' retorted the chevalier.

'We shall have the advantage of surprise. They're not expecting us to attack them. If we wait here over the crest of the hill, we'll have the high ground. Soon it will be dusk. We can fall upon them from above as they climb the hill, when they're least expecting us,' insisted Piers. 'It's our only hope. We've got to break out of the trap before it's too late.'

But Robert de Vere wasn't even listening. 'The King is expecting me to join him before the month is out,' he muttered. 'He'll be furious if I don't do what he wants. We can't take on Arundel on our own. If we can but meet up with the King, we'll be a match for them all. We must cross the river.'

'Better to fight Arundel on our own terms with an element of surprise than be hacked to pieces by both armies while we're crossing the bridge,' remonstrated Piers.

'There are only a few of them. Our archers could keep them busy while the knights force a way across.'

'The bridge has been partially demolished. We could not risk a charge, there's no room. The only way you'll take that bridge is in single combat.'

'By the Rood, Piers, you have it,' exclaimed de Vere, delighted. 'I seem to remember you distinguished yourself in the tourney at Christmastide. Now's your chance to put your skill to the test in battle. Isn't that what you want?'

'No,' said Piers, but at the back of his mind an idea was forming.

De Real supported the plan wholeheartedly. 'Our archers can keep theirs busy while you dislodge the men on the bridge,' he said. 'As soon as you're across I'll follow and we'll set about those three knights. It should be a splendid mêlée.'

Piers turned away sickened by the expression of jaunty confidence on the young man's handsome face. It's just a game to him, he thought in disgust. The charming young chevalier seemed to think all fighting was like a tournament. He didn't realise that in war there weren't the same chivalric rules.

Grimly Piers beckoned to Esmon to bring the horses.

Robert de Vere cupped his hands to his mouth and hailed the waiting column. While it came squeaking and creaking up the hillside in a wave of colour and steel, Piers dismounted from his gelding. Esmon helped him don his great steel helmet with the winged unicorn on its crest.

'Now heed me well,' Piers said and heard his voice boom inside the helmet. 'Keep out of range of the archers. Don't attempt to cross the bridge until the Chevalier de Real has reached the other side. If I fall, you're not to come to my aid. Do you understand?'

'I understand you don't think I'm good enough to go with you,' Esmon muttered.

'Nonsense,' Piers snapped. 'It's a fool's errand we're on and I want to limit the damage.' He thrust his hands into his mailed gauntlets and mounted the impatient destrier who was snorting and pawing the ground, sensing that the moment had come for him to play his part. Once in the saddle, feeling the great strength of the animal beneath him, Piers felt a surge of confidence.

'What if your horse is brought down? You could take mine if I was behind you.'

Piers turned away quickly from his squire's beseeching eyes. 'And block the bridge with fallen horses,' he retorted harshly. 'This is no time for heroics. You'll be more use to me if you do as you're told. You can join me when the bridge is secured. In the meantime, look after my gelding. I don't want to walk all the way to London if the destrier is killed.' The disappointment in the boy's face was plain to see and Piers felt a pang of anguish as he slipped his left arm through the leather loops on the inside of his shield. Esmon would have much more to break his heart over before the day was done.

The Chevalier de Real rode up. 'Good luck, Piers,' he said. Was there a malicious twinkle in his merry eyes? Piers inclined his helmet briefly in de Real's direction and took up his lance, resting the steel-capped butt on his right stirrup. The debonair Chevalier of the merry eyes and charming smile could always best Piers in the games of love they played at court. Piers envied him his ability to engage in easy, witty conversation with Nicolette as much as he resented his public attentions to her, which he continued even after she had become the established mistress of that blackguard Brembre.

That de Real knew Piers to be a rival for Nicolette's favours there was no doubt; the chevalier lost no chance to tease him whenever an opportunity presented itself.

'Ready, Piers?' asked Robert de Vere.

'Ready,' replied Piers.

De Vere raised his arm in an absurdly arrogant gesture. 'Forward in the name of King Richard,' he cried, reining back to let Piers pass.

Slowly Piers rode down the hill. The stallion was prancing and shifting restlessly from side to side and he had to keep a tight hold on the rein. The beast's excitement was exhilarating and, despite everything, Piers could not help feeling an answering excitement of his own. Both man and horse had been bred and trained to the work they were about to do.

Peering through the narrow slits of his visor, Piers surveyed the scene before him. The archers were in place ready to keep the bowmen on the other side busy. The pikemen had stopped their work of destruction and were gathering together behind the knights, ready to defend the bridge. Piers felt a deep calm. Seen through the limited eye-slit of his all-encompassing helmet, the world seemed wonderfully concentrated. His mind was made up. He knew what he had to do. All his doubts and uncertainties had been conquered by the simple imperative of immediate action. Out of the corner of his eye he saw a lance tip moving forward level with his shoulder and swung round with a curse.

'Stay back, Esmon,' he shouted. 'By Christ's mercy, can't you do as you're told?' The lance tip disappeared.

Not far now. Soon he would be within range of their arrows. Piers shifted his grip on his lance, feeling for the hook fixed to the right side of his breastplate which helped to bear some of the weight of the weapon and to absorb the shock of impact. The destrier, as soon as the lance was couched, tensed his great muscles in anticipation of the charge. Uttering a swift prayer to St Michael, patron saint of soldiers, Piers released his iron grip on the rein. The stallion surged forward. With a bloodcurdling cry Piers spurred the horse at full tilt towards the bridge.

A hail of arrows fell, bouncing harmlessly off his armour but pricking the stallion through the wildly flapping caparison and staining its cream background with bright specks of crimson. Hurtling down upon the bridge, Piers saw a gap two paces wide and glimpsed rushing water even as the charger shortened his stride. He dug his spurs mercilessly into the stallion's flanks and braced himself as the animal hesitated and then leapt, landing with a mighty clatter of iron-shod hooves on what remained of the bridge. Piers's helmet slammed down on his head with the shock of landing but he hardly registered the jolt, he was too busy steadying the destrier as a knight came charging towards him from the far end of the bridge.

The two knights met in the middle of the bridge with a crash of steel and splintering wood as their lances shattered. There was no room to pass or wheel for a second charge; Piers drove his destrier forward and as his opponent lowered his shield the merest fraction to balance himself Piers thrust at his throat with his broken lance finding the fine line between helm and hauberk. Standing up in his stirrups, he lunged relentlessly with such strength the knight toppled sideways and with a gurgling cry disappeared over the parapet of the bridge into the river below. Piers hurled his broken lance after him and pulling his sword free charged across the bridge.

Three men leapt at him. Piers reined the stallion back on to his haunches. A pike streaked for his shoulder and the horse reared even as Piers slashed at the pike with such force it spun out of the man's hand. The horse came down knocking the man backwards with his front feet and Piers caught a glimpse of his mouth opened to scream as he disappeared beneath the destrier's hooves. Sword blades crashed against Piers's shield. He pulled the horse round in a tight circle as he swept his sword in a blind slash at the assailants behind him. He looked down and saw a pikeman thrusting for the stallion's belly. He wrenched the animal sideways and the pike stroked the horse's shoulder, ripping the caparison as Piers struck. Such was the strength of his wrist and forearm that his short, quick sword stroke sliced through the man's shoulder, severing his arm from his body as cleanly as a knife through bread.

A pike hit Piers's shield with such force the blow numbed his arm right up to the shoulder. He raised his shield, knocking the pike upwards, and before the pikeman had time to recover or see the blow coming, Piers leant forward and thrust beneath his shield, catching the man full in the face with the point of his sword. A shriek and he was gone.

In the brief respite that followed Piers had time to look for the other two knights. Neither of them seemed anxious to engage him in combat. Seizing his opportunity, he sliced the badge with the King's white hart from the sleeve of his surcoat with his sword, rode up and threw it in the mud at their feet.

'I've come to join you,' he said. Then without waiting any further he wheeled his horse round and before the astonished gaze of the defenders galloped back across the bridge to meet the Chevalier de Real hesitating on the bank.

Crouching forward behind his shield and with his sword held high above his head, Piers spurred the stallion at the gaping chasm. The horse leaped it confidently and landed to continue full tilt at the bewildered chevalier. Instinctively de Real raised his lance tip to strike, but Piers dodged it easily; the lance passed over his shoulder and he brought his sword down with a ringing blow on the chevalier's shield as the two destriers passed each other. Piers wheeled and checked the excited stallion, carefully measuring the ground through the slits of his visor.

The chevalier, lance couched, was ready now for battle. Piers charged again, taking de Real's lance thrust on his shield at such a speed that the long wooden pole was bound to break. He reined the horse back even as he thrust his shield up against de Real's with a crash of steel against steel. For a brief moment the two knights were locked together so close that Piers looked straight into the other's eyes through the narrow eye slits. They weren't quite so merry now. Then Piers brought his sword down on de Real's helm with a stunning blow and while he was still reeling, heaved until his muscles cracked. Slowly the chevalier toppled backwards, and as his horse surged forward again he somersaulted gracelessly over his tail. Without waiting to see him fall, Piers spurred once more for the bridge and the stallion cleared the hole in the ground effortlessly. This time no one came hurtling across to impede his progress. Piers reined back to a trot. At the foot of the bridge he came to a halt and surveyed the men gathered there warily.

At first no one moved. Piers raised his visor and waited, listening to the sound of his own heavy breathing and the stallion's heart pounding beneath him as sweat trickled down his face and into his eyes. Finally one of the knights rode up.

'Do you yield to me and give me your word as a knight not to try to escape until the ransom be paid?' he asked.

'I yield to no one,' replied Piers. 'If you'll provide me with a lance I'll fight a course with you and any others who care to come forward. I've come to help you hold the bridge, but of my own free will and not as your prisoner – as all those here will witness.' To prove his point he turned his charger and stationed himself facing the King's men he had just deserted so flamboyantly. They might try to kill him now, he supposed, but it wasn't very likely. Knights did not get put to the sword, they were too valuable as prisoners.

He waited, willing himself not to look round, while the charger fidgeted restlessly and behind him Bolingbroke's men argued what was to be done with this troublesome new recruit. He noticed that the Cheshire archers, bewildered and discouraged, were retreating aimlessly to the higher ground out of range. The Chevalier de Real's squire was helping the fallen knight to his feet. He did not seem unduly harmed. Relieved, Piers allowed himself to relax a little. He could not resist a thrill of triumph at his success, coupled with satisfaction at having taught the chevalier a well-deserved lesson. Suddenly from halfway down the hillside a horse and rider came hurtling towards the bridge, and Piers swore angrily. It was Esmon. A hail of arrows flew over Piers's head and de Real began to run, cumbersome in his armour, scrambling out of the way like a startled crab. At any other time Piers would have sat and watched the chevalier's discomfiture in amused delight but now he swung round.

'Don't shoot,' he called to Bolingbroke's men in ringing tones. 'It's my squire, come to join me.'

Esmon had reached the foot of the bridge. His charger, a heartbeat away, saw the gap. All four feet came down together on the brink of the bank as the horse slithered to a violent halt. Esmon, taken by surprise, was pitched straight over his shoulder head first into the river below.

'God have mercy,' cried Piers throwing himself from his horse and running across the bridge as quickly as his armour would permit. At the edge of the gap he knelt and peered down in despair. But there was no sign of Esmon. Weighed down by his heavy chain mail the boy had already disappeared beneath the muddy waters of the Thames. What could he do? He could not plunge in after the boy in all his heavy armour.

'Come and help me,' he shouted across the gap to the retreating archers. But nobody came. For a long time Piers knelt there on the edge of the bridge staring down into the river's murky depths in helpless disbelief. Neither side attempted to come near. He was roused at last by the sound of cheering behind him. Looking round, he saw Bolingbroke's men holding their weapons aloft and pointing in jubilation to the crest of the hill he had not long ago left, where through the gathering gloom he could distinguish a line of pennants advancing slowly over the hill. Arundel had arrived sooner than any of them had expected.

What happened next ought to have satisfied Piers that he had made the right choice. The King's forces, spread out haphazardly over the hillside, were already in disarray. Perhaps if Robert de Vere had acted quickly something might have been accomplished, but as Piers watched appalled, he saw de Vere spurring away from his army as fast as his horse could gallop. His already scattered forces began to dart hither and thither like a flock of frightened sheep, some trying to follow their leader, others spurring in the opposite direction, the rest waiting to be taken. Further down the river bank, de Vere was throwing off parts of his armour.

With no one to lead them and no identifiable target to attack, the archers laid down their arms and surrendered without a blow being exchanged, even as the King's favourite was plunging his horse into the river in a last desperate attempt to cross in safety. Piers saw him clinging frantically to the animal's flowing mane as the charger began to swim, but in the falling dusk was unable to see what became of horse or rider. It was a deplorable spectacle and Piers ought to have been relieved that he had changed sides not a minute too soon. But he was overwhelmed by Esmon's pointless death. With that on his conscience, he could take no pride in anything. It seemed to him that what he had done was little better than de Vere's cowardly desertion.

The Earl of Arundel did not seem to think so when later that night Piers was brought before him. The Earl was in his tent, quaffing wine from a leather jug, with no armed men to guard him and no quick-witted young courtiers to flatter and amuse, just a squire busy polishing the rust from his armour. Broad of shoulder, strong of neck, the Earl was built like an ox. He was still dressed in the padded leather gambeson he had worn under his armour, and with his close-cropped hair and ruddy complexion, he looked every inch the hard fighting man he was.

'You've cost Henry Bolingbroke dear,' Arundel announced as Piers entered the tent. 'Three pikemen killed and Sir Roger Malfeasant dead as well.' To Piers's surprise he was smiling at him quite pleasantly.

'I'm sorry about Sir Roger,' said Piers. 'I only meant to unhorse him. It was bad luck he fell over the side of the bridge.'

'Yes, it's a pity about Sir Roger, but that's the price of war,' said Arundel handing the leather jug to Piers. 'Sir Roger's not an easy man to unhorse. In fact he's one of the best knights in Henry Bolingbroke's retinue, which is probably why he put him in charge of holding the bridge. I hear you unhorsed the Chevalier de Real as well, in little more than a paternoster time. The chevalier's always been a pretty jouster, his fighting is almost as nimble as his dancing.'

'I had to vanquish the chevalier to prove the seriousness of my intent,' replied Piers as he raised the jug and poured a stream of wine into his mouth. It was sharp and vinegary but welcome nevertheless. Arundel took the empty jug from him and handed it to the squire, bidding him go and refill it. Then he looked Piers up and down appraisingly.

'Why do you want to desert the King?' he asked when they were alone.

'I don't want to desert the King,' replied Piers. 'To the King I'm still loyal, as I'm sure you are too, Your Grace.' In the flickering light from the torches it was difficult to read Arundel's expression but it seemed to Piers that he was no longer smiling. 'Civil war destroys a land,' Piers added to emphasise his point. 'I saw enough of that in Tuscany with all the warring city republics.'

'So you've been in Tuscany, have you? I suppose you learnt to fight so effectively with Sir John Hawkwood's White Company,' Arundel said approvingly. 'If you've been a mercenary I wouldn't have thought you'd mind who you fought for.'

'I don't mind fighting the French or the Spanish but I

don't like fighting fellow Englishmen. If there were civil war I might have to fight against my own father.'

'After what we have seen today I don't think there's much danger of civil war,' replied Arundel with a shrug. 'The King's friends do not seem very anxious to fight on his behalf.'

'The King's friends are many and legion. The people support him, of that I'm sure, but the ministers who serve the King are not worthy of the trust he puts in them and it has alienated the sympathies of his subjects.'

'Well said, young man, by the Rood,' replied Arundel, slapping Piers heartily on the back. 'The King surrounds himself with as evil a bunch of advisers as any in the land. You did the right thing changing sides when you did. I could use a good fighter such as you. You can join my retinue and help us see this thing through to the end.'

Piers was not at all convinced that the end Arundel had in mind was the same as his. But he had made his choice and for now was stuck with it. Only then did he think about Nicolette. The events of the day had crowded out even her memory. For so long he had believed her to be beyond his reach, but now he might be able to claim her at last.

That night he lay down on the cold ground to sleep, warmed by bright visions of his lady smiling down upon him, and woke in the grey light of dawn eager to get to London as quickly as possible.

CHAPTER 13

On the second day of Christmas the armies of the five lords appellant arrived at Clerkenwell and encamped in the fields. The city of London closed its gates and the King remained safely celebrating Christmas behind the impregnable walls of the Tower of London. Early in the morning William Gryffard went to Mass at St Peter's Cornhill, not so much to celebrate the joy of Christ's birth as to try and discover what was happening.

The church was alive with the most alarming rumours. Desperate to find out the truth, William hurried to the Guildhall where he tried to see the Mayor, but the Mayor was not seeing anybody and it was said that Nicholas Brembre had already fled the city. All that William could discover for certain was that the city was besieged and the King had taken refuge in the Tower.

Outside the Guildhall the crier was issuing a proclamation forbidding anyone to sell arms or victuals to the army besieging the city, who were to be treated as rebels. William studied the crowd of anxious men and women gathered around the crier. Some of them were nodding in approval of the proclamation, others muttered and grumbled. It was bitterly cold and snowflakes were beginning to fall. William mingled with the crowd, listening intently, collecting seeds of information like a poor widow following the reapers at harvest time and gleaning for corn. Would the Londoners support the King and the Mayor? That was what William had been trying to find out all morning. He knew that the city was divided and suspected that there were those who might take advantage of the present crisis to settle scores of their own. He had seen it all before back in 1381. Then the city had been besieged not by powerful magnates and their retainers but by an undisciplined army of peasants, yet London had opened its gates and for days and nights chaos had reigned.

The crowd outside the Guildhall was beginning to disperse. If only he knew what had happened to Piers. William shivered and wrapped his fur-lined mantle more closely round him. The men encamped in the open by Clerkenwell would be cold and might soon be hungry if the Londoners obeyed the Mayor's proclamation. Was Piers one of them? In an agony of uncertainty William mounted his palfrey. He could do no more here.

He rode home through a fine curtain of small, wet snowflakes. Should he run now, before it was too late? He could still leave by London Bridge, slip away to Gravesend and from there take a ship across the Channel to Calais. If what he had heard this morning after Mass and later outside the Guildhall were true, then all the King's friends had already fled. He alone was left. He should run. If only he knew what had happened to Piers. Was he out there besieging the city or had he fallen at Radcot Bridge? Somehow, William did not think Piers would have fled.

At home, walking into his magnificent hall, William's agony was increased by a stab of possessive pride. He looked at his wall paintings, the envy of every merchant in London, his gleaming silver vessels on the cup board, his expensive tiled floor, the new coloured glass in the window at the far end. He could not take all these things with him to Calais.

Adam Stickleby, the steward, came hurrying to take William's wet cloak. His face was grey with fear. William could not bear seeing his own doubts so plainly mirrored, and so he hurried away to his counting house, shaking his head in silent confirmation of the steward's worst imaginings.

In the counting house he sat down on his high stool and drew the abacus towards him, moving the beads swiftly to and fro, unable to resist the compulsion to calculate how much he might lose. He was interrupted in this depressing task by the sound of a brisk, firm step and a familiar, confident voice.

'Don't tell me, he's in his counting house as usual – I know the way.'

Sir Nicholas Brembre! William leapt from his stool not knowing whether to be pleased or sorry, but certainly afraid.

'By the Rood, William, I'm glad to see you're still here,' said Brembre, clasping him warmly round the shoulders. 'I thought you might have made a run for it like all the others.'

'Where have you been?' William demanded uneasily.

'In the Tower, celebrating Christmas with the King,' replied Brembre, grinning at him with what William considered most untimely confidence. Unless of course things weren't quite as bad as he had heard.

'It's not true then, what they're saying, that the King's advisers have all deserted him?' he asked cautiously.

'Suffolk and the Archbishop have fled to France, Tresilian I know not whither.'

'What of Robert de Vere? They say he was captured at Radcot Bridge.'

'Robert de Vere escaped from that disaster by swimming his horse across the river. He managed to reach Windsor disguised as a groom, where he spent a little time with the King. He should by now be across the Channel in safety, seeking help from the French. You and I are all that are left – except for poor old Simon Burley.'

Then it was every bit as bad as he had feared; yet Brembre seemed not to mind, thought William. He began to wonder whether Brembre's arrogance was so overweening he was unable to contemplate the possibility of failure.

'Don't look so frightened William,' Brembre teased. 'The King is determined to resist. He has refused to see any of the rebel magnates. Do you know what he told the Bishop of London? "Let them lie there with their great multitude of people in the winter cold till they have spent all they have and then I trust they will return poor enough and needy whence they came. Then I shall talk with them and see that justice may be done." That ought to make his uncle of Gloucester think about his soul's repose. It's treason, after all, to take up arms against the King.'

'Men with armies at their back don't take seriously the threats of an unarmed man,' William muttered, crossing himself fearfully as he thought of his own soul's unreadiness.

'But he is still the King, divinely appointed by God. There are five lords encamped at Clerkenwell with their forces. Each one guards his own power jealously. They are an uneasy coalition. If the King refuses to see them and the city stands firm by the Mayor's proclamation, time and the weather will be on our side. Men who are bored and hungry and cold will soon start quarrelling among themselves.'

'You still think London will do as you bid it?'

'I don't think. I act. I must ensure that London does not let the rebel army in.'

'That was not what you advised back in the fourth year of the reign, when the peasants' army lay outside the walls,' William could not resist taunting him.

'We all learn from our mistakes. As you know, the city is still divided between the victualling and non-victualling guilds.' Brembre fixed William with a challenging stare. 'Exton will support the King and the victualling guilds will stand by him, but I'm not so sure about the non-victualling guilds. I don't trust them not to use this crisis to get the better of us again, just as they did after the Peasants' Revolt. That is where you can help, William.'

'You know I have never played any part in city politics,' objected William hastily.

'I know you are always careful to keep in the background but that you always have friends in both camps. I want you to use your influence to persuade the mercers and goldsmiths to support us. They're important guilds. If they back us, enough of the rest will follow.'

'Your sister-in-law is married to Adam Bamme, the goldsmith,' William reminded him. 'I have no influence as strong as family.'

'But you have friends among the mercers and drapers and goldsmiths. I need everyone, if we are to survive,' declared Brembre.

'I never rely on friendship for that,' William said.

'No, but you have your secrets. You do not have a friend without knowing something you can use against him. The time has come for you to put your treasury of secrets to good use. It is not enough for you to be my eyes and ears; you must also be my voice. I don't need to tell you how to manipulate people.'

William stared about him at the ledgers, the tally sticks, the letters of credit, the deeds of partnership, the bills of lading, the letters of advice and bills of exchange which represented his daily toil, and felt his spirit quail.

'I won't,' he said. 'I can't. There's not enough time.'

'What's the matter? Are you afraid? It's time you stopped running away to Calais every time the pace gets too hot for you. If you want the fruits of victory, you have to bear the pain.'

William fumbled with the papers on his desk. He would have to begin again, in another city, in another country, pitting his wits and his cunning against new adversaries, getting to know their strengths and their weaknesses, weaving a new web of delicate intrigue and leave behind all that he had built up here in the city of London, maybe never to return. Could Brembre still do it? If only he could.

'Think what it means, William,' Brembre continued as if he had read his thoughts. 'All the King's friends have deserted him. If we can but save him now there will be no limit to his gratitude. I'll be Chancellor or Treasurer at the very least and you'll be knighted at last, I promise.'

William remembered another time, at the height of the Peasants' Revolt, when Brembre had promised him a knighthood. He shuddered. They had been in the Tower of London with the King, surrounded by a mob of angry peasants baying for the blood of the King's advisers. They had ridden out of the Tower with the young King at their head and William could well remember the sheer terror he had felt that day. Memories of it still came back to haunt his dreams. He had run away back into the city – to more horror and fear and almost death. Brembre had stayed with the King and triumphed eventually and been knighted. Could he do it again?

'If you're so sure of victory, why did you make over all your London property to Henry Vanner and others?' William asked.

'Perhaps because unlike you I wanted to leave my property in good hands if I had to flee. But you have no one to leave your beautiful house to, William.'

The stapler darted a quick glance at Brembre, wondering if by any chance he had news of Piers.

'You'll have to stand up and fight for it, like a man.' Brembre was still brutal even when asking for favours. 'You know what you have to do. Use your influence to persuade the waverers and I'll make sure the Mayor doesn't lose his nerve. Courage, my friend. If we can just hold out until de

Vere brings help from France we'll triumph yet.'

Brembre left and for a long time William sat where he was, trembling with rage and fear. France indeed. Would France come to the help of an English king? Invade perhaps, but not help! It was playing straight into the magnates' hands.

William began flinging papers together and piling his ledgers one on top of the other. Brembre had no sense of self-preservation, that was the trouble. He went on riding hell-bent into danger blinded by his own ruthless arrogance. He was too used to getting his own way in the city; too spoilt by the King's trust and protection; he had come to believe in his own invincibility. Perhaps he always had. As clear as if it were yesterday William remembered how he had been dragged from his house, made to kneel in the gutter while the peasants threatened to kill him. How he had had to part with a precious deed belonging to one of his creditors while the man held a knife to his throat. Brembre had let the peasants into London; the prisons had been broken into and every criminal and debtor in the city had taken the law into their own hands. Brembre was nothing but trouble and now he was determined to drag him, William, with him all the way. It would end in disaster – ruin at best, execution almost certainly. He must run while there was still time.

He was interrupted in his frenzied packing by his steward who came to inform him that Sir Piers Exton was in the hall and anxious to see him.

'Sir Piers Exton?' William stared at Adam Stickleby blankly, trying to readjust his fear-crazed mind to a glimmer of hope. 'Have food and wine sent to my chamber,' he commanded when he had collected his scattered wits. 'The young man may be hungry.'

The steward left to do his bidding, and William sat down on his high stool to calm himself. Carefully he searched through the papers still lying on his desk. He extracted an important-looking document and read through the closely written script on the parchment. He smiled grimly to himself. Then slowly he went up to the hall to meet his visitor, all his faculties sharpened at the thought of parting with his most valuable asset.

Piers was waiting in the hall, standing in front of the fire in his armour, his head encased in a close-fitting leather cap and one hand resting on the hilt of the long sword hanging from his waist, the perfect symbol, William thought, of self-denying chivalry. He studied the surcoat Piers wore over his armour; it was so muddied, the cream and red markings were barely distinguishable.

'Where is your badge of the King's white hart?' he asked without preamble, fixing the knight with a piercing stare.

'I lost it at Radcot Bridge,' Piers replied, holding the merchant's gaze steadily.

'Is that all you lost there?' asked William.

'No. I lost Esmon, my squire. God rest his soul.' Piers's face was bleak.

'And your honour?' William persisted softly.

'That too,' said the knight.

To hide his elation William went over to the cup board and studied the array of costly silver drinking vessels arranged upon it. 'Have you come to me for succour or reward?' he demanded over his shoulder.

'I've come to be of service to the Damoiselle de Saint Pierre – if I can,' was the reply.

Carefully William selected the finest drinking vessel in his collection. 'Then you are not a prisoner? You have not come to me to help find a ransom?' He turned to face the knight with the silver goblet in his hands.

'On the contrary, I'm serving in the Earl of Arundel's retinue now. I came with the messengers from the other lords to find out what the leaders of London intend to do.'

William was impressed. He had not really believed that Piers could do it. 'Come to my chamber,' he said, smiling quite openly. 'We can talk more comfortably there.'

He led the way into the chamber off the hall. It was a large room painted like the hall with scenes of gods and goddesses in brilliant colours. The large bed in the centre was curtained in rich vermilion velvet and as William closed the door carefully behind them, he watched Piers closely for a reaction. But Piers gave the room no more than a cursory glance. He was looking at William, rather like an eager hound waiting to be released upon the quarry.

'The Earl of Arundel must value you highly to send you on so important an errand,' William said walking over to the table beside the fire, which had been laid with food and wine. 'What did you do to win his trust so speedily?' He filled the precious silver goblet with red wine and handed it to Piers.

152

'The Earl chose me, I think, on account of my knowing Richard Whittington,' said Piers, taking a long deep draught from the cup and then handing it back. William's long nose twitched as he raised the goblet to his lips.

'Ah yes, Richard Whittington, the mercer. He befriended you, didn't he, when first you arrived in London.' He peered expectantly at Piers over the rim of the cup.

'He was very kind,' agreed Piers.

'Sit down and eat,' said William waving his hand towards the laden table. 'You must be hungry – or did Whittington share his dinner with you?'

'We're not starving yet,' said Piers suddenly grinning at him. 'In spite of the Mayor's proclamation. We can hold out until the citizens succumb.'

'Does Richard Whittington think that they will?'

'I don't know. I shall carry his message back to the Earl of Arundel.' Piers was not to be drawn and William was even more impressed. The knight, for all his shining honesty, knew how to guard other men's secrets. But if the Earl of Arundel was already negotiating direct with such influential men as Richard Whittington, then things looked bad for Brembre.

William made up his mind. He had to save himself today, before it was too late, and here was Piers already a trusted retainer of the Earl of Arundel, sitting at his table wolfing his food. William did not know how the knight had managed to change sides to such advantage but it was the last opportunity he might have of saving his property from confiscation. William believed in grasping opportunities whenever they presented themselves, however inopportune the time.

From inside his long fur-lined sleeve he extracted the deed he had brought with him from the counting house and began to read out loud to Piers as he ate. Halfway through, he paused.

'Do you understand what this is?' he asked.

'I understand Latin,' said Piers through a mouthful of capon, 'but no, I cannot make sense of that.'

'It is the deed to my house and all that it contains. I have had it ready and waiting to make over to you. All it needs is your signature.' William held out the parchment.

But Piers shook his head. 'I don't want it,' he said.

'If you can't write, a thumb print will do, as long as it is witnessed,' William reassured him, mistaking the knight's reticence.

'I can write well enough,' Piers told him. 'But I care nothing for your fine house. All I want is to be of service to the Damoiselle de Saint Pierre. To rescue her from Sir Nicholas.'

'Of course, of course,' said William soothingly, 'and so do I. But to do that you must marry her and you cannot marry her with nothing.'

Piers pushed away his half-finished food, got up from the table and seized the parchment. For one terrible moment William was afraid that he was going to tear the precious deed to pieces.

'You don't think much of a knight's service, do you, Master Gryffard?' Piers said looking down at the merchant with a wry smile as he tossed the deed on to the table.

William let out his breath in relief. 'On the contrary I think so much of a knight's power of protection that I am trying to give you all that I hold most dear to look after for me.' He retrieved the parchment and examined it carefully once more. 'Now, will you not sign?'

'Why not give it to the damoiselle? It's her dower, isn't it?'

'Only if she marries you.'

'She might refuse.'

'I'm relying on you to see that she doesn't.'

Piers looked at him in puzzled bewilderment. 'You mean she doesn't know? Aren't you going to send for her and tell her yourself? She is your ward, is she not? You can command her obedience whereas . . .' He broke off, looked at William, his brown eyes full of helplessness. 'I can only plead.'

'How can I send for her? The damoiselle does not live here with me any more. She's living in Brembre's house at Westminster. I can't go there now. I must leave this night for Calais before your friends take over the city. If Sir Nicholas Brembre is arrested, I shall be in the most deadly peril.'

'But what am I to say to her?'

'I'm sure your love will make you eloquent,' William smiled cynically. 'But I will give you a letter, if you like, making my wishes plain.' Quickly he went to the door, shouted for the steward. It would have to do, he thought, watching Adam Stickleby come hurrying through the hall. He did not like having to trust any man with anything; never before had he done so, but never before had he been in such danger of losing everything. Piers was trustworthy and honest, and he loved Nicolette.

It had been a mistake putting Nicolette in Brembre's way, a grave mistake. I've made too many mistakes recently, thought William in an agony of self hate. The biggest mistake was removing Nicolette from the convent in the first place. She had proved far more spirited and hot-blooded than a girl schooled in self-denial, chastity and obedience had any right to be. She had defied him but he wasn't finished with her yet. Through Piers he would maintain his grasp on his daughter, and his house, and Piers would be grateful; as would Nicolette, once she realised the extent of her folly. A little adversity would soon bring her to her senses; she would thank her father for saving her in spite of herself and when he came back she would make it up to him – he would see that she did. It was a thought worth clinging to, a glimmer of hope to dispel the darkness of fear and despair as he prepared to flee into exile once again.

On the fourth day of Christmas, Nicolette stood at the window of her chamber in the little house at Westminster and watched the snow falling. It was very quiet. The work of the staple was suspended during Christmastide and nobody came to the house. She had given up trying to find out what was happening; the news was too confused and contradictory and most of it was bad. Instead she had tried to celebrate Christmas and resign herself to waiting. She had not seen Nicholas for over a month. She did not know where he was, but she believed that he was still in London ensuring the city's support for the King.

'The snow looks as if it means to stay this time. It's getting quite thick,' she said.

'It'll be cold for the soldiers out in the fields by Clerkenwell,' said Lisette. 'Not much of a Christmastide for them.'

'Serves them right, taking up arms against the King. Maybe they'll give up and go home,' said Nicolette, watching the snow. It's not been much of a Christmas for us either, she thought sadly. Not like last Christmastide, that enchanted magical time at the palace when it had all begun. She had tried hard to recapture some of that magic. She had gone to the shrine of St Edward the Confessor with all the other pilgrims on Christmas Day. She had made her vow and lit her candle and said her prayers for Nicholas's safety and then come home to the quiet little house which she had tried to make look festive with holly and yew and all kinds of green branches. She had hoped that somehow Nicholas would come to her and she wanted to be ready for him with a happy smiling face and the house full of festive cheer. But he did not come.

The snow was pretty but it was blowing in through the open window and settling on the wooden window seat. Nicolette closed the shutters across the window and sat down on the wide step running round the bed.

'Shall I read to you from the Lives of the Saints?' she asked Lisette, picking up a book lying open on the floor.

'You'd be better to rest than to tire your eyes with all that reading,' replied the maid. 'Why not lie down now and let me bring you a tisane to make you sleep. It be better for the babe.'

'I can't rest at a time like this. If you don't want me to read to you, I'll read to myself.' She picked up the book but dropped it almost immediately as from below came the sound of knocking. It was an ominous sound. Nicolette and Lisette looked at each other wordlessly, then Nicolette flew to the window, flung open the shutters and peered into the street below. A knight was dismounting outside her door but she could not make out his colours or the shape of his crest through the falling snow.

'Quick, Lisette, it may be him. I can't tell for sure.' She ran to the polished steel on the wall, peered at herself appraisingly. 'Help me get ready.'

'There be no need, mistress. You're always ready – for him.'

Nicolette smiled at her image in the polished steel. It was true, she thought, and besides, there was no time, already she could hear the measured tread of someone approaching the chamber. The door opened.

'Sir Piers Exton craves permission to speak with the damoiselle,' announced the servant.

Piers! Nicolette stared at the servant while disappointment threatened to engulf her. She did not want to see Piers. She was about to tell the man to send him away when she suddenly remembered Piers was a retainer of the King's. He would have news. Maybe Nicholas had sent him.

'I'll see him in the hall,' she said. The servant withdrew and she was about to follow, but Lisette held her back.

'You'd best take a mantle. It be colder in the hall.'

'I'm never cold,' Nicolette replied, shaking off the maid's restraining hand. 'Let me go to him. Perhaps he brings good news.' But Lisette was stubborn.

'No good flaunting your condition at a time like this,' she said. 'Best wear a cloak.'

'If I must, but it won't make any difference, Lisette,' said Nicolette turning once again to study her image in the polished steel. Although her gown had been cleverly altered by Lisette, who was now a talented seamstress, it could no longer disguise the fact that she was pregnant. Lisette arranged the cloak so that it swirled about her in voluminous velvet folds, hiding the telltale contours of her swollen belly. Then she fastened it at the neck with a jewelled clasp, picked it up by its heavy fur-trimmed train and accompanied her mistress into the hall.

The hall was dark and shadowy but Piers was standing clearly visible in the light from the fire. Small rivulets of water ran off his armour and dripped into the rushes at his feet.

He watched her come in, gazing at her as if he could not believe his eyes. She waited, bracing herself for whatever he had to tell, hardly daring to breathe for the agony of uncertainty and hope, while Lisette rearranged the mantle's sweeping folds and withdrew into the shadows.

'Tell them to bring candles, Lisette,' said Nicolette. When the maid had gone, she turned to Piers eagerly. Surely now he would speak. But still Piers said nothing, just gazed at her longingly, his brown eyes with their thick lashes devouring her intently.

It made her feel uncomfortable. 'You have news for me?' she asked when she could stand the silence no longer.

'News?'

'From Sir Nicholas perhaps?'

'I have a letter from Master Gryffard.'

'Why did he write to me? Why did he not come himself?'

'He had to go away to Calais on urgent business.'

'To Calais? On urgent business? At Christmastide? He's

run away! That's it, isn't it? Sir Nicholas,' she cried in an agony of fear. 'What has happened to Sir Nicholas Brembre?'

'I don't know what has happened to him, I expect he's fled?'

'Fled! I don't believe it. Sir Nicholas would never run away.'

'London has opened its gates to the forces of the five lords and all the King's supporters have fled. There is no reason to believe that Sir Nicholas Brembre has remained in the city. He would not dare, not now it has defied him and supported the rebel magnates.'

'But you are here,' she pointed out. 'You are one of the King's retainers, are you not? Why have you not run away with the rest of them?'

'I am no longer a retainer of the King,' Piers said. 'I'm with the Earl of Arundel now.'

'Traitor!' she shouted at him. 'So much for all your fine talk. You deserted the King in his hour of need. Coward! Was your King not worth fighting for? Or were you too afraid of losing?'

'I discovered, when I had to choose, that I would rather fight for you than for the King,' he said, still staring at her intently.

She hardly took in his words. They meant nothing to her. All she could think of was Nicholas. She turned her back on Piers, walked over to the window, stared out at the falling snow. Her lover was a fugitive; somewhere out there in the snow he would be cold and hungry and hunted.

Piers came to stand beside her. 'Did I not say that if ever you should need me I would come? Well, here I am.'

She turned to him in bewilderment. 'But what can you do?' she asked.

'Here, you'd better read the letter from Master Gryffard,' he said, thrusting it at her.

As if in a trance she took the letter, sat down on the window seat, watched while the servant lit the wall torches. Then finally she held the letter up to the light and began to read. Her eyes followed the neat spidery writing without difficulty but her mind refused to make any sense of it. Only one thing leapt off the parchment at her and she seized on it, to use against Piers as a weapon to wound him.

'He has made over his house to you?' she accused.

'For you,' he pleaded. 'It is your dower. I have it in trust for you.'

'You sold yourself after all. You did well – better than Judas anyway. He only got thirty pieces of silver. But you have a fine house in the city and all that it contains.'

'I did it for you, damoiselle. I would do anything for you,' he pleaded. 'I did it because I love you, more than friends, more than honour, more than life itself.'

'Well, I don't want your love,' she flung at him. 'And I don't need your protection either. Save Sir Nicholas Brembre for me. That is what I want. You say you will do anything for me. Save him. He is dearer to me than life itself.' Even through her pain and anger she was aware that he looked completely stunned.

'I don't understand. I thought Master Gryffard had forced you . . .' he broke off, staring at her miserably.

'You thought Master Gryffard forced me to become Sir Nicholas Brembre's mistress,' she interrupted unable to bear the bewildered accusation in his eyes. 'You thought that I would sell my body to help make Master Gryffard prosper.' She was so angry she scarcely knew what she said. 'What I have done I have done for love – just as you did.' He was silent and she got up, began to pace hurriedly back and forth thinking not of Piers and his shattered illusions but of Brembre. 'Where do you think he might have gone?' she asked.

Piers shrugged. 'Who knows. Perhaps he followed Robert de Vere to France. If he is in France he has gone to seek help from the French. To betray us to our enemy.'

'We must try and persuade the Mayor not to give in,' she said, ignoring him. 'The city is divided. Sir Nicholas was always saying that only the victualling guilds were reliable – the fishmongers and the grocers and the others who supplied food.' She was trying to remember something about Piers, something important.

'The Mayor is trying to save his own skin,' said Piers. 'He's afraid of being too closely connected with Brembre. His only hope is to co-operate with the five lords, so Dick Whittington says.'

Whittington. That was it. She remembered Brembre time and again cursing the mercers and saying that they were being led by the nose by an ambitious man who would stop at nothing until he was Mayor. Richard Whittington.

'Isn't he a friend of yours?' she asked. 'Couldn't you persuade Whittington to help?'

'It's too late for anything like that now. You don't understand how unpopular Sir Nicholas Brembre and his friends are in the city. The ordinary citizens of London welcome us, they want to rid themselves of their unpopular leaders. The authorities had to open the city gates for fear that the mob would do so by force if they refused and then proceed to loot the houses of the rich. No one can hold London for the King now.'

'I don't believe you. The Londoners loved Sir Nicholas. They elected him Mayor year after year. You must find him for me – help him.' In her desperation she barely knew what she was saying.

He stood in front of her, blocked her frenzied pacing. 'Leave Sir Nicholas to look after himself. It's you I've come to save,' he declared.

'You don't know much about love,' she said scornfully, 'despite all your fine words. Do you think I'd abandon him now when everyone else has? Won't you go to Whittington for me?'

'What can Whittington do? He has no power in the city. It is the Earl of Arundel and Gloucester and the other three who rule there now.'

'What about the King?'

'The King is a prisoner in the Tower.'

'A prisoner?'

'He is safe inside the Tower, but what can he do? He has no power, no army. Sooner or later he will have to agree to see the five lords and accept their terms.'

'What are they?'

'I don't know, but certainly impeachment for Suffolk and for de Vere and Brembre, of course.'

'But you say they have all escaped.'

'Yes, they have all escaped. The time has come to think about yourself. Let me take you to your house in the city. You will be safe there.'

'I'm perfectly safe here,' she said. 'And I'm going to stay here until I know what has become of Sir Nicholas. Are you going to force me to go with you like the chivalrous knight you are?' He was beaten, she knew by the hurt look in his eyes. She was not afraid of Piers Exton. He was too much her slave. If only she could think of some way in which he could help her to help Nicholas.

As soon as Piers had gone, Lisette materialised from the shadows shaking her head dolefully like a cow newly deprived of her calf. 'Whatever be you adoing, sending off a good man like that for?' she chided. 'What is to become of you now that Sir Nicholas Brembre has upped it? What is to become of that poor unborn babe? Here you are adrowning in a sea of trouble and he holds out a hand and you haven't the sense to grab it. You don't deserve to survive, you don't.'

'Please, Lisette, not now. Don't berate me when I feel so miserable.'

'Poor young man,' muttered Lisette. 'As good and true a knight as any lady ever was lucky to get. It makes no sense, that it don't.'

Nicolette sank down upon the window seat overwhelmed by a sense of loneliness. Her father had abandoned her to Piers who had become his stooge. Nicholas was a fugitive, she knew not where and now even Lisette had turned against her. She felt a familiar movement and put a hand on her swollen belly. The baby was kicking furiously, as he always did at this time of day. She was not entirely alone, she thought. She still had something of Nicholas to cling to. 'I'll not leave him,' she vowed to herself. 'He's not finished yet. I know him. I know he'll never fail. Not while he has life left in his body. He'll triumph still, if I go on believing enough, and I will, for he is all I care about now.'

CHAPTER 14

Piers left Westminster feeling baffled and humiliated. What did a knight do, he wondered, if a damsel in distress refused to be rescued? Did he carry her off anyway? It was a tempting idea but it wasn't chivalry. If he did that he would be no better than Brembre – who had carried her off against her will and then woven an evil spell over her.

Piers dug his heels savagely into his horse's flanks and the surprised animal set off down the Strand at the gallop, upsetting a train of heavily laden packhorses and a party of monks on their way to the shrine of St Edward the Confessor at Westminster Abbey. Piers drew rein and continued at a more sedate pace, his mind much disturbed. For not only was he baffled by Nicolette and what to do to help her, he was anxious about the fate of the King. With the capitulation of London, the King had been persuaded by the Bishop of London to place himself at the mercy of his uncle Gloucester and the other four lords – Warwick, Arundel, Derby and Nottingham. But Piers knew that mercy was not something on the Earl of Arundel's mind and he wondered if any of the others could be trusted to stay loyal to their King. His own disloyalty lay on his conscience like a scourge and Nicolette's scorn had done nothing to ease it.

On the sixth day of Christmas Piers rode with Arundel and the rest of his retinue when the five lords appellant went to the Tower of London to take counsel with the king. They clattered over the drawbridge and in through the narrow stone arch beneath the gatehouse, one after the other, like a river of steel that flowed without interruption for as long as it might take the Bishop of London to preach a sermon. The courtyards rang with the clash of iron-shod hooves, the battlements bristled with archers, and the square, indomitable fortress of the White Tower where the King held counsel was ringed with knights three deep. Piers looked about him at the glistening armour, the colourful pennants, the glorious panoply of war displayed so forcibly and felt ashamed; all this might was ostensibly for the King's protection but it looked far more like intimidation. But when he voiced his unease to his neighbour, the knight just shrugged.

'Gloucester wants to be King,' he said. 'And we're here to see he gets what he wants.'

'Henry Bolingbroke won't allow that,' retorted another. 'John of Gaunt's son isn't going to let his father's younger brother snatch the crown so easily.'

Piers listened to them arguing and hoped they were wrong, that whatever it was that was going on inside the white walls of the inner fortress, his worst fears might not be realised. For however much harm the King might have done, he did not deserve to be deposed. He was King by divine right. I should not have deserted him, thought Piers.

Perplexed, baffled, cold and depressed, he waited for the King's fate to be decided while he examined his conscience. It did not help him that Nicolette was alone in thinking the worse of him for having deserted the King. The Earl of Arundel seemed pleased with him, his new companions in arms were impressed by his prowess. Henry Bolingbroke had even asked him to take Sir Roger Malfeasant's squire in place of Esmon. The boy was a good, hardworking squire who carried out his duties with punctilious efficiency but Piers felt two deaths, Sir Roger's and Esmon's, lay between them. Once he had tried to find out whether the boy held the death of Sir Roger against him.

'Isn't death in battle something a knight has to be prepared for?' the squire had replied, polishing Piers's armour relentlessly, in a manner that discouraged further discussion. He was obedient and seemed loyal enough but he had none of Esmon's eager desire to please. Piers missed Esmon sorely, perhaps because he was the one person who had truly loved him for himself, and Esmon's death weighed heavily on his soul. He saw himself through Nicolette's eyes and his image

163

was tarnished. Only through winning Nicolette could he make his sacrifice worth while, but how could he win her when he was so unworthy?

When many hours later the five lords came out of the White Tower at last, Piers was relieved to learn that Richard was still King. He had agreed to call Parliament and allow his friends and favourite ministers to be impeached. It was capitulation but not deposition. Arundel, Gloucester and Warwick were withdrawing with their forces until Parliament met at Westminster but Bolingbroke and Mowbray were to remain in the Tower with the King by his request. He doesn't trust his uncle of Gloucester not to murder him in his bed, thought Piers and shivered.

Parliament met on 3 February, the day after Candlemas. The King's palace at Westminster was surrounded by the armed men of the five powerful magnates who had joined together to challenge the King's authority. The White Hall, which was used for administrative purposes, was filled with rows of men seated on benches, the representative knights, two from each shire, and the burgesses, two from each borough, who had come to Westminster for the Parliament. King Richard seated himself on the throne and the Chancellor Thomas Arundel, Bishop of Ely, on the Woolsack, flanked on either side by earls and barons and mitred bishops. But when the great door at the opposite end of the hall was flung wide and Gloucester, Arundel, Warwick, Derby and Nottingham entered, dressed in cloth of gold and walking arm in arm in a rough and overbearing display of power, it was very plain who was really in charge of Parliament's deliberations. They stood at the foot of the flight of stone steps leading up to where the King sat and demanded the death of the King's five servants: Michael de la Pole Earl of Suffolk, Robert de Vere Duke of Ireland, Alexander Neville Archbishop of York, Robert Tresilian Chief Justice of the King's Bench, and Sir Nicholas Brembre.

Piers on guard in the White Hall agreed with some of the arguments being put forward, that for instance the King's ministers bore some responsibility not only to the King but to the nation as represented in Parliament; but he could not help remembering the other occasions when as a retainer of the King he had sat at table eating and drinking in this very hall; now his presence there, and the large forces surrounding the Palace of Westminster outside, were a show of strength designed to demonstrate to all those who attended Parliament that they had no choice but to follow their King in bowing to *force majeure*. It worried him also that since most of the accused had either escaped or were still in hiding they would not be present to answer their accusers in a court of law. Only Brembre was available for trial. He had been captured in Wales on 4 January, imprisoned in Gloucester and removed two weeks later to the Tower.

But what most concerned Piers was Nicolette. She was so close; he could walk to her house in King Street in less time than it took to put his armour on. Each day when his duties in the palace allowed he went and stood outside the little house in King Street; but he had only once dared seek admission and that was to tell her about Brembre's capture, to warn her of his impending impeachment and to try to prepare her for the inevitability of his fate. He had hoped that once she realised that Brembre was truly ruined she would allow him to help her. But all she would do was to beg him to save her lover. In vain had he protested that no one could save Brembre now. Nicolette refused to listen. So Piers stayed away.

Sir Nicholas Brembre's trial began on 17 February. His case was to be examined by the King's uncle the Duke of York, his half-brother the Earl of Kent, and ten other great tenants-in-chief, for it was the custom in cases of impeachment for the Commons to act as accuser before a group of lords as judges.

As soon as the first day of the trial was over, Piers went to see Nicolette. She welcomed him almost eagerly and invited him into her chamber. She sat down on the ledge by the bed and raised candid eyes to his face.

'Tell me,' she said, 'how does he look?'

Piers was embarrassed. He noticed for the first time that she was big with child. It made him even more confused.

'He looks well, confident, his usual arrogant self,' Piers told her. 'He has pleaded not guilty and claimed knight's privilege of trial by battle. Of course it was refused.'

'I'm glad,' she said, clasping her hands together tightly above her swollen belly. 'He might be killed in battle.'

'You don't believe in his innocence then?' he asked sharply, unable to bear the sight of her large misshapen body, a reminder, if such were needed, of one of Sir Nicholas Brembre's many sins.

'I only know he will get the better of them,' she declared confidently. 'Of what do they accuse him?'

'Firstly of having agreed with and supported Archbishop Neville, de Vere and de la Pole in alienating the King from his subjects, particularly the great lords.'

'What is wrong with helping the King stand up to his overbearing subjects? Nobody is going to condemn a man for that.'

'Except a Parliament dominated by those overbearing subjects,' Piers said. There was no doubt in his mind that the outcome of this Parliament had been settled long ago at Radcot Bridge and that the King's friends and advisers would be found guilty. That was the intention of this show of strength. But how could he make her understand?

She looked at him coldly. 'What else?'

'That he used his position at court to make his own fortune by gifts of land and jewels and issues from the taxes; that he procured land and offices for relatives and also those who would give him a commission on the grant.'

'They cannot hang a man for that surely?'

'Damoiselle, Sir Nicholas Brembre stands accused of corruptly using the King's favour to grow rich at others' expense; he has taken bribes and misappropriated taxes to reward his own family and supporters; he has betrayed the King's trust. How can you love such a man?'

'Master Gryffard was one of those who grew rich through Sir Nicholas and you have accepted his house and all it contains,' she countered. 'Are you going to give it back to the Crown?'

He stared at her dumbly, wishing he did not feel so tainted, that he could win her through some great glorious deed of his own, that he could be more worthy of her, that she did not look so big with child, or so beautiful still.

'Won't they have to find him guilty of treason before he can be put to death?' she asked him.

'They have not accused him of seeking French help in

exchange for the surrender of Calais as de la Pole, de Vere and the Archbishop have been accused,' Piers admitted reluctantly.

'Of course they have not,' she retorted indignantly. 'They could not find him guilty of such a charge. He would never have agreed to such a thing, and nor would Master Gryffard. Master Gryffard would never have gone back to Calais if he thought it was to be sacrificed. Does the King say Sir Nicholas knew about such a plan?'

'The King defended him valiantly, protesting that he had never known Brembre to be a traitor and that he did not recognise him as appreciably guilty of anything,' replied Piers. 'But it doesn't much matter what the King says while the magnates have their forces surrounding the palace. The King can do nothing to protect his friends and advisers.'

'Sir Nicholas Brembre is not a traitor,' she insisted stubbornly. 'They cannot hang him for having used his power to increase his fortune. Half the burgesses in Parliament have done that in their time. What treasonable acts is he supposed to have committed?'

'They say that he attempted to raise the city of London in arms against the lords appellant and to put them to death, and aided and abetted the efforts which the rest of the accused were making in other parts of the country, particularly Wales and Chester.'

'Is that treason?' she asked him, frowning. 'Was he not doing his best for the King? You went to Chester to help raise troops, did you not? Why is he being tried for treason and not you?'

'Perhaps because he is now on the wrong side,' replied Piers bitterly, walking away from her to the window, unable to bear her cold blue eyes turned on him with such scorn. For a while there was silence in the chamber.

'Don't let us quarrel,' she said softly. 'Let's think instead of some way to help him.'

He swung round. 'Have you no idea what sort of man Sir Nicholas is?' he said fiercely. 'Don't you know what he did when he was Mayor of London? How he stayed in power year after year? The murders without trial of those like John Constantine the cordwainer who dared to oppose him, the delays in allowing others to be brought to trial, the bribes he has taken, the charters of pardon he has obtained for people

167

guilty of felony and treason. He imposed a reign of terror on the city. Why do you think the ordinary Londoners almost rioted when we were outside their gates and their leaders dared not open them? They summoned two members of every London guild to Parliament today to give evidence. If you had heard what some of them had to say, you could not still love him.'

'I don't want to know what he has done. It only matters to me what he is. I know him to be fearless and clever and despite what you say I believe that even now he will still triumph over his enemies. When that happens I shall be here, waiting for him, and nothing you can say will change me.'

It was useless. Piers wished he could hate her for being so wilfully misled but instead he loved her all the more for a constancy so noble and selfless.

She got up and came gliding across the floor on her slippered feet with so much dignity and grace despite her laden stomach, that just to watch her gave him joy.

'You will come tomorrow and tell me how the trial goes?' she begged, touching his arm lightly with her fingertips. Her touch was like a firebrand. Of course he promised; he could not keep away.

By the end of the second day of Brembre's trial Piers began to wonder whether Nicolette's confidence might be justified after all, for the noblemen who were examining his case found him not guilty.

Nicolette was overjoyed when Piers brought her the news. 'There, you see. I knew it. When will they release him, do you think?'

'Tomorrow the Mayor, the aldermen and the Recorder of London have been summoned to give their opinion,' said Piers.

'The Mayor will stand by him, I know,' she said, still confident, but he was not so sure. He wondered whether to let her go on hoping, or try to disillusion her a little to lessen the final blow should it come. 'You look so solemn, Piers,' she said. 'What is it that you are afraid of? That he will be acquitted? Surely you do not begrudge an innocent man his freedom.'

'I don't think you can count on all the aldermen,' he said reluctantly.

'Then we must make sure of them, that is what Sir

Nicholas would do. He did it once before when he got them to promise to support the King back in October before you went with de Vere to raise the north. And they would have gone on supporting the King, I'm sure, if you had not lost to the lords appellant at Radcot Bridge.' She looked at him accusingly but Piers refused to be drawn. He did not want to quarrel with her; more than anything he wanted her to understand why he had done what he had done. 'Will you take me to London?' she asked him suddenly. 'If we are quick we can still be there before the gates are closed at curfew.'

'I cannot take you to London,' said Piers horrified. He had all too little experience of women but he imagined that ladies who were big with child could not ride about the countryside, especially not in a hurry.

'But I must go. I've got to help him. His life may depend upon it.'

'I will not take you to London in your condition. It would be madness. Nothing you can say will make me.' She looked at him haughtily and he wondered if she was going to order him out of the house then and there. But in an instant her mood changed. She moved closer. Laid her hand on his sleeve. Looked up into his face with imploring eyes.

'Then will you go for me?'

'You forget I'm a retainer of Arundel's.' With his flesh burning with desire from the merest touch of her fingers he scarcely knew what he said. 'I can't get involved in city politics.'

'You are pledged to fight for Arundel but that doesn't stop you dining with whomever you like,' she pleaded.

'But I don't know any of the aldermen, they're not going to invite me to dine with them,' he objected.

'What about that mercer, Whittington? He's a friend of yours, isn't he?'

'He was kind to me once,' agreed Piers. 'But I don't think Whittington is an alderman.'

'If you loved me you would go. You keep saying that you love me. Prove it, by helping me now to save Nicholas.'

'I have already proved it,' he said. 'I sold my honour for love. You'll never know that I love you if you don't know now.'

She did not hear him. She was lost in an obsession of her

own and he could not reach her. To his horror she knelt down at his feet, threw her arms round his legs.

'Please,' she said.

It was more than he could bear. 'If I go,' he said lifting her up, 'what do you want me to do?'

She began to pace up and down the hall, frowning thoughtfully. 'Go and see his wife,' she said. 'The lady Idonia. She helped him before. Her family is very powerful in the city. She will know what to do. Only don't say you come from me. It would be better not to upset her. You could say ...' Suddenly she smiled and Piers caught his breath. 'You could say the King sent you.'

The radiance of her smile drove out all his remaining ability to think. Unable to speak for the emotions churning in his breast, he stood and gazed at her, spellbound by her beauty.

'Go quickly then,' she said, giving him both her hands to hold. 'And if you can, come back and tell me the outcome before Parliament sits tomorrow.'

Piers left the house with his senses reeling and no thought in his head save one. He would go to see Whittington and place before that wise merchant the terrible dilemma he was in.

CHAPTER 15

When Piers had gone, Nicolette felt almost confident again. The worst was over, she was sure of it. If the lords who examined Nicholas's case had found him not guilty and they had heard the representatives of all the guilds in London, what was there left to fear? The Mayor and aldermen were the city's leaders. Nicholas was one of them. They would not condemn one of their own. As for the other dreadful things Piers said he was supposed to have done, Nicolette refused to let herself think about them. She loved him. She could not help loving him. He could not be guilty of all that they said he had done. Some of the lesser guilds feared and hated him for political reasons. They would say anything to bring him down. But they had not succeeded. He was going to win, she knew it. Had always known it. Sir Nicholas Brembre could not fail.

Buoyed up by hope, she ate a good supper and went early to bed.

The next day as she waited for Piers, she resolved to be especially nice to him. Perhaps she'd been just a little cruel to him; if she had, it was because she was so unhappy, but if Nicholas was freed she would never be cruel to anybody ever again.

She was up early waiting in the hall in case Piers came before the third day of the trial began. She had all the candles lit and the fire burning brightly to welcome him and some wine and fresh-made tartlets laid out on the trestle board.

But Piers did not come. She waited all day, as patiently and as calmly as she could, telling herself that if Nicholas had been released then Piers would not like to come back. Perhaps instead of Piers it would be Nicholas who came. As soon as it entered her head, the thought would not go away. It was now more than three months since she had seen her lover and she longed for him with an insatiable appetite that frightened her by its intensity.

All day she waited, until the candles burnt down to their sockets and the supper dishes grew cold upon the table; she had new candles brought and sent away the supper dishes untouched, trying not to notice Lisette's disapproving, anxious face, refusing to give up hope, sitting by the window until the candles once again burnt down and she could no longer see to sew. She heard the watch calling the hour and all's well and knew that Piers would not come now.

Utterly exhausted she allowed Lisette to help her to bed, but she was unable to sleep. Her body craved rest but her mind would not be still. She lay alone in the big bed cocooned by the heavy bed curtains in stuffy darkness, plagued by memories of the passionate hours she and Nicholas had spent there together. The darkness had not been stifling then. It had been intimate, secret, a welcome velvety mantle for the wild, unrestrained antics of two bodies urgently pleasuring each other.

The baby began to kick and Nicolette lay on her back and savoured his vigour, remembering how he had been conceived. Into her mind came suddenly unbidden some of the terrible things Piers had told her Nicholas was accused of. But he was innocent, she reminded herself fiercely. She would never believe he could be guilty of such things, but sometimes she wondered whether she was the only one. What had happened to Piers? Why had he not come? Would the Mayor stand by his friend and former leader? Would the aldermen? It was very quiet in the chamber. She could hear Lisette, lying on her pallet by the foot of the bed, snoring steadily. She heard the abbey bell calling the monks for matins and then for lauds. She imagined them stumbling sleepily out of their dorter and into the cold dark chapel. She tried to say the night office to herself, and felt very much alone.

Towards dawn she could stand it no longer. She would go to early Mass. She was no longer sure if God would hear the prayers of an unconfessed sinner, but she was prepared to leave no stone unturned. Lisette when she heard where they were going looked surprised.

'Aren't you going to wait at home in case Sir Piers comes?' she asked.

'If Sir Piers comes, he can wait until we get back. We won't be long,' replied Nicolette and felt relieved to be out of the house at last.

But when they arrived at the abbey and went in to St Peter's, they found the church in an uproar.

'What is it?' asked Nicolette, frightened. 'What has happened?'

'Sacrilege,' a monk, white-faced and trembling, told her. 'One of those on trial for his life at Westminster sought refuge here in the church but they dragged him out, violated the sacred laws of sanctuary and took him away to hang him on Tyburn Hill.'

'Who was it?' Nicolette asked, shaking all over as if with an ague.

'Chief Justice Tresilian. He'd been hiding in the church these two days past,' said the monk. 'They'd no right to take him. While he remained in Saint Peter's, he was under God's protection. The priest told them but they wouldn't listen.'

Nicolette let out a small sigh of relief. She felt sorry for the judge but he was a cold, cruel man and at least Nicholas was still safe.

'Did they hang him without trial?' a woman asked.

'The men-at-arms announced that the Chief Justice had been tried and found guilty by assent of Parliament and condemned to death,' replied a burly woolman.

'Never mind,' replied another. 'They should never have dragged him from the altar. It's an attack on Holy Church, that is.'

'I followed them to London and saw the judge die,' the woolman said. 'He didn't die well.' Everyone within earshot was eager to hear what had happened. 'He were drawn on a hurdle all the way from the Tower to Tyburn.' The woolman, pleased to have such an attentive audience, launched into his tale with gusto. 'At the end of each furlong he were allowed to rest – to confess to the friar who accompanied him. When he arrived at Tyburn, he refused to go up the ladder which led to the gallows.' He paused and Nicolette knew she ought to leave, but she was transfixed like the rest of them by the horror of what was to come. 'They had to beat him with clubs to get him to climb the ladder. Then when at last he stood upon the scaffold, he says to the hangman, "You cannot hang me as long as I am still wearing anything."' The audience gasped. Nicolette, unable to bear any more, turned to flee but was hemmed in by the crowd avidly awaiting the gory details. 'They took off his clothes and found in his pockets – guess what?' asked the woolman, spinning out his tale. The crowd shook its collective head. 'Charms to protect himself against a violent death. He must have known he were guilty. So the hangman removes the charms and they hang him naked.' The crowd recoiled in horrified wonder and Nicolette, appalled, managed to escape. In an agony of apprehension she fled back to the house in King Street. If only Piers was there with good news.

When she got back to the house, she found on entering the hall not Piers but a strange woman she had never seen before. She looked like a prosperous merchant's wife.

'Good morning, mistress,' said Nicolette much mystified. It was not often that any woman called at Brembre's house in King Street. 'Can I be of service to you? I'm Nicolette de Saint Pierre,' adding with a glance at the bread and ale which had been set upon the trestle board for the visitor, 'and mistress here.'

'I'm Agnes Fraunceys,' replied the woman. 'Widow of Adam Fraunceys, the friend and partner in some ventures of Sir Nicholas Brembre. I've come to take over the rent of this house and must ask you to leave as soon as you can find it convenient.'

'Leave? I can't leave, not yet,' exclaimed Nicolette. 'Not until the trial is over. Sir Nicholas is innocent. I must be here for him when they let him go.'

'The trial is over,' the woman told her shortly. 'Sir Nicholas has been found guilty and condemned to death.'

'No, no, you must be mistaken,' Nicolette told her quite calmly.

'He has been found guilty of treason and is to hang this day,' replied Agnes Fraunceys, shaking her head sadly.

'Treason? But he's not a traitor,' cried Nicolette. 'He was not accused of trying to buy help from the King of France by the surrender of Calais. Not like some of the others. They cannot hang him for a crime he did not commit. What did the Mayor say?'

'Nicholas Exton was asked whether he thought Brembre

had known about such treasonable matters, and replied that he thought he did and was worthy of death. The aldermen and Recorder of London agreed.'

'No, no, it's not true. The Mayor and the aldermen, they would never let him down, not now. They have followed him wherever he has led. He has been their leader all these years. They would not condemn him now.'

'The Mayor is in a difficult position. His downfall is being sought by certain guilds as much as Brembre's is. He was the champion of free fishmongers in the city. The fishmongers are very unpopular now.'

'Merciful Jesus, Sir Nicholas Brembre has been betrayed and by his closest friends. How could they? After all he has done for them, how could they betray him?'

'We all of us have to save ourselves as best we can. You must think of yourself now. Once Sir Nicholas is dead, it would be much better for you not to be found here.'

Nicolette heard nothing save the fateful words, once Sir Nicholas is dead.

'When?' she whispered, barely able to speak. 'When will they hang him?'

'Today. After noon,' said the Widow Fraunceys. 'Having persuaded Parliament to find him guilty, the lords appellant are anxious to have the sentence carried out forthwith.'

'I must go to him,' cried Nicolette wildly. 'I must be with him at the end. He cannot die alone.' She turned and ran from the hall. At the top of the flight of stairs leading down into the courtyard, Lisette caught up with her, held her in her arms.

'No, mistress,' she cried. 'You can't go. Think what you be doing. You can't go arushing off to London and you so near your time. God have mercy on us all.'

'I can and I will and there is nothing you or anyone can do to stop me,' replied Nicolette.

'How are you going to get there then?' demanded Lisette. 'You can't ride nor bump about in a litter, not if you don't want to have that poor little babe somewhere along the way. Our Lord have mercy. Much better wait here and let Sir Piers Exton take care of you now.'

At the mention of Piers's name, Nicolette shuddered. Piers had failed her once again. She did not ever want to rely on Piers.

'I shall go by river,' she said, shaking off Lisette's restraining hand and slowly, carefully walking down the steps into the court below. After the first shock, she felt quite calm. 'There are always plenty of watermen at Westminster Steps. It's early yet. Not long past prime. It shouldn't take too long to row down the river to the Tower.' She fished in the purse she wore hanging from her girdle, brought out a handful of coins, counted them carefully. 'It should be enough to pay the waterman.' Thus occupying her mind with the practical problems of how to get there, she was able to avoid thinking what she was going to.

'What about her that's taking over the house? Are you going to leave her free to help herself?'

'What does it matter? She can have anything she wants,' replied Nicolette, beginning to walk quickly across the court. 'Sir Nicholas won't need them. You can keep her out of my coffers, I dare say.'

'I'm coming with you, mistress,' Lisette declared stoutly. 'You don't think I'd let you go where you're going all on your own, do you? Only I wish we had that good man Sir Piers Exton with us. He'd know how to look after you better nor I.'

'Don't mention his name to me again, Lisette. He promised to serve me and all he ever does is make matters worse – much worse.'

The journey by river was tortuously slow, as the tide had turned and the waterman had to row against it. But Nicolette was not aware of how long it took. Lisette fussed and fidgeted and plagued the waterman with questions, unable to keep a still tongue in her head, but Nicolette heard nothing. She was haunted by the description of Judge Tresilian's terrible end, determined that Nicholas should not have to go through such public humiliation, desperate to see him once more. She did not notice the passing scene as the boat headed downstream through open fields until it reached the ruins of the Duke of Lancaster's Palace of Savoy. They rowed on, past noblemen's houses, bishop's palaces and convents until the well-tended gardens sweeping down to the water's edge gave way to a jumble of wharves and warehouses and tall wooden houses crowded together along the river bank. Dimly Nicolette was aware of pain, stabbing with a kind of questing insistence, like a beggar who will not be turned away, but her whole being was so full of pain she did not dare think about it, else she would be totally engulfed and unable to help Nicholas in his last hour.

Skilfully the waterman guided the little boat through the turbulent waters swirling round the great stone arches of London Bridge and entered the deeper, calmer pool beyond, where the bigger ships anchored. The river now was dotted with craft of every sort: colourful sailing barges tacking to and fro as they delivered their cargoes to the busy wharves; small rowing skiffs carrying passengers; large galleys and sailing ships at anchor loading or unloading or just waiting for the wind and the tide. But Nicolette saw none of them. Her mind seemed frozen. She watched the waterman's oars dipping in and out of the water as she had done all the way from Westminster, numbed and calmed by the rhythmic beat, unaware of anything save the tiny silvery trail which dripped from the blades of the oars as they skimmed the surface of the water before plunging in once again for another pull.

The waterman brought his boat up to a flight of steps beneath the great walls of the Tower and Nicolette climbed carefully out of the boat and on to the cobbled public way, catching her breath sharply as another stab of pain took her unawares. She looked up at the forbidding walls towering above her and became aware suddenly of a noisy tumult like the roar of the sea swelling all around her. The drawbridge over the moat round the Tower was being lowered.

'Merciful Jesus, mistress, we never ought to have come,' exclaimed Lisette. 'Hanging's a great spectacle, the more so as he's such a public man. This is no place for you, with all these people. Come away, by Our Lady, do, before it's too late.'

'No, no, we're not too late – see,' exclaimed Nicolette, unable to think of anything but her desire to see and speak to him just once more. 'God in his mercy has sent us in time.' She stood and watched, hardly daring to breathe, as slowly the portcullis was raised and a horse and cart surrounded by mounted men-at-arms and pikemen on foot came out of the Tower. Standing up in the cart bareheaded and clad simply in doublet and hose stood Sir Nicholas Brembre and, at his side, a priest.

At the sight of him, Nicolette's calm deserted her. She broke into a stumbling run and pushed her way through the

177

cheering crowd towards the cart, desperate to reach him. A woman with two sturdy boys was before her, running along beside the cart.

'Remember John Constantine,' the woman screamed. 'This day is he avenged at last.'

'Forgive me,' Brembre mumbled. 'Jesu have mercy.'

Nicolette hardly recognised him. His head was bent, his hair was blowing wildly in the wind, and his face – she could not bear the desolation in his beloved face.

'You can think yourself lucky,' yelled the woman. 'You had a fair trial but you killed my John without trial or priest to hear his confession. Was that mercy? Was it justice?'

He didn't deny it. Just crossed himself and fell to his knees in the cart.

The woman dropped back and Nicolette took her place, stumbling along beside the cart, clutching the rough wooden edge for support. To her horror he was not praying as she had thought, but babbling incoherently in terror.

'Nicholas,' she cried, 'my own dear love. I am here. I love you. I regret nothing.'

He gazed at her blankly and she saw in his face not arrogant certainty or resolution, but fear, naked and terrible.

'Forgive me,' he said, crossing himself with a hand which trembled so much he could barely make the sign of the cross. 'I have sinned.'

'Don't you know me?' she cried again. 'It's me, Nicolette. I'm here with you. I love you. Don't be afraid. I've come to be with you, to help you.'

'I have sinned, forgive me.' He stared at her wildly. 'Mary Mother of Jesus have mercy, for I am on my way to hell.'

A man pushed past Nicolette declaring he was John of Northampton's son and challenging the prisoner to deny that his treatment of his father had been unjust. Dazed, struggling to keep up with the cart, Nicolette watched while her lover shook his head like a baited bear. The cart was moving more slowly now as the crowd pressed in on all sides. Others came to castigate him, hurling his sins in his face, their hatred for him venomous. Nicolette was stunned. He was not a giant among men but a sinner whose many misdeeds had caught up with him. Stripped of his power and the King's protection, her wonderful lover was nothing. He had no pride, no dignity, no excuses to offer for all that he

178

had done. In despair she looked at the man now kneeling in the cart, the man she had been so proud to serve. He was clinging to the edge with whitened knuckles, tears of remorse and terror streaming down his face.

She plunged towards him, determined to make one more effort to bring him love and consolation and it was then that the pain struck much stronger than before. She gasped and sank to the cobbles. The crowd gathered round, peering at her curiously. All she could see was a forest of legs. She took a deep breath. The pain receded, but she seemed to be sitting in a puddle of water. She tried to get up but the crowd hemmed her in on every side.

'Help me,' she cried. 'Somebody!'

The pain was back again, twisting through her body like an eager, hungry rat. She struggled for air.

'Here, you bastards, let her breathe.' Through the mist of pain a face swam in front of her eyes, a pale thin face framed by a hood of blue. 'What's the matter, my child?' a voice asked.

'I don't know.' The pain came again and she closed her eyes; darkness threatened to engulf her.

'It be the babe.' When Nicolette opened her eyes again, Lisette had appeared from nowhere and was kneeling by her side. 'The bag of waters has burst. It won't be long now before she gives birth.'

'Well, she can't do it here. Get her off the street so the wagon can pass,' said a harsh voice. She was picked up and dumped unceremoniously at the side of the road and the cart began again rumbling over the cobbles on its long way to Tyburn, where the gallows were waiting to claim the father of her child.

'Blessed Lord have mercy on him,' she prayed and gasped as a contraction gripped her anew. For a while the pain blotted out everything, even the terrible fate of the man she loved with such destructive passion. Then as it receded she was picked up, more gently this time, and she saw again the man in the blue hood peering at her with evident concern.

'Where are you taking me?' she asked.

'To Billingsgate. I have a house there. It's not far,' he replied.

'Who are you?' she asked, bewildered.

'Richard Whittington,' he replied with a thin smile.

PART II
1388–1390

He was a devotee of chivalry
Of honour, faith and generosity.
Through Christendom, and heathen lands as well,
His fame was spread – though heathen cities fell.
Yet he behaved with manly modesty
To anyone, however low of birth.
He was a brave, true knight of sterling worth.

Geoffrey Chaucer, *The Knight's Tale*

CHAPTER 16

1388

Almost immediately Dick Whittington began to regret what he'd done. He told himself wryly that he was a mercer not a knight in shining armour; he never did anything except for profit. It was just that she was so very beautiful; even *in extremis* there was something about the delicate purity of her face that had made him for once act impulsively. So now here he was hurrying down Thames Street with a young woman who seemed about to give birth at any moment, her ugly maid gabbling hysterically in a French patois so broad he found it difficult to understand one word in ten, when he should have been on his way to Tyburn to watch Nicholas Brembre hang.

The young woman stopped and to his horror crouched down in the gutter moaning and straining in total disregard of her surroundings while again a small crowd of would-be helpers gathered round. He could have abandoned her then, would have liked to have done so, only she suddenly looked up at him with an expression so beseeching, he thought better of it.

'I'm sorry,' she said, panting. 'I'm being a great trouble to you. Is it very much further?'

He looked down Thames Street. He could see the spire of St Bodolph's. The shop he owned in Billingsgate was close by the church.

'Not far now. Do you think you can walk or shall we carry you?'

'I can walk,' she said but as she tried to rise she screamed in pain. 'I'm sorry,' she said a moment later. 'That was a very bad one. I don't think I can walk much further.'

An old crone pushed her way through the crowd. She

fumbled about among the folds of her capacious skirts and finally brought forth a vial of lard darkened with blood and filth. Scooping out some of the rancid grease she began to cover her hands and forearms with it. Then she knelt down on the cobbles beside the straining young woman. She was old and dirty and probably drunk; Whittington guessed that she was a midwife. He looked away in disgust while she plunged her greasy hands under the girl's skirts; but the wretched child screamed so loud he turned back in alarm.

'You can't deliver her here!' he exclaimed, horrified. 'Can't you wait until we get her indoors out of sight of all these curious onlookers? My shop's barely a bowshot away.' But the old woman paid no attention; she just went on with her work while Whittington gazed about him helplessly, wishing he was at Tyburn watching the hanging. The girl screamed again. 'By the Blessed Virgin,' he muttered, 'she'll have it now, and then what am I to do with her?'

'There be no hurry, sir,' replied the old woman sitting back on her haunches and wiping her hands on her filthy skirts. 'The poor creature's got a long hard time ahead of her. The silly bugger wants to come into the world wrong end first. Now where's this place of yourn? Best have her carried there before she frightens every poor child-laden woman in Billingsgate with her caterwauling.'

They picked Nicolette up and Whittington led the way swiftly, trying not to listen to her ragged screams, uncomfortably aware that not only was their progress attracting the attention of the few people in the street, but that others were leaning out of the overhanging windows above to see what all the noise was about. The fishmonger who rented the shop in Billingsgate was standing outside staring in open-mouthed curiosity; to Whittington's relief his wife was at his side.

'Here's a poor child I found trying to give birth in the street,' Whittington said to them. 'Will you give her shelter and see that she's safely delivered?' The fishwife looked unenthusiastic. 'Do this for me, Dame Storey,' he said fixing her with a hard stare, 'and I'll forget that you're behind with the rent again.'

'Who is she?' demanded the woman.

'I don't know,' replied Whittington with a shrug. 'But

she's in need of your Christian charity. Will you do it?'

'My name is Nicolette de Saint Pierre,' the girl gasped and clutched Whittington tightly as she tried not to scream. Jesu, he thought, cursing anew, Piers Exton's lady! He glanced at her again and even as he wished more fervently than ever that he had not succumbed to the sight of such loveliness he acknowledged that Piers had true cause for his infatuation.

'Help me!' she cried, digging her fingers into his arm, and he wished that he could, that Piers had not seen her first, and that Piers was not such a trusting friend.

'You'll be all right now,' he said, prising her clinging fingers with difficulty from his arm. 'The women'll take care of you.' Then without waiting for further demands on his goodness, he hurried away, back to his own house in the Royall in search of Alice his wife who would, he felt sure, be able to provide help and succour.

Alice was in the pantry with a batch of new-baked bread. 'You're back early,' she said. 'I thought the hanging wasn't until noon.'

'I didn't go to the hanging,' he replied. 'I got led astray, rescuing a young lady who was about to give birth to what I fear is Brembre's bastard right outside the Tower. I took her to my shop in Billingsgate. The Storeys are looking after her now. But they won't want to keep her after the baby is born.'

'Why can't she go back to her husband?'

'She hasn't got a husband.'

'I suppose she's very beautiful' she said, laying a round, warm loaf on the shelf beside the others.

'She's Piers Exton's lady,' he said. She had her back to him and was carefully arranging the loaves neatly on the shelves. 'I couldn't in Christian charity leave her lying there, poor child, now could I?' he said to justify himself. 'Of course I didn't know then who she was.'

Alice turned round to face him. 'She was Brembre's mistress, wasn't she? You were a fool to get involved. What are you going to do with her now?'

'I don't know. I thought you might go and see how she does.' From her expression he knew she did not welcome the idea. 'The midwife seemed to think the birth would be long and difficult,' he added. 'She might even die.'

'And if she doesn't she'll be ruined. Sir Piers Exton won't want her now. Not after Brembre.' He wished she would not always give her opinions as if they were irrefutable fact, that just occasionally his good, practical Alice might be more troubled by imagination.

'Piers is a very noble young man,' he said. 'Sees himself as a second Sir Galahad. It's just the kind of thing he might do. He certainly ought to be given the chance. I'd better go and see if I can find him.'

'I can't understand why you take so much trouble over that young man, Dick. He's not extravagant like some of your other customers. Not likely to borrow from you, nor rich enough to afford any of your fine wares. He's nothing but a landless younger son.'

'Just as I was when I first came to London and was apprenticed to your father. Don't you remember?'

'I remember you were a cheeky young scamp of barely thirteen summers always trying to get the better of the other apprentices and usually succeeding. Not a bit like Piers Exton.'

'Perhaps that is why I like him,' said her husband. 'He's what I might have been but chose not to become.'

Alice merely tightened her lips and asked, 'Where are you going to start looking for your knight errant?'

'Tyburn's as good a place as any,' he said. 'There's bound to be some of the retainers of the five lords appellant on guard at the hanging.'

When Whittington got to Tyburn the hanging was over. The lifeless body of Sir Nicholas Brembre was dangling from the gibbet and it seemed to Whittington that there was something almost obscene in its helplessness. Listening to the crowd of curious spectators all still excitedly talking about the hanging, he judged that it was not long over. On the edge of the crowd a group of knights mounted on their horses sat watching as the citizens of London jostled each other to get a better look at the body of their former leader. Recognising Piers's red and cream blazon Whittington pushed his way through the crowd towards him.

'I thought you'd be here, Master Whittington,' said Piers when he reached his side. 'What did you think of the hanging?'

'I wasn't here in time for the main spectacle,' said Whittington. 'Did he die well?'

'Better than the Judge Tresilian, but no, I wouldn't say he died well. No better than he lived to my mind.'

'He started off well,' commented Whittington. 'He defended the city's right to its own independence against several attempts to take it into the King's hand. For years he was the most powerful man in London, whether Mayor or not, and it made him a great favourite of the King.'

'And that was his undoing,' said Piers staring up at the gibbet.

Thoughtfully Whittington studied the body suspended from the gallows, as limp as any rag doll. 'No man ever allied himself to great lords without losing his feathers in the end,' he said. 'A wise Italian merchant told me that once. I've often wondered if he was right.'

'But how can a man prosper without allying himself to some great nobleman?' asked Piers. 'A knight's not much use on his own in this world.'

'I wonder,' mused Whittington. 'Brembre need not have fallen if he'd shown more regard for London's freedom. But he'd stopped listening to the other voices in the city – the aldermen, the Common Council. In the end he heard only his own and it made him dangerous. He became as big a despot as any magnate. The city made him what he was and the city destroyed him in the end. That was his mistake. He underestimated the collective power of the city of London merchants.'

'He was too proud, if you ask me,' replied Piers scornfully. 'Too sure of himself, always arrogant. He was over-ambitious, power hungry and a bullying coward to boot. It was inevitable that one day he would overreach himself, and he did, and there he hangs.'

'A salutary lesson to us merchants not to fly too high,' replied Whittington with a wry smile. 'Come back to my house for dinner. I want to talk to you.'

'I can't. I must go to Westminster to see the Damoiselle de Saint Pierre and break the news to her, if she hasn't heard already. I don't know what I'm going to tell her. She thought I was going to save him.'

'And I believe you might even have been fool enough to try if I hadn't stopped you,' declared Whittington. 'The question is, are you fool enough to marry her now Brembre is dead?'

'Of course, if she'll have me. But I'll not force her against her will,' declared Piers.

'You're a romantic idiot,' Whittington informed him. 'Of course she'll have you. She's ruined else. But you don't have to have her. That fine inn of Master Gryffard's is yours whether you have her or not. He made it over to you outright. Gryffard has exiled himself like the rest of the King's friends. He'll be lucky if they don't try him in Parliament with all the others. The lords appellant are making a clean sweep while they can.' He looked up at the young man sitting on his horse in all his bright armour, like a vision of chivalry. 'You're free to enjoy the fruits of Master Gryffard's labours without having to burden yourself with a wife,' he reiterated wondering if Piers could be tempted.

'But in honour bound,' said Piers, smiling down at him.

'Ah, Piers, Piers, that honour of yours – is it real or is it merely a disguise for your baser instincts? Is it honour or is it passion which drives you to rescue your lady from her folly?' The smile disappeared and Piers looked so incredulous that Whittington for once felt ashamed of his cynicism. 'You'll have to come back with me, Piers,' he said, 'for I've been doing some knight errantry of my own today. While you've been here watching the dragon's death throes I have rescued your fair lady for you.'

'What!' exclaimed Piers, sitting bolt upright in his saddle. 'By the Rood, I'll not believe it!'

'And have hidden her away where you'll never find her,' added Whittington, enjoying himself.

'I don't believe it,' Piers repeated. 'You haven't been to King Street, have you?'

'No, I haven't been to Westminster. I found her nearer, much nearer than that. But I'm getting hungry and the noonday bells are ringing. Alice will have a good dinner waiting and we don't want it to spoil. She knows hangings always make me hungry. I'll tell you all about it on the way. It's why I was too late to see Sir Nicholas go to meet his Maker – the intervention of Divine Providence wouldn't you say?'

When the pain stopped, Nicolette thought she must be dead and was glad. The agony had for so long ruled her with its

188

relentless demands, twisting her tortured body out of all knowledge of itself, that it had seemed to her pain-crazed mind that she was pursuing Nicholas Brembre through eternity on his journey into hell. Desperately she had been trying to catch up with him, but always he fled from her. In vain she cried out for him to wait, but he wouldn't wait and he never turned round. She screamed and screamed at him but he kept running and no matter how hard she struggled she could never reach him. The pain was holding her back, an army of demons seemed to have hold of her and to be stoking their flames with her tortured flesh. Then, unbelievably, when she thought that this was hell and she condemned to dwell in it for evermore, the pain was gone and so was he.

She lay still. Not daring to move. Scarcely daring to breathe. Slowly she became conscious of little things: her aching body – if she was dead, why did her body ache so? The smell of fish – she didn't expect heaven or hell or even purgatory to smell of fish. A thin mewling sound – like a cat or a peacock perhaps. She opened her eyes and saw Lisette holding in her arms a small bundle from which came that thin mewling cry.

'Your son,' she said, holding out the bundle.

All Nicolette could see of the creature which had given her so much agony to bring into the world was a puckered red face and tiny open mouth from which came that insistent, irritating cry.

'Take him away, I don't want him,' she said, turning her head away.

'He's hungry. Will you not suckle him?' Lisette laid the baby down beside her on the bed and disappeared. Nicolette peered at the wailing bundle of misery beside her and was shocked to see that the little face looked just like Nicholas. Not the triumphant powerful master of London but the helpless frightened sinner who had gone to his death with so much last-minute repentance. She did not want to be reminded of Nicholas. She frowned as she studied the tiny form swaddled in what looked like a pudding cloth. She had vowed to give this baby to God – if He would only spare the father. To bring him up to be a monk or a priest, that is what she had promised when she had lit all those candles for Nicholas in St Peter's. But quite clearly God did not want her baby or He would have answered her prayers. She closed her

189

eyes again and oblivious of the baby's feeble crying slept the sleep of exhaustion.

All too soon she was woken again by Lisette smoothing away her tangled hair from her breast.

'The baby,' said Nicolette pushing the maid's hand away. 'Can't you stop him crying? He makes my head ache so.'

'He'll not stop crying unless you feed him,' said Lisette as she began to bathe the breast with a cloth soaked in warm water. 'That'll bring a bit of peace to you both.' She leant across the bed and picked up the bundle, holding the baby with his face against Nicolette's warm breast. At first the crying continued but helped by Lisette the little mouth found her nipple and fastened by instinct on it. The crying stopped. But he did not suck for long. Soon his eyes closed and he lay so limp and helpless, Nicolette was afraid he must be dead.

'What's the matter with him?' she said, feeling confused and rejected.

'You're both of you weak from the prolonged birthing,' pronounced Lisette, removing him. 'We'll try again later when you've slept.'

Relieved Nicolette closed her eyes and almost immediately fell into deep sleep again.

It seemed no time before Lisette woke her once more. 'Dame Storey is here to see you,' she said.

Dazed, Nicolette stared in surprise at a red-faced woman standing by the side of the bed. She was fat and badly scarred by the pox, and she too smelt of fish.

'We'll send the boy to fetch your husband, if ye'll tell us where he's to be found,' she said

Alarmed, Nicolette tried to gather together her scattered wits. 'Where am I?' she asked, looking about her at the small mean chamber in dismay.

'In our bed,' replied the woman, staring down at her somewhat belligerently.

Nicolette studied her surroundings for the first time. The room was without adornment but functional. A chest, a stool, a smoking fire, a small window with a trestle table beneath it, rushes on the floor, and the bed with its hard horsehair mattress and cloth bed curtains.

'It's very kind of you to have helped me,' said Nicolette with her most winning smile.

190

'It's Master Whittington you must thank for that,' said the woman with a sniff. 'It's his house – we only rent it off him. He brought you to us day before yesterday when your labour started.'

'So long?' Nicolette was startled. She wanted to ask the woman if she had been to the hanging, to find out if Nicholas had died bravely, but Dame Storey looked so fierce she did not dare. Instead she tried to placate her. 'I know I must be a dreadful nuisance to you. If I could just sleep a little now – to get back my strength, you know.'

'You are a nuisance and that's a fact,' declared the woman.

Nicolette gazed up into the fishwife's uncompromising stare. She wasn't wanted here. A wave of panic swept over her. 'Can't I stay just a little longer?' she pleaded. 'I'm not strong enough to get up yet, I don't think.'

The woman looked away uneasily. 'It's not me, mind,' she said. 'It's my husband. He wants his bed back. He doesn't like sleeping on the floor with the apprentice under the counter, and we've too many mouths to feed as it is. Your husband can fetch a straw-filled wagon to you. You'll do well enough in that.'

Nicolette stared at the woman in dismay as the true nature of her plight hit her. She had no home. No husband. Where was she to go, now that Nicholas was dead and the Widow Fraunceys had taken over the house in King Street? The fishwife, gazing down at her implacably with her arms folded across her chest, did not look as if she knew nor cared.

'If you're not out of here by nightfall I don't know what's to be done,' the woman said.

Nicolette shut her eyes again. 'I'll send to him presently,' she promised, feigning sleep. She was so tired she didn't want to think, just wished they would leave her alone. First it was Lisette pestering her to feed the baby. Now it was Dame Storey come to see what was to be done. Nicolette did not know what was to be done. She did not want to think about it. She did not want to think about anything. All she wanted was to be left alone to sleep; to escape into oblivion and wake up to find all her troubles miraculously resolved.

She slept. But all too soon, Lisette was back with the baby who was crying again.

Nicolette took the tiny bundle and held him against her

breast and this time a shock of pure pleasure shot through her as he fastened immediately on her nipple.

'The fishwife's creating something terrible,' Lisette informed her. 'She wants us out, Holy Mother protect us. I told her you wasn't strong enough to walk, let alone ride, and that you'll catch your death being rowed in a boat all the way back to Westminster. The river's full of nasty damp vapours like as not, what'll bring on the fever – that's what I told her.'

'We can't go back to King Street, the Widow Fraunceys turned us out. Don't you remember?' Nicolette said wearily.

'Where then?' demanded Lisette. 'Us can't stay here. She's having none of it.'

Nicolette looked at the little creature in her arms. He had already given up trying to suck and was lying limply against her breast. She felt a fierce protective rush of love for him. Poor little bastard child, she thought. He was not even a lusty, healthy babe, but a mewling sickly thing, too weak to suckle while she, who had tried so hard to please everyone, lay in a fishmonger's shop, unwanted and alone.

'She says as how you can have the fish wagon lined with straw,' went on Lisette, 'take you wherever you wishes to go. She means it. She wants the bed for her man.'

Nicolette stared helplessly at Lisette's worried, ugly face and was afraid. She was a failure. Just like her mother. What had happened to change everything so quickly? She had disobeyed her father, the still small voice of her conscience told her. Defied him when he had wanted her to leave Nicholas and marry Piers.

She had been so sure that Nicholas would always triumph; blinded by her love for him and convinced by his belief in his own invincibility, she had clung to him for too long. Now he was dead and she was alone. She wanted to go back to the beginning, to the innocent days before Nicholas when everything was simple. Through the small chamber window she could hear the bell of St Bodolph's tolling the Angelus. All over the city the bells rang out in clamorous welcome for the end of the day.

Hail Mary full of Grace
The Lord is with thee
Blessed art thou among women

Hail Mary full of Grace
The Lord is with thee
Blessed art thou among women

Hail Mary full of Grace
The Lord is with thee
Blessed art thou among women

Instinctively Nicolette repeated the familiar words as she always did when she heard the bells, only this time longing with an aching sadness for the days when she could pray with a clear conscience, days when she could confess. 'Father, I have sinned.' 'Go in peace, my child.' Peace, that was what she wanted now. Peace from them all.

Alice Whittington paused outside the door of St Bodolph's to listen to the bells and wished she could go to vespers instead of having to pick up the pieces of her husband's knight errantry. The church looked very inviting. Inside she could see the priest preparing for the last service of the day, smell the incense. 'Blessed Mother, aid me,' she prayed, walking swiftly on past the open church door. Better to get it over quickly, she thought, and then go to Mass, if there was time.

The fishmonger who rented Whittington's shop was putting up his shutters and wasted no time telling Alice that he was not prepared to put up with a fallen woman in his respectable house one day longer. Nothing Alice could say would change his mind and she entered the living chamber above the shop in no mood to treat the young mother gently.

Nicolette was lying in the bed in the middle of the room feeding her baby. She was pale and there were dark shadows of exhaustion beneath her eyes. Her hair, neatly plaited, lay in two long ropes of gold on either side of her breast. She is certainly beautiful, thought Alice, impressed in spite of herself. But then she would have to be beautiful to have caught Dick's attention enough to distract him from his purpose.

'I'm Alice Whittington,' she said. 'My husband tells me he rescued you the day before yesterday and brought you here. He sent me to find out how you are.'

'That was very kind of him,' murmured the girl.

'Not kind, necessary. The fishmonger and his wife are not prepared to keep you here any longer.'

193

'I have a little son – see, is he not beautiful?' Nicolette held out the baby like a peace offering. 'I think perhaps I shall name him Richard after Master Whittington in tribute to his having come to my rescue.'

'The question is what is to be done with you?' said Alice, unappeased. The baby began to cry.

'I thought they were your tenants,' replied Nicolette trying to get him to feed again. 'If Master Whittington wishes it, they'll have to keep me, surely.'

'But I don't think he does wish it,' announced Alice, exasperated by the girl's naivety. 'There's only one man can help you now.'

'Who?' asked Nicolette her eyes wide and bright with hope.

'Sir Piers Exton.'

'Oh, Piers. He's always plaguing me with his offers of help, but when I need him he's never any use.'

Alice wondered whether she had been counting on Dick to come to her rescue. If she had, then she was a sad judge of men, a fact which her present predicament bore out all too plainly.

'Piers is all you have,' Alice told her firmly. 'And you can thank God that he'll have you. He has told my husband that he is prepared to honour his pledge to Master Gryffard and marry you as soon as maybe.'

'But I don't want to marry Piers. I don't love him.'

'Love,' scoffed Alice. 'What has love to do with marriage?'

'I'm sure Master Whittington must have loved you when he married you,' said Nicolette and Alice felt sickened by her desperate desire to please.

'My husband married me because I was the daughter of Sir John Fitz Warren, a mercer, to better himself,' she said harshly, 'and my father gave me to him because Dick was his star apprentice.'

Nicolette was silent. Down below, Master Storey was swearing at his apprentice and his wife, and Alice knew that it would not be long before one of them came to them to find out what arrangements had been made to remove the unwelcome cuckoo in their nest.

'Couldn't I go into a convent?' asked Nicolette suddenly.

'You need a dowry for a convent,' said Alice. 'Sir Piers Exton has your dowry, Master Gryffard made it over to him, it seems. A foolish move, but then he was a man in a hurry to flee before it was too late and men in fear for their lives cannot be expected to make sensible marriage settlements. It's fortunate for you that Sir Piers is honourable enough to stick by his word even though there was no betrothal vow to hold him to it.'

'Oh, Piers is full of noble principles except when he wants to save his own skin.'

'I don't know him well, but I wouldn't have thought that Sir Piers Exton was a coward,' replied Alice. 'But coward or no, it doesn't much matter, you'll have to marry him, you have no other choice. The world is a cruel place and gives no shelter to a woman on her own. Marriage is a woman's survival.'

'I can't leave here, not tonight. I'm too weak from the birth,' protested Nicolette.

Alice was relieved that at least she appeared to have accepted the inevitability of her fate. Her task was almost done. 'I've arranged for you to go back to Master Gryffard's house in Cornhill. It belongs to Piers now, of course, but he is at Westminster where Parliament is still sitting. You will be safe and well cared for by Master Gryffard's people; all the servants remain in the house. The Storeys will take you in their wagon. It's not very far.'

Nicolette clutched the sleeping baby tightly against her breast and gazed at Alice soulfully, her eyes very large and bright with unshed tears.

'Couldn't I come home with you?' she asked.

'I'm afraid that would be quite impossible,' replied Alice swiftly. 'You have a maid, my husband said. I will go and find her. She must make you ready for the journey.' So saying she whisked herself out of the chamber before Nicolette could make any further appeals to her hospitality. Nicolette de St Pierre might be a fallen woman but she had an artless innocence about her which went well with her fragile beauty, and Alice was afraid of being beguiled by it, just as her husband had been. She had no intention of doing more for the girl than she deserved.

CHAPTER 17

The sun had already set and it was beginning to get dark as the fishmonger and his wife helped Nicolette into the wagon. She thanked them prettily and Dame Storey actually smiled and wished her well, now that she was on her way; but her husband just stared contemptuously and Nicolette suddenly felt glad to be leaving.

The wagon was attached to a bag of bones on four legs with the dejected air of a beast of burden whose work is never done, attended by a scrawny lad who looked similarly underfed and whom Nicolette guessed must be the apprentice. The fishmonger ordered him roughly to get the horse moving and the boy yanked on its bridle, but the animal hung its head obstinately, clearly determined that its work for the day was over like everybody else's.

'Get on, you whoreson lazy bastard,' shouted the fishmonger, bringing a hand the size of a small sledgehammer down on the horse's bony backside. The boy leapt out of the way as the horse plunged forward and Nicolette, who had been sitting upright trying to maintain some appearance of dignity, fell backwards on to the pile of straw. They set off at a lumbering walk with the boy at the horse's head and Lisette walking alongside the wagon carrying the baby.

Once started, the horse kept up a steady plodding pace through Billingsgate. The wagon lurched over the uneven cobble stones on iron-clad wheels and Nicolette could feel every jolt and bump despite the cushioning of straw. When they reached Bridge Street their progress became even slower as the way was crowded with all those entering the city by London Bridge before the gate was closed for the night. Carts and horsemen and people on foot jostled together in the narrow street and the fishwagon with its reluctant nag was always the first to go to the wall. The boy did his best but he was small and easily bested by more impatient travellers. It was a clear frosty evening and Nicolette shivered. She pulled her travelling cloak more tightly round her and resigned herself to being the last to leave Bridge Street that night.

By the time they reached Gracechurch Street, Nicolette could see one or two stars beginning to appear in the narrow gap of sky just visible above the overhanging upper storeys of the houses on each side of the street. The ground floors were closed and shuttered and as they passed the Church of St Benet de Gracechurch, Nicolette spotted the chantry priest hurrying away to his supper. There was more room now but their horse was a one-pace animal and plodded steadily along at the same slow walk, ignoring the boy's half-hearted attempts to make him go any faster.

'Not much further now,' Lisette kept saying. 'You'll soon be in a nice soft bed.' But Nicolette was not concerned with the tedious discomfort of the journey so much as the indignity of it all. She was worrying about what the steward and the other household servants would think when they saw her arriving at Gryffard's fine house in a fishwagon. She could not bear to let them know she had come home in disgrace.

'Not much further,' Lisette said again. 'There be Saint Peter's by Cornhill.'

Nicolette sat up and peered through the gloom. 'Stop!' she shouted at the boy. He looked round in surprise and the horse, recognising if not the word at least the tone, shuffled to a halt. 'I will walk from here,' said Nicolette.

'Please no, mistress,' objected Lisette. 'We'll be there in a paternoster time. Have patience just a bit longer.'

'I know how far it is from the church,' replied Nicolette, annoyed with Lisette for being unnecessarily protective. 'I can walk it easily.' But Lisette continued her protests in a stream of voluble French while the horse took advantage of the argument to investigate the contents of the gutter running down the centre of the street. The boy, unable to understand one word, stood with his mouth agape.

'Do you think you could help me out of the wagon?'

Nicolette asked him in English, smiling sweetly. He continued to stare at her in bewildered alarm, so she added more sharply, 'Or are you afraid I'll be too heavy for you?'

'I doubt if ye'd be heavy as a basket of wet fish,' he said coming to the side of the wagon and gazing at her as if weighing her up.

She stood up and put her hands on his shoulders, not at all amused to be likened to a load of fish. He lifted her out of the wagon with ease and set her on her feet.

'I'll be getting back then,' he said and tugged ineffectually at the horse's bridle. He looked so small and tired and half-starved that Nicolette forgot her own troubles for the moment as she thought of the long weary walk through the dark streets he had in front of him. She fished in her purse and found two groats – all that was left. She gave them to him, to make up for his delayed supper. His mouth dropped open again as he gazed at the two small coins with as much wonder as if they had been florins. It was not much, she thought, but it was probably the first money he had ever been given. Feeling better for having been able to give him pleasure, she left him still staring at his unexpected wealth and walked towards her father's house.

It was not a long walk, but it seemed much further than she remembered. By the time she reached the door she was quite out of breath and her legs were trembling. The steward himself opened the door and she walked past him, her head held high and her travelling cloak clutched about her tightly, through the carved entrance screen and into the hall. It was cold and dark and unusually cheerless with damp logs smouldering in the hearth, billowing smoke.

'If I'd known when you were coming I'd have prepared a better welcome,' said Adam Stickleby. She glanced at him suspiciously, wondering if he meant it as apology or criticism, but his face was expressionless.

'No need for that, Master Stickleby,' she said as he went to kick the fire into life. 'I'm tired and I shall go straight to the solar. Have some water heated and sent up. We'll talk in the morning.'

With a nod he disappeared to do her bidding and she slowly mounted the wide stone stair to the solar, feeling confused and somehow disappointed. Not one word of welcome, or query, or even condemnation had she received.

No doubt Stickleby had been trained by her father in the utmost discretion and she supposed she should be thankful for that.

The solar, too, was cold and dark. Nicolette sat down on the ledge running round the bed to feed the baby who by now had started to cry. A servant brought candles and kindled the fire; soon the flames were leaping in the hearth. Watching the chamber come to life again, Nicolette was struck by how beautiful and comfortable and luxurious it all was. For the first time since leaving Nicholas's house in King Street, she felt a glimmer of hope. She was home and glad to be here. She had forgotten how pleasurable such comfort could be.

Lisette appeared carrying jugs of steaming hot water and Nicolette laid the now sleeping baby on the bed.

'Oh, Lisette,' she said getting up, 'how I long to be clean and sweet-smelling again. You can throw away everything I have on.' She began stripping off her clothes, standing in front of the fire and dropping them on the floor one by one. 'My surcoat, my kirtle, my coif, everything. Burn them. They smell of fish. I never want to see them again.'

But Lisette was frowning and shaking her head.

'What's the matter?' said Nicolette, adding her linen shift to the pile and stepping naked to look at herself in the polished steel hanging on the wall. 'Give them to the poor at the gate if you think it wasteful.'

'There are no clean clothes here, mistress,' Lisette reminded her. 'All your things are in your coffers and them still in the house at Westminster.'

'Holy Mother, I had forgotten!' exclaimed Nicolette. 'Now what am I to do?'

'Go to bed and rest, that's all you can do,' said Lisette, picking up the discarded clothes. 'Tomorrow the laundry maid can have them. You won't want no clothes whiles you're resting and bed rest is what you needs most now. Lucky it be Lent and the custom to wear old clothes. By the time Eastertide be here, doubtless Sir Piers can fetch your coffers back from Westminster for you – if the Widow Fraunceys hasn't sold them all already.'

Always Piers, thought Nicolette wearily, always it comes back to Piers. She stared at herself in the mirror and was shocked at what she saw, her face was so pale and her hair lifeless and dirty; her eyes seemed sunk in the back of her head and her lips which once had been so full and rosy now looked pinched. Piers would not want her now. No man would want her.

Depressed, her body aching from the jolting she had received in the wagon, cold and afraid, she felt suddenly drained. Wearily she let Lisette bathe her and then climbed into bed and lay there shivering, convinced she had been rejected by everyone. Her father had run away and left her, the fishmonger had thrown her out of his house, and Richard Whittington, whom she had thought so kind, had sent his wife who had been severe and cold. Even Piers had not bothered to visit her or inquire after her. No one wanted her, it seemed, only little baby Richard who had once more started to cry.

'What's the matter with him, Lisette?' she asked. 'Why does he keep crying all the time?'

'He's hungry, poor little mite.'

'Always you say he's hungry,' complained Nicolette, 'but I've only just fed him; he won't suck any more.'

'You haven't enough milk for him, that's what it is. He needs a wet nurse.'

Nicolette felt more of a failure than ever. She could not even feed her own baby. Lisette took him, washed and changed him, then walked about the chamber with him crooning and singing to him tunelessly until at last he stopped crying. Nicolette lay in the centre of the large bed overwhelmed by the hopelessness of it all, by the collapse of all her certainties, by grief for Nicholas. Hope, fragile as a beam of sunlight, had gone again. She was alone, and unloved. A failure.

She could hear Lisette moving about the chamber, undressing, extinguishing the candles. Then she came to draw the curtains round the bed, and stood with her hand on the bed curtains looking down. Nicolette could not see her face in the dark, all she could see was a shapeless mass of naked flesh illuminated by the glow from the fire. Nicolette was so cold her teeth were chattering and she was shivering uncontrollably now. Without a word, Lisette lifted the covers and got into bed beside her, pulling her into her arms. She was neither clean nor sweet smelling but she was warm and comforting. Nicolette burrowed into the mounds of ample flesh like a small puppy, and began to weep. Lisette held her, crooning and soothing in much the same way as she had done with little Richard. Warmed and comforted Nicolette felt a little of her desolation lift and with her head pillowed on the maid's ample breast she fell asleep at last.

Lisette went out early in the morning in search of a wet nurse and came back triumphant.

'I've found someone,' she said, 'a woman whose milk is two months old and she vows that if her babe, which is on the point of death, dies tonight, she'll come as soon as it be buried.'

Nicolette looked down at the baby in her arms and tears sprang to her eyes in pity for the poor woman whose babe was not expected to live another day. 'Her'll have to be paid, of course,' added Lisette, looking at Nicolette inquiringly.

'Just her keep, surely. One more mouth to feed is nothing in a household such as this,' Nicolette said, stroking her baby's head gently with her finger. He had such soft skin and so little hair, just fluffy down on top of his head. 'Clever Lisette has found you some more milk, my angel,' she crooned. 'Soon you will be a big strong healthy babe and not need to cry all day and all night.'

Piers did not come that day, or the next day or the next. Nicolette stayed in bed, tended by Lisette. It was very comfortable in the large feather bed; with the velvet bed curtains drawn round her, she was cocooned from the world outside and all its difficulties. Sometimes she began to wonder whether perhaps being a failure was not such a bad thing after all.

She lay staring up at the painted tester above her head with its picture of Christ being carried up to heaven. Perhaps Piers would never come and she could stay here in her father's house. The thought was followed almost immediately by another one. If Piers did come and she refused to marry him, he would not turn her out. He would not dare. The house was hers really. Her father had only made it over to Piers so that it would not be confiscated. The more she thought about it, the more she came to believe that she did not need Piers. She would give a great feast, she decided, when she had regained her strength. At midsummer perhaps, on the eve of St John. Perhaps by then it would be safe for her father to come home and she could help him to re-establish himself in the city.

She lay in bed planning who to invite – the Mayor and all

201

the most important merchants in London. Would they come? Richard Whittington might but the rest, all the important men in the city whom Nicholas had been so sure would support him, they would not come to a feast given by the mistress of the man they had betrayed. And William Gryffard when he returned would make her marry Piers.

Perhaps she could go to court, become one of the Queen's ladies. That would be much more fun than being married to Piers. Only without Nicholas's influence, how was she to get into the Queen's household? She threw herself face down in the feather bed and wept for all that she had lost the day that Nicholas was hanged.

She was aroused out of her self-pity by Lisette who brought the unwelcome news that Adam Stickleby wanted to see her.

'What does he want?' asked Nicolette, drying her tears with the corner of the linen sheet.

'He won't say but it be better you should see him, mistress,' said the maid. 'It be time now for you to be leaving your bed. The danger of fever be over and you'll feel better when you're up and about with less time to brood.'

Nicolette sighed. She did not want to leave the security of the solar and face the steward. She did not know what he wanted but she felt sure he was going to be difficult. 'Not now, not today, Lisette. I'll get up tomorrow,' she said. She did not want to have to explain or justify herself. She wanted to be left alone, with her grief and her baby, in peace.

'You can't stay in that there bed for ever, not if you don't want to lose the power of your legs,' said Lisette, drawing back the curtains round the bed with a purposeful tug. 'Little Richard should be churched. He's so weak and sickly he might slip off back to God at any time and we can't have that happening, not afore he's baptised.'

'Blessed Saint Mary, no!' cried Nicolette, sitting bolt upright in bed. She would never forgive herself if her poor babe should die and go straight to join his father in hell because she had been too weak to make provision for his immortal soul. She swung her legs over the side of the bed. She would take him to church that very day and light a candle to the Virgin too, to ask Her to make him healthy and strong. 'The wet nurse is coming, isn't she?' she asked.

'Today, she promised,' Lisette replied. 'But best you see

the steward first, mistress. I don't trust that one not to turn her away from the door.'

Nicolette got out of bed and was surprised how weak her legs felt. 'Are my clothes ready?' she said, clutching the bedpost for support.

'As good as new again,' Lisette assured her.

It took some time getting dressed and when she was finished, Nicolette studied her image in the polished steel anxiously. She was still pale but at least she looked clean and presentable once more.

'Tell Master Stickleby that I'll see him now,' she said sitting down carefully on the stool by the fire.

The steward's problem was quite straightforward. There was no more money.

'Oh, money,' said Nicolette with a little shrug. 'Surely that's not much of a difficulty, not in a house like this. A letter of credit should suffice.'

'We've been living on credit ever since Master Gryffard left. Now the vintner declares he won't supply us with any more wine for bits of paper; he wants money or payment in kind.'

She stared at him blankly. 'Give him wool then,' she said.

'There is no wool, the warehouse is empty.'

She knew nothing of her father's business except that he traded in wool, but she did not want to display her ignorance. If Stickleby said there was no wool then she believed him. He was the steward.

'We don't need wine, not in Lent. We can manage with ale,' she told him, still unperturbed.

'The ale won't last for ever.'

'Then sell something. One of the silver cups in the hall, if need be.'

He was looking down his long nose at her and she could tell from his expression that he did not at all approve of the idea.

'Master Gryffard told me once that he bought so many silver vessels because they were easy to turn into money when it was needed,' she told him, feeling rather pleased with herself. 'Well, it's needed now, so sell one of the drinking goblets. That's what they're for.'

'Master Gryffard took all the silver cups with him to Calais when he left,' the steward informed her.

'Can't you write to Master Gryffard and ask him for a letter of credit or a bill of exchange or something?' She could not understand why he was pestering her with problems which it was his duty to solve.

'I have written, and received a letter in return saying that since the house belongs now to Sir Piers Exton, he is responsible for our keep – and our wages.'

Always Piers! Sweet Mother of Mercy, thought Nicolette, why did everything always come back to Piers? The steward was looking at her now with an expectancy that made her uneasy. 'I don't see what I can do about it,' she said hastily.

'I understand, damoiselle, that you are to be married to Sir Piers. If you could tell me when the marriage is to take place, then I am sure the traders will be prepared to wait – if it's not too long.'

She couldn't believe it. She couldn't believe that her father who had abandoned her, run away to Calais and left her to face ruin alone, could treat her so.

'I don't think we can be married in Lent,' she said stiffly, determined not to give in.

'There's no rule of Holy Church says you cannot,' he told her solemnly.

'Sir Piers has no money!' she exclaimed, wanting to shake him.

'He is a retainer of the Earl of Arundel,' replied the steward smoothly. 'He will have his retainer's fee and the Earl's protection. That's what I tell our creditors and it makes them very happy. A retainer of the Earl of Arundel is in these times a very useful man to have as master.'

She refused to believe that she could be beaten by such a silly, unimportant thing as money. 'Can't you borrow?' she asked at last. 'Isn't that what merchants do all the time? Why, even the King does it. I know because Sir Nicholas Brembre was always lending money to the King.' She stared at him defiantly, but his face was as expressionless as ever. 'With a magnificent house like this as surety, I am sure you would have no difficulty in borrowing,' she added.

'Not without Sir Piers Exton's permission,' explained the steward almost apologetically.

'But it is my dower,' she said angrily.

Stickleby was unmoved. 'I was not privy to what passed between Sir Piers Exton and Master Gryffard,' he said.

Now she hated his unyielding discretion! She sat staring

into the fire utterly at a loss to know how to answer him. She wondered, for a brief moment, whether she could ask Richard Whittington for money, but she remembered that Whittington was Piers's friend. He was unlikely to help her – Alice had made that very clear. She felt trapped. Her father had been too clever. She had been sure of herself when he had first conceived his idea of marrying her to Piers, and she had defied him. She wasn't so sure of herself now. She looked up at the steward. Perhaps she should appeal to his sympathy.

'What am I to do?' she whispered, her blue eyes wide and helpless.

He stared back at her as grave and stern as ever. 'Once Sir Piers comes, I am sure he will be able to make all good,' he replied reassuringly.

She was not sure of anything any more, that Piers would come, that he would still want to marry her, that he would want to spend his money on keeping all her father's servants. He might in one of his noble gestures decide to give it all away to the poor. All she knew was that they needed Piers. Her father had seen to that. William might be a wanted exile, but she could feel his power even from across the Channel, relentlessly bending her to his will.

'When Sir Piers does come, I don't want you to plague him with worries about money,' she said to Adam Stickleby at last. 'Time enough to settle all that after we're married.'

'Of course,' he said with far too knowing a look. 'I understand very well, damoiselle.'

'Until then we'll all have to make what sacrifices we can,' she told him, determined to re-establish her authority. 'Since it is the season of Lent, the household must make do with just one meal a day.'

'We could always cut down on the number of servants,' he offered helpfully. 'That would make fewer mouths to feed.'

It was not at all what she wanted. 'But not the wet nurse,' she said. 'You'll be able to find room for her, won't you?' She could not bear the calculating look in his eye. 'If there's not enough for her to eat, she can have my share,' she added, determined to make him feel at least a little guilty.

'Oh, we're not as hard up as that yet,' he said with a thin smile.

Piers did not come until the seventh day of March. Nicolette saw him riding down Lime Street from the window of her solar where she spent much of her time, for want of any better occupation. Immediately she saw him, she flew to the polished steel and examined her image critically. 'If only I had a better headdress or something,' she cried, pulling a face.

Lisette came into the chamber at that instant to inform her of the knight's arrival, beaming happily and displaying all her few remaining teeth. 'The Lord bless you, Sir Piers doesn't care what you wear,' she said. 'He fell in love with you that very first day when all you had was that grey serge from the abbey. He's a true man, Sir Piers is, what knows how to see beneath all them fancy feathers.'

Nicolette wasn't sure she wanted Piers seeing more than he was supposed to see. 'You can tell him I'll see him here,' she said. 'And don't come back. I'll see him alone.'

'I'd best take little Richard with me then,' said Lisette, scooping the sleeping baby out of his cradle. 'You won't want 'im upsetting Sir Piers like.'

'Yes, take him to the wet nurse,' said Nicolette, sad that she should be made to feel ashamed of her beautiful son. 'It must be almost time for his feed.'

Lisette picked up the baby, grinned at her again and hurried away full of so much obvious good cheer, Nicolette felt resentment welling inside her. All very well for Lisette to be so certain of a happy outcome. She did not know how difficult it was. If only Piers were like the other young knights at court, with their quick repartee and languishing glances. She knew how to deal with them, but Piers was different. The very intensity of his devotion frightened her at times. His honesty was embarrassing.

She sat down on the stool by the fire, fighting down panic. She remembered all too clearly the last few times he had visited her in Nicholas's house in King Street. She had spurned him, rejected his love and tried to use all his offers of help for Nicholas. How could she now throw herself on his mercy? It was humiliating.

But when Piers came he looked at her with such love she did not feel in the least humiliated.

'We were wondering what had become of you, Sir Piers,' she felt confident enough to say.

'I did not come before because I heard you had not been

206

well,' he said, glancing at her quickly and then looking away in obvious embarrassment.

'That is true, but I'm better now,' she said.

'I didn't want to be a nuisance,' he explained.

She could not think of a suitable reply so she sat and gazed at him in what she hoped was an encouraging manner. He was dressed in chain mail with his tabard of cream and red over it and the Earl of Arundel's badge on his sleeve. He did not seem to know what to say to her so she asked him for news of the city. He told her that Parliament was now trying Robert de Vere in his absence and that it was a foregone conclusion that he would be found guilty. Then he suddenly reddened, looked at her awkwardly. 'I'm sorry, it must be painful for you.'

In the silence that followed she had a sudden vivid recollection of Nicholas on his knees in the cart, and stared very hard into the fire, willing herself not to think of him.

'How is the King?' she asked.

'Fearless in defence of his friends,' he said.

'But unable to protect them,' she replied before she could stop herself.

'I'm sorry,' he said again.

She bit her lip and clasped her hands tightly in her lap, unable to think of anything to say to him which was not trespassing on dangerous ground.

'I did not come here to quarrel with you, damoiselle,' he said at last.

'What did you come here for?' she asked, seizing her chance and looking up at him with her blue eyes wide and appealing.

'I came to find in what way I could be of service to you.'

She looked away, down at her hands. How could he be so obtuse!

'There is something you can do,' she said to punish him for being so slow-witted. 'My coffers with my jewels and clothes and trinkets are in the house at King Street. The Widow Fraunceys has it now. Do you think you could go there and rescue them for me?'

'Of course I can, why did you not ask me before?' he replied, clearly delighted to have a straightforward task to perform for her. She got up, went to stand in front of him, laid her hand lightly upon his tunic.

'Because you did not come to see me before,' she murmured, head bent. She heard the sharp hiss of his indrawn breath and glanced at him quickly from beneath her lashes. The telltale colour was sweeping over his face once more. She waited with her hand still resting lightly against his chest. She could feel his heart hammering beneath the chain mail. He was trembling like a nervous horse at an unfamiliar touch. Surely he would ask her now. But he turned away; he strode to the window and stood looking out.

'The wind has gone round into the east,' he said with his back to her. 'I think it's going to snow later.'

She wanted to give up then, to tell him she was tired, to send him away, but she thought of Adam Stickleby and all the servants waiting eagerly for news. They would be in the hall laying out the trestles for dinner but watching the stairs to the solar like a lot of eager hounds waiting for the appearance of the huntsman. She could not go down to dinner today alone.

Piers had turned to look at her. The hunger on his face was plain to see. There was no doubt at all that he wanted her. So why did he not speak?

'Master Gryffard has reached Calais in safety,' she said. 'Our steward Adam Stickleby has received a letter from him.' Perhaps William's name would remind him of his obligation.

Piers opened his mouth to say something and then seemed to think better of it.

'When do you think it will be safe for him to come home again?' she asked.

'Not for some time yet, I fear.' At least he had found his tongue.

'Oh dear, then what is to become of me?' she said pitifully. Surely that would do it.

He gave her an agonised glance, leant back against the stone frame of the window as if trying to put the greatest distance possible between them. She sank down on her stool again and stared dejectedly into the fire. He cleared his throat loudly, and she held her breath, waiting.

'You know that I am yours for ever,' he said at last from the window embrasure. 'That I love you. That I will fight for you, to my last dying breath.'

'I know that,' she said, impatience making her bold. 'But do you love me enough?'

'Enough? By Saint Valentine, have I not already proved it?'

'Enough to marry me?' she whispered, shame and indignation and doubt struggling together in her breast.

He left his refuge by the window and came to stand looking down at her. 'You did not want to marry me,' he said. 'You made that very plain when I asked you before. I do not want you to be forced into marrying me against your will. I love you far too much for that. Whatever you do, I will love you and serve you in every way I can, whether married or not.'

'And if the only way you can be of service to me is to marry me?' she asked him softly.

'Then gladly, joyfully I will do it,' he said. 'If that is what you wish.'

She looked into the fire. She did not want his honest gaze to see into her heart. Then she took a deep breath. 'That is what I wish,' she said.

He knelt in front of her, took her cold hands in both of his. Silently bent and kissed them. She wished he would say something light and carefree, or sweep her into his arms, as Nicholas would have done. Resolutely she pushed all thought of her dead lover out of her mind. Piers was still kneeling holding her hands against his heart. She jerked them away and stood up.

'Will you make all the arrangements?' she asked him. 'I'm afraid I don't know what to do.'

'I'll ask Master Whittington,' he said, getting to his feet. 'I'm sure he'll be pleased to help us.'

'Dinner will be ready soon,' she said. 'Will you stay and share it with us?'

'I'd be honoured,' he replied. 'And afterwards I'll ride straight back to Westminster to see the Widow Fraunceys about your coffers.' He smiled at her with so much happiness that she felt quite desolate. He was so young and innocent and in love. She did not see how she could possibly live up to his expectations. She knew love, had been badly burnt in its fires and would never be the same again. She also knew she was nothing like the image Piers carried of her in his heart. She could not be the woman he thought her, did not want to be. Piers was in love with an image of perfection and she told herself she could never be that. Not any more. She had tried to be perfect and failed. She did not want to have to try again.

CHAPTER 18

They were married on the Feast of the Assumption of the
Blessed Mary. It was a cold, blustery March day with a great
bullying wind sweeping along Cornhill, seizing loosened
shutters and banging them carelessly against the windows,
pouncing on any weak tiles and sending them crashing into
the churned mud and pools of fetid water lying in the gutter
below.

It was the sort of wind that brought work for tylers and was
no respecter of wedding finery, thought Alice Whittington,
trying to control the wildly flapping tails of her headdress.
She looked up at the huge banks of dark cloud looming above
the spire of St Peter's and hoped the bride would arrive
before the rain.

The small grass churchyard was empty. None of the
merchants, knights and noblemen who lived in the neigh-
bouring houses set apart by their fine gardens and orchards
had come to this wedding. Once William Gryffard had
entertained them all in that magnificent big house of his;
even the King had gone to his feasts. It was a sign of
the times, a measure of the fear inspired by the five powerful
magnates who were hounding the King's friends to their
deaths. William Gryffard had been rich and powerful but
now, thanks to the work of this Parliament which people
had come to call the Merciless Parliament, the girl he had
taken under his wing was getting married alone and
unsupported. It was frightening how quickly a person could
fall from grace. Alice glanced at her husband, calmly talking
to Piers by the lych gate. She hadn't wanted to come to
this hurriedly arranged wedding but Dick had been quite
undisturbed.

'We're doing it for Piers,' he had told her this morning when she had tried to dissuade him. 'Piers is a retainer of the Earl of Arundel, there can be no harm in it.'

Are you sure you are doing it for Piers? Alice had wanted to say, but she didn't. 'It's sad that the girl has no family at a time like this,' was all she said. 'No one save William Gryffard, and he in exile.'

'William Gryffard has nevertheless managed to look after her in spite of his own troubles,' said Dick, arranging his long-skirted velvet houpland carefully into symmetrical folds under his leather girdle. 'He's a clever man, one of the wiliest in the city. It's not the first time he's found himself on the wrong side and had to run for it, but he always comes back victorious while other men go to their ruin.'

'Who is she, Dick?' asked Alice. 'I can't believe this story that she's some sort of distant family relative. A man like Gryffard does not make over his splendid mansion which he has taken so much time and trouble to build to a poor relation.'

'The talk in the Mercery is that she's his mistress or his natural daughter,' replied Dick, examining himself in the polished steel as he settled a beaver hat on his head. 'Perhaps both.'

'By the Blessed Virgin,' exclaimed Alice, shocked. 'I hope for poor Piers's sake that's not so. He's far too noble a knight to find himself married to a whore.'

'I told him he was a fool not to take the money and run, but the boy's an old-fashioned knight who takes his oath of chivalry seriously, it would seem. Gryffard's a master craftsman in the trade of survival; he knows how to choose his tools well.'

'Couldn't you have warned Piers?'

'I could but he wouldn't hear me. There's none so deaf as those who are in love. Besides, "poor Piers" is doing well enough. He couldn't have hoped to have married so beautiful a girl with such a dowry in the normal course of events.'

Alice had said no more.

She looked at Piers now and guessed that he was not listening to a word Dick was saying. From here it was just possible to see the entrance to Gryffard's magnificent inn and Piers was anxiously watching the distant doorway, like a dog

211

waiting for the reappearance of a beloved master. Was he afraid, even now, that she might not come? She would be a silly girl if she didn't, thought Alice, appraising the knight dispassionately. Piers had the strong sturdy figure of a warrior, which looked its best in chain mail, but today he was dressed for his wedding in a short tight-fitting jupon and bright particoloured hose. Broad-shouldered, thick in the waist and with strong powerful legs taut with muscle, he wasn't handsome in the way that Sir Nicholas Brembre had been handsome, but he was still an attractive young man, with his close-cropped curly dark hair and vulnerable eyes the colour of beech leaves in autumn. Nicolette was lucky to get him.

Piers's anxious gaze suddenly softened and Alice saw, with a sense of relief, that Nicolette was coming at last, walking along Cornhill on her wooden pattens, carefully avoiding the puddles. She was wearing a dark cloak with the hood pulled up over her head and was clutching it tightly to protect her from the wind. She did not look at all like a bride, more like the chief mourner at a funeral. With her was the ugly little peasant woman who seemed to fulfil the ubiquitous role of serving woman, companion and nursemaid, and a tall stooping man dressed in sombre fustian whom Alice guessed was Gryffard's steward come to stand in for his master. How sad, thought Alice with a twinge of compassion, to have only a steward to give you in marriage.

When she reached the shelter of the church porch, Nicolette took off her cloak and handed it to her maid, revealing a low-cut gown of sapphire blue velvet trimmed with miniver; round her swelling hips she had a girdle of silver set with bright jewels and on her head a garland of tiny white and yellow flowers. Her hair was loose, hanging down to her knees as was the custom for brides in token of virginity. An absurd token under the circumstances, thought Alice, as Nicolette slipped off her pattens, revealing small neat feet in slippers of softest cordwain. All the same Alice found it hard to reconcile this poised and lovely girl with the bewildered, exhausted creature she had visited in the fishmonger's shop and her sympathy for Nicolette's lonely plight diminished. Anyone as truly beautiful as that, thought Alice, with a pang of envy, did not need any sympathy.

Piers made his vows slowly and deliberately, gazing at his prize with such hungry longing that Alice had to swallow hard to get rid of the lump in her throat. Nicolette kept her head bent and said her vows quickly in a low murmur that was drowned by the howling of the wind. Then the priest opened the door and led them into the church.

After the noisy windswept porch, it was very quiet in the empty church, and dark and gloomy and cold. All the images were covered for Lent with painted cloths; some depicted the Day of Judgement with the devils receiving souls and hurling them into the fire, others showed souls plunged to the neck in yellow flames suffering unspeakable and endless torment, their bodies unconsumed and indestructible. The only brightness was Nicolette's hair, falling to the floor like a train of cloth of gold as she knelt beside Piers at the altar. Alice glanced at her husband. He was gazing round the church, his face expressionless. He was a good husband, she thought. He had worked long and hard to build up the mercer's business he had taken over from her father. Now it was twice as prosperous as it had been in Sir John Fitz Warren's time. She was proud of him and knew that she was lucky to be married to such a man. He never beat her, never once complained of their lack of children. She had respect, security, friends, and was surrounded by beautiful things. Dick loved beautiful things; it was his trade, after all.

The church grew darker and above the intoning of the priest came the distant rumble of thunder, followed almost immediately by the sound of heavy rain drumming on the roof. Piers was helping his wife get up from her knees. He gave her a smile so radiant with love it pierced the darkness like a bright sunbeam and made Alice feel inexplicably forlorn.

Once again she glanced at her husband, hoping he would smile at her. Dick had such a sweet smile. It was the only time his pale, shuttered face came to life. But he was staring ahead of him with the concentrated appreciative look she had seen so often when he contemplated a particularly fine piece of workmanship. Piers was leading his wife down the nave. When she drew level, Nicolette looked straight at Whittington and smiled, but he remained impassive.

Outside in the porch they took their leave. As it was Lent,

there was to be no wedding feast. Nicolette put on her pattens and her cloak. Piers thanked them for coming.

As husband and wife set off with their attendants to walk through the rain the short distance to their home, Alice felt unaccountably depressed. 'Such a dismal wedding,' she said. 'If only it had not had to be in Lent we could have given at least a little feast to celebrate.'

'Piers didn't want to wait until Eastertide,' said Whittington. 'The Earl of Arundel might suddenly have to leave to fight the French.'

'I wish it had not been quite so quiet,' said Alice with a sigh. 'Or that the sun could have shone for them, even for a paternoster time. This storm breaking now, it's a bad omen.'

'But a good day's work,' replied Dick, pulling his fur-lined cloak round him as he stepped out into the rain. 'A young girl's future has been secured today. You can take comfort in that.'

At least her wedding night will not be a horrible shock, thought Alice, following him out of the porch as she remembered her own.

The wedding night was all that Piers had been thinking about for days. He had made love to Nicolette so many times in his mind that he thought he knew exactly what he wanted to do to her. But he was surprised when she led him into the great chamber off the hall, saying, 'I thought we'd have our supper in here by the fire instead of with the rest of the household.'

Nervously he followed her, not quite prepared to have his dreams fulfilled so soon. An enormous fire blazed on the hearth and a dozen candles burned in their iron prickets, illumining the gambolling gods and goddesses chasing each other round the brilliantly painted walls. The floor was strewn with sweet rushes and a small damask-covered table in front of the fire was laid with cups and trenchers. But the chamber was dominated by the large bed in the centre of the room. It had vermilion velvet bed hangings and the bed covers were turned down to reveal fresh linen sheets strewn with all kinds of herbs to bless the marriage bed and make it fruitful.

Piers hardly noticed any of it. He had eyes only for Nicolette. She sat down on a low stool by the fire and Lisette came in bearing a basin of warm water. She curtseyed as she held it out to Piers.

'Ah, Lisette,' he said, smiling at the maid while he washed his hands. 'How are you? Are you taking proper care of your mistress?'

'Oh sir, yes, sir, thanking ye,' said Lisette curtseying once more and displaying her terrible teeth. 'Here's a joyful day to thank the Blessed Mother for and it's glad I be that you'll be taking care of my lady from now on.'

'Thank you, Lisette,' said Nicolette, dipping her fingers in the basin of water, 'you can go and join the rest of the household in the hall now.'

Lisette turned and waddled off, but not without a jerk of her head in the direction of the bed and a broad wink at Piers. She looked so lewd and comical he turned to Nicolette to share the joke with her, but she was staring pensively into the fire and he felt more nervous than ever.

They supped together at the table near the fire, waited on by Crispin, Piers's squire. Piers hardly noticed what he ate he was so fascinated with everything Nicolette did. She glanced at him occasionally as she ate and it occurred to him, seeing the watchful, hesitant look in her eyes, that she was nervous too, for all her poise. What to say to her? He had no eloquence with which to persuade a woman to trust him. All his experience was with men. A hawk he could tame, a horse he knew how to gentle, even a dog he could enslave. But a woman was a complete mystery. Nicolette's very beauty made his throat clog up. So instead he talked to Crispin about stupid things like horses and tourneys until, when Crispin retired to the serving table, Nicolette lent forward and said softly, 'Piers, could we not be alone? I can serve you.'

'Of course,' he said, and instantly dismissed Crispin, delighted that she should prefer to be alone with him.

She got up and he marvelled at the graceful way she went about the business of serving him, so much more exciting to watch than the squire. But then he thought that perhaps she did it so well because she was much practised. Had she done it for Brembre?

'You don't dislike Crispin, do you?' he asked more harshly than he intended as he pushed the unworthy thought hurriedly away.

'No, but I'm not sure he likes me all that much,' she said.

'It's Crispin's way. I thought that too when first he came to me. He's not much of a talker and shows no emotion, but he's a good squire, none better and will make a fine knight one day.'

'It's just that I'm not used to being waited on by squires on bended knee,' she said sitting down once more at the table. 'I have so much to learn. You must be gentle with my ignorance.' She was all beauty as she sat there in her blue velvet, her hair falling round her like a curtain of gold and her skin white and lustrous as a pearl in the gleaming candlelight. He trembled and, leaning across the table, covered her small white hand with his large callused one.

'You know I will be gentle with you always,' he said fervently. 'I swear by Christ's body on the Cross that I shall never do anything to hurt you. You know that, don't you?' He would like to have swept her up into his arms, thrown her on to the bed and started to do all the wonderful things he had imagined so often. Only she was so still and quiet and unresponsive. It was hard to make a girl realise you loved her when she wouldn't look at you, didn't seem to hear you and made your throat close up.

He took a great draught of wine from the goblet. She wasn't eating, just sitting there gazing at the fire and occasionally shooting perplexed glances at him. He drained his cup. What did she do with Brembre? What did they talk about? He took a huge mouthful of eel stew and followed it with a hunk of trencher bread, swallowing vigorously, as if he could bury the pernicious thought. She had married him willingly, hadn't she?

She got up and filled his cup again while he desperately cast about in his mind trying to think of something to say to her, but all he could think about was Brembre. Resolutely he thrust the thought of her former lover away and, greatly daring, picked up a tendril of her long shining hair.

'It's like spun gold,' he said. She smiled at him, a small wistful smile which did not reach her eyes. What should he do next? The only women he had slept with before had been whores who were easy enough to lay. There were those who said Nicolette was a whore, but it wasn't true. She had loved Brembre with a constancy which was noble in its own way. She had followed him to the scaffold, remaining true even unto death. Did she love him still? It was impossible. She must know by now the man Brembre was, must have seen his true self the day he went to his death.

The silence in the chamber was almost tomb-like. Piers wished she hadn't sent away his squire. At least he could talk to Crispin about something. A log crashed to the hearth and he got up to put it back. Nicolette too got up, yawned, stretched her arms above her head gracefully like a sleepy cat.

'Are you not tired?' she asked. He would like to have seized her then, to have thrown her sapphire blue skirts up over her head and forced her back on to the table, scattering half-eaten food and wine and taken her, only he could not treat her like a whore. Instead he gently took hold of her little pointed chin and kissed her tentatively on the mouth. She shuddered. He looked into her clear blue eyes and was reminded of a terrified palfrey bitted for the first time.

'I swear I shall not hurt you,' he told her.

She dropped her eyes and slowly, carefully began to undo the row of buttons down the front of her gown. He held his breath, while the blood coursing through his body seemed all to be flowing to his loins and he trembled like a stallion just before the charge, straining to hold himself back. Carefully she stepped out of her gown and laid it on the chest at the foot of the bed. He gazed, spellbound by the sight of her in her linen shift. She looked at him, a tiny frown creasing the white smoothness of her brow.

'Are you not coming to bed, my husband?' she asked him. Then without waiting for an answer she dropped her shift and slipped beneath the covers of the bed. Confused, delirious with desire, yet wishing it had been at his prompting not hers, Piers struggled out of his clothes and climbed into the large comfortable bed beside her.

Her naked flesh was soft and smooth as silk against his and almost he lost control then, but she was lying so still, with her glorious hair spread in a billowing cloud about her, and her eyes so wide open and watchful, he forced himself to be patient. Somehow he must gain her trust. He kissed her but her lips were cold and unresponsive. He stroked her hair, winding it carefully round his huge powerful wrists, to distract his mind from the urgent demands of his senses. He kissed her again, harder this time, but still she did not respond.

217

'What's the matter, Nicolette?' he asked. To his horror two tears slid out of the corner of her beautiful eyes and rolled down her cheek on to the pillow. 'I thought you wanted me,' he said. Then could not help asking the question he dreaded. 'Is it Brembre? Are you still in love with him?' The tears came faster now and he wiped them away carefully with her hair. 'Tell me,' he prompted.

'You don't love me enough,' she whispered into his shoulder.

'I do, I do,' he groaned.

'Then show me,' she demanded looking up at him almost fiercely.

But to his shame and disgust he could not. He had wanted her so badly for so long, had forced himself to wait for her, to be gentle, had wanted so much for it to be perfect that now when it was time, his body defied him.

'You don't love me enough,' she said again with a sob and turned away from him.

'Too much, my darling Nicolette,' he cried, flinging himself on his back and staring up at the deep purple tester in despair. 'I love you far, far too much.'

Next day Adam Stickleby caught Piers as he was leaving to ride to Westminster and asked to speak to him.

'Can't it wait?' said Piers. 'My Lord Arundel needs all his retainers at Westminster when Parliament reassembles at noon.'

'Just a word about the household, Sir Piers, if it please you,' replied the steward with a deferential grimace.

'I'm quite happy with the way you run the household,' said Piers with his winning smile. 'It all seems remarkably comfortable. Well done.'

'The thing is I'm not sure how much longer I can go on running it well,' replied the steward, looking more apologetic than ever.

'Crispin, you go on and see to the horses,' said Piers, stifling his impatience. 'I'll be with you as soon as I can.' He had learnt that it was better to lose time listening to men's grievances early on rather than to wait until it was too late to do anything about it. 'You're not thinking of leaving, are you, Master Stickleby?' he said when they were alone in the empty hall. 'I'm sure Lady Exton would be lost without you.'

'No, no, not that. It's just that we've run out of money, Sir Piers.'

'Run out of money?' exclaimed Piers looking round the sumptuous hall with its wall paintings and tiled floor and piled-up logs burning brightly in the hearth. 'I don't believe it.'

'For the everyday necessities. I have applied to Master Gryffard in France, but he has pointed out that the house belongs to you now and so it is your responsibility.'

Piers was completely at a loss. He had served as a page in larger houses than this; from the age of six he had been taught all the complex niceties of life in a well-ordered household; as a squire he had learnt how to carve roasted meats elegantly, pour wine without spilling a drop on white damask cloths; he had lived in castles and slept on hall floors with the rest of the retainers; on campaign he had learnt how to go without; he had been fed and housed and clothed all his life without ever having to use money to pay for it. He had no idea how a large household was paid for.

'Tell me,' he said, ashamed of his ignorance, 'what is it you need?'

Stickleby embarked on a long explanation of the provisioning of the household. Piers tried to follow it all but he found it hard to concentrate. 'Fish has got more expensive again since the free fishmongers have been given back their rights,' said the steward, while Piers wondered what he was going to use for money, 'and the pepperers are greedier than ever but you can't keep food without salt and we're almost out of spices.' Stickleby paused and looked at Piers inquiringly.

'I wasn't expecting – Master Gryffard did it all so quickly . . .' By the Rood, it wasn't as if I even wanted this great inn, Piers longed to shout.

'I understand your difficulty very well, Sir Piers.' The thin lips curved into a sympathetic smile. 'I know that knights are not accustomed to keeping large sums of money readily to hand. But you could borrow. The house is a very valuable asset. Master Whittington, I'm sure, would be happy to lend you the money. He lends to many noblemen, including Sir Simon Burley, I've heard.'

Piers frowned. 'I don't hold with borrowing money,' he said.

'Just until you can get your hands on some spoils of war,'

the steward urged him. 'You won't be tied up with this Parliament much longer, I dare say, and the Earl will be anxious to continue the fight against the French. There'll be booty and such to be won. You'll be able to pay it back soon enough.'

Piers looked him up and down thoughtfully. 'No,' he said.

'What then? I've only been able to go on provisioning the household up until now because our creditors thought you would see them right. You being a knight and a retainer of the Earl, they thought they were safe. But if they don't get paid soon, we shan't be able to feed the household.'

'There's my retaining fee, I'll have a word with the Earl and see if he will advance me what you need,' said Piers. 'Bring me your bills and we'll go through them when I return.'

The steward seemed instantly relieved. He escorted Piers to the door, holding it open almost reverently and following him out into the street, where Crispin was waiting with the horses.

As he rode away, Piers cursed himself for a gullible fool. He saw it all now. Nicolette had not married him of her own free will. She had been forced, or manoeuvred, into it by William Gryffard. The stapler was behind this withdrawal of funds, the steward was only the tool. Almost Piers could see the wily William rubbing his hands with glee at the success of all his plans. He felt angry at the way he had been used. Angry with himself and angry with Nicolette. It seemed to him now as if he were being asked to buy her, like a whore.

His anger lasted until he reached the Lud Gate and rode out of the city. He crossed the narrow bridge over the River Fleet and trotted briskly along the Strand towards Westminster. At his side Crispin kept pace and his thoughts to himself. Piers was glad of the squire's habitual reserve. It allowed him to think.

They passed the turreted manor of the Bishop of Salisbury and the high stone walls of the Convent of the White Friars. By the time they came to the ruin that had once been John of Gaunt's Palace of Savoy, Piers was beginning to feel sorry for Nicolette. He understood now the pressure the poor girl had been subjected to. Pity for her drove out his anger. Pity and an immense sadness. He was not what she wanted after all. As he thought back over the shambles of the previous night, he realised how difficult it had been for her. No wonder she had wept. She was not a whore. She could not give her body where her heart was not engaged. And he did not want her to. He wanted her love, her willing surrender not her dutiful cold compliance.

He made up his mind as he rode on towards Westminster, past open fields with the cold March wind blowing in his face, that he would never force her, but would wait for her heart to heal. Then he would win her for himself.

The Earl of Arundel was at first surprised when Piers, full of embarrassment, mentioned his retaining fees.

'Money? Don't I feed and clothe you well enough, provide good horses for you to ride? Knights need not concern themselves with money – leave that to the merchants, it's what they're good at.'

'I've never concerned myself with money before,' said Piers. 'When I had nothing but a suit of armour and a horse and a sword, it was enough. But now I'm the owner of a splendid mansion filled with servants and it seems I need money.'

'Yes, I heard you got married,' chuckled the Earl. 'To a beauty, well dowered, they told me. You aren't the first man to discover that the rich and beautiful come more expensive in the end. Do what I do, borrow the money. We all do.'

'I'd rather not,' said Piers. 'It's borrowed money which comes more expensive in the end.'

'I'll have to borrow it to pay you,' declared Arundel. 'The cost of keeping all you knights with me is well-nigh ruining me. If it weren't for the merchants, I'd be beggared by now. But as soon as this plague-ridden Parliament is over we'll be off to have another go at the French. That should replenish all our coffers.'

'The French knights are not very anxious to come out and fight,' said Piers. 'And I'd rather not be beholden to a city merchant for want of a ransomed Frenchman.'

'Damned merchants think they can hold us to ransom because they've got the money bags, but we've shown them this time,' said the Earl. 'Brembre's fate should have taught them a lesson. Hang one just to frighten the rest.' He laughed – unpleasantly, Piers thought. 'After this I doubt if they'll start interfering in the King's business. You'll see. Already the city's lent us a thousand pounds to be spent on naval defences and safeguarding the seas. We'll have ourselves a fine time laying siege to the coastal towns of France – it could be quite profitable.'

'In that case, my lord, you'll not mind paying me what's due,' Piers persevered doggedly. 'Otherwise I'll take my sword and hire it out to some other master.'

'The devil you will. You've sworn fealty to me,' exclaimed Arundel, his good humour disappearing quicker than scraps of food thrown to the poor.

'But I owe you no knight's service. The oath of allegiance I swore was to the King, the same as you did.'

'Trouble with you, Piers, you spent too much time fighting for that pirate Hawkwood,' grumbled the Earl. 'In your soul you're nothing but a hard-hearted mercenary, despite all your fine talk of chivalry.'

'John Hawkwood taught me more than how to couch a lance,' agreed Piers with a grin, 'which is why, my lord, you value my sword.'

The Earl paid him in the end, but when Adam Stickleby produced his bills, Piers realised that it wouldn't last very long.

'You'll have to economise,' he said, fixing the steward with a forbidding stare.

'I'm practically starving them as it is,' complained Stickleby. 'Soon Lent will be over and we'll have no excuse for living the way we do. It's not at all what we're accustomed to.'

'Then you'll just have to get rid of some of the servants.'

'Lady Exton wouldn't like that. They all have a job to do here.'

'What about you?' Piers shot back. 'Now that Master Gryffard is no longer running his business from here, there can't be very much work for you to do, and what there is I'm sure could quite easily be done by Lady Exton. Perhaps we should start with you.'

Stickleby looked shaken. Mumbling something about seeing what he could do, he took himself off and Piers hoped he had got the measure of the man.

The Merciless Parliament dragged on until 4 June, by which time Piers was heartily sick of the whole distasteful business, particularly by the treatment of Sir Simon Burley. The King's old tutor was so ill he had to be supported by his friends when he appeared before Parliament. The King's youngest uncle, the Duke of York, rose in full Parliament and testified that Burley had been faithful in all negotiations to King and kingdom. But the Duke of Gloucester, without presenting evidence, gave his brother the lie and belligerently offered to prove Burley's falseness by trial of combat. Burley was condemned to death and executed on 3 May, although the Queen went down on her knees to plead for his life and the King did everything he could to defend the old man.

To Piers it seemed that the lords appellant were abusing their power, and Parliament's, in a vengeful attack on every one of the King's friends whether guilty or not. He recognised that he was himself a part of that power which was being so misused; he felt tainted and unworthy and helpless to do anything about it. Once he had told Nicolette that he used his skill to defend the weak not to prey upon the defenceless, yet he could no longer feel that was true. From the moment when he had changed sides at Radcot Bridge he had lost his innocence. It was hard to live with the knowledge that Esmon had died out of too much loyalty and love while he, Piers, had sold his honour for the woman he loved. It was even harder to live with the thought that Nicolette didn't want his love and had been forced to marry him out of financial need. It was hardest of all to sleep in the same bed with her when he burned to take her in his arms and could not. Nicolette continued docile and compliant but her very submissiveness was an insult to his chivalry. He felt that William Gryffard's cunning had somehow tarnished them both, that in paying the merchant's price he had lost not only his honour and his innocence but his proud and perfect lady. So since sleeping with her was torture, he took to spending his nights at the Palace of Westminster, whereupon Nicolette moved back to sleep in her solar above the hall.

Piers felt uneasy helping to guard Parliament, and when he went home to his wife there was no comfort for him there either. Nicolette was cold and dutiful, the steward unhelpful, the battle over expenditure unresolved. Every time Piers won a victory with Stickleby over some small measure of saving, he would lose it again to Nicolette to whom he could deny

223

nothing. One way and another, he was relieved when Parliament ended and the Earl of Arundel took his retainers off to ravage the coastal towns of France.

CHAPTER 19

In the second week of May 1389, William Gryffard dined at the castle in Calais. During the year and a half that William had been based in Calais he had made himself very useful to the Captain, supplying provisions and exchanging information. Frequently he was asked to dinner with the garrison, and he always went, although he seldom enjoyed it. The castle was a grim fortress built to withstand invasion rather than to provide comfort. The great hall was a high-vaulted stone barn with windows no wider than a crossbow bolt. Even at midday it was dark and gloomy; the torches thrust in their iron prickets flared fitfully in the swirling draughts, casting long fretful shadows on the stone walls.

The Captain was as grim as his castle. Calais was commanded by a Constable – a nobleman of rank who was given the title as a favour from the King. The actual work of commanding the garrison was done by the Captain, a knight who had to endure much in the way of sporadic interference from a variety of different overlords, since the constables changed as frequently as the King's favour. He had become adept at keeping his loyalty available to all, and in secret serving only himself.

'I have some news for you this time, Master Gryffard,' the Captain greeted William as he entered the hall. 'King Richard seems to have broken free again since he has come of age.'

'Free?' William dipped his hands into the water of the lavabo. 'What of the lords appellant?'

'Dismissed by the royal prerogative,' the Captain told him. 'Our young King is not a Plantagenet for nothing. He's proclaimed in a manifesto delivered throughout the country that since he's now twenty-one he intends to rule without help from his uncles. The Chancellor and Treasurer have been dismissed and the King has appointed Bishop William of Wykeham instead.'

'I can't see the magnates accepting the King's manifesto just like that.' William watched the Captain from beneath hooded lids as he dried his fingers carefully on a linen napkin proffered by a page.

'The magnates have fallen out among themselves, it would appear,' the Captain said as he too washed his hands in the lavabo. 'Henry Bolingbroke and Thomas Mowbray are supporting the King.'

'Now why would they do that?' mused William, who had heard the rumours from his various sources but had not known whether to believe them.

'I hear that King Richard has recalled the Duke of Lancaster to England and is granting him the governorship of Gascony for life,' replied the Captain drying his hands carefully. This was indeed news to William. 'I expect Henry Bolingbroke is afraid of what his father might have to say when he gets home if he goes on supporting Gloucester.'

'Lancaster's not always been in King Richard's favour,' murmured William.

'I doubt if he wants the crown now,' replied the Captain. 'But he'll make sure his brother of Gloucester doesn't take it and he's more powerful than any of the magnates.' He led William towards the long high table at the dais end of the hall and left him with the lesser clergy seated below the salt. William did not mind. He had come, not for self-gratification, but for information, and had not been disappointed.

The noise in the hall increased as the wine flowed freely. Men shouted and laughed as they stretched across each other with their daggers to spear pieces of food from the dishes laid out upon the trestle tables. Dogs quarrelled ferociously over the bones tossed into the rushes. Behind the knights, squires waited on their masters patiently, flitting backwards and forwards with flagons of wine, hungrily watching the dishes on the table growing ever colder and congealing in their sauces. William sliced off a capon's leg with his dagger, chewing on it absently as he pondered the Captain's news and its implications. Was it safe now, he wondered, to go back to London?

He might have gone back the previous autumn when Sir Nicholas Exton and the others had received pardons for all treasons and felonies, but he hadn't dared, even though he himself had never been officially accused. Brembre's downfall had been so horribly final that it had left William shaken to the root of his soul. He felt he had had a very narrow escape. He helped himself to a lamprey from the dish in front of him, put it in his mouth, chewed and swallowed it without tasting it at all.

Under Brembre's protection he had grown rich easily. He had been able to take short cuts and evade tax knowing that his powerful patron would protect him. There had been ways in which he had been able to cheat and it enabled him to surpass his rivals. He had grown used to making large sums of money without the constant, tireless, painstaking effort the acquisition of wealth usually required but now that Brembre was gone, William knew it would not be so easy.

He had not been idle all these months in exile. But he had not been entirely successful either. He traded in anything he could make a profit out of but so did the great Italian houses, the Venetians, the French and the Flemish. While the Earl of Arundel was attacking the coastal towns so effectively, an Englishman who travelled through France did so at his peril. Since he did not dare leave the security of Calais, William had to leave it to his agents to buy and sell for him. He had made a mistake with some Spanish jewels which he had sent to Paris only to discover there was already a glut of all but the highest quality. His network of informants was no substitute for his own nose. He needed to be there himself to be able to compete with the foreigners.

He left the castle still undecided and went in search of Giles de Bourdat. He found his partner at home in the counting house writing up the books.

'The King has dismissed the lords appellant and appointed a moderate ministry,' William told him.

'A bold stroke,' exclaimed Giles de Bourdat. 'Does the King have the support of the people this time, I wonder?'

'Too bold, perhaps,' William replied. 'It reminds me a

little too much of how the King behaved when he was being advised by Sir Nicholas Brembre. But the King has recalled Lancaster from Spain, so the Captain informs me. With his father coming home, Henry Bolingbroke will have to support the King. The appellants are in disarray. It looks as if it might be safe for me to return to England again.'

'Better wait until Gaunt is safe home from Spain. The Duke of Gloucester might take it into his head to do something foolhardy.'

'Always you err on the side of caution, Giles,' William sighed. 'It must be many months before Gaunt can hope to reach England and I don't think I can afford to wait. The seas are much safer for English ships since Arundel's successful raids on the French. There will never be a better time for taking goods across the Channel. If I'm going I ought to go now. There's no point in being first with the news if I don't act on it speedily.'

'Why go back to London at all?' asked Giles. 'Haven't you learnt your lesson yet? How many times have you had to flee from London at a moment's notice? How many more times do you think you can count on God's good grace to save you from calamity?'

'Each time I've had to flee it was caused one way or the other by that devil Brembre,' said William with a shudder. 'Now Brembre's dead, the city of London should be much more peaceful. I shall be free to get on with what I know best.'

'Wool is what you know best,' said Giles. 'Calais is where all wool and cloth exported from England has to pass. You should stop taking so many risks and be content being a stapler.'

William hitched himself up on to a stool beside his partner. 'You don't get rich administering taxes imposed by Parliament,' he said frowning down at the neat columns of figures in the ledger. 'The wool tax is killing the trade, as you know very well. Besides I don't take risks. I'm very careful.'

'You are worn down with care, William,' Giles told him. 'But you take no account of time. You count on your fingers and say in so much time I shall have made so much and shall have so much time left and when I am rich indeed I shall have time to rest. Why don't you retire now and live here in Calais in a way that will make you happy?'

'I'm not old, I'm only thirty-nine,' William said indignantly. 'I've plenty of time left.'

'You'll be forty before the year is out.' Giles smiled at him. 'I'm not much older than that, but I know it's time to give more thought to how matters will go after my death than to those of this world.'

'Well I have given thought,' William protested. 'I've endowed a chapel in the Convent of the Sacred Heart where my poor Mariota died. I give more to the poor than any other merchant in Calais, which is why there are so many poor here at my gate. God's poor will be more certain of getting what is theirs if I prosper, whether it be Calais or Bruges or London.'

'I can see you've made up your mind to go.'

'I have to go.' William stared out of the open door of the counting house, at the goods lying carefully stacked in the warehouse beyond. There were Tuscan silks, embroideries, pictures, fine enamels from Paris inlaid with gold, Flemish and French painted stuffs for bed curtains and wall-hangings – treasures which it had taken him time and much toil to come by. 'A London mercer will give me a knight's ransom for some of the goods we have here,' he said. 'But I don't want the same thing to happen to them as happened to those Spanish jewels. I must be there myself to know when the time is right.'

'Remember, you can't take it with you to the next world,' said Giles, shaking his head sadly.

'London is where I can make the most money,' went on William, ignoring him. 'It's where the Venetians, the Florentines, the Italians all have branches. How can I compete with them without going to London?'

'You don't have to compete with them, William. You're a rich man already. Can't you be content with what God in his goodness has given you?'

'What of my beautiful inn in Cornhill? I didn't go to all that trouble to build the finest house in London to end my days here in Calais,' retorted William.

'Your house belongs to Sir Piers Exton now,' Giles reminded him.

William picked up a quill lying on the desk in front of him and held it between his fingers. 'Sir Piers can't afford a house like mine,' he said. 'Nicolette is living in it all alone like an anchoress in a cell. I must go back to London for the sake of my poor Nicolette.'

'If the Earl of Arundel has been dismissed by the King I dare say he will be disbanding his retainers and Sir Piers will be free to go home and look after his wife.'

'That's not something I'm prepared to leave to chance,' said William, stroking the quill absently. 'Do you think Nicolette would have married Sir Piers if I had left it to him to persuade her? Of course she wouldn't. He hasn't the least notion how to get what he wants.'

'Perhaps he was too honourable to force her against her will,' suggested Giles.

'She only married him because they were running out of money. Adam Stickleby told me. And I saw to that. I knew the romantic young fool would fail to carry his damsel off without my help.'

'You think you can control everyone with money.' Giles looked sad. 'Can't you find a better use for it?'

William took out his dagger and began carefully scraping one end of the quill to make a point. 'How else am I to control Nicolette?' he demanded. 'It didn't take her long to forget all that goodness and obedience she was taught in the abbey. She will have learnt to obey me through this.' Lovingly he stroked the columns of figures in the ledger with the feathery tip of the quill.

'You think you can buy her, William? Nicolette isn't another of your silver goblets or fine Flemish tapestries.'

'She's a work of art,' said William, smiling at his partner. 'I'm proud of her and I want the whole of London to be proud of her too. She should be seen and admired, not hidden away.'

'She's flesh and blood, William.'

'I know that.' He put down the quill. 'She's my flesh and my blood – my base-born daughter. You knew that, didn't you?'

'Jeanne told me – she guessed.'

'Now she is a knight's lady. My bastard is a knight's lady! Do you know what that means to me, Giles? And it's all my doing. Mine.' He paused. Giles was shaking his head sadly and William knew that he could not make him understand. Giles did not know what it felt like to be constantly creeping under men's feet, bowing and scraping, flattering and humbling oneself in order to gain their confidence, learn their secrets, get the better of them. But Nicolette did not have to do that. Nicolette would be his revenge on all of them.

He smiled at his partner, feeling a glow of quite unfamiliar happiness as he thought of his daughter waiting for him in his house in Cornhill. 'Perhaps you're right, perhaps I am getting old,' he said. 'I want to spend what time I can with my beautiful daughter – she needs me.'

'Only two things are needful when you grow old – to do what is pleasing to God, and to spend the little time that is left to you giving back to God what He in his goodness has lent you. Let her go, William. You have done what you can to provide for her and it was well done. Let Piers take care of her now.'

'Sir Piers Exton is a knight,' William said, 'and knights are necessary for our protection but they are stupid and ignorant. Piers is a useful tool, no more.'

'Because Sir Piers is honourable you are in danger of thinking him weak. But honour has its own strength. You cannot use an honourable man like Piers the way you use the captain of the garrison here.'

William was startled. He had thought that the various ingenious schemes he had devised with the captain for their mutual profit was a secret known only to themselves. He did not want his partner's conscience troubled by dishonest dealings.

'A man who will sell his honour once will sell it again,' he said pretending not to understand. 'I think I know Piers's price.'

'I wonder if you do. He has courage and he has gentleness and he is very much in love with Nicolette, which has made him vulnerable. But if she should ever cease to deserve his love, you might find him less easy to use.'

He was wrong, thought William as he got down from the stool. Poor Giles was always wrong. He was good and honest and hardworking but he was far too trusting. He was prepared to hope for the best whereas he, William, knew that nothing was achieved without expecting the worst and being fully prepared to overcome it.

Nicolette was in the garden when William arrived home. She

was sitting by the carp pond, holding her small son by the hem of his cote-hardie while he leant over and beat at the water with his chubby hands. So engrossed were they both that they did not notice William.

For a while he stood and watched them. The garden which he had created with so much laborious care was a haven of peace and tranquillity and the girl playing with her child by the carp pond fitted into the scene most perfectly. He was home at last. This was where he belonged and they were all his, the child, the girl, the garden and the house. He had made them and saved them.

The child shrieked and almost toppled into the water but Nicolette scooped him up and held him close against her breast. She was dressed in a mantle of blue with her hair covered in a netted mesh of gold, and as she cradled the child tenderly, William had a bright vision of the Virgin Mary. Swiftly he crossed himself in fear that such a thought might be blasphemy.

She looked up and all the tenderness was instantly wiped from her face. She clutched the child so close he screamed in protest. William felt suddenly cold, as if a shadow had fallen across his grave. He wanted her to look at him the way she had looked at her child.

'Well, my daughter, you make a fine sight for a weary traveller to come home to,' he said. 'Are you not going to bid me welcome at last?'

'Welcome,' she said, still clutching her child who began to wriggle in her arms. It occurred to William that amidst all the colourful scenes he had had painted on the walls of his house, there was no Virgin and Child. He decided to rectify the omission immediately and wondered which painter would do justice to so perfect a subject. An Italian, perhaps. With Nicolette as inspiration, it would be the finest wall painting in the city.

Nicolette said nothing, just sat looking at him with that wary look in her eyes.

'Aren't you going to put that child down? He doesn't seem very happy where he is.' He walked over to her.

'I don't want him to fall in the water,' she said, dropping a kiss on his head. Then at last, as if suddenly becoming conscious of her lack of good manners, she said, 'Did you have a very tiring journey in all this heat?'

'It was hot but it was trouble-free, Saint Christopher be praised.' William leant forward to catch hold of one of the child's flailing fists. 'It's a pretty babe.'

She got up, moved away from him across the garden to the orchard with the child in her arms.

'How old is he?' asked William following her.

'A year and four months almost,' she said, turning to stare at him defiantly. 'He was born on the day that his father was hanged.'

'Does your husband mind?'

She set the struggling child down in the shade of an apple tree. 'I don't know whether he minds or not,' she said. The infant set off back towards the carp pond, staggering along on his little fat legs in a kind of tottering run, and she ran after him, catching him at the edge of the pond. He shrieked as she picked him up, but she held him high above her head, laughing and tossing him up and down until he gurgled with glee. She looked even more beautiful when she laughed, so happy and alive, and William was struck again by the contrast between how she was with her baby and the veiled hostility with which she greeted him. He told himself it would take time for her to learn to appreciate all that he had done for her.

'Don't you want to see if there are any birds in the dovecote, my little love?' she said, setting the child on his feet again only this time keeping a firm hold of his hand. Determined not to be ignored, William bent down and grasped the child by his other hand.

'My grandson,' he said. 'My bastard's bastard.' He shot a quick look at her to see if the barb had gone home, but she was bending over the child and he could not see her face.

'I thought you didn't want it known that you're my father.'

He shrugged. 'Since you're safely married now it doesn't much matter. Piers is happy with his bargain, is he?'

'Piers is hardly ever here,' she said straightening up. 'He's been fighting the French with the Earl of Arundel most of the time.' She seemed quite composed. He let his gaze slide over her with calculated deliberation. Beneath the flowing blue mantle she wore a clinging sheath of ivory silk, her body was as slender and shapely as ever it had been.

'You should be childbearing again,' said William. 'Give Piers an heir of his own.' She blushed and he thought he detected a hint of shame in her lovely eyes. Had Piers not succeeded in bedding her? The knight must be even more of a fool than he'd thought.

'What use an heir if there's nothing for him to inherit?' she said quickly. Ah, thought William pleased, so my little falcon is growing hungry. Soon she will be ready to come to the lure. 'Hasn't Piers managed to bring back any spoils of war?' he asked. 'The Earl of Arundel's ravaging of the French coast has been very successful, so I've heard.'

'A little but it doesn't go far, not with a house like this one. He took no rich prisoners. There were no French knights defending the towns they attacked and Piers does not like to rob the poor, even in war.'

'Piers has a very costly conscience, I'm afraid,' said William. 'But you and I must indulge him in that. He is our protection, after all.' She frowned. 'Where would we be without Piers?' he added, and saw that this time the barb had gone home.

'I don't think being married to Piers has done anything for me at all,' she said sulkily. It was music to his ears.

'Don't you go anywhere? See anybody?' he asked then. 'I thought by now you'd have been taking the city by storm, have had the Mayor and all the city knights to your feasts.'

'I've been looking after Dickon. He wasn't very strong at first. The birthing was long and it left him very sickly. He needed everything I could give him.' She was turned away from him, watching the child who was squatting on the ground pulling grass up in small handfuls and scattering it over his embroidered tunic.

'He's strong and healthy enough now, and a bundle of mischief. A babe to be proud of, even if he is a bastard.'

'Yes, he's thriving, thanks be to God.' She bent and picked him up. 'I couldn't bear to lose him now,' she said showering kisses on his face.

'He has the blood of the best merchant capitalists in his veins,' said William, surprised by a sudden surge of possessive pride. 'Shall we make him Mayor, do you think? Or perhaps we should give him to God and he can become Chancellor of England like Bishop William of Wykeham.'

'It will be for Piers to decide,' she said quickly. 'I expect he would like Dickon to be a knight.'

'But Piers has nothing to do with him,' said William

sharply. 'He's yours and mine. It is our blood which runs in his veins.'

She moved away from him with the child clasped protectively in her arms. 'In the eyes of the world Piers is his father,' she insisted.

William did not argue. If that was what she wanted to believe, let her believe it. But the child was the mirror image of Brembre; the eyes of the world, which were not blind, would see that!

'And what does Master Whittington think?' he asked, setting off on a new tack.

She stared at him in startled surprise. 'Master Whittington hasn't even seen him,' she said.

'Yet you named him Richard. Is Dick Whittington not your friend?'

'He's Piers's friend, not mine,' she said. 'I have no friends.'

'That is a great pity.' He shook his head gravely. 'It's not what I planned when I gave you the house. It was built to be fit for kings to feast in. A knight's lady can do better than staying at home being a perfect mother to her babe.'

'How can I make friends and give expensive feasts without money?' she retorted, pouting at him.

'Wouldn't Whittington lend you the money?' he asked, drawing a bow at a venture.

'Piers doesn't like to borrow.'

'But didn't you try, when Piers went away? Didn't you ask Whittington to help you?' He kept his eyes on her averted face. It was a beautiful profile. She really was quite enchanting, he thought, especially when she was a little unsure of herself, like now.

'No, of course not!'

'Don't lie to me, Nicolette. I've told you that before. I know you went to see Whittington. How much do you owe him?'

'I don't owe him anything. Whittington refused to lend me his money.'

It was easy really, he thought, well pleased. Properly handled, she would be as good and obedient as on the day she left the convent, and it would give him so much pleasure, indulging her, laying at her feet all the fruits of his hard-won success. The child of the convent who had been brought up to regard poverty as a virtue now knew what want was. She was susceptible to the temptations of the flesh despite her early training. She was his daughter after all. All that self-denial and restraint which were supposed to bring you closer to God were all very fine in Lent but it became less uplifting if you were forced by necessity to practise it all the time. She had learnt her lesson well and now knew that poverty was the ultimate failure.

'I'm glad you are not in debt to Richard Whittington,' he said softly as he kissed her cheek. 'I have some merchandise I think he might be very interested in and I wouldn't like our bargaining to be prejudiced by any sense of obligation.'

CHAPTER 20

As soon as William was back, all the irksome shortages in the household miraculously disappeared. There was wine again for dinner, beeswax instead of tallow for candles, fresh white bread for all, lamb and capon no longer had to be saved for feast days. In addition, William showered Nicolette with small trinkets – an ivory comb, a purse of embroidered wool, some silver buttons, and a beautiful rosary of coral with a gold cross and pearl beads. It ought to have made her feel good. She knew she ought to be grateful. Instead she was annoyed that her father thought he could win her over with his money. She told herself that he was her father and that in marrying her to Piers he had only been trying to protect her; she tried to see her marriage from his point of view, not as a disastrous failure but as a perfectly acceptable business arrangement. But she could not help wishing that it was Piers who was giving her all these things, not William Gryffard who had used Piers and her for his own ends, and who had now slipped back into his old role as master of the household as if nothing had changed.

The house which had been so empty and cheerless was filled now with music and feasting. The people William invited to the house were mainly merchants and their wives. Some of them were foreigners – Hanse merchants from the steelyard, Italians buying wool for the Vatican. These Nicolette did not mind for they were full of courtesy. Some were knights, but she suspected they only came because they owed her father money, for they treated him with such veiled contempt it would have made her angry if she had not felt so ashamed. Some were aldermen or members of the Common Council. Richard Whittington was one of these and he too treated her with courtesy. Nicolette would like to have got to know Whittington a little better but he never came to the house without his wife and Alice saw to it that there was never an opportunity. It was the women Nicolette found the hardest to like, particularly the aldermen's wives, for they all seemed to be friends or relatives of Idonia Brembre and her family and it seemed to Nicolette that they never missed an opportunity to make her feel wretched – especially Margaret, Idonia's sister.

'Must we have that woman here?' Nicolette asked William. 'She goes out of her way to tease me with her mischief-making and her grand airs and her cat's tongue.'

'I'm afraid we must,' William replied. 'Margaret is married to Adam Bamme the goldsmith who in all likelihood will be Mayor one day. Sir Nicholas Brembre may have perished but his wife's family still run this city.'

'She spent the whole time we were in the solar telling the other women what a wicked bad man Sir Nicholas was. I hate her.'

'Sir Nicholas was a wicked man and you, my child, were a fool to be taken in by him. But that is all over now. What you have to do is to make a friend of Margaret Bamme. If she likes you, the others will too.'

'Never. She goes out of her way to make me feel inferior. I could never be her friend.'

He took her chin in his hand. 'You've had your own way for too long, my dear,' he said, gazing into her face. 'The world is a hard place and you have to learn to make your enemies like you. It's the art of survival.'

'I know how to make people like me,' she said disdainfully. 'Everybody liked me – when I was the mistress of Sir Nicholas Brembre.'

He smiled. 'But you're a knight's lady now and can hold your head up with the best in the city.'

All very well for him to say that, she thought bitterly, when all the time he kept reminding her that she was still a bastard. How could she ever succeed again when she had to fight against his constant criticism and doubt?

Piers came home at the end of August and Nicolette did not know whether to be glad or sorry. When he was at home she felt confused because she did not know quite what to make of him. She admired his strength – not just his physical strength although that was impressive enough, but his inner strength, the way he never seemed to have to prove anything to himself. He did not seem to suffer from guilt and regrets as she did. He wasn't like her father with his fears and his worries, endlessly trying to anticipate and so avoid disaster before it struck. Piers seemed content to meet trouble head on. Nor did he seem to care what people thought of him; she couldn't help being impressed by that. What annoyed her was his slavish devotion. He was so considerate and chivalrous and kind. It made her feel guilty. He had sold his honour for love and got a very bad bargain for his pains, and yet he did not seem to hold it against her at all. When he was at home she felt angry with him but when he was away she missed him. With William in the house she was afraid that it would be even more difficult. Her father would lose no chance to mock and deride her husband and where would her duty lie then? Besides, she did not want her father to know how bad things really were between them.

'Well, Piers, what do you intend to do with yourself?' asked William the first night as they sat down to supper.

'I thought I'd go to Smithfields,' said Piers. 'I might find a knight to ride a course against or get some practice at the archery butts. If all else fails, Crispin here's longing to unhorse me, aren't you, Crispin?'

Crispin blushed. 'I'd like to try, but I doubt if I'll succeed,' he muttered, pouring wine into Nicolette's silver cup.

Nicolette smiled up at him warmly. 'If you unhorse him you can have one of my ribbons to wear in your helm as a favour,' she promised him. He blushed an even deeper shade of red and she gave her husband a quick provocative peep through her long lashes to see whether he minded. But Piers was busy dismembering a capon with his dagger.

'It's the duty of all squires to be in love with their knights' ladies,' put in William, and Nicolette looked down at her trencher, ashamed. 'I didn't mean what are you going to do tomorrow,' William went on. 'I meant what are you going to do now that you are no longer a retainer of the Earl of Arundel?'

'I don't know,' said Piers, as he sliced off the wishbone and a long thin sliver of breast and laid it carefully on his wife's wooden trencher.

'Shouldn't you be looking for another worthy cause to fight for? Or another magnate perhaps. What about the Earl of Warwick? He keeps a fair-sized retinue, so I'm told.'

'I don't want to ride about the country in an armed band preying on the weak, that's not what my sword is for.' Piers was indignant. 'I had enough of that with the Earl of Arundel.'

'I thought you were fighting the French,' said William.

'I was, most of the time. But the Earl of Arundel had some private grudges he didn't mind using his retainers to settle. It's not my idea of chivalry.'

'Is that why you left the Earl's service?' asked Nicolette, turning sideways on the wooden bench the better to look at him.

'Partly.' But his eyes slid away from hers as if embarrassed.

She turned away, to hide her irritation. Why couldn't Piers learn to flirt a little, like other men? Why couldn't he at least pretend in front of the ever watchful William that everything was all right between them?

'Perhaps you should offer your sword to the King again,' suggested William. 'He has offered to abolish all liveries including his own.'

'The King has my loyalty, of course,' Piers replied. 'But he's not a good judge of men, in my opinion, and I'd sooner not end up under the command of someone like Robert de Vere.'

'The King's a great deal more clever than you give him credit for,' Nicolette said, to needle him. 'Look how he's triumphed once more over his powerful uncles. You shouldn't underestimate the King, he'll always win – in the end.'

'Nicolette's right,' said William smiling at her quite warmly now. 'The King has an uncanny knack of triumphing over his enemies. He's not a fool. He knows that his people want peace, and so he promises to negotiate peace with the French and therefore lower taxation. Peace and prosperity, that is what we all want – except you, Piers. What can you do, now that peace has descended over the land?'

'I can help to keep the peace,' replied Piers. 'Peace does not last long without knights to enforce it. The trouble is that the great lords are using their retainers to stir up trouble instead of putting it down. What I should like to see is a company of white knights dedicated to fighting for the weak and oppressed.'

Nicolette gazed at him. He had such noble visions, she thought, and a clear idea of doing good. It was just that the world seemed full of more successful men who were wicked or cunning or more willing to compromise than Piers.

'I have a better idea.' William said. 'I have to go to the Cotswolds for the autumn woolclip. I'd be happy to have your protection on the way. I can teach you a great deal about buying wool. It might come in handy one day, when you have manors of your own.'

Nicolette clenched her hands together beneath the damask tablecloth. If only Piers could do something truly heroic to win the King's favour, then they might not be so dependent on William Gryffard's bounty.

'I thought perhaps I might stay at home and get to know my wife better,' said Piers smiling at last at Nicolette. 'Since we've been married I've hardly spent more than a month with her at any one time.'

Nicolette looked up quickly. The hunger was there in his liquid brown eyes. She held her husband's glance over the rim of her goblet and somewhat to her surprise she found herself blushing like a foolish virgin. Piers grinned at her sheepishly. She began to hope that he would come to her chamber tonight, and not just because of William's presence. Perhaps tonight it would be different, perhaps tonight Piers could lay the ghost of Nicholas Brembre.

'I fear I may not have been entirely honest with you about Nicolette,' said William. She dropped her eyes quickly, aware of her father's watchful scrutiny and suddenly afraid. 'I let you think she was my ward, a distant kinswoman, whereas in truth she is my daughter – my bastard daughter. I hope that does not make you feel any differently towards her.'

Nicolette burned with shame. How could he be so cruel as to taunt her with the secret now in front of the squire and the steward, and for no reason at all? William's eyes were not only watchful, they were calculating, as if he was trying to measure her pain. She clutched the stem of her goblet tightly and looked away, not wanting him to know the extent of her hurt and distress at his betrayal.

'Nothing either in heaven or on earth would make me feel

any differently towards my lady wife,' Piers replied quietly.

Nicolette stared down into the contents of her drinking cup, feeling too ashamed to meet his gaze.

'That's good,' William continued. 'As my own flesh and blood I naturally want the best for her – and for my grandson too, of course, poor little bastard. Although I cannot expect you to feel the same way about him since he is not your own.'

'The child cannot help the sins of his father,' replied Piers. 'He has my name and I will do my best to bring him up as if he also had my blood.'

'So chivalrous,' murmured William. 'A very perfect, gentle knight. You see, Nicolette, how wise I was to make you marry him.'

Nicolette, drank her wine and said nothing. For some reason her father was angry with her and she did not know why. But she sensed that it had something to do with Piers. Piers was being very noble and patient, refusing to be provoked. Why did he not fly to her defence? She did not want to be married to a man who allowed someone like William Gryffard to ride roughshod over him. Unable to bear it any more, she got up from the table and went to her solar.

It was a fine summer evening and the sky was pink from the setting sun. She sat by the open window in the solar, letting the evening air cool her cheeks, watching the pink fade from the sky and thinking about Piers. Would he come to her solar tonight? He must come. He would not shame her in front of her father by sleeping in the hall with the servants. The trouble was, with Piers anything was possible. He said he loved her. She remembered his eyes devouring her. Why then did he come so seldom to her chamber? And when he came why did he not take her as Nicholas had done? She looked at the canopied bed standing in the middle of the chamber, its heavy damask curtains hanging at all four corners ready to guard its secrets, and in spite of herself felt a thrill of expectant pleasure. She wanted someone to conquer her fears, to take her in his arms and sweep her off her feet and make her feel wonderful again, as Nicholas had done.

She leapt up and began to pace about the chamber, her arms tightly folded across her chest. Nicholas was a wicked man and her love for him was sin, doomed from the very first time when she had fallen from grace on the Feast of Epiphany. If only she could forget him, perhaps she could give Piers what he wanted. Piers wanted their marriage to be something more than William had meant it to be. He kept going on and on about love and trying to do better. But Nicolette knew that William was right. There was no such thing as love. She did not love Nicholas, she knew that now. She could not love a man as wicked as that, surely. No, she had been bewitched, possessed by the devil. Nicholas had been a devil. The nuns had warned her that the devil came in many tempting disguises and Nicholas had been temptation incarnate. She was still possessed by him. In spite of all her prayers and penances and confessions and absolutions, her body still hungered for him. Piers did not love her; if he did he ought to be able to cast out the devil that possessed her; he was good enough surely. But Piers was in love with his vision of a perfect lady. Every time he came to her bed, it was disaster. He was too chivalrous to force himself upon her when he thought she did not want him and she was terrified of what he might think of her if he knew what she was really like.

Slowly she began to undress, her hungry flesh tingling with expectancy. If only Piers would let her come down from her pedestal and be a woman, she felt they could do better.

Piers came when it was almost dark. He stood inside the door and she could see by the dancing of the candle flame that his hand was trembling. She walked across the chamber towards him, the rushes whispering softly beneath her bare feet. She was dressed only in her shift, her glorious hair hanging to her waist in a curtain of gold. She reached his side and blew out his candle. He groaned and pulled her against him. She tilted her head and his mouth found hers. She was surprised at how good it felt. His kisses were warm and sweet and his breath perfumed with wine. She kissed him back, her mouth opening instinctively, while her body, so long starved of sensual pleasure, clung to his with a will of its own. He raised his head and held her at arm's length, trying to see her face. She was glad that it was so dark.

'Shall we try again?' he murmured, his voice hoarse with desire.

She took him by the hand and led him to the bed, praying that this time it would be different.

In the dark confines of the closely curtained bed, naked

243

and aroused, with Piers so warm and hard and powerful on top of her, she abandoned herself to her senses, longing to soar once again to impossible heights, to recapture the ecstasy and the wild exhausting passion, to escape the clamouring insistence of her flesh into bliss. But before she came near that wonderful feeling of release, Piers suddenly gave a long shuddering sigh. Kissing her tenderly, he asked if he'd hurt her.

'No,' she said, desperately trying to contain her disappointment. 'You didn't hurt me.' She lay still and prayed that he would leave her alone, ashamed of her need and determined that he should not discover it now. If only he would go to sleep and forget as Nicholas would have done. But instead he picked up her tangled hair where it lay spread out on the pillow and lay down beside her.

'Teach me how to please you,' he begged.

'You don't have to please me,' she said twisting away from him in the darkness. 'You have given me your name and your protection. I must give you sons. Isn't that so? Marriage is for security and for taking care of the future, it's not for pleasure.' She lay with her back to him, curled up in a resentful ball.

'But I love you,' he said, tugging at her shoulder insistently. 'All the time I have been away I have been dreaming of this moment and I have not lain with any other woman since I was last with you.'

'It's a pity you did not get more practice!' She flung herself on to her back and lay staring up into the darkness.

'I'm sorry if I didn't do it right. I love you so much it makes me over-anxious. But I will improve.' He was laying her hair reverently over her body to cover her nakedness. 'The first time I tried to hit the quintain with a lance I was knocked clean off over the tail of my horse by the bag of sand,' he said. 'But I got the hang of it eventually. I'm very good at it now. My timing's almost perfect.'

'Well, don't come practising on me,' she said, pushing his hands away. 'I'm not a bag of sand.'

'I know, my beloved,' he said burying his face in the nape of her neck. 'You're my lady and I cannot lie with anyone but you. So you will just have to bear with me while we learn to love one another.'

'Love!' she retorted turning her back on him in disgust.

'Love's for fools. Why can't you just take your own pleasure and be content with that?'

'Because that wouldn't be love,' he said, drawing her against him. 'And it wouldn't last.' He had a powerful body, she thought, feeling him against her back. A knight's body, lean and hard with muscle, honed to physical perfection by the disciplines of fighting. It was a pity he did not know how to use it in bed. Through the heavy damask bed curtains she heard a faint familiar cry. Dickon was having a nightmare.

'The only love which lasts,' she said getting out of bed, 'is the love of a mother for her child.'

Dickon stopped crying as soon as she picked him up. She held him close and he snuggled sleepily against her breast. She took him back to bed with her, as she was wont to do when he cried. 'Goodnight, my best beloved,' said Piers, as she laid the child in the centre of the big bed between them. 'Sleep well.'

It was infuriating, she thought, such unselfishness. He ought to have been jealous of the baby. He ought to have forced her to make love to him again. She wanted to believe he loved her but she could not. Love was fire, love was passion. It was uncontrollable consuming flame, not this tentative unsatisfactory search for perfection. She lay on her back and stared into the impenetrable darkness above her head. Sweet Mary, Mother of Jesus, don't let me think of him any more, she prayed, tormented by the memory of Nicholas Brembre's demanding embraces.

Next day Piers rose early to go jousting at Smithfields. Nicolette watched him leave the house in his armour, a strong stocky figure moving with a slow but powerful vigour and she thought of that hard muscular body pressed against her in bed with a quickening of the senses. Crispin brought the horses and Piers swung himself into the saddle with practised ease. He looked up at the window and saw her. She leant far out to wave to him and he raised his lance in acknowledgement, then rode away down the street, the red and cream markings rippling on the caparison covering the stallion's powerful flanks. Crispin, carrying his shield and helm, rode in his wake. Just for that moment she felt a glow of pride. She was a knight's lady, after all. Now Piers was home, perhaps that bitch Margaret Bamme would treat her with respect.

The rest of the morning Nicolette spent preparing for her husband's return. First she went to the kitchen to see what was for dinner. It was a round wooden building standing on its own in the middle of the garden. It had a large open fire in the centre with a hole in the roof to let out the smoke. A large pot hung on a hook above the fire and a heavy oak table ran down the middle. The heat was intense. The spit-boy turning the long pole above the fire was stripped to the waist and his skinny little body glistened with sweat. The cook was sitting at the table pounding spices. Nicolette lingered just long enough to taste the contents of the pot and inspect the small charred bodies of the conies revolving on the spits, and to pronounce them good.

Emerging thankfully into the cool of the garden, she picked an armful of roses. She arranged them artfully in a pitcher and set them on the high table in the hall. By the time she was finished, she felt hot and sticky. The servants were beginning to set up the trestle tables for dinner so she hastened to her solar to change her crumpled dress. The noon day bells were pealing when she re-entered the hall, clad in a sheath of blue silk which clung to her slender body, with her hair braided and coiled round her head like a crown and a jewelled girdle encircling her hips. William was already seated in the carved master's chair, waiting for his dinner.

'You look very beautiful, my dear,' he said, studying her carefully. 'Are we expecting visitors today? Or is this in celebration of our hero's return?'

'It was hot in the garden this morning,' she muttered, feeling foolish. 'I thought this would be cooler.'

'I doubt whether Piers and his squire will be back from their games of war before dark,' said William. 'I've told the steward we won't wait dinner.' She took her place beside him and smiled sweetly, determined not to show her disappointment.

'You don't like Piers, do you, Father? If you despise him so, why did you go to such trouble to make sure I married him?'

'We needed Piers, don't you remember? To save you from your folly and my house from the lords appellant.' He poured wine into her goblet. 'You need not worry. He'll not be here to plague you long. I'll take him off with me to the Cotswolds and leave you in peace.' He smiled at her knowingly and she looked away. Why was her father trying to keep Piers and her apart? Was it because with Piers home everything was so confusing and difficult? Her eyes wandered to where Lisette sat with Dickon, spooning pease pudding into his mouth. Nicolette smiled.

When dinner was over, she took the child from Lisette and went out into the garden to spend a happy afternoon playing with him in the sunshine. Her love for Dickon was pure and uncomplicated. She could love him with all her heart and nobody disapproved.

The bells were ringing for the Angelus when Nicolette saw Crispin wandering somewhat aimlessly in the herb garden. She went across the grass towards him feeling unaccountably light-hearted, and ready to put him at his ease should he be overcome with confusion at being alone with her. He looks downcast, she thought. Piers must have proved invincible.

'What's the matter, Crispin?' she asked, feeling proud of her husband. 'Did you not manage to unhorse Sir Piers after all? Never mind. I'll give you one of my ribbons to wear in your helm anyway. It may bring you better luck.'

'But I did unhorse him, my lady,' said the squire, 'that's what's worrying me. Sir Piers has never been unhorsed by anyone, not since I've been his squire.'

'Perhaps he let you unhorse him to encourage you. It's just the sort of thing he would do.'

'Sir Piers would never insult me like that,' said the squire. 'He fell off his horse not by intent and not by any skill on my part, I'd swear by the Rood. It's my belief he has a fever and if I knew which of these herbs to use I'd make him an infusion to bring the heat down.'

'It's probably just too much fighting in all that armour in the heat of the day,' she said. 'He seemed well enough this morning. A tincture of aconite should help cool him. I'll make one and bring it to him presently.'

'I left him lying in the solar,' said the squire. 'I'd better get back there to see how he is.'

Nicolette watched him hurry away, amused and at the same time a little put out that Crispin's dedication to his master should be so much stronger than his interest in her. Piers seemed to inspire great devotion in his squires.

When she went to her solar with the potion some time

247

later, she found Lisette anxiously trying to get little Dickon to sleep in his cot and Piers lying in the middle of the bed moaning and struggling while the squire tried to hold him still.

'Jesus have mercy,' she said, staring at her husband in dismay. 'You didn't tell me he was out of his senses.'

'He's getting worse all the time,' said the boy. 'I don't know what ails him. Do you think we ought to send for a doctor?'

She stared helplessly at Piers tossing restlessly in the bed. She had no idea how to find a doctor. The squire was watching her anxiously, his young face full of fear. She must do something.

She twisted up her long floating sleeves, hoping she looked more confident than she felt, and sat down on the bed to make Piers drink her potion. He muttered something unintelligible and flung an arm out sideways, knocking the cup from her grasp. She watched the liquid running down the front of her silk gown, annoyed and at a loss to know what to do. Lisette came with a wet cloth and Nicolette held it to Piers's burning head. He opened his eyes and for a moment recognised her.

'I'm sorry, my angel,' he croaked.

'What's the matter with you, Piers?' she asked, dismayed at how difficult he seemed to find it to speak. 'Where does it hurt?'

'All over,' he groaned. She leant over him, bathing his hot skin with the cloth, not knowing what else to do. 'I didn't mean to be a nuisance to you,' he whispered. 'Crispin will look after me.'

'Hush,' she said. 'Lie still and try to sleep.' His eyes clouded over again and he tossed to and fro in the bed, muttering in a thick, hardly recognisable voice about siege engines. Occasionally he gave a groan and seized the bed cover, clenching it tightly in his fist. It was clear that he was in great pain. She watched him helplessly, overwhelmed by a feeling of inadequacy.

'He needs a doctor,' said Lisette coming to stand by the bed. 'The sooner the better. I'll go now if ye'll only tell me where.'

'No, you stay with Dickon,' Nicolette said, unable to bear the sight of Piers's suffering any longer. 'I'll go.' She ran

248

from the chamber down the wide stone staircase into the hall, where the servants were laying the trestle tables for supper as if nothing had happened. William was waiting by the high table and looked her up and down disapprovingly. For once she did not mind. William would know what to do. He knew everything.

'Piers is sick. We need a doctor,' she said.

'Christ Jesu, not plague?' He crossed himself, turning pale.

'I don't know what ails him. But he looks bad. I don't know what to do, Father.'

He sent a servant immediately to fetch his own doctor. Then he made Nicolette sit down in the cool hall and poured her a goblet of wine which he made her drink to steady herself. By the time the doctor came, Nicolette felt sufficiently restored to accompany him to the solar and her sick husband.

'It is what they call the scarlet sickness, my lady,' said the doctor when he had examined Piers. 'They mostly go out of their heads with it for a while. It's very painful and the throat swells up, making it difficult to breathe.'

'Will he die?' she asked.

'It's possible, but he's very powerfully built. If we can get him to the stage when the skin turns red, he might pull through. I'll bleed him now to try and cool the overheated blood and you must keep him wrapped in cold cloths.' He looked round the solar and frowned disapprovingly. Nicolette was not surprised. It was very untidy. Piers's clothes lay in a heap in one corner where the squire had thrown them. She opened her mouth to apologise for the disorder.

'I should get that child moved from the chamber,' the doctor said, forestalling her. 'This disease isn't like the plague, there's little danger for older people, their humours are strong, but children are much weaker when it comes to infection.' The cold hand of fear gripped Nicolette somewhere in the pit of her stomach. She snatched up the sleeping Dickon from his cot and rushed out of the chamber with him without another thought for her husband. On the stairs she encountered William.

'You can have my chamber,' he said, backing away from her down the stairs when she told him what the doctor had said.

'But where will you sleep?' she asked, standing at the top of the stairs with the child in her arms.

'I'm not staying, I'm leaving for the Cotswolds.'

'Now? But it's nearly dark. You can't go tonight.'

'There's a party of woolmen leaving at first light tomorrow. If I hurry I can catch them at their tavern and spend the night with them there. If Piers is not to accompany me then I'd better go with them. It will give me added protection on the road.'

'I wish you didn't have to go so soon,' she said. 'How am I to manage here without you, with Piers so ill and only his squire to help with the tending of him?'

'There's Lisette. Let her look after Piers, she's a good, capable woman. Your duty is to your child. Stay away from your husband.'

'The doctor doesn't think he will die,' she said.

'He's a good doctor, very skilled. I paid for his training myself, sent him to study at the medical school in Florence. He's the best that money can buy. If anybody can save your husband, he can. There's nothing I can do for you by staying here.'

'Can't you wait until Piers is better? I thought you wanted him to go with you,' she said.

'My business can't wait that long. All the best wool will have been sold if I wait until Piers recovers – if he recovers.'

Always money, she thought, clutching her sleeping baby to her. He wanted to buy her with his money but he wasn't prepared to stay and help her when she needed him. Always he ran away at the first hint of danger.

On Sunday, when William had been gone three days, Piers was better. The fever persisted but now his body was covered with a mesh of tiny dots and he seemed to feel less pain. The doctor said that though he was still in danger, there was hope for his recovery. Nicolette began to feel more cheerful. Until Dickon wouldn't eat his dinner.

'What's the matter with him, Lisette? He doesn't seem hungry.'

'It's probably just the heat. It often puts a child off his feed.'

Nicolette took her son on her knee, determined not to panic. She dipped a piece of bread in sauce, coaxing him gently, but Dickon turned his head away. She gave him her finger to suck but he began to cry, fretfully. Fear gripped her. She held him in her arms, crooning to him softly, but he struggled restlessly. It wasn't like him to be so difficult. He was a good, contented, docile child most of the time. Suddenly he vomited all over her fine damask gown. She looked at Lisette, her throat so choked with fear she could not speak.

'No, no, don't fret, my lady,' Lisette soothed. 'He's just eaten something. Give him to me. I'll take him to lie down while you cleans yourself up.'

But Nicolette did not care about her spoilt gown. 'No, I'll take care of him. You fetch the doctor, Lisette, quickly. I'm afraid, so afraid.' She took the child to the big chamber off the hall and laid him in his crib. He was hot and fretful and disinclined to sleep. She tried singing all his favourite lullabies but he was tossing feverishly and didn't seem to hear.

When the doctor came, he told her that the child had succumbed to the scarlet sickness. Nicolette already knew. The child's throat was so swollen and dry he could barely cry. The doctor did his best. Nicolette did not leave her son for an instant, holding him for the doctor to take his precious blood, cradling him in her arms while he thrashed and whimpered and struggled for breath, his little limbs beating the air ever more feebly, his hot skin burning however many times she changed the cloths. She prayed, how she prayed, with her sick child clutched tightly to her breast – to the Virgin, Mother of Jesus, to St Nicholas the children's saint and St Christopher who had carried the Christ child over the river. But her prayers went unheeded. Within twenty-four hours Dickon was dead.

Nicolette was inconsolable. She clung to the little body of her son now so limp and still, spurning all Lisette's efforts to comfort her and refusing to let him go. Piers, pale and gaunt from his own battle with death, came and tried to reason with her.

'It won't do, Nicolette,' he said. 'You'll wear yourself out. One day you'll have other babes, if God wills. I love you so much, Nicolette. Let me comfort you.' He held out his arms to her, but she jumped up.

251

'No,' she screamed. 'Don't touch me. It's all your fault. You brought this sickness here. Why, oh why did God let you live and not my baby?'

'Perhaps it's God's punishment for loving you so,' said Piers bitterly as he turned away from her. She was so distraught she scarcely paid heed to what he meant. Not then. But she remembered later that night, as she kept vigil by her son's cradle, praying for his innocent little soul. She remembered, and knew that she was wicked. God knew, which is why he had forsaken her, and William knew, which is why he despised her so. She remembered Nicholas shaking with fear and unable to recognise her as he went to his death. It was a vision she had pushed ruthlessly away, buried deep beneath all her other resentments, but now it rose to taunt her. Only someone who was wicked could have so loved a man like Sir Nicholas Brembre.

CHAPTER 21

In the spring of 1390 the sailing cog *Saint Agnus* arrived in Calais. Nicolette leant over the rail watching the ship being tied up, glad to be out of the stuffy cabin. The wharf below was a jumble of people drawn by the arrival of the ship like bees to a honey pot. Merchants, beggars, priests got in the way of the sailors busy seeing to the ropes securing the ship, while a long line of mules, heads hanging patiently, waited to bear away the contents of her hold. Suddenly Nicolette caught sight of a familiar face.

'Look, Lisette,' she cried, 'there's Giles de Bourdat come to meet us. Master Gryffard must have told him we were coming.' But Lisette was on her knees with her rosary clutched tight against her ample chest, fingering her beads in heartfelt relief at having crossed the treacherous Channel in safety. Nicolette smiled, feeling for the first time in months a lightening of spirit. It was good to breathe the fresh salt-laden air, to see the sparkling waves breaking against the shores of her native land, to hear from the crowded dock below the babble of French, spoken not as a courtly accomplishment but by those who had been born to it. Then she saw Piers, looking pale and drawn, weaving his way carefully towards her through the clutter of ropes and dropped sails and busy cursing seamen.

'You don't look very well, Piers,' she said. 'Don't tell me you were sick all the time. I would have thought you'd have got used to the sea after all that time you spent attacking the French coast with the Earl of Arundel.'

'I'm used to it, but my stomach isn't,' he replied with a wry grin. 'It's hard, isn't it, Lisette? My squire and your mistress seem to feel nothing but it's not like that for us.'

'Some people weren't created by God to journey by sea,' declared Lisette getting up with difficulty from her knees and crossing herself for good measure.

'No matter,' replied Piers. 'We're here safe and sound and you'll soon feel better when you have dry land under your feet again.'

'I'm not on land yet,' retorted the maid, 'and I doubt if I can climb down that there ladder without breaking my head in a fall. My legs is shaky as a lambkin's tail.'

'I'll go first and catch you then,' promised Piers. 'There's nothing to fear.'

'That'll be a comfort,' said Lisette winking at him lasciviously as she hitched up her skirts and approached the ladder. 'I'm ready, young master, when you are.'

Nicolette was not amused. Lisette's affection for Piers was genuine, she knew, but it never ceased to annoy her the way her maid flaunted her devotion at every opportunity until it became a subtle form of accusation. She followed Lisette over the side and down the ladder into her husband's arms without feeling in the least comforted. Physical contact with him was something she had shunned after the death of her baby and Piers had given up all too soon, accepting her coldness with a patient forbearance she found infuriating.

He lifted her off the ladder and set her carefully on her feet, turning quickly away to greet Giles de Bourdat who was waiting for them. Stifling the familiar forlorn feeling, Nicolette smiled graciously at Giles and then caught sight of his wife coming towards them, her arms outstretched in welcome.

'I can't tell you how much we've been looking forward to this day, to seeing our little Nicolette again,' said Jeanne enfolding her in a warm embrace. 'I've got quite a feast prepared even though it is Lent. Salmon caught fresh from the sea this morning. Giles went down at dawn to buy it from the fishermen.'

'How kind,' whispered Nicolette, clinging to Jeanne as a wave of quite unexpected emotion swept over her and rendered her voice unsteady.

'Piers won't want to leave until he has seen his stallion safely unloaded,' said Jeanne, squeezing her tightly in return, 'and Giles has Master Gryffard's cargo of cloth to see to, so we might as well go home and wait for them out of this cold wind.'

Gratefully Nicolette allowed Jeanne to lead her away from the hubbub on the wharf, glad to be in the company of this warm, loving woman once again.

'How beautiful you are, and married to Sir Piers as I prayed you would be. Giles and I are so happy for you,' said Jeanne as they walked through the busy streets of Calais.

'Yes,' said Nicolette. 'My father is a very clever man.' Jeanne looked at her sharply. 'You knew, didn't you, that Master Gryffard was my father?'

'I didn't think he wanted it known,' replied Jeanne.

'It doesn't matter. Now that I'm married to Piers I'm respectable. Master Gryffard managed it well, didn't he?'

'Piers is a husband any girl would be proud to have,' said Jeanne warmly. 'And he loves you, that's very plain to see. You're a lucky girl.'

'Piers is going to try his luck at the jousting at Saint Inglevert,' said Nicolette. 'Three French knights have undertaken to joust for the honour of France for sixty days against all comers. It seems that since the truce has prevented him from fighting our enemies, Piers needs some other excuse to be at the Frenchman's throat.'

'Of course, everyone in Calais knows about it. Some of the best knights in the world will be there,' said Jeanne.

'And some of the worst,' said Nicolette. 'All the weak-minded young nobles who spend vast sums in pursuit of vanity and honour pretending to fight one another when they would not dare do it in defence of their country.'

'Is that what Master Gryffard believes?' asked Jeanne stopping to let an ox-drawn wagon pass.

'My father did not want me to come, but Piers insisted.'

'I dare say William Gryffard hasn't much time for tournaments,' said Jeanne, walking on.

'He hasn't much time for Piers,' replied Nicolette. 'He never loses a chance to put Piers in the wrong, to mock and degrade all his ideals of chivalry and knightly glory.'

'Piers is everything William Gryffard is not,' said Jeanne stoutly. 'Brave, noble, generous and self-sacrificing. I expect Master Gryffard can't forgive him for that.'

'If only Piers would stand up for himself more,' complained Nicolette.

'But Piers got his way in the end,' said Jeanne. 'You are here and Master Gryffard let you come without him.'

'Only because of the spring woolclip. Master Gryffard couldn't leave England before he'd bought all the wool,' explained Nicolette. 'Of course Piers doesn't understand about wool. There was a bitter row. My father thinks it's bound to end in disaster. Everything Piers does always ends in disaster.'

They had reached the house. Jeanne de Bourdat put her arm round Nicolette and led her up the outside stairs saying, 'Try not to see Piers through your father's eyes. He cannot best William Gryffard in the marketplace. Don't be too hard on him for that. He's a knight, remember. He only wants to show you what he can do.'

Nicolette turned at the top of the stairs and confronted Jeanne. 'Just because he's a knight you think Piers is very noble and good but he's not been very successful finding a cause to fight for.'

'It's difficult for a knight when there's no war on,' said Jeanne, leading the way into the house. 'What does Piers want to do?'

'He wants to go about the land with a band of knights protecting the weak but he hasn't done anything about it.' The hall was smaller than she remembered and the rushes on the floor clung to the fur round the hem of her gown. She picked up her skirts holding them carefully above her ankles.

'A band of retainers costs a great deal of money to feed and house and mount,' said Jeanne, pulling Nicolette down beside her on the window seat. 'And I can't see William Gryffard financing such a venture. You must be patient with Piers. It can't be easy for him.' Nicolette stirred restlessly on the seat but Jeanne was looking at her with nothing but friendly concern in her eyes.

'Piers has been kicking his heels in London for almost nine months now and all to no avail. He just rides practice bouts all day at Smithfields and then comes home and argues with William. I'm not surprised my father's tired of him.' Once started, Nicolette found she was unable to stop. It was such a relief to be able to confide in Jeanne. 'He doesn't like the people William has to the house. So he leaves me to entertain them and I don't like them either. I need his support.'

'You can't expect a knight to get on with a lot of merchants,' put in Jeanne soothingly.

'He gets on well with Richard Whittington – he's a merchant. He's rich and successful and I know my father would like me to know Master Whittington better only Piers doesn't take me when he goes to see him and Whittington doesn't come to the house very often. I don't think he likes me very much.'

'I can't believe any man not liking you. I expect his wife is jealous. You're too beautiful.'

'My father says it's because Piers is ashamed of me because of my birth. And I think he is. He's always trying to make me better than I am.'

Jeanne put her arms round her. 'My dear, of course he's not ashamed of you. You're beautiful and good and he's proud of you, so proud he's taking you to Saint Inglevert. Don't be silly.'

'I'm not good,' said Nicolette hanging her head. 'I'm wicked. You don't know what I've done.'

'I know that you were for a time the mistress of Sir Nicholas Brembre. I find it hard to forgive William Gryffard for letting that happen. It wasn't your fault, my dear. You were very young and very innocent and you did not know what you were doing. William Gryffard used you. He's like that. He brings out the worst in people. You'll be better away from him.'

'The trouble is,' said Nicolette pulling away, 'my father is so often right – that's why he's so successful, isn't it, Jeanne? He's always prepared for the worst.'

'May the Blessed Mother have mercy.' Jeanne crossed herself, appalled. 'My poor little Nicolette, don't let William Gryffard's twisted vision corrupt you. When you came here first you were pure and good and full of confidence. I know that it's there still, hiding beneath this new cynicism. Trust to Piers. He's good, let him bring out the best in you. Once you're away from William you can be more what Piers wants you to be.'

Can I? thought Nicolette. She had never had much hope of living up to Piers's ridiculously high ideals and she wasn't at all sure she wanted to be his perfect lady anyway. Life would be very dull. Only she couldn't tell Jeanne. Jeanne wouldn't understand; like Lisette, she could see no wrong in Piers.

St Inglevert was a little town situated on the pale of Calais, halfway between that port and Boulogne. They arrived on a Sunday and found the whole town completely given over to the great festival of jousting.

As they rode up and down the narrow streets in search of lodgings, it was like a lesson in heraldry. In every street the shields and banners of knights participating in the tournament hung from the windows of their lodgings and Piers pointed out to Nicolette the ones he recognised – the Earl Marshal of England Lord Huntingdon, the Lords Beaumont and Clifford, Sir Peter Courtenay. They found two rooms above a cook shop in a street already bedecked with banners. They were small and cooking smells pervaded them from the shop below but they were lucky to get anything at all now that the town had been almost taken over by the great lords and their retainers. It made Nicolette feel more insecure than ever. Piers had no great overlord to protect him and find him lodgings. She looked at the small cramped chamber in disgust. It contained a bed, a small table with a pitcher on it, a stool and nothing else. Not even a piece of polished steel hanging on the wall. As usual, her father had been right. Piers should never have brought her.

Crispin hung Piers's shield bearing a device of three red trefoils on a cream background from their window and Piers went down to look at it from the street below. Nicolette heard the sound of a horse trotting on the cobblestones. It slowed to a walk and a voice in foreign-sounding French called out, 'There's something familiar about your banner. Could I have seen it before somewhere?'

'It's unlikely,' she heard Piers reply. 'We're from England, just arrived today.'

'Another English knight – you're a bloodthirsty lot, you English,' was the reply. 'There must be well-nigh a hundred of you. I'm from Lombardy. Stephano Corsini.'

'Piers Exton.'

Nicolette leant out of the window to get a look at the Italian knight and was deeply impressed by his elaborately decorated armour, his splendid horse, and most of all by the gold-embossed helm hanging from his high-fronted jousting saddle.

'By the Virgin!' he exclaimed, his eyes raised to her in

startled surprise. 'Now the lady I can swear by the Blessed Virgin Herself I have never seen before! Such beauty a man can never forget. Will you give me a favour to wear on my helm, *Bellissima*?'

'My wife,' Piers said curtly, 'and I'll wear her favour until delivered of it by any knight who wants to challenge me. You're welcome to fight me for it.'

The Italian was frowning as he studied Piers's shield again. His hair, Nicolette noticed, was long and glossy and black, curling down below his ears.

'I'm sure I've seen that shield somewhere before,' mused the Italian. 'Have you ever fought in Italy, Sir Piers?'

'For a time I was with the White Company,' Piers admitted.

'Fair lady, I must resist your favour,' Corsini kissed the tips of his mailed fingers to her. 'There are knights aplenty for me to fight without my having to risk being knocked off my horse again.'

'I'm sorry,' she smiled down sympathetically from her window.

'Who unhorsed you today?' asked Piers. 'Was it Jean de Boucicaut?'

'The champion isn't fighting today. He's been injured and is resting. I had the honour to ride a course against the Earl of Nottingham. You English are all the same – too brutal by half.'

'And what of the French?' asked Nicolette.

'The French have the most beautiful women,' replied the Italian, gazing up at her with a knowing smile, 'and they are very good hosts. As it is Sunday and we can break our Lenten fast, there's to be feasting in the castle tonight. All the visiting knights are welcome – and their ladies. Just a little feast, alas no dancing until after Eastertide, but then we shall see.'

'How do I enter the tournament?' asked Piers.

'It's easy. The defenders have hung their shields outside their pavilion on the tournament ground. All you have to do is touch a shield belonging to one of the defenders to give notice of your intention to fight the next day and to indicate which lance is to be used. The shield of war is for sharpened lance, the shield of peace for blunted.'

'Have you touched one yet?' asked Nicolette.

'Not yet, fair damoiselle, and now that I have seen you I'm not sure that I shall. I don't want to be unable to dance. If your husband is to keep guard over that favour of yours, you may need a champion, fair loveliness, to dance with in the evenings.' So saying he waved merrily and rode off down the street.

'What a peacock,' said Piers watching the Italian ride away.

'He has very splendid armour. Do you think he wears that magnificent gold helmet to fight in?' she asked.

'It's tournament armour,' replied Piers. 'He may have won the helm in a tournament, but I would judge it more likely that he had it made specially to make men think he had won it. I'm not surprised Mowbray vanquished him.'

'Wasn't Mowbray one of the lords appellant?' asked Nicolette with a tiny shiver.

'He was,' Piers told her, 'but he and Henry Bolingbroke have fallen out with the others. I like to think it was for the way Gloucester and Arundel misused their power. He's a good fighter, Mowbray, one of the bravest knights in England. Crispin, I think we just have time to inspect the tournament ground before nightfall. I'd like to strike the shield of one of the defenders so I can fight tomorrow.'

'You'll come back in time to take me to the castle for supper?' Nicolette called out as Crispin ran hurriedly down the stairs.

'Don't worry, we won't be long. Just long enough for you to make ready,' Piers replied and rode away.

Nicolette turned back into the small mean chamber feeling excited at the thought of the feast. Lisette was already on her knees attacking the contents of the panniers and Nicolette joined her in laying out her clothes on the bed, trying to decide what to wear. She wanted to make a good impression on this her first evening, but if they were to be here for some time and there were bigger and better occasions to come, it was important to keep something for later. Her eyes roamed over the coifs and cauls, the jewels and girdles arrayed upon the bed. The brilliantly coloured silks lavishly trimmed with fur of which she had been so proud when she had set out from London did not seem quite so fine now. There would be people of great wealth at the castle tonight – the Italian's armour had been only a foretaste. Then she remembered the startled appreciation in the Italian knight's eyes and felt more confident. She would not try to compete with the other ladies' jewels and fur trimmings but would let her beauty speak for itself. Tonight people would want to know who she was and so she would wear a surcoat embroidered with the red unicorns and trefoils of Piers's arms. To go under it she chose a simple sheath of rose taffeta. Her head she left uncovered. Lisette rebraided the long silky tresses and wound them into two perfectly matched bosses on either side of her head, and fixed a narrow band of gold on her brow.

'How do I look?' she asked, standing in front of Lisette and longing for a piece of polished steel to see herself in. 'Ought I to wear just one jewel perhaps?'

'You look like an angel,' replied Lisette, nodding her head fervently. 'They'll be lighting candles to you if you looked any better.'

'Hush, Lisette,' Nicolette rebuked her. 'That's blasphemy.' But she wasn't angry. 'There'll be many fine ladies at the castle this evening and I don't want to let Sir Piers down.'

'You'll not do that. Sir Piers is proud of you even if you was to go in your shift,' Lisette told her smiling.

Nicolette sighed. That was the trouble with Lisette, she was so easily pleased. She looked down at the device on her surcoat. At least now she was a knight's lady and entitled to wear a coat of arms. Her past was behind her and she could take her place among the other ladies without feeling ashamed.

Later, when she and Piers arrived at the castle, she was not quite so sure. The castle was ablaze with torches and the lower court full of horses and servants as the knights and their ladies arrived.

'Goodness,' said Nicolette gazing in awe at the ladies in their lavish dresses weighed down with fur and jewellery. 'If this is just a little feast, what will it be like at Eastertide?'

'Don't worry,' said Piers. 'You're the loveliest by far. I shall have my work cut out defending your favour.' He did not look worried, she thought, watching him. He seemed happier than he had been in months.

They followed the stream of people through the castle's outer bailey and into the great hall, where a harassed steward was busy trying to seat everyone according to their rank and station. Waiting with Piers until such time as the steward might deign to notice them, Nicolette stared about her in fascination at the serried ranks of knights in their colourful tabards. Some were young and handsome, others old and grizzled and battle-scarred, some lean and sinewy, others thickset and bull-necked from a lifetime spent couching a lance in peace and in war. The one thing they all had in common was a hardness of body and keenness of eye so different from the stooped and fleshy-jowled merchants who came to her father's house in Cornhill.

At last the steward found them a place at a table low down in the hall and Nicolette stifled a feeling of disappointment as she took her place on the hard wooden bench beside her husband.

The feast began with a huge lion made of wood being wheeled into the hall out of whose depths came the sound of singing. On his back rode a dwarf who released richly painted birds. Music played and a long line of pages carried a great many dishes to the high table. Crispin, like the other squires, stood behind his master and kept the wine flowing.

Nicolette sipped her wine and gazed about her eagerly as she waited for the food to come down from the high table. She noticed a man with a bushy dark beard and a mass of black hair falling on to his fur-trimmed collar sitting above the salt at the high table. He was arguing hotly across the table, stabbing the air with his dagger to thrust home each point, and there was something about the ruthless vigour of his every action that reminded her irrepressibly of Nicholas Brembre. He tossed off his wine and turned round with the empty cup, looking for his squire, and in so doing caught her watching him. The stare he gave her was bold and long. She returned it coolly, but her heart skipped a beat. She wondered who he was and glanced at Piers, but he was too occupied with the selection of dishes which had now reached their table to notice anything. She, too, applied herself to the cornucopia spread before her, determined not to show any further interest in the black-haired knight.

While Piers ate his way in silence through the many elaborate and varied dishes laid upon the table, Nicolette watched the poor birds flying about the high-vaulted roof, blundering into the rafters in their fright and swooping at the flaring torches in terrified confusion. The dwarf had dismounted from his lion and was running about the hall, in and out and under the trestle tables, much to the amusement of the assembled company. Nicolette looked round the hall for the handsome Italian and once again her eye was caught by the knight who reminded her of Nicholas. This time he raised his silver goblet in salutation. She quickly looked down at her trencher. What should she do if the knight approached her? Would Piers be angry if she were to flirt with some of these delightful young men or would he simply be ashamed of her? She was tempted to make him jealous, to see if she could provoke him enough to make him abandon his impeccable behaviour towards her. How far would Piers go, she wondered, if he were really angered?

With the dishes of the third course a troubadour came to entertain the company. The tale he sang was of a knight who went on a crusade in his lady's service to win her love. She glanced at Piers sitting beside her. He smiled at her with such sweetness that she instantly felt remorse. No, it would be very wicked to make him jealous. That was not the way to prompt him into action. She sighed and picked delicately at her food, keeping her eyes lowered.

The dishes of the third course were removed from the table; the squires, released from their duty of waiting upon the knights, darted off to share the broken meats and the rest of the company left the tables and began to mingle. Nicolette rose from her bench and found the young Italian at her side. For a time she chatted to him easily, and he kept her amused with extravagant compliments and languishing looks from his long-lashed, soulful eyes. Piers stood silently at her side and she wished that just for once he would leave her on her own. Suddenly, without any preamble, the Italian bade her a swift farewell.

'What did I say to frighten him away?' she said laughing up at Piers.

'It wasn't anything you said but the prospect of meeting Mowbray that frightened your champion away,' replied Piers. Over his shoulder she saw the black-haired knight coming purposefully towards them.

'I'm Mowbray,' he announced with what she thought the most perfect arrogance.

'I know,' replied Piers. 'I hear you unhorsed Corsini today. Well done.'

Mowbray's eyes swept over Nicolette, lingering on the low-cut front of her gown then back to her face to hold her eyes with a promisingly wicked gleam. 'The Italian's not a bad jouster if he could only control his horse,' he said with a shrug.

'How do you rate the French champion, Jean de Boucicaut?' asked Piers.

'That I can't tell you, since I only arrived a few days ago and haven't been able to fight him yet.'

'Oh, I am disappointed,' said Piers. 'I thought it must have been you who gave him the injury that put him out of the fighting today.'

Nicolette looked at her husband sharply. He grinned at her but she looked away, embarrassed for him. Mowbray was looking quite put out.

'My husband tells me you are the bravest knight in England,' she said smiling at him.

'Only one of the bravest,' retorted Mowbray modestly. 'Who is your husband?' He was looking at her very hard and she recognised the challenge in his eyes. He was definitely trouble, she thought, delighted.

'Sir Piers Exton,' she said, laying a proprietary hand on Piers's sleeve.

Mowbray grinned down at her. 'He's a lucky man.'

'Did you come with Henry Bolingbroke?' asked Piers.

'With Bolingbroke and eight other knights,' he said, 'including John Beaufort and Thomas Swynford. I hear you've offered a private challenge of your own. Any knight to take your lady's favour from your helm – is that right?'

'That's right.'

'And if I win, do I get to keep the lady or just the favour?' said Mowbray looking not at Piers but at Nicolette. He was almost a head taller than Piers. Strong and bull-necked and powerful – a giant of a man. It was not difficult to imagine him being invincible.

'You won't win,' Nicolette told him, lifting her chin and staring at him defiantly. 'My husband's a mighty jouster. The Italian was frightened of fighting him.'

Mowbray swung round to Piers. 'I've heard of your prowess at Radcot Bridge,' he said. Nicolette blushed with shame. At Radcot Bridge Piers had run away, hadn't he? She glanced at Mowbray and found him staring down at her intently.

'Well, Lady Exton,' he said, 'if I do win the favour, I shall be honoured to fight on your behalf in place of your husband.'

'A fine offer, but I don't think it will be necessary,' said Piers quietly.

'À outrance, Sir Piers?' said Mowbray.

'À outrance of course.'

'What is à outrance?' asked Nicolette.

'Combat fought under war conditions, that is using the normal weapons of war and wearing the normal armour of warfare – no coronals and blunted swords,' explained Mowbray.

'Isn't it dangerous? Why do you have to fight each other? I thought you'd come here to fight against the French.'

'So we have, fair lady,' Mowbray replied. 'But there's no harm in having a bit of sport while we're waiting. It'll be well into Eastertide before the three French defenders get through the English, let alone the rest.'

'And if one of you is injured?'

'Then there'll be one fewer for the French to worry about.'

When the feast was over they rode back through the town to their lodgings in company with many others. Looking at the knights in their multi-coloured tabards and the ladies in their wondrous headdresses and flowing mantles, Nicolette felt a mixture of pride and fear. Pride to be part of so gallant a throng, fear that she should not have encouraged a man like Mowbray to fight her husband. For there was no doubt in Nicolette's mind that Mowbray was fighting Piers to make an impression on her, and she was impressed, and excited, that he might become her champion. But she did not want her husband to be hurt. An innocent flirtation had somehow become a dangerous confrontation and it was all Piers's fault for making it a question of honour.

They reached their lodgings and bade goodnight to what remained of the company. Nicolette slid quickly off her palfrey and ran up the steps to their rooms above the cook shop. Lisette was already asleep on her straw pallet in the room adjoining and Nicolette did not bother to wake her. She did not want Lisette's searching questions tonight. She undressed, slipped into the hard narrow bed and prepared to feign sleep. Piers now always waited for her to be asleep before he came to bed, and she had encouraged his self-denial with her own pretence, although it often left her feeling unaccountably forlorn. But this time when he came to bed at last, instead of remaining stiff and resistant on the edge of the narrow bed, she raised herself on one elbow and let her long silky hair fall across his naked chest like a kiss. He pushed her down almost roughly and turned away from her.

'Don't you want me to love you?' she asked, hurt.

'You don't have to love me just because your conscience is troubling you,' he said. 'Love me tomorrow when I have earned it.'

She lay and contemplated his unrelenting back feeling more guilty than ever. 'I just don't want you to get hurt,' she said quietly.

'Try and have a little more faith in me, Nicolette,' he said to the wall.

'Why do you have to fight *à outrance*? I thought jousting was only a game, why do you have to take it so seriously?'

'I shall always fight for you seriously,' he said.

'You'll make me look such a fool if you lose. What do I say to Mowbray if he insists on becoming my champion?'

'You don't have any confidence in me at all do you?'

'And you don't have any confidence in me,' she retorted, turning her back too. 'How can I show you I'm to be trusted if you're always at my side picking fights with anyone who so much as gives me the time of day?'

'Trust is something you have to earn,' he muttered.

She lay back to back with him, feeling the cold draught of misunderstanding and ill will blowing through the gap between them. So many nights they spent like this, so close together in the darkness yet separated from each other by an invisible portcullis of resentment. It made her feel lonely and unloved.

CHAPTER 22

The tournament was in a meadow outside the walls of the town. It was a scene of such chivalric splendour Nicolette could scarcely believe her eyes. Gaudy pavilions were dotted about the grass like a crop of colourful mushrooms. The largest and most elaborate had the banners, shields and crested helmets of the three French knights, the Chevaliers de Boucicaut, de Roye and de Sempy, who were defending the field. In the centre of the meadow stood the lists, 150 yards long by 100 yards wide with a brightly decorated padded wooden barrier down the centre. The whole was surrounded by a stout fence of stakes. Outside the stockades were booths selling food and drink and goods of every sort, armourers to perform running repairs, blacksmiths to shoe the horses, pedlars with trays of trinkets, friars begging, and even tumblers entertaining the crowds. For those who had not been fortunate enough to find perches on top of the barrier round the lists, there was plenty to do and see apart from the jousting. It was better than a fair, more mercenary than most tournaments. To Nicolette it seemed as if a whole industry had been constructed around the honour of France and she wondered what William Gryffard would have made of it all. Probably money, she thought.

Crispin found her a place in the stands which were already filling up and she took her seat aware that the other ladies were looking at her curiously. She knew that she was well worth a second glance, having dressed to live up to the part she was to play in the elaborate artifice of the tournament. Her pale gold hair was twisted into an elaborate frame of gold wire, over her gown of bright green she wore her surcoat emblazoned with Piers's arms, and jewels.

She sat down calmly, staring out at the spectacle below with serene indifference. She had had much practice in bearing the curious stares of women when accompanying Nicholas Brembre to court. But then she heard someone calling her name. Peering round, she saw Gisela, the flaxen-haired Bohemian who had once been lady-in-waiting to the Queen in London. She was sitting a few rows away and beckoning with a heavily jewelled hand. Surprised but delighted to find at least one familiar face among so many strangers, Nicolette got up and with many gracious apologies clambered carefully past the irate ladies seated between her and Gisela.

'What are you doing here, Nicolette de Saint Pierre?'

'I'm here to watch my husband fight,' she replied. 'And you? Surely the Queen isn't here, is she?'

Gisela explained how she had left the Queen to go back to Bohemia and marry a very good friend of her father's, whose wife had died. 'He's old but he's kind and very rich. He has a great big castle and I have ladies waiting on me now. We've come to watch the Bohemian fight de Sempy. It's his first proper tournament but he's very good. It should be well worth watching.'

When Gisela heard Nicolette was married to Piers, she clapped her hands together gleefully. 'So it's you he's fighting Mowbray for. I might have known. Piers never had eyes for anyone else that Christmas at Westminster. How lucky you are to have a husband like that.' She squeezed Nicolette's hand affectionately and added without a trace of rancour, 'It must be nice to be beautiful.'

Nicolette sighed and turned away from Gisela's placid gaze. It was depressing that everyone thought she should be so happy to be Piers's wife. It made it so much worse that she wasn't.

The day's jousting was opened by the novice Bohemian knight against de Sempy. As the two knights rode at each other time after time from opposite ends of the lists Nicolette watched at first in awe and then, as very little happened save a broken lance from one or the other, with impatience. She began to wonder what all the fuss was about. The Bohemian acquitted himself well for a beginner, breaking nine lances in eighteen courses, but de Sempy was declared the winner for reasons which none of the ladies in the stand seemed to know. What they were far more interested in was the splendour of the two knights' tournament armour.

It was as nothing to the elaborate artifice of the next challenger, a bastard son of Philipe the Bold of Burgundy who arrived in a castle with four towers which opened to reveal him fully armed and on horseback. He had come, they were told by the heralds, in the guise of a knight held prisoner by a self-imposed vow to wear an iron collar as a symbol of his love enslavement. The defenders at St Inglevert, apart from holding the field for the honour of France, had also offered to deliver from their vows any knight who challenged them. Gisela and Nicolette were much impressed by the magnificence of the challenger's arrival; they agreed that he seemed more the heir to one of the greatest lordships in the world than just a bastard of the Burgundian house. His horse, however, flatly refused to come up to the barrier and run the course, so he had to retire without having encountered his opponent.

'Poor young man, now he will have to wear the iron collar until the next tournament,' said Nicolette giggling as she began to enjoy herself.

'He should get a new horse,' said Gisela. 'Or perhaps it would be easier if he were to marry the lady he's sworn to love. He's magnificent enough, I'll swear by Our Lady.'

'But a bastard,' said Nicolette softly.

Gisela did not hear her. Her blue eyes were on the field as two heralds with trumpets marched solemnly towards each other. They announced a joust between Thomas Mowbray, Earl of Nottingham, and a Cheshire knight, Sir Piers of Exton. The challenge was for the favour worn in Sir Piers Exton's helm which the Earl sought to win by a successful combat in courses *à outrance*. If he failed, he was to give Sir Piers a gold rod for his lady.

The crowd cheered as the two knights rode into the arena and took up position at either end of the lists. 'Which one is Piers?' asked Gisela clutching Nicolette's arm in her excitement.

'The one with the leaping unicorn on his helm,' replied Nicolette, gazing at her husband in mingled pride and terror. What had possessed him to make such a foolish, proud challenge? she wondered, terrified that he might disgrace himself – and her – in front of all these people. Impossible to tell if he saw her. The huge helmet hid him from her completely. Tied round the unicorn crest of his helm was the scrap of bright green silk she had given him to wear that morning and despite everything she felt proud to see it fluttering in the wind. Without thinking, she raised her arm to wave to him; the crowd caught sight of the green of her hanging sleeve, which matched the streamer in Piers's helm, and cheered again. She clenched her hands in her lap, dismayed. Now they all knew who she was. Suppose his horse refused to come up to the tilt like the Burgundian bastard's. Her humiliation then would be complete.

The trumpets sounded, the squires released the stamping destriers and the two knights galloped down the field, lances levelled at each other's helms. They drew level on either side of the barrier and barely checked as each lance was skilfully deflected; then they were at the far end of the stockaded rectangle wheeling their chargers and returning to attack again. They met with a resounding crack of breaking wood as lance met shield, and swept on to the far end of the lists to exchange their nine-foot wooden poles for swords. This time they met with a crash of steel as they hacked at each other's shields with their swords.

The restless gossiping crowd suddenly became very quiet. Here was proper fighting. Nicolette saw the rapt expressions on the faces of the watching knights and knew that the struggle being fought out for their entertainment was something different from the morning's sport. She held her breath as the two knights swept down upon each other again and the ferocity of their onslaught was so terrible it brought both horses down in a whirling confusion of flashing hooves and steel. Nicolette leapt to her feet. Crispin and Mowbray's squire were pulling their knights free. Surely it would be over now. Piers had acquitted himself honourably. Both of them were on their feet and apparently unhurt. Then to Nicolette's horror the squires handed them each a battle-axe and they started hacking at each other on foot. She sat down again, feeling weak. Then Mowbray brought his battle-axe down and caught the open end of Piers's gauntlet. Bright blood spouted from his arm. Nicolette closed her eyes. Now it would finish. He had lost, but he had fought well.

She opened her eyes again and could not believe what she saw. Piers was attacking Mowbray ferociously with his shield held in his injured hand and his battle-axe in his left, forcing his opponent relentlessly towards the barriers. Mowbray seemed to have lost his balance and was unable to recover it in the face of such a determined onslaught. He fell and Piers pinned him by his shield to the ground. As the crowd cheered, Nicolette let out her breath in a long sigh. Piers had won!

She waited, while the trumpets sounded, not sure what would happen next but expecting Piers to come to her in the stand and ready to receive him proudly, to weep perhaps a little over his injuries. In front of all these people he had defeated one of the bravest knights in England and she was ready to love him for it. But Piers wasn't coming. He was walking away towards the wooden tilt in the centre of the lists and only then did she notice that one of the horses still lay on the ground where it had fallen. The horse was struggling to rise, kicking with its front legs at the red and cream caparison but its hindquarters dragged on the ground helplessly. Once, twice, three times the animal tried to lurch to its feet and around it a crowd of knights and squires and heralds pulled and shouted at it in vain. Piers pushed them all away and taking his sword from Crispin, held it above his horse's head for an instant. Before Nicolette had time to comprehend what he was doing, he plunged it up to the hilt in the stallion's breast. Blood spouted everywhere, the animal gave a grunt, its limbs thrashed once more in sudden frenzy and finally lay still.

Appalled, Nicolette watched Piers walk away, his armour red with blood, and made to rush out after him, but Gisela's hand on her arm restrained her.

'Let me go, Gisela,' she said. 'I must find out how he is.'

'It's better you wait for his squire to bring you news,' advised Gisela.

'But he loved that horse. I must comfort him.'

'Comfort him tonight, when the leech has had time to dress the wound and he has recovered a little. Men are much better left to themselves at times like these.'

Nicolette had to acknowledge that it was good advice. She would make it up to him tonight. At the thought, her senses quickened. 'Love me tomorrow,' he'd said, 'when I've earned it.' Well he had earned her love now and she would show him how she could love. 'Sweet Mary, Mother of Jesus, let him not be too hurt for it,' she prayed.

A knight came riding back into the enclosure and Nicolette hoped it might be Piers. But then she noted the red and gold mulberry trees embroidered on the caparison and the crouching lion on the knight's helm and knew it to be Mowbray. He rode up to the front of the stand and saluted her. She froze, not knowing what to do.

'Go on,' Gisela pushed her forward. 'He brings the ransom he has to pay.'

Carefully Nicolette walked down to the front of the loge, all too aware that she was once more the centre of attention. Mowbray leapt from his horse and on bended knee presented her with a baton of gold in recognition of his defeat.

'Is my husband badly hurt?' she asked him, stooping to receive it.

'No need to worry, my lady. The leech has staunched the bleeding. He may have a broken bone or two in his hand. He'll live to fight another day and then I shall be waiting to get my revenge.' He rose to his feet and stood towering over her, his eyes glittering through his visor. 'I've taken a liking to that favour of yours.' He rode off and she went back to sit by Gisela feeling far from triumphant.

The last challenge of the day was between Henry Bolingbroke, Earl of Derby, and the French defender de Roye. The two knights were well matched and fought with panache but although the honour of England and of France was at stake, the battle lacked the ferocity of the previous fight.

When it was over, the prize of a pearl on a golden chain for the best fighter of the day went to Piers. Watching him walk up to the dais to receive the prize, Nicolette was all the more proud for not having expected him to be quite so victorious.

That night, as they lay in bed alone together at last, Piers did not behave at all like a victor.

'I'm sorry, Nicolette,' he said kissing her tentatively. 'I seem to have made a mess of it as usual.'

'But you won,' she said kissing him back. 'You defeated Mowbray, the bravest knight in England. You have the prize for the best fighter of the day. I'm so proud of you.'

'But I don't know when I'll be able to fight again,' he said, drawing away from her. She bent over him and brushed his bandaged arm gently with her lips.

'Your hand, is it very bad?' she whispered.

'Never mind the hand, it will mend,' he said. 'But where am I to find another war horse in a place like this?'

'Surely you can buy another horse?' she said. From the light of the moon shining through the unshuttered window she could see him lying on his back staring up at the raftered ceiling.

'You don't understand, Nicolette,' he said. 'Good horses trained to battle are as scarce as water in the desert.'

'You can have the gold rod you won for me from Mowbray,' she offered with what she thought was generous self-denial.

'The knights here can't be bought with that paltry piece of gold,' he said scornfully. 'They're men of substance.'

'They can't all be. Look at you,' she retorted, stung.

'I'd never sell my horse at a tournament,' he said, 'no matter how much I was offered for it. Without a horse a knight is no better than an archer or a pikeman.'

'Every man has his price,' she said. 'That's what my father always says.'

'Master Gryffard thinks he bought me, doesn't he?' Piers turned towards her at last. 'Is that what you think too?'

But she was not going to be drawn into a fruitless argument over William Gryffard and his opinions. Not here, not tonight. Tonight she was trying for a victory of her own. 'What about the Bastard of Burgundy?' she said, snuggling up to him. 'I'm sure he doesn't want that horse of his that refused to come up to the tilt.'

He pulled her to him with his good arm. 'By the Virgin, I believe you've got something there,' he exclaimed, kissing her. 'You're as clever as you're beautiful.'

'Is that why you love me?' she asked, kissing him back. Now perhaps he would make love to her.

'I'd love you if you were neither,' he said returning her kisses almost absently. 'I'll make him an offer tomorrow while he's still smarting over the indignity of today's defeat. I just might get him to sell it to me then.' She slid down on to his chest and kissed him until he forgot his horse and his aching wound and kissed her back in earnest. She felt her body come alive after months of stupid self-imposed abstinence. His kisses were sweet and her flesh was beginning to tingle with joy. But all too soon he was groaning in ecstasy and then he was holding her tenderly in his arms telling her how much he loved her.

She lay listening to his protestations of love, trying to subdue the feeling of restless resentment which threatened to overwhelm her. His love was a disappointment. Where was the fire, the passion of love which she longed for? That was merely lust, William Gryffard would say, and lust was a deadly sin. She laid her head on her husband's breast and wished she did not feel so sinful. He stroked her hair gently, murmuring endearments. All too soon his caressing voice ceased, his breathing became deep and regular. Despondency swept over her. Piers had shown plenty of fire today in the lists. Did he only care then for fighting? Was all his talk of love just an excuse for that?

The next day Piers was burning with fever, the wound on his arm so swollen and angry Nicolette did not dare touch it. The leech when Crispin fetched him to their lodgings told Nicolette it was nothing to worry about. Wounds were inclined to fester but as long as they were left open to the air to let the poison out and the patient kept still until the fever abated, they would heal with God's good grace. He then produced some balm to smear on the wound, bled Piers and told Nicolette he would return on the morrow. No sooner had the leech departed than Piers was struggling to get out of bed.

'I must find the Burgundian – get him to sell me his horse before it's too late,' he muttered.

'I'll go,' she told him, pushing him back on to the bed. 'If you don't do what the doctor tells you that arm will never heal and then what use will it be to have a horse?'

'You're right,' he said lying back with a grimace. 'But don't give too much for him. The horse needs a great deal of work before he'll be much use.'

'I'll get the best bargain I can. Am I not my father's daughter, after all?' she retorted, unable to resist the taunt.

But he was too exhausted from the leech's ministrations to argue with her. 'Take Crispin, he'll look after you in my place,' he said, protective to the last. He looked so pale and ill, Nicolette doubted very much if he would be able to take

274

any more part in the tourney but she thought it best to humour him. She dressed carefully and went in search of the natural son of the House of Burgundy.

Nicolette found him as charming as he was flamboyant and agreeably susceptible to her beauty. He even went so far as to promise, if he could succeed against either de Roye or de Boucicaut and rid himself of his love enslavement, to don the iron collar again and become her vassal instead. Since without his splendid armour he was older, fatter and altogether less romantic than he had appeared at the tournament, she was alarmed by the prospect of such homage and only encouraged him enough to get his horse for nothing.

After a week, Piers's fever subsided. The wound on his arm looked terrible to Nicolette but Piers dismissed it as of no account and began riding practice tilts on the new horse with Crispin. As the tournament went on from day to day all through March and on into April, Nicolette grew bored watching knight after knight charging each other. Sometimes Gisela's husband joined them in the stands. He had been a jouster of some renown in his day and was delighted to explain to Nicolette the significance of every blow given and received. It did not seem to Nicolette to add up to very much – a hit or a miss, a lance broken or dropped, a knight unhelmed or unhorsed, a horse out of control, or even a refusal by both horses to charge again. She felt sorry for Gisela, for he was very old and very dull and yet remarkably robust.

If Piers had been jousting, it might have been different. But Piers was preoccupied with his battle to make the horse a bolder charger and determined to ignore the pain from his injured hand. In vain she urged him to stop the daily practice tilts, to wait at least until his hand had healed, but he was obdurate.

'You want me to win, don't you?' he would say and she felt unjustly accused. If only Piers did not expect so much from her all the time. Thomas Mowbray had no such illusions. He was wicked and all he offered was temptation.

After Mowbray jousted against the great de Boucicaut and broke several spears and upheld the honour of England, Nicolette forgot all her good intentions and congratulated him warmly.

'I can see your husband's not making much headway with

that horse of the Bastard's,' said Mowbray. 'Does he fight in the mêlée on Easter Monday?'

'I didn't know there was going to be a mêlée,' said Nicolette.

'Henry Bolingbroke is getting it up – the English against the rest – to celebrate Eastertide, with feasting and dancing in the castle at night. Hasn't he asked Sir Piers?'

'Piers isn't ready yet to fight,' she told him.

'Well of course Bolingbroke doesn't want a man with an injured sword arm on his side and everyone knows that horse of the Bastard's is useless. I'd offer to lend your husband one of mine, but he's an impetuous devil and needs a pretty strong hand on the rein.' He was looking at her boldly, his dark eyes full of a most exciting devilment. 'As do you, Lady Exton, I shouldn't wonder,' he added. She glanced over her shoulder and saw Piers standing on his own watching her. She felt a pang of pity mixed with pride. Piers was as good as any of them; it wasn't fair that Mowbray should belittle him just because he'd been unlucky.

'Be careful, my lord,' she said, resentment making her rash. 'Piers is so very protective.'

'He has much to be protective of,' Mowbray told her.

'And has proved himself a staunch protector,' she told him, lifting her chin and gazing at him with challenge in her eyes.

'I doubt if he could do it again, so don't provoke me too far,' said Mowbray.

'What would it take – to provoke you?' She knew she was playing with fire but she couldn't resist it. She was so bored and he reminded her so much of Nicholas. She was sure Mowbray would be exciting in bed.

'A kiss perhaps?'

She pouted at him prettily. 'Then I must be sure not to provoke you too far. I would not like my husband to have to vanquish you a second time.'

'It was by the merest ill fortune he vanquished me the first time. If I had not been distracted by that cut I gave him I would never have been taken off guard. I didn't like to take advantage of him, it's not usually done in friendly jousts.'

'I didn't know *à outrance* was all that friendly,' she said, disappointed. For all his splendour he was a bad loser. Abruptly she left him to join Piers, determined not to encourage Mowbray any more. Piers was dressed in his old leather gambesons, stained and dark with smudges where his armour had left its mark, and his face was streaked with sweat. He said nothing, just looked at her with such disappointment in his eyes that she turned away hurriedly, besieged by guilt. She told herself that it did not matter. He was not fighting in the mêlée and if at the last hour Bolingbroke chose him, he would be on the same side as Mowbray with the English. It was only a game – she and Mowbray were playing. It was silly of Piers to take everything she did so seriously.

The night before the mêlée, Nicolette found Crispin busy polishing Piers's armour in their lodgings and discovered that Piers was to fight after all, on the opposite side to the English. The Italian had invited him because there were too many English.

Crispin was very worried. He sat on the bare wooden floor with his back to the wall, pursuing specks of rust with relentless zeal, and told Nicolette that Piers was not yet fit to fight. The horse was useless, his sword arm too weak to hold a lance properly, and he wouldn't be doing it if it weren't for her. Of course she chastised him but she knew in her heart that he was right. It did not help when Lisette, too, shook her head and told her that beauty was a gift from God, a responsibility as well as a boon. She tried to persuade Piers not to fight.

'What else can I do except fight?' he told her. 'I didn't bring you all the way to France to lose you to Thomas Mowbray.'

'Piers, it's a game, can't you see? Everyone plays it – except you. Mowbray is only interested in me because he knows it inflames you.'

'I know that, Nicolette,' he said, much to her surprise. 'Tournament fighting is not interesting enough for the spectators unless we dress it up a little. That's why we need you ladies to give us something worth fighting over. I have the most beautiful lady at the tournament and the worst horse. It's the sort of challenge I enjoy.'

She was somewhat shaken. Did he not care for her at all then? Was it all some chivalric dream and she just a symbol? Was Piers, too, playing games? She went to bed that night feigning sleep as she used to do and to her fury he made no attempt to wake her. He didn't love her. It was all make-believe, like the Burgundian's ridiculous vows, the gilded turrets, the elaborate pageants at mealtimes. Piers was a different man here among all these other knights; among his own kind he was stronger, tougher than she had suspected, and she was proud of him. But his slavish devotion which once she had thought so tiresome wasn't real. She lay against the warm naked body of her sleeping husband and vowed to make him sorry. If Piers wanted to play games then so could she.

CHAPTER 23

Through the slits of his visor Piers studied the twenty knights lined up at the far end of the lists. They were packed so close together it was impossible to see the colours on their horses' caparisons, and the crests on their helms were too far away to identify, for all their flamboyant idiosyncracy. Nor could he see the stands on either side; the all-encompassing helmet shut them off from his view, but he knew Nicolette was there watching.

She was too beautiful for her own good, he thought, but that was why he had to fight for her. He was well aware that as an unknown knight without a noble patron he would never have been given the chance of a fight *à outrance* against no less a knight than Thomas Mowbray, Earl of Nottingham, had it not been for Nicolette. Her beauty and her mischievous tricks had ensured that every knight of any consequence was anxious to accept his challenge. He should be glad, he told himself angrily, to have the chance to prove himself against so many worthwhile opponents, and he was glad, he just wished that he did not have to go on proving himself to Nicolette, that he could count on her loving support in what he was trying to do.

He lowered the lance carefully and raised it again, testing the weight of it, hoping that his injured arm would stand up to the work it would have to do. He wanted to give a good account of himself today, not just for his wife's sake but because de Boucicaut, the young French champion, was leading their side against the English.

The horse Achilles was trembling so much, with fear or excitement, that the red trefoils on the flowing caparison were dancing. Piers ran a gauntleted hand down the

279

creature's powerful neck. 'Easy, boy, easy,' he soothed. 'This is always the worst time – the waiting.' Achilles was a good horse, strong and well balanced with all the agility so important in a war horse, but he wasn't very bold. The trembling continued unabated. Pray God it was excitement. Beside him Stephano Corsini's horse was pawing impatiently at the ground and Piers wondered if the Italian would be able to hold his splendid destrier in check when the trumpets sounded.

The mêlée was the form of jousting most like real warfare and Piers liked it best for that reason. In a mêlée it was important not to charge too fast and to fight in close order in disciplined groups; Jean de Boucicaut specialised in waiting until the opposing group had broken up before attacking and would then charge them on the flank and hunt down any isolated knights. It was a good tactic for a mêlée. Piers hoped the Italian would not prove to be one of those knights who launched himself like an arrow down the lists and hoped to make contact.

The trumpet sounded the signal to begin and Achilles backed nervously. Piers dug his spurs in mercilessly. The horse bounded forward but Piers checked him with a jerk of the reins as he lowered his lance. If they broke ranks now, or tried to be first into the fight, their action might result in defeat for their side. He swung round awkwardly to get a glimpse of de Boucicaut. Through the corner of the visor he saw the French champion had not moved. Piers held his lance loosely in his injured hand and stared down the lists, his body tingling with expectancy but not yet tensed for action. To brace too tightly caused the lance to deviate from its target and so he always waited until the point of impact before tightening his grip.

They were coming. A wall of bristling steel, charging head on, each knight aiming for his opposite number to the left, the lance couched across his horse's neck and aiming for his opponent's shield. Piers squeezed Achilles forward, keeping pace with the Bohemian knight on his left, but on his right he caught a glimpse of the Italian surging past, whether by intent or because his horse was out of control, Piers did not know. But he could not hang back and let Corsini take the brunt of the English attack. He plunged his spurs relentlessly into Achilles and galloped after the Italian.

A knight was charging down towards him and he felt the shock of impact on his injured arm as his lance hit the other's shield, but the first pain was always the worst; he ignored it and concentrated on parrying the knight's lance with his own shield. But instead of surging forward, Achilles hesitated just too long and what should have been a glancing blow on Piers's shield landed with such force he was only saved by the high jousting saddle from being swept off over the animal's tail.

Seeing a gap open in front of him and obedient at last to the spurs raking his flanks, Achilles was galloping from the fray. Piers turned him with a vicious pull on the rein, peering through the narrow slit of his visor to survey the field. De Boucicaut was holding the line steady in the centre, the far left was wavering but locked in combat; on the right all was chaos, out of which a knight came charging at Piers like a steel thunderbolt. Piers urged his horse forward and this time took the other's lance first on his shield before thrusting his own lance towards the knight's helm. It was parried by a shield and shattered with the force of the blow. Piers threw away the broken lance, whirled Achilles round as he tugged at his sword and next thing he knew he was lying flat on his back on the ground with all the breath knocked out of him, braced for a kick from a flying hoof. Instead he was yanked upright; he caught a glimpse of a golden helm and recognised the crest of Corsini, fighting far better without his horse.

In the brief respite the Italian had won for him, Piers again surveyed the field. He saw the blue and white plumes of France fluttering from de Boucicaut's helm; he was still mounted and riding a course with a knight with the red and gold of England on his caparison – Bolingbroke. Suddenly Piers received a numbing blow on his arm just above his gauntlet, right on his wound. Pain made him dizzy as his sword spun from his hand and he recognised the lion on the crest of his opponent's helm. Desperately he groped for a weapon and found a sword thrust into his hand by Corsini. Piers leapt at Mowbray, a blinding vision of Nicolette looking up at the man, her eyes full of mischief, driving from his mind all reason. He was so fuelled with rage he was unaware of pain or danger or tactics. It was as if he was exorcising all the frustration and bitterness of the last months, hacking at his enemy with the blind fury of a man demented.

When at last he returned to his senses several knights had a hold of him and Mowbray was being helped from the field, his armour covered in blood. Piers looked about him in dazed surprise and became aware that the battle was over; his arm was aching abominably and his sword was gone. Jean de Boucicaut and Henry Bolingbroke, both still mounted but without their huge helmets, were staring down at him. Bolingbroke held a sword, its naked point bloodied. 'To substitute a sharp weapon for a blunted one in a friendly tourney is a foul,' he said as he threw the sword at Piers's feet. Piers picked it up appalled but did not recognise it for his own. He opened his mouth to object and then remembered fumbling for his sword in the heat of the battle. Corsini had come to his rescue. He looked at the weapon in his hand. If it were the Italian's sword then Corsini had broken the tournament rules. The Italian was unworthy of his knighthood. It was unforgivable to try to gain advantage by cheating. Of course his squire may have given him the wrong sword by mistake. Piers did not want to believe ill of a man who had come to his rescue. But then Corsini should have noticed the sword's sharp edge. But so should Piers. The moment he attacked his adversary he should have known. He would have noticed, if he had not been lost to all reason. He stared at the ground, covered in shame. He was no better than Corsini. It was unforgivable for a knight to lose his temper in a tournament. A fully armed knight could so easily kill an opponent in the heat of the moment. It did not help that he had wounded unfairly a man of higher rank, an earl, one of the all-powerful lords appellant.

'No doubt he was sorely provoked,' he heard the Frenchman say.

'A knight who breaks the rules of a tournament has to be punished,' replied Bolingbroke.

'Agreed.' De Boucicaut was not going to plead any further for an Englishman. 'Will you pronounce sentence?'

'I think perhaps he should not be allowed to attend the dancing this evening.' Piers could not believe his ears at so lenient a sentence. He looked up in surprise and found Bolingbroke smiling down at him. 'You fight well, Sir Piers. I'd like to have you by my side in real warfare.' Piers, relieved and grateful, smiled back. Henry Bolingbroke was a man he would willingly follow wherever he might care to lead.

As soon as he could, Piers hurried to Bolingbroke's tent where they had taken Mowbray. He met the leech coming out. 'You're keeping me busy, young man, one way and another,' he said with what Piers felt was macabre cheerfulness. To his anxious inquiries the leech replied that Mowbray had lost some blood but he had staunched the bleeding with the application of powdered blue vitriol and he would recover provided he did not succumb to a fever. Piers left feeling relieved. He had sinned, albeit unwittingly, but he had got away with it. Then he remembered Nicolette. She would be so disappointed not to go to the dancing.

The disrobing tent was crowded with knights and their squires, all full of the kind of comradely high spirits that come to men who have shared violent action and survived unscathed. Crispin was waiting, his eyes full of accusation.

'I found your sword on the tournament ground,' he said. 'It's blunted, as I knew it was.'

'Good,' said Piers, and held out the sword the Italian had given him. 'You can give this to Corsini's squire and, Crispin, do it quietly, will you? If it had not been for Corsini coming to my aid, we'd not have been able to bring my lady's favour back a second time.' Crispin opened his mouth to protest. 'You'll obey me in this, Crispin,' Piers added sternly. 'And not a word to anyone as you value my friendship.' Crispin flushed a dull red but said nothing as he began to strip Piers of his armour.

Piers paid no attention to the teasing and the boasting of the other knights as they relived the excitement of the mêlée, comparing tactics, claiming conquests, each man anxious to have his own part in the fighting acknowledged or justified. Piers did not need the flattery of frightened men released from fear. As a fighter he knew his own worth. It was as a husband he felt himself to be wanting. What should he do? Let his wife go to the castle without him tonight? That would be the noble way. Did he dare? She accused him of not having enough confidence in her. Should he test her now? He hoped so much that when he gave her the chance she would choose to stay with him. He had proved his worth. Brought her favour out of the battlefield a second time against all the odds. Surely she would love him now.

But when Nicolette was offered the choice of sharing his punishment or going dancing without him, she chose to go to the castle.

'Crispin will be my protector, won't you, Crispin?' she said, smiling radiantly at the startled squire and if Piers had not felt so wretched he would have been amused at the look of dismay on Crispin's face. Instead he felt sick with disappointment. His noble gesture had been in vain.

Lisette fetched food for him from the cook shop below and Crispin brought a flagon of wine. Piers bore their concern ungratefully. His arm was throbbing abominably, and he was bruised all over from his fall. He wanted to shout at them to be gone if they were going and to leave him to bear his sorrows alone. Instead he lay on the bed and watched Nicolette make ready. She was wearing a sheath of some silky damask with a sweeping train trimmed with fur. Round her white neck she wore the pearl on the golden chain he had won at the tournament and round her slender hips a girdle of chased silver.

'Will I be a credit to you, my husband?' she asked, turning slowly in front of him, so self-absorbed in pleasurable anticipation that she seemed incapable of comprehending his pain.

'Take care of your mistress, Lisette,' he said, levering himself up off the bed, his muscles aching.

Lisette watched him with her head on one side, like a faithful hound intuitively sensing his distress. 'I'd sooner stay here and take care of you, young master,' she said, beaming at him. 'She'll not want me there, not among all those grand people.'

'But I want you there,' he told her. 'My lady needs someone to carry her train and Crispin needs his sword arm free to fight off all her admirers.' Even in his own ears the joke sounded bitter. He went with them down the stairs and out into the street where Crispin had the horses waiting.

'I shall be good, you'll see,' said Nicolette, flinging her arms round his neck and kissing him lightly on the cheek. He lifted her on to her palfrey without a word, too depressed to trust himself to speak, then seized Lisette and hoisted her up behind Crispin, his wounded arm stabbing with pain in protest. Even then he wanted to plead with Nicolette not to go, to stay with him and share his punishment as she had shared his triumph. But he clenched his teeth until she was gone, riding down the street with her mantle floating out behind her over the palfrey's rump and her head in its elaborate headdress held high.

Returning to the small chamber above the cook shop, Piers threw himself down upon the bed again, sunk in gloom. What had happened to his perfect lady? He had thought that her innocent goodness had been tainted by Brembre. That once that dragon was slain, his lady would become perfect again. Then he had concluded that it was William Gryffard who was corrupting her. He lay on the bed and stared up at the raftered ceiling above his head. He had done everything he could to win her. He didn't see what else he could do. Perhaps it wasn't Brembre who had corrupted her, perhaps she had loved Brembre because she was evil. Sweet Jesus. Piers sat up suddenly and groaned aloud. She was so vulnerable at times, so selfish at others and looked so impossibly beautiful always that even if she was evil he could not stop wanting her. He was bewitched.

He ate the meat pasties Lisette had fetched for him and drank all the wine. Then he lay down again and fell into an uneasy sleep. When he awoke he was lying in a shaft of moonlight as bright as the day, but Nicolette still had not come back. He got up and leant out of the window. A full moon was riding high in the sky, bathing the town in white light. He looked up and down the quiet street with its banners hanging lifeless in the still air. There was no sign of her.

He felt suddenly wide awake and restless, unable to remain cooped up in the small deserted chamber any longer. He took his sword and ran down the stairs into the street. A terrible sense of foreboding gripped him. He began to run down the street in the direction of the castle until his throbbing arm and bruised and aching limbs got the better of him. He paused at the end of the street for breath and heard horses' iron-shod hooves ringing on the cobblestones. He waited, panting, until they came within sight. Two horses, one with a pillion passenger, the other a palfrey with a lady in a flowing mantle, came trotting towards him. With a sigh of relief he recognised Nicolette.

'What are you doing out here in the middle of the night?'

she asked, reining in beside him while the other horse with its burden of two continued down the street.

'I was worried about you. It's late,' he said, feeling foolish.

'There was no need. Crispin looked after me very well.'

Piers took hold of the palfrey's bridle and began to retrace his steps towards their lodgings, not looking at her, his eyes on the squire and the maid riding ahead. Some awkwardness in the way Crispin dismounted made him instantly alert.

'What's the matter with Crispin?' he demanded as he lifted Nicolette out of the saddle.

'It's nothing, he's tired. Leave him alone.' She turned away from him quickly as soon as he set her on her feet and Piers knew she was lying.

Crispin was waiting to stable the horses and Piers threw the palfrey's reins at him carelessly. The boy lunged to catch them with his right hand, winced, missed and with a sheepish air bent down and picked them up from the ground with his left.

'Your right arm, let me see it!' Piers exclaimed.

'It's nothing, the merest scratch,' muttered the boy.

'I'll be the judge of that,' snapped Piers, grabbing his squire by his hand and holding it none too gently. The boy's face was white but he gripped Piers firmly enough. Then Piers noticed a long tear in the emerald sleeve of his doublet, from the elbow to the wrist. Gently he probed beneath with his finger and found it wet with blood.

'A dagger did that. You've been careless, Crispin,' he said trying to hold back his anger.

'Not careless, brave,' Nicolette's voice sounded all too proudly in his ear.

'Mowbray?' he demanded, so angry he forgot that Mowbray was in no fit state to seduce anyone.

'No, not Mowbray. The Burgundian Bastard,' she said and he thought he detected a tiny note of pride in her voice.

'You whore!' Piers rounded on her furiously. 'You're not content to have me fight for you. Your vanity is so gross you must have Crispin too.'

'It wasn't her fault. The Burgundian kept pestering her. I didn't think you would want him to think that because you weren't there he could make a nuisance of himself. But he's no fighter, the Burgundian. He's done me no harm.' As Crispin prattled on with his excuses, Piers could hardly believe his ears. Crispin, the silent, efficient, practical soldier-in-waiting, she'd bewitched him too. It was the last straw.

'See to the horses as best you can,' he ordered. 'And you, Lisette, go help him. Then tend that wound.'

The maid folded her arms and looked mulish. 'What of my lady?' she demanded.

'You can leave my lady to me,' he promised. 'I'm going to beat her.' Ignoring Lisette's protestations, he seized Nicolette by the wrist. 'I should have done it a long time ago.'

He dragged her up the stairs, kicked open the door of their chamber and hurled Nicolette across the room so roughly that she fell across the bed. She lay staring at him like a wounded hind while he slammed the door shut and looked about him for something to beat her with. All he had was his sword belt. It took him some time to unbuckle the leather girdle and disentangle his sword. Finally, holding the strap in his hand, he turned to the bed, fully intending to use it to good purpose. But Nicolette had taken off her finery and was sitting bathed in moonlight on the edge of the bed, her hair hanging in long silky tresses about her nakedness, like some sort of goddess of the night.

Desire ripped through him fuelling his anger. He dropped the sword belt and hit her across the side of her face with the flat of his hand. 'Whore!' he shouted, demented with rage. She fell backwards across the bed, her eyes blank with shock. He leapt on her, crushing her mouth so fiercely he tasted blood on his tongue. Then he took her as he would a woman he had paid for, using her body mercilessly as he strove for release. But anger had him in its grip and would not let go. She struggled and he crushed her with his powerful body. He had no thought of pleasing her. Fury drove him, to hurt, to punish; he did not care, hardly knew what he was doing. She moaned and he paid no heed. She moaned again and cried out.

This time he paused, looked into her eyes. They were wet with tears. His anger changed to passion; he drove on and on and on, encouraged by her smooth, agile body, her mouth filling his with fragrance, her hunger matching his, until at last he was within sight of the Holy Grail, reached for it and was rewarded with a fleeting sense of immortality as he clutched her to him. He was angry no more, but blissfully, totally in love as he held her, and she clung to him, murmuring his name and moulding her body into his. All night long he made love to her tenderly, passionately, endlessly, until at last she fell asleep in the dawn with her head cradled on his shoulder and her abundant hair strewn across his body like a curtain of silk.

Nicolette awoke to bright sunlight still cradled within his arm. For a while she lay there, relaxed and at peace, savouring this strange new feeling of security. Piers had killed her demons for her, exorcised the ghost of Nicholas Brembre. She turned her head to look at her husband and found him gazing at her with troubled eyes.

'What's the matter, my beloved?' she asked, leaning back against his encircling arm the better to see his face.

'Nothing,' he said smiling down at her. 'You looked so pure and innocent. I thought perhaps I must have dreamt it all.'

She wasn't disturbed, not then. She was only conscious of her glowing body, already tingling with renewed anticipation. 'No, you didn't dream it,' she said trailing her hand down his strong thigh and marvelling at the feel of the hard muscles beneath her fingertips, 'but I never dreamt you could be such a wonderful lover.'

He groaned and pulled her against him. 'Teach me how to love you better,' he murmured hoarsely and she took him at his word and showed him how to make even their two satiated bodies catch fire again.

At first Nicolette was so filled with happiness she was unaware that anything was wrong. Piers still guarded her jealously, but now she revelled in his possessiveness. He was a success at last and she was content to be his slave. Once he had thrown off his fear of hurting her with too much ardour, he proved an apt and willing pupil at learning how to give her pleasure. She taught him much for she was well practised in the art of love but he brought something else which she had never known before. A tenderness and unselfishness which had been entirely missing from the animal passion she had aroused in Brembre. What she had felt for Brembre had been lust as destructive as it had been evil. William Gryffard had known and tried to warn her. All too often her father proved to be right in the end, but he was wrong about love, she thought. William did not believe in love because he had never found it.

Love made her more intuitive and it was because she now loved Piers truly that she gradually became aware that he was troubled about something. He hid it well and she did not dare upset their new-found pleasure in each other by asking him dangerous questions, but deep down in her heart she was afraid of what troubled him. Then one day she learnt that Henry Bolingbroke was going to join the Duke of Bourbon's crusade against the infidel on the Barbary coast and had invited Piers to go with him.

'You won't go, will you?' she asked, her fear leaping out at her and making her stupid.

'Of course I shall go,' he replied almost harshly. 'It's a great honour. Bolingbroke is a terrific soldier. The more I see of him, the more I like him. At last I've found a cause worth fighting for and a man worth fighting with. It will be a fine crusade.'

'But what about me?'

'I'll see you safely back to England of course.' Piers was deliberately misunderstanding her, she knew; he would not meet her gaze. 'Bolingbroke is going back to England to raise troops and horses. We can travel with his train. It will be far more comfortable for you than our previous journeyings.'

She turned away from him to hide her disappointment. She did not want him to know how much he had hurt her.

'Louis de Clermont isn't setting out until late in the summer,' he went on. 'We're going to attack Tunis, the lair of the Barbary corsairs. It should be a great adventure.' Piers seemed determined not to recognise her dismay. He loved her, she knew that, but he was ashamed of his love which was why he was going on a crusade. It made her feel terribly afraid. She could not bear to lose him now.

Piers knew he had failed her but he was so confused he could do nothing about it. On the day that he had won his lady, he had lost control of his emotions. Twice in the same day he had totally lost his temper, broken every instinct of chivalry. Nicolette was his prize, yet he felt tainted. He could not reconcile the wanton, sensuous woman who drove him mad with delight each night with the perfect lady he wanted to love with blind, uncritical devotion. He knew he had won a pearl beyond price, that every knight at St Inglevert envied him. He was proud of her, so proud he was bursting with it, but he was frightened too, frightened of the tide of passion which swept him away every night when they made love in the small mean chamber above the cook shop, afraid that his perfect lady was far from perfect and that he was too enslaved by his passionate nature to want to change her. He was no longer his own man and it frightened him. And so it seemed like the answer to all his difficulties when Henry Bolingbroke asked him to go on this crusade. Here at last was a cause worth fighting for, better than all these tournament games, a chance to prove his real worth and find inner peace away from the distraction and confusion of women.

CHAPTER 24

Alice Whittington walked in her garden, savouring the spring sunshine. It was quite a small garden but large enough to hold a little fishpond and some neat beds of pot herbs and scented flowers.

She sat down on a stone seat to enjoy the view of the river and the bridge just visible beyond the bulk of the Church of St Michael Paternoster. She bent down and picked a sprig of rosemary and gillyflower, holding it to her nose to banish the smell from the privy pit behind the dovecote. It was a pity that Dick did not want to buy land – to return to his roots in Gloucestershire, for instance, now that he was doing so well. She sighed. It would be a fine thing if they could have escaped from the city in summer to enjoy the fresh air and cool peaceful quiet of a manor in the country like all the other rich and successful merchant families. But of course Dick was not like other merchants, she thought a little sadly. She had known he was destined for great things when he was just one of her father's apprentices. He used to talk to her about how one day he would be Mayor and change the city, how he would help the poor and conquer injustice; it wasn't lover's talk but she had listened enthralled by his vision and when at last he was admitted to the freedom of the Mercers' Company and her father had arranged for him to marry her, she had been the happiest girl in the Mercery.

That was thirteen years ago. She was no longer an innocent impressionable girl but a married woman of twenty-eight. She was growing old, with no children to comfort her. Dick now had four apprentices learning their trade through him; he lent money to noblemen, sold cloth of gold to the King;

had shops in Castle Barnard Ward near the King's Wardrobe and in Billingsgate; and yet he did not seem any nearer to being Mayor. Why, he was not even an alderman. She did not mind for herself. But she knew that Dick was still striving, that having set his heart on something he would never give up. London was what he wanted and he would never be happy building castles in the country.

She was so absorbed in thought she did not hear the faint jingling of spurs or notice the knight walking into her garden until his shadow fell across the grass in front of her. She looked up startled. It was Piers.

'I'm sorry to come barging into your garden to disturb you,' he said. 'I was looking for Master Whittington and your steward sent me out here.'

'The steward knows Master Whittington has gone out,' she said abruptly, knowing that she looked hot and untidy from having spent most of the morning in the kitchen. He was obviously taken aback and she realised that as usual her shyness had made her sound rude. 'Dick will be home for dinner, won't you stay and have it with us?' she said more gently. 'I know he will be longing to hear all about your adventures at Saint Inglevert.'

'With pleasure,' he replied, grinning at her with disarming openness. 'How did you know that was what I really came for? Some horses are for sale out at Cripplegate. I'll go now and look at them and call in again on my way back.' He looked happy, she thought, and was glad because she liked him.

'Did it go well for you then at the jousting?' she asked.

'Yes, it did go well. Very well.' He smiled at her so joyfully she guessed that it was not only the jousting that had gone well. She felt pleased knowing that it had been her suggestion that he should take Nicolette with him to France. Perhaps the marriage which had begun so inauspiciously would turn out blessed in the end. It ought to, she thought, for Piers had the gentle courtesy and steadfast courage but none of the overbearing arrogance of a knight.

'How is your wife?' she asked. A shadow crossed his face.

'I'm going on crusade with Henry Bolingbroke,' Piers told her. 'Nicolette doesn't want me to go. I thought,' he hesitated, looked at her beseechingly, 'would you look after her for me? She may be lonely while I'm away.'

'I doubt whether any girl as beautiful as your Nicolette will be lonely for very long,' retorted Alice.

He looked troubled. 'That's what I mean. She's so beautiful and impulsive. She can't help it, I know. But it might make a difference if she had someone to guide her a little, a companion of similar background and breeding. She's well educated and intelligent and would benefit so much from your company.'

Alice could not help feeling pleased. The compliment he paid her was all the more beguiling because she knew he meant it. Piers would never try to get his way with false praise but he knew instinctively how to bring out the best in people.

'Can you not find a gentlewoman to wait upon her?' she suggested. 'Her tiring woman is only a simple French peasant, hardly a suitable companion for a girl such as Nicolette.'

'Lisette is devoted to my wife and speaks her own language. I could not possibly replace her,' he said.

It was hard to resist the appeal in his eyes. Alice was not accustomed to being begged for favours by young knights as personable and unassuming as Piers Exton, yet she was determined not to take Nicolette into her household. She did not want to become another Idonia Brembre. So she promised nothing and watched him leave, her pleasure in the bright May morning a little sullied, as if a small dark stain had suddenly appeared on an otherwise snowy white cloth.

Richard Whittington returned home at noon and seemed pleased that Piers was to dine with them. 'We'd better have the Burley cups to drink from as it's a special occasion,' he said.

He walked over to the trestle at the side of the hall and picked up two of the biggest silver goblets, laying them one at a time almost reverently on the table. Alice told him about the crusade that Piers was going on with Bolingbroke.

'I'm glad to hear it,' he said. 'The merchants of the Italian seaports have been suffering so much damage to their shipping it's become almost impossible to insure a cargo.'

Piers arrived shortly afterwards, having successfully purchased some useful rounceys and mules.

'You'd have been proud of me, Dick,' Piers told him. 'I

beat the rascal down to less than half what he was asking at first.'

'I'm surprised Bolingbroke left such a task to a knight,' Dick said. 'Hasn't he got some cleric to put in charge of the provisioning?'

'He's appointed the Archdeacon of Hereford to be Treasurer for Wars, but the horses and stores are to be purchased in London. I'm quite good with horses,' said Piers modestly, 'so he's put me in charge of that. I thought you might be able to help.'

'What about Master Gryffard? Shouldn't you give him the chance to make some money to keep up that expensive house of yours?' Dick poured wine into one of the silver goblets and handed it to Piers.

'Gryffard's still in the Cotswolds buying wool,' said Piers. 'As soon as we have all the horses and stores we need, we'll be off again to Calais.'

'I shall be happy to do what I can.' Dick held his silver goblet up to the light with both hands and watched Piers almost wistfully before he drank. He so wanted Piers to notice his beautiful cups, thought Alice.

'The *viande de cipre* I made specially because it is May Day,' she said laying sugared chicken and rich flour on to Piers's trencher bread. 'But the cups Dick has chosen to drink from in honour of you.' Thus prompted, Piers picked up his goblet and studied it admiringly.

'It's very fine,' he said holding it up to peer at the device engraved on the silver. 'Isn't that Burley's coat of arms?'

'It is,' said Dick, much gratified. 'I lent Sir Simon four hundred marks before he got in trouble with the lords appellant and the cups were his surety for the loan. After his fall he could not pay me back, which is how they came into my possession. Are they not lovely? The best in my collection.'

But instead of being impressed, Piers looked shocked. 'Doesn't it worry you when you benefit from other men's misfortunes?' he asked putting his goblet down almost guiltily.

'How else is a merchant to prosper in this troubled world except by other men's misfortunes?' retorted Dick. Piers frowned and Alice glanced at her husband anxiously. 'We cannot all go off and fight the infidel for the good of our souls,' Dick added, dipping his spoon into the shallow wooden bowl he shared with his wife.

'I may be saving my soul but I'm also clearing the Mediterranean of the Barbary pirates so that you and your fellow merchants don't lose so many cargoes.'

'Well, Sir Galahad, if you find the Holy Grail on the Barbary coast and get killed by the infidel, promise to send me down manna from heaven when I am still in purgatory paying for my sins,' teased Dick laughing.

'Certainly,' replied Piers, 'if you will look after my wife for me while I am away.' He smiled disarmingly at Alice and she warmed to him even more. He was shy, like her, but only with women was he tongue-tied and she guessed it was because he knew so little of them. Beneath his shyness lay a gentle sense of humour and a degree of sensitivity unusual in a knight. With men Piers was quite at ease, able to hold his own with someone like Dick, who was as sharp as a sword of war. Alice selected a date from a dish of dried fruits and took a careful bite. She felt ashamed of herself for worrying about Nicolette and Dick. Once Nicolette came to know Piers better, she would not look for love from any other man, least of all Dick who was Piers's good friend. Dick was no Brembre. He was like Piers, searching for some Holy Grail. It was what made them such friends.

The conversation turned to St Inglevert. When Piers confessed how he had lost his temper in the mêlée and unfairly wounded Thomas Mowbray, Dick was not so much shocked by this breach of chivalry as fascinated by Henry Bolingbroke's treatment of Piers.

'So Bolingbroke is not too particular what happens to his fellow appellant,' Whittington said. 'What does it mean, I wonder.'

'It means that Bolingbroke is a true soldier at heart as well as being generous with his forgiveness,' said Piers. 'He knows I never meant to commit a foul.' Dick was silent. Alice, watching her husband toying with his trencher bread, arranging the small rectangular shapes into a neat triangle, realised that he made no promise to Piers to look after Nicolette. He was far more interested in the relationship between Mowbray and Bolingbroke.

Dick was not tempted by Nicolette. He did not believe in

love and he did not have time to waste amusing spoilt beauties. But he loved beautiful things, which is why he had avoided Nicolette ever since the day of her wedding to his friend. He did not want to covet Piers Exton's lady. But when William Gryffard invited him to his house in Cornhill a few weeks after Piers had left for Calais, Dick went, taking Alice, for Piers's sake.

'It won't do you any harm to make a friend of Nicolette,' he said to his wife as he helped her from her litter outside William's inn. He could see from Alice's face that she didn't think much of the idea. The trouble was, Alice was a home-loving woman. She showed little interest in gadding about the city or gossiping with the other wives. Perhaps they could sew or read or do whatever women did in their solars together.

'I suppose I could ask her to see the Marching Watch with us,' said Alice.

'An excellent idea,' he agreed. 'You get a far better view of the procession from the Royall.' The Watch – to which each guild contributed a certain number of men – was the responsibility of one of the aldermen in each of the City Wards. The setting up of the Watch for the ensuing year took place on the Vigil of St John. For two days and nights the city celebrated midsummer; bonfires burned, balconies were hung with garlands of flowers, and on the eve of St John tables were set outside the houses with cakes and ale as everyone took to the streets to witness the great procession of the Marching Watch.

As they entered William's fine hall Dick thought how fortunate he was to have Alice. She was an admirable wife, good, dutiful and quick to obey. He rarely had to command her in anything. He feasted his eyes on the brilliant colours of William's painted walls, the array of silver goblets gleaming on the trestle against the walls, noting with the eye of a connoisseur that William seemed able to afford the best of everything. Mingling with the other guests, Dick was not surprised to see Adam Bamme the goldsmith and one or two leading fishmongers and grocers as well as some drapers and skinners. William was trying to be all things to all men as usual, he thought, and today he seemed to be succeeding. What he was not prepared for was the vision of Nicolette acting the part of hostess with consummate ease.

296

She was dressed in a tight-fitting gown of blue and gold with long, hanging sleeves trimmed with miniver which swept the tiled floor. Her elaborate headdress emphasised the perfect oval of her face and the pearl she wore on a gold chain round her neck was no whiter than the expanse of unblemished flesh it rested upon. She really was a beauty of quite rare quality, thought Dick, watching her greet Margaret Bamme. Beside Nicolette the most powerful woman in the city looked overblown and weighted down with too many jewels.

A servant proffered a basin of water and Dick dipped his hands into it, watching Margaret Bamme with new insight. She was laughing too much at something Nicolette had said, her malicious eyes roving the hall for her next victim. Margaret was the spoilt beauty, he thought in surprise, shaking water from his fingertips. She bent and whispered something in Nicolette's ear and Dick knew it must be hurtful from the way Nicolette flushed and looked about her helplessly. Catching his gaze, she sent him such a look of desperate appeal that before he knew it he was crossing the hall to her rescue.

'Lady Exton, let me congratulate you on having been the heroine of Saint Inglevert,' he said, deliberately ignoring Margaret Bamme. 'Sir Piers tells me he had to fight a great many noble knights on your behalf.' As he had hoped, Margaret flounced off in high dudgeon, leaving them alone.

'You are being very hard on me,' Nicolette sighed as she looked at him shyly.

'Not at all,' replied Dick studying her perfect profile with detached delight. 'I was slaying your dragon for you in Piers's absence. Mistress Bamme does not like to be outclassed by any woman or overlooked by any man, even a mercer.' She laughed then and he felt pleased with himself.

'Shall I give you my favour to wear?' she asked, extending a small white hand for him to kiss. It made him feel noble. It was a long time since a woman had treated him like a knight.

'I doubt if I could do justice to the honour,' he said as he raised her hand to his lips.

'You're just like all the others then.' She removed her hand. 'You're frightened of Margaret Bamme and the trouble she can make. Master Gryffard wants me to make a friend of her but it's so difficult.'

'William Gryffard is a master of expediency,' he said.

'And you're not?' she countered.

'I'm not frightened of Margaret Bamme,' he said, smiling at her, 'just because she'd like to be Mayoress again. Her second husband, John Philpot, was Mayor more than once and it gave her a taste for it. Now it looks as if Adam Bamme will be the next one. She has a great instinct for survival, but she likes to be liked. We all of us have to be friends with her.'

'Margaret Bamme hates me for what I did to her sister.'

'If she hates you at all it is because you're younger and more beautiful than she is,' he said.

'And you are an accomplished courtier, Master Whittington,' she replied, fluttering her eyelashes. He was disappointed. He had hoped she was better than that.

'Piers asked me to look after you while he's away,' he said to put her in her place.

A shadow crossed her lovely face. 'Do you always do what Piers wants, Master Whittington?'

'No, but in Piers I always see my better self, the man I might have become if I had not pursued my ambition so wholeheartedly.'

Her eyes widened and she looked up at him in genuine bewilderment. 'Can't you be good and successful?' she asked.

'I don't know about goodness,' he replied. 'If you want to succeed you have to be selfish. Are you selfish enough to succeed?' She looked startled and he was amused. She had clearly never thought of herself as selfish.

'I don't think I'm good enough to succeed,' she told him. He picked up one of her hanging sleeves. Ran his fingers along the soft fur trimming.

'I tell myself that when I am successful I shall be able to do more good,' he said looking down into her eyes.

'Are you very wicked now?' she asked and her eyes sparkled suddenly with challenge.

'Sometimes I have to do things I'm not proud of,' he said. 'We all of us have to do that, don't we, my lady?'

'Piers has gone away to fight the infidel because he thinks I am not good enough for him to love.' Her eyes which had been so full of mischief a moment before were large and tragic. 'When he comes home, will he be cured do you think of loving me?'

He was shaken, touched in spite of himself by her vulnerability. While he was still trying to decide how to respond, her mood changed again.

'Is that what you want, Master Whittington?' she asked, but so seriously that he wasn't sure whether she was flirting or not.

'I want,' he paused, unsure of himself, at a loss to know how to answer her, 'I want you to come to the marching watch with us,' he finished lamely.

'Your wife has already invited me,' she said with great dignity. He felt irritated with himself and her. She thought he was like all the others, lusting after her. But it was not so. He did not want to steal Piers Exton's lady. But there was something about her which interested him. Her sudden changes of mood were intriguing. She could be an exciting woman, he thought.

He watched her putting the Venetians and the Flemings at their ease and acknowledged that she did it far better than Alice could. It was not just Nicolette's natural fluency in French, their common language, but the gracefulness and poise that was a part of her beauty. She was a swan among geese. No wonder Margaret Bamme was so cruel. Among these squabbling merchants and their ambitious wives, a beautiful creature like Nicolette was wasted. Her beauty was undeniable but she had spirit too, and a certain amount of guile, unless he was much mistaken. She was not William Gryffard's daughter for nothing. He suspected there was a streak of wickedness lurking somewhere in Piers's perfect lady, a dark enthralling beast of which she was afraid. While he ate the excellent dinner provided by Gryffard, he wondered if Nicolette was not also wasted on a good man like Piers.

On the morning of St John's Day, Alice was dispensing cakes and ale in the Royall outside her house. The whole city was celebrating midsummer. The buildings were decorated with garlands and in every street trestle tables were set up outside to feed the hungry spectators who had come to watch the procession. Alice, filling a cup of ale, looked up to see Piers standing grinning at her.

'Well, here's a fine surprise,' she said handing him a cup of ale. 'We didn't expect to see you again till winter had come and gone.' At his side was Nicolette, wearing a sheath of rose-coloured silk with a fine Venetian veil, and glowing like a newly lit candle.

'Bolingbroke changed his mind and sent us home,' Piers explained. 'Is Master Whittington taking part in the marching watch?'

'He is,' said Dick appearing at Alice's side dressed in his mercer's gown and hood, ready for the procession. 'What's all this then, Piers? You haven't let us all down, have you? I was counting on you to get rid of the Barbary pirates for us.'

'John Beaufort, Bolingbroke's half-brother, left with twenty-four knights and one hundred archers for the Barbary crusade, but Bolingbroke's decided to go to Prussia later in the summer and I decided to go with him.' Piers handed his cup to Nicolette and she drank from it, looking up at him with such fervour Alice was embarrassed.

'I hope you know what you're doing, following Henry Bolingbroke,' said Dick.

'I like Henry, he's an honest soldier.'

'But indecisive it would seem. All this changing his mind is going to cost someone a deal of money. The provisioning for Prussia will be far costlier than the expedition to the Barbary coast. Who's paying for it all?'

'John of Gaunt, from the six hundred thousand gold francs the Castilians paid him for relinquishing his rights to the Spanish throne. Master Gryffard found that out from the Treasurer for Wars.'

'Gryffard would want to know,' said Dick, 'if he's helping with the provisioning. When are you leaving?'

'The day after tomorrow. I only stayed because I wanted to see the marching watch with Nicolette.'

'I still think you'd have done better with John Beaufort. If Bolingbroke is anything like his father, he'll lead you a merry dance all over the Continent and you'll never get to fight the infidel. You'll be back here a year or two from now with nothing to show for all your soldiering.'

'I'm not going for spoils of war,' said Piers. 'I'm going to fight the infidel for the good of my soul.'

'Of course you are, I had forgot.' Dick was put out about something, thought Alice as she offered them cakes. He was always at his most cynical when he was cross. 'What about you, Lady Exton?' Dick turned to Nicolette who was clutching her husband's arm, a vision of fragile dependence. 'Wouldn't you like him to come home with some booty?' She shook her head and looked at the cobblestones and Alice wondered if she was truly so submissive or if it was for Dick's benefit. If so, it wouldn't do any good, she thought, with relief. Dick was unimpressed by submissive women.

'Henry Bolingbroke will have plenty of manors to bestow upon those who serve him well, when Lancaster dies,' said Piers looking not at Dick but at his wife's bent head. 'If I serve him well I'm sure he will not be ungrateful.'

'Will his gratitude go so far as to pay your ransom should you be taken captive by the pagans?' demanded Dick.

'There's not much chance of that,' said Piers frowning.

'No chance at all,' retorted Dick. 'Not with the infidel. They'll kill you if they can.' Nicolette gave a little gasp and Alice wondered if Dick had deliberately meant to frighten her, and if so, why.

Dick was cross because he felt a fool; he had been looking forward to Nicolette's visit and now he was disappointed. Seeing her with Piers, the way she looked at him, was unsettling. No woman had ever looked at him like that. As he set out to join the procession, he suppressed a stab of envy tinged with guilt. Nicolette was Piers Exton's wife, he told himself. He must forget her. Walking through the gaily decorated streets, with the banners of the Mercers' Company in front of him and the torches and music and cheers ringing in his ears, he told himself that London was his mistress. He coveted it for its power and its independence. He would go a long way to guard its magic from harm, which is why he so much wanted to be Mayor. London is my lady, he thought, smiling wryly as he marched in the procession. How far would I go for her? Beyond honour as Piers once did for Nicolette? And where is my honour? It was an interesting thought, one that kept him pondering as the procession wound its slow way through the city. But then he chided himself for having caught a dose of sentiment from Piers. The sooner the knight left on his crusade and they could all get on with the murky business of making a living, the better.

PART III
1397–1398

There is a Bush that is overgrown
Crop it well and keep it low
Or else it will grow wild
The long grass that is so Green
It must be mown and raked clean.
For it hath overgrown the field.
The great Bag that is so mickle
It shall be cut and made little,
   Its bottom is nearly out . . .

Song popular at the end of the fourteenth century.

CHAPTER 25

1397

The King lolled in his chair frowning down at the long tapering points of his shoes. It was a fine day at the beginning of June and the soft breeze blowing through the window ruffled the end of his hanging sleeve almost playfully. From the grassy courtyard below he could hear occasional shrieks from his new bride, playing tag with her ladies. He looked out of the window. The sun was shining in a clear blue sky above the crenellated battlements. What was he doing, shut up in his apartments in the Tower of London on such a beautiful day when he could be out in the woods hawking? He leapt up and began to pace restlessly about the room while the nobles waiting in attendance watched him expectantly. As well they might, Richard thought, pleased with himself, as well they might! It had taken a long time but soon now he would have all the pieces in place upon the board.

From the far end of the chamber a page approached to tell him that Richard Whittington was waiting to see him.

'Good,' said the King. 'Send him in.' The last pawn! Soon the game could begin.

'You sent for me, Sire?' said Dick going down on his knee with easy grace. Too easy.

'The white s-silk for the Queen's mantle, where did it come f-from?' demanded Richard, to tease him.

'From Florence, Your Grace,' replied Whittington. 'Does it not please you?'

'The Queen doesn't like the marbling of vine leaves and red grapes,' replied Richard. 'You'll have to take it back, f-find her something more elaborate.' Did Whittington guess why he had been sent for? he wondered. You never could tell what Dick Whittington was thinking. He was too good a mercer not to seize the opportunity to tell him about a blue cloth decorated with white lilies and white and red stars and compasses that would make an unusual surcoat although he must know he had not been summoned to the Tower of London to discuss silks and velvets. The Keeper of the King's Wardrobe did that. It amused Richard to keep the mercer guessing, while the attendant nobles yawned with boredom.

'Of course you'll have to lend me the money to pay f-for it,' Richard said. 'You know I cannot possibly afford it.'

Dick smiled. 'Your Grace knows I am always ready to be of assistance. The six hundred pounds I lent in March is proof of that.'

'A timely reminder, Master Whittington, but didn't you get a tally of assignment issued upon s-some s-source of royal revenue? You're so much better at collecting my money than I seem to be. My s-s-subjects don't like paying their taxes, it would s-seem.'

'It all depends what the taxes are for, Sire. The Londoners do not mind paying for the defence of the realm. But the Queen's coronation last January was very expensive.'

'Well, what else could I do? The Queen is almost as extravagant as I am. But what can you expect from a daughter of F-F-France. She is used to having the best of everything.' Almost Richard lost his temper. He hated to be reminded of his extravagances. He glowered at the mercer who smiled back, unperturbed, and Richard remembered that it was Whittington who had encouraged him to make so much of the Queen's coronation. He sighed. His beloved wife Ann had been dead three years and a year ago he had married, for the sake of peace, the seven-year-old daughter of the King of France.

'They s-still don't like my little Queen, in s-spite of all that money I s-spent on her coronation. They'd rather we were still at war, I s-s-suppose,' he said.

'The merchants in the city of London like it well enough. You, Sire, understand our needs and priorities far better than your warrior barons who are only interested in an excuse for making war.'

The King felt better. He took Dick by the arm and drew him over to the window where they were out of earshot of the bored courtiers.

'I am thirty years old, Whittington,' he said, 'and I have no heir.'

'You have the Earl of March, whom you have officially appointed your heir. The people like him.'

'But no s-son, no direct successor and my cousin Henry is very fond of telling me what I can and cannot do.' Moodily Richard stood looking down at the court beneath, where Queen Isabella ran about in her rich gown shrieking with glee.

'You must have patience, Sire,' said Dick at last. 'As soon as the Queen becomes a woman you will be begetting an heir.'

'Patience!' exclaimed the King. 'F-For too long have I been patient. Twenty years now I've been on the throne and never really been allowed to rule.'

'I too have waited long and made many false starts. But all the time I've been waiting I've been gaining experience,' said Dick.

He really had a very sweet smile, thought the King, and made up his mind. He would wait no longer. The time had come to move his first pawn.

'So the Mayor has died in office,' he said, 'and left London leaderless. We can't have that.'

'No, Sire,' replied Dick calmly.

'Adam Bamme's been Mayor how many times? Twice? Thrice? It's been too heavy a burden, it would s-seem. Or perhaps it was the hand of God. May his soul rest in peace.' He crossed himself and Dick followed suit. 'I think perhaps it's the hand of God. Bamme's death is most timely. I have need of a Mayor I can trust just now.' He paused. Stared hard at the mercer. Dick returned his gaze serenely. 'I can trust you, can't I, Whittington?'

'Completely, Sire.'

The King felt a warm sense of comfort. He liked Whittington. The man understood him. For all his cold manner, he had a great love of beautiful things which Richard shared. It was much easier to get on with Whittington than the domineering, fractious members of his own family.

'You can be Mayor,' he said. 'I need to know that London is with me in the coming months.'

'Sire!' Whittington fell on his knees. 'You do me too much honour. I am all unworthy.'

'You're appointed from this day. You can tell them. No need for elections.' The King was delighted. The mercer seemed quite overcome with gratitude. It was good to be able to please somebody for once. 'Do you want me to s-send you back to London with my Cheshire archers to reinforce your authority?'

'No, no.' Dick shook his head. 'There's no need for a bodyguard. A royal warrant will suffice. The Londoners are law-abiding citizens.'

'They weren't always. And they don't always do what I want them to do. I'm relying on you, Whittington, to s-see to it that this time they do.'

'You can trust me, Sire,' promised Dick, getting to his feet. 'I love London and I love you. We will serve you faithfully, the city and I – that I swear.'

Dick walked out of the Tower filled with elation. His moment had come. It was twenty long years since he had been admitted into the freedom of the Mercers' Company and married Alice his master's daughter, and now in his fortieth year the moment he had worked so hard for had come. He was Mayor of London. He was so excited he did not go home immediately. He wanted to savour his moment of triumph alone.

He wandered through the city, a slightly built man in a flowing gown of rich damask, his straight brown hair cropped just below his ears. He walked past the fine houses of the rich merchants with their gardens running down to the river and the busy wharves along the water's edge; for a while he stood by Billingsgate watching the fishing boats unloading their catches, then left Thames Street and the river behind him and plunged into the heart of the city, taking his time, listening to the raucous sounds of apprentices crying their wares, the clangour of iron being hammered into shape in Lothbury, the soothing plainsong of a chantry priest through an open church door in Ironmonger Lane. He loved it all – the noise, the smells, the whole bustling colourful fight for life and livelihood that went on each day in the city.

When he came to the Guildhall he stopped to gaze at the wooden building which guarded the city's secrets and was its seat of power. It was here the members of all the different guilds in the city came to elect the Mayor every year, sometimes amid scenes of disorder and confusion. Dick smiled grimly to himself, remembering when more than once armed men had packed the hall to coerce the voters. He was Mayor now, without the help of armed men but by the King's command. The King had ignored the city's right to elect its Mayor.

Dick walked on, his excitement tempered by wariness. The King feared his cousin Henry. Ought he to warn Piers? But Piers would only warn Henry. Already, it seemed to Dick, he was being asked to choose. What compromises would he have to make in order to carry out the King's trust? Could he serve London and the King without betraying either?

He found that his wanderings had brought him to Cornhill and Gryffard's Inn. He was hot and tired after his long walk and ready now to share the news of his good fortune. Nicolette would be the ideal person to tell. Nobody knew better how to appreciate success.

Nicolette was in the garden and to his delight she was for once without her two little boys and her companion, Jeanne de Bourdat. She got up to welcome him, walking a little awkwardly for she was childbearing again. She was far lovelier than the day on which he had first seen her when she had collapsed in labour at his feet. But even then he had been able to appreciate her beauty. She had been a helpless victim then, a burden upon his charity; now she was a woman of twenty-six, a knight's lady, wiser, more sure of herself, but without losing the hint of vulnerability that was part of her appeal.

She led him to a stone seat beneath a shady walnut tree. He sat down beside her and told her his news. 'How proud of you I am,' she exclaimed, her eyes shining, and he glowed with pleasure. Then she clapped her hands and looked at him mischievously. 'Can I take precedence now over Margaret Bamme? You will ask me to your Mayor's day feast, won't you, Dick?'

'I will ensure that poor Margaret Bamme is invited so that you can queen it over her if you wish,' he promised. 'You can sit at my right hand and keep me awake, for I shall be in grave danger of falling asleep in the middle of the feast after the long walk from Saint Paul's.'

'Alice must sit at your right hand,' she said quickly, with the sudden switch from mischievous beauty to cool lady that he found so tantalising. 'I shall be quite happy as long as I am at the high table above the salt.'

Piers had done his work well, Dick thought watching her. She was almost as good as she was beautiful. It was tempting to discover if there was any trace left of the woman who had been Nicholas Brembre's mistress lurking beneath the impeccable surface of Piers's perfect lady. It was a temptation Dick had so far managed to resist. He had fallen into the habit of visiting her when Piers went away, pretending he did it for Piers's sake, but in reality because he enjoyed her company. When Piers came home, he kept up the pretence, accepting his thanks with a twinge of guilt, knowing that his first instincts had been the right ones and that he should have avoided Nicolette not sought her out.

'Be careful, Dick,' she said suddenly with another of her swift changes of mood. 'The King can be a dangerous friend. Don't let him embroil you in his schemes to take London into his own hand. The city may destroy you in the end.'

'I am already embroiled,' he said frowning down at his dust-covered shoes. 'My appointment by the King is in breach of the city's right. But I love the city more than my own life, which is why I have taken the King's appointment. If I had refused, the King would only find another who might love London less. At Michaelmas I'll stand for election and they can throw me out then if they want to.'

'They wouldn't dare,' she said and the pride in her eyes made him feel better.

'The King needs London's support and he's clever enough to know that he won't get it if he attacks our rights and liberties.'

'The last time the King needed London's support it was to fight the lords appellant,' she said, growing thoughtful. 'Do you think he means to move against them now? You don't think Piers is in any danger, do you?'

'Why should he be in danger?'

'Because he serves Henry Bolingbroke and Bolingbroke was one of the five lords appellant. If Bolingbroke were arrested, would his retainers not be taken too?'

Dick took her hand and looked down into her eyes. 'There is no danger to Bolingbroke while the Duke of Lancaster his

310

father is alive to protect him,' he said giving her hand a fatherly squeeze. 'Piers is safe enough.'

'You are such a comfort to me, Dick,' she said withdrawing her hand. 'My father is always fearful. He's terrified that the King means to get his revenge one day for what they did to him all those years ago. But you know what my father is like. He sees disaster like a beggar waiting outside every rich man's gate.' Dick knew William Gryffard to be a man who spent a great deal of time and money in pursuit of accurate information. If he was fearful, perhaps he had good reason, but Dick kept this thought to himself.

As he walked home an hour later, Dick considered the danger to Piers. If the King was bent upon revenge, would Piers find himself on the losing side? And if he did, would Nicolette drop into his lap like a ripe plum? Was her love of success greater than her love for her husband? He quickened his step, afraid of where his thoughts were leading. He had always thought that if he could just be Mayor, he would be content. Now that he was, he wondered whether there were other kinds of contentment within his grasp.

William received the news of Dick Whittington's success with his customary suspicion. There were rumours that the King was plotting revenge upon his enemies. Arundel had shut himself up in his castle of Reigate, Warwick in Warwick, and the Duke of Gloucester had taken to his bed at his stronghold Pleshey in Essex. William prided himself on his ability to anticipate trouble. When on 8 July he watched the King riding out of London from the Tower with a large body of armed men, he felt fairly sure that trouble was on its way, only he couldn't discover who it might strike and when. A few days later he was down in the docks anxious for news of a ship of his which was overdue at Genoa, and discovered that there was a ship lying ready in the Thames waiting to take the Duke of Gloucester, a prisoner, to Calais.

William quivered from head to foot with alarm. Gloucester arrested! 'On whose orders?' he demanded in a voice that shook.

The seaman shrugged. 'I know not. All I knows is that the ship's been taken by Thomas Mowbray.' William digested this morsel of news with care and began to feel a little better. If Gloucester had been entrusted to Mowbray then perhaps the King's vengeance was not directed against all five of the men who had defied his royal prerogative all those years ago. All the same the King must be very sure of himself to have moved against his powerful uncle. William nosed about the busy wharf questing for further information, like a dog searching the rushes for discarded scraps of meat, but all he could discover was that Mowbray was leaving for France with the Duke of Gloucester in his care, as soon as the wind and tide would permit.

William went home unhappy with his discovery. He knew that the King had recently made Thomas Mowbray Constable of Calais. It now appeared as if there had been a sinister reason for Mowbray's appointment. He entered the hall to find the household already at supper. At first nobody noticed him. The brilliant colours of the painted walls glowed in the soft evening sunlight slanting through the narrow windows, the array of silver goblets on the cup board gleamed reassuringly. At the far end of the hall, Nicolette and Piers presided over the high table laughing with the most senior members of the household. It looked the picture of prosperity and domestic bliss. He ought to have been pleased, for he had created it all, but he wasn't; he could not forget that the house now belonged to Piers and he felt excluded.

William moved out of the shadows and Nicolette saw him at last. She smiled and beckoned to him, patting the vacant chair at her side invitingly. If only she had leapt to her feet to welcome him, waited supper until he had come home.

'The Duke of Gloucester's been arrested,' he told her bluntly, wanting her to share some of his fear. 'I knew when the King chose Whittington to be Mayor he was up to something.'

She looked anxiously, not at him, but at her husband.

'Whittington doesn't think there's any danger,' said Piers, smiling down at her reassuringly. 'He told me so.'

'You knew? Why did you not tell me?' exclaimed William, furious that he should have been kept in ignorance by his own family.

'I knew the King had invited Arundel, Warwick and Gloucester to a great feast,' Piers said laying a protective hand on his wife's arm. 'Warwick complied and found himself arrested. Arundel suspected something but, relying on a promise of safety, went and was also arrested. I thought

Gloucester had escaped by pleading ill health.'

'How could you keep such a . . .' William searched angrily for the right word, 'calamitous piece of news from me?' he demanded.

'I didn't want to frighten Nicolette,' replied Piers calmly. 'There is nothing to be afraid of, my angel.' Nicolette looked relieved. It irritated William all the more. He wanted them to be afraid, to share with him his terrible anxiety for the future.

'You are Bolingbroke's retainer,' he rounded on Piers accusingly. 'If anything happens to Bolingbroke, we'll be done for.'

'Henry Bolingbroke isn't like Gloucester,' said Piers, unruffled. 'He and Mowbray have always been on the side of moderation, the King knows that. It was his cousin the King relied on to protect him from the others when he was at their mercy in the Tower.'

'Then it's probably Henry and his father the Duke of Lancaster that the King will be relying on now to help bring the three he has arrested to trial,' said William. 'It's after the trial is over that we should be afraid.'

'Dick Whittington says the King only wishes to hold the three lords to show that he can control his nobles,' said Piers. 'It seems that there's some plan to elect our King Richard emperor but the German envoys say he lacks power over his lords. When he's held them long enough for their detention to be known abroad, he'll probably restore them to their former dignity.'

'If that is the case, why has Gloucester been sent to Calais?' asked Nicolette, wrinkling her brow.

'Dick's a friend. He wouldn't lie to me,' said Piers.

'And you believe that, do you?' retorted William. 'How can you be so trusting?'

Piers shrugged as he picked up a chicken leg and began tearing at it with strong white teeth. Nicolette, too, applied herself to her trencher again, seemingly unconcerned.

William drank a deep draught of wine. Things had not been going well for him. Giles de Bourdat had died and William wasn't at all sure he could trust his new partner completely. It wasn't getting any easier to make money despite the last seven years of peace and prosperity. The best money was to be made out of calamity and other men's misfortunes. Good times only made it easier for everyone else. He picked up a chicken leg and dabbed it in a bowl of spiced sauce. Everything Nicolette had she had from him. He had wanted to bind her to him with chains of gold but it was Dick Whittington who was doing that. He had watched Whittington buying Nicolette's friendship over the years and knew that he could neither compete nor prevent it. Whittington was a useful friend for his daughter to have, William knew that, especially now that the mercer was Mayor. But it didn't make it any easier to bear. He sucked at the chicken leg, letting the sauce dribble down his chin while he tried to pluck the flesh from the bone with his rotten teeth.

William had no friends. The nearest he had come to friendship was with Giles de Bourdat. When Giles had died William had brought Jeanne into his household to keep Nicolette company and to solve the problem of what to do with Giles's widow. But Jeanne and Nicolette and Lisette, chattering together in French all day long, made him feel more excluded than ever. He suspected his daughter was getting away from him, that it was she who ruled his household now and that all of them, Piers, Whittington and himself, were dancing to her tune. She did it so cunningly, with so much charm, he wouldn't have minded if only he could rid himself of the fear that beneath all her studied efforts to please she despised him.

CHAPTER 26

Parliament met at Westminster in September and the first of
the King's magnates to be tried was the Earl of Arundel. To
Piers, armed and on guard as a retainer of Henry Bolingbroke's, it was all too horribly familiar. The procedure
followed in almost every detail the impeachment of the
King's friends during the Merciless Parliament nine years
before. It worried Piers that Henry Bolingbroke had to
take so prominent a role in the attack on Arundel, and
that Henry's father, the Duke of Lancaster, presided at the
trial as Seneschal of England. It seemed to Piers that there
was no such thing as simple loyalty any more; he was
confused and sickened by the conflict of interests, the
betrayals.

On the day of Arundel's conviction, he escaped the
menacing atmosphere of Westminster Palace and hurried
home to find Nicolette. She was seated in her solar sewing
with Jeanne de Bourdat, while the children played at her feet.
It was a scene of such domestic tranquillity Piers felt soothed
just watching them. But he was not allowed much peace. The
two boys flung themselves at him – six-year-old Christopher
wrapping his arms round Piers's waist and Tarquin, three
years younger, clinging to his legs.

'Jeanne, take the children down to the hall,' said Nicolette,
laying aside her embroidery. 'They can help get supper
ready.'

The two boys began a vociferous protest, but Jeanne de
Bourdat silenced them with a stern command and shooed
them out of the chamber. When they had gone, Nicolette
looked up at Piers questioningly.

'Something's happened,' she said.

'The Earl of Arundel is to be hanged, drawn and quartered,' he told her. 'The Duke of Lancaster pronounced sentence today.'

'May God have mercy,' she whispered, crossing herself.

Piers nodded gravely. 'He was a violent man at times, I know, and something of a bully but he was a good soldier and deserves at least a soldier's death.' He walked over to the window and stood looking moodily out into the street below. 'I wish I could ride out and fight against the Earl,' he burst out fiercely. 'I wouldn't mind that, even though I was his retainer for a time. There's something clear cut and honest about trial by combat, not like this game they're all playing in the name of justice. It sickens me.'

Nicolette rose somewhat ponderously to her feet and came to stand by him, winding her arms round his neck. 'It isn't your fault, you know, Piers,' she said. 'The Earl of Arundel brought it on himself by becoming too powerful.'

'Arundel offered trial by battle.' Piers kissed her cheek absently. 'It was refused.'

'Just like Sir Nicholas,' she said, releasing him and sinking down on the window seat. 'He was so proud of being a knight, but they wouldn't let him die like one either.'

'It's a barbaric sentence for a man who did so much for England,' he said. 'You'd have thought the Duke of Lancaster might have put in a plea for mercy – or Henry. Sweet Jesu, they were comrades in arms.'

'They're only trying to preserve their own heads,' said Nicolette. 'Be thankful to God it isn't Henry on trial and that his father Lancaster is Seneschal of England. At least we are still safe.'

'Be careful, my lovely,' he said rounding on her bitterly. 'You're beginning to think like your father.' Instantly he regretted it. She looked at him reproachfully, two large tears trembling on her long lashes, ready to fall.

'You don't really think that, do you?' she said looking at him anxiously. 'I'm not at all like William Gryffard. I have to try and pretend to be – a little – just to please him.'

He took her hand and kissed her fingers one by one. 'You ought to know by now that William Gryffard can never be pleased. Isn't it enough that you please me?'

She gave a little sigh. 'Of course, but I have to keep the

peace between you. My father likes to think he can control me with his money. But I care nothing for it. Does that surprise you?'

'You are full of surprises but after so many years you must expect me to know you better than that.' She gazed up at him with such a hungry longing in her beautiful face he felt a surge of love all the stronger now that it was tinged with compassion and understanding.

'If you knew everything about me you wouldn't love me any more.'

'What makes you think that? I'll always love you.'

'That's how men are.' She glanced down at her swollen belly and then gazed mournfully at him. 'I mean one day I'll be old and even fatter than I am now and my hair will be grey and my teeth will be worse than Lisette's. I'll have nothing new to say to you and you'll be bored silly.'

'What nonsense you do talk, Nicolette. The love I have for you is nothing whatever to do with the way you look.' He stroked the swelling mound beneath the blue damask gown. 'My clever, fertile, perfect wife,' he said. 'I'll always love you.'

'Promise.'

'I swear by the Rood.' He kissed her warm red mouth and tingled at the swift, sweet certainty of her response.

That evening at supper William was full of gloom. 'The rumour from Calais is that the Duke of Gloucester has died in captivity,' he announced.

'May God have mercy on his soul.' Nicolette crossed herself and Piers did likewise. 'All the same,' she went on looking at him uneasily, 'it makes it easier for Bolingbroke, doesn't it? At least he doesn't have to send his uncle to his death.'

'A little too easy,' replied William darting one of his shrewd glances at her from beneath his hooded eyes in the way Piers had come to dislike. 'In Calais it's believed that Gloucester was murdered – with Thomas Mowbray's contrivance.'

Nicolette shook her head, puzzled. 'I can't believe Thomas Mowbray capable of murder. Can you, Piers? He was rash, hot-tempered, even cruel perhaps. But murder? Surely not.'

'He may have had no choice,' William mumbled, pulling at his straggly beard. 'Of the five appellants who accused the King's friends back in the eleventh year of his reign, only Bolingbroke and Mowbray have now escaped arrest. Perhaps Gloucester's murder is the price of their freedom.'

'Of course not.' Piers was indignant. 'Bolingbroke doesn't have to dishonour himself in such a way. His father is much too powerful. Lancaster would never stand by and see his son arrested and the King knows it.'

'But Mowbray has no powerful father to protect him,' William said. 'And neither do you. That father of yours in Cheshire wouldn't be much use to you if you fell foul of the King. Would you be able to survive, like Mowbray has, or has all that crusading with Henry Bolingbroke made you too good for such work?'

Piers told himself that William was a frightened man, that he must make allowances; he himself was not afraid but he glanced anxiously at Nicolette.

'Piers would never stoop to murder, would you, Piers?' said Nicolette, looking at him with such trust in her beautiful eyes that he felt immensely proud. She had plenty of courage, he thought, and an instinct for goodness.

'Even for love?' William persisted, bent on picking a quarrel. 'He sold his honour once before, remember?' Nicolette was silent, her face pale.

If only William would leave her alone, Piers thought angrily. But he seemed to delight in taunting his daughter, picking at her fragile confidence, always criticising, throwing past misdemeanours in her face, playing on her fear of failure for no good purpose that Piers could see. He longed to strangle his father-in-law. But William was one dragon he could not slay for her. Tonight he would reassure her. It would take time and patient loving but in the end she would feel safe and happy. He was fortunate that among so many conflicts of interest he still had Nicolette who loved and needed him. At least he could be true to her.

At the end of September the King adjourned Parliament for a second session to meet at Shrewsbury after Christmas. As a dramatic climax to a dramatic session, a grand review of the armed bands of the Londoners was held by the King and Lancaster on horseback, but Nicolette was unable to watch the splendid procession. She had just given birth to another son. She lay in her curtained bed listening to the bells of St Peter's Upon Cornhill ringing for the King's benefit and thought of what he had done. Richard had been merciful only in so far as the more barbaric part of Arundel's sentence was concerned and the Earl had been executed on Tower Hill. Warwick was punished with a sentence of perpetual imprisonment and was banished to the Isle of Man. The Constable of Calais, Thomas Mowbray, appeared before Parliament and certified that his prisoner the Duke of Gloucester had died in captivity. Sentence was passed nevertheless and the King's uncle attainted guilty of treason.

The pealing of the bells swelled into a continuous joyful sound as churches all over the city paid homage to the King's triumph over his enemies. Nicolette closed her eyes, remembering the day Sir Nicholas Brembre had gone to his death. Never would she forget that first lying-in above the fishmonger's shop, the despair and hopelessness and sense of failure. Could it all happen again? Was her father right to be so fearful? Was the King's vengeance satisfied, or was today's great show of strength just a preliminary for more trumped-up charges and false accusations?

She opened her eyes and stared about the chamber, at the painted coffer from Italy, the arras cloths, the Venetian mirror hanging on the wall. It was all so lavish; she was surrounded by everything that William Gryffard's money could buy. Before the hearth stood the cradle in which her newborn babe, washed, rubbed with honey and wrapped in linen cloth, lay sleeping. She knew in her mother's heart that no matter how much was done for this puny little infant, he was unlikely to survive. Only the strong survived. Christopher and Tarquin had been lusty babes yelling heartily as soon as they came into the world but this one was a sickly little thing who whimpered feebly, just like the little daughter she had lost at Pentecost when Piers was away on one of his crusades. So much for Piers and his fight to win God's favour. Nicolette moved her head restlessly on the pillows. She no longer believed that God could be bought with vows or that illness could be banished by confession and exorcism. It was God's punishment, that was all.

She searched her heart wondering in what way she had displeased Him this time. Her eyes lighted on the wall painting of the Virgin and Child of which William was so proud. She had been proud too when the painter had sung her praises as she sat for him in her blue mantle with little Christopher in her arms. Perhaps it had been blasphemous to be thought to resemble the Virgin. Perhaps she had been wrong to allow her father to use her thus. Had she been guilty of the sin of pride? Once she had known with simple certainty what was right and what was wrong but now she knew nothing any more. The Virgin's face so like her own stared down at her almost accusingly. Nicolette groaned aloud.

'What's the matter?' The round, trustworthy face of Lisette appeared between the bed curtains.

'Nothing, just nightmares again. Oh, Lisette, I'm so tired but I dare not sleep.'

'It will pass,' said the maid, 'when the little one can suck better. The rush of milk makes you feverish, I dare say, and them dratted bells will be giving you the headache.'

Nicolette sighed, hot and uncomfortable with the throbbing pain in her breasts. Her weary body lay beneath the coverlet worn out with the effort of giving birth. But more exhausting still was the effort she would have to make once Piers went away. She had tried hard to make friends with all the people William wanted her to impress but even after seven long years, she knew in her heart of hearts that she had failed. It was not just Margaret Bamme and her sisters, who no longer counted since the rise of Dick Whittington. It seemed to Nicolette that she would never be accepted here in the city of London. They did not like her because of her French accent and her convent education; none of them liked her, not even Alice Whittington. Yet she would have to go on trying, for Dick Whittington's sake if not for her father's. Dick had been so kind and she could not let him down. She began to sink into a deep pool of exhaustion.

'Well, my darling?' It was Piers this time and she welcomed the sound of his voice. She opened her eyes.

'Back so soon,' she said examining him anxiously. 'Is anything wrong?'

'Nothing's wrong.' He smiled at her reassuringly. 'The King has made Bolingbroke Duke of Hereford and Mowbray Duke of Norfolk as a reward for their support. It's all over now.' He looked very strong and chivalrous with his brightly coloured tabard over his armour and Henry's white swan on the badge of his sleeve. 'The procession went very well but I wanted to be back here with you so I asked Henry if I could be excused from the grand feast the King gives tonight.'

'Was that wise?' she asked.

'I don't much mind whether it was wise or not, I wanted to be with you.' He sat down carefully on the side of the bed. 'I was worried about you.'

'I shall be well enough once I've rested,' she said. 'But I'm not so sure about the babe.'

'I'll light a candle for him,' Piers promised. 'But you've no need to be so anxious. I've found a learned doctor who casts horoscopes. He says the child was born under a lucky star.'

For the first time that day hope pierced her troubled mind. Always he knew just how to soothe and comfort her. Once she had despised him for being so easy to please. Now when she was surrounded by people who were never satisfied, she knew how to appreciate her husband better.

'I wish you weren't leaving so soon,' she said. 'How am I to manage here without you?'

'I wish it too, my own,' he said stroking her cheek gently. 'But Henry Bolingbroke needs me in Hereford.'

'When will you be back?' she asked.

'I don't know – as soon as I can. I promise I'll be with you at Christmastide.' For once she did not mind too much. She needed time to get over the exhaustion of childbearing to be able to respond to his ardent lovemaking with the proper enthusiasm. When he came back, she would be ready for him, her beauty restored, her hunger as sharp as his.

She smiled at him lovingly. 'I know you're really longing to get back to Henry Bolingbroke, that you're ill at ease in this magnificent house of ours which is still under my father's hand.'

He bent and kissed her tenderly on the mouth. 'I'm never ill at ease as long as I'm with you,' he said. 'But I have my duty to do, as you have yours.'

She clasped his hand and pressed his fingers to her breast. 'Don't let Henry lead you into trouble with the King,' she said.

'That's all over now,' he said. 'The King has what he wants, God have mercy. Today Lancaster and Bolingbroke were at his right hand.' Just for a moment his face looked grim. She squeezed his hand more tightly and he smiled at her. 'I believe the King to be good at heart,' he said. 'It's just he listens too much to bad advice. Now that he has Lancaster and Bolingbroke and Whittington to guide him, all should be well.'

She released his hand and lay back against the pillows. She wanted so much to believe in Piers, to be able to trust to his strength and goodness to keep them all from harm.

'Don't let William upset you with his fears and worries,' Piers said, and it was as if he had read her thoughts. It made her feel warm and comforted. 'You are my perfect lady. Nothing William Gryffard can say or do will make you any better than you already are.' He kissed her hand and she lay gazing at him longingly. 'Adieu, my angel.' She closed her eyes. 'Sleep well now,' he said. He stepped easily down from the dais, his armour creaking. She heard him saluting the women, then he left the chamber.

At first it seemed as if Piers was right. At Michaelmas Dick Whittington was elected Mayor by the Londoners for a further year. Nicolette was both touched and flattered when he asked if he could be godfather to the new babe. The child survived and was christened Michael in honour of his godfather's election on the Feast of St Michael. As the baby grew in strength, Nicolette believed it was a good omen. Dick had brought them luck.

The weeks passed and Nicolette felt stronger every day; the baby lived on; Christopher and Tarquin were full of health and high spirits. By the second week of Advent, winter arrived with premature severity. The Walbrook was frozen and the laundry maids had to break the ice to do their washing. But it did not matter, for by then everybody in the household was cheerfully preparing for Christmas and looking forward to Piers's return. Until the day William burst into the solar and shattered all Nicolette's happy security.

'Ruin!' he cried, throwing himself down on the dais round the bed. 'Henry Bolingbroke's been arrested.'

Nicolette looked around her like one in a dream. Jeanne de Bourdat was amusing the two older boys, little Michael was sleeping peacefully in his cradle.

'What's happened? What's he done?' Nicolette could hardly take it in.

'He's accused Thomas Mowbray of treason.'

'There must be some mistake,' she said, trying to gather her scattered thoughts together.

'There's no mistake. I heard it this morning at the Corn Market. It was the only topic of conversation. Prices of corn rose so sharply I couldn't buy so much as a bushel. The Londoners are afraid the city might be besieged if Lancaster goes to war for the sake of his son.'

Always he thought first of money. 'It might be just a rumour,' Nicolette suggested, clutching at straws, 'got up by the corn merchants.'

'It's true enough,' he said. 'Whittington has Mowbray under his custody confined in the King's Wardrobe. I've just come from there. Mowbray's story is that he met Bolingbroke on his way to London, they quarrelled and now Henry has falsely accused him of treason.'

'Henry would never do anything so stupid. If he's accused Mowbray, it's because he is guilty.' She was assailed by a vision of Thomas Mowbray of the wicked eyes going to his death on Tower Hill and began to shake.

'We are ruined for certain if Bolingbroke is found guilty.'

'No, Father, no. It won't come to that, surely.'

'Henry Bolingbroke and Thomas Mowbray are the only two of the five lords appellant left,' said William pulling fretfully at his beard. 'Now they are both under arrest. Piers would do well to flee abroad while there is still time.'

Nicolette sank down on to a stool by the fire. The thought that had been chasing round her head ever since William had blurted out his terrible news now struck at her heart like a crossbow bolt. Piers was in danger.

'I don't know where he is. Where to reach him. He promised he would be home for Christmastide,' she babbled.

'Then I expect he will keep his promise.' Jeanne de Bourdat's calm voice steadied Nicolette a little. She bit her lip and fought to control the dismay that was threatening to overwhelm her.

'If Piers has fled already then we are ruined!' William interjected.

Nicolette frowned at him. 'Piers would never run away,' she said indignantly.

William jumped up and began to wander around the chamber, ignoring the children who stared at him silently.

323

He kept darting to the window to peer out as if he could conjure Piers out of the air by magic. 'Where is he then? Why has he not sent word?'

'You needn't be afraid that he will desert us,' Nicolette said, clinging to the thought of his strength and his goodness.

'Little fool!' William burst out suddenly, coming to stand in front of her. 'Don't you understand what it means? The inheritance of anyone exiled for treason falls to the Crown. If Piers is impeached with Bolingbroke, then we'll lose our house.'

Still money, she thought impatiently. That's all he ever worried about. 'He'll be home for Christmas,' she said. 'He promised.'

'He can't keep his promise if he's under lock and key,' retorted William. She wished that just for once he might pretend that he had hope, might throw her a crumb of comfort, but he always feared the worst. Piers was not like that. He kept his worries to himself, only ever told her the good news. Oh Piers! How was she to bear it if he did not come?

'If he does come back you'd better persuade him to make the house over to me, while there's still time,' William said.

'Piers must do as he thinks best,' she replied. Tarquin began to cry, unable to understand what was the matter but sensing with a child's sharpened intuition that disaster was at hand. Christopher, his eyes round and dark with anxiety, tugged at her sleeve. 'Is Papa not coming home for Christmas after all, Mama?' he asked.

She swept him up into her arms and hugged him tightly. 'Yes, of course Papa's coming. This evening we'll all go to Saint Peter's and light a candle to Saint Nicholas, shall we?' To discourage any more of William's doom-mongering and to distract her own tangled thoughts, she settled Christopher on her knee and started to read to him from a book of saints, but he soon grew restless.

'He's getting too big for us women to teach,' said Jeanne. 'Just as well he's to go into Henry Bolingbroke's household as a page after Christmas.'

Jeanne was only trying to be sensible, Nicolette knew, but it was these simple words which brought the true nature of the disaster home to her. She sat down on the bed and burst into tears while William shook his head in despair and Jeanne set about trying to comfort the frightened children and their weeping mother.

Piers came on Christmas Eve. He strode into the hall just as the household was sitting down to midday dinner, mud-splattered, vigorous, and very much alive. Nicolette leapt from the dais and ran down the hall to welcome him.

'Careful, my darling,' he said as she threw herself into his arms. 'You'll get mud all over your fine surcoat.'

She drew back while he threw off his heavy travelling cloak and sent servants to help Crispin with the horses, thinking she had never loved him so much as now. His chain mail was rust-speckled and his face smeared with grime and dark with several days' growth of beard, yet his eyes with their incredibly long lashes were so warm and tender and loving she felt completely safe. He was her champion, her perfect gentle knight. He would not run away and leave her unprotected.

'Aren't you going to finish your dinner before it's quite cold?' he demanded, grinning at her. 'Crispin will wait on me when he comes.'

But she would have none of it. She waited while a servant brought a basin of water for him to wash his face and hands and then led him up to the high table like a conquering hero. William was still sitting hunched over his trencher, waiting to pounce.

'Where have you been? What's happened? Is it true that Bolingbroke's under arrest?' William fired his questions one after the other, his eyes dark with anxiety.

'Henry's at Lancaster, safe in his father's castle. He's been released on bail,' replied Piers seizing a poulet's leg and tearing the flesh ravenously with his strong teeth. 'By the Rood, this is good. I haven't eaten since daybreak the day before yesterday.'

'Why not? You're not a fugitive are you?' Nervously William picked at the bread of his trencher with his long thin fingers.

'No, nor like to be,' said Piers through a mouth full of pasty as he turned to Nicolette and winked. 'I was in a hurry because I wanted to be home in time for Christmas, as I promised.'

Nicolette's spirits soared. Everything would be all right

now that Piers was back. She had been dreading Christmas but now that he was safe and home at last she was determined to make it the best Christmastide ever.

'Is Bolingbroke to be impeached or what?' demanded William.

'Their quarrel is to be referred to Parliament when it meets in Shrewsbury after Christmastide,' replied Piers. He took a deep draught of wine and looked at William. 'You needn't be afraid, Henry's no traitor. The King knows that.'

'He may know it, but he hasn't forgotten Radcot Bridge.'

Piers tossed off his wine. 'The King has pardoned all who took part in that battle.'

'Including Arundel, Gloucester and Warwick, and look what happened to them.' William leant forward across the table and pointed his eating knife at Piers. 'You'd best flee while there's still time.'

Nicolette held her breath and looked at Piers sitting beside her calmly wolfing quince tartlets. 'Piers would never run away,' she said defiantly. Then greatly daring and because her father had frightened her, added, 'Unlike you.'

William shrugged. 'Only a fool makes no effort to save himself,' he said. 'I thought you would have learnt that by now, Nicolette.' A cold tremor ran through her as she remembered that time when she had defied him before, when Nicholas had been in danger. She had not believed it possible that anything could happen to him. She began to shake and clasped her hands tightly together under the table, determined not to let him see that his arrow had found its mark.

'Have no fear.' Piers covered her trembling hands with one of his. 'Lancaster, York and Albermerle have provided Henry's bail. With those three supporting him, the King dare not proceed against him. The truth will come out in Parliament and you'll see then that it is Mowbray who is the real traitor.'

She held the warm, comforting hand imprisoned in her lap, gently tracing the hard calluses on the palm, the fighting man's insignia. She wanted to believe him. Piers always hoped for the best and William always feared the worst. Her heart wanted to put her trust in Piers and leave everything to him, but bitter experience had taught her that William was more often proved right in the end. Her head told her she should listen to her father.

326

That night their lovemaking was as intense and passionate as danger and long abstinence could make it. Afterwards as she lay in Piers's arms, warm and at peace and satiated with love, Nicolette dared to make a suggestion.

'Do you think you should go and see Richard Whittington?' she asked.

'Why? Why do you want me to see Dick?'

'He's your friend. And he has Thomas Mowbray in his custody. He might be able to tell you Mowbray's side of the story.'

'I don't need to hear Mowbray's side. Bolingbroke's not a liar. I'd trust him with my life. Whereas Mowbray's got no idea of chivalry. He murdered Gloucester, I'm sure of that now. He's frightened his sins have caught up with him and so he's turned traitor.' She felt his body tense beneath her hand. She stroked the warm flesh delicately with her fingertips, choosing her words with great care.

'Maybe it's not just a case of who is right and who is wrong. Maybe my father is right and the King means to take his revenge. Ought you not at least to consult Dick?'

Piers raised himself on to his elbow, peered down into her face. 'What can he do?' he demanded, almost roughly.

She reached up to him, wound her arms round his neck. 'He's very close to the King. They say the King consults him over many things. He might know what is in the King's mind.' He was frowning still. She pulled his head towards her, kissed him tentatively. 'Go and see him,' she begged, her lips working slowly along his clenched jaw to the hard line of his mouth. 'To please me.'

Swiftly he responded, pulling her to him and returning her kisses with ardour. 'You know I'd do anything,' he said as he paused for breath, 'to please you.' He covered her aroused and tingling body with his and her heart sang as she abandoned herself once more to his fierce proof that he loved her.

On the third day of Christmas Piers went to see Dick Whittington but the Mayor had little consolation to offer.

'I don't know what Bolingbroke's game is,' he told Piers, 'but whatever it is, it's a dangerous one. You ought to leave him while you can.'

'I don't abandon a man because he's in trouble,' retorted Piers.

'Not even for that beautiful wife of yours?' Dick replied.

Piers glared at him. 'Am I going to have Radcot Bridge thrown in my face for the rest of my life?'

Dick shook his head. 'Nobody but you blames you for what you did. It was the right thing to do at the time. We all have to learn to live with our unpalatable choices. The question now is, what are your choices? Isn't that why you came to see me?'

'I came to see you because Nicolette wanted me to.'

'Ah, the beautiful Nicolette,' Dick sighed. 'She has a good head on her shoulders, your perfect lady. You should listen to her more, my friend.'

'She thought you might know what is in the King's mind,' persevered Piers, ill at ease for the first time in Dick's company and beginning to wish he had not come.

'None of us know what is in the King's mind. What I do know is that your Henry Bolingbroke has played into the King's hand. If the King refuses to believe Bolingbroke, and Bolingbroke is unable to substantiate his charges, he will be branded and disgraced as a perjurer. If the King does believe him and Bolingbroke proves his charges, Thomas Mowbray can be disposed of as a traitor without public complaint.'

'Do you believe Mowbray is guilty?'

'I'm his gaoler not his confessor,' said Dick.

'Gloucester died in his care. If he's not a traitor he's a murderer.' Dick looked uneasy. 'Or was Gloucester murdered by the King's command?'

But Dick was not to be so easily drawn. 'The King's younger friends are daily urging their master to secure his position by disposing of the last two survivors of the original five lords appellant,' he said, subtly changing ground.

'And is that your advice too?' Piers was determined to hit his target somewhere.

'You should know me better than that.' Dick looked at him with a half smile. Piers did not return the smile.

'I know that the King takes your advice, as he once took Nicholas Brembre's,' he accused. There was something about Dick that he could not quite grasp, but he sensed that power had changed his old friend and was disappointed.

'The King doesn't need my advice, just my money.' Dick

was unabashed. 'I believe that the King has a much clearer idea of what he wants than any of us have given him credit for. If it's vengeance, then I'm afraid I can't help you, my friend. Not if you won't desert your liege lord. But I could perhaps do something for the lovely Nicolette which would help your cause. I might be able to get her taken into the Queen's household. One of her ladies-in-waiting died on Christmas Eve. Nicolette is French, she has many delightful accomplishments. The little Queen could well take to her. If she does, I think I could persuade the King to indulge his wife in this. He is very fond of the child.'

All Piers doubts dissolved in a sudden rush of gratitude. 'If you could do that I would be eternally in your debt,' he said, seizing Dick by the hand and shaking it enthusiastically. 'She'd be far happier in the Queen's household away from William Gryffard's constant carping. You're a true friend, Dick.'

'Once in the Queen's household, it will be up to your wife to make herself popular,' said Dick, flexing his fingers gingerly. 'Something which I'm sure she will be able to accomplish easily. Then when you bring down the King's wrath upon your head by your misplaced chivalry, your wife may be able to rescue you from ruin,' he added with his cynical smile.

CHAPTER 27

On the twelfth day of Christmas it began to snow. Nicolette stood by the window of the solar watching the flakes floating down into the street below and shivered.

'What a day to be going to court,' she sighed.

'It don't much matter,' Lisette said brightly, 'since Master Gryffard's got a litter for you to go in.'

Nicolette turned her back on the window as panic seized her. They all of them set such store by this day. Jeanne and Lisette had laboured since prime to get her dressed and looking her best for this most important occasion. William had spared no expense. Even Piers had new clothes for the occasion. So much was expected of her – what if she should fail?

She studied her reflection critically in the polished steel hanging on the wall of the chamber. The gown she wore was of blue velvet with a train of white cloth of gold. The trumpet-shaped sleeves were lined with crimson silk and trimmed with white miniver. But her breasts which once had peeped provocatively now hardly dared to show themselves above the edge of the low-cut bodice; her body beneath the flowing folds of blue velvet was no longer willowy. She was twenty-six, an old married woman, who had borne five children. But she still had her unblemished skin, her eyes and her white teeth. Her hair, tucked out of sight beneath the wonderful artifice of her headdress, was just as long and silky, if a darker shade of gold. She sighed. Her beauty was her most cherished weapon, but it was becoming harder to keep it shining and sharp.

'Still preening!' Piers appeared in the doorway. 'There's

no need. You could go in your shift and still turn all the heads at court.'

'Why Piers, you're becoming quite a courtier,' she said, turning to look at him. He was dressed in a short doublet of purple velvet, tightly belted at the waist, whose long trailing sleeves were also lined with crimson and almost reached the ground. His muscular legs showed off their bright red hose magnificently and his thick black hair curled vigorously round the brim of his high-crowned beaver hat. He was a handsome man, she thought proudly, full of vigour and strength. 'I shall have to keep a careful watch. There will be many ladies at court ready to steal you from me,' she teased.

'You know there's none can do that,' he replied, smiling at her foolishness and she praised God that it was so, that he was all hers and that she had no need to worry on that score. To Piers, she would never be a failure. It was one of the reasons she loved him so.

Christopher was doing somersaults to attract his father's attention, tumbling off the bed on to the platform and bouncing up on to his feet as he hit the floor. It was nimbly done.

Piers caught him firmly by the neck of his tunic and cuffed him lightly. 'You can fetch your mother's cloak, Christopher,' he said. 'We ought to be going.'

'Can I come with you and carry your train, Mama?' the child pleaded, wriggling out of his father's grasp like a playful puppy.

'Not today, Kit,' she said, bending down to kiss him.

'Soon you'll be doing all the fetching and carrying you want,' Piers told him, 'when you go into Henry Bolingbroke's household. Make the most of your freedom while you can.'

Nicolette swallowed nervously. She hoped that they would not all of them have to make the most of their freedom while they could.

In the hall, William was hovering. He studied her anxiously, from the crown of her elaborate headdress to the long pointed toes of her fashionable shoes. She bore his scrutiny calmly, as she had done so many times in the past. It would be too much to expect a word of praise, she thought, glad that Piers was standing at her side full of love and confidence.

'Have you a New Year's gift for the Queen?' William asked.

Her face fell and she glanced helplessly at Piers. How could they have forgotten! William darted a look of triumph at her before he hurried to the trestle where his gold and silver cups were displayed.

'I could give a dog, or a cat, or even a monkey,' said Nicolette, ashamed and at the same time angry that he had found her wanting. 'Something to play with. She's only a child. Not much older than Kit.'

He did not answer. For a while he stood staring at the cups arrayed on the board. Nicolette bit her lip, thinking of his eternal vigilance, the ceaseless watchful anxiety which resulted in no detail ever being overlooked. Finally he picked up a silver-gilt cup and cover.

'This ought to please the Queen's Grace,' he said, gazing at it lovingly. 'I'm told she has an eye for beautiful things remarkable in one so young. Take it.' He held it up in front of her. It was bell-shaped, embossed with oak leaves which glinted in the light from the fire.

'But that is the finest cup in your collection!' she exclaimed.

'I'm sure the Queen will know how to appreciate its worth,' he said almost smugly as he placed the cup carefully in her hands. 'Look upon it not so much as a gift as an investment in our future.' Nicolette clutched the cup to her and fought down rising panic. So many people were relying on her to find favour with a spoilt, imperious child of eight. What if she should fail?

Piers put his arm round her waist. 'Come on,' he said, 'We'd better get started. We don't want to miss any of the fun.' She leant against him gratefully. He was right. They were invited to the palace for a great Twelfth Night banquet. Why should they not enjoy themselves?

As Nicolette alighted from her litter in Westminster Palace, she looked through the falling snow at the great cluster of buildings. Memory swept back to her first visit that Christmas so long along. What an innocent, silly girl she had been then. As if sensing her fears, Piers put an arm round her waist, squeezing it gently.

'Courage, my darling,' he said. 'You're as good as the best of them.'

She handed the cup to Crispin. 'Guard it well, Crispin, until the Queen sends for me.'

The squire took it from her, tucked it dexterously under his arm and bent to pick up her train. 'You can rely on me, my lady,' he said with perfect grace.

'I know that, Crispin,' she said smiling at him. He should be a knight by now, she thought, but they had no rich manors to give him and he could not win his spurs when the country was at peace.

At the entrance to the central hall, a bowing chamberlain informed them that the ladies were to eat in the Queen's chamber and summoned a page to show Nicolette the way. The page led her up a narrow stone stairway; she clutched the precious cup in one hand and held up her skirts with the other, getting her wide trailing sleeves tangled and wishing she could have kept Crispin with her to carry her train.

The stairs led into an antechamber. Music played, flames leapt in the hearth, candles blazed. The tapestries covering the walls rippled in the draught and the figures woven on it danced. As Nicolette stood in the doorway listening to the babble of French, she felt excitement rising within her. Here among all these French noblewomen was where she belonged. She remembered her mother, the poor faded beauty who had fallen from grace because of her. If Margarite de St Pierre had not become pregnant, she would not have had to go into a nunnery. She might have been like one of these ladies here.

Nicolette clutched the silver-gilt cup more tightly to her. This was how she could repay her mother for the curse of her birth. Blessed Mary, Mother of Jesus, let them like me, she prayed as her name was called by a herald in ringing tones. The babble of French ceased, curious eyes examined her, the music played on. A stern-looking woman detached herself from a group by the fire and came sweeping across the chamber.

'I am the Dame de Courcy, the Queen's Mistress of Ceremonies,' she announced and Nicolette, not sure of the procedure, swept her a curtsey. Looking pleased, the Mistress of Ceremonies took her across the chamber and presented her to the other ladies; Nicolette was delighted to find that some of them she had already met – at St Inglevert. Soon she was happily chatting to them in her native tongue and blushing becomingly as they teased her for the way her husband had defended her favour what seemed a lifetime ago. They stood about in little groups, pretending to be engaged in conversation but in reality watching each new arrival.

When Alice Whittington arrived, she was welcomed graciously by the Dame de Courcy as befitted her rank as Lady Mayoress, but she looked uncomfortable in these surroundings. Nicolette smiled at her across the chamber and was touched when Alice came and joined her. To put her at her ease, she showed her the gift she had brought for the Queen and asked if it would be acceptable.

'It's very fine,' said Alice, turning the cup round in her hands with care. 'William Gryffard must be very anxious to get rid of you.' All Nicolette's elation vanished like early mist on a summer's morning. It had never occurred to her that her father might want her out of his way. 'Don't look so stricken, my dear. I was only joking,' Alice soothed. 'But won't you miss your children in the Queen's household?'

'I shall just have to get used to being without them,' Nicolette said, wishing Alice did not always make her feel so guilty. 'Other women do and Kit will be leaving us soon anyway to go into Henry Bolingbroke's household.'

'If he has a household left to go into,' said Alice.

Nicolette repressed a shiver of fear. 'That's why it's so important I should succeed today,' she said. 'William is very much afraid, although Piers says there is nothing to fear.'

'Like all brave men, Piers fears nothing except fear itself. It sometimes makes them blind to danger. But you too have courage, Lady Exton, or you would not be here today.'

Nicolette wanted to ask Alice what she meant but her words were drowned by the sound of a trumpet.

'Make way for the Queen of England,' declaimed the herald. With a rustle of silk, all the women sank into deep curtseys as a small procession entered the room. All Nicolette could see as she rose from her curtsey was a gleam of gold above a floating veil as the Queen, surrounded by her ladies-in-waiting, walked through the chamber. The ladies stood back while the Queen held her fingers above a basin for a page to pour scented water. Her gown was stiff with embroidery, the golden crown heavy for so small a head. The ceremony of washing completed, the Queen processed regally to the high table in the adjoining room.

Nicolette was overwhelmed with panic once more. How could she possibly hope to reach so precocious a little creature, so spoilt and formal and aware of her own importance? How find favour with a child such as that in the short time available to her?

By the time all the ladies had been seated according to their rank and station, the Queen had eaten all she wanted of the first course. Nicolette, bewildered by the multiplicity of dishes littering the table, had barely begun when the trumpet sounded again. The Mistress of Ceremonies announced that the Queen would watch the entertainment in the hall. The benches were pushed back, the ladies scrambled to their feet and processed out in the Queen's wake, to a long gallery hung with tapestries and scattered with silken cushions upon which the ladies settled with a flutter of their colourful draperies like birds of paradise taking over a pigeon loft.

Nicolette looked down into the great hall at the noisy, colourful scene. In the centre was a long rectangular table decorated with tapestry and covered with a dazzling display of gem-studded gold and silver work. She thought of the gift she had brought the Queen and wondered whether the most prized item in her father's valuable collection was of any significance at all amid so much splendour. The men were sitting at tables ranged along either side of the hall, watching an allegorical scene – a spectacle of costume so costly and elaborate that no one had much attention to spare for its meaning. When the entertainment was over, a fanfare of trumpets paved the way for a long line of pages with more food, and the Queen led her ladies back to their own chamber for the second course.

The feasting continued throughout the afternoon, with repeated sallies to the gallery to watch the various entertainments which took place between each course. There were dwarves, a wooden painted whale containing musicians, a troupe of mummers dressed as savages besieging a castle filled with live birds. It was while returning from one of these trips that Nicolette found herself summoned by the Mistress of Ceremonies to the Queen who was seated in a large, carved chair, barely visible above the top of the table. Nicolette curtseyed low to the ground and waited for permission to rise.

'They tell me you want to take Mariete de Tigonville's place. What makes you think you can?' the high-pitched childish voice demanded. Nicolette was taken aback by such a direct attack and tried desperately to think of a winning reply. 'She was my favourite, you know.' Just for a moment the childish voice trembled. 'She grew big with child, so big that she died.'

'I know that nobody can take the place of a loved and trusted friend,' said Nicolette, feeling her way carefully, 'but I would do my best to serve Your Grace in whatever way I can.'

'Do you have a husband?'

'Yes, Madame, an English husband, just like Your Grace.'

The Queen toyed with a pink sweetmeat in the shape of a deer, holding it delicately in her small bejewelled fingers. 'You won't get big with child and die like the Dame de Tigonville?' she asked.

'No,' promised Nicolette, crossing herself furtively beneath the edge of the table. The Queen bit the head off the deer and chewed it thoughtfully. Nicolette, still kneeling, tried to ignore the ache in her legs.

'Can you tell good stories?' the Queen asked presently. 'Geoffrey Chaucer tells me stories, he's a friend of the King my husband.'

'I'm afraid I can't tell stories like Geoffrey Chaucer's,' said Nicolette. It was not easy to look at the Queen crouched as she was on the floor, but she managed to get a glimpse of the sullen little face peering at her over the top of the table.

'You speak French like a Frenchwoman,' the child told her.

'I am French,' Nicolette replied, 'and often I am homesick for France, which is why, Madame, I so much wish to join your household.'

The Queen's face grew sad. 'I too am homesick for France.' She began to dig about in the dishes in front of her, searching for a morsel of something to tempt her jaded appetite. 'If you can't tell stories, can you play games?' she asked, stifling a yawn.

'I was born and brought up in the Abbey of the Holy Trinity at Caen, Madame,' Nicolette said. 'We were not permitted to play games.'

'A nun!' The Queen stared at Nicolette over the edge of the

table. 'You don't look like a nun. Chaucer knows a nun that tells stories.'

Desperately Nicolette searched her wits for some way to dispel the Queen's languid ennui. 'Perhaps, Madame, you could teach me how to play games,' she said. The Queen stopped eating and stared at Nicolette. 'Would that not be fun? Better than lessons.'

Suddenly the Queen smiled and clapped her hands together. 'All the time they want me to learn things. I'm tired of all the things I'm supposed to know.'

'Do you know some pretty French songs?' asked Nicolette pressing home her advantage. 'In the abbey we only learnt how to sing plainsong. I think perhaps I would not miss France so much if you, Madame, could teach me how to sing.'

'Can I really?' The Queen squinted at Nicolette over the top of the table. 'You won't scold me if I sing flat?'

'I'm sure Your Grace never sings flat,' Nicolette replied and then because the child looked doubtful added quickly, 'I have brought Your Grace a New Year's gift. If you will permit me, I shall fetch it.'

The Queen graciously gave her leave to rise and Nicolette brought William's cup and placed it on the table; beside the ornamental silver-gilt salt cellar it looked a poor gift for a Queen.

'For me,' cried the Queen, picking it up and turning it round in her little hands, examining it carefully. 'It's good. We like it.' She handed the cup to a page. 'You can be my lady-in-waiting if the King likes you. He should be pleased, he wants me to have ladies from England in my household, but I won't have anyone who is not French.'

When at last the tables in the central hall were dismantled the Queen and the ladies went down to join in the dancing. As they arrived in the hall, the King walked down the flight of stairs from the high table to greet his young wife. It was an act of singular condescension and Nicolette watched the child turn quite pink with pleasure. Richard bowed over her hand, treating her as if she were a full grown adult, and Isabella drew herself up to her full height with regal dignity.

'Sire, may I present for your approval my new lady-in-waiting, Lady Exton?' she said.

The King turned to look at Nicolette and she sank into a deep curtsey, keeping her head bent, suddenly fearful that he might remember her. She had been at court several times when Nicholas Brembre had been advising the King and although never officially presented to him, she had attended the evening meals and spent many a happy hour in his last Queen's apartments. Would he remember her, and if he did, would he deem the woman who had been Brembre's mistress unsuitable to attend the innocent child he was married to now?

'You may rise, Lady Exton,' he said. 'Exton!' He frowned, staring at her. 'S-Surely I know that name.' The frown turned to a scowl and her heart missed a beat. 'Of course, Nicholas Exton. He was that rascal of a mayor when the Londoners let me down. You're not married to him, are you?'

She shook her head. 'No, no – a distant cousin.' She was terrified that he might begin to question her about Piers, but Richard Whittington came to her rescue.

'Ah, Whittington,' said the King as Dick bowed low before him. 'Do you not like my new roof? Is it not a masterpiece?'

'A work of art for which you, Sire, will still be remembered when many other deeds are long forgotten,' said Dick, looking up at the delicate carving high above his head.

'S-So I don't waste money on everything.' The King was beaming with pleasure.

'No, Sire,' replied Dick, bowing now before the little Queen. 'The King's Grace is a great lover of beautiful things and it is never a waste to spend money on beauty. Is that not so, Madame?' The Queen smiled and dimpled at him prettily.

What a courtier he is, thought Nicolette, impressed by the way he managed to delight both King and Queen. It was hard to believe sometimes that he was a mercer and not a knight.

Dick caught her glance and smiled a little mockingly. Then he took her hand in an almost proprietary way and turned to the Queen. 'Does she please you, Madame?' he asked.

'Very much. But of course I won't take her unless my husband also wishes it,' said the Queen. Nicolette held her

338

breath, terrified lest the King should suddenly recognise her and send her away.

'Have her by all means – whatever you want,' said the King.

Nicolette let out her breath in a long thankful sigh but it was some time before she dared to look up. By then the King was taking his young wife to dance and Nicolette found herself alone with Dick.

'A singular victory, Lady Exton,' he said, raising her hand to his lips. 'The Queen is no easy conquest.'

'I couldn't have done it without you, my Lord Mayor,' Nicolette responded, twinkling at him as elation bubbled inside her. 'I had no idea you were such a silver-tongued charmer.'

'I've had some practice of late,' he said. 'But don't think it will be all music and honey from now on. The Queen's a capricious little minx and her household a hotbed of gossip. You'll have to be very careful.'

'It can't be easy for her,' said Nicolette. 'What must it be like for the proud daughter of the King of France to be thrust so young into the role of consort, to be expected to uphold the honour of France all on her own in a foreign land, especially one that is the natural enemy of her own country? It's no wonder she is so full of airs and graces. She must feel threatened on every side.'

'I thought I was doing my Nicolette a favour today,' said Dick smiling at her, and this time there was no mockery in his smile. 'But perhaps it is the Queen who will be rewarding me for finding her such a sympathetic lady-in-waiting.' Nicolette was warmed by his approval but took care not to show him how much. She looked about for a sight of Piers and noticed that the King had already grown bored with his wife and restored her to her ladies-in-waiting. The Queen yawned – a small yawn, quickly suppressed behind her jewelled fingers. Nicolette's heart went out to her new mistress. Isabella looked exhausted by the long day's festivities. There would be many more before Christmastide was over. Then she became aware that Dick was looking at her somewhat expectantly and realised that she had not yet thanked him properly for what he had done for her. But before she was more than halfway through a very pretty speech, he interrupted her.

'You can show me your gratitude by dancing with me, my lady.' He took her by the hand but she drew back. She did not quite trust the gleam in his eye. Was it desire or was it amusement? With Dick it was impossible to tell what he was feeling.

'I must find Piers,' she said. 'I haven't seen him since we arrived.'

'Piers is in hiding.' Dick drew her arm through his and Nicolette gave a little gasp of fright. 'I told your husband to keep out of the King's way. He was mad to come to the palace at all. I offered to escort you here, but that noble husband of yours insisted that he must bring you himself.'

'You don't think Piers is in any danger, do you?' asked Nicolette, terrified that he might not be joking.

'After what happened when the King asked Arundel and Warwick to a banquet?' Dick shook his head sadly. 'I'm surprised at you, Nicolette. I thought you had sense as well as beauty. You won't last long at court if you can't keep your wits about you better than that.'

Nicolette suddenly remembered what Alice had said. Piers was so brave it made him blind to danger. He had bolstered her courage and supported her and she had never given a thought to what it meant for him. He was risking his life for her and all she could think about was her own puny success.

'I must find him,' she said, abruptly breaking away from Dick.

She found him dancing with one of the Queen's ladies and not in hiding at all. As soon as the dance was finished, he excused himself with easy grace and came to her side.

'We must leave at once,' she said plucking at his hanging sleeve. 'Where's Crispin?'

'Why, my beloved? What has happened to upset you?'

'Suppose the King recognises you? Remembers what you've done? It's not safe for you here. And I've been a stupid fool not to realise it before.'

He laughed. 'Don't worry, my angel. The King isn't going to concern himself with me. Come and dance. I haven't danced with you in a long time.' But she wouldn't hear of it. She hurried him away out into the now clear and frosty night. It was only then, as he lifted her into the litter, that he asked how she had fared with the Queen.

'The Queen liked me, thanks be to God,' Nicolette told

him. 'And the King has agreed that I may be taken into the Queen's household.'

'The saints be praised. You'll be safe now.' He said it so low she guessed she was not meant to hear. She felt a great weight descend upon her. The Whittingtons were right. Piers was brave and strong but he courted danger. She could not rely on him for protection. Dick had also made her see that if she wanted to succeed she must look after herself. But how was she to do that without being selfish? Was it better to be brave and true and ride headlong into trouble like Piers, or to try to see trouble coming and avoid it like her father with his fears and endless anxiety? She did not want to be like William Gryffard but she did not dare to be like Piers.

CHAPTER 28

William tossed in his sleep and came up against warm, soft flesh. He drifted back to consciousness and the sound of snoring. I must be getting old, he thought, to have fallen asleep immediately. He didn't usually. He liked to kick them out before that point.

He poked and prodded her. The whore took some waking, but she climbed out of his bed eventually, muttering curses. He was glad it was too dark to see her ugly body. He lay in bed listening to her stumbling about on the other side of the bed curtains and wondered why he bothered with the Widow Wendegoos when he could have someone younger and more flavoursome for his money. Of course he could always get married again, and then he would not have to rely on whores for comfort. But marriage, he had found, created as many problems as it solved. Once he had had a wife as beautiful as Nicolette and he had lusted after her. She had been good and dutiful, but cold, and he had bedded all the female servants in the household because she made him feel so unwanted. Nicolette also made him feel unwanted, although she was warm and loving enough with Piers.

With sleep slipping away from him, William cursed the whorish widow for having proved so difficult to arouse and burrowed down beneath the bed covers. What if he were to get married again? It was lonely here in the big house without Nicolette. He thought of his second wife. She had brought him much-needed outlets for his trading empire and some useful property. He cast his mind over all the widows he knew. None of them were wealthy enough for his needs.

The Widow Wendegoos stuck her head through the bed curtains and demanded payment. She was getting old and fear made her greedier, but the information she gleaned from her other clients and passed on to William had sometimes proved very useful. This time, however, she had nothing new for him; he haggled with her until he was wide awake again and finally sent her away with a curse.

When she had gone, he sank back into the warm softness of his feather mattress, vainly seeking sleep, but the peace her undesirable flesh had bought for him had proved even more fleeting than usual. Behind the tightly drawn bed curtains, he lay wide awake and worrying, alone with his fears.

What had gone wrong? When had his carefully fortified financial castle started to crumble? He cast his mind back to the day he had learnt about the ship overdue at Genoa. It had never arrived. He had many ships at sea, carrying much merchandise. One ship missing was a pity but it shouldn't be a disaster, except that he had not insured the cargo. He told himself that the reason he hadn't was that it was so difficult to collect the insurance money, but he knew that wasn't true. He had taken a chance, because he needed to make a greater profit. One step on the road to ruin. Risk was all part of his daily toil, as inevitable as death to life. The secret was to balance the risk. He'd had a run of bad luck lately, but he knew, none better, that only fools were ruined by bad luck alone. Bad luck came when you took too many chances, and he had taken too many chances trying to get rich quickly. Money was not made by chance but by effort.

William flung himself on to his back and stared up into the velvety blackness above his head. If he didn't do something soon to stem the tide he would be facing ruin and a debtor's prison. He must devote himself anew to the onerous task of making money, as many hours as it took, as many hours as God gave. Misunderstandings had arisen because he had not kept in sufficiently close touch with all his agents. That would have to change, starting with Calais. Something would have to be done about his partner in Calais. The man was robbing him, he was sure of it, only the rogue was being so clever, William could not quite work out how he was doing it. He must go to Calais and take over the business himself. Get rid of his partner. Except he couldn't leave England, not now, not until he'd managed to get Piers to make over the house to him. The house was worth an earl's ransom. If only he could wrest it back. At least if Bolingbroke was disgraced

Piers might be prepared to give up the house to safeguard Nicolette and the children's future. One of the few things Piers could be relied upon for was his chivalry.

William sat up in bed grasping handfuls of the soft fur of the bed cover in exasperation. The adjourned Parliament had met in Shrewsbury on 28 January. Bolingbroke had publicly accused Mowbray of plotting to kill him and his father at Windsor. But the King had dissolved Parliament before it could investigate the matter further. Parliament had only sat for three days – long enough for the citizens of Shrewsbury to be beggared by the expensive privilege of providing for the King and his court and for Parliament to secure the King's own finances by granting him the duties on wool, woolfells and leather for life. To conclude unfinished business, a committee had been appointed made up of the King's uncles Lancaster and York, the King's heir the Earl of March, and the Earl Marshal, Northumberland, plus six knights of the shires and the Earls of Worcester and Wiltshire as clergy's proctors. William suspected that the committee would do as the King willed, which is why he had been in such a hurry to dissolve Parliament. William groaned with frustration. There was nothing he could do except wait for Nicolette to send him word.

At the thought of his daughter, he became calmer. At least with Nicolette in the Queen's household he knew what was happening at court. He wrote to her frequently and she kept him well informed.

In the second week of Lent, William received a letter from Nicolette full of tidings that struck fear into his heart. Her letter came from Bristol where the court had gone in March. Bolingbroke and Mowbray had met face to face at Oswestry in the King's presence and each had accused the other of treason. Henry had challenged Mowbray to trial by battle and accused him of the murder of Gloucester and misappropriating funds while Constable of Calais. The committee appointed by Parliament was looking into the case. William let the letter fall and sank down on to the stool in his counting house. If they started investigating Thomas Mowbray's financial dealings while Constable of Calais, what else might they find. He leapt up and searched through his ledgers until he found the one he wanted. He rifled through the pages. There it all was, carefully recorded in his own neat hand. He tore at the parchment but it was too strong for his trembling fingers. He seized the eating knife he kept tucked into his girdle and began hacking at the pages in the ledger. When he had cut them free he held them up to the candle flame and watched them burn. Only when they were a pile of ashes among the rushes at his feet did he breathe freely again.

But not for long. He could destroy the evidence but he could not prevent the captain telling his tale to Mowbray and Mowbray would be looking for a scapegoat. Deny it as he might, they would not take the word of a merchant against that of a knight and a nobleman. He longed to run back to Calais. He was needed in Calais. He could go tonight. Take his partner by surprise, find out what the rogue was up to and get rid of him. Only he did not dare. He picked up Nicolette's letter, sat down on the stool. Composed himself to read the rest of it. She told him that the court would be at Windsor in April where the King was to celebrate Easter.

He laid the letter carefully on the table in front of him and wondered whether he could not use Nicolette to help with more than just information. If he was to rescue his crumbling castle from ruin, he needed to find a new source of revenue. He thought with longing of the lucrative new taxes the King had been granted at Shrewsbury. If Nicolette was well thought of at court, she might be able to help put in a word for him with the King. Of course the surest way to the King's favour was to lend him money, but William was not in a position to lend money to anybody just at the moment.

He stared round at his counting house, his eyes travelling lovingly over the ledgers; there was no merchandise here, no money. Just an intricate network of promises and trust which he had woven so carefully over the years. It was like a spider's web, and as easily broken. Nothing would be solved by running away to Calais. Calais was not the cause of his financial sickness, it was merely a symptom. So for once he decided to do what he had never done before: meet trouble head on.

On 2 April, William set off for Windsor, reaching it the following day. As he approached the castle, he found he had to compete with farmers from the surrounding countryside bringing in their produce, much of it on the hoof. Ducks and geese waddled by the roadside, pausing to pick at the trampled grass, swine and milking cows and oxen, pulling carts filled with every sort of provision, straggled all over the road. Inside the town of Windsor it was no better. Shopkeepers stood in the middle of the streets crying their wares or ran panting towards the castle laden with them; men on horseback jostled those on foot. William's own retinue was somewhat cumbersome since he had decided that if all was well he would continue westwards into the Cotswolds to buy wool. He had with him two men-at-arms, a train of packhorses and a wool brogger, who would supervise the packing of the wool he bought. The packhorses were cursed by everybody as they plodded placidly through the gutter in the middle of the cobbled road, scattering its unsavoury contents to right and left.

'We'd better not go no further,' said the brogger. 'There won't be room for us, not up at the castle.' The wool brogger was the best in the trade, one who knew every trick a farmer might try. He could spot a sack of wool which had been unfairly weighted quicker than a hawk a mouse. But he liked to be comfortable when he could. 'Best if I was to start looking for lodgings here in the town. With all this lot here, we'll be lucky if we can find a stable to sleep in, let alone a bed.'

'No,' said William. 'Wait for me by the castle gate. I want to be able to find you and don't mean to go looking for you all over the town.' He did not say that if the news was bad he wouldn't be staying.

A knight came riding up the street clad from head to foot in steel with his squire at his side. The knight's charger struck out with its forefeet at the docile pack animals in its path and they scattered with a squeal, sending pedestrians flying and panicking William's amiable rouncy who blundered into an armourer's stall and sent the whole crashing to the ground with enough noise to waken the dead.

'By Christ's thorns!' swore William rubbing his knee which had caught the corner of the stall. 'No need to ride down every street as if into battle.' But the knight, supremely indifferent to the chaos in his wake, was fast disappearing through the portcullis into the castle. William followed, suppressing his anger. It was useless, he knew, to expect a knight to show chivalry to the lesser orders. Chivalry was something they only showed to each other.

The great paved courtyard in the lower ward was as full of

confusion as the streets outside. William surveyed the scene in dismay as he dismounted.

'Wait here inside the gates,' he told the brogger. 'See if you can water the animals. There should be a trough somewhere if you can find it in this mêlée.'

He pushed his way through the milling throng past the Round Tower and through another arched gateway into the upper ward. Here he paused, not sure where the Queen's apartments lay. A page came darting over the grassy courtyard and William caught hold of him by his hanging sleeve. 'Do you think you can find Lady Exton for me?' he asked.

The page grinned. 'I'd be delighted,' he said. 'Who shall I say sent me?'

'Master Gryffard,' replied William, pleased that Nicolette's name had such a good effect. 'I'll wait here.' The page bowed – a cursory nod of the head, but a bow nonetheless. William began to feel better.

People came and went – pages running to and fro on innumerable errands, two squires with hawks on their fists, deep in conversation, a lady, her train held by two pages and her veil floating out from a high headdress. She passed him by without so much as a glance. He watched as he waited, unable to let his busy mind rest, while the sound of music and occasional laughter drifted down from the turreted walls above his head and the soft April breeze caressed his hot cheeks.

Presently the page returned. Behind him hurried Nicolette. She was dressed in a blue robe trimmed with fur and her pale gold hair was looped in a net of fine gold mesh which sparkled in the last rays of the spring sunshine. She held out her hands to him with a worried smile.

'Master Gryffard, why did you not send me word that you were coming? The castle is so full I don't know where they can house you.'

'No matter. I dare say I can find lodgings somewhere in the town.' He was suddenly aware of how much he had missed her. 'Are you behaving yourself? Serving the Queen as you should?' he demanded. 'Is the Queen pleased with you?'

'I think so.' She looked at her feet doubtfully. He wished she had seemed more pleased to see him, showed at least some interest in why he had come. He gazed at her proudly.

His little bastard had done well for herself, married to a knight and lady-in-waiting to the Queen. But she could not have done it without him. Without him she'd be penniless. But if he wasn't careful he would lose her. It was Whittington who had got her into the Queen's household, after all. Whittington and Piers between them thought they were taking care of his daughter for him, but only he, her father, really knew how to look after her properly. If he left everything to Piers, they'd all be penniless. Let Nicolette find out then how much Whittington was prepared to do for her.

'Your children – don't you want to know how they are?' he asked harshly.

She looked at him, startled. 'They're not ill, are they?' she asked anxiously.

'Only Tarquin's cough,' he said. 'He's had it ever since you left.'

'Jeanne de Bourdat writes to me regularly – she doesn't seem worried by Tarquin's cough.' There was something about the calm almost defiant way she looked at him that made him feel spurned. She thought she didn't need him any more.

'They may be well, but they miss you,' he told her. 'They need a mother.' He hadn't meant to say it, but he wanted her to feel spurned too. Her eyes filled with tears.

'I'll ask the Queen if I can ride back to London with you to see them. As an Easter boon,' she said.

'I'm not going back to London. I'm on my way to the Cotswolds.'

'Isn't it early for the woolclip?'

'Spring is early this year and I like to get ahead of the rest. I may even buy while the wool is on the sheep's back.' She was looking so crestfallen he regretted his tiny victory. 'Piers can take you to London,' he said, relenting. 'If the Queen grants you permission.'

'Piers isn't here. He left yesterday with Henry.'

'And Mowbray?' William demanded.

'He's still here,' she said. She looked uneasy and William cursed himself for a fool. He should have come earlier, then he might have caught Piers, persuaded him to make over the house. 'Has Bolingbroke retired to his castle in disgrace?' he asked as he fought down panic.

'No, no. He's got what he wanted. Trial by battle. Piers is delighted. He says it's the best way, a good clean fight. If Henry is innocent, God will see that right prevails.'

William breathed a sigh of relief. Trial by battle meant that nobody was going to begin delving into Thomas Mowbray's financial dealings in Calais. He was for once glad that between noblemen might was right and no other evidence was deemed necessary to prove innocence.

'When is it to be?' he asked.

'In September at Coventry.'

'That's a long time to wait. Why can't they fight here and now and get the matter settled one way or the other?'

'There's a lot to arrange. A Court of Chivalry is a splendid occasion. Two of England's most famous knights equal in rank and prowess in a *curia militaris*. It'll be a rare treat.' Her eyes were shining with excitement. 'Knights will come from far and wide to be there, just like Saint Inglevert. It will take time to arrange such a spectacle.'

'Will it be such a spectacle when one of them is killed?' asked William. 'Trial by battle is a fight to the death, is it not?'

She gave a little shiver and glanced over her shoulder nervously. 'I can't stay much longer,' she said. 'The Queen may need me.'

He caught hold of her wrist. 'When will I see you again?'

She looked down at his fingers almost disdainfully. 'I'll have a word with the steward to see if he can find a place for you in the hall for supper tonight,' she said. 'But I don't know if I shall be there; the Queen may sup in her own apartments.' He knew she was slipping away from him; the hawk he had taken such trouble to tame was being fed by another, more generous, hand and soon she would no longer come to the lure.

'There is something you can do for me,' he said tightening his grip on her wrist. 'Something which would help me a great deal, as I have helped you, my daughter,' he reminded her. 'I've had a run of bad luck – fortune's wheel. It happens to us all at times.' He wished that she would not stand with averted gaze as if he were some sort of beggar. 'The really successful men are those who can keep going when trouble comes, who can turn it to advantage. With your help I shall do that.'

She was clearly startled. 'How can I help you?' she asked.

'The Queen,' he murmured.

'I cannot ask the Queen for money.' She looked appalled.

'Not money, a boon. The Shrewsbury Parliament granted the King duties on wool, woolfells and leather for life,' he said, ignoring the distaste on her lovely face. 'He will need a man to collect the customs for him. I could be that man. I'm ideally suited to the task.'

'Why can't you ask the King yourself?'

'Think of your children, if not your father,' he urged, ignoring her question. 'And your husband. What will he be able to do for you if Bolingbroke is defeated in September?'

'Piers says Henry will win,' she said. 'There's nothing to fear.'

'Help me in this,' he begged, 'and I shall be able to feed and shelter you and your husband and your children whatever happens at the Court of Chivalry in September.'

She was silent, biting her lip and staring down at her feet, while he held fast to her wrist, thinking with a detached part of his mind that even in perplexity her face was still lovely.

'The King is fond of his child bride, I'm told,' he said. 'Indulges her in much. Will you not try for me?'

'The Queen is but a child, she knows nothing and cares less about such matters.'

'Then speak to the King,' he demanded, losing all patience with her. 'Use your wits, Nicolette, or your beauty. I don't have to instruct you how to charm men. But I tell you, if you cannot get me the wool customs I don't know how I am to provide any longer for you and your children.'

She stared at him, aghast. 'But I thought you were so rich, so successful.'

'I was and I will be again.' He pinched her cheek. 'You're my flesh and blood, after all. It's not much to ask.' He released her then and she backed away from him nervously.

'I'll try,' she said. 'But I cannot promise to succeed.'

'Yes you can, my dear,' he said. 'You were not born to fail – not like your mother.'

She shot him a glance of pure fear before darting away down the long passage that led to the Queen's apartments.

He watched her, knowing that he had found the goad that would spur her into battle on his behalf. But he wished he did not have to ask it of her. Then he shook himself angrily.

Feelings were dangerous. Women were the very devil if you allowed yourself to become fond of them. He had lost his heart once, to Mariota, but recovered when he discovered how cold and poor-spirited his wife was. Then he had transferred his passion to Mariota's half-sister and made a fool of himself. Now he was in danger of growing too fond of Nicolette and she was likely to be the worst of them all, for she could twist a man round her little finger and break him if she had a mind to it.

CHAPTER 29

The Queen was having a tantrum. As Nicolette hurried towards the Queen's bedchamber, she could hear the high-pitched childish voice screaming in French and her heart sank.

'Where is the Dame d'Exton?' the Queen was demanding. 'You're so clumsy, Marie de Saint Pol, I shall never be ready in time.' Nicolette slipped into the chamber and threw herself down on her knees in front of the little Queen, bending so low her brow almost brushed the brightly painted floor tiles.

'Forgive me, Madame,' she said.

'Where have you been?' demanded the Queen. 'I need you here.'

'I was called away on an errand of mercy.' Frantically Nicolette racked her brain for some sort of fantasy to proffer as an excuse, which might fire the child's imagination. 'A dragon flew into the upper ward, blowing great puffs of smoke so that day was turned into night and every time he opened his mouth a great flame shot out of it.' She paused for effect, raised her head and caught the disapproving eye of the Dame de Courcy.

'It's not true, is it? There isn't really a dragon in the upper ward?' said the Queen, staring wide-eyed at Nicolette.

'No, Madame, it isn't true,' said Nicolette. 'Have I your permission to rise?'

The Queen nodded. 'Tell me more about the dragon. What happened to him? Did they catch him?' Isabella fidgeted restlessly while Marie de St Pol rubbed her thick brown hair with a silk cloth to increase its shine.

'Well, the poor dragon was lost, you see, and had only

come to ask his way home but everyone was so terrified of catching fire, they all ran away.' The Mistress of Ceremonies was frowning horribly. Nicolette picked up a comb and a handful of hair from Marie. 'Madame, how would you like your hair braided, tonight?' she asked. 'Will you wear your new headdress?'

'Not the new headdress, idiot.' The Queen stamped her foot. 'My crown.'

'The Queen will take her meats in the hall,' the Mistress of Ceremonies announced as Nicolette began the elaborate braiding of her mistress's hair. 'Everyone who is anyone will be in the hall for supper tonight.'

'The King wants me to be there beside him. To show them all,' explained the Queen, twisting round and looking up at Nicolette with an expression half defiant, half afraid. 'So I must look my best, my very best. The honour of France is at stake.'

'The King is very proud of you,' said Nicolette as she wound the thick braids round the small head to make a cushion for the crown. 'He wants to show all his nobles what a very fortunate man he is to be married to a daughter of France.' She pinned the braids carefully in place.

Marie brought a fine Venetian veil which covered the Queen's hair and tightly hugged the small childish face. Two other ladies brought a casket of jewels. Isabella took a long time choosing which ones she would wear. When her fingers were covered with rings and her flat child's chest decorated with a large ruby pendant, she seemed satisfied. Then the Mistress of Ceremonies brought the crown and carefully set the thin gold circlet on top of her veil. Ready at last, the Queen stared at herself in the Venetian glass mirror. The tantrum was over. She had herself well under control now. She would behave throughout the evening with the dignity and restraint she had been taught since birth.

Nicolette, looking at her own reflection, wished she'd had time to dress properly for the grand company in the hall tonight. But William's appearance had put paid to that. She caught the Queen's eye in the mirror and smiled reassuringly. The Queen did not return the smile.

'We are ready,' she said, her small head with its gold burden proudly erect. 'We shall go down to supper.'

Nicolette bent and picked up one corner of the Queen's

heavily embroidered train while Marie de St Pol picked up the other. The Mistress of Ceremonies led the way out of the chamber. Preceded by heralds, they walked out of the Queen's apartments, across grass-covered courts, down winding stone stairs, along passageways until they reached the entrance to the great hall.

A fanfare of trumpets announced the Queen's arrival as they entered through a carved wooden screen. Slowly they processed between the long trestle tables. Nicolette walked close to Marie, keeping in careful step with her fellow lady-in-waiting, her eyes on the train they held between them until they reached the dais at the end of the hall. Solemnly the Queen mounted the steps, washed her fingers in the scented water presented to her by a page. Nicolette and Marie helped her into one of the two carved arm chairs in the middle of the table, arranging her train, her fur-trimmed hanging sleeves, the floating ends of her veil. Then the trumpets rang out again. The King was coming. The Queen had to be helped to her feet, her chair pulled out so it would not interfere with her train. The King received a deep curtsey, the Bishop of York said Grace, and then the Queen was ready to resume her seat and it was all to do again. Nicolette and Marie stood back behind the Queen's chair. Not until Isabella released them would they be free to go and eat their own supper lower down in the hall.

The King and Queen sat in the middle of a line of glittering, gorgeously jewelled men and women at the high table while pages and squires came and went with wine and food like busy drones flying in and out of a beehive. Nicolette tried to keep out of their way and yet be ready to attend to her mistress if she should need her. Tonight it did not look as if she would be needed, for the King was being very attentive, picking choice morsels out of the dishes in front of him and placing them on his wife's trencher, sharing the bowl of more liquid food with her and from time to time passing her his wine goblet. The Queen was delighted. She ate carefully and drank sparingly, as poised and dignified as always. But Nicolette could tell from the pink flush in her usually rather pale cheeks that she was much gratified.

Nicolette studied Richard, sitting so near and bending forward a little so he could hear what his wife was saying above the noise of the music. He was a handsome man, still in

354

his prime and tonight he was being very kind. It was not surprising that Isabella was so devoted to him. He was so near, Nicolette had only to reach out to tap him on the shoulder. 'Your pardon, Sire, but please will you let Master Gryffard collect the customs on the wool subsidies for you?' Nicolette turned cold at the very thought. How could she possibly misuse her position in the royal household to intrude on him thus? It was unthinkable.

She gazed out over the Queen's head at the packed tables in the hall below. From up here on the dais it was a splendid sight, the blazing torches on the walls, the colourful banners hanging from the vaulted roof, the rows of richly dressed men and women seated at table, the music, the heraldic symbols, the occasional bright flash as a silver goblet or a dagger caught the flickering candlelight. The heraldic symbols prancing on banner and surcoat were like a jungle of wild beasts waiting to pounce – like Thomas Mowbray, thought Nicolette. For a time he had been a prisoner in the castle's dungeons, but he was now out on parole, free within the precincts of the castle. She must avoid him at all costs. Especially now that Piers had gone. Dear God, if only Piers were here. If only she could see his faithful gaze looking up at her from the body of the hall. If only he was here at her side to protect her and not on his way to Hereford protecting Henry Bolingbroke.

She shrank back a little further behind the Queen's chair. Up here she was safe, from Mowbray, from William Gryffard and his impossible demands, but not from her troubled thoughts. How could her father, the fount of so much plenty, be running out of money? It was frightening. It was impossible to contemplate. William who was so wily, so careful, who always knew what to do and where to turn, was in trouble, or so he said. She couldn't believe it, wouldn't believe it. Always he worried about things, imagined the worst.

The Queen twisted round in her seat and beckoned. Nicolette glided forward. 'You may go and have your supper now, if you wish,' she said with a wave of her hand. Nicolette and Marie slid unobtrusively to the table where the other ladies-in-waiting were sitting. The food on the table was cold, the highly spiced sauces congealing in their own grease. Nicolette picked at it half-heartedly. She wasn't hungry

355

anyway. William had taken away her appetite.

When supper was over, the trestles were cleared away and there was dancing. Nicolette, hurrying back to the Queen for shelter, was waylaid by Thomas Mowbray. She looked up into his dark swarthy face and stifled a stab of fear. What had she ever seen in him?

'Come and dance with me, my pretty little bird,' he said.

'I can't, I must go back and wait on the Queen. I am on duty tonight,' she told him firmly.

'The Queen doesn't need you just now, her husband is dancing with her.'

'The King is very kind to his young wife. I think he must be fond of her,' she said, striving for some sort of neutral topic as she edged away from him.

'The King's not kind. He's not a kind man,' retorted Mowbray, staring down at her moodily. 'The King wants to show her off tonight, in front of all his most powerful barons. He is determined to rub their noses in his unpopular French marriage, to let all us warriors know there will be no war with France.' She looked about her nervously to see if anyone was within earshot. He was being dangerously indiscreet. 'What's the matter?' Mowbray teased. 'Are you afraid to be seen with me? You weren't once, were you, my angel? At St Inglevert you led me a merry dance.'

'St Inglevert was a long time ago. I was young and foolish and but newly married. I know better now how to behave,' she said, wondering if there was anyone who could come to her rescue; even William would be welcome.

'But not a whit less beautiful. Your youth may be gone but you've still got your eyes and your lovely white teeth and your glorious hair which I can see through that fetching jewelled snood is as golden as ever. By the Holy Grail what would I give for just one night with you.' For a brief heartbeat she wondered whether he could help her get the wool customs for her father. People said he was the King's tool, that even now the King used him to do his dirty work. She looked up at him appraisingly. He certainly did not seem the least bit ashamed – not at all like a man in disgrace.

'I hope you're not going to take advantage of me just because my husband is away,' she said, pouting at him a little.

'I'd fight him for you again and willingly,' he grinned

down at her. 'What do I have to do for one kiss from those lips?' He was so close she could smell the mixture of sweat and wine and sheer maleness. Then she remembered that Henry Bolingbroke had accused him of murder. She backed away, horrified at what her father had brought her to, that she should have even considered seeking help from such a man. He caught hold of her hand and pulled her gently but firmly towards him.

'Come, my treasure, come and dance with me and maybe we can think of some quest I can perform for you.' She shook her head and tried to draw her hand away. But he was very powerful. With a quick jerk of her hand, he pulled her against him, holding her fast. She put both hands against his chest and tried to push him away.

'No, no. I cannot. Please let me go. If the Queen should see me . . . if I'm not there when she needs me . . . Already I am in trouble for having been late this evening.' She was babbling excuses, terrified of what he might do next.

'Trouble!' He laughed, throwing back his head like a defiant stallion. 'Am I not in trouble up to my neck? But it makes life seem all the sweeter – when you dice each day with death.'

He was mad, she thought, but he had both hands round her waist and although she struggled he seemed determined not to let her go. She looked about her wildly, beating her fists against Mowbray's chest, while he looked down at her in delight.

'You're even more beautiful when you're flustered, my fair lady,' Mowbray said.

'And you, my lord, even more of an opportunist than I thought,' Dick Whittington said, appearing at Nicolette's side.

'Sweet Jesu! Here's my gaoler.' Mowbray looked ruefully down at Nicolette and she could not help being a little impressed by his nerve. 'What the devil do you want to come butting in for, Master Whittington?'

'It seems to me that Lady Exton is not enjoying your attentions as much as you believe,' said Dick.

'And so you've come riding out of the forest to rescue her from me,' mocked Mowbray. 'It's a pity you're not entitled to bear arms in a tourney, my Lord Mayor. I'd be happy to break your lance – or your head, for that matter.'

357

'I know I'm not much of a knight in shining armour,' said Dick, smiling at Nicolette, 'but Thomas Mowbray need not feel that because your husband is absent you are without protection.'

'Going to lock me up again, are you?' said Mowbray with a bitter laugh. 'You'd better tread more carefully. The Court of Chivalry will prove my innocence, you'll see. When I kill Henry Bolingbroke in battle, there'll be nothing more they can hold against me.'

'Molesting one of the Queen's ladies against her will is scarcely the sort of behaviour for a Court of Chivalry,' said Dick, quite unruffled.

'What makes you so sure it was against her will?' retorted Mowbray and Nicolette felt the hot flush of shame stain her cheeks.

'No man of honour would assume otherwise.' Dick turned to Nicolette. 'Lady Exton, will you allow me to escort you to the Queen?' He held out his arm and bowed with surprising grace. Nicolette laid her fingertips on his sleeve and let him lead her away.

'You know, Nicolette,' he said when they were out of earshot, 'you don't have to encourage Thomas Mowbray when you have me to pay you homage.' She glanced at him nervously, not sure whether he was teasing her or not.

'I didn't encourage him,' she said, eyes downcast. She had not meant to flirt with Mowbray, indeed was almost sure that she had not. Yet she had a sneaking feeling at the bottom of her heart that she could, if she had been more ladylike, have prevented his advances.

'My dear, you have learnt a great deal since you have been at court but I don't think you will ever learn to be a very good liar.' He was looking at her challengingly and Nicolette knew that he expected some quick-witted response, but tonight she didn't feel quick-witted, she felt weighed down by her father's request. It suddenly occurred to her that Dick Whittington might be the very man to help her father. He was Mayor of London, he advised the King just as Nicholas Brembre had done.

'You're right,' she said, looking up at him. 'I think perhaps you understand me almost better than anyone. I thought, just for a moment, that perhaps Mowbray might be able to help me. But it was foolish to seek the help of such a dangerous man.' She gave him her most beguiling smile.

'Very foolish,' he agreed.

'So much better if I asked you to help me instead.' She paused. Dick's face was inscrutable. 'There seems to be nothing you cannot do.' Flattery did not seem to move him either. 'William Gryffard is anxious to make himself useful to the King,' she finished in a rush and looked at her feet, feeling embarrassed.

'The King needs money. Is William good for a loan?' replied Dick. Blessed Mother, she wished she had never started. What could she say now? She could not admit to Dick that her father was in financial trouble. She knew he wouldn't want anyone to know that.

'William Gryffard is always good for a loan,' she said. 'But he's very careful who he lends money to, as I am sure you are.' She peeped at him through her lashes. Dick did not smile. 'Everyone knows that the King is very extravagant.'

'The King's finances are not so bad now that he has been granted the wool duties,' said Dick, playing into her hand.

'But he'll need someone to collect the taxes, won't he?' She grasped the straw he flung her gratefully. 'Someone especially qualified in such matters, with a lifetime's experience of the wool trade.'

'Like William?'

She knew she should not seem too eager. 'William Gryffard is very busy with his work with the staple in Calais and then he exports a great deal of wool from England himself. I don't know whether he would be able to find the time,' she said.

'A merchant can always find time to make a profit,' said Dick with his rare sweet smile.

She looked up at him, her eyes clear and guileless. 'Is there profit in collecting taxes?'

'If you know where to look,' he replied. She could tell nothing from his expression and rather to her relief she saw the Queen had grown tired of dancing.

'The Queen needs me. I must return to my duties,' she said.

He bowed. 'Thank you for the pleasure of your company, my lady.'

She hurried away to attend to the Queen feeling unaccountably disturbed by Dick. He was her very good friend, full of sympathy and understanding, but just for once she wished that he did not understand her quite so well.

Two days later William caught her again. She could tell something was wrong by the way he looked her up and down as if she were some sort of a rodent.

'What did you tell Whittington?' he demanded without preamble.

'Nothing,' she snapped. Blessed Mother of Mercy! Was she never to be able to please him?

'If I'd needed Dick Whittington's help I'd have gone to him myself,' he told her.

'Did you get the subsidy?' she asked, determined not to be intimidated.

'I got it. But he dragged a fat loan out of me.'

So what had she done wrong? He had what he wanted and if he could lend the King money, he couldn't be on the brink of ruin after all.

'Why did you not ask Thomas Mowbray to help?' William suddenly asked. The question took her by surprise.

'Mowbray's a traitor, Father!' she said angrily. Had Dick told him about that scene in the hall with Mowbray?

'Henry Bolingbroke says he is a traitor,' William corrected her. 'Mowbray has the free run of the castle here at Windsor and has made himself very useful to the King in the past. I do not think you should spurn his friendship.'

She turned away from him. Why must he always try and use her? And now that he had the wool customs, why try and curry favour with Thomas Mowbray? 'If I were to make a friend of Thomas Mowbray,' she said acidly, 'it would be a very short-lived friendship. When the Court of Chivalry meets in September, if Bolingbroke does not kill him, Piers most certainly will.'

'Ah, the mighty Piers,' sneered William. 'Always so ready to ride into battle on your behalf, but what does he do in the meantime to feather your nest, my beautiful bird of paradise?'

Too hurt and angry to reply, she walked away from him. Her father mocked Piers because he envied him his courage and strength. Piers had no fear, because he did not believe he could lose. But if he is proved wrong, she thought with a terrible sinking of the heart, what will become of us then?

CHAPTER 30

Piers lowered his lance and galloped to meet the knight charging towards him, his concentration focused on the exact spot where he would have to strike the other's shield. As the stallions closed Piers gripped the lance tightly, holding it steady for the impact. But then the knight veered to the right. Piers was dismayed. Surely his opponent hadn't lost his nerve. Instinctively, Piers turned his stallion to intercept him. He had him now. But just as suddenly the other horse abruptly swerved back to the left and Piers found himself bearing down on the wrong side of his enemy, unprotected by his shield and unable to alter course. He was at the mercy of the lance which came at him with blinding speed, catching him squarely in the chest and sweeping him from the saddle. He landed with a great metallic crash and lay on his back, all the breath knocked out of him. Helplessly he lay on the ground, trying to get some air back into his lungs. He waved his arms and legs, like an upturned wood louse, vainly trying to right himself, at the mercy of the mounted knight who now advanced upon him and deliberately pinned him to the ground with the point of his lance.

'Do you yield, Sir Piers?' said Henry Bolingbroke, panting.

'Not if I'm Mowbray, I won't,' gasped Piers, managing to raise himself on to his elbows. 'Could you run him through with that lance?'

'If you were Mowbray, you'd already be dead,' said Henry, backing away his horse.

Piers sat up. His stallion had galloped off the field and his shield and lance lay six paces away. He was well and truly vanquished. 'That was a rare trick you played on me,' he said. 'I've not seen you use that before. And now that I've seen it I still don't quite believe it.'

'It's a French invention,' said Henry, grinning down at him through his raised visor. 'I learnt it from Jean de Boucicaut. You need a very good horse. If my charger had reacted an instant too late, you'd have run me down.'

'And to swing the lance to the offhand side and strike the target in one motion,' said Piers, getting unsteadily to his feet. 'By the Virgin! The impact should have wrenched the lance from your hand.'

'You think it'll do for Thomas Mowbray tomorrow?' Henry removed his helmet.

'You'll beat him without a doubt,' replied Piers. 'You're the better jouster by far, with or without such a trick as that.' Crispin was bringing his horse.

'Mowbray's a bold desperate fighter and he'll be fighting for his life. It might make him more cunning. I'd like to think I had a surprise in store for him if I should need it.' Henry handed his helmet to his squire. 'Now I must go and pay my respects to the King.'

Piers clambered stiffly back on to his horse. 'Do you want me to come with you?' he asked, thinking that Henry, too, would be fighting for his life tomorrow.

'Not today,' said Henry. 'Today I go to bend my knee and kiss the King's hand and take my official leave. Better not to go with any show of strength. I'll take Thomas Rempston and John Dabrichecourt and our squires. Go and tend your bruises.' He rode off, grinning cheerfully. Watching him ride away, Piers felt disappointed. He had hoped that he might have a chance to see Nicolette. It was now several months since he had set eyes on his wife and he was hungry for a glimpse of her. He was used to long separations, of course, and consoled himself with the thought that she was safe enough in the Queen's household, whatever the outcome of tomorrow's combat. The King was lodged in the castle of Baginton nearby; it belonged to his friend Sir William Bagot and Piers knew that the Queen had accompanied her husband. Knowing Nicolette was so near made him restless. Suddenly he became aware that Crispin was gazing at him reproachfully.

'Well, what is it?' he demanded more harshly than he intended.

'Are you hurt, Sir Piers?'

'Only my pride,' said Piers. 'Don't look so damned ashamed of me. I'd sooner be unhorsed by Henry Bolingbroke than any other knight in England.'

'I'm not ashamed,' said Crispin, looking more reproachful than ever. 'I just didn't think you could be unhorsed, that's all.'

'The knight that says he can never be unhorsed is a liar. It comes to all of us at some time, and those that learn from it are all the better for it. If you're afraid of being unhorsed, you'll end up swerving from the target. Now, were you watching carefully? Did you see how it was done? It's the neatest trick I've seen for many a long time. We'll have to practise it.' Crispin grinned and they rode out of the tournament field which was as busy as an anthill with carpenters putting the finishing touches to the stands and painters at work upon the tilt and heralds running about seeing to the correct positioning of the silken banners.

The next day, 16 September, as soon as the first light crept up over the battlements of Baginton Castle, the Queen's ladies were astir in the small round turret they occupied above the Queen's chamber.

Nicolette felt proud to be one of them even though it wasn't easy when half a score of well-born ladies were trying to make themselves look their best with only one piece of polished steel and one harassed tiring woman to share between them. They flitted about the chamber, chattering and laughing excitedly as hair was brushed and braided, elaborate headdresses donned over smooth white brows, jewels fixed round white throats or hung on low-cut bodices, kirtles smoothed over hips. When Nicolette took her turn at the mirror, she felt satisfied that she could hold her own in this elite band of Frenchwomen, with her jewels and her fur-trimmed mantle and Piers's arms embroidered on her surcoat. Her beauty was her talisman but it was enhanced by the fine costliness of her apparel.

A page came knocking at the chamber door to tell them that the Queen was awake and ready to rise. They floated out of the little round tower and down the winding stone stairs in their colourful silks like a cloud of brilliant butterflies, confident that in the great pageant of English chivalry that was to be enacted today, France would not be outdone in beauty or in splendour.

In the Queen's chamber, the Mistress of Ceremonies was beginning to panic.

'Can you not hurry?' she whispered to Nicolette who was on her knees in front of the Queen, trying to ease the royal feet into pointed slippers of red satin embroidered with gold thread.

'Don't be so impatient, Madame de Courcy,' said the Queen, whose ears were sharp. 'They will wait until we are ready.'

'But the King, suppose he should overtake us on the way?'

'He won't,' replied the Queen.

The Mistress of Ceremonies darted across to the window to look out for the seventh time that morning and Nicolette tried not to smile, amused that the severe matron who controlled all their lives should be so agitated. The Queen was excited and everything seemed to take longer than usual. It was hardly surprising. Today the flower of English chivalry would be on display in all its magnificence, and the Queen and her ladies were eager to appear worthy of the occasion. The lists of Coventry had been heralded throughout the country. The King had been generous to both combatants, placing at their disposal royal painters of escutcheons, and armourers had been summoned from the Duke of Milan to assist Bolingbroke and from Germany to assist Mowbray. Talk in the Queen's apartments had been of little else for weeks.

When they arrived at the tournament ground Piers was waiting, dressed in blue and green with Henry's badge of the white swan upon his sleeve. Nicolette clung to him as he lifted her out of the litter and she longed to stay and talk to him. It was so long since she had seen him and there was so much to say, but the red and gold toe of the Queen's little foot was emerging from her litter and the Mistress of Ceremonies was beckoning. Nicolette dared not linger.

'When will I see you?' she asked hastily.

'When it's all over. It'll be easier for us to be together once Henry has cleared himself,' Piers replied and kissed her swiftly on the mouth. She had to hurry to catch up with the other ladies-in-waiting and had no time to look about her as she climbed the steps into the Royal loge, holding the Queen's train and her own sweeping skirts, keeping her head up and her eyes down and praying that she would manage it all without fault.

At last the Queen was safely installed in her chair beneath the canopy of red and gold silk. She waved away her ladies with her small jewel-laden hand and they withdrew decorously to the bench reserved for them in an adjoining loge. Then Nicolette saw the banners, the serried ranks of spectators in their different stands, and the splendour of it all. She held her breath and marvelled at such magnificence; it rivalled anything the French had produced at St Inglevert.

Henry Bolingbroke, as the challenger, was the first to enter the lists. He was mounted on a white courser banded with green and blue velvet embroidered sumptuously with swans and antelopes. His armour shone with gold. After him came King Richard accompanied by all the nobility of England. They processed down the field, a ribbon of brilliant colours stretching from one end of the lists to the other. The King seated himself on his throne on the great dais beneath a silken canopy. There were more trumpets.

'Here is Thomas Mowbray, Duke of Norfolk,' the herald cried. 'To do his devoir against Henry of Bolingbroke, Duke of Hereford Appellant, upon pain to be found false and recreant.'

Nicolette watched Mowbray riding into the lists, his horse banded with crimson velvet embroidered richly with lions of silver and mulberry trees, and felt a rush of overwhelming revulsion that all this glory, this elaborate ritual and costly display was for a fight to the death. Here before all these eager, beautifully dressed spectators a man was going to die.

Across the field she saw Piers climbing into the Lancastrian loge on the opposite side of the field with the rest of Henry's retainers. He was very confident that Henry would win. Was Mowbray really doomed? It was all so unreal. She could not believe that these two men in their bright and costly armour were about to fight each other until one of them was dead.

The two challengers were now at either end of the lists. Their squires handed them their lances. A trumpet sounded and the squires let go of the impatient destriers. But as the horses pounded down the lists, the trumpet blasted a

warning. The King was on his feet and had cast down his
staff. The heralds ran on to the ground, the two knights
rocked back in their saddles as the horses slithered to a halt.

'What is it? What does it mean?' Nicolette asked in
dismay.

'The King has stopped the joust,' replied the Dame de
Courcy.

Lances were being reclaimed by the Marshal, the two
knights were dismounted and ordered back to their loges,
and the King left his dais.

For two hours they had to wait while first one baron and
then another was summoned to the King in a tented pavilion.
Rumour and counter-rumour, disappointment and specula-
tion ran through the ranks of spectators. Nicolette longed to
be allowed to leave her seat, to get up, walk away from the
chattering and laughing ladies to be reassured by Piers whom
she could see waiting with Henry and his other retainers in
the opposite stand. The Queen remained where she was, a
small, dignified figure, sitting upright in her chair, holding
her head with its heavy band of gold erect and proud, waiting
with the composure born of rigorous training and discipline
for her husband to finish his deliberations. With the Queen
setting such an example, Nicolette felt ashamed.

Sir John Bushy, the King's secretary, at last appeared.
Henry of Bolingbroke, Duke of Hereford, he announced,
was sentenced to exile for ten years. As was Thomas
Mowbray, Duke of Norfolk.

Nicolette sat stunned while the crowd roared its disapproval.

'The blood lust of a holiday crowd disappointed to the
point of fury,' remarked the Dame de Courcy with a sniff,
'but such emotions do not last. We must attend the Queen.'

The King, surrounded by his nobles and men-at-arms,
was leaving amid more howls of protest from the crowd.
Calmly Nicolette followed the other ladies-in-waiting to
attend the Queen, too bemused to be frightened.

'I don't know why they are all so cross,' said Isabella. 'The
King has acted with wisdom and forbearance. To save
bloodshed. And in doing so he has cleverly got rid of both his
enemies.'

Nicolette tried not to think, forcing herself to perform her
duties with grace and charm. This was why she was in the

Queen's household, to be safe in case disaster should strike. But had disaster struck? Was Piers in danger? She did not know and could not find out until she had spoken to her husband.

Two days later Henry Bolingbroke arrived at Baginton Castle to take his leave of the King. Nicolette watched him ride into the courtyard with his retainers and recognised Piers's red and cream blazon from the Queen's chamber window. She thanked God that she was helping to oversee the packing of the royal valuables and not on duty keeping the Queen company.

'Madame de Courcy, may I have permission to go down to speak to my husband?' she asked. 'Henry Bolingbroke is here to take his leave and I must know what my husband intends to do.'

'If he has any sense he'll seek service with the King,' said the Dame de Courcy. 'His Grace is taking on Lancastrian knights, they say.'

Nicolette's heart leapt. If the King could be persuaded to take on Piers, she would be able to see him all the time. It was the answer to all their problems. 'May I go down now and tell him?'

'Yes, you may. I can manage here without you. I know it has been a difficult time for you since the Duke has been in disgrace. Good luck.'

She wasn't such a bad old stick after all, thought Nicolette as she raced out of the turret and across the cobbled yard to the lower court where Henry's entourage was waiting. Piers saw her and came striding over the grass. She threw herself into his arms.

'Oh, Piers, I'm so glad you've come. I've been so worried about you.' He held her close for a moment and something in the way he gripped her so tightly made her fearful. 'What is it, Piers?'

'Nicolette, you must be brave. I know that you have courage and tenacity, that when you love you can be blind to all wordly considerations, that when Brembre was brought down you followed him to the scaffold even.'

'The Blessed Virgin have mercy! What do you mean, Piers?' she exclaimed.

He took both her hands in his, held them tight against his

heart. 'I must go into exile with Henry,' he said.

'No, no,' she said smiling up at him, full of joy that she could be the saving of him this time. 'The King is taking on Lancastrian knights. I have it from the Queen's Mistress of Ceremonies. You could be one of them. I'll ask the Queen to speak to the King for you.'

'No, my angel. I go with Bolingbroke.'

'But no man goes willingly into exile,' she exclaimed. Surely just for once, she thought he would show some sense of self-preservation.

'You want me to sell my honour a second time?' he demanded, staring down at her.

'You did it before, why not again?' she flung at him, disappointment making her angry.

'It's different now.'

'I'm your wife now, that's what's different. You'd have done anything for me then when I was your perfect lady. But now I'm your wife I've become a burden.' She pulled away from him, blinking back tears of frustration and disappointment.

He put a hand beneath her chin, raised her head. 'If my wife is worthy of my love she'll come with me into exile,' he said. His eyes, dark and sorrowful, were looking at her with such pleading she could not bear it.

'How can I?' she demanded. 'What about the children?'

'Bring them too.'

'What can you do in France with three small children and a wife in tow?'

'Take shelter in the abbey in Caen then.'

She looked out across the busy courtyard with a shudder at the thought of all that she would have to forgo shut up in the Abbey of the Holy Trinity.

'It won't be for ever,' he said and she felt ashamed that he had read her thoughts so well.

'It will be ten years. I shall be an old woman by the time you're allowed back!'

'John of Gaunt has persuaded the King to commute Bolingbroke's sentence to six years. Monastery life will do the younger boys nothing but good. Kit can come with me. It's time he learnt to use a sword.'

'The Abbess would never take us without a dower,' she said.

'There's your jewellery. You could sell that, or the house in Cornhill. Predictably, William Gryffard wants me to make the house over to him again. He's very anxious it might be confiscated.'

'Well, so it might,' she said, 'like Mowbray's estates. I think perhaps you should listen to William.'

'But I could make it over to the abbey instead. It's your dower. It's for you to decide.'

He means it, she thought, panic sweeping over her. He really means to take us away from all this and bury us in a monastery for six whole years while he enjoys himself with Henry Bolingbroke fighting all over Europe.

'Why can't you stay behind and look after your family?' she burst out, looking up at him imploringly. 'What is so dishonourable about that? If you loved me as much as you say you do you'd put aside your stupid principles and become a retainer of the King's.'

He looked down at her sadly and she was afraid she'd lost him. Tears welled and she let them fall one by one. He never had been able to resist her tears.

'You don't love me any more, is that it? You've grown tired of me, just as I knew you would.'

'I'm going, Nicolette, because I have to stay true to myself, otherwise how can I ever be true to you. If you knew how to love me you would understand that.'

She was crying now in earnest, unable to speak. Through a blur of tears she saw Henry come striding out into the courtyard. A squire brought his horse. She flung her arms round Piers's neck, clung to him. 'Don't go,' she whispered through her tears. He prised her clinging hands loose and held her away from him. As he looked down into her face, his eyes were bleak, his mouth grim.

'I swear by the Rood I shall stay true to you for as long as I am away. I love you, Nicolette, whatever you may think. Remember that.' Swiftly he bent and kissed her hands. Crispin was bringing his horse. She could not beg and plead in front of the squire. Piers was in the saddle now. Henry Bolingbroke was riding towards the portcullis. Nicolette stood benumbed with shock, the tears streaming down her face.

'I wonder,' said Piers, 'will you stay true to me?' Before she could promise he had wheeled his charger and was trotting after Henry, out of the castle and out of her life, perhaps forever.

CHAPTER 31

Within a fortnight, Bolingbroke was in London making preparations for his departure. Ships had to be found to carry him and his retinue overseas; attorneys appointed to look after his estates in his absence; horses purchased; armour, weapons, stores, clothes, fodder collected and packed into wagons for the journey.

Not an hour was wasted. Henry was hard at work from sunrise to sunset, driving himself, his retainers and everyone in his household into a frenzy of efficient activity. Piers was glad to be kept so busy, he was trying not to think of Nicolette. He kept hoping against hope that she might change her mind and decide to join him in exile after all. He knew it was too much to expect of her, but he could not stop himself from hoping. When the longing became too much to bear, he obtained permission from Henry to go and bid farewell to his children, not admitting even to himself that he was going there in one last despairing hope that she might be waiting for him.

Henry was sympathetic. 'It's hard, I know,' he said, 'to say goodbye to one's children. They will be much changed by the time we see them again. Take as long as you need.'

'My lord is gracious,' said Piers.

'Not as gracious as I should like,' replied Henry, shaking his head. 'I haven't been much use to you as an overlord, I'm afraid.'

'You've provided me with adventure aplenty, which is all I look for,' said Piers. 'That and a chance to fight in God's cause. Six years will soon pass. Just about time enough for another crusade to the Holy land.' He smiled, but Henry was not so easily fooled.

'Your loyalty is the only gleam of light in one of the darkest days of my life,' he said, grasping Piers's hand in both of his. 'One day, when I come into my inheritance, I shall be able to show you my gratitude. In the meantime, all I can do is thank you for sharing my disgrace, knowing that in some ways it's worse for you in that you leave a wife behind as well as children. At least poor Mary's death has spared me that.' Piers was surprised. Henry was a soldier, with a soldier's reticence. His wife Mary had died in childbirth several years ago and Henry seldom mentioned her.

Henry turned to issue more orders to the clerks bent over their tables and Piers left him to his letter writing, warmed by appreciation.

He hurried to the house in Cornhill impelled by foolish hope, but as soon as he entered it, he knew his quest was in vain. William Gryffard was lying in wait for him in the hall.

'A word with you, Piers,' he said, grasping him by the arm. Piers longed to go to the solar and confirm that Nicolette was not there, to linger in the chamber where they had spent so many happy hours together, to catch perhaps the last lingering echoes of her fragrance trapped in the bed curtains. For one brief instant of madness he considered crushing the fingers clinging tenaciously to his mailed sleeve like a predator's claw. But he restrained himself, thrust his disappointment deep down inside himself where William might not detect it, and followed him out to his counting house.

William ferreted about among the ledgers and pieces of parchment and letters piled on his table in the counting house. Piers remembered with vivid clarity that time when he had made over the deeds of the house. Then it had been William who was fleeing from the city. Piers watched his father-in-law sharpening the point of the quill, listened with detached disinterest as he explained what was in the document. Just such a scroll had brought Nicolette within his grasp; was he to lose her now, like the house? William was talking of the need to take the long view, to be prepared for the worst, darting quick nervous glances at him, but Piers did not care.

'If it helps Nicolette, of course I'll sign,' said Piers, interrupting William's careful explanations. 'Give me the pen.' He felt revulsion at the relief on the other's face and signed his name quickly where William indicated, without even bothering to read what was in the document. He had not wanted the house then and he did not want it now. He had never felt it was truly his home.

'The children,' he said, throwing down the quill. 'I should like to bid farewell to my children.'

'Of course.' William examined the parchment carefully, threw sand over the ink and waited until it was dry. 'I'll have them brought to the hall.' Piers would like to have taken leave of his children in their mother's bower, away from William's prying eyes, but he was too depressed to make a fight of it.

He waited patiently while William rolled up the parchment and carefully stowed it away. He was anxious to be done with the whole sorry business of leavetaking as quickly as possible but determined not to show how much he cared. He followed William back to the hall, ate the cake and drank the ale a servant proffered, forcing himself to stay calm, staring into the fire and ignoring William, until the women came with the children.

Lisette carried baby Michael in her arms and her round peasant's face was as miserable as a stone gargoyle's on a church wall.

'Oh, sir,' she wailed, 'here's a bad day for us all. When shall us ever set eyes on 'ee again?' Four-year-old Tarquin, running across the hall in joyful welcome, stopped in his tracks and his face crumpled.

'That'll do, Lisette,' Piers admonished her more harshly than he meant. She looked even more woebegone. He wagged a finger at the babe in her arms and the infant seized it, smiling and gurgling happily at him, understanding nothing. But Tarquin was now clinging tearfully to his legs. Piers bent down, picked up his small son, kissed him swiftly and handed him to Jeanne de Bourdat.

'Take good care of him, won't you, Jeanne?' Over her shoulder, Piers caught the eye of his eldest son regarding him solemnly. 'Kit will help you, he's the head of the household now in my place.'

'Can't I come with you?' Kit demanded.

'No, I'm afraid not.'

'But I thought I was to go into Bolingbroke's household

after Christmas last year. It's almost Christmas this year and I'm a whole year older.' The disappointment in his son's voice reminded Piers all too poignantly of Nicolette when unable to get her own way. 'Soon I'll be too old to be a page at all.' It was true, thought Piers with a shock of dismay. By the time I come back, Kit will be thirteen. The six years which he had tried to pretend were so trifling suddenly seemed all too long. He caught William's eye watching him over the top of his goblet as he sipped his ale. Kit might soon be too old to be a page, thought Piers, but he was not yet old enough to be an apprentice. William Gryffard could not turn his son into a scribbling wool counter in his absence.

'You need not worry about the children's education,' said William, almost as if he had read his thoughts. 'I shall see that they learn to read and write and use the abacus.'

'Knights don't read and write,' scoffed Kit, staring up at his grandfather belligerently. 'Who's going to teach me to use a sword?'

'I shall, when I return,' Piers promised, scowling at William. 'Meanwhile, here's my longbow for you to practise with.'

The boy seized it joyfully, his anxious face transformed by this unlooked-for prize. He tugged at the fine line of gut that stretched from one end of the pole to the other, and Piers watched as he struggled without success to bend the long, thin pole and blessed the inspiration which had made him bring the bow with him today.

'I shall need some arrows,' Kit said.

'You can have arrows when you can bend the bow,' replied Piers, smiling at his son. 'It's not as easy as it looks. It takes great strength and much practice. When I come back, I want you to be the best archer in Cornhill Ward.'

'You're going to be away a long time then?'

'Long enough for you to learn how to use the bow,' replied Piers.

The boy's face fell. Suddenly Piers could stand no more. Jeanne and Lisette had begun to weep and the younger children too. Swiftly Piers took his leave.

William walked with him to the end of the hall, flung open the heavy oak door. 'They'll be safe in my care,' he said. Piers could not trust himself to speak. He strode out of the house feeling that honour carried a high price upon its head.

374

Crispin was waiting outside with the horses.

'Sure you don't want to change your mind, Crispin?' Piers demanded harshly as he mounted his placid gelding. 'It's not too late to find you a new master, even at this late hour.'

'By the Rood, no!' exclaimed Crispin. 'I reckon I'll see more adventure with you and Henry overseas than here in England. Another crusade maybe. I'd like to win my spurs fighting the infidel.'

'You should have been knighted in the last one,' replied Piers. 'Although what I should do without you, I don't know.' He dug his spurs into the horse's side.

'There's one man who's not sorry to see us go,' said Crispin as they rode off. Piers turned for one last look at the house he had given up. William stood in the open doorway smiling in triumph, master once again of his domain. But Piers did not care. Let William have his house. It was a burden he was glad to be rid of.

On 12 October, Henry Bolingbroke left to go into exile and all London turned out to see him on his way. Listening to the cheers as they rode down Chepeside, Piers could hardly believe that they were leaving England in disgrace. Ahead of him he could see the aldermen dressed in their cloth of scarlet bobbing up and down on their sturdy palfreys like little fat robins as they cleared a way for the steel-clad knights in their wake. Behind came Henry and the Mayor riding side by side, Dick Whittington's beaver hat inclined deferentially towards Henry's crested helm. The cheers rang in Piers's ears, echoing from wall to wall in the narrow streets, drowning the sound of the horses' shoes on the cobbles. He looked up and from the balconies above, women and children smiled down at him, cheering and waving. Some blew kisses, others threw flowers. It was more like a victory procession than a banishment.

They reached the city wall and passed through Cripplegate. The horses broke into a steady trot as they rode out into the open fields beyond. Gradually the running figures who escorted them on either side began to fall back as they left the city behind. But still the Mayor and aldermen rode with them.

When they reached Dartford, Piers found Dick riding beside him.

'How far are you coming?' asked Piers. 'You and the aldermen? Do you mean to accompany us all the way to Gravesend?'

'We might as well, having come this far,' replied Dick with his enigmatic smile. 'It's a fine day for a ride. I don't get out of the city often enough.'

Piers studied the scarlet-clad figures ahead of him. One or two of the bright red robins who had bobbed so jauntily through the city streets were showing signs of dropping off their perches. Whatever they were here for, it was not for the ride.

'What is it all for, this splendid show?' he asked. 'What has my liege lord done to merit London's approval in so marked a manner?'

'Henry Bolingbroke has always been popular with the Londoners,' Dick replied. 'They supported him before, remember, when he was one of the five lords appellant.'

'And they'll support him again – is that it? If the King becomes a tyrant?'

Dick brought his horse closer, so that his knee almost touched Piers's. 'A lot can happen in six years. Old men die. Henry is heir to vast estates all over England.'

'The King has promised Henry that he shall enjoy his father's possessions should they fall to him in his absence.'

'Maybe when he made the promise the King forgot the vast powers enjoyed by the Palatinate estates,' replied Dick. 'When he remembers, he may be tempted to break his promise.'

'He has allowed Bolingbroke two thousand pounds per annum in exile. Would he do that if he meant to confiscate all his estates?'

'Six years is a long time. People forget. Who knows what might happen? You're a fool to be going. Much better to stay here and serve the King. It's not too late. You could ride back with me and I'll put in a word for you with the King.'

'I know you mean it well, Dick,' said Piers, patting him on the knee with his mailed fist. 'But no. I've been that road before and I don't want to go down it again.'

'You're an idealistic fool,' retorted Dick. 'I thought marriage to Nicolette would have cured you of some of that nonsense, or are you running away from your perfect lady?'

He was smiling his old cynical smile and it annoyed Piers that Dick seemed incapable of seeing good in anything. 'Do you perhaps prefer the simplicity of loving an ideal?' Dick continued. 'Are the agonies of unrequited love preferable to the demands of a beautiful wife who loves you in return?'

'I'm not running away,' Piers retorted, angry that his friend could be so unfair. 'I'm going into exile out of loyalty to my liege lord.'

'No man goes willingly into exile.'

Nicolette had said the same thing, Piers remembered. It made him feel angrier than ever. 'Not willingly,' he said. 'But I cannot, with honour, change sides again.' He had to make Dick understand how hard a choice it had been, because if he didn't, he wasn't sure that he could trust his old friend any more.

'Even for Nicolette?'

'You look after her for me,' he said.

'Piers, Piers, always so trusting. You asked me to do that for you before and I did my best. But she's very beautiful. You're putting temptation in my way.'

'But you'll resist it, won't you? An honourable man isn't honourable until he resists temptation.' Piers wanted to believe that Dick's cynicism was just a cloak for his finer feelings.

'What temptation are you resisting, Sir Piers?' asked Dick. 'Are you sure you're not choosing honour because it's more exciting?'

'I thought you were like me, trying to bring justice and honour to London's corrupt government,' retorted Piers.

'So I am,' replied Dick, staring out over his horse's ears at the road ahead. 'Which is why I have not attempted to win re-election as Mayor like some of my predecessors.'

Piers was taken aback. 'But I thought you were still Mayor,' he said.

'This is my last act as Mayor,' replied Dick. 'It doesn't do to get too fond of the position. Drew Barantyn the goldsmith has been elected and will succeed me after Mayor's Day on the Feast of Saint Simon and Saint Jude. The old monopoly of the city's governance by the victuallers or the mercantile crafts is finished. Freedom to elect our own Mayor is a privilege to be fought for and guarded well. I'm afraid that now the King has no restraints on his power, he may be tempted to take the city into his own hands again, unless we pay well for our privileges.'

Piers wasn't really interested in city politics. All he knew was that Dick was here today, riding with Henry as far as Gravesend, an act that even he could see was above and beyond the call of civic duty. 'What do you mean to do,' he asked, 'if the Duke of Lancaster dies while we're in exile and the King succumbs to temptation?'

'It's not what I intend to do that should concern you,' said Dick, looking more enigmatic than ever. 'It's what will become of your wife and children if the King starts confiscating the property of Henry and all his supporters, as he has done already to Mowbray's.'

'Nicolette is safe in the Queen's household and I've made over the house to Gryffard. The King cannot confiscate it on my account.'

'Isn't that what Gryffard's always wanted, to get his house back?'

'I can't help that. It's safer. One thing William Gryffard excels at is surviving.'

'In that I entirely agree,' said Dick. 'He's a wily old rogue is William Gryffard; he manages to get back on the winning side however many times the wind of fortune changes. Go and find the Holy Grail for us, while we merchants look after your dependants for you.'

Piers knew then it was no use. If Dick did not understand now, it was too late to make him.

In the Queen's great chamber at Westminster Palace the ladies-in-waiting were sewing while the Queen sang in her high-pitched childish voice:

> In serenest spring you'll see
> Julie by the greenwood tree
> in her sister's company —
>   Dulcis amor!
> who pass you by when spring is nigh
>   care nothing for!

Nicolette bent her head over her embroidery and tried not to think about Piers. But he was never far from her thoughts. She could not help hoping that perhaps he would have a

378

change of heart, that he would suddenly appear at court with the King's white badge again upon his sleeve, that his love for her would triumph over his desire for honour and glory, as it had before. Not until she knew for certain that he had left England with Henry would she give up hope.

She stared out of the window at the towers and thatched roofs and secret inner courtyards, at the sprawling jumble of buildings that was Westminster Palace. Surely someone here in the palace could tell her what was happening in the world outside. If Henry had gone. If Piers went with him. But Bolingbroke's name had not been mentioned at court since he had taken his leave of the King at Baginton Castle. Nor Mowbray's. Nicolette felt helpless and alone. If only she knew for sure then she could kill the small flame of hope that burned within her.

> Now that lilies bloom again
> to the gods in heavenly train
> girls direct their hearts' refrain –
>   Dulcis amor!
> who pass you by when spring is nigh
>   care nothing for!

Sometimes the Queen sang flat and the small fingers plucking at the lute strings missed a chord or two. Nicolette gazed around the chamber, at the silken draperies round the bed, the glorious tapestries hanging on the walls, the ladies in their beautiful clothes sewing peacefully by the glowing fire. The Queen was weighed down, as ever, with embroidered finery. It was all so lovely and comfortable. She ought to be so happy.

> Could I clasp whom I adore
> on the forest's leafy floor,
> how I'd kiss her – Oh and more!
>   Dulcis amor!
> who pass you by when spring is nigh
>   care nothing for!

The words filled Nicolette with an aching sense of loss. What was all this expensive lavishness compared with love? She placed another immaculate stitch in the red silk draped

379

across her knee and thought of all the springtimes to come without Piers. Once again she had lost the man she loved. Why? Where had she gone wrong? Nicholas Brembre had been evil and their love a sin; she understood that well enough now. But Piers was goodness incarnate. Why did he have to desert her? Was it because she was too selfish?

The Queen stopped singing, laid aside the lute. 'You look sad, Nickie,' she said. 'Does my singing not please you?'

'Forgive me, Madame,' said Nicolette wiping away a furtive tear with the corner of the red silk she was embroidering.

'I know I sometimes sing flat,' said the Queen. 'But I don't want to make you weep.'

'On the contrary, Madame,' said Nicolette, quickly collecting her wits, 'your singing is so beautiful it brings tears to my eyes.' But the Queen was not so easily reassured. She persisted in trying to make Nicolette tell her what was wrong with her singing until the Dame de Courcy came to the rescue.

'I daresay Lady Exton is pining for her husband, even as I often miss my own lord left behind in France when I came with Your Grace to England,' she said.

The Queen stared at Nicolette haughtily, while Bolingbroke's name hung unspoken in the air between them.

'You should be happy, Nickie, that I took you into my household in good time,' Isabella said at last. 'If it were not for me, you would be an outcast like your husband.'

'Indeed, Madame,' murmured Nicolette.

'You mustn't be sad. I too miss my native land, but I am never sad.'

'Perhaps if you were to go on a pilgrimage,' suggested the Dame de Courcy, 'you would learn to bear your burdens with more cheerfulness.'

The Queen clapped her hands together gleefully. 'A pilgrimage!' she exclaimed. 'What a delightful idea. We shall all go on a pilgrimage in the spring. To Our Lady of Walsingham in Norfolk, or to Canterbury perhaps. There now, doesn't that make you feel better?'

Nicolette bent once again over her needlework, feeling more miserable than ever. The Queen rebuked her for lack of self-control, the Dame de Courcy thought she lacked sanctity. Perhaps that was it. Perhaps Piers had been taken

380

from her as a penance because she had turned away from God. But it wasn't true. She prayed and lit her candles and bought a great many indulgences, but it was no use. She had not turned away from God; she no longer knew where to find Him.

The days passed slowly and it seemed to Nicolette as she went about her many tasks, hiding her sorrow beneath a forced gaiety, that for all its luxury and comfort, the Queen's household, with its rigid formality, its discipline and its rules, was sometimes a little like being back in the abbey at Caen, except that the Dame de Courcy was stricter than the Abbess and the Queen much more demanding.

About a week after Piers's departure she was walking in the Queen's garden in a brief respite after dinner when she encountered Dick Whittington.

'Well met, my lady,' he said. 'I was just coming in search of you.'

'Of me?' Nicolette gazed up at him full of breathless hope. Perhaps he had a message from Piers.

'Yes, the last time I spoke to the Queen she was wanting some fine French enamels on a gold ground. You may tell her that I have found some, but that it is very expensive.'

Nicolette looked down at her feet in disappointment. He was teasing her, she felt sure. If he wanted to make a sale he could do it through the Queen's Wardrobe and not come directly to one of her ladies. 'I thought perhaps you had brought me news of my husband,' she said full of gentle accusation. She did not feel like playing games with him today.

'Your husband, my lady, has gone into exile with Henry Bolingbroke. I thought you knew that,' he said.

'So he has gone.' She sat down on the low wall round a pond filled with fat carp, unaware of the cold stone, or the chill wind nipping across the court, or Dick Whittington, standing studying her gravely with his head on one side. 'Why can't he stay behind and look after his wife and children instead of being honourable all the time!' she cried out.

'I told him he was an idealistic fool,' replied Dick.

'And what did he say?'

'That he had made over the house in Cornhill to William Gryffard before he left.'

'The fool! What is to become of him now?' Her disappointment was so great she was careless of what Dick thought of her.

'He will doubtless slay a great many of the infidel and come home in a state of grace when the six years are up.' Dick was smiling.

'But a landless knight,' she said, staring into the water of the pool. 'No better off than the day when I first encountered him on the road outside Caen.'

'He has done everything in his power to ensure that you will not suffer for his principles.'

'Not suffer!' She looked at Dick, thinking of the lonely nights ahead of her. Her hungry flesh, her aching heart. Six years. She would be thirty and more before he came home. Too old for love maybe. 'I'm a failure again,' she said in despair.

'We're all of us failures from time to time.' Dick sat down on the wall beside her. 'It's nothing to be ashamed or afraid of. Many, many times along the road I have failed and had to start again. Failure is just a natural consequence of trying.'

'It's different for you,' she said. 'Of course there are risks and setbacks in the marketplace. I know that. William Gryffard is always telling me how difficult it can be. But why does everyone I love always leave me?' She watched a large fat carp lazily circling the pool. 'I've tried so hard to be what Piers wanted,' she said. 'But it's so difficult. If I'd been a better wife, he would never have left me now.'

'It's no use trying to be perfect,' said Dick. 'The perfect wife, the perfect daughter, the perfect mistress. To do that you have to compromise your own soul. Why don't you try to be true to yourself, like Piers. That is why he's gone off with Bolingbroke.'

'Piers isn't selfish!'

'No,' Dick agreed, 'he's not – and you and I are.'

She looked at him, shocked. He was frowning at her almost disapprovingly. 'Do you think it was selfish of me not to go into exile with Piers?' she asked.

'If it was, it's time you thought of yourself.' He took her hand, held it in both of his. 'Piers wants a saint. Your father wants a tool.' She tried to draw away, afraid that Dick might be about to take advantage of Piers's departure to make an embarrassing declaration of love. He smiled knowingly into her eyes. 'You're neither of those things, are you, my lady? Why don't you try to be yourself?'

She looked at him with relief and gratitude. Here was a man who understood her. A man who did not want her for her beauty, her outward appearance, but who wanted to help her find her inner soul. 'You're such a good, true friend Dick,' she said, letting her hand rest confidently in his. He raised it to his lips.

'I shall count it an honour to be allowed to serve you, my lady,' he said. Then deliberately he kissed her fingers.

PART IV
1398–1400

'Oh ye noble and engaging hearts, longing to win sweet favors and joyful gratitude from the God of Love and your Lady, do not waver in your resolution, never abandon your first love but be true to her, unchanging from one day to the next . . .'

From Duke René of Anjou's *Le Cueur d'Amours Espris*

CHAPTER 32

November, 1398

'I need money, Whittington,' said the King. Dick was gazing out of the window of the White Tower at the men in chain mail lounging on the battlements and his spirit quailed. Resolutely he turned his back on the window.

'Parliament granted Your Grace duties on wool, woolfells and leather for life,' he said, trying to play for time. 'Is William Gryffard not proving able at collecting them for you, Sire?'

'It's not enough.' Moodily the King kicked a dog which was licking the wine spilling from his carelessly held goblet. The animal yelped. Dick watched it retreat to the corner of the chamber and wondered uneasily if he would be next. The King scowled into the contents of his goblet. Dick allowed his gaze to wander about the chamber, feasting his eyes on the costly furnishings, the glorious wall paintings, the evidence everywhere of the King's love of the highest culture, a taste which Dick shared and which made him his living. It was in his own interests to encourage his extravagant King to indulge his tastes. He noticed a fine new tapestry hanging on the wall.

'That's a wondrous work of art,' he said, walking over to study it more carefully. 'From Arras, I don't doubt.'

'Do you like it?' the King seemed pleased. 'You s-should. It cost a f-f-fortune.'

Dick fingered the tapestry lovingly, praising it with genuine admiration and was relieved when the King smiled. It was hopeless having a serious conversation about money with a man in a temper.

'The Earl of March is dead,' Richard said suddenly, interrupting Dick's fulsome praise. 'S-slain in battle in

Ireland in July. The news has only just reached us. I have lost my heir.'

'What do you intend to do?'

'I have recognised his young s-son Edmund as heir presumptive. I think it's time I went to Ireland with a proper army and taught those wild bogmen a lesson. Don't you?'

'War is expensive,' cautioned Dick.

'But Parliament will vote new taxes for a war.' The King looked pleased with himself. 'Isn't that what all my barons want? A chance to get their s-s-squires knighted and to test their own prowess with s-s-sword and lance without all the rules and restrictions of the tournament, a chance of getting rich booty, a f-f-fine new arras like mine to bring back and hang in their castles? Yes, I think it's time I gave them s-s-some f-fighting. Otherwise they might s-start f-fighting each other again, don't you think, Whittington?'

'Ireland's not the same as France,' said Dick uneasily. 'France is a rich country. An army can live on plunder from the countryside; France also has a wealthy aristocracy – plenty of prisoners who can be held to ransom to make victory a paying proposition. But across the Irish Sea there is nothing but bog and forest and a half-savage clan system which will yield no worthwhile spoils. An ill-provisioned army might easily starve and there's no terrain for the sort of pitched battle you need to win honour and glory.'

'That's why I need more money,' said the King. 'Are you going to tell me I can't have it?' Dick cursed himself for letting his merchant's mind overrule his courtier's cunning. The King was scowling at him again. 'I must remind you I have already f-fought one successful campaign in Ireland,' Richard said. 'I s-see no reason why I might not f-fight another.'

'I grant that there may never be a better time for Your Grace to leave England,' Dick hurriedly reassured him. 'The baronial opposition is finally overthrown, all the lords appellant dead or in exile. Around Your Grace are able men of Your Grace's own choosing and a court which shares the cultural tastes which elevate Your Grace above any other ruler in Christendom. Now is the time to achieve that martial glory which every knight of chivalry is expected to pursue.'

'And to avenge the death of my heir,' put in the King much mollified. 'If with God's grace we are victorious, we'll make

388

Ireland for the f-first time a profitable appanage to the Crown.'

'If Your Grace succeeds in that, then, however much it costs, the venture will have been well worth it,' conceded Dick.

'Good for you, Whittington. You make me f-feel better. F-find me the money for this campaign and you can have whatever you ask. Perhaps you s-should come with me. We'll make a knight out of you yet.'

Dick smiled and shook his head. He didn't want a knighthood. He wanted to save London from the King's rapacious hand. 'I'm not really a fighting man, Sire,' he said.

'Well, I've got plenty of knights and barons eager to f-fight. You can stay and see that London remains loyal in my absence.' The King was in high spirits again. 'Just think of all those barren Irish castles in need of costly furnishings,' he went on eagerly. 'The cloth of gold, the damasks, the silver goblets you'll be able to sell them. You'll make a whole new fortune when I've conquered the King of Leinster and his followers.'

The King's violent swings of mood were exhausting, and now that he had succeeded in casting off all restraints upon his power, he was becoming dangerously unpredictable. It was with relief rather than elation that Dick made his way out of the White Tower a short time later.

Before he had ceased to be Mayor, the King had made him, together with the Archbishop of Canterbury, sign a blank charter on behalf of all the citizens of London placing them and their goods at the King's pleasure in acknowledgement of their guilt at the time of his imprisonment at the hands of the appellants. The Londoners had had to buy the charters back. It was a device for getting money out of them, a very successful device, but Dick was not proud of his part in it. He had once told Nicolette that he wanted to be successful to do good but here he was, the King's friend and adviser, and all he seemed to be doing to London was harm.

He was all too aware of the men-at-arms on the Tower battlements and in the corridors, guarding every door and even patrolling the gardens; their arrogant stares followed him as he walked across the grass court towards the outer bailey. For the first time since he had become the King's friend, Dick felt afraid. Only a tyrant had to surround himself with so many armed men when he was secure upon his throne. Dick hurried on, not daring to look to right or left until he reached the gatehouse and passed beneath the raised portcullis and crossed the lowered drawbridge. Once outside the great fortress, he breathed a sigh of relief. It was good to be safely outside again.

He turned his mind towards the King's enthusiasm for Ireland. It was true that if he were successful, and a lasting peace could be imposed on that troubled land, there would be huge profits to be made by any merchant intrepid enough to take civilisation to that poor and barren land. It was what every merchant dreamed of. Yet Dick was far too much of a realist to believe that such a dream could be accomplished with one more successful campaign. Whatever the outcome, it would cost a great deal of money. How was the money to be found? Not in the city, that was certain. The King had already extracted all that he could with his blank charters and forced loans. That particular well was dry. Parliament then? Another tax – but on what? The King already received all the wool dues.

At the thought of the wool customs, Dick remembered William Gryffard, just as the bells in the city began to ring out the Angelus. Dick bowed his head in prayer. The end of another day's work. The apprentices could lay down their tools and look forward to their supper. Dick thought longingly about his own supper which Alice would have ready for him. He was tired and longed to go back home to the comfort and peace of his well-ordered household. But he could not go home yet. There was still one more task he must perform before he could rest.

When Dick entered the Customs House in Thames Street the clerks were just finishing for the day. There was no sign of William Gryffard or his fellow collector Andrew Neuport. Dick knew there was no reason to suppose that a collector of customs actually did the collecting. No matter, he thought. I'm sure I can find the answer for myself. It will be here in the ledgers.

He sat down and began to look through the carefully kept ledgers while the deputies who were engaged in the day-to-day toil of the Customs House waited respectfully, hiding their impatience as best they might.

'No need for you to wait,' said Dick, when the nearest man's stomach had rumbled quite audibly more than once. 'I don't want to keep you from your dinner.'

As he had anticipated, no one was anxious to put too many difficulties in the way of a man who until recently had been Mayor of London and was known to be close to the King. Dick promised to close the Customs House himself when he had found what he wanted and so the deputies bade him goodnight and departed, leaving Dick alone with his candle.

It took him a long time and much careful checking and cross-checking, for William Gryffard was very skilled. But then so was Dick. At last his labours were rewarded and he sat back, easing his cramped limbs. What he had discovered would not make much difference to the King's need for money. That was an everlasting problem. But from small acorns great oak trees could grow, and attention to detail was how Dick had built up his own riches. Should he make Gryffard pay back what he had stolen from the King? He sighed. He was tired of money. Everyone needed money – except Nicolette.

Carefully, Dick set about putting everything back in its proper place and allowed himself to think about Nicolette. Piers had been gone for over a month now and Nicolette was showing no sign of falling into his lap like a ripe plum. He had tried once or twice to pierce the armour of her goodness, but she knew too well how to turn an attempt at seduction into an idle flirtation, to make a game of his interest. She teased him and called him her true knight but with such light artistry that he was left in no doubt that all he was being offered was a lifetime of unrequited love. Once it might have amused him a little, the absurdity of a hard-headed mercer playing games of courtly love. But not now. He was tired of games and he had no illusions about love. He snuffed the candles one by one. She would not do it for money. He had tried, in the subtlest way possible, to tempt her with gold, but she had been quite unmoved and he was glad. He did not think he would have wanted her if she could be bought with gold. But now he had William Gryffard in his power if he cared to use it. Should he force Nicolette into his bed?

He closed the Customs House and went out into the mild, humid November evening. A fine vapour hovered in the air;

Dick coughed and pulled his cloak closer about him as he started walking, wrapped in thought. What was it about Nicolette that attracted him so? Was it her struggle to be good, to live up to Piers's impossible image of perfection? Or was it that she belonged to Piers? Did he want to punish Piers for his noble certainties, his foolish trust? Dick did not know. He only knew that he was tired of the role of courtly lover and very much wanted to seduce Piers Exton's perfect lady, to discover if the dark enthralling beast of wickedness Nicolette feared and believed vanquished could be tempted from its lair. Dick smiled wryly to himself. Nicolette did not love her father. Would she risk losing her husband's love to save her father from ruin? Would Piers approve of such a test of unselfishness? Dick doubted whether Piers knew what true temptation really was.

So absorbed was he in his delicious thoughts, it was some time before Dick became aware that there were torches in the street ahead. Then a loud cry sounded from an adjoining alley. A stumbling figure came running down the street, hotly pursued by a group of men. Dick shrank back against the wall of one of the houses, cursing himself for wandering about the city alone and unprotected after dark. 'Help me!' The voice was shrill with fear. Dick remained frozen in the shadows. The men caught their prey and knocked him down with a brutal blow from a spear not far from the arched doorway where Dick stood, pressed against the stone lintel.

'Why are you doing this?' the unfortunate man cried out weakly as he slumped to his knees in the middle of the street, raising his arms to ward off another blow.

Dick could see from the flickering torches that all the attackers were in chain mail and wore the badge of the King's white hart upon their sleeves.

'Help me!' screamed their hapless victim again as the armed men descended upon him.

Dick withdrew further into the shadows. What could he do? He had only his dagger. He ought to have tried to stop them; he was, until lately, the Mayor after all, responsible for law and order in the city. But he knew it was useless, even foolhardy, to try; the King's privileged bodyguard was beyond the reach of the law. So he waited and watched while they bent over the body now slumped in the street, robbing him of his jewels, his purse, his high-crowned beaver hat, stripping from him even his blood-soaked velvet mantle. Then they ran off laughing. Dick waited until the sound of their laughter had died away and the flickering torches had vanished out of sight. Then and only then did he leap from his hiding place and shout, 'Murder!'

Soon men came hurrying with torches and before long the street was filled with people. A monk knelt down in the mud beside the body. The man was still alive. They laid him on a cloak under the arched doorway of the house that had sheltered Dick and called for the watch and a doctor.

Dick melted away into the darkness. He could do nothing to help. The wounded man was in good hands. Piers would have ridden to the rescue. The thought came unbidden and unwelcome to Dick's troubled mind. That's what knights are for, he told himself, to defend the weak and succour the oppressed. But not these knights, who beat and robbed the King's subjects everywhere, committing rape, murder and other evil without hindrance. The King was his friend but Dick did not dare ask him to punish the perpetrators of this attack. He had tried once before to advise the King to keep a strong hand on his bodyguard, reserving it solely to put down baronial opposition should it arise. But the King would not hear one word spoken against the men who wore the badge of the white hart. Was that why Piers had preferred to go into exile rather than serve King Richard?

Dick went home sickened and ashamed. He knew he was no saint; he had made many compromises in his time. Now he was afraid that he was becoming the tool of a tyrant.

Nicolette lit a candle and placed it in front of the picture of St Nicholas in the chapel in the Tower. It was her saint's day, 6 December, and she had stayed behind in the chapel after Mass to snatch a brief moment by herself. She knelt in front of the saint's shrine, pretending to pray but in reality thinking about Richard Whittington.

Dick was a great favourite in the Queen's household and since the court had been in London, his visits had become frequent. Some of the ladies-in-waiting teased Nicolette that he came not to see the Queen but to see her. Certainly he came more often than he needed. Nicolette could not help being pleased and flattered but at the same time she was beginning to be alarmed by his growing ardour. She told herself that she should stop encouraging him, but he was so much more charming, kind, intelligent, and interesting than any other man at court. She said an Ave, counting her beads without thinking. The rosary had been a gift from Dick. She had made it clear that she meant to stay true to Piers, that she could not be bought. Perhaps it would be better not to accept any more gifts from him.

A footfall on the stone floor behind her made her start. Afraid that she had lingered too long in the chapel and now would be in trouble for neglecting her duty to the Queen, she scrambled guiltily to her feet. But it was Dick who had disturbed her. Relieved, she greeted him perhaps a little too warmly.

'I was just thinking about you,' she said.

'And I think of you far more than I should,' he murmured.

'I thought you were someone come to summon me to the Queen,' she explained quickly. 'I mustn't linger too long.'

'Is the Queen very demanding?' he asked with what seemed like genuine sympathy in his eyes.

'It's not just the Queen, I'm fond of her,' Nicolette said. 'She's very young and has much to learn and is so far from home. It's just that we never have any time for ourselves, no freedom at all. We're at someone's beck and call every minute of the day.'

'But you're happy here in the Queen's household?'

'Of course. I know that I am lucky to be here, and that I have you to thank for that.' She gave him a warm, bright smile. 'I don't like the Tower, though. Whenever we lodge here it makes me feel uneasy.'

'I would not like to think that I had done you any disservice.' The words were innocent enough, but the way in which he was looking at her was far from innocent.

'I'm as happy here as I would be anywhere – without Piers,' she said, turning away from his ardent gaze.

'You're too beautiful to be by yourself, too lovely to be lonely. Let me comfort you a little.'

'I'm not lonely,' she declared hastily. 'How can anyone be lonely here in the Queen's household?' She made to leave the chapel, dismayed by this sudden bold approach which was quite unlike Dick. She could not believe that he meant to force his attentions upon her. He was far too chivalrous for that. All the same, in the quiet solitude of the empty chapel he just might be tempted to seize his opportunity.

He barred her way. Her dismay turned to anger. How dare he! She looked at him icily. To her relief he stepped aside. Then before she could sweep past him, he told her he had discovered that William Gryffard was cheating the King.

'Are you telling me my father is a thief?' she exclaimed.

'Not a thief exactly, oh no, but he has been using his position as Collector of the Wool Customs to put a bit by for himself.'

'But you said it was profitable being a tax collector.' She could not understand what he was trying to tell her.

'There is profit and there is corruption. Gryffard has been a little too greedy. Perhaps he was financially stretched. Took a risk or two too many. An unusual run of misfortune. It can happen to us all. It's very easy to be tempted.'

Nicolette stared past him out of the door of the chapel. The walls of the Tower were very high. She shivered and pulled her fur-lined cloak closer. 'Will he go to prison? Perhaps I should warn him. What will happen to him?'

'That rather depends,' replied Dick.

'Depends?' Her thoughts were chasing round in her head like leaves in an autumn gale.

'At the moment I'm the only one who knows,' said Dick.

'That's all right then,' she gave a sigh of relief. 'You'll not betray him, will you?'

'I ought to tell the King.'

She stared at him. 'And then what?'

'Gryffard could be impeached by Parliament. If found guilty, he will be fined, his goods confiscated perhaps; he may even be imprisoned. The King is desperate for money. I should think he would welcome an excuse to confiscate that fine house in Cornhill.'

'Ruin!' She raised her lovely eyes to his face. 'But you won't tell the King.'

He captured her hand and raised it to his lips. 'Not if you don't want me to.' His meaning was very plain. She withdrew her hand gently and moved away from him.

'Poor Father. He's done so much for me'. She gazed at Dick piteously. 'Don't be too hard on him.'

'Perhaps it's your turn to do something for him.'

'What can I do to help him?'

He took possession of her hands once more, both of them

this time, and gazed into her eyes. 'You know what you can do.'

She could not possibly mistake him. 'How can I? Here in the Queen's household I am never alone,' she hastened to point out.

'We are alone now,' he said, holding her hands against his chest. She could feel his heart pounding beneath his velvet doublet.

'It's too dangerous. I just couldn't – the Mistress of Ceremonies . . . the Queen . . . No, I couldn't.'

'I can always find a way,' he said. She detected a look of hardness creep into his face. He was no longer the charming, cultured friend but a merchant driving a hard bargain. What was she to say to him? How reach his better self?

'I cannot be untrue to Piers,' she said at last. She tried to withdraw her hands but he held them with a grip that bruised and for the first time she felt frightened. 'If you love me truly, you would not ask it of me,' she whispered.

'Did I say I loved you?' He bent to kiss her and she remained quite placid, yielding her lips to his without returning any of his fire. He released her, panting a little, and she regarded him in silence with accusing eyes.

'I thought you were Piers's friend,' she said at last.

'I am also a friend to the King.' The hard look in his face became more marked. 'But if you will give yourself to me, I promise your father's little discrepancies shall be our secret, yours and mine. No one else shall ever know of it. I give you my word.'

'But I cannot be untrue to Piers, I love him,' she pleaded.

'Either that or see your father ruined,' he insisted.

'Let me think about it,' she said. 'I'll let you know at Christmastide. I promise.'

'And I give you my word that your father will be safe if you wish it. You believe me, don't you? That I can and will protect him?'

'Yes, yes, of course,' she murmured.

His face softened. 'Don't keep me waiting too long.' He stooped to kiss her hands. His hot lips lingered long on her soft, cool palms. 'You're driving me mad with longing.'

The King celebrated Christmastide at his palace at Westminster with extraordinary lavishness. Twenty-eight oxen, three

396

hundred sheep and innumerable fowls were consumed daily as the pomp with which the King surrounded himself became wondrously extravagant. Nicolette and the other ladies-in-waiting were kept busy from morn until night. But this did not mean that Nicolette was able to avoid Dick Whittington. The Queen spent much of the festival at the King's side, which meant that her ladies were in the hall every day to enjoy the many exciting entertainments. Nicolette knew that she was lucky to be part of such a wonderful celebration, and if it had not been for Dick, she would have enjoyed it all hugely. The irony of it was almost unbearable. It was here that she had first been tempted to stray from the abbey's strict upbringing; to sin – for it was nothing less than mortal sin – with Nicholas Brembre. Then she had been impressed by Brembre's success and power. She had let him take her because she wanted him to. She had loved him for his power and his arrogance and because he always got his own way, but she knew now that he had been evil. Now she loved Piers who was good. She remembered Piers's parting words: 'I wonder, will you stay true to me?' Sweet Mary, Mother of Jesus, she could not be untrue to Piers.

Then she remembered her father choosing his most cherished silver-gilt cup for her to give to the Queen; an investment in her future, he had called it. Poor William with his ceaseless vigilance, the desperate feints and ruses he employed to stay out of trouble. William would fail and fail utterly unless she helped him. She could not stand by and let her father go to his ruin. And her children, what would become of her children and Jeanne and Lisette if the house in Cornhill was confiscated by the King?

She tried to avoid Dick. All her pleasure in his company had gone since he had confronted her with his impossible choice. She realised that she had been interested in him because he was the one man she thought unimpressed by her beauty. That was all. But Dick was like all the rest and he was using his power to force her to do his will. Power was a dangerous elixir; it had changed Dick from a kind friend into an impatient lover who was impossible to avoid amid the riotous Christmas merriment in the hall every night. The more Nicolette tried to evade him, the more inflamed he became.

On the Feast of St Stephen when the court was drunk with food and wine, the Lord of Misrule was getting bawdy and the little Queen was asleep on her throne, Dick managed to get Nicolette on her own.

'I will not wait for you much longer, my beloved. The King is ceaseless in his demands for money. If I could give him Gryffard, it would make it so much easier for me.'

'I thought you were my friend, that you wanted me to be true to myself,' she pleaded.

'I do want you to be true to yourself,' he replied, 'and I want to be more to you than a friend.' He caught hold of her arm and drew her into the shadows. 'That is why I am prepared to run such a risk for your sake.' He looked about him cautiously, bent closer. 'The King is all-powerful and it has made him dangerous. None of us know where he will strike next.' He was so close, she could feel his breath on her cheek. But she did not try to move away. He slipped an arm about her waist, held her against him. 'Tonight?' he asked. 'My lodgings are close by. We could go now and never be missed.'

She bent her head in mute acquiescence. What else could she do? It was not as if she had ever been perfect. She was already a sinner. At least she could do something unselfish for a change.

He was not without skill, or tenderness, and her body was hungry. While she was in his arms, Nicolette managed to forget the hard bargain which he had driven and surrendered herself to his undoubted passion, deriving pleasure from his groans of satisfaction and her own expertise. But afterwards he withdrew from her quickly and leapt out of bed as if she had suddenly become a leper. Blessed Virgin have mercy and forgive me for what I have done, she thought.

'What's the matter, Nicolette?' he said pulling on his particoloured hose. 'You're not afraid of Piers, are you? He must know you cannot live like a nun for six years or more.'

She lay watching him arrange the folds of his flowing velvet gown, feeling the weight of sin lying heavy upon her. Once she had been drawn to Dick because she thought he understood her. Now she was afraid that he understood her too well to love her. He sat down on the side of the bed and she gazed at him sorrowfully. 'Better get dressed,' he said.

'We don't want them to miss us in the hall.'

She got out of bed, smoothed down her damask gown. 'I don't believe you wanted me to find my true self. I think all you want is to lead me to eternal damnation.'

'Evil has its own intense pleasure, my dear,' he said buckling the clasp of his girdle. 'Wickedness is exciting. You can fight it or you can give in to it. But until you learn to stop being afraid of the wickedness that is in you, you'll never learn to enjoy being good.'

He stood impatiently by the door, but she was no longer upset that he was in such a hurry to leave. She knew she had to keep him wanting her, as Nicholas had, as Piers did. Whatever happened, she had to keep Dick happy. She was in his power, she and her father and her children. She must not fail them now.

CHAPTER 33

The court remained at Westminster until Candlemas on the second of February and Nicolette flung herself into the enjoyment of Christmastide with a wild abandon as she tried to put Piers out of her mind. Dick, as the King's friend, was often at the palace and Nicolette found him surprisingly adept in the art of dalliance despite the public life of the court. Every evening there were mad romps in the great hall and merry games devised by the Lord of Misrule; Nicolette allowed Dick to kiss and fondle her, pretending it was all part of the general bawdy behaviour; she discovered to her surprise that beneath his cool, reserved manner, he was both resourceful and daring in creating opportunities for a quick liaison. When a long day's feasting reached its height, he would withdraw suddenly into some well-placed recess behind the arras and she would slip in unobtrusively a little later.

'My perfect little accomplice,' he murmured breathless with desire as he drew up her fine skirts. 'Does anyone know that you go naked beneath your kirtle?'

'The tiring women assigned to the Queen's ladies are too busy to be interested in who goes about in the middle of winter without linen undergarments,' she said, deftly untying the strings and lacings beneath his doublet; his ardour became more urgent and he groaned with pleasure. Quickly he took her, his half-stifled moans of triumph drowned by the raucous merriment in the hall beyond the arras. She pretended to share his excitement as he took his pleasure. It was not what she wanted, this hasty, fervent gratification of the senses, but he did not seem to notice that she was not entirely in tune with him.

'You're a true courtesan, my beauty,' he said smiling at her knowingly, when he had recovered his breath. 'Far too experienced in the art of love for a romantic idiot like Piers.'

She did not rise to the bait. She knew it would do her no good to show how much she still hankered after Piers. So she shook out her mantle, adjusted her veil, twinkled at him coquettishly. 'I've kept my part of the bargain,' she said. 'As you have kept yours.'

'Yes, indeed. William Gryffard prospers, so they tell me.' He peered out into the hall. 'It looks safe for me to go – they're all drunk or busy playing one of the Lord of Misrule's silly games.' He slipped away without so much as a gesture of affection.

She waited, smoothing her surcoat carefully over her kirtle, peering cautiously out from behind the arras. Men and women lay sleeping off the after effects of the long day's feasting. Some of the more agile were still racing around with the King who was teasing a tame monkey; the Queen, her crown tipped over her ear, had for once forgotten her dignity and was shrieking with laughter at her husband's antics. Dick stood with his back to her, watching the merriment. Nicolette picked her way carefully across the disordered hall. Nobody showed the slightest interest in where she was going or where she had been. She sat down on a bench by a disordered table, feeling unaccountably lonely as she watched a pool of spilt wine dripping drop by slow red drop on to the floor.

'I've brought you a present,' said Dick, coming to join her on the bench.

'You don't have to bring me presents,' she said. 'I'm running out of lies to explain them away to the others. The Queen's ladies are very envious.'

'I like to bring you beautiful things,' he said with his mocking smile. 'It's what I'm good at.' She sighed. He was a realist. Once his hunger was satisfied, the mantle of his cool reserve fell upon him like a bishop's cope. He did not want her to pretend, he was far too cynical for that. Just her swift, willing obedience whenever he needed her, that was what he wanted.

When the weather permitted, the King went hawking. The Queen was a keen huntress and had a merlin of which she was very proud. On a clear January day, bright with frosty sunshine, a great cavalcade left the palace and rode into the surrounding fields. Dick released his goshawk and watched complacently while it flew into a dense thicket. 'Come and help me find her,' he said to Nicolette.

She looked over her shoulder. 'The Queen may need me,' she said.

'The Queen has her falconer, her grooms, and her husband to distract and attend her, as well as all her other ladies. You'll never be missed.'

She looked about her anxiously. The hounds had flushed a hare. The King had released his hawk, the hunters were galloping in pursuit. Dick was growing impatient; when he took a risk, he took it boldly, she thought, intrigued to discover courage in a merchant.

The thicket was small but dense enough to hide two people. Dick tied the horses to a tree, calling loudly for his hawk as he helped Nicolette to dismount. Then he pushed his way further into the thicket and Nicolette followed obediently. He laid his cloak carefully on the ground and sat on it, pulling her down beside him.

His lips were cold and hard, his hands impatient. She lay on his fur-lined cloak and closed her eyes, all too aware of the hard ground beneath, of the cold, of the sound of voices receding into the distance as the hawking party pursued its prey, of the tinkling of bells from a hawk's jesses nearer at hand. Dick was all over her, his mouth clamped upon hers, his tongue probing, his breath far from sweet.

> Could I clasp whom I adore
> on the forest's leafy floor
> how I'd kiss her – Oh and more . . .

The lines of the song popped into Nicolette's head unbidden and she stiffened involuntarily. Oh Piers! her heart cried, remembering with an aching pang the warm wonderful feeling when she lay in her husband's arms after their lovemaking.

'What's the matter?' Dick demanded, breathing hard as he rocked back on his heels, straddling her, his face flushed despite the cold.

'Nothing. The sound of the bells startled me. I thought

perhaps someone might be coming this way. Better be quick.'

He needed no urging. He plunged into her and she closed her eyes again and clasped her arms round his waist while he groaned in ecstasy. She strained against him feverishly, desperately trying to hold him to her, to find some warmth, some consolation, some comfort, but the brief moment of pleasure was already gone. She opened her eyes, gazed at the bare black branches above her head, then at her lover kneeling on the ground, his head cocked, listening to the sound of voices far away.

'Better get back before they miss us,' she said, sitting up.

He turned to look at her, a gleam of triumph in his eyes. 'Not yet. I want to remember you as you are now, to gloat a little over my treasure.' She scrambled to her feet. 'It gives me great pleasure sometimes just to look at you, my lady,' he added, with none of his customary self-mockery, 'knowing that you are mine.'

'I don't see how I can be yours while I am married to Piers and you to your Alice,' she said, unnerved by his unusual possessiveness.

'You will have to learn to forget Piers when you're with me,' he said, pulling her hood up over her head and arranging it with care.

'I didn't think you wanted love from me,' she said, too surprised to dissemble.

'Not love,' he replied with the devastating candour she found so repellent. 'But I'd like to think I give you at least a little pleasure. That what you do, you do because you enjoy it.' So he was not such a total realist as he made out, she thought, like all men, he had his vanity. Perhaps what Dick really wanted was to win her away from Piers.

'Maybe I would enjoy it more if it were not for the risk we run,' she said, afraid that she might have offended him.

'That's part of the excitement, don't you see?' He was brushing the twigs from her mantle of Lincoln green like a well-trained squire. 'The fascination of danger makes even a merchant's heart beat faster sometimes.'

'All very well for you, you get the excitement but it is I who will be ruined if we're found out,' she retorted.

'We won't be,' he said, walking to the edge of the thicket and peering out, 'not if we're careful.'

'And if I were to get with child?'

He swung round, stared at her, suddenly eager. 'It would make me very proud.' He stroked her cheek almost tenderly. 'Are you with child?'

'Not yet,' she crossed herself hastily, 'the Blessed Virgin be praised. But it can only be a matter of time.'

'I've never fathered a child,' he said, gazing at her wistfully. 'If you bear my child, he will want for nothing, I can promise you that.'

She said no more. It was easy for him to talk about provision and being proud. If she were to become with child, her days in the Queen's household would be finished. And Piers would cast her off forever; even his love was not strong enough to conquer being made a cuckold by his closest friend. Sweet Jesus! Nicolette shivered as she tugged her cloak tighter round her. Was Piers lost to her now? Or would he, when he was allowed back, find enough love in his noble heart to understand and forgive her?

On the Feast of the Purification of the Virgin Mary, the King and his court trooped to church bearing tapers, a long colourful snake winding from the palace through the streets of Westminster to the abbey. Nicolette clutched her taper and looked through the candle-lit gloom to the sanctuary guarding the mysteries of the Confessor's tomb. The tapers were to ward off ghosts, lightning, storms and tempest. Nicolette's heart felt heavy within her. She wanted to ask the Virgin to preserve her from childbearing. But she knew that until she confessed and received absolution she could not expect divine protection of any kind. Candlemas was the last day of Christmastide. Tomorrow the Queen was leaving for Windsor Castle and the King was going north on tour. With the King away it would be much more difficult for Dick to find good reasons for visiting one of the Queen's ladies. Nicolette knelt on the cold stone floor and counted her beads thankful that she had escaped so far without detection and with no sign of a child. The candles pricking through the darkness seemed full of a mysterious magic. Perhaps everything would be all right in the end. All she could do was to live from day to day and trust that somehow, someone, perhaps God, would protect her.

* * *

At Windsor Castle there was respite of a kind for Nicolette. She spent the days singing or sewing in the Queen's apartments, hawking in the royal chase beyond the castle gates, and going to Mass. It was a privileged, pampered existence and Nicolette was aware that many women would envy her her good fortune. Once she would have thought so too. But the peace and tranquillity were superficial, like the unruffled calm of a deep and treacherous moat; beneath the calm ran strong undercurrents.

The extensive Christmas jollification had been as exhausting as it had been fun; for a child of nine it had all been too much too soon, and the Queen grew bored and irritable, teasing her tutors and constantly losing her temper with her ladies-in-waiting. The child missed the King who was unfailingly kind and affectionate to his young wife. The Dame de Courcy tried to distract her royal mistress with expensive toys. The chefs in the kitchens tried to tempt her palate with new and different dishes, mocking the season of Lent with ever more ingenious devices to make fish look like meat. Nicolette bore the Queen's sullen fits patiently, trying to be the perfect lady-in-waiting; if she could win the Queen's particular favour, it might stand her in good stead one day.

A month after they had arrived at Windsor, news reached the Queen's household that John of Gaunt, Duke of Lancaster, had died on the day after Candlemas. The news caused a frisson of excitement in the Queen's apartments; with so little to divert them, even a death was exciting in its way. It was something to enliven the season of Lent; it provided an excuse for new mourning clothes, a fresh topic of conversation. For Gaunt himself there was little sorrow. He had been an old man, if still a powerful one. The King had always been afraid of his uncle, although he had come in later years to rely on Gaunt's strength to keep the peace between his warring barons. But the King was his own master now. No one in the Queen's household believed that Richard was in need of Lancaster's protection. It was as if an ogre, tamed but still capable of an occasional roar, had suddenly been slain.

Nicolette, listening to the ladies chatter as they sat sewing in the Queen's chamber, did not believe that Lancaster's death was likely to affect her much one way or the other; at least that was what she thought until the Dame de Courcy asked her one day if she was relieved to know that her husband would never be coming back.

'Not coming back! Why, what has happened to him?' exclaimed Nicolette, aghast.

'The King has seized his uncle's lands and exiled Henry Bolingbroke for life,' explained the Mistress of Ceremonies. 'His revenge against Bolingbroke is now complete.'

'What will happen now?' asked Nicolette, stunned.

The Dame de Courcy shrugged. 'The King will go to Ireland, I expect, now that he has the money for his Irish expedition.'

'I mean to Piers.'

'If Henry Bolingbroke has been exiled for life, I don't see how your husband can abandon him and come home, do you?'

Nicolette felt her heart stop. 'Piers said ... the King promised that Bolingbroke's inheritance would not be confiscated.' Henry banished for life. Piers never coming back. She could not accept it. It was too dreadful.

'The King is all-powerful, my dear. If he wants to break a promise, he can do so with impunity. He needs money for his Irish expedition – the Lancastrian estates are very large and very lucrative. The King has fallen prey to temptation, just as you have done.'

Nicolette stared at her, the blood draining from her face.

'What's the matter?' The Dame de Courcy smiled quite pleasantly. 'Did you think we did not know? You cannot keep secrets among so many women shut up together. We have nothing better to do than to gossip all day.'

Terrified, Nicolette looked about the chamber, wondering if the others could hear what the Mistress of Ceremonies was saying. The Queen was with her tutor frowning over her books, her ladies were stitching serenely at a large tapestry on a frame. Nobody showed the slightest interest in her and the Dame de Courcy sitting in the window embrasure with their embroidery.

'The Queen! Does she know?' whispered Nicolette.

'Have no fear, the Queen knows nothing. The little one is an innocent about such matters.'

Nicolette looked out of the window at the grassy sward beneath, trying to gather her scattered wits. Somehow she had to keep this formidable and powerful woman on her side.

'Whittington has given me many beautiful things,' she began tentatively. 'He is very generous. A fine reliquary – I'm sure you would think it very beautiful.'

The Dame de Courcy smiled and patted Nicolette. 'Good,' she said. 'You may need them one day.'

So she was not to be bought, thought Nicolette. Perhaps she should try asking for advice – all powerful women enjoyed telling others what to do.

'What should I do?' she asked humbly.

'Give him up, of course. Oh, I know how tedious it is for a woman as beautiful as you to be shut up with a lot of ladies like nuns in a convent. And Master Whittington is a great favourite of the King. While your lover has the King's protection, I doubt whether anyone would dare to criticise you. The King is very loyal to his friends. But if Dick Whittington should fall, as others before him have fallen, then you'd better be ready to dump him quickly. But I don't need to tell you that, you've been down this road before, have you not?'

Was there nothing this woman did not know? Nicolette bent once more over her embroidery, unable to meet the Dame de Courcy's worldly eye. She concentrated on sewing neat even little stitches, pleased to see that her hand hardly shook at all. 'You don't understand, it's not what you think,' she said at last.

'Oh, I understand very well. You like to please and you succeed. You're everybody's favourite. Almost I would say that you had been fashioned by nature for the role of courtesan. But favourites fall further and faster than the rest of us when their luck runs out and no one will come running to pick you up.'

Nicolette raised her eyes to the Dame de Courcy and smiled her most beguiling smile. The Mistress of Ceremonies returned the smile knowingly. 'The only joy for those who cannot succeed is to rejoice in the failure of those who do,' she said with a little nod of her head.

There it was again – the dreaded demon, failure. Dick said not to be afraid of failure. But how could she not be when there were so many people around her who wanted her to fail?

'Much better to end it now,' went on the Dame de Courcy, 'before the secret gets to the wrong ears.'

Nicolette gazed at her. 'You would not betray me.'

'Your secret is safe with us, here in the Queen's apartments. We are all of us foreigners, are we not? We French must stick together. But Whittington is an Englishman and you cannot rely on him for ever. Better finish with him before he finishes with you.'

If only she could! Almost she was tempted to confide in the Dame de Courcy. Sometimes Nicolette had thought about what would happen if she and Dick were discovered; when her sinful reliance on him weighed especially heavily on her soul or when life in the Queen's household was particularly irksome, she had contemplated bringing about her own disgrace. She would be dismissed from the Queen's household, she supposed. If that happened, she could go back to her father's house and look after her children, waiting until Piers came home. At times the thought of the peace and solitude of her father's splendid home was wonderfully reassuring. But now Piers was never coming home and her father could still be ruined if Dick betrayed his secret. Nicolette told herself she could not afford to think of Piers. Not now, not yet. What mattered was to keep her wits about her and do nothing to upset Dick. While he was the King's favoured adviser, he was her only protector. Whatever way she looked at it, she did not see how she could afford to take the Dame de Courcy's advice.

With the coming of spring, the King's Irish expedition gathered momentum. Men and provisions were slowly assembled at Milford Haven. After Easter the King came to Windsor to say farewell to his child Queen. From the moment the King arrived with his retinue, the peace and tranquillity which had caused the ladies such ennui through the long months since Christmastide was replaced by turmoil.

The morning after the King's arrival the ladies-in-waiting were summoned to the Queen's bedchamber an hour before her usual time of rising. Nicolette was dismayed to find the child sitting up in her big bed with tears flowing down her cheeks. Whatever had occurred to upset her must have been very grave. Isabella threw tantrums, but she hardly ever cried. She was far too well schooled in what was expected of the daughter of a French king to give way to weakness.

The ladies gathered about the bed offering sympathy but all their efforts to comfort their little mistress seemed to no avail. The child continued to sob brokenheartedly. Finally Nicolette threw herself down on her knees in front of the bed.

'Have I done something to offend you, Madame?' she said.

The Queen stared at her wildly. 'Not you, the King. He has made his will before he goes to fight the Irish.'

Nicolette had to bite her lip hard to prevent herself from laughing at the absurdity of the Queen's distress. 'Naturally the King makes a will. What prudent man does not?' she soothed. 'But no harm will come to him. He takes a formidable army with him to Ireland. His knights and nobles will see that he runs no risk in battle.'

'Of course I know that.' The Queen glared at Nicolette angrily. 'He's a Plantagenet and invincible in battle. The English always win against the Irish.' Nicolette was relieved that at least the tears had ceased and were about to be replaced by a royal tantrum. Tantrums she could cope with. She waited, still on her knees beside the bed, while the other ladies hovered anxiously, like nuns awaiting their bishop's blessing. From outside the chamber came the sound of the chapel bell ringing for prime and Nicolette dared to suggest that perhaps it was time they began to get the Queen dressed for the day.

'Your Grace will want to look your best to bid farewell to His Grace, the King,' she suggested, knowing that the child loved dressing up in all her finery. But the Queen's bottom lip began to tremble again.

'It doesn't matter what I wear for him since he cares nothing for me after all. In his will he has asked to be laid to rest beside his first Queen, the revered Ann of Bohemia.'

So that was it! Nicolette's heart went out to the child. For a moment she almost forgot Isabella was the Queen of England and went to gather her up in her arms to soothe away her hurt pride. But she remembered in the nick of time. Such behaviour would be frowned upon by the Mistress of Ceremonies and the Queen herself would regard it as an unpardonable liberty. Then Nicolette suddenly realised that the Dame de Courcy was not in the Queen's bedchamber.

'Is the Dame de Courcy ill?' she asked, hoping to distract the Queen a little from her unhappy thoughts.

'The Dame de Courcy has been dismissed. They say she is

too extravagant; she is going back to France.' The Queen was sitting on the end of the bed in her smock, her hair hanging down her back in two untidy braids, her small child's face bewildered and lost. 'The King's Grace has appointed Roger Mortimer's widow Mistress of Ceremonies in her place. It is all very unsettling.'

So in the end it was the Dame de Courcy who had fallen from favour. Nicolette's consternation must have shown in her face for the Queen's mouth suddenly twitched into a brave ghost of a smile. 'You liked her too, didn't you?' she said.

'Yes, I liked her,' said Nicolette. 'She was kind to me, in her way.' She felt frightened. If the formidable Dame de Courcy could be so swiftly sent packing back to France for extravagance, what would happen if a lady-in-waiting was found guilty of adultery?

The business of getting the Queen dressed in her stiffly embroidered clothes and ready to make a dignified and regal farewell to her warrior husband was sufficiently taxing to keep Nicolette busy and by the time she went down to the hall with the Queen and the rest of the ladies-in-waiting, she had recovered something of her poise.

William Gryffard was among the throng waiting in the great hall with the King. The sight of him looking so incongruous in his merchant's gown and hooded cowl among all these knights in their chain mail threw Nicolette into fresh turmoil.

'What are you doing here?' she asked him.

'The King has sent for me,' he replied. Her fear turned to panic.

'God in His mercy spare me, then the King knows,' Nicolette exclaimed.

'Knows? Knows what? That you are Richard Whittington's mistress?' She blushed to the edge of her Venetian veil. The way he looked at her made her feel so ashamed. 'I doubt whether the King cares very much who consoles you in your husband's absence.'

The injustice of it cut her to the quick. 'I had to do it, Father. To save you from disgrace. Dick Whittington knows about the wool tax.' He seemed quite unmoved. 'He knows how much profit you take,' she added, determined that he should accept some of the blame for her behaviour.

'It doesn't matter,' he said. 'What matters is that the King has asked me to keep an eye on Whittington while he is away. The King doesn't trust him.'

'But Dick is his friend.'

'The King has learnt not to trust even his friends these days. He knows that Whittington rode all the way to Gravesend with Henry Bolingbroke when he went into exile, that the citizens of London can be very disloyal. The King wants to be kept informed of what the Londoners are up to while he is away fighting the Irish. You can help me in this.'

'I can't. Dick doesn't confide in me.'

'Why not? He's your lover, isn't he? Brembre confided in you when you were his mistress.'

'Dick isn't like Brembre,' she said.

'He's more cunning,' retorted William, his watchful eyes scanning the hall. 'But you're a clever woman now. You're not the silly lovestruck idiot who let Brembre break her heart – are you?' He turned to stare into her face knowingly. 'You're not in love with Whittington?'

She blushed furiously, feeling shame and disgust and self-hatred for what she had done. 'Of course I don't love him,' she murmured. 'What I did I did for you.'

'I know that.' He seemed pleased with her. 'You've learnt at last how to let your head control your heart. Now I have found a way for you to get rid of Whittington if you want, without endangering either of us. If Whittington is plotting with Henry, the King wants to know and will reward whoever brings him the news. You must find out what Whittington is up to.'

'But I know nothing of city politics. They're no concern of mine. He knows that, he's not a fool.'

'But Henry Bolingbroke is very much your concern. Your husband, if you remember him at all, is a retainer of Henry Bolingbroke.' She looked down at her feet; she did not want his watchful eyes to see how he hurt her. 'The King is leaving England with a formidable army, leaving the very heart of his kingdom exposed to easy attack. If Henry Bolingbroke is tempted to return and take back his sequestered lands by force, the Londoners might be tempted to support him. They did so once before. The King needs to know, and you and I need to know, if they intend to do it again.'

If that happened, Piers would be coming back, she

thought, her spirits lifting in spite of everything.

'If that happens,' added William, 'we may all be ruined.'

'Why should we be ruined?'

'Whittington, you, me, we are all of us dependent on the King's favour now. You might ask yourself what Piers will do if he comes home victorious and finds he has been made a cuckold by the man he counts his friend.'

She wanted to walk away from him. Tell him that she had sacrificed herself for him for the last time. But it seemed that wickedness had a momentum of its own. One sin led to another and another. To save her father and herself, she now had to spy on Dick. She clenched her teeth and willed herself to meet William's searching gaze.

'Surely Dick wouldn't send for Henry Bolingbroke. It's against his interest,' she said.

'I believe it is.' He smiled at her sardonically. 'I know for a fact that he has personally lent the King up to one thousand pounds. No one, not even Whittington, can afford to lose that sort of money.'

'Then there is nothing to be afraid of,' she said.

'That is what the King feels or he wouldn't be going. But in this world there is one thing you can always count upon and that is that nothing is ever quite as straightforward as it seems. I find it pays to check and doublecheck and never to believe oneself safe from disaster.'

She felt the weight of his uncertainties fall over her like a mantle. She wanted to believe that Piers would be coming home, that he loved her enough to save her from herself and forgive her, that he would understand that she had done what she had done because she had had no choice. Yet she could not. She could not believe that Piers was her best champion. Always it was her father with his constant nervous vigilance, his depressing habit of expecting the worst, his fears, his diabolical cunning, who had the last word. So she promised him to do her best to get Dick to confide in her and prayed that she would not be caught committing adultery in the process.

CHAPTER 34

'The bay tree that withered on the day Lancaster died has as suddenly broken into leaf again,' said Alice Whittington.

'Don't trees usually?' replied Dick, who had come into the garden to find her.

'Not in June they don't. Trees lose their leaves at Michaelmas, not Candlemas, and break into leaf again in the spring. It's all wrong.' She held up a small bunch of glossy, pointed green leaves. 'Besides, bay trees don't usually lose their leaves at all. Could it be a sign?'

'Perhaps.' He had heard this tale of the bay trees elsewhere. He did not want to worry her, but he could tell from her face that she was worried already. 'It's not only ours,' he said. 'It's happened to bay trees all over the city, I'm told. Whatever it means, it's not some personal disaster. Some momentous upheaval is about to fall upon us all.'

'And you expect me to take comfort from that?' she said, but she was smiling at him.

'Not comfort, courage,' he replied as he sat down in the shade of an apple tree beside her.

'Perhaps it means the House of Lancaster is about to rise again,' she said. He frowned. 'That is what they were saying after Mass this morning,' she added.

'That would be a momentous upheaval indeed.'

'You would not subject us to that, surely.'

He shook his head. 'Not me,' he said. 'The Mayor and aldermen.'

'You're still an alderman and they listen to you.' She looked at him proudly. 'You've always been different from the rest. They know that, which is why they'll follow wherever you care to lead.'

He knew that she was right, which is what made him feel afraid. 'King Richard is very unpopular in the city. His forced loans and blank charters were an interference with our freedom. His punitive taxation makes it very difficult for all of us. I doubt if the citizens of London will endure any more. Now Henry Bolingbroke has written from Paris saying that the King is plotting to put to death the chief magistrates and intends to impose a burden of taxation greater than ever before.'

'And you believe him?'

'After what the King did to his own uncles, I believe him, yes,' said Dick. 'All morning I've been with the Common Council, listening to confused and frightened men trying to decide whether to send messages to Henry in Paris inviting him to come and set us free from tyranny.'

'Henry Bolingbroke has good reason to think ill of the King, he has lost his inheritance and his country. He's a fighter like the rest of the Plantagenets. But there is no need for you to become embroiled in his schemes. Stay out of it. You're a mercer not a kingmaker. Leave that to the great barons.' He had never known her so vehement. Fear had broken down her habitual reserve. 'Remember Nicholas Brembre,' she went on. 'He was a great leader and the city's hero, but look what happened to him.'

'I'll try not to end up at the end of a rope,' he said. She did not respond to his joke and looked so anxious that he felt compelled to try to convince her. 'Nicholas Brembre came to grief because he defied the city, tried to use it for his own purposes, to support the King. I shan't do that.'

'Perhaps you're more like Nicholas Brembre than you'd have me think,' she said.

'The Mayor is no Brembre,' Dick replied swiftly, afraid of where the conversation might be leading. 'Barantyn is a good goldsmith but he's not anxious to take the lead and nor will any of the others.'

'Then why should you? We have so much to thank God for, Dick. You have worked so hard, built up so much. Why go looking for trouble now?' She twisted round on the hard stone bench to look him firmly in the eye.

He took her square, practical hand in his. 'The King has become a tyrant.' It was important to him that she should understand. 'I've known it for a long time. He's determined

414

to rule in his own right on principle, to impose his will through his own ministers.'

'What of the money you have lent him?' she interrupted swiftly. 'If you bring him down you'll lose all hope of ever getting it back.'

'If he can seize Henry Bolingbroke's rightful inheritance despite all his promises to the contrary, who knows what he will take next?' Dick retorted. 'If the King should come home from Ireland empty-handed, as he surely must, then no man of property in the land is safe.'

'But the King is the King, divinely appointed by God. I would not be happy being married to a man who has betrayed his King.'

For a moment he wondered whether perhaps it was not fear but anger which made her so outspoken, whether she knew about Nicolette, whether she meant to accuse him. But Alice was no fool. She would not bring out into the open anything which it was better to keep dark.

'What of our hard-won privileges, our civic freedom?' Somehow he had to make her understand, to overcome her anger, get her to share the burden of the decision he had to take. 'Don't we owe it to the men who fought so hard for London's rights in the time of King John, and to the men who came after who battled to preserve our independence, to continue the fight now? Freedom cannot be taken for granted, it has to be tended like your garden here, day in, day out, in good times and in bad or else it'll wither and die.'

'You men can always justify what you do with fine words, but it is we women who have to keep the food on the table whatever happens,' she retorted, pulling her hand away and getting to her feet. 'As I must do now if we are to have any dinner today.' She stalked off towards the kitchens and he watched her, convinced that somehow she must have learnt about Nicolette. It was not like her to be so unreasonable.

Dick looked about him at the peaceful garden, at the bright June sunshine dappling the ground beneath the apple trees, the splash of water falling from the fountain. If they sent for Henry, Piers would come back with him, and if Piers came home, Nicolette would be lost to him. Or would she? The very thought made his pulses race. Just thinking of Nicolette, of the pleasure she gave him, made his flesh tingle. He did not want to lose her. What had begun as an exercise in power had become a dangerous addiction. In seeking to rouse the dark beast which lurked beneath Nicolette's aura of goodness, he had roused a dark beast of his own. He visualised her as he had last seen her at Windsor, cool, elegant, well bred, walking in the Queen's garden among the high, clipped hedges which provided such excellent hiding places for adulterers. His loins ached with longing as he remembered the swift transformation from cool beauty to willing slave. He had no idea that any woman could be so exciting. But he remembered something else, how she had shown a great interest in the Mayor and the aldermen. She did not usually show any interest at all in the affairs of the city. He smiled to himself now as he sat in his garden. He understood her so well; there was a great deal more of her father in her than she was prepared to admit. But her ability to please, which made her such a delightful mistress, also made her a dangerous confidante. Not for anything would he discuss his difficult decision with Nicolette. Unlike Alice. He sighed. Alice was dutiful and her reserve made her dull but it also made her discreet. She, too, was her father's daughter, shrewd, hard-working, strong in adversity. In any crisis he could depend upon Alice, and it was a crisis they faced now.

The bell of St Michael began to ring. It was noon, time for dinner. Dick sat and listened to the bells all over the city pealing in joyous harmony. He loved them; they directed the hours of the day from prime which got him up in the morning to the Angelus which when he was an apprentice brought the good news that work had ceased for the day. His work never ceased now. The bells pealing triumphantly would not let him rest. He had to decide. There was no time to be lost. If they were to take advantage of the King's absence, messages would have to be sent to Henry this day.

It seemed to him, sitting in his garden with his mind in turmoil, wondering what to do, that the bells were calling to him. Turn again, Whittington, they seemed to say. He sat bolt upright on the stone seat. Could he turn? Encourage the Mayor and aldermen to back Henry Bolingbroke against the Lord's anointed? Could he betray his friend the King? The sound of the bells beat in his head. Turn again, Whittington, they insisted with awful clarity. Compromise, desert your friend, survive.

Once before he had listened to the bells. It was not long

after he had arrived in the city, when he hated his apprenticeship and the longing to be a knight was almost too much for him. He had been on the point of running away then, was in fact on his way out of the city when the bells had called him back – back to a life of hard work and compromise and finally great financial success. Now they were calling him again, to forget his money, his mistress, his honour, and to send for Henry to come and save the city.

The city was still his first love, and it was threatened by the King's determination to take it into his own hand. It was the city that needed him most. Dick sighed. She was a demanding mistress but more rewarding than any brief gratification of the senses.

His mind made up, he went in to his dinner with the sound of the bells still ringing in his ears.

Henry came. He landed at Ravenspur just north of the Humber on 5 July. When the news reached London, it threw the Mayor and aldermen into a frenzy of excitement verging on panic.

'We must find out what Bolingbroke intends to do,' declared Dick at a meeting of the city's leaders hastily gathered at the Mayor's house.

'Do? What can he do?' asked the Mayor. 'The force he has with him filled no more than three small ships. He cannot take over the country with that.'

'Not if no one in England supports him,' agreed Dick. 'But we invited him to come to our rescue, we must support him. We'd better send a deputation to assure him of London's sympathy.'

'Would it not be better to wait until we see what the barons do?' objected one of the other aldermen.

'The barons must be waiting too,' said Dick. 'If we show them that we mean business, it will encourage them to come out on Henry's side. No man wants to go to the Tower on his own.'

They argued hotly among themselves; some were for playing safe, others wanted to show their support for Bolingbroke. In the end, Dick carried the day.

Fifty of the city's most influential leaders, including two other aldermen and Dick himself, left for the north that same day. Five days later they caught up with Henry at Doncaster.

417

The crowded lower bailey of the castle was filled with activity. Dick dismounted gingerly. His limbs were stiff and sore, for he was not accustomed to so many days of hard riding. He looked about him nervously at the shining armour, the bristling spears, the longbows, the colourful escutcheons and snorting destriers, all the weapons and panoply of war. This was Piers's world, he thought a little apprehensively as he wondered not for the first time what the knight would have to say at his appearance here with London's deputation. Armed men arrived and departed with a great deal of noise and Dick braced himself nervously when he recognised one of them as Piers.

'I didn't expect to see you here, Dick,' said Piers, seizing him by the hand and shaking it heartily.

'What did you expect? That I would be like Nicholas Brembre and stick to the King when the rest of London is determined to have none of him?'

'I should hope not – Brembre was a scoundrel,' said Piers, grinning at him without a hint of malice. 'Whereas you're a good man, Dick, for all the cynical nonsense you talk. The fact that you're here today proves you have London's best interests at heart.'

Was it possible, thought Dick, that a man could be so generous in spirit? Not a word about honour or loyalty, not a quibble at my having changed sides.

'I knew you'd come to see it my way in the end,' Piers beamed at him.

Would he prove so noble when he found that he had been cuckolded and by whom? Dick wondered. Or would his belief in the goodness of others make him impervious to the truth? It was a fascinating idea but one which he thrust firmly away for consideration when he had leisure. He had far more important matters than the beautiful Nicolette to worry about now. 'So, your principles have brought you back a hero.' Somehow Dick could not keep the bitterness out of his voice. 'Nicolette should be proud of you.' Her name sprang from his lips despite all his good intentions and he realised that he must get a better control of himself.

'I've done nothing yet,' said Piers. 'It's all been so quick, so easy. I can hardly believe it's scarce three weeks since we set sail for England with barely three hundred men. Since then we've occupied the castles of Pickering, Knaresborough and Pontefract without striking a blow. Thousands have come rallying to Henry's standard.'

'Where will it all end?'

'End?' Piers looked surprised. 'With Henry being restored to his estates. What else?'

'It's what Bolingbroke would have men believe,' replied Dick quietly. 'Not many men will have the stomach for a fight against a lord who has merely come to claim what is so obviously his own. But when he has England under his control and the King at his mercy, what then? It takes a man of great self-restraint to stop short at the Crown when it is within his grasp.'

'He has given his word – to the Percies. The Earl of Northumberland and Henry Hotspur would not have thrown in their lot with him if they thought he meant to be King.'

'And Henry Bolingbroke is a man of his word?' inquired Dick.

'I would not have served him so long or gone into exile with him if I had not believed him to be an honourable man,' replied Piers.

'Good for you.' Dick was unable to help envying Piers a little. He was so eager and so full of the boundless energy which confidence brings. 'Will you help us to see Boling-broke?' he asked. 'The army seems to be spread out all over the town. It's taken us the whole morning just to get this far and it's far too hot a day.'

'Of course, come with me. The message you bring ensures that you'll get a warm welcome.'

'I'm afraid there are rather a lot of us,' said Dick, drawing Piers's attention to the rest of his party.

'Can't you speak for them? The chamber's very crowded. There's a great deal to do at a time like this.'

'They've come a long way in a hurry, an arduous journey fraught with danger with so many armed men on the move, and I think I owe it to them to make sure they see Henry Bolingbroke in person, that they do not feel they have endured so much peril and discomfort for nothing.'

'Wise and prudent as ever, Dick,' said Piers, cuffing him a little too vigorously on the back. 'You don't want to accept sole responsibility and have them desert you as they did Brembre if it all goes wrong. But it won't this time. Henry knows what he's about. Bring them then, if you must. I'll see if I can get Henry to come down to the great hall and speak to you there.'

In the great hall of the castle, trestles were being set up for dinner; at the dais end a number of scribes were sitting at the high table writing busily while merchants, armed men and clerics came and went. Dick watched the activity with a knowing eye.

'Quite a job feeding all these people,' he said.

'Indeed it is,' replied Piers. 'We've had so many recruits we've had to send some of them home for lack of provisions for them. Wait here. I shan't be long.'

Dick was impressed by the orderly, efficient manner in which everything was being done. There was none of the extravagant show and elaborate luxury with which King Richard surrounded himself. Henry Bolingbroke was a man who knew about campaigning, that was certain. But how far was he intending to go? Dick frowned. It was important to know whether he was dealing with his future King or merely a powerful overlord such as Henry's father had been. Anxiously Dick thought of all that was at stake. Would Henry take on the burden of repaying Richard's debts if he became King? Would he guarantee London's privileges? An ambitious man on the threshold of power might promise much to those who helped him. Was Henry the man to honour his pledges?

'So you've finally made up your mind which way to jump, Master Whittington,' said Henry an hour later when Piers brought him into the hall.

Dick spread his hands deferentially, managing as he did so to include the other merchants with him. 'I am merely the mouthpiece of the city of London.'

'You were the King's friend, you know him – better perhaps than I who share his blood. Why did he run away to Ireland?'

The rumour Dick had heard on his journey from London was that the King had fled to Ireland to avoid the reckoning with so famed a knight as Henry Bolingbroke. Ugly rumour was a mighty ally and Henry was no doubt capable of exploiting it to the full. All the same, Dick suspected Bolingbroke was not the man to value flattery rather than the truth.

'The King is no coward,' said Dick. 'But he often listens to the wrong advice.'

'Not yours this time, then,' said Henry fixing Dick with a piercing stare.

'I only advise the King on financial matters and for that reason alone I was against the Irish venture. Alas I could not satisfy the King's need for money and so he seized Your Grace's estates.'

'The Duke of York has called up the shire levies of the Midlands and the south and summoned them to Saint Albans. They've responded well, so my informers tell me.'

'But not the gentry,' Dick pointed out.

'You're well informed, Master Whittington,' Henry suddenly smiled. 'I should have enough men here to defeat what the Regent can bring into the field against me. But the King took a formidable army with him when he went to Ireland. Do I march to Saint Albans to take care of the Regent and then occupy London, which you say will support me, and wait for the King there?'

'It is not for me, a mere mercer, to advise an experienced soldier like yourself how or where to fight battles,' said Dick. 'But I can tell you that the Londoners have already taken the law into their own hands. Even as we left, certain citizens had gathered in Westminster to search the abbey for the King, thinking he had in secret fled there. When they did not find him, they shut up three of the King's special counsellors instead. The Londoners are already putting actions to words.' Henry was watching him closely. 'Experience has taught me, Your Grace, not to try to fight the will of the ordinary citizens of London.'

'Or of England,' returned Henry.

Dick looked into those shrewd, hard eyes. Henry would go as far as he could in the end. He was no slave to chivalry as Piers was.

A month later, William Gryffard stood looking up at the rotting heads impaled above him on the Drawbridge Gate of London Bridge. There was not enough flesh remaining to recognise them, but he knew who they were well enough. They were Bushy, Green and Scrope, three of the King's ministers. William had feasted with them, lent them money and profited by it. The last time he had seen them was on

20 July at Wallingford, where the Queen had taken refuge with her household. The three ministers had been with the Duke of York's army when the Regent had visited the little Queen to reassure her that she had nothing to fear. William had been visiting Nicolette, in a desperate quest for good news, and he too had been reassured – by the size of the Duke of York's army and his vow to deal swiftly and harshly with any rebellious lord who dared to challenge the King's authority in his absence.

Reassurance had turned to dismay when William learnt that the Duke of York had deserted to Henry as soon as he encountered the Lancastrian army – somewhere between Berkeley Castle and Bristol on 27 July. The King's ministers had fled to Bristol Castle which in turn had surrendered without a blow; the three ministers were summarily executed without even pretence of a trial and their heads sent to London in a white basket with a letter from Henry to the Mayor. Henry had been encamped at Bristol with a large and jubilant army.

William had grown very frightened. He was unable to make up his mind what to do. Then the King had landed at Milford Haven with his army from Ireland and London had been besieged by rumour: the King had fled north abandoning his personal baggage, plate, chapel furniture and other encumbrances; the Earl of Salisbury, loyal to the King, had amassed a substantial army of Welshmen and Cheshire archers; the King was expected to make a stand in Wales and it would be impossible for Henry to dislodge him.

Throughout the long hot month of August, William stayed in London, dithering and sick with worry. He realised with a dreadful sinking of the spirit that he was in trouble whether Henry or the King triumphed. If Henry, then he would lose his valuable position as Collector of the Wool Taxes and the money he had lent to the King. If the King, he would be in danger of losing his head for having failed to warn Richard of London's betrayal and for robbing the King of his just dues – if Whittington chose to expose him. He ought to run – back to Calais where he would be safe from impeachment, imprisonment and death. But he was tired of running and there was profit to be made out of war and uncertainty. Besides, he could not leave Nicolette's children, his grandchildren. Nicolette had begged him not to take them away with him to France, insisting that the King would win if he reached Wales in safety. The Welsh were loyal to Richard and so were the Cheshire levies. If the struggle went on for long, Henry's cause would be lost, his support would fade and Richard – who was the King, after all, appointed by God – would triumph in the end.

William stared up at the heads impaled upon the gate. If what he had heard today proved to be true, he would be glad that he had listened to Nicolette. Today his quest for news had taken him to the whorehouse of the Widow Wendegoos on the other side of the river from London. Only a pressing need for information would have sent him into the stews of Southwark in the heat of midsummer. But his persistence had been rewarded. A customer of the widow's, a mercer who was one of those who represented the city in Parliament, had let slip that Parliament was to be held at Westminster on 30 September. When the Widow Wendegoos had refused to believe such an unlikely tale, the mercer swore the writs had been sent out from Chester in the King's name. William had paid her well for the information.

As he rode across the bridge back into London, he wondered if he might allow himself once more to hope. If the King had called Parliament, he must still be in control of the country. Did he mean to use Parliament to have his revenge? A cloud of well-fed flies rose sluggishly from the rotting contents of the gutter in the middle of the street and William brushed them impatiently away as he thought about the effects of the King's revenge. Dick Whittington would be impeached, that was certain, impeached and executed for treason. Piers would be executed or banished if he had not already been killed in battle. But Nicolette would be safe in the Queen's household – and free.

William reined in to allow an ox cart to pass in the narrow street. The city was hot and airless, not a breath of wind stirred the putrid air. Perhaps with Nicolette's help the King could be persuaded to overlook his failure to inform him of Whittington's treachery. William buried his nose in a posy of gillyflowers he always carried when he visited the stews and let the sweet scent of hope banish the odour of defeat. He was going to survive. There was no need to run away to Calais.

By the time he reached Cornhill, his mind was on the wheat he had stored in his warehouse. The price of wheat would soon begin to fall once the corn merchants realised the city was not going to come under siege. Or would the city try to resist the King? Should he hold on to his wheat a little longer? Wrestling already with this new fear, William reached the fine stone-arched entrance to his house. Outside, a small group of men-at-arms sat waiting, their horses' heads hanging listlessly in the heat. One of them was dressed not in chain mail but a gown of bright blue camlet and hope died as William recognised Dick Whittington.

'We're here by order of the Mayor and Common Council to take you into custody until my lord Henry's pleasure,' said Whittington, fulfilling William's worst fears.

'Why me? What have I done?' he demanded, his voice squeaking with terror.

'The Mayor and aldermen feel that as one of the few friends the King has left in the city, it's better we know what you're up to and where you are.' Whittington had the good grace to look discomfited.

'The King will make you answer for this,' William protested, his voice a little stronger. 'Parliament has been summoned at Westminster. The King would not have summoned Parliament unless he was on his way south.'

'The King is on his way to London, it is true,' replied Dick, 'but as a defenceless prisoner of Henry Bolingbroke. Parliament has been called by Henry in the King's name. The city is anxious to show its support for Henry in every way we can. A special deputation is on its way even now demanding Richard's instant execution.'

William was stunned, but he had been anticipating disaster for so long that he was almost prepared for it. Even as he was led away, his devious brain was busy trying to see a means of escape. He had done nothing wrong, he thought, apart from that little matter of the customs. Nothing treasonable, nothing that could be proven in Parliament. Then he remembered the King's three ministers who were executed without trial and began to tremble. But he was not a minister, he was not even a very good friend. He had not warned the King of Whittington's betrayal. Whittington! It suddenly occurred to William that his arrest might be Whittington's doing, a wicked attempt by him to keep some hold over Nicolette perhaps. As they entered the Royall and began to ride down the broad cobbled thoroughfare towards

St Nicholas' Church, William gripped the reins of his horse so tightly the animal threw up its head in fright. Somehow Whittington had to be removed.

William's head ached and beads of sweat dripped off the end of his nose on to his heavy damask gown. There was always Piers. The knight was a trusted retainer of Henry's. He would have power and influence. Suppose Piers were to be told about Nicolette and Dick Whittington? Hope, like an errant hound, came creeping back into William's troubled mind. If Nicolette's husband killed her lover and then deserted her, William would be rid of them both. His daughter would be totally reliant on him again. Would Piers desert her? No man as idealistic and noble as Piers could bear the pain of knowing that his perfect lady had cuckolded him with his trusted friend. It would kill his love for ever.

They had reached Whittington's house. William dismounted, so engrossed in his cunning scheme that his limbs scarcely trembled at all. Nicolette must be freed from Whittington's power. Somehow, he must get a message to Piers.

CHAPTER 35

'There is a Bush that is overgrown,
Crop it well and keep it low,
Or else it will grow wild . . .'

Nicolette shut the window hastily so the Queen would not
hear. 'The Bush' was King Richard. It was a scurrilous song
and if someone was singing it here in the palace at
Wallingford it showed how very bad things must be for King
Richard. Nicolette looked anxiously at the Queen, but she
was at her prayers and had not heard. Isabella and her ladies
spent a great deal of time now going to church and praying
that the King should triumph over his enemies. The little
chapel was bright with the innumerable candles lit daily in a
vain attempt that fate, in the shape of Bolingbroke, should be
placated. Nicolette went to church and lit her candles like the
others, although she did not know what to believe or pray for
any more.

As the bad news slowly reached the Queen's household –
the Duke of York's defection to Henry, the capture of the
King, lured out of the stronghold of Conway Castle by false
promises of safety – the Queen's ladies drew away from
Nicolette. They were French women, foreigners in a foreign
land, bound together by their fear and isolation. But
Nicolette was married to an English retainer of the victorious
Henry. She was no longer one of them. Then one morning
the Queen told Nicolette to send someone else to dress her;
that was after they had heard how King Richard was being
treated by his victorious cousin Henry. The Queen had wept
when she was told how her husband had been mounted on a
tiny nag and clothed in a plain black gown like a penitent. He

426

had been allowed to hear Mass in Westminster Abbey for the last time before being taken to the Tower of London. Nobody knew what Henry intended to do next. The Queen and her ladies prayed for Richard's soul, terrified that Henry might already have deprived the King of his head and his crown.

The Queen rose from her knees. Nicolette stood up, waiting with hands folded and eyes downcast in case the Queen should summon her. But the Queen summoned Marie. 'Will you not sing to us, Marie,' she said, seating herself on the step running round the bed. 'Sing about Marie de France, she's your namesake and her song is sad enough for our mood.' The ladies settled themselves like flowers about the chamber. Marie plucked the strings of the lute and began to sing, about the lady who had loved four knights, all so handsome, brave, worthy and generous that she could not choose between them and so had made them fight for her love.

> Alas, she said,
> whatever shall I do?
> I shall never again be happy!
> I loved these four knights
> and desired each one
> for his own sake . . .

Nicolette sat down on the window seat and picked up her embroidery again, thinking about Piers. The Queen's household was not under siege. Isabella had received a message from Henry Bolingbroke assuring her of his protection. It had brought on a right royal tantrum. So why had Piers not sent his wife a similar message? Or better still brought Henry's message to the Queen himself. She told herself that Piers could not come. He was too busy helping Henry make England his. Nicolette did not know what rebels did when they took over a country but she was sure it kept them very, very busy.

> 'I made them compete for my love,
> not wishing to lose them all,
> to have just one,' sang Marie.

Nicolette's hands lay idle in her lap, her thoughts bleak.

No news had reached the Queen's household about the fate of Dick Whittington and the rest of the King's friends, but everybody feared the worst. Nicolette felt an enormous sadness. The same fate awaited Dick as had befallen Nicholas Brembre. But she was also conscious of a feeling of relief. If Dick had been arrested with the rest of the King's friends, she would be free from the burden of lies and pretence, free to love Piers as she wanted to love him, truly and faithfully.

> 'I do not know which of them to mourn the most
> but I can no longer disguise or hide my feelings.
> One of them I now see wounded
> and three are dead.'

Nicolette watched her little mistress wipe away a tear, but for once her sympathies were unmoved. What did the spoilt but innocent child she served know of the agonies of guilt and sin and remorse? She picked up her embroidery. The white hart she had been embroidering on a cushion for the Queen was nearly finished. It glowed with a radiant purity against the purple satin. It had taken Nicolette most of the month of September to do. She had begun it to show the other ladies that she loved the King as much as any of them. Now it no longer mattered what they thought. Piers would be coming soon to take her away from the Queen's household. And when he did, what would she tell him? Did she dare tell him the truth? Perhaps he knew already. But who would tell him? Not Dick, surely. Not me, she thought, unable to bear the thought of confessing such a terrible sin to her husband. Never me. She made two more little white stitches on the purple satin, feeling deeply depressed about the lies she would have to go on telling.

'Why did you shut the window?' The Queen's high-pitched querulous voice interrupted her melancholy thoughts.

'I'm sorry, Madame. I thought Your Grace might be in a draught.'

'Well, we're not. We're too hot,' came the irritated rejoinder.

Nicolette threw the window open again and as she did so she looked down into the court below. There, waving her arms about and arguing with one of the men-at-arms, was Lisette. Blessed Mother, some terrible calamity must have befallen them at home! Nicolette lent further out of the window, managing to knock her embroidery out as she did so. Turning back into the room with a small cry, she humbly asked the Mistress of Ceremonies for permission to go down into the court below to retrieve the cushion she had been working on. Lady Mortimer assented grudgingly. Nicolette slipped out of the room, raced down the spiral stairs into the courtyard and caught hold of the man-at-arms who was trying to drag Lisette away to the guard chamber.

'It's all right, she's my tiring woman from London. I'll look after her,' she panted. He looked dubious but she smiled at him sweetly and he gave in instantly. Nicolette turned to Lisette without even waiting for the man to leave them alone. 'What is it? What has happened? Is it one of the children?'

'No, no, the Blessed Virgin be praised, the children are all well and as full of spirit as spring lamb.' Lisette paused, waiting until the archer had withdrawn. 'It's Master Gryffard. He's been arrested,' she announced dolefully.

'My father arrested?' In all her worries and doubts, Nicolette had never once thought that anything might befall her father. How could such a wily old bird be taken? 'What has he done?'

'He's the King's friend, that's crime enough nowadays,' said Lisette. 'The Londoners have seized anyone they thought likely to support the King and locked them up. Some in the Tower. Master Gryffard's lucky, Master Whittington has him in his charge under house arrest.'

'Whittington? But he was the King's friend too. Isn't he in the Tower with the King?'

'Dick Whittington knows which side his bread's buttered,' said Lisette with a sniff. 'He's advising Henry Bolingbroke now.'

Nicolette gasped. A cold hand clutched at her heart. 'Piers?' she asked.

Lisette shook her head sadly. 'Changed – success has changed him. I never thought a good noble creature such as that could have his head turned so easy. Him what'd give away his last shilling to the poor and think nothing of it, who bore knocks as they was gifts not curses from above.'

'Lisette, tell me,' Nicolette interrupted impatiently. 'Have you seen him?'

Lisette was silent.

'Has he not been to see the children even?'

'No, him ain't, but after what happened to the master I took it upon me to go and find him. So I tracks him down to Westminster. There I tells him. That Master Gryffard's in prison and the house is besieged each day by his creditors. There's no money to buy food and his children be starving if something isn't done soon. And what does he say, my noble knight that used to uphold the weak and the oppressed?' Lisette folded her arms and looked so outraged Nicolette would have laughed if she hadn't been so much afraid. 'He says go and ask Dick Whittington to help.'

'Sweet Jesus have mercy!'

'They're your children, says I, and he rounds on me fierce as a wild boar. Are they? says he.'

'So he knows!' said Nicolette, bursting into tears. 'Oh Lisette, what am I going to do now?'

'Now then, my lady, there's no use crying. It's too late for that. Whatever you've done, ye'll have had your reasons. But if you've been playing your silly games with that Dick Whittington, then the fat's in the fire good and proper. Sir Piers'll never get over being cuckolded by the man he trusts most.'

Nicolette looked at her maid standing in the grassy court with the late September sun bathing her ugly peasant's face and felt a tiny glow of comfort seep into her heart. Lisette was not shocked, only worried. If Lisette was prepared to forgive without even knowing the whole story, perhaps Piers who was so noble would understand when he knew it all.

'I didn't want to, Lisette. Dick Whittington made me. He could have ruined Master Gryffard and then what would have happened to you all?'

'I might've known you'd get into a hogswash of trouble without me or Sir Piers here to watch out for you. When Master Whittington got you taken into the Queen's household I knew it'd come to no good.'

When she had heard the whole story, Lisette shook her head more dolefully than ever. 'That Whittington's betrayed you, my lady. Be sure that he's behind this arrest of Gryffard. Wanting to keep you in his power, that's what the whoreson son of a pot-bellied pig is about. Not but what I'd like to put Sir Piers across my knee like I do little Kit when he's being above himself. Sword Bearer to Henry Bolingbroke now,

430

that's what he is, my lady. Thinks he's too grand for the likes of us.'

'Not too grand, too good,' said Nicolette sadly.

'Well, I'd like to tell him it's time he stopped being a knight in shining armour and started being a human being,' said Lisette indignantly. 'What are you going to do, my lady? You've got to get him back.'

Nicolette looked around the sun-lit courtyard. Just for a moment she considered taking the easy way out and playing into Dick's hands. She knew so well how to please him. It would be easy to send Lisette to him, ask him to contrive to have her father released. She did not know why or how he was still in power, but he had been very clever. Cleverer by far than Piers or her father. She looked up at the window of the Queen's chamber.

'Lisette, I must go back to the Queen. You stay here for a day or two while I think of something. You can help the other tiring women.' Impulsively she seized Lisette's hands, held them tight. 'It will be so good to have you here with me. I can't tell you how much I've missed you.'

For the rest of the day Nicolette tried to behave normally while her thoughts raced. She had to do something. To rescue her father, to protect her children, to win back her husband. She had not expected Dick to be so devious or Piers so harsh. He must be deeply, deeply hurt, yet he had passed judgement on her without hearing her side of the story, was prepared to believe she had betrayed him with Dick from the very beginning, that all their love had been a sham. How was she to fight that? Did she want to fight it? Would it not be easier just to let Dick take care of her? He must surely love her a little, and he expected nothing from her except willing participation. Just for a while, Nicolette was tempted to let him win.

But in the dorter, helping Nicolette get ready for supper, Lisette was full of plans to appeal to Piers again.

'Let me go to Sir Piers,' she said. 'Tell him it's not true. It's your word against that cuckolder Whittington, him that's proved he's not to be trusted – changing sides every time the wind changes. I'll see your knight comes riding out here on his white charger soon enough to beg your pardon and make it up.' She paused, comb in hand, as a sudden thought struck her. 'You're not childbearing, are ye?'

'No,' said Nicolette.

'The Blessed Virgin be praised.'

Nicolette knew then she could not lie to Piers. If they were ever to have any sort of life together again it must be founded on trust. Lisette's simple-hearted loyalty made Nicolette realise that she had been worshipping false gods all these months at court. Wickedness was not something to be played with; it had to be fought and conquered, otherwise it was like an insatiable dragon devouring more and more innocent maidens until none were left. She had an idea. Suppose she were to be thrown out of the Queen's household for what she had done with Dick? The one thing Piers could not resist was a damsel in distress. Love was what mattered and Piers had loved her, and perhaps still did beneath his hurt. Did he love her enough to come to her rescue or was he like all the rest of them? If he was, then she might as well go into a nunnery straightaway.

She went down to the hall for supper thinking about the penalty for adultery and wondering what it was. In London, she rather thought there was something about having to do public penance in a white sheet. In minstrels' tales, Queen Guinevere was tied to the stake and Lancelot came galloping out of the forest to rescue her. Piers would enjoy that. Nicolette wondered if the little French Queen could be persuaded to tie her to a stake and smiled to herself almost cheerfully. Strange, she thought, dipping a piece of chicken into a sweet sticky sauce, once she had feared discovery more than anything. Now she was prepared to embrace shame, failure even, in the attempt to win her husband back. Would he understand and would it work?

As soon as supper was over, Nicolette went to the Mistress of Ceremonies and made a full confession. Lady Mortimer was horrified.

'How could you dishonour your husband so – when he was in exile?'

Nicolette hung her head. 'I know,' she whispered. 'I have been very wicked. But I thought my husband was never coming back and Master Whittington was so kind and good to me. He was kind and good to the Queen too. Everyone loved him. But now he has deserted the King and become Henry's friend and I realise what a fool I've been.'

'Of course you can no longer remain in the Queen's

household. An innocent child still unaware of the temptations of the flesh should not be tended by a woman who has proved herself wantonly unable to resist them.' The Mistress of Ceremonies was exceedingly shocked. The other ladies giggled and whispered, delighting in Nicolette's downfall. The way they felt about her just now, Nicolette thought ruefully, they might not only tie her to the stake but light the fire if Piers did not come.

The Queen did not know what adultery was but she threw a tantrum. 'They cannot send you away,' she screamed, forgetting her former displeasure and clinging to Nicolette in a way that almost broke her resolve. 'They cannot make me. I forbid it.'

Lady Mortimer, who had still not learnt how to handle Isabella when she was in one of her tantrums, looked nonplussed and for a moment Nicolette was afraid that her sin was to be overlooked, which was not at all what she wanted.

'Perhaps a public penance,' suggested the Mistress of Ceremonies. 'If the Lady Exton truly repents of her sin and will do public penance, then perhaps there is no need for her to be dismissed from Your Grace's household.'

The Queen was delighted. 'You can dress in a white sheet – or should it be sackcloth and ashes? And we will attend with all our court.'

Nicolette rushed to find Lisette. 'You must ride to London at once. Find Sir Piers and tell him if he loves me to come and save me.'

'I can't ride.'

'How did you get here then?' Nicolette demanded.

'I walked, of course. Begged a lift on the back of a packhorse when I could.'

'Well, you must ride back. I'll send you with one of the Queen's men-at-arms.'

The day for Nicolette's public penance was set for 29 September, the Feast of St Michael and All Angels. It dawned bright and sunny. Early in the morning a colourful procession left the castle. First came the Queen and her attendants, brilliantly attired. Behind on a mule rode Nicolette dressed in a white sheet with her hair bound and braided in two long ropes of gold. She was escorted by priests carrying their scourges.

At the cross at Wallingford they halted. Nervously Nicolette looked down the street, convinced now that he would not come. She would have to go through with it; in front of all these townspeople who had turned out in force, she would have to walk barefoot through the town with the priests whipping her all the way. Merciful Saviour, I have sinned, she muttered. Have mercy. The bishop read out the indictment. 'The Lady Exton, wife of the knight Sir Piers Exton who at that time having displeased the King Richard and having been banished from the realm, did commit adultery with one Richard Whittington, a mercer in the city of London, for which mortal sin she is now accused and if no one comes forth to do battle for her honour she will be acknowledged guilty. The punishment for her crime...'

His words were drowned by the roar of the crowd. A knight in full armour was riding down the street. A scrap of green silk fluttered from his helm. Nicolette could barely see the red and cream marking on his caparison, her eyes were so blurred with tears. Piers had come. He cantered up to the cross and reined back in front of the Queen.

'I proclaim this lady's innocence before any who dare challenge me. In a trial by battle to the death.' He swung his horse round in a circle, his armour bright in the sun. Never had Nicolette felt more proud of him or more triumphantly in love. Nobody came forward to do battle. Piers rode up to the foot of the cross where Nicolette stood shivering in her white sheet, bent forward and swept her off her feet and up into the saddle in front of him. The horse fidgeted nervously and she clutched the high front of the saddle with both hands while her heart beat fast with joy.

'Madame.' Piers bowed to the Queen. 'I proclaim my wife to be an innocent victim of malicious intrigue and gossip. Since you do not know how to appreciate such a jewel in your household I am taking her with me where she will be better appreciated.'

The Queen's small face crumpled and her bottom lip began to quiver. Nicolette felt a pang of remorse as she leant against her husband's steel-clad body. He was wheeling his charger and soon they were galloping out of the town with the cheers of the townspeople ringing in their ears.

Beyond the city wall, a squire was waiting with a warm travelling cloak and a sedate-looking palfrey for Nicolette.

'You're new,' Nicolette said to him as he helped her down. 'What's happened to Crispin?'

'This is Guy de Luval, a French nobleman's son. My lord Henry knighted Crispin when we landed at Ravenspur,' said Piers, removing his helm. The squire, averting his eyes, wrapped Nicolette in the travelling cloak. Piers ripped the scrap of faded green silk from his helm.

'That's my old favour,' said Nicolette with a smile of joy. 'You kept it.' Everything was going to be all right. He still loved her.

'I wore it next to my heart all the time I was away. But I have no need of such things now.' Piers tossed the scrap of silk on to the ground where the stallion's hooves stamped it into the mud. 'Not now that I have my own true wife with me again,' he said bitterly, handing the helmet to his squire. Nicolette grew cold. 'Are you ready? We'd best be going.'

The squire helped her on to the palfrey and a glance at the boy's face told her that she could expect no mercy there. They set off at such a punishing pace, further talk was impossible. Nightfall found them in the abbey at Medmenham where there was no chance of a private word with Piers. He treated her with elaborate but distant courtesy and she was at a loss to know how to behave with him. Once he had been tongue-tied with love, often he had remained silent if he had nothing worth saying, but now he gave every sign of never wanting to speak to her again. Somehow she had to reach him, now while they were on the road, before he left her in her father's house and went back to Henry Bolingbroke.

She slept badly in the communal dormitory at the abbey and next morning she begged Piers to go more slowly.

'What's the matter, Nicolette? Did you not go hunting and hawking when you were in the Queen's household? You should be used to riding by now. You used to be determined to put up with all kinds of aches and pains without complaint. Don't you want to be the perfect wife any more?'

Blessed St Mary, she thought, his angry silence was better than words so cruel. Lisette was right, he had changed. This was not the man who went away for honour's sake.

'Piers,' she pleaded, 'won't you at least hear what I have to say? Don't judge me so harshly. You don't understand.'

'You're right, I don't understand you. I tried, by God's truth I tried, and I thought at one time that I did, but I was wrong. Now I don't want to understand you.'

'Piers, for the love you once bore me, will you not let me have one last chance?' she pleaded.

'Love!' He laughed harshly. 'What a monstrous trick love is!'

'But you must love me just a little or you wouldn't have come to my rescue.'

'No knight can let his wife be publicly accused of infidelity. I was in honour bound to come to your rescue.'

His accursed honour, she thought. Dear God, was his honour all that he had?

CHAPTER 36

It was with a guilty conscience that Dick Whittington went into his warehouse where his prisoner was confined. He was conscious that he had used his power to arrest William Gryffard not because the merchant was a danger to Bolingbroke, or indeed to anyone, but for reasons of his own, which had nothing to do with expediency; he had for once allowed emotion to rule instead of sense and he regretted it. He would not last long in the swiftly flowing currents he had chosen to immerse himself in unless he was totally in control of his every action.

A bed had been set up in one corner and William was lying on it in his fur-trimmed velvet gown, his eyes closed. From the very first day of his arrest, he had feigned sickness. He had pleaded to be allowed his own doctor to attend him and Dick had permitted it, even though he suspected that William was not half as ill as he made out.

Dick walked up to the bed and looked at William a little anxiously. If he had not been ill at first, he most certainly was now, in spite of all the ministrations of the learned doctor from Florence. William's eyes opened.

'I've been trying to get you released,' said Dick. 'But it's proving more difficult than I thought.' William had been his prisoner now for over a month and he was finding it quite difficult to be rid of him.

'A bad deed is always easier to do than to undo,' replied William, 'which is why I don't often try to mend my mistakes.'

'That probably explains how you've made so many enemies in this city,' Dick retorted. 'I can't get any of the common councillors to agree to let you go free.'

William stirred restlessly on the bed. 'What will happen to the King?' he asked.

'King Richard has been deposed. He is a prisoner in the Tower. He will abdicate.'

'And Henry? Has he claimed the crown?'

'Naturally.'

'So the usurper has shown his true colours,' muttered William, tossing on his narrow pallet. 'It did not take him long to change his mind.'

'He had no other choice. He has been swept into power from exile with astonishing speed, by the people of England. He may not have sought such power, but he is a man of quick action and decisive thinking. If he were to hesitate now and leave the throne vacant for too long, the whole country would soon be plunged into turmoil. There are too many barons with retinues of their own eager to seize power for themselves. Bolingbroke has to keep them under control and the only way he can do that is if he is King.'

'Justify him, since you must,' William replied. 'It was you who helped him to his crown.'

Dick sighed. 'We need stable government,' he said patiently. 'You know it as well as I. Henry is our only hope.' But if he expected to be exonerated by William Gryffard, he was disappointed.

'A fine land this is, which has exiled, slain, destroyed or ruined so many kings, rulers and great men,' declared William. Suddenly his claw-like hand shot out and clutched Dick's velvet sleeve. 'Be careful, for it is tainted with strife and envy. Henry has seized the crown by force. There will be others who will try the same. Is that the stability you hanker for?'

William was really looking very ill, thought Dick; his skin was dry and blotchy, his eyes, usually so watchful, were wild, sure sign of a troubled mind. The grip on his arm tightened.

'You lent King Richard over a thousand pounds, so I heard,' William whispered. 'How are you going to get the money back?'

So that was it. Poor William was tormented by the thought of the money he himself had lent King Richard. Dick smiled. 'Don't worry,' he said almost indulgently. 'I'll soon have you back in your own house with Lady Exton to tend you. Your arrest was a mistake. Our new King has nothing against you.'

The grip on his arm slackened. 'My daughter? Isn't she still with the Queen?'

'Sir Piers has rescued her.'

'Sir Piers!' Suddenly a crafty look crept over the sick man's face. 'From what? Surely the Queen is safe enough at Wallingford. Even Bolingbroke wouldn't make war on defenceless women.'

'Lady Exton has been falsely accused of adultery. But thanks to her husband's conspicuous chivalry she is now at home without a stain on her character.'

'Sir Piers Exton is the kind of man who can always be counted upon to gallop to the rescue. Lady Exton is very fortunate,' said William. His wild eyes had grown watchful and Dick began to suspect who it was who had told Piers. William must have used the doctor, he thought, and he had somehow managed to get word to Piers. What warped purpose did William think such a deed might serve? Whatever the purpose, it had miscarried. Nicolette had been too clever for both of them.

'Sir Piers is a good man in a fight,' croaked William. 'Are you not afraid that he might be after your blood?'

'Why should I be afraid?' Dick shrugged, hiding his anger behind a thin smile. 'I'm glad, not for the first time, that I did not choose to become a knight, and that I do not have to prove my innocence by riding out to do battle. I think I can count on Sir Piers's chivalry not to murder me in the street.'

William was lying back in his narrow bed pulling at the ermine round the sleeve of his gown with nervous fingers. 'Sir Piers must have learnt how to compromise with his conscience by now if he's come thus far with Henry Bolingbroke. No man who sees the Lord's anointed King duped, betrayed and deposed by his cousin within so short a time can still remain a slave to romantic notions of honour.'

'I used to think that part of Piers's great charm was that he saw the world as we should like it to be,' said Dick, 'and not as it really is, but success has no doubt changed him, as it does the rest of us.' His anger drained away and he felt suddenly sad. 'The romantic idiot who rode away with the disgraced Henry Bolingbroke has, I fear, become a survivor. A few years of power and success and Piers will be just like me.'

'But will he abandon her?' demanded William.

Dick knew exactly what he meant. Then suddenly he realised that this was precisely what William hoped for. Almost Dick was tempted to throw him to the wolves after all. There was no doubt that the merchant of the staple deserved to be arrested, if not this time then for all those other times when he had been so skilful in escaping his just deserts. There were enough citizens of London who had suffered at William Gryffard's hands to ensure he had a very speedy and unpleasant end. But Dick knew such a deed would be unworthy. He was determined to uphold justice, freedom, the city's rule of law. In the midst of such violent upheaval, it was very important not to revert to the rule of the jungle.

'No need for you to worry about Lady Exton. She has been very clever. With one bold stroke she has won back her husband, and the hearts of all the people of London. The little French Queen has always been unpopular with the Londoners, as you know, and Sir Piers's gallant rescue is all of a part with Henry's coming to save the ordinary people of the land from King Richard's tyranny. He cannot abandon her – not yet. He has behaved with honour and she, thanks to his chivalry, is now considered to be pure as driven snow. Oh yes,' he reassured the anxious father with a wry smile, 'Nicolette has become quite a heroine.'

Nicolette did not feel like a heroine, even though she had been welcomed back into her father's house like some sort of saving grace. In the hall they had all lined up to welcome her, Adam Stickleby, the servants, Jeanne de Bourdat, Lisette and the children. Tarquin threw himself at her. 'Don't go away again, Mama,' he said clinging tightly to her legs. 'Promise.'

'I promise,' she said kneeling down to hug him.

'Is the King really going to go to prison?' asked Kit, when she did the same to him. 'Will there be a battle here in London if he doesn't?'

'All these questions.' Nicolette kissed his dark curly hair so like his father's. 'Nobody knows what will happen next. We have to be brave.' He wriggled out of her arms, trying to pretend he did not like being hugged and kissed.

The baby, now a vigorous toddler, came staggering across

the tiled floor on sturdy fat legs, towing Lisette by the hand. Nicolette held out her arms but Michael suddenly stopped and hid his face in the maid's serge skirts. 'He doesn't know me,' said Nicolette in dismay.

'Well, he was but three months went you went away,' Lisette said. 'He'll remember in time when he hears your voice some more.'

'Is Papa coming home now that my lord Henry has won?' asked Kit. 'Will I be able to be a page now do you think?'

Nicolette wished she knew the answers to his questions. There was so much that was uncertain, she felt overwhelmed by exhaustion and fear.

'Your father's busy making kings and things,' Jeanne de Bourdat came to her rescue. 'Men don't pay much attention to us women at times like these. We'll just have to wait and see what will happen when it's all over. Now don't pester your mother, she's tired after her long journey.'

Nicolette let herself be led away to the solar by Lisette, looking forward to the luxury of being washed and dressed by her own maid in the privacy of her own chamber without having to battle with a dozen other ladies in an overcrowded dorter. But when the solar door was shut firmly behind her, Lisette leant against it with her arms folded and a long face.

'No clothes again,' she said, shaking her head. 'All your things'll be in the Queen's household at Wallingford still. That's the second time ye've landed up in this chamber with nothing but the clothes ye stand up in and this time it be a bedsheet 'neath your travelling cloak. Ye're not learning from your mistakes in life, my lady.'

'Don't scold me now, Lisette,' pleaded Nicolette. 'I have enough to bear without you turning against me.'

'Bless you, my lady, I'll not turn 'gainst thee no matter what sort of a mess you goes and makes of it. Haven't I been with you now more nor ten years past? Maybe Jeanne can let you have a gown and kirtle, until Sir Piers gets your coffers back – like last time. He'll be getting good at it with such practice.'

Nicolette felt too dispirited to smile at Lisette's attempt at a joke. She was not at all sure that Piers, having rescued her, would give her another thought. Jeanne de Bourdat was right. With the whole country in a state of upheaval, Piers could not be expected to think of his wife, let alone her missing coffers.

On the day that the King's abdication was announced, the citizens of London went mad with joy, dancing in the streets and acclaiming Henry Bolingbroke their King and saviour. But Nicolette was thrown into new despair. The date of Henry's coronation was fixed for 13 October and Nicolette was terrified that Piers would be too ashamed of her to let her go. Then everyone would know that she was guilty.

Her fears were proved groundless when her coffers were delivered intact, together with a message from Piers. She was to go to Henry's crowning in Westminster Abbey and Guy de Luval, his squire, would escort her. Immediately Nicolette felt better. If Piers had found time to arrange to have her clothes and jewels collected from the palace at Wallingford and brought to London, at least he had not put her out of his mind completely; such thoughtfulness at a time like this gave her reason to hope. It was not much to cling to but she needed something.

The day before the coronation Henry rode bareheaded through streets which were thronged with cheering Londoners, on his way from the Tower to Westminster. With him went his four sons, six dukes, six earls, eighteen barons and a great procession of more than six thousand mounted men. The rain pelted down on this great show of strength with unrelenting impartiality.

From the house in Cornhill, Nicolette could hear the cheers and the music but she did not go to watch, turning a deaf ear to the pleas of her children. She was far too busy with preparations to look her best next day. The servants were kept running with an endless stream of jugs filled with hot water from the kitchens; Lisette washed and combed her mistress's hair, rubbing it with silk cloths until it shone like burnished gold; she scrubbed Nicolette's body from head to toe and anointed it with fragrant oils, grumbling all the time. 'No need for all this costly preparation,' she said. 'Sir Piers always loved you for yourself, my lady.'

'Not any more, he doesn't – at least, I cannot count on it,' said Nicolette busy plucking the hair from her brow to make it look higher and whiter. 'Tomorrow the most noble men and women in the land will all be at Westminster. I must be able to hold my head up high, make him proud of me.'

'Fine feathers'll not win him back. It'll take time and God's grace for the wound to heal.'

Nicolette knew that Lisette was probably right but she also felt it might hasten the process a little if Piers could be visually assaulted by her beauty. The last time he had seen her she had been dressed in a bedsheet with her hair hanging in two ropes like a peasant woman. She wanted him to see her again as his perfect lady.

Next morning she was up long before dawn, and so were Lisette and Jeanne, struggling in the light of the candles to braid and pin her hair into the gold wires of her elaborate headdress. Jewels hung round her throat and her hips and flashed from her fingers. Her gown was of scarlet velvet trimmed with white ermine, her hanging sleeves cloth of gold sweeping to the ground, her train decorated with Piers's arms. Kit was to carry it and he was bursting with pride, dressed in a new short doublet and particoloured hose. Then all the finery had to be carefully covered with a voluminous travelling cloak to protect it from the dirt of the road on the ride to Westminster.

By the time the bells were pealing for prime, the squire had arrived, Nicolette was mounted on her palfrey with Lisette clinging on behind, Kit was riding pillion with Guy de Luval and they were on their way.

Guy managed to find a seat for Nicolette in the abbey chancel with the other ladies. Carefully she sat down on the narrow bench, and was surprised when the other ladies smiled and made room for her most graciously. Her heart swelled with thankfulness to Piers – for his gallantry, his loving kindness, his steadfast devotion over the years. She longed to make it up to him if only he would let her.

The long, splendid ritual of the coronation began with Henry Percy, Earl of Northumberland, carrying the Lancaster Sword which Bolingbroke had been wearing on the day he landed at Ravenspur. In front of the new King walked his handsome young son, Henry of Monmouth, bearing aloft the Curtana naked and without a point, the emblem of the execution of justice without rancour. All the ladies craned forward to see the victorious Henry clad in white walking beneath a canopy of blue silk borne by the barons of the Cinque Ports. Already he looked like a King, thought

Nicolette, although he was not nearly as handsome as Richard. Behind him came all the peers of the realm robed finely in red and scarlet and ermine.

The solemn ceremony of the crowning took a long time, but Nicolette did not mind. She was used to elaborate ceremony. Everything that was performed here in the abbey was filled with symbolic significance and awe, yet Nicolette noticed that the ladies kneeling beside her in the chancel had the same patient endurance on their faces as she had often seen on those of the ladies in the Queen's apartments. The nobles gathered around Henry had different symbols on their colourful banners, but it was the same pomp, the same display of power, the same mantle of majesty which was transforming Henry from a brave and effective soldier into a king.

As the service dragged on, Nicolette could not help thinking of the little Queen Isabella and her insistence on the most rigid formality over everything she did. What would become of Richard's child wife now? she wondered sadly.

At last the coronation of Henry Bolingbroke as Henry IV of England was over. They processed out of the abbey church of St Peter to the white hall of the palace for a celebration feast. Piers was waiting at the great stone arch leading into the hall. It was the first time Nicolette had seen him since her flight from Wallingford. Then he had been dressed from head to foot in steel; now he was splendidly attired in fashionable short doublet, belted at the waist, and tight-fitting, brightly coloured hose; on his head he wore a wide-brimmed jaunty cap with long liripipe carelessly thrown over his shoulders. She wanted to tell him how handsome he looked but was restrained by the distant look in his eyes.

'Kit has been managing my train quite beautifully,' she said instead. 'He will make an excellent page.'

Piers stared past her shoulder at his small son who was holding Nicolette's train and looking longingly at his father. 'Come and let me present you to the King,' was all Piers said.

Kit bit his lip and Nicolette could see he was bitterly disappointed that his father had refused even to acknowledge his presence. But there was nothing she could do except smile encouragement at her son and follow Piers. Her heart was wrung by the hesitant, uncertain smile Kit gave in return as he clutched the fur-trimmed hem of her train, holding it carefully out of the mud as he walked after her.

The newly crowned King sat alone on a dais at one end of the hall receiving a stream of guests come to do him honour. When Piers presented Nicolette, she sank down before him in her deepest curtsey and waited, head bent, for permission to rise.

'Now I know what a sacrifice Piers made for me in leaving such a beautiful wife behind,' said Henry stretching out a ringed hand and raising her to her feet. She kept her eyes demurely cast down while he talked of making it up to her – of the manors in Lancastrian strongholds he had given Piers. 'Not very rich ones, no castles I'm afraid. But since he's to be my Sword Bearer he will be with me for most of the time. I hope you can spare him for a little longer, Lady Exton.'

She looked up swiftly. In his coronation robes and crown he was a stranger. It was hard to think of him as her husband's friend and companion in arms.

'It's fortunate I have a house in London in Cornhill. Master Gryffard gave it to me as part of my dower. So at least I can be near my husband when Your Grace is at Westminster, as now,' she said with a swift, imploring glance at Piers. His face was expressionless.

'Master Gryffard?' said the King and he was suddenly frowning.

She had forgotten that William had been imprisoned for being a friend of Richard II. Cursing herself for a tactless fool, she glanced again at Piers who was now staring over her shoulder, his face set. Thoroughly disquieted, she followed his gaze and caught sight of Dick Whittington. Blessed Mary, Mother of Jesus, let me be calm, she prayed instinctively. She was terribly conscious of Piers standing at her side, as stiff as if he'd been encased in steel instead of purple velvet. The King was looking at her inquiringly but her mind was blank. Piers came to her rescue.

'My wife is a kinswoman of William Gryffard's,' he explained. 'She is naturally anxious to obtain his release. Perhaps Your Grace would grant it as a coronation favour?'

'I have nothing against the man,' said Henry. 'He is Whittington's prisoner not mine.' To Nicolette's horror, the King beckoned and Dick came forward to stand at her side. Henry said, 'Lady Exton has asked that her kinsman William Gryffard be released as a coronation boon. But I don't mean to interfere with the affairs of London – that isn't what you want, is it, Whittington?'

Nicolette did not hear Dick's answer. She was concentrating her whole being on staying calm, not blushing, composing herself to look Dick in the face as if nothing had ever happened between them. Slowly she raised her eyes and stared at him coolly, just as a lady whose fair name had been unjustly sullied would look at a man who was a stranger to her. Dick smiled at her, an amused and admiring glance.

'How is my kinsman, Master Whittington?' she asked. 'I hope that you are treating him with kindness for he has done nothing to deserve his fate, of that I am very sure.'

'I am doing my best to have him returned to you, my lady,' he replied, 'but as the King's Grace appreciates, it is a matter for the citizens of London to decide.' Only then did she dare to look at Piers, but he was still looking at Dick and his face was grim.

When the feasting was at its height Sir Thomas Dymmok the royal champion entered the banqueting hall mounted on a destrier, clad in full armour and bearing a sword with a golden hilt. Before him rode two squires; one carried a naked sword, the other a lance. A herald came forward and from the four sides of the hall proclaimed that if any man here should say that his liege lord and King of England was not the right crowned King of England, the royal champion was ready to prove the contrary with his body then and there or when and wheresoever it might please the King. Henry stood up. 'If need be, Sir Thomas, I will in mine own person ease thee of this office.' Cheers rose to the rafters and nobody stepped forward to contest Henry's right to the throne.

Throughout the feasting and dancing that followed, Piers treated Nicolette with impeccable courtesy. She tried once or twice to break through his icy reserve but met with such little success that she decided perhaps Lisette was right. Piers needed time. It would be better to wait patiently and to hope that when he came to the small chamber they had been allotted in the palace that night, the spell of her beauty or the wine he had drunk would be enough to conquer his disillusion. Then once he was a slave to his passions again, she could set about the hard task of winning his love.

When Nicolette retired to the chamber, Kit was curled up

on a pallet in a corner of the chamber, fast asleep after the excitements and exertions of the day. While Lisette brushed her hair and prepared her for bed, Nicolette tried to think what she would say to win Piers back.

She knelt down by the small shrine of the Blessed Virgin in a corner of the chamber, fumbling with her rosary and remembering all the many, many mistakes she had made here in the Palace of Westminster. She lay awake long into the night praying she would not make a mistake now with Piers. But he never came.

In the morning Lisette told her that Piers had spent the night sleeping on the floor of the great hall with the other knights and their squires as he had so often done in the past. With a heavy heart, Nicolette dressed for the journey back to London. Piers was waiting with his squire and the horses in the outer court.

'Aren't you coming home with me?' she asked, disappointment making her forget her strategy. 'The children are longing for a glimpse of you. They are plaguing me to death.'

'I'll come as soon as I can,' he said walking her firmly towards her palfrey. She could see Kit trying not to mind as the squire lifted him on to his gelding while Piers ignored the boy completely.

'Something must be done about Kit soon,' she said, angry with him now. 'He's expecting to be taken into the royal household as page. Wouldn't this be the right moment to approach the King?'

A muscle quivered in his cheek. He swung round, glared at her. 'Why don't you ask Whittington to speak to the King?'

She almost lost patience with him then. 'Punish me if you must,' she said. 'But don't take it out on the children. I swear by the Blessed Virgin herself that they are yours. If you don't believe me, look at them. Kit is the very image of you. Don't you ever look in a mirror? All he wants is to learn how to fight, to be a brave warrior like his father. Will you deny him that?' The palfrey, waiting patiently, threw up its head nervously. Piers picked her up and dumped her in the saddle.

'I can't possibly pester the King with requests for pages, there are too many important things on his mind just now. Try to understand, England is in the midst of a great upheaval.' She understood. All too well. He did not want her near him.

William Gryffard was released at the end of October. Nicolette was shocked at the change in his appearance.

'You look ill, Father,' she said. 'Let me send for your doctor.'

'Send for him if you must, but it won't do any good,' said William sitting down in his big carved armchair. 'I've had him torturing me with all his tricks this past month, ever since I was arrested, and it's done me no good in spite of the expensive training I gave him. I dare say Whittington thought he was doing me a good turn, letting me have my own doctor attend me, but the leech'll doubtless ruin me in the end for he's the most expensive in the city.'

'You don't have to worry about money now, Father,' she said pouring wine into a goblet for him. 'Piers is Sword Bearer to the King and has been given Lancastrian manors. I'm sure he'll be glad to repay you for everything you have done for us.'

He took the wine she handed him and peered up at her witheringly. 'Piers has never taken care of anything,' he grumbled. 'You're better off with Whittington.'

She felt sorry for him, sitting hunched up in his master's chair, holding his treasured silver goblet in hands which trembled. He would go on trying to use her until the day he died, she thought. She would never succeed in pleasing him, because he only valued her for the use she might be to him. It made her feel sorrier for him than ever. He was watching her over the rim of his goblet with the familiar calculating look in his eye.

'Did you borrow money from Dick Whittington?' she asked, as a sudden horrible thought struck her.

'A little, nothing significant.' He was suddenly very interested in the contents of his drinking cup. 'Whittington is a very patient man, he'll wait until I come round in time. We all have our setbacks, you know.'

'I thought it was Whittington who had you arrested – so Piers says,' she persevered.

'I have many enemies. Whittington's not the worst and he took good care of me while I was in his charge. It was he who had me released, that I do believe.'

'Does it mean . . .' she paused, stared at him angrily. William was drinking noisily and would not meet her gaze.

'Father, does it mean Whittington still believes he has some sort of a hold over me?'

'I don't know. But the city leaders must have thought it was safe to let me go.' He set down his cup with a clatter on the table in front of him. 'And if that is so, it probably means that King Richard is no longer in the Tower. Henry must have had him smuggled out and sent to some northern stronghold, where he'll be more easily forgotten.'

'Surely the Tower is a secure enough prison,' she said with a shiver.

'But too close to London. Our new King will be afraid that while Richard of Bordeaux lives there will always be those who are anxious to rescue him.'

'But not you, Father!'

'You're right, Nicolette. I've never been a man of action. Whittington knows that, which is doubtless why they thought it safe to release me.'

'Did you tell Piers about Whittington and me?' she demanded.

'I did it for you. I meant it for the best.'

'But why? Do you want to destroy my life?'

He shook his head, drew the cup towards him, caressing the slender stem in his shaky fingers. 'A hot-blooded woman like you should not have to live the life of a nun,' he said. She blushed scarlet with shame and wondered if he had guessed that Piers had not laid a finger on her since his return. 'A man like Piers can't live with your imperfections. You lost him the day he went into exile with Henry. When he left he made everything over to me – a severing of all ties. You're only an embarrassment to him now.'

She could not bear his eyes, watchful as ever, noting her pain. 'Suppose Piers sends me to his manor in the north?' Her fear which had lain dormant in her heart since the moment Henry had told her about the land he had given to Piers rushed at her like a rudely awakened bear.

'My illness will prevent him. A man as noble and good as that husband of yours would not be so unfeeling as to leave me here to die alone. You have learnt to play on that noble nature of his. You can play on it again. It was a brilliant stroke having Piers rescue you in that way. A bold move, and brilliant.' He sat back in his chair, gazing up at her admiringly. 'You've been very clever, my dear. A sign of true greatness is the ability to convert failure into success.'

It was almost the first time he had ever praised her, but she did not feel successful, she felt bitterly ashamed. 'The trouble with Piers is that he's too good for me,' she cried.

'Piers wants a saint and you'll never be that,' William retorted. 'You're a woman of the world despite your convent upbringing. You've become a survivor – like me.'

Nicolette knew she had much to atone for, but she could not accept that she was like her father. All the same as the weeks passed and Piers did not come she was haunted by what her father had said. She went to church, confessed her sins and was shriven. She lit candles, prayed, fed three beggars three Fridays in a row. Sooner or later Piers would come for her and she must be ready to show him that she had changed. She was sure that beneath the hurt, the anger and the bitterness, he still loved her and wanted her.

William watched all her preparations and mocked her. The doctor came and talked about a wasting disease and purged him and bled him and gave him foul medicines to take. He talked about the humours of the blood and the conjunction of Saturn and Uranus being unpropitious. Nicolette did not understand any of it but she could tell that her father was not going to get better. His face was marked with the greyness of death and everything the doctor did was like a Christmas mumming, to entertain and reassure the patient.

Just before Christmas, Nicolette believed her prayers might be answered when Piers came to tell her that the King was to spend his first Christmas in the royal castle of Windsor. A magnificent 'mumming' was to be held on Twelfth Night. Piers needed his wife with him and Kit was to come too. He was at last to be a page in the royal household. Nicolette was overjoyed. Here was the chance she needed to get close to Piers again. But she was thrown into a turmoil of guilt and confusion when her father begged her not to go and leave him alone at Christmastide.

'Piers, what should I do?' she asked, wanting him to know that she had changed, that she was no longer selfish.

'Please yourself,' he replied. 'You've always done what your father wanted.'

'I want to do what you want now,' she said. 'If you say I should go, then I will.'

450

He turned on her angrily. 'Your father has always done what he has done for your sake. He's in debt up to his ears because he lavished so much money on you. Now he's very ill and very frightened. I think you should stay and comfort him in his last hours. They're not likely to be easy ones for him.'

How could he be so blind? she wondered. Could Piers not see that even now her father was trying to use her? She so longed to go with him to the palace. For Piers to want her as always in the past he had wanted her.

'It won't be much of a Christmas here without you,' she said sadly. 'So many Christmastides without you. Couldn't you stay here with us instead of going to the King at Windsor?'

'No, Nicolette, I couldn't. I'm sure you'll manage very well without me. You've always done so in the past.'

It was useless. She tried to hide her disappointment getting Kit ready to go. The child was full of so much happy excitement Nicolette could not help remembering that first Christmas when she had gone to Westminster Palace with Lady Brembre. If only she had known how to appreciate Piers then, she thought miserably. What heartache and pain she would have saved herself. Piers was now the successful one and William the failure. She could have gone with Piers, insisted on it. But she could not leave her father; he needed her. Piers was successful and no longer needed her.

She watched him ride away, with Kit proudly riding pillion behind Guy de Luval. For once she thought she had done the right thing, the unselfish thing. But what was the point of it if Piers no longer loved her?

CHAPTER 37

On the tenth day after Christmas a raven flew into the garden of Gryffard's Inn. Nicolette was crossing the garden from the kitchen; she heard its unwelcome voice and crossed herself. A raven croaking near a sickbed meant death of the ailing.

A cold wind from the east was sending flurries of icy rain. She pulled her hood tighter round her head and huddled into her warm fur-lined cloak as she hurried back into the house. The hall was dark and cheerless. The branches of holly and yew they had brought in for Christmastide looked forlorn and out of place. She walked quickly through the hall and quietly entered William's chamber at the far end. It was lit by a great many wax tapers burning brightly on the wall sconces and the smell of incense mingling with the dried herbs which she sprinkled everywhere still could not mask the sickly sweet stench which permeated the chamber.

She closed the door softly. From behind the bed curtains came the low murmur of voices. William was confessing his sins, had been since early that morning. The hoarse voice paused often as the sick man struggled for breath then, prompted by a word of encouragement from the priest, resumed haltingly. Nicolette walked over to the fire; she stood and listened to the rain falling down the chimney, concentrating on the hiss and spit as water and flames fought each other, anything to shut out the poor tortured voice of her father with its litany of repentance. Day after day he had made her read his will to him, the bequests, the gifts to the poor, the chantries through which with his great wealth he would buy his way into paradise. She was not sure where it was all to come from but she supposed it was there somewhere bound up in all those mysterious bits of paper in the counting house.

At last the voice was quiet. In its place was the measured, assured voice of the priest reciting in Latin. Nicolette knelt on the hard tiled floor, her rosary in her hand, but the sick man was interrupting, his voice growing more agitated. He had remembered another sin. Nicolette sighed and waited for him to finish. The priest began again, she knelt counting the beads on her rosary until the priest pronounced absolution. There was silence in the chamber, even the rain seemed to have ceased for a while. The priest came to her and she got up from her knees.

'He wants to speak to you,' he said.

She approached the bed quietly, drew aside the red velvet bed curtain. 'What is it, Father?' she asked.

He pointed a bony finger at the priest. 'Pay him,' he croaked.

'Not now, later.' She did not want him to be worried any more about money. 'I'm sure Father Paul will not insist on payment today.'

But William was not to be deflected. 'Pay him now,' he said, glaring at her over the top of the sheet which was pulled up to his chin. She did not know what she was to pay him with and did not want to call the steward. She was afraid that Adam Stickleby would only tell William what he knew already – that there were no more golden coins in the treasure chest in the counting house. It did not matter. She was sure that the Church would be prepared to give its services on tally like everyone else. Piers would see to it when he could, his honour would ensure it, whatever he might feel about his wife. She smiled at Father Paul over her shoulder, hoping he would understand. But he shook his head and mouthed the words, 'Best humour him.'

William was plucking at her hanging sleeve. 'Bring the cups,' he whispered, his tongue wetting his dried lips nervously. She could see that he was becoming frightened again. Soon all the good of the absolution would be undone.

Swiftly she went out into the hall to do his bidding. The great array of silver cups that had once stood on the board in the corner had dwindled to just two. She picked them up carefully and carried them back into the chamber. She held first one and then the other before William, remembering the time he had given his best cup as a New Year's gift to Queen Isabella. That had been Christmastide too. Now it was Henry who was celebrating Christmas at Windsor and Piers was there enjoying himself without her. Was he being beguiled by one of the beautiful ladies at court? Fruitless to worry, she told herself firmly, when there was nothing she could do about it. Not while she was here with her father, whose last hours on earth she was struggling to make easier.

William eyed the silver glinting in the light from the candles. 'That ought to do,' he said, pointing to the second cup, then while the priest mumbled his heartfelt thanks he added with a hint of his old cunning, 'And buy a thousand Masses for my soul.' The priest looked disappointed even as he concurred. 'Give it to him,' William ordered. She gave the cup to the priest who tucked it into his belt with a little too much alacrity. William lay back and closed his eyes in exhaustion. Nicolette let the bed curtain fall closed and drew the priest away.

'Do you think you should administer the last rites now, or will it frighten him too much?' she asked.

'The last rites are meant to comfort not to frighten,' the priest admonished her. 'William Gryffard has made his peace with God.'

Paid for it, she couldn't help thinking, but meekly she bowed her head. She knelt once again while the priest busied himself with the mysteries of the sacred pyx, the wine and the bread, listening to the comforting Latin, hoping that now her father's troubled mind might rest, that he might stop trying to make arrangements for his soul's swift passage through purgatory and wait for death in peace.

When the priest had gone, she went to sit beside her father. He lay in the middle of the bed, his breathing shallow and irregular, his eyes open – watching her.

'Just you and me now,' he said quite distinctly. 'That's how I always wanted it to be. But there was always Piers. The house belonged to Piers. Now it's in hock to Whittington. There won't be much left when all my bequests are paid for.' A ghost of a smile quivered about his sunken mouth. 'I've been clever, haven't I? One of them will look after you – when I'm gone.'

She tried not to mind. Tried not to think what it would

mean. Tried to tell herself that he was her father, that he was on the edge of the abyss and that he was much afraid. She laid her cool, soft hand against his cheek. 'You've always looked after me, Father.'

His skinny fingers groped for her hand, held it. 'Will you do something for me?' he asked.

'If I can,' she said. She was not going to make any deathbed promises to William Gryffard. He was too cunning even in his last hour and she did not want him finally taking advantage of her.

'There's a convent called the Sacred Heart. On the edge of the forest not far from Reading. My first wife Mariota is buried there. I built a fine chapel for her and endowed it well. Will you go to the convent and ask the nuns to pray for me as well as for Mariota?'

She was surprised, it was not the kind of request she had been expecting. Even as she promised, she felt dismayed for him. Still he was making sure and doubly sure. Faith, the Church's last blessing, was not enough. He had to go on checking and doublechecking to be certain of salvation.

There came a knocking at the door. Nicolette glanced at her father. He seemed to have drifted off to sleep. She got up and opened the door.

'There's a woman here, wants to see the master,' said the steward. Over his shoulder Nicolette saw a sturdy-looking female in a hood of scarlet ray. A whore, she thought, shocked that the steward had not sent her away at once. 'My father is sleeping, I can't disturb him now,' she said.

'She says she has important news for Master Gryffard's ears alone,' explained Stickleby, adding apologetically, 'I thought it better to find out what it is.'

Nicolette stared at the woman in disdain. She had probably come to try to extract money from her father for past services. 'You can tell me,' she said to the woman.

'I'll tell it to him or no one,' the woman declared. 'He always wants to be first with the news.' It was a raucous voice, one more used to crying wares than whispering secrets.

'Who is it?' William called out.

'Nobody.' Nicolette shut the door in the woman's face and hurried back to his bedside.

'Don't lie to me, Nicolette,' he said. 'I told you that, didn't I, the first day I saw you. I taught you how to lie, but not to me. Bring the woman here. If she has news, I want to hear it.' His voice which had been so weak and hesitant when confessing to the priest now had much of its old authority again. Reluctantly, Nicolette did as she was bid.

The woman entered the chamber and walked straight up to the bed as if she had been there many times before.

'Well, what is it?' William asked and from the way he looked at her Nicolette knew that the woman was no stranger to him.

'You'll have to pay me,' said the woman.

'Don't I always?' he retorted.

'My news is worth a King's ransom this time.' She laughed but it was not a merry sound and Nicolette felt her flesh grow cold.

'I'll be the judge of that.' William fumbled beneath his pillow and to Nicolette's surprise produced a money bag. So he still has some hard cash left, she thought, the old rascal. He had rallied and was enjoying himself haggling with the woman.

'I'll tell it, then, for old time's sake,' said the whore. 'If ye'll promise to be generous, like it or no.'

'I'll give you what's in here,' he said shaking the bag, 'if it's worth it.'

The woman cocked her head and listened to the chink of coins then nodded as if satisfied. 'The rightful King is being set upon his throne again,' she said. 'There's a plot to storm Windsor Castle and capture Henry and his eldest son dead or alive.'

'I'll not believe it! It's a lie,' declared William.

The woman shrugged. 'Believe what you will. Now pay me.'

'Who plans such a daring deed?'

'Rutland, Huntingdon, Kent,' the woman ticked the names off her fingers as if they were men who had been in her bed. 'Salisbury and Despenser, the Bishop of Carlisle, Walden lately Archbishop of Canterbury, the Abbot of Westminster and Sir Thomas Blount.'

Nicolette believed her. The woman was too sure of herself to have made it up. But it was impossible. 'Windsor Castle is invincible,' she said to reassure herself. 'Nobody can storm it. It's far too well guarded.'

The woman smiled knowingly. 'They've got it all worked

out. They're going to get into the castle, some of them, with carts of harness and armour in readiness for the grand tournament which King Henry is holding on Twelfth Night to welcome the new century. Once inside the castle they'll overpower the guards, admit their friends outside and then, once Henry and his family have been killed, they'll proclaim the restoration of Richard.'

Nicolette sat on the side of the bed, stunned, thinking of Piers and Kit even now feasting and dancing and celebrating Christmastide, unaware of the danger they were in.

'How do you know this?' William croaked.

'One of their men lay with me last night and told me. He had drunk too much mead and reckoning it was too late for the knowledge to be much use, he told me – though I had to worm it out of him, mind. I came to you because I knew you to be a friend of King Richard's.'

'Not any longer,' groaned William.

'Was I not right, isn't it worth a King's ransom?' The woman cackled at her own joke.

'Throw her out of the house,' ordered William. 'She's made it up to extort money from me. It's all a lie.'

'If you don't believe me, it doesn't matter.' The woman stood with her arms folded across her ample chest and there was no love in the baleful stare she gave him. 'It's God's truth I've told you. I thought you'd be pleased, you who always wanted to be first with the news.'

'Pleased?' William struggled to sit up in bed, his money bag clutched to his chest like a talisman. 'If it's true then I'm ruined. May God curse you for the whore that you are. You'll get nothing from me.'

'What's it matter if you're ruined now?' she demanded. 'You can't take your money with you where you're going.' She spat contemptuously on the fine tiled floor of the chamber and rounded on Nicolette still sitting stunned on the edge of the bed. 'At least I've spoilt his last hours on earth, him that's driven more than one man to his ruin,' she sneered and stormed out of the chamber. The banging of the heavy door behind her brought Nicolette out of her trance.

'We must warn them,' she cried, leaping to her feet.

'It's too late. They'll already be in the castle.' William's sickly pallor was now a greyish green. 'Ruin, ruin,' he muttered, his hands tearing at the bedsheets in a frenzy. So

457

great was his terror that for a moment Nicolette forgot her own fear.

'Why will you be ruined?' she asked in a desperate attempt to calm him. 'You were Richard's friend. You went to prison for him. If King Richard comes back . . .'

'Then he'll find me out for sure,' he groaned. 'Whittington will be done for. He can't protect me any more. I'll be impeached, fined. Don't you see, there'll be nothing left.' He clutched her arm, babbling with fear. 'King Richard always triumphs in the end. If he can take Henry of Lancaster's lands he can take anyone's.'

'They won't find you out. I won't let them,' she promised soothingly, just as she did when little Tarquin had a nightmare. 'Whittington will be at Windsor too. If he is killed, your secret must die with him.'

'But I have many enemies in the city.' He looked at her wildly. 'You can't lie with all of them.' He was so panic-stricken she ignored the jibe, too horrified by his abject terror to mind what he thought of her. Instead she thought of his will which he had laboured over so carefully, of the innumerable bequests which would expiate the wrong he had done to so many little men in his time. All his life he had toiled in pursuit of material possessions, had robbed and cheated and betrayed anyone for the gleam of gold, had come to worship money for itself, thinking that it could protect him from life's uncertainties, even from death and the awful reckoning in the world to come. All that the Church had to offer by way of redemption was as nothing compared to the money which was to buy his way into paradise. 'I will pray for you,' she said as pity for him overwhelmed her. 'And today is only the tenth day after Christmas. There's still time to warn them before Twelfth Night.'

She hurried out of the chamber to find the steward. He was waiting anxiously in the hall. He listened carefully while she told him the terrible news.

'It may not be true,' he said. 'The Widow Wendegoos is not a very reliable source of information.'

'True or not, the King must be warned,' she insisted. He was being so calm and dignified as always. 'Sir Piers and Christopher are in danger. If the castle is attacked, they will be in the thick of the fighting.' He was standing with his brow furrowed, lost in thought. She wanted to shake him, rouse him out of his stupor. 'We must act,' she said. 'Warn them. You must find me someone we can trust; someone who can ride hard enough to get there in time and who has the authority to get past the guards at Windsor Castle and speak to Sir Piers in person.'

'I'd better go myself then,' he said, much to her surprise. She doubted whether he was a sufficiently good horseman for the job, but there was no one better to send.

'Do you think you can get there in time?' she asked.

He smiled. 'I too have much to lose if Sir Piers, or any of them, are killed,' he said. 'Best say nothing of this to anyone,' he cautioned. 'If it is indeed true and I am too late to warn them and King Richard regains the throne, he may remember that William Gryffard was his friend.'

Even in her fear for Piers and her young son she was able to appreciate his caution and instinct for survival. 'Thank you,' she said, laying her hand on his sleeve. 'You do well to remind me. You are a good friend as well as a good steward and I ask your forgiveness that I did not always appreciate your care for us.'

He bowed and hurried away, and she went upstairs to the solar and her children.

The chamber was bright and cheerful in contrast to the gloom downstairs. Nicolette took Michael on her knee and buried her face in his warm, chubby neck so that Jeanne de Bourdat and Lisette would not see that anything was amiss. Better that they should be left in peace as long as possible.

'How is Master Gryffard?' Lisette asked.

'Much troubled in his mind still,' replied Nicolette.

'He won't die in peace, that one,' said Jeanne, shaking her head. 'He has too much on his conscience.'

'The priest has been. I don't think it will be long now,' said Nicolette. 'I heard a raven croaking in the garden earlier.' From the window she saw Adam Stickleby riding away down the street and she crossed herself and prayed that he might be in time. Tarquin was tugging at her skirts.

'Will you read me a story, Mama?'

'Not today, angel.' She stroked his soft hair. 'I must go back and look after Master Gryffard.'

'Would you like me to sit with the master for a while?' asked Jeanne. 'You're looking very peaky. It's almost as hard helping them out of this life as helping them into it.'

459

But Nicolette didn't hear her. She was listening to the sound of men running and shouting in the street outside. She handed Michael to Lisette and leant far out of the window. 'What has happened?' she called.

'The Earl of Huntingdon's men says to raise the city. King Henry and his sons have been taken prisoner in Windsor Castle. It's time to restore Richard of Bordeaux anointed by God to his rightful throne.'

Nicolette slumped on the window seat. 'Too late!' she cried. 'Our Blessed Lady have mercy, they may be dead.' Then she told Jeanne and Lisette about the Widow Wendegoos' visit.

'Sir Piers'll find a way out, never fear,' Lisette soothed. 'He'll not let any harm come to the little one.' But Nicolette feared that Piers would be much more likely to die honourably in defence of his liege lord.

'Have courage, my lady,' Jeanne said. 'Sir Piers is one of the best knights in Lancaster's retinue.'

'Then why is Henry taken prisoner?' Nicolette looked round the chamber wildly. 'Piers must be dead.'

Tarquin climbed on to her knee, peered into her face anxiously. 'Has something happened to Papa?' he asked.

She could not bear it. Could not find the words to reassure him, her throat was so tight with tears. She hugged him but he only wriggled away from her. 'Tell me, Mama.' She swallowed and did her best to smile.

'It's nothing, just a silly rumour,' she said, wishing it were true. Then unable to bear having to keep up the pretence in front of them, she said, 'I'd best go back to Master Gryffard.'

With dread she entered her father's chamber again. How was she to tell him? How comfort him on the threshold of eternity, when her own heart was filled with so much terror for Piers and Kit? In the chamber all was quiet. Merciful Jesus, let him be sleeping, she prayed.

She crept across the floor and approached the bed, drew aside the bed curtains. William was lying on his back, his eyes wide open. He was dead and the terror in his face was so horrifying Nicolette fell to her knees in despair. Desperately she tried to pray for his soul but the familiar words would not come. All she could think of was the futility of it all. William had devoted a lifetime to accumulating money but it could not buy peace; at the end he had nothing. Piers was right and it was her father who was wrong. Then she groaned out loud. What had become of Piers and little Kit? Death, which never makes less than three visitations to a community, could have struck at them too.

Her father's terrified eyes seemed to be watching her still. She tried to close them but without success. She got up and sat shivering by the fire, putting off the moment when she would have to leave the chamber and face all the trouble that awaited her outside. She could not believe that her father had gone. She had never loved him. She could not love a man who had been so utterly unscrupulous, who had used her for his own ends ever since he had removed her from the convent at Caen. But she had allowed him to use her, she realised suddenly, because she depended upon him for security, for all the things he had taught her to value. Always he had somehow rescued her from her own folly and now he was gone, and Piers and Dick Whittington also. What was she to do? What was there left for her now if King Richard should be restored to power? She had burnt her boats with the little Queen. She would never be allowed back into the Queen's household. Piers, if he was not already dead, would be at best exiled for life. She would go with him this time, willingly, if he would have her, if he was spared. Strange that what had once seemed an impossible sacrifice was now the best that she could hope for. With that straw to cling to, she nerved herself to face the household.

She assembled the servants in the hall where they huddled together like hungry beggars at feeding time. None doubted the reason why she had summoned them. The laundry maids were weeping, the cook with his bloodstained apron looked hot and uncomfortable, the other men were muttering among themselves.

'Your master is dead,' Nicolette told them, 'God rest his soul.'

They knelt and crossed themselves. But it was not for William's salvation they were primarily concerned. 'What is to become of us now?' asked the cook, voicing the fears of all the rest.

Nicolette was so drained by all that she had gone through that day she was unable to think of an answer that would allay their fears. It was Jeanne de Bourdat who came to the rescue.

'The priest must be sent for,' she said. 'The locks, bolts

461

and staples released, doors and windows opened to allow his soul to pass unhindered.'

Good practical Jeanne, thought Nicolette, while the servants were despatched upon their various tasks. One to reverse the mirrors so that the reflection of the dead man's soul would not be trapped in the glass; another to bring fresh candles to light beside the corpse to drive away evil spirits, who were afraid of light.

'What would I do without you to look after things for me, Jeanne?' said Nicolette. 'I'm so hopeless in times of trouble.'

'Bless you, my dear lady, I've had more practice, that's all.' Jeanne went to throw open the door. 'We must not give up hope.' Outside it was raining, a heavy downpour drowning hope.

When Adam Stickleby came back, he had nothing to report. He had ridden as far as the city wall and found the gates closed and the Mayor and aldermen anxiously waiting inside the city. Nobody seemed to know anything except that Windsor Castle had fallen to Richard's supporters. Realising that he was too late, the steward had returned speedily. On his way back through the city, he had seen nothing. No men marching. No bells ringing. There was no sign that the city was responding to Huntingdon's call to arms and every reason to believe that the Mayor and aldermen would refuse to let Richard in, when he came.

Jeanne set the household about the task of getting supper since there was nothing to be gained by fasting, but none of them had much appetite. They came into the hall when the trestles were laid and sat upon the benches subdued and listless. The sense of fear and impending doom was as heavy and relentless as the rain outside.

Suddenly through the open door came the sound of horses clattering down the street, the creaking of armour and the jingle of spurs. Nicolette sat very still. Was it Richard of Bordeaux's men come already to arrest them? Into the hall came a knight in full armour. Nicolette gave a shriek and jumped up from the table, scattering cups and trencher bread.

It was Piers with Kit and Guy de Luval. Nicolette bent and scooped up Kit, smothering him with kisses. But he wriggled away from her uncomfortably and went to stand beside his father.

'Oh Piers!' she cried, throwing her arms round his neck. 'We thought you were dead.' He looked down at her and she held her breath, as for a heartbeat his arms tightened round her. Then he thrust her from him almost violently.

'Nobody has died, not yet.' His face was grim.

'My father is dead,' she said. 'Oh Piers, he died in such terror. We heard about the plot from one of his informers. He died convinced that Richard was coming back in triumph again and that he would lose everything.'

'Serves him right. He always prided himself on his ability to be first with the news. If he got it wrong at the end he has only himself to blame.' He was changed, she thought. It was unlike Piers to be so harsh and unsympathetic.

'It wasn't supposed to be until Twelfth Night. Adam Stickleby was going to come and warn you. Then we heard that the King was a prisoner and I was so afraid for you.'

'We were warned and escaped in time,' said Kit. 'We crept out of Windsor Castle in the dead of night with the King and his sons and galloped all the way to London. I was on the front of Papa's saddle.'

She held out her arms to him. 'Oh Kit, my angel. I was so worried about you. I should never have persuaded your father to take you with him.'

But he did not rush to her as once he would have done. 'I wasn't afraid, not once,' he said looking proudly up at Piers. 'Not even when we got to the city gates and found them all closed against us.'

'It was Huntington who made the city bar its gates,' said Piers, his face softening as he looked at the boy. 'It worked for a while. But the Mayor came out and met us outside the city walls. As soon as he saw that King Henry was with us and he was unharmed, he welcomed him in. He and your friend Whittington are busy raising the city trainbands.'

She longed to tell him that Whittington didn't matter. Nothing mattered any more. Money and possessions and success, all the things she had thought so important, were of no account. But she could not tell him here in the hall in front of so many people. 'You must be hungry,' she said instead. 'Come and eat.' But he wasn't listening.

'There's no time to lose,' he said. 'I only came to bring Kit home and to collect some men. The news is that the rebels have six thousand men in the field. I shall need every man in the household who can hold a spear.'

To Nicolette's amazement, Adam Stickleby immediately started selecting who was to go. Guy de Luval had already dragged out the chest full of small arms and was handing them out. They ate on their feet, wolfing the food down while the men put on leather jerkins and helmets. Nicolette was overcome with a sense of uselessness. Piers was leaving her alone with nothing but women and striplings; even Adam Stickleby was going.

'Not Adam, surely,' she said. 'He's more used to a pen than a sword.'

'Adam is a good organiser and knows how to read and write. The King needs such men to get his army into the field quickly and efficiently,' explained Piers patiently.

'Don't go,' she pleaded, knowing she was being unreasonable but unable to stop herself. She had thought him dead and he had been miraculously restored to her. She wanted to tell him everything that was in her heart. 'I have a terrible sense of doom. Just before my father died, there was a raven croaking in the garden. Death never visits a community but in threes. It's an evil omen.' She held out her hands to him, tears running down her cheeks.

'I'm a knight. Fighting is my duty. I have to go.'

'But I need you here. What am I to do with my father not yet cold and all the servants gone with you?'

'Christ Jesus, there's a rebellion. The rebels have thousands of men out there. The King has to act swiftly if he's to cut them off. If I don't go with every able-bodied man I can find, we'll all be finished.'

'I don't care,' she cried, throwing discretion to the wind. 'I don't care whether you succeed or fail. I love you, have always loved you, only I've been foolish. I thought . . .' His expression showed impatience; he was eager to be off. Desperately she clung to his mailed fist. 'The only thing that matters now is you and me.' She saw that he had already gone from her in his thoughts. The men were all waiting outside for him to start. She flung her arms round his neck.

'What matters is that all our work is to do again,' he declared as he took her hands and pulled them down from his neck. 'While Richard lives, the King will never sit safely on his throne.' She felt a cold shiver run down her spine. He

464

looked so fierce and resolute. So unlike the kind, gentle man who had loved her with such devoted persistence, who had been blind to all her faults.

'Piers,' she said, afraid of him, 'don't do anything dishonourable – anything you might regret when you come to the end of your life. No success is worth the guilt and fear my father faced on his deathbed.'

'I'll do whatever I have to do to serve King Henry,' he told her. 'Give my life if necessary – there's no dishonour in that.' She wanted to beg him to be careful, to forgive her, to try to make him understand about Whittington. But she knew it was useless. Possessions meant nothing to him; she had bartered her honour, loyalty and faithfulness for the sake of material security and to him that was unforgivable.

He strode out of the hall and she followed, watching forlornly while Guy de Luval held the stallion for him to mount. The rain had stopped. Brightness filled the sky. Piers spurred his horse forward into Cornhill, the motley cavalcade of the household's servants running after him. She watched them disappear out of sight behind St Peter's Church.

Quiet fell on the house after that. She left the door open in case her father's restless spirit was still about and walked with dragging step up the wide stone staircase to her solar. Piers did not want her. She was his wife and he would honour and protect her but that was all. The love he had once had for her was gone. As a wife she had failed and as a daughter too. At the last, William had died not only alone but terrified. She was a failure but, worse than that, she was worthless.

CHAPTER 38

Piers rode away angry that her beauty still had the power to move him so much. Of course it was all part of the spell she cast over men. She was cunning as the serpent, a temptress like Eve, and greedy as her father William Gryffard had been. She wanted him now because he was successful at last. Furiously he dug his heels into his horse's flanks and charged up Cornhill, until Guy shouted at him to slow down.

'The men on foot are far behind,' the squire said. 'I'd best go back for them.'

Piers reined in, struggling to get a hold over himself as he waited. Resolutely he pushed the thought of his wife's soft clinging form, her piteous tears, out of his mind. There was work to be done; a rebel army to be confronted and defeated. This was no time to be thinking about women.

Henry had taken refuge in the fortified tower at the top of the Royall known as the Queen's Wardrobe. It was a stronghold which had once sheltered Richard when he was besieged by the revolting peasants at the beginning of his reign. Piers guessed that Henry had chosen it rather than the Tower of London because the Queen's Wardrobe was in the middle of the city; judging by the journeymen and apprentices all armed to the teeth and eager for battle who were swarming about in the courtyard, it was the city that was going to provide most of Henry's much needed forces.

Piers was ushered into the great chamber and found the King taking counsel with the Mayor and other anxious aldermen, including Dick Whittington. At the sight of his erstwhile friend and protector who had stolen his wife, Piers felt his anger take hold like an impatient stallion. He gripped his sword hilt compulsively but forced himself to let it remain in its scabbard. Since he could not kill Whittington honourably, he had to learn to let him live. The worst of it was that the King seemed to value Whittington quite as much as his predecessor had done and Piers could only marvel at the mercer's ability to make himself indispensable so easily. It was money, he thought scornfully. Whittington was made of money.

Henry was busy signing documents. He looked up and noticed Piers. 'The Earl of Huntingdon's attempt to stir up a rising in London failed, by the grace of God. The city has stood by me. Now I must see that the rest of the country follows their lead. The Mayor here tells me that London can provide at least ten thousand men.'

'I've brought you half a score,' said Piers. 'It's not very many and they're all unskilled, not a decent archer among them, but they're all stout fellows and should stand firm. Our steward is a good writer and efficient organiser. I brought him too.'

The King looked pleased. 'Good,' he said. 'I need men who can organise. You'd better take him to Hounslow Heath with your foot soldiers, that's where I shall review the troops. The aldermen say they can have their men out there by noon. It'll take a good deal of work getting that number into order, ready to march. See to it, will you, Piers. As soon as I've finished here, I'll join you.' He turned away and addressed himself to Whittington. 'I want all Richard's friends who were arrested in October kept under close guard. Those who've been pardoned should be rearrested.'

Piers and Whittington left the chamber together.

'I'm afraid that means William Gryffard,' said Dick to Piers, without so much as an averted glance to show that he had cause to be ashamed of himself.

'Gryffard's dead,' Piers told him, clenching his teeth.

Dick smiled wryly even as he crossed himself. 'Trust Gryffard to escape punishment,' he said. 'I wouldn't give any of Richard's friends much of a chance after this rebellion has been crushed.'

'You were once a friend of Richard, when he was King,' Piers declared angrily and just for a moment Dick had the grace to look uncomfortable. 'Gryffard died thinking King Richard was coming back to seize his house and his goods, that there would be no money for all the bequests he had made,' Piers went on, staring at him icily. 'He may have escaped punishment by dying in time, but he didn't believe he had escaped eternal damnation.' Dick's face was inscrutable and Piers knew he was wasting his time trying to make him feel guilty. Since he could not kill him in battle, the only thing left was to better him at his own game, to show him, and Nicolette, that he was more successful, more indispensable to Henry, more powerful.

He rode off with his troops to Hounslow filled with a sense of purpose. If ever there was a time to show his mettle it was now. Action and danger were things Piers perfectly understood. Not all Whittington's money could buy Henry victory; it was brave knights the King needed now and Piers intended to show that he was the bravest and the best.

On Hounslow Heath he found Crispin, his shield bright with its quarterings of green and gold and the crest of a flying fox upon his helm.

'The King believes that the rebels will try to make a stand somewhere between Windsor and London,' said Piers. 'It looks as if you'll soon have the chance to show how good a knight you can be, Crispin.'

'God send I find you fighting by my side then,' responded Crispin. 'All morning I've been trying to get these ignorant craftsmen into some sort of marching order; they've got about as much idea of proper warfare as a pack of wild dogs.'

'The King will have to make the most of what troops he can find. Time isn't on our side if we're to catch the rebels before they can do real damage. The trainbands of London are composed of journeymen, apprentices, cooks, pantry boys – willing amateurs like my own men, whose only experience of battle is street brawls. But their numbers may be enough to frighten the enemy.'

'They certainly wouldn't frighten me,' grumbled Crispin.

Looking about him ruefully, Piers felt inclined to agree. But when Henry appeared on his white charger in full armour and rode up and down their ranks, a cheer went up which flowed across the open heath like a tidal wave. Hearing that cry and witnessing the forest of spears raised in greeting, no one could be left in any doubt that King Henry had the support of the people. It made Piers feel better. He wanted to believe that what Henry had done he had done because he had no choice. That the people of England had called to him in their need to rid them of a tyrant and that what had been done to Richard had been done in the name of freedom.

They left Hounslow Heath that afternoon. The King's scouts brought back news that there was a huge army waiting at Colnbrook. A pitched battle seemed inevitable. But when they reached Colnbrook, the army had fled, whether because they'd lost heart after the disappointment at Windsor or were overawed by the size of Henry's army and the speed with which he had mustered his forces, nobody knew, only that they were retreating westwards.

'They may be making for Wales, or even Cheshire,' said the King grimly. These were Richard's traditional strongholds; if Wales with its innumerable fortified castles and wild inhospitable terrain welcomed the rebels, it would be impossible to dislodge them; if Cheshire rose in support of Richard's cause the contagion might spread and they would not be facing a battle against six thousand men but civil war. Piers thought of his father and elder brother and wondered which way they would fight if the choice had to be made.

Relentlessly Henry pushed on as fast as those on foot could go, marching them through the night, which by the mercy of God was bright with a full moon. The laden packhorses plodded stoically through the mud, sometimes stumbling over unseen holes. The wagons creaked and groaned, all too frequently becoming stuck in the mud. But each time they did, a hundred willing men leapt to lift them clear. Henry rode up and down, encouraging, urging, driving them forward. Piers had seen it all before; on the dash from Bristol to Conway, they had covered a distance of 250 miles in ten days. Henry was renowned for the speed with which he could move an army. This time their swift progress was brought to an abrupt halt when they reached the bridge over the River Thames at Maidenhead and found it defended by Richard's half-brother the Earl of Kent.

'Well, Piers,' said Henry, 'are you going to clear the way for me? You're a bit of a specialist at taking bridges, if I remember.' The King smiled for the first time that morning. 'Men still talk about how you fought that day at Radcot Bridge when this all really began, which is why I'm choosing you to lead today.'

Piers studied the stone bridge, filled with joy at having

been singled out by the King. He could see the defending force drawn up on the far bank. There were only two knights and about a score of foot soldiers with spears and battle-axes crowded about the foot of the bridge.

'I'd be glad to try, Sire,' he replied. 'It shouldn't be too difficult.'

'The bridge is wide enough for two knights to make a charge side by side, but there may be archers in that wooded knoll to the right – it's barely a bowshot from the bridge,' warned the King.

'As soon as we're across, we'll deal with those two knights waiting on the bank and then drive on through the wood to scatter the archers,' promised Piers.

'Do you think you can manage without archers of your own?' asked Henry.

Piers nodded. 'I should think so. They can't shoot while we're engaged with the men on the bank – they'll kill their own men.'

'We can't afford to waste any time.' The King was frowning. 'The longer we're held up here, the more time it gives them to make an orderly retreat. I want the way clear by the time the foot soldiers catch up, so choose who you want to go with you and get on with it.'

Piers chose Crispin and four other knights. They all looked keen. As Guy brought the destrier Piers would ride into battle, he could see that both stallion and squire were full of excitement, the horse pawing the ground and snorting, the squire grinning from ear to ear as he handed Piers his helm.

'I suppose you think you're coming with me,' said Piers, donning his helm.

'I'll try not to let you down,' said Guy. Piers looked into the eager young face and felt the old familiar reluctance to expose the boy to danger. Guy was brave and showing prowess at the quintain but he was still young and inexperienced. Remembering another bridge and another squire, Piers was about to refuse. But then he saw Crispin with his own squire helping him get ready. Crispin had had to wait a long time for his knighthood. Piers asked himself if he had perhaps valued him too much as a squire, kept him out of danger because he could not bear the responsibility of his death. The French nobleman who had entrusted his son to him expected Guy to be taught how to be a knight, and to be

470

given the chance to win his spurs. No squire became a knight without risk.

Piers mounted his trembling destrier. 'You'll not let me down,' he told Guy. 'Not if you do what you've been taught and keep out of the way of the opposing knights. Remember, this isn't a tournament. Their swords are sharpened and their lance points deadly, and they're just as anxious to stay alive as we are.'

The boy swung into his saddle looking suitably serious, and Piers hoped that he would prove equal to the task ahead. If he did, knighthood could be his reward.

They rode towards the bridge, the pale January sun glinting on their armour, the pennants on the tips of their lances streaming in the wind. On the river bank Piers reined in and surveyed the scene. The defenders were closing ranks.

'They'll be easier to mow down, packed together like that,' said Crispin as he ranged his horse alongside. The other knights fell in behind, two by two, with the squires bringing up the rear.

Piers lowered his visor, clapped spurs to his warhorse and charged over the bridge. The foot soldiers scattered in panic before the stallion's plunging hooves; the destrier's ravaging teeth closed on a man's face, laying it open to the bone. Piers laid about him with his sword, each downstroke sheathing itself in flesh and bone; the agonised faces he occasionally glimpsed through the slits of his visor meant nothing. Dead foot soldiers were simply the refuse of battle.

He swept onwards, the momentum of the charge carrying him too far. With a quick jerk of the reins he wheeled his horse, peering through his visor towards the bridge they had just crossed: the others were all still mounted and busy making short work of the rest of the defenders. Everything was going according to plan. But it was all too easy. Something was wrong, Piers felt it in his bones. He had fought in too many battles not to know when something wasn't right and now every instinct was screaming a wordless warning. He squinted through the narrow slits of his visor, searching for the two knights in charge of the defenders. There was no sign of the Earl of Kent's crest. Perhaps he had already fled. Still, it didn't feel right.

Through the corner of his visor he glimpsed a battle axe descending towards his destrier's flank and swung his sword down fiercely. It cleaved the man's arm from his shoulder. Guy was acquitting himself well, he noticed, pleased. The battle for the bridge was almost won. A shower of arrows fell but they bounced harmlessly off his armour, all power spent. The bowmen must be barely in range. It was time to do something about the archers in the wood.

Suddenly out of the wooded area to the left of his line of vision five knights came charging, their lances levelled. Piers knew that the sheer force of impact would be enough to knock any knight out of his saddle unless he met the charge head on. No time to warn Crispin, no time to get the others into line, no time even for a quick plea to the Almighty.

'Attack!' he yelled, instinct and training and love of combat spurring him forward to meet the charging knights at full gallop. They met with a mighty crash. The impact was so great it lifted the stallion off his front feet. Piers's weight crashed into the back of his high saddle and he was almost swept off and over its tail. Almost, but not quite. The opposing knight had lost his shield; Piers swung his lance tip to the other side, caught him on his undefended shoulder and prised him from the saddle like a sack of bran. He swung viciously at a knight on his right with a backhand blow across the side of the helmet, denting the steel plate and sending the man reeling. Blades struck at him from all directions at once, careening off his shield and ringing on his helmet with deafening clangs.

Where were the other knights? Piers desperately tried to manoeuvre for position in the midst of the plunging, thrashing horses. He finally managed to wheel his horse about and saw that four of Henry's knights were on the ground, knocked clean out of their saddles by the first charge. He wheeled again, spurring mercilessly to get between them and the opposing knights. Somehow he had to give them time to get to their feet to continue the fight. It was the last coherent thought he had.

A sword blow from behind rang off his helmet and he clenched his teeth as it bit into his shoulder armour. Before he could react, two more jarring blows struck his helmet. The next thing he knew, his charger was galloping furiously towards the river. His head was swimming and there was a drumming in his ears. Someone shouted, 'Give me your reins, sir!' Piers thought it was the voice of Guy, but he

472

couldn't give him his reins, he needed them to control his stallion. The maddened charger was running away with him. He knew he must act fast but his usual lightning reflexes seemed somehow slowed. As if in a trance, he saw the muddy waters of the river coming closer; the stallion was gathering himself together. Jesus! thought Piers. The bastard believes he can leap straight over. No horse could leap that river. The charger, frightened out of his wits, had lost all sense of self-preservation.

Piers's mind recognised his danger but utterly failed to convert the knowledge into action. Suddenly the reins were torn from his grasp. The stallion slewed violently, crashing to his knees as the bank of the river crumbled beneath his scrabbling hooves. Piers was thrown clean out of the saddle, pitched over the horse's shoulder into the river. It happened too quickly for him to feel fear, but he knew he would sink like a stone. As the water closed over his head, he had a bright vision of Nicolette and a poignant stab of regret, then a hand seized the back of his mail coif and lifted him to the surface. 'I've got you, sir,' he heard Guy cry, and he was dragged coughing and choking through the water to the river bank.

He sat on the bank, gulping precious life-giving air, unable to believe that he was still alive. Guy was standing holding his horse, staring at him in concern. 'Get back, Guy,' Piers gasped. 'We've got to drive them from the foot of the bridge.'

'We've done that, sir,' replied Guy, mounting again. 'I'll see if I can't catch your horse.'

'Forget my horse. Try and dislodge those buggers of bowmen from the wood,4' commanded Piers.

The squire galloped off and Piers struggled to his feet, his head ringing and water dripping from his armour. He had lost his shield and his sword and his helm. His excited destrier was in the river, swimming downstream with determination. Piers could see little of the battle from where he stood. He began trying to clamber up the river bank like a drunken tortoise in his armour. From time to time the pernicious mud would take hold of a leg like an importunate beggar and he would lose his balance and fall with a terrible clatter, cursing and swearing as he struggled to right himself again. Ignoring the pain in his head and the ringing in his ears, he battled on until eventually he reached the foot of the bridge.

The main body of Henry's army had started to arrive and the foot soldiers were pouring across the bridge to help in the fierce hand-to-hand fighting. The Earl of Kent was trying to rally his men, shouting until his voice failed him. But the overwhelming numbers were beginning to tell. In vain, Richard's half-brother spurred his foam-drenched, blood-spattered destrier back and forth, striking about him with the flat of his sword at his fleeing soldiers, but courage was not enough. Wave after wave of armed men were running over the bridge. The Earl of Kent could see the battle was lost. All around him his men cast aside their weapons, sought only to save themselves. Their leader, too, finally acknowledged defeat and galloped from the field. Piers stood impotently cursing at the foot of the bridge and watched the Earl escape.

Henry rode across the bridge. 'You've lost your helm, Sir Piers,' he said.

'And my senses for a time,' replied Piers ruefully. 'If it had not been for Guy de Luval here, I'd have been drowned in the river.'

Crispin was riding out of the wood, his armour stained with blood, his caparison in tatters and his horse white with sweat. He had Guy de Luval with him. They both seemed unharmed. Perhaps the King would take the hint and knight the squire now.

'The Earl of Kent has escaped, I see,' said Henry.

'His horse is spent, he'll not get far. I could catch him easily, Your Grace,' offered Piers.

'Better not. There's a whole army of rebels somewhere out there. Kent's brave defence has bought them time to withdraw in good order. Until we know where they are, we shall have to proceed carefully. Caution as well as valour makes the best soldiers.' Piers could tell that the King was not pleased. 'We've wasted too much time crossing the river, I fear. All we can do now is to make with what speed we can for Oxford. You, Sir Piers, can ride on ahead with caution – if your squire can get your horse back. Find out for me where their army is. See if you can do better than you did today.'

An hour later Piers set out. Crispin had found his horse peacefully grazing further down the river. Guy had retrieved his shield, his sword and his helm. Piers rode through the cold January countryside with but one thought in his aching head – to win glory for himself and somehow for Guy too.

The squire had saved his life, he had shown presence of mind and courage and resourcefulness, the three most useful attributes in the heat of battle. He deserved recognition.

At Oxford it began to rain and they were told that the army had passed through a day or two ago. At Fairford they met a travelling pedlar who had seen a large party of armed men barely a few hours ahead. 'They'll be making for Cirencester,' said the pedlar. 'It's a market town at the meeting of the Fosse, the Icknield Way, Ermin Street and Ackman Street. Four good roads to escape by, should the need arise.'

Piers knew he should hurry back to Oxford to tell the King. His head was swimming; the horses needed food and water; it was still raining steadily. Even if he were to kill the horses on the way it would be dark by the time he reached Cirencester.

'Is there an abbey within an hour's ride of Cirencester?' he asked the pedlar.

'There's Malmesbury Abbey not ten miles distant,' was the reply.

Piers rode on wearily, determined to win glory somehow. By the time they reached Malmesbury, night had fallen. The Abbot made them welcome and told Piers that some men wearing the white hart had sought shelter earlier, but he had barred his gates. It was then that Piers realised how easily he could have walked into the arms of the enemy had the Abbot been more disposed towards Richard of Bordeaux, and he cursed himself for a careless fool; fatigue and that blow on the head were making him behave like a simpleton.

He left the abbey with his squire at dawn next day. The rain had stopped and there was a cold light in the sky. The night's rest had cleared his head; his senses were alert and he was ready for action. He set a brisk pace, keeping a sharp watch for enemy forces on the move. When they came in sight of Cirencester, a thin column of smoke was rising into the sky from the town.

Piers took his helmet and shield from Guy. The horse, sensing battle, fidgeted nervously. They rode on, approaching the partly walled market town cautiously. From the square close by Cirencester's abbey came a roar of voices chanting and shouting.

'Something's up,' said Piers, 'but it's not a siege.' He lowered his visor, couched his lance and trotted purposefully

475

towards the sound of the shouting. A great cheer went up when he was about a bowshot away from the open rectangle in front of the abbey which formed the marketplace. The townspeople were so engrossed in what was happening that no one took any notice of his approach.

The stallion snorted and tried to charge as another stupendous roar filled the air. Piers held him back firmly. They had reached the marketplace. Standing up in his stirrups, he glimpsed over the crowd two headless bodies lying spreadeagled on the cobblestones, their limbs still twitching involuntarily. One of the burghers was holding a severed head aloft for all to see. Piers recognised the features of the Earl of Kent. Anger swept over him, not because he had been robbed of his prey but because a brave knight who had shown so much courage in defending the bridge only yesterday had been so brutally beheaded.

Piers raised his visor, sickened and disgusted by the scene. It was one thing to be killed in battle, quite another this butchering without trial.

A knight with a small contingent of armed men was marshalling the crowd. Piers pushed his way forward. 'What is the meaning of this outrage?' he demanded.

'I am Thomas Lord Berkeley, Captain of the Guard. What has been done here has been done in King Henry's name,' the knight replied, holding up a scroll. Piers recognised the hand of Adam Stickleby. Lord Berkeley explained that the sheriffs had received orders from the King to arrest the rebel leaders and seize their property.

'I am Sir Piers Exton, Sword Bearer to the King,' Piers informed him. 'The King empowers you to arrest and seize, not to butcher without proper trial or benefit of clergy.'

'They had a priest – one of the monks from the abbey,' Berkeley protested. 'Salisbury refused his ministrations and preferred his own prayers as he waited for death. He was a Lollard to the end. Lollard and traitor – he was bound to die.'

'They were knights who chose to fight for the wrong side,' replied Piers uncomfortably as he remembered how loyal Salisbury had proved all his life to King Richard.

'I did my best,' Lord Berkeley insisted. 'I tried to protect them. We agreed that if Kent and Salisbury would surrender without a fight, they could be lodged under house arrest in the abbey. But then some fool tried to fire the town, hoping to

476

draw off the citizens to the protection of their homes, I suppose. But the burghers weren't having it. They dragged the two Earls into the street and beheaded them. There was nothing I could do to stop the mob.'

Piers looked at the people in the market square. They were no different from the humble citizens of any small market town. The people were loyal to Henry. They'd had enough bad government and extravagance. They had been taxed too much. Richard had been a tyrant and the people did not want him back on the throne.

'What shall we do with these?' asked the Mayor, pointing to the heads still dripping blood.

'Send them to the King at Oxford,' replied Piers. He watched while the heads were carefully packed round with straw and put in a basket, like fish for the market. Already the excitement was beginning to fade. The bodies lying on the cobblestones had stopped twitching. The burghers stood muttering together in little groups.

'You'd better ride back to Oxford with me,' Piers told Lord Berkeley.

That night Piers stood with the King above the gatehouse of Oxford Castle listening to the wind moaning round the battlements.

'Well, Piers, you'll have to find a new squire now that I've knighted Guy de Luval. It shouldn't be difficult to find one – you're getting a reputation for always being in the thick of the fighting.' Henry's words sounded brave enough but Piers could tell by his voice that he was depressed. The rebellion was over; the remaining lords, when they heard what had happened to Kent and Salisbury, had lost their nerve and fled for safety. Twenty-six knights and their squires had already been caught and executed here at Oxford.

'I'll take whoever you wish,' replied Piers, leaning against the cold stone of the parapet.

Henry nodded and continued to stare down into the court below at the bloodstained block which had seen so much grisly work that day. Piers was struck by the contrast between Henry now and when the first hint of the rebellion had reached him at Windsor Castle. Then he had been full of vigour and resolute action. Now that the danger was past and victory his, he seemed depressed and drained.

'I was too lenient,' the King muttered. 'I tried to keep too many men in their old places. I thought I could undo all the wrongs Richard did without shedding blood, but I was wrong.'

'The people know better,' Piers tried to comfort him. 'They'll always be behind you. Remember the way the whole of London turned out to see you crowned and again when you reviewed the army on Hounslow Heath. You have the support of the people, Your Grace.' The King continued to stare morosely at the scene of the executions. 'And in Cirencester the mob set upon Kent and Salisbury unafraid of the troops in the surrounding countryside. You've got the whole country behind you, Sire.'

'There'll be others – I can't reward every baron, ennoble every knight. Sooner rather than later there will be those who have not grown as powerful as they hoped; discontented, ambitious men are the curse of kings. While Richard lives there will always be the temptation to challenge my authority.' Lightning flickered silently on the horizon.

'Surely not. No one with any sense would try again. Twice in a short time you have quelled all opposition with hardly a blow struck. They'll have learnt their lesson by now, Sire.'

Henry straightened up and swung round to face Piers. 'You think so? Men never learn. While Richard lives, the temptation is always there, like a burr under the saddle. There will be more blood shed, more scenes like this we've had to witness today, more brave knights sent needlessly to their death. We must not destroy ourselves. France is the enemy we should be fighting but I fear that while my cousin lives, it will never be done.' The wind was gusting heavily now, ruffling their hair. Henry sighed deeply, looked up into the darkening sky. 'Have I no friend who will rid me of this living fear?' he said. The words were carried away on the wind; the lightning flashes were coming closer, accompanied by the rumble of thunder.

'Better get off this parapet, Your Grace,' said Piers. 'I'd hate to have lightning undo all our hard work for us.'

'You're a good friend, Piers, as well as one of the best knights in my kingdom, even if you did get taken by surprise at Maidenhead.'

As he followed the King down to the great hall for supper, Piers's heart began to thump and his skin grew clammy.

'Have I no friend?' the King had said. 'You're a good friend.' His meaning was unmistakable – so unmistakable it was almost a command. Now he knew how to render the ultimate service to his sovereign; after that, no prize would be too great, no honour too high it would not be his for the asking. He suddenly thought of Nicolette. Whittington had bought her, William Gryffard had bought her. Did he want to buy her? Or punish her or get rid of her? He did not know. All he wanted was to show Dick Whittington that money wasn't everything. He sat down to supper that night with murder in his heart.

CHAPTER 39

On 15 January Henry re-entered London with his army. The next day, the Feast of the Epiphany, Nicolette went to Chepeside with Kit and Lisette attending her to watch the King's triumphant progress through the city. It took them a long time to travel the short distance between Cornhill and Chepeside, for although it was still early in the morning, the streets were already lined with people eager to see the procession. The permanent stands overlooking Chepeside by Bow Church were already almost full and Nicolette began to wish that she had got here earlier. But as soon as she gave her name to the steward in charge, he ushered her into the stand with great deference. She took her seat unmoved by her success.

It was cold waiting for the procession to come; the wind came from the east, whipping down the wide thoroughfare of Chepe and plucking at the shivering spectators like an uneasy conscience. Nicolette clutched her velvet fur-trimmed mantle round her tightly. In the stand the ladies tried to keep warm, exchanging gossip, chattering and laughing and huddling close together on the hard wooden benches.

'Will Papa be with the King, do you think?' asked Kit.

Nicolette could not answer him. The men who had left with Piers had all returned safe and sound, full of their adventures and brimming with pride over the important part Piers had played in the skirmish at Maidenhead. But nobody knew where he was now. Nicolette clung to the hope that soon she would see him.

From the direction of the river came the sound of cheering. The procession was on its way. Nicolette felt her heart begin to pound. She could hear music now above the cheers.

Craning forward, she saw the heralds coming into sight and behind them a great parade of knights, brightening the January gloom with their brilliant banners and gay caparisons. At last the King entered Chepeside. He was riding a white charger, the coronet of gold round his helm glinting. The people cheered and cheered, drowning the music; women leaned from the overhanging balconies throwing garlands and ribbons which were soon crushed into the mud beneath the destriers' hooves. 'God bless our King Henry and God bless my Lord the Prince,' came the cry repeated over and over from a thousand throats.

Nicolette strained her eyes for Piers's arms, for a caparison with red and cream trefoils and a helm crested with a leaping unicorn.

'Look,' shouted Kit, 'there's Crispin.' He leapt to his feet waving frantically and Crispin swivelled round in his saddle and raised his lance in recognition.

'He saw me! He saw me!' Kit plumped himself down again in great delight at having been recognised by his hero. 'Papa must be here. Can you see him?' he demanded.

Nicolette fought down rising panic. Where was Piers? She had been so sure he would be here today with the King.

'Can we go to London Bridge now to see the heads and quarters of the executed traitors?' asked Kit, his interest in the procession beginning to wane as soon as the King and his chief barons had passed.

'Most certainly not,' replied Nicolette with a shudder.

The King's Council rode by, among them Richard Whittington in the scarlet gown of an alderman, a fine beaver hat pulled well down over his hood. At the sight of him, Nicolette suddenly remembered her debt-ridden inheritance. She had no idea how much money her father had borrowed from Dick. Would he take the house away from them? Or would he offer to cancel the debt – at a price? Somehow it no longer mattered what Dick intended. She did not need him any longer. Where was Piers?

'Papa hasn't been killed in battle, has he?' Kit's sudden anxious question voiced her own gnawing fear.

'Of course not, my angel,' she reassured him. 'If anything bad had happened to your father, Crispin, Master Stickleby, Guy de Luval – someone – would have told us by now. We must just wait and see.' It was the hope she clung to.

On the day that Henry rode in triumph through the streets of London, Piers reached Pontefract. He rode along the Fosse, a good, straight Roman road, sparing neither himself nor his steed. He dared not stop to think but rode on through blizzard and torrential rain, driven by a dreadful urgency that would not allow him rest.

An hour before dark on the Feast of the Epiphany he first saw the turreted towers of Pontefract Castle, reaching above the town like a vision of chivalry – at least that was how Piers had thought of it those few short months ago when Henry's army had taken the castle without a blow struck against them. Now as Piers pushed his tired horse up the steep hill towards the castle, it appeared more like an impregnable fortress. Henry had been lucky the castle had offered no resistance, he thought, staring up at the stone walls rising like cliffs above his head. It would take months to subdue a castle like this if properly defended. He stared across the moat and the raised drawbridge at the gatehouse. The portcullis was down and there was no sign of life. He craned his head back and thought he saw movement on the battlements high above the tower of the gatehouse.

'Open in the King's name,' he shouted at the top of his voice.

A helmeted head appeared above the battlement. 'Who goes there?'

'Sir Piers Exton, Sword Bearer to the King.'

'No one is allowed into the castle without the constable's say so,' the gatekeeper replied.

'Then fetch him out here – and hurry.'

The keeper disappeared and Piers waited outside, trying not to notice the cold. Banks of cloud were scudding across the darkening sky above the castle's great cluster of towers, driven by a wind strong enough to rattle the gates of Hell. By the time the gatekeeper returned with the constable, Piers was chilled through in spite of the thick padding beneath his armour.

'Is it you then, Piers?' the constable shouted peering down at him from the gatehouse tower. Piers removed his helm and looked up so that Sir Thomas Swynford could see his face clearly. Piers knew him well enough, he had fought beside him on Henry's various crusades. Swynford was Henry's stepbrother, the son of the Lady Katherine Swynford, John of Gaunt's third wife. He was a dour Saxon knight, a staunch fighter, if not a very jolly comrade in arms.

The drawbridge came rattling down. Piers urged his exhausted horse into one last effort and rode across it as the portcullis was slowly raised on squeaking hinges.

'Got to be careful,' said Swynford coming down from the gatehouse to greet him. 'I heard what happened at Windsor Castle. Can't have anyone breaking in here and rescuing the prisoner.'

Piers swung down from the saddle.

'Did the King send you?' asked Swynford. 'Doesn't he trust me to carry out his orders?' It occurred to Piers then that whatever deed was done here at Pontefract, it would be difficult to do without Swynford's connivance.

'The King sent me,' Piers replied. 'I've come to see your prisoner. There've been rumours that he'd escaped – was leading the rebellion.'

'I heard there'd been a battle.' Thomas looked rueful. 'Is that where you lost your squire?'

'Not much of a battle – a bit of a skirmish at Maidenhead. After Kent and Salisbury were killed by the mob in Cirencester, the rest of them ran away. The King knighted my squire for the part he played at Maidenhead. He saved my life when I fell in the river.'

'The King must value you highly then,' said Thomas. In the gloom of approaching nightfall it was difficult to read his expression.

'The rebellion's over,' Piers said. 'Twenty-six knights and their squires were executed at Oxford and there'll be more when the King gets to London, I don't doubt.'

'He'll not sit safe upon his throne until our prisoner is dead,' Swynford said, looking at his visitor closely. Piers felt cold. His teeth began to chatter. 'I'll take you to him, now if you like,' Swynford went on. 'It's Richard of Bordeaux all right, but you may have difficulty recognising him.'

Piers nodded, not trusting himself to speak.

Swynford led him through the huge fortress in silence, down far below ground into dungeons so dank and miserable that it was impossible to tell day from night, summer from winter. Like eternal purgatory, thought Piers with a shiver.

'There he is. You can see for yourself it's Richard of

Bordeaux.' Swynford held up the flaming cresset he carried.

'Sweet Jesu!' Piers swore softly, shocked when he saw the man who had been King. Richard was chained to the wall muttering to himself, clad in filthy robes of some coarse grey cloth, gaunt and haggard. Piers couldn't believe it was the same man whose court had been so lavish and who had once been so powerful.

'He's out of his senses most of the time,' said Swynford. 'Doesn't eat, doesn't sleep. Raves a bit – that's why we have to keep him chained up.'

Piers stared at the bowl of unappetising gruel untouched by the King's side and fought down horror. This was the man he had once sworn allegiance to. The prisoner began to cough, a hoarse wracking sound which convulsed his whole body in agonising effort.

'The King wants him dead, doesn't he?' said Swynford, not even bothering to lower his voice. 'Have you come to kill him?'

'He'll be dead soon anyway if you keep him in these conditions much longer,' Piers said bitterly. 'It's cold enough down here to kill any man, let alone a poor half-starved wretch with a broken heart.'

'Not him, he's a Plantagenet and they're a tough lot, the Plantagenets, though of course if he refuses to eat . . .' Swynford bent and picked up the plate of gruel.

Richard looked up and Piers knew him by his eyes – the piercing blue of the Plantagenets. He had seen those eyes when they were cruel and mischievous and petulant. Now they were full of helpless misery. 'He hasn't finished his supper,' Piers muttered, appalled at Thomas Swynford's callous indifference.

'He never does,' Swynford replied. 'I'd better take this away or the rats'll have it.' He led the way out of the dungeon, leaving the prisoner in darkness. 'Time for supper. You'll be hungry after the journey you've had.' His sour smile was positively ghoulish in the flickering light from the cresset.

'Aren't you going to leave him at least a candle's end?' demanded Piers.

'What for? It'd burn down soon enough in draughts like these. Then he'll be worse off than before. Better snuff the candle quick – that's what I say.' He winked at Piers knowingly and stalked out of the dungeon without so much as a backward glance to see if Piers followed. Piers knew he could have killed Richard then and the constable would have done nothing to prevent it. One blow with a sword, a clean downward thrust would cleave his head like a piece of cheese, put an end to his misery once and for all. He would know nothing. It would be a kindness.

Richard's coughing had ceased, but the sound of his breathing seemed to fill the silent dungeon. Piers gripped his sword until his knuckles turned white, but he could not draw it from its sheath. One thing to kill a man in battle, quite another to murder in cold blood a helpless victim chained to the wall. He ran after Swynford as if afraid of being alone in the dark, pursued by the terrible hoarse rattle of Richard's struggle for breath.

The great hall, for all its spartan gloom, was almost cosy after the chill of the dungeons. Piers sat down to supper with his appetite gone. He was haunted by the spectre of the deposed King. There was no doubt in his mind that Richard was on the point of death. If he were an animal, I'd put him out of his misery, he thought. He caught the eye of Thomas Swynford. He knew what the constable was doing. He was starving Richard to death. Piers knew he could insist that the fallen King be brought out of the dungeons and kept in comfort and warmth, properly fed and tended by a doctor. He was not afraid of Thomas Swynford. Richard came of strong stock, there might still be time to save him. But that was not what he had come here to do. Piers imagined himself riding back to London, confronting Henry. 'Your cousin is alive and well, safely incarcerated in Pontefract Castle.' Was that the message Henry was waiting to hear? Piers knew that it was not.

He looked round the gloomy hall at the men in their chain mail, the weapons of war decorating the walls. Here was no colour, no music. It was a fortress built to withstand a siege. Richard who loved beauty, music, art, would have to spend the rest of his life in fortresses such as these – either that or be rescued. Sooner or later another rebellion would be begun in his name.

Piers drank some wine. It was bitter and sour for having been kept too long. What was he to do? He thought of Dick Whittington, of the choices he had made to stay at the top; he remembered Richard of Bordeaux's acts of tyranny when he was King, of the Duke of Gloucester murdered at Calais by Thomas Mowbray. The thought of Mowbray brought Nicolette unbidden into his mind. Mowbray, Brembre, Whittington – these were the men Nicolette was fascinated by. All of them ruthless in pursuit of power. If he wanted power, Piers told himself fiercely, he must be ruthless too.

These thoughts churned through his head as he tried to eat. He could try to save Richard's life; or he could put the poor sufferer out of his misery and so earn King Henry's gratitude for evermore. Wasn't that what he had come here to do? He told himself that he would wait until the morning when he would not be so worn out. He would be more fit then to decide what to do.

He was so exhausted that when he lay down in the hall with the other men-at-arms, he fell instantly into a heavy sleep. But he was plagued by nightmares, by battlefields and frenzied killing; he was chasing a white hart covered in blood, and every time he raised his hand to strike, his adversary had the face of Richard of Bordeaux.

He was woken an hour before dawn by a hand on his shoulder.

'I hope you're sufficiently rested, Piers,' the voice of Thomas Swynford sounded in his ear. 'You'll have to ride again today. Get back to London as soon as you can.'

'Why? What has happened?' Piers struggled up. 'Is it another rebellion?'

'Richard is dead.'

'Dead!' exclaimed Piers. 'Who killed him?'

'By his own hand,' replied the Saxon. 'He starved himself to death. You'd better take the news to Henry – he'll be pleased with us.'

Piers stared at the constable of the castle, appalled. Swynford was determined to implicate him in Richard's death. I am guilty, he thought savagely, for though I lacked the courage to do the deed, I did not actively prevent it either.

'I'd come with you, if I could,' Swynford said. 'But I'd better stay here, to make sure nobody tries to steal the body. The King will want proof positive to show the people, I expect.'

'You'd better let me see him then,' said Piers, his mind numb with shock.

Piers was used to death; he had seen too much of it on the

battlefield to be afraid to look upon it now. But when he stood in the dark cold of the dungeon and stared down at the emaciated body of the man who had once been a king, he felt terror such as he had never known. Could he have saved Richard if he had insisted last night on his being moved and cared for, fed and kept warm? He did not know, would never know. He began to shake as if with an ague. If he had not killed him, he had come close, so close he doubted he would ever be able to believe in himself again.

'See for yourself.' Swynford propelled Piers forward. 'No marks. He died by his own hand. You'll tell King Henry?'

Piers promised – he couldn't get out of the castle fast enough. Swynford gave him a fresh horse and escorted him to the gatehouse. 'I know I can trust you not to take all the credit for yourself – you're a man of honour, Piers. I know that. We'll both be well rewarded for this day's work.'

Piers rode across the drawbridge with the words echoing in his ears. As the portcullis squeaked and rattled shut behind him, the word honour mocked him. 'Where is my honour now?' he wondered as he set spurs to his horse.

If he had ridden hard on the way to Pontefract, he rode as if pursued by the very devil away from it. But however hard he rode, he could not flee his thoughts. Honour! Once he had thought that honour was all. But it was as much an illusion as the rest – love, honour, duty, he had pursued all three and where had it brought him? To the brink of the abyss.

As always the thought of Nicolette entered his head suddenly, without his being able to prevent it. He swore fiercely at the top of his voice, his words carried away on the wind. Nicolette would never be his perfect lady but compared to him she was white as driven snow. What she had done, she had done for love. Piers squirmed in the saddle, anger rising to the surface once more. His wife whom he adored had fallen in love with Whittington, as she had with Brembre, as she had with him. Love was all-important to her, he knew that, having tried so hard to win it and succeeded too. But Whittington was far more clever and accomplished and successful, the kind of man Nicolette admired.

Piers rode on at the gallop, unconscious of hunger or cold or the fading of the light, glad that he had no squire with him to hold him up, no one to consider save himself.

He entered Sherwood Forest still riding hard. His noisy passage startled a deer which broke from the deep undergrowth and fled in panic across his path. The horse shied but Piers hardly bothered to check him. The fleeing deer was a poignant reminder of Richard's badge of the white hart – the badge Piers had once been so proud to wear upon his sleeve, the badge he had abandoned in order to win Nicolette. A wolf howled mournfully and the horse laid his ears back nervously. The King had become a tyrant, Piers told himself he had been right to desert him. The people had begged Henry to come and set them free; everything Henry had done had been with the support of the ordinary people of England. Did that make it any better, the compromises, the betrayals, the blood which had been shed in the name of peace?

The horse stumbled and Piers, so deep in despair, failed to hold the animal up. The horse, too exhausted to save himself, lurched awkwardly a second time, fell forward on to his knees and buried his nose in the soft mud beneath his feet. Piers was pitched head first over the animal's ears. 'I do not deserve her,' he thought as his helmeted head hit the trunk of a tree with a resounding clang. It was his last thought before darkness enveloped him.

CHAPTER 40

Dick Whittington was not a little ashamed of the advantage he had taken of Nicolette; ashamed, and frightened too – not so much of Piers but of the empty hollow feeling in his heart since he had been forced to give her up. He was plagued by vivid memories of their time together, by the desire to see her again, to feast his eyes on the perfect oval of her face. But it was not until Candlemas that he dared visit her at home. He told himself that he was doing it out of compassion.

She was in the solar with her women and children. The shutters were closed against the raw February cold, a fire blazed in the hearth, candles burnt in the wall sconces. After the chill outside, the room was pleasantly snug and smelt of beeswax, fresh herbs and wood smoke. No sign of penury here, his merchant's mind could not help noting.

'Have you come to make an inventory of the house?' she asked him almost pleasantly. She was seated at her spindle and made no attempt to get up and welcome him. 'You did that when the Duke of Gloucester was attainted for treason, didn't you?'

'That was when I was Mayor,' he said. 'I'm not Mayor now and there's no question of William Gryffard's being impeached. God will be his only judge now.' He crossed himself perfunctorily.

'Gloucester was tried after his death,' she reminded him. 'But of course that was when poor Richard of Bordeaux was still King.' She was dressed simply in unadorned black velvet, her head covered with a veil of Brabant linen. The severe mourning only accentuated the whiteness of her skin; he thought she had never looked more beautiful or more unobtainable.

'Have you news of Papa?' demanded Kit.

'I hear rumours, but no direct word,' Dick replied, not to the child but to the bent head of his mother. 'I came to find out if you had received a message from him.'

'Sir Crispin told us that he left Oxford on an important quest,' the boy said, clearly bursting with pride. 'The King sent him.'

Dick frowned.

'That's what Sir Crispin says,' Kit insisted defiantly. 'When I grow up I'm going to be Sir Crispin's squire.'

Nicolette looked up at last from her spinning, to smile indulgently at her son. 'He's very bored at home. The few short weeks he spent in the King's household have made what we do here seem all too dull.'

'I could arrange for your son to go back into the King's household,' Dick said, smiling at the boy. 'He will be quite safe there, now that everything has settled down again.' Kit's face was so wreathed in smiles that Dick felt a stab of quite unexpected pleasure.

'As soon as Piers returns, he'll take Kit back,' said Nicolette, staring at him coldly.

'It may not be quite as easy as that.' Dick's joy quickly evaporated as he remembered his errand. He peered through the haze of smoke hanging in the chamber. The ugly little tiring woman was in one corner brushing mud from the hem of a velvet mantle. Jeanne de Bourdat was seated on the step running round the bed, with his godson Michael on her knee. Deliberately he crossed the chamber to where Nicolette sat spinning, stood close to her, so close he could not help but be aware of her fragrance. 'It is rumoured that Richard of Bordeaux is dead,' he said, 'that he has been killed,' he whispered into her small, well-shaped ear.

'God have mercy on him,' she murmured, crossing herself instinctively. 'May his soul rest in peace.'

'Amen.' As he made the sign of the cross, Dick hoped that now she would realise that he had news to impart, news for her ears alone, but she seemed not to have appreciated the significance of what he was trying to tell her.

'If I could have a word with you in private,' he said quietly. She stopped spinning and raised her eyes to his face with a detached calm that made him feel uncomfortable.

'I would have thought,' she said, 'that we had nothing left to say to each other in private.'

'I very much fear that Piers may have killed Richard.' Angered by her scorn, he blurted it out more brutally than he had intended.

'We heard that Richard of Bordeaux had escaped and was leading his forces,' she said. 'If Piers has killed him it must have been because he could not help doing so. Piers always says that war is not like a tournament, you know.'

'The rebels used Richard's secretary, Maudelyn, who resembles him, to pretend that he had escaped and was leading them,' said Dick, 'but Maudelyn has been captured and executed with the rest of them.'

'Is his head up on London Bridge? Will you take me to see it?' demanded Kit.

Dick frowned, wondering how much the boy understood. 'The late King Richard has been kept closely guarded at Pontefract Castle since before Christmas,' he went on. 'The rumours are very persistent that he has been killed.' Perhaps now she would see how necessary it was that she should speak to him in private. But Nicolette was bent over the spindle, spinning for all the world as if her life depended upon it.

Jeanne de Bourdat came forward and stood by Kit, one hand on his shoulder. 'You can come with me to the hall and help lay the tables for dinner,' she said.

Kit's chin jutted defiantly. 'If Sir Richard of Bordeaux is dead,' he said to Dick, 'King Henry will be pleased.'

'He will indeed,' Dick agreed. 'For now he sits secure upon his throne.'

'No more battles?' Kit was looking almost disappointed.

'No internal strife,' Dick said. 'Now go and practise laying tables – you'll have to, you know, if you are going to be a good page.'

Kit looked as if he was about to object but Jeanne had taken a firm hold of his doublet. Propelling Tarquin before her and dragging Kit in her wake, she left the chamber.

'That young son of yours has a remarkable understanding for one so young,' Dick remarked when the door closed behind them. 'One day he will understand the service his father has done the King.'

'Piers has served King Henry faithfully ever since St

Inglevert. He has proved his loyalty in good times and in bad,' she replied sulkily. 'Piers may not be as clever as you, Master Whittington, but his loyalty is beyond question.' She was looking directly at him at last but her eyes were full of accusation.

'Perhaps this time he has gone too far to prove his loyalty,' retorted Dick, tired of being found wanting. He had not come to justify his own behaviour to such as her. He had come to warn her, to prepare her for the consequences of her husband's folly, to help her if he could, but she was making it so difficult for him. He looked around him and found his eyes drawn irresistibly to the splendid bed which filled so much of the chamber. The baby had fallen asleep in an untidy heap, like a puppy, curled up in the folds of the bed curtains. Nicolette was busy once more with her spinning. The ugly peasant woman watched him suspiciously as she laid the brushed and folded mantle carefully in the coffer at the foot of the bed.

Suddenly Lisette straightened up and confronted him. 'What are you trying to tell us, Master Whittington? That Sir Piers is a murderer? I'll not believe it. He that's never done a dishonourable act in his life.' She folded her arms over her chest, a belligerent look in her eye, for all the world like Cerberus guarding the entrance to Hades, thought Dick wryly.

'It's all right, Lisette,' said Nicolette with a sigh. 'Whatever Sir Piers has done, he has done for honour's sake, you can be sure of that.' Lisette opened her mouth to say more but quickly Nicolette forestalled her. 'You had better go down to the hall and help Jeanne with dinner. I expect Master Whittington will be joining us.'

'Regrettably I cannot – not today,' Dick said. 'The Council meets after noon and the King expects me at the palace.'

'There's those as know how to turn with the prevailing wind,' announced Lisette waddling towards the door, 'and there's those as is too nice to do the fighting and the killing; but a man's soul stays the same however many times he changes his coat.'

Dick showed no emotion. He was used to hard words; they only hurt if you let them. As the door closed behind Lisette's indignant back, he dismissed the maid from his mind.

492

He had got what he wanted. He was alone with Nicolette at last and found that he was excited as a stallion going into battle. His body, which had enjoyed her and remembered every delicious incident with keen pleasure, was beginning to disobey his heart and mind. She was still spinning, the flickering light from the wall sconces shining down on her bent head. A gust of wind blew a great billowing cloud of smoke into the room. Dick put a hand on her shoulder. She tensed.

'You need not think,' she said, 'that because we are alone I am unprotected. I have only to call and a servant will come running.'

He could feel the warmth of her flesh through the heavy velvet of her padded surcoat. 'I have never taken you by force, my dear. You always came willingly,' he drew a deep breath, filling his nostrils with the scent of her, 'as I hope you will again.'

'Why? Why should I ever have to pretend to love you again?'

He winced and his hand dropped from her shoulder as if it had been a live coal.

'Is it because you lent my poor father money? Will you take this house in payment of the debt as you took Simon Burley's cups?'

'I would not turn you out into the street, surely you do not think that of me,' he replied, horrified. She was looking into the fire, and he feasted his eyes on the small square of exposed flesh between her throat and the low-cut bodice of her surcoat. 'I had hoped to be able to offer you my protection,' he murmured and his voice was husky despite all his efforts to stay calm and detached.

'Piers will protect us,' she said. 'Whatever I have done, he will do his duty.' She turned to look at him and her eyes were full of appeal. 'Piers is the King's friend, he will have his just reward.'

As Dick returned her gaze, his loins began to throb with an urgency of their own. To distract himself, he crossed the chamber and from the safety of the window embrasure said, 'There is no reward for the man who kills an anointed King. Especially the King's friend. Can't you see?' Angered by the clamouring of his rebellious body, he clasped his trembling hands together in the folds of his velvet sleeves. 'The King cannot afford to be in any way associated with Richard's murder,' he almost shouted at her. 'He must seem shocked, avenge the killing. If he is seen to approve, he signs his own death warrant; if he condones the death of Richard, he will be the next to be put to the sword. Piers has made a mess of things, as usual.'

'Piers doesn't care about riches,' she said, shaking her head. 'But he thinks I do. He thinks that you bought me – you and my father between you. He has done this for me, I know it, and it means I must share the burden of his sin.'

Dick stared at her lovely face in exasperation; only a true beauty could be capable of such vanity. He would have been amused if he had not felt so angry. 'He has ruined himself! Are you prepared to share his ruin?' he demanded. It was not what he meant.

'Piers has a talent for doing the wrong thing for all the right reasons,' she said, ignoring his question. 'It's what makes him so very difficult to love,' and then added almost to herself, 'yet so well worth loving.'

Anger had hold of him now, driving away his lust. 'Like the rest of us, Piers has his price,' he said. 'He too has been corrupted by power and position. He thinks that if he performs this service for King Henry, it will make him rich.'

'Is that what makes you so angry?' she asked suddenly. 'Are you afraid that Piers is going to win after all? That the King might value loyalty more than all your money?'

'Piers has ruined himself,' repeated Dick. 'That is what makes me so angry. The King cannot possibly condone murder.'

'Why not?' Suddenly she seemed full of confidence. 'What about Gloucester? He was murdered in Calais, was he not? You were Mayor and advising King Richard then, if I remember.' Dick looked quickly away. 'Gloucester's death was very convenient and Mowbray his gaoler was shown nothing but special favour thereafter.'

She would remember Thomas Mowbray, he thought, quelling the desire to seize her by the shoulders and press his lips to that small white triangle of naked flesh. 'Have you forgotten that less than a year later Norfolk was banished for life and has since died in exile?' he said instead. 'I'm very much afraid the same fate awaits your husband.'

She got up from her stool and came to stand in front of him. His flesh began to tingle anew.

'Do you think I have learnt nothing from you?' she asked. 'I am a good apprentice, quick to learn – that is my talent.' She smiled and his heart began to pound. In another minute they would be in the big bed, the curtains closed tightly round them, snatching a brief interlude of happiness together. 'You taught me that,' she said.

He was so carried away with his vision he had not been listening to what she was saying. 'Taught you what?' he asked, smiling at her indulgently.

'Not to be afraid of failure,' she said. 'To be myself. I'm not afraid of failure any more, I've seen what success can do.'

He could not believe what she was saying. He tried to grasp her by the wrist, to pull her into his arms, but she moved away quickly.

'I'm not for sale.' She shook her head sadly at him. 'There is nothing you can give me that I want any more. For a while I thought you could help me find my true self, but you can't, can you? I have to do that for myself.'

He knew then that he had lost her. He drew a deep breath, took hold of his dignity, found his cool head and his iron self-control. 'What will you do?'

'Go on a pilgrimage,' and from the way her face lit up he knew the idea had only just occurred to her. 'A pilgrimage to Canterbury. It will help me to learn to do without things.'

'Nobody goes on pilgrimage in the dead of winter,' he exclaimed.

'The mortification of the flesh will be all the more severe,' she was glowing with resolution, 'it will make me learn all the quicker.'

Dick felt sudden impatience; it was all very well, this sudden piety, but it was totally impractical. He found himself offering advice and help and protection and being gently but firmly refused.

'But what about your children?' he asked. 'At least let me help you with them.'

'God will protect us,' she told him serenely.

There was nothing he could do, so he took his leave. Outside, it was cold and bleak. His servant stood shivering in the raw wind, holding his horse. Dick gathered his fur-lined cloak tightly round him and mounted his gelding. A great sadness settled on him, dark and heavy as the banks of cloud gathering above the spire of St Peter's. He'd lost Nicolette. He'd lost Piers. Gryffard was dead. Richard, once his King and his friend, was probably dead also.

Slowly he rode down Cornhill making for the Lud Gate which would lead him out of the city towards Westminster where King Henry had summoned him to his Council. He could at least do one last thing for Piers and Nicolette. He could persuade Henry to send Piers home to Cheshire. The King would need a man whose loyalty he could depend upon to keep watch in Richard's stronghold, and who more loyal than a knight who would endanger his immortal soul with murder to serve his King. Dick rode on up the hill towards St Paul's Cathedral. If he could help them without their knowing, he would feel better. Would Nicolette be able to live with a murderer? He didn't know. If she believed that Piers had done it for love then she might. All she really wanted was love, he thought, and that he had not been able to give her. Piers and Nicolette deserved each other, he thought sadly.

The bell of St Paul's began to toll and others took up the clarion call. Dick rode on past the great cathedral, listening to the bells of the city calling to him. He was still on top. London needed him. But he felt lonely.

Nicolette began to tremble. She had controlled herself in front of Dick, determined that he should not know how afraid she was for Piers. If what he had said was true and Piers had killed Richard of Bordeaux, then the sin was hers for driving him to do it. She was an evil, cursed woman. No penance was too harsh, no indulgence too costly to pay for such a sin. A pilgrimage was her last hope of salvation, but she must be gone before Piers returned. She felt unable to face him.

In an excess of piety, she began her penance. While Lisette wept and Jeanne beseeched her not to be so hasty, she took a knife to the glorious wonder of her hair. 'There,' she said, watching the long silky tresses fall in heaps of gold upon the rushes. 'Beauty is a temptation of the devil. I have been vain and proud of my body, worshipping it like a false God and encouraging others to worship it too.' She bound a pudding cloth about her cropped head and donned a garment of coarse serge with a knotted rope tied loosely about her waist. Then she smeared ash from the fire on her high white brow and looked for the last time in the polished steel on the wall. 'Nobody will want me now,' she said with a little shiver of revulsion. But it was the first step on the road to redemption.

Elated by the act of self-sacrifice, she set forth immediately, believing in her heart that it would not be long before Piers would come looking for her. Her penitence would move him as her beauty had failed to do and when he realised that she was no longer evil he would surely forgive her at last. Her elation carried her through the first few difficult days of pain and discomfort. She did not mind the mud oozing between the toes of her bare feet, discovering with pleased surprise that once her feet were wet and muddy, it no longer mattered how many puddles she walked in.

At first she could not force herself to eat the greasy scraps that were tossed into her begging bowl, but after she had fasted for several days, she discovered the pleasure of hunger satisfied. She was afraid as she walked across the wild wasteland of Hounslow alone and unprotected, until she encountered a party of bandits and realised that she had nothing they wanted – no money, no jewels, and in her sackcloth and ashes no feminine allure. Indeed, they were kind to her, and generous. They put more in her bowl than any prosperous citizen, for they understood poverty. The weather turned unseasonably mild. Nicolette, plodding barefoot, hungry and penitent along the road to Canterbury, took it as a sign that God approved of her pilgrimage.

But once she had grown used to her bodily discomforts, she found that her thoughts, instead of turning to God, were occupied more and more by Piers. Where was he? Why did he not come? What was she to say to him when he caught up with her?

She walked each day in expectation and fear, always looking over her shoulder when she heard hoofbeats on the road behind her. But although she was passed many times by other travellers – and showered with mud in the process – none of them was a knight with red trefoils on a cream shield. Slowly she began to face the truth that all her penitence and remorse had been for no other purpose than to win her husband's forgiveness, to appeal to his chivalry. After that came despair and the realisation that Piers was not coming to rescue her from the task of repentance. Fiercely she reproached herself for being so weak, for clinging so tenaciously to the things of the flesh. In each abbey she passed along the way she tried to recapture the feelings of peace and conviction she had known all those years ago in the abbey at Caen. She spent the night not resting in the pilgrim's hostel but in the chapel in silent vigil upon her knees. But God was still displeased. She could not find him. She prayed, she scourged herself, she spent hours questioning a hermit in his small wayside sanctuary. But all that she discovered during the long solitary hours of painful walking was that she was lost. All her life she had been guided by her mother's dying command. In renouncing success, she had found nothing to put in its place.

By March she was well on the way to Canterbury, but no nearer to finding God. When the steady clip clop of horses' hooves sounded behind her, she did not look round. She had long ago become too tired and dispirited and footsore to pay attention to other wayfarers. The horses slowed to a walk. With her head bent and leaning heavily on her staff, Nicolette limped on. She became aware of the jingle of chain mail, the creaking of harness. She looked over her shoulder. A knight was reining his horse in beside her. On his shield were three red trefoils on a cream field. Her eyes flew to his face.

Piers!

'Your feet are bleeding,' he said. The sun was in her eyes and she could not see his face properly.

'Are they? I hadn't noticed,' she stammered, all too aware that her face was filthy, her body stank and her head was shaven.

'Are you going to walk all the way to Canterbury?' He did not sound very pleased to see her.

'People do.' She stood in the middle of the road looking down at her swollen feet, terrified that he might not want her any more. She had thrown away all the outward trimmings of success – her jewels, her beautiful clothes, her glorious hair; all she had left was her failure. Would he ride on and leave her to seek her own salvation?

'You always take everything you do to extremes, even penitence,' he said angrily.

He was right, she thought miserably, even now she was

trying to be the perfect pilgrim. 'Perhaps that's why I'm finding it so difficult to find God.' She looked up at him imploringly.

He swung down from his horse. 'Then I'd better come and help you,' he said.

She was trembling from the shock of his sudden appearance. 'You can't walk to Canterbury in those ridiculous shoes,' she said, trying to get her breath back.

'I shall walk barefoot,' said Piers. 'If you can do it, so can I.' He sat down on the ground, tugging at the long tapering points of his fashionable shoes while his squire watched baffled. The squire, Nicolette noticed, was new, and didn't seem to know whether he should be helping his master undress on the roadside or holding the horses. The poor boy must be utterly bewildered, she thought. Piers looked so ridiculous sitting on the ground in his chain mail and emblazoned surcoat, struggling with his bright blue hose while his sword became entangled in his long spurs.

'You can't come dressed like that,' she laughed, joy bubbling up inside her. 'Not with your sword.'

'How can I protect you without a sword?' he demanded.

'We don't need protection.' She smiled at him tenderly. 'When you've got nothing to lose you've got nothing to fear.'

He stared at her intently, then got carefully to his bare feet and shuffled towards the waiting squire. 'Ride on to Canterbury, Martin,' he said, handing him the sword and spurs. 'Find some tavern or abbey to stable the horses. Then come and find us in the cathedral.'

'When do you think you'll get to Canterbury?' asked the boy, clearly not happy with his task.

'How should I know? You'd better visit the shrine daily until we come – it will be good for your soul.'

Listening to her husband's voice which she had at times thought never to hear again, feasting her eyes on his vigorous, beautifully controlled body, Nicolette's heart overflowed with thankfulness. It did not matter what he had done, or why. He was here and he was coming with her to Canterbury. This time she was determined not to let anything come between them again.

The squire rode off, with one last perplexed and embarrassed glance at Nicolette. There was none of the instant leaping admiration she was used to seeing in male eyes of whatever age. The poor boy must be sorely disappointed in Sir Piers Exton's lady, she thought, without a twinge of regret.

She turned to Piers. He was looking lost and forlorn, not at all like the courageous champion who fought all her battles for her. She knew then that before they began their pilgrimage together the truth had to be wrestled with.

'What happened to Guy de Luval?' she began tentatively.

'The King knighted him. Martin was a page in the royal household and the King gave him to me in de Luval's place. I don't know whether as punishment or reward.'

Nicolette detected a harsh, defiant note in his voice that she had never heard before. She drew a deep breath. 'Richard of Bordeaux,' she murmured.

'Is dead. I could have killed him – I meant to.'

'But you didn't. Oh Piers,' she said relieved, but something in his face made her careful. 'I would still have loved you even if you had.' He was staring down at her intently.

'I was afraid you loved Whittington.'

'What I did with Whittington I did because I had to – to save my father from ruin. Dick had found out how William was robbing the King and threatened to expose him. It would have meant ruin, death maybe.' She could not bear the way he was looking at her. 'Forgive me, Piers,' she begged.

'You don't have to beg my forgiveness,' he said turning away from her. 'What I have done – or failed to do – is far worse.' He wasn't going to tell her, she thought. She would have to draw it from him slowly, like poison from a festering boil.

'Whatever you have done, or might have done, it was for Henry's sake,' she tried to comfort him. 'He knows that, even if he cannot afford to acknowledge it.'

'Whittington has persuaded King Henry to be lenient,' Piers said bitterly. 'I've been made Sheriff of Cheshire with manors and a fine castle in need of fortification. The King wants me to hold the north for him.'

Her spirits leapt at the news. It was just what they needed, a new start far from London, where Piers would be able to shine, doing what he did best. Clever, clever Dick.

'So you see, I can provide for you at last – thanks to Whittington,' said Piers as if reading her thoughts. 'Although you'll miss the excitement of the court, you'll want for nothing.'

Mary, Mother of God, let me help him, she thought, pierced by the agonising uncertainty in his face.

'I find it hard to forgive Whittington,' Piers went on. 'The monks at Rufford Abbey said I would find it easier to forgive him if I prayed for him. They said it's hard to go on hating someone when you are beseeching God nightly for their redemption. I try to pray for him.' He was standing staring fiercely at the ground kicking the dirt of the road with his bare foot. His honour, she thought, his precious honour. Somehow she had to draw the poison out of him, get to the truth that was troubling him so.

'Tell me about Rufford Abbey. What were you doing there?' she asked.

'I had a fall in Sherwood Forest,' he said. 'I was riding carelessly and the horse came down. A party of monks from Rufford found me lying senseless. When I came back to my senses, I was in the abbey. I was in a terrible state for a while, broken in body and in spirit. But the Abbot helped me – he is a man of great holiness. He told me that in order to forgive others it is necessary first to be able to forgive oneself. It's something I'm not finding very easy to do.' He looked at her then and the pain in his eyes made her heart twist.

'I too have been searching for forgiveness,' she said, choosing her words carefully. 'All the way from London I have been looking for God to ask His forgiveness and I have been unable to find Him.' She felt as if she was groping towards the truth like a benighted traveller stumbling through the dark night with only one poor little candle. 'Oh Piers, perhaps I couldn't find Him because in my heart I was looking for you.' Piers looked at her in astonishment. She drew a deep breath, took a few more hesitant steps towards the truth. 'God is not hiding His face from us, it is we who are hiding from Him, because we cannot forgive ourselves.'

He stretched out his hand and his face had lost its bewildered, haggard look. 'Like Adam and Eve in the garden,' he said. Then suddenly he grinned. 'Except Eve had a fig leaf instead of sackcloth and ashes.'

Timidly, still fearing rejection she placed her hand in his. He gripped it tightly, looked down lovingly into her anxious eyes.

'Shall we try and find God together?' he said.

With a sigh of heartfelt thankfulness she leant against him, glorying in his strength. It would not be easy, she thought, but at least they were setting out on this quest together. Always in the past Piers had tried to be good enough for both of them. Now at last he was prepared to trust her with his honour.

AUTHOR'S NOTE

King Richard II died at Pontefract Castle. The Lancastrian story was that he had starved himself to death; Adam of Usk says that he perished heartbroken, fettered, and 'tormented by Sir Thomas Swinford with starving fare'; the French chroniclers give the story of his murder by one Sir Piers Exton, which Shakespeare followed. The truth will never be fully known, but in 1871, when Dean Stanley examined the skeleton of Richard in the tomb at Westminster Abbey, he found no marks of violence on skull or frame.

No historical record of Sir Piers Exton is known, therefore I felt justified in making him a fictional character.

Richard Whittington actually existed. But he was not so poor as legend will have him. He was the younger son of a Gloucestershire knight, who went to London aged about thirteen and was apprenticed to Sir John Fitz Warren, a mercer, and married Alice Fitz Warren, his boss's daughter. What is strange is that of all the colourful characters who fought to be Lord Mayor of London it was Richard Whittington who became the hero of nursery fables and pantomime. Was it because he lived for such a long time and was Mayor under three different kings? Richard II in 1397, Henry IV in 1406 and again under Henry V in 1419 when Whittington was sixty years old. Or was it because unlike nearly all other prosperous city merchants Whittington did not buy land but kept his money liquid. Perhaps it was because he had the kind of personality and charisma that breeds a legend; it is known that he was the sort of man who could make at Thomas Spital (St Thomas's Hospital) 'a new chamber with 8 beds for young women that had done amiss in trust of a good mendment And he commanded that all the

503

things that be done in that chamber should be kept secret with out forth in pain of losing their living for he would not shame no young woman in no wise for it might be cause of her letting [preventing] of her marriage'.

This is a work of fiction and Dick Whittington's liaison with my heroine is pure imagination. I like to think that he was a man subject to many complex temptations which helped him acquire much wisdom. That he should leave money for young women that had done amiss makes me think that perhaps he understood the frailty and vulnerability of such women and his understanding could well have been acquired through first-hand experience.

He was certainly a survivor and there is reason to believe that he felt guilty for having forsaken Richard II, for at the end of his long life he left money in his will for prayers to be said for Richard, and also for the Duke of Gloucester, which may mean that he knew Richard had Gloucester murdered at Calais.

Dick Whittington had no children. He left a piece of ground beside his house in the city on which to build an almshouse for thirteen men or women who were poor citizens of London. He endowed it with land and money from the bulk of his fortune and entrusted it to the Mercers' Company on the death of his executor. The value of the whole at that time was about six thousand pounds. Over the centuries the almshouses have sheltered countless poor folk and the income from the money is still growing. So the old legend has a grain of truth in it after all, because the land Whittington left in the city of London has indeed turned into gold.